LOVE & OTHER DETOURS

INCLUDES

LOVE & GELATO  LOVE & LUCK

∞ JENNA EVANS WELCH ∞

SIMON & SCHUSTER BFYR

New York London Toronto Sydney New Delhi

SIMON & SCHUSTER BFYR

An imprint of Simon & Schuster Children's Publishing Division
1230 Avenue of the Americas, New York, New York 10020
This book is a work of fiction. Any references to historical events,
real people, or real places are used fictitiously. Other names, characters, places,
and events are products of the author's imagination, and any resemblance to actual
events or places or persons, living or dead, is entirely coincidental.

For information about special discounts for bulk purchases, please contact
Simon & Schuster Special Sales at 1-866-506-1949 or business@simonandschuster.com.
The Simon & Schuster Speakers Bureau can bring authors to your live event.
For more information or to book an event contact the Simon & Schuster Speakers
Bureau at 1-866-248-3049 or visit our website at www.simonspeakers.com.
Interior design by Mike Rosamilia
The text of this book was set in Adobe Caslon Pro.
Manufactured in the United States of America
2 4 6 8 10 9 7 5 3 1
This SIMON & SCHUSTER BFYR bind-up paperback edition September 2020
Library of Congress Control Number 2020931583
ISBN 9781534478145 (bind-up pbk)
ISBN 9781481432566 (*Love & Gelato* ebook)
ISBN 9781534401020 (*Love & Luck* ebook)
These titles were previously published individually.

CONTENTS

LOVE &
GELATO

To David,

for being my love story

Prologue

YOU'VE HAD BAD DAYS BEFORE, RIGHT? YOU KNOW, THE ones where your alarm doesn't go off, your toast practically catches on fire, and you remember way too late that every article of clothing you own is soaking wet in the bottom of the washer? So then you go hurtling into school fifteen minutes late, *praying* no one will notice that your hair looks like the Bride of Frankenstein's, but just as you slide into your desk your teacher booms, "Running late today, Ms. Emerson?" and everyone looks at you and notices?

I'm sure you've had those days. We all have. But what about really bad days? The kind that are so pumped up and awful that they chew up the things you care about just for the fun of spitting them back in your face?

The day my mom told me about Howard fell firmly in the *really bad* category. But at the time, he was the least of my worries.

It was two weeks into my sophomore year of high school

and my mom and I were driving home from her appointment. The car was silent except for a radio commercial narrated by two Arnold Schwarzenegger impersonators, and even though it was a hot day, I had goose bumps up and down my legs. Just that morning I'd placed second at my first-ever cross country meet and I couldn't believe how much that didn't matter anymore.

My mom switched off the radio. "Lina, what are you feeling?" Her voice was calm, and when I looked at her I teared up all over again. She was so pale and tiny. How had I not noticed how *tiny* she'd gotten?

"I don't know," I said, trying to keep my voice even. "I feel like I'm in shock."

She nodded, coming to a stop at a traffic light. The sun was doing its best to blind us, and I stared into it, my eyes scalding. *This is the day that changes everything*, I thought. *From here on out there will only be* before *and* after *today.*

My mom cleared her throat, and when I glanced at her, she straightened up like she had something important to tell me. "Lina, did I ever tell you about the time I was dared to swim in a fountain?"

I whipped around. "What?"

"Remember how I told you I spent a year studying in Florence? I was out photographing with my classmates, and it was such a hot day I thought I was going to melt. I had this friend—Howard—and he dared me to jump into a fountain."

Now, keep in mind, we'd just gotten the worst news of our lives. The *worst*.

"... I scared a group of German tourists. They were posing for a photo, and when I popped out of the water, one of them lost her balance and almost fell back into the fountain with me. They were furious, so Howard yelled that I was drowning and jumped in after me."

I stared at her, and she turned and gave me a little smile.

"Uh . . . Mom? That's funny and everything, but why are you telling me this now?"

"I just wanted to tell you about Howard. He was really a lot of fun." The light changed and she hit the gas.

What? I thought. *What what what?*

At first I thought the fountain story was a coping mechanism, like maybe she thought a story about an old friend could distract us from the two blocks of granite hanging over our heads. *Inoperable. Incurable.* But then she told me another story. And another. It got to the point where she'd start talking and three words in I'd know she was going to bring up Howard. And then when she finally told me the reason for all the Howard stories, well . . . let's just say that ignorance is bliss.

"Lina, I want you to go to Italy."

It was mid-November and I was sitting next to her hospital bed with a stack of ancient *Cosmo* magazines I'd swiped from the waiting room. I'd spent the last ten minutes taking a quiz called "On a Scale of One to Sizzle: How Hot Are You?" (7/10).

"Italy?" I was kind of distracted. The person who'd taken the quiz before me had scored a 10/10 and I was trying to figure out how.

"I mean I want you to go live in Italy. After."

That got my attention. For one thing, I didn't believe in *after*. Yes, her cancer was progressing just the way her doctors said it would, but doctors didn't know everything. Just that morning I'd bookmarked a story on the Internet about a woman who'd beaten cancer and gone on to climb Mt. Kilimanjaro. And for another, *Italy?*

"Why would I do that?" I asked lightly. It was important to humor her. Avoiding stress is a big part of recovery.

"I want you to stay with Howard. The year I spent in Italy meant so much to me, and I want you to have that same experience."

I shot my eyes at the nurse's call button. *Stay with Howard in Italy?* Did they give her too much morphine?

"Lina, look at me," she said, in her bossiest I Am the Mother voice.

"Howard? You mean that guy you keep talking about?"

"Yes. He's the best man I've ever known. He'll keep you safe."

"Safe from *what*?" I looked into her eyes, and suddenly my breath started coming in short and fast. She was serious. Did hospital rooms stock paper bags?

She shook her head, her eyes shiny. "Things will be . . . hard. We don't have to talk about it now, but I wanted to make sure you heard my decision from me. You'll need someone. After. And I think he's the best person."

"Mom, that doesn't even make sense. Why would I go live with a stranger?" I jumped up and started rifling through the drawers in her end table. There had to be a paper bag *somewhere*.

"Lina, sit."

"But, Mom—"

"Sit. You're going to be fine. You're going to make it. Your life will go on, and it's going to be great."

"No," I said. "*You're* going to make it. Sometimes people recover."

"Lina, Howard's a wonderful friend. You'll really love him."

"I doubt it. And if he's that good of a friend, then why haven't I ever met him before?" I gave up on finding a bag, collapsing back into my chair and putting my head between my knees.

She struggled to sit up, then reached out, resting her hand

on my back. "Things were a little bit complicated between us, but he wants to get to know you. And he said he'd love to have you stay with him. Promise me you'll give it a try. A few months at least."

There was a knock on the door, and we both looked up to see a nurse dressed in baby blue scrubs. "Just checking in," she sang, either ignoring or not noticing the expression on my face. On a Scale of One to Tense, the room was at about 100/10.

"Morning. I was just telling my daughter she needs to go to Italy."

"Italy," the nurse said, clasping both hands to her chest. "I went there on my honeymoon. Gelato, the Leaning Tower of Pisa, gondolas in Venice . . . You'll love it."

My mom smiled at me triumphantly.

"Mom, *no*. There's no way I'm going to Italy."

"Oh, but, honey, you have to go," the nurse said. "It will be a once-in-a-lifetime experience."

The nurse ended up being right about one thing: I did have to go. But no one gave me even the tiniest hint about what I'd find once I got there.

Chapter 1

THE HOUSE LOOMED BRIGHTLY IN THE DISTANCE, LIKE A lighthouse in a sea of headstones. But it couldn't be *his* house, right? We were probably just following some kind of Italian custom. *Always drive newcomers through a cemetery. That way they get a feel for the local culture.* Yeah, that must be it.

I knit my fingers in my lap, my stomach dropping as the house got closer and closer. It was like watching Jaws emerge from the depths of the ocean. *Duuun dun.* Only it wasn't a movie. It was real. And there was only one turn left. *Don't panic. This can't be it. Mom wouldn't have sent you to live in a cemetery. She would have warned you. She would have—*

He flipped on the turn signal, and all the air came rushing out of my lungs. *She just didn't tell me.*

"Are you okay?"

Howard—my dad, I guess I should call him—was looking at me with a concerned expression. Probably because I'd just made a wheezing noise.

"Is that your . . . ?" Words failed me, so I had to point.

"Well, yes." He hesitated for a moment and then gestured out the window. "Lina, didn't you know? About all this?"

"All this" didn't even come close to describing the massive moonlit cemetery. "My grandma told me I'd be staying on American-owned land. She said you're the caretaker of a World War II memorial. I didn't think . . ." Panic was pouring over me like hot syrup. Also, I couldn't seem to finish a single sentence. *Breathe, Lina. You've already survived the worst. You can survive this, too.*

He pointed to the far end of the property. "The memorial is that building right up there. But the rest of the grounds are for the graves of American soldiers who were killed in Italy during the war."

"But this isn't your *house* house, right? It's just where you work?"

He didn't answer. Instead we pulled into the driveway, and I felt the last of my hope fade along with the car's headlights. This wasn't just a house. It was a *home*. Red geraniums lined the walkway, and there was a porch swing creaking back and forth, like someone had just gotten up. Subtract the crosses lining the surrounding lawns and it was any normal house in any normal neighborhood. But it wasn't a normal neighborhood. And those crosses didn't look like they were going anywhere. Ever.

"They like to have a caretaker on-site at all times, so they built this house back in the sixties." Howard took the keys out of the ignition, then drummed his fingers nervously on the steering wheel. "I'm really sorry, Lina. I thought you knew. I can't imagine what you're thinking right now."

"It's a cemetery." My voice was like weak tea.

He turned and looked at me, not quite making eye contact. "I know. And the last thing you need is a reminder of everything you've been through this year. But I think you'll find that this place grows on you. It's really peaceful and it has a lot of interesting history. Your mother loved it. And after being here almost seventeen years, I can't imagine living anywhere else."

His voice was hopeful, but I slumped back in my seat, a swarm of questions taking flight in my mind. *If she loved it so much, then why didn't she ever tell me about it? Why didn't she ever talk about you until she got sick? And for the love of all that's holy, what made her leave out the teeny-tiny detail that you're my* father?

Howard absorbed my silence for a moment, then opened his car door. "Let's head inside. I'll get your suitcase."

All six foot five of him walked around to the back of the car, and I leaned over to watch him in the side mirror. My grandma had been the one to fill in the blanks. *He's your father; that's why she wanted you to live with him.* I probably should have seen it coming. It's just that good old buddy Howard's true identity seemed like the sort of thing my mother would have at least *mentioned*.

Howard closed the trunk, and I straightened up and started rifling through my backpack, buying myself another few seconds. *Lina, think. You're alone in a foreign country, a certifiable giant has just stepped forward as your father, and your new home could be the setting for a zombie apocalypse movie. Do something.*

But what? Short of wrestling the car keys from Howard, I couldn't think of a single way to get out of going into that house. Finally I unbuckled my seat belt and followed him to the front door.

Inside, the house was aggressively normal—like maybe it thought it could make up for its location if it just tried hard enough. Howard set my suitcase down in the front entryway, and then we walked into a living room with two overstuffed chairs and a leather sofa. There were a bunch of vintage travel posters on the walls, and the whole place smelled like it had been soaking in garlic and onions. But in a good way. Obviously.

"Welcome home," Howard said, switching on the main light. Fresh panic smacked me in the face, and he winced when he saw my expression. "I mean, welcome to Italy. I'm so glad you're here."

"Howard?"

"Hi, Sonia."

A tall, gazelle-like woman stepped into the room. She was maybe a few years older than Howard, with coffee-colored skin and rows of gold bracelets on each arm. Gorgeous. And also a surprise.

"Lina," she said, enunciating my name carefully. "You made it. How were your flights?"

I shifted from one foot to the other. Was someone going to introduce us? "They were okay. The last one was really long."

"We're so glad you're here." She beamed at me, and there was a thick moment of silence.

Finally I stepped forward. "So . . . you're Howard's wife?"

Howard and Sonia looked at each other and then practically started howling with laughter.

Lina Emerson. Comic genius.

Finally Howard got himself under control. "Lina, this is Sonia. She's the assistant superintendent of the cemetery. She's been working here even longer than I have."

"Just by a few months," Sonia said, wiping her eyes. "Howard always makes me sound like a dinosaur. My house is on the property too, a little closer to the memorial."

"How many people live here?"

"Just us two. Now three," Howard said.

"And about four thousand soldiers," Sonia added, grinning. She squinted at Howard, and I glanced back just in time to see him frantically running one finger across his throat. Nonverbal communication. Great.

Sonia's smile vanished. "Lina, are you hungry? I made a lasagna."

That's what that smell was. "I'm pretty hungry," I admitted. Understatement.

"Good. I made my specialty. Lasagna with extra-garlicky garlic bread."

"Yes!" Howard said, pumping his arm like a housewife on *The Price Is Right.* "You decided to spoil us."

"It's a special night, so I thought I'd go all out. Lina, you probably want to wash your hands. I'll dish up and you can meet us in the dining room."

Howard pointed across the living room. "Bathroom's over there."

I nodded, then set my backpack on the nearest chair before practically fleeing the room. The bathroom was miniature, barely big enough for a toilet and a sink, and I ran the water as hot as I could stand it, scrubbing the airport off my hands with a chip of soap from the edge of the sink.

While I scrubbed, I caught a glimpse of myself in the mirror and groaned. I looked like I'd been dragged through three different time zones. Which, to be fair, I had. My normally tan skin was pale and yellowish-looking, and I had dark circles under my eyes. And my *hair.* It had finally figured out a way to defy the laws of physics. I wet both my hands and tried to smash down my curls, but it seemed to only encourage them. Finally I gave up. So what if I looked like a hedgehog who'd discovered Red Bull? Fathers are supposed to accept you as you are, right?

Music started up outside the bathroom and my nervousness kindled from a flame to a bonfire. Did I really need to eat dinner? Maybe I could go hide out in a room somewhere while I processed this whole cemetery thing. Or didn't process it. But then my stomach roared in protest and *ugh*. I did have to eat.

"There she is," Howard said, getting to his feet as I walked into the dining room. The table was set with a red-checkered cloth, and an old rock song I sort of recognized was playing from an iPod next to the entryway. I slid into the chair opposite them, and Howard sat down too.

"I hope you're hungry. Sonia's such a great cook, I think she missed her calling in life." Now that it wasn't just the two of us, he sounded way more relaxed.

Sonia beamed. "No way. I was destined for life at the memorial."

"It does look good." And by "good," I meant *amazing*. A steaming pan of lasagna sat next to a basket of thickly sliced garlic bread, and there was a salad bowl piled high with tomatoes and crisp-looking lettuce. It took every ounce of willpower I had not to dive right onto the table.

Sonia cut into the lasagna, placing a big gooey square right in the center of my plate. "Help yourself to bread and salad. *Buon appetito*."

"*Buon appetito*," Howard echoed.

"*Buon appe* . . . something," I mumbled.

The second everyone was served, I picked up my fork and attacked my lasagna. I knew I probably looked like a wild mastodon, but after a full day of nothing but airline food, I couldn't help myself. Those portions were *miniature*. When I finally came up for air, Sonia and Howard were both staring at me, Howard looking mildly horrified.

"So, Lina, what kinds of things do you like to do?" Sonia asked.

I grabbed my napkin. "Besides scare people with my table manners?"

Howard chuckled. "Your grandmother told me you love running. She said you average about forty miles a week, and you're hoping to run in college."

"Well, that explains the appetite." Sonia scooped up another piece, and I gratefully held out my plate. "Do you run at school?"

"I used to. I was on the varsity cross-country team, but I forfeited my spot after we found out."

They both just looked at me.

". . . When we found out about the cancer? Practice took

up a lot of time, and I didn't want to leave town for all the meets and stuff."

Howard nodded. "I think the cemetery is a great place for a runner. Lots of space, and nice smooth roads. I used to run here all the time. Before I got fat and lazy."

Sonia rolled her eyes. "Oh, please. You couldn't get fat if you tried." She nudged the basket of garlic bread toward me. "Did you know that your mother and I were friends? She was lovely. So talented and lively."

Nope, didn't tell me that, either. Was it possible I was falling prey to some elaborate kidnapping scheme? Would kidnappers feed you two pieces of the best lasagna you'd ever had? And if pressed, would they give you the recipe?

Howard cleared his throat, snapping me back to the conversation. "Sorry. Um, no. She never mentioned you."

Sonia nodded, her face expressionless, and Howard glanced at her, then back at me. "You're probably feeling pretty tired. Is there anyone you want to get in touch with? I messaged your grandmother when your plane arrived, but you're welcome to give her a call. I have an international plan on my cell phone."

"Can I call Addie?"

"Is that the friend you were living with?"

"Yeah. But I have my laptop. I could just use FaceTime instead."

"That might not work tonight. Italy isn't exactly on the cutting edge of technology, and our Internet connection has been pretty slow all day. Someone's coming by to take a look at it tomorrow, but in the meantime you can just use my phone."

"Thanks."

He pushed back from the table. "Would anyone like some wine?"

"Yes, please," Sonia said.

"Lina?"

"Uh . . . I'm kind of underage."

He smiled. "Italy doesn't have a drinking age, so I guess it's a little different around here. But no pressure either way."

"I'll pass."

"Be right back." He headed for the kitchen.

The room was quiet for about ten seconds, and then Sonia set her fork down. "I'm so happy you're here, Lina. And I want you to know that if you need anything, I'm just a stone's throw away. Literally."

"Thanks." I trained my eyes on a spot just over her left shoulder. Adults were always trying too hard around me. They thought that if they were nice enough they could make up for the fact that I'd lost my mom. It was kind of sweet and horrible at the same time.

Sonia glanced toward the kitchen and then lowered her voice. "I wanted to ask you, would you mind stopping by my place sometime tomorrow? I have something I want to give you."

"What?"

"We can talk about it then. Tonight you just focus on set-tling in."

I just shook my head. I was going to do as little settling in as possible. I wasn't even going to unpack my bag.

After dinner Howard insisted on carrying my suitcase upstairs. "I hope you like your room. I repainted and redecorated it a couple of weeks ago, and I think it turned out really nice. I keep most of the windows open in summer—it's a lot cooler that way—but feel free to close yours if you'd prefer." He spoke quickly, like he'd spent all afternoon rehearsing his welcome speech. He set my bag down in front of the first door.

"Bathroom is right across the hall, and I put some new soap and shampoo in there. Let me know what else you need and I'll pick it up tomorrow, okay?"

"Okay."

"And like I said, the Internet's been pretty spotty, but if you decide you want to try it out, our network is called 'American Cemetery.'"

Of course it was. "What's the Wi-Fi password?"

"Wall of the Missing. One word."

"'Wall of the Missing,'" I repeated. "What does that mean?"

"It's a part of the memorial. There are a bunch of stone tablets listing the names of soldiers whose bodies were never recovered. I can show you tomorrow if you'd like."

Nooo, thank you. "Well, I'm pretty tired, so . . ." I edged toward the door.

He took the hint, handing me a cell phone along with a slip of paper. "I wrote down instructions for dialing the States. You have to put in a country code as well as an area code. Let me know if you have any trouble."

"Thanks." I put the paper in my pocket.

"Good night, Lina."

"Good night."

He turned and walked down the hall, and I opened the door and dragged my suitcase into the room, feeling my shoulders sag with the relief of finally being alone. *Well, you're really here*, I thought, *just you and your four thousand new friends*. There was a lock on the door and I turned it with a satisfying *click*. Then I slowly turned around, steeling myself for whatever Howard had meant by "really nice." But then my heart practically stopped, because *wow*.

The room was perfect. Soft light glowed from this adorable gold lamp on the nightstand, and the bed was antique-looking, with about a thousand decorative pillows. A painted desk and dresser sat on opposite sides of the room, and a large oval mirror hung on the wall next to the door. There were even a bunch of picture frames standing empty on the nightstand and dresser, like they were waiting for me to fill them up.

I stood there staring for a minute. It was just so *me*. How was it possible that someone who hadn't even met me had managed to put together my perfect bedroom? Maybe things *weren't* going to be so bad—

And then a gust of wind blew into the room, drawing my attention to the large open window. I'd ignored my own rule: *If it seems too good to be true, it probably is.* I walked over and stuck my head out. The headstones gleamed in the moonlight like rows of teeth, and everything was dark and eerily silent. No amount of pretty could make up for a view like that.

I pulled my head back in, then took the slip of paper out of my pocket. Time to start plotting my escape.

Chapter 2

SADIE DANES MAY BE ONE OF THE WORST PEOPLE ON THE planet, but she'll always have a special place in my heart. After all, I owe her my best friend.

It was the beginning of seventh grade. Addie had just moved to Seattle from Los Angeles, and one day after gym class she'd overheard Sadie make a comment about how some of our classmates didn't actually need bras. Which, be real— we were in seventh grade; only about one percent of us actually needed bras. It's just that I was *particularly* less in need of one, and everyone knew she'd meant me. While I'd just ignored her (i.e., stuck my twelve-year-old head in my locker and blinked back tears), Addie had taken it upon herself to clothesline Sadie on her way out of the locker room. She'd stuck up for me that day and then never stopped.

"Go away. It might be Lina." Addie's voice sounded distant, like she was holding the phone away from her face. "Hello?" she said into the speaker.

"Addie, it's me."

"Lina! IAN, GET AWAY FROM ME." There was some muffled yelling and then what sounded like a Mexican knife fight going on between her and her brother. Addie had three older brothers, and rather than baby her, it seemed they'd unanimously agreed to treat her as one of the guys. It explained a lot about her personality.

"Sorry," she said when she was finally back on the phone. "Ian's an idiot. Someone ran over his phone, and now my parents say I have to share mine. I don't care what happened. I am not giving his caveman friends my phone number."

"Oh, come on, they're not *that* bad."

"Stop it. You know they are. This morning I walked in on one of them eating our cereal. He'd poured an entire box into a mixing bowl and was eating it with a *soup* ladle. I don't think Ian was even home."

I smiled and shut my eyes for a moment. If Addie were a superhero, her power would be Ability to Make Your Best Friend Feel Normal. Those first dark weeks after the funeral, she'd been the one to get me out of the house on runs and insist I do things like eat and shower. She was the kind of friend you knew you couldn't possibly deserve.

"Hold up. Why are we wasting time talking about Ian's friends? I'm assuming you've met Howard."

I opened my eyes. "You mean my father?"

"I refuse to call him that. We didn't even know he was your father until like two months ago."

"Less," I said.

"Lina, you're killing me. What's he *like*?"

I glanced at my bedroom door. Music was still playing downstairs, but I lowered my voice anyway. "Let's just say I need to get out of here. Right away."

"What do you mean? Is he a creep?"

"No. He's actually kind of okay. And he's like NBA tall, which is surprising. But that's not the bad part." I took in a deep breath. She needed the full dramatic effect. "He's the caretaker of a cemetery. Which means I have to live in a cemetery."

"WHAT?"

I was ready for her outburst, holding the phone a good three inches from my ear.

"You have to live in a *cemetery*? Is he like a *gravedigger or something*?" She whispered the last part.

"I don't think they do burials here anymore. All the graves are from World War II."

"Like that's any better! Lina, we have to get you out of there. It isn't fair. First you lose your mom, and then you have to move halfway across the world to live with some guy who suddenly claims to be your father? And he lives in a *cemetery*? Come on, that's too much."

I sat down at the desk, scooting the chair around until my back was to the window. "Believe me, if I'd had any idea of what I was getting into, I would have pushed back even harder. This place is *weird*. There are headstones all over the place, and it feels like we're really far from civilization. I saw some houses on the road coming in, but besides that it looks like there's just forest surrounding the cemetery."

"Shut up. I'm coming to get you. How much does a plane ticket cost? More than three hundred dollars? Because that's all I have after our little run-in with the fire hydrant."

"You didn't even hit it that hard!"

"Tell that to the mechanic. Apparently the whole bumper had to be replaced. And I blame it on you entirely. If you hadn't been jamming out, I probably wouldn't have had to join in."

I grinned, pulling up my feet to sit cross-legged. "It is *so* not my fault that you can't control yourself when old-school Britney Spears comes on the radio. But do you need help paying for it? My grandparents are in charge of my finances, but I get a monthly allowance."

"No, of course not. You're going to need your money to get home from Italy. And I really do think my parents will be on board with you living here again. My mom thinks you're a good influence. It took her like a month to get over the fact that you put your dishes in the dishwasher."

"Well, I *am* pretty remarkable."

"Tell me about it. Okay, I'll talk to them soon. I just have to wait until my mom chills out. She's in charge of this big football fund-raiser for Ian, and you'd think she was throwing a debutante ball. Seriously, she is stressing out *way* too much. She totally lost it last night when none of us ate her noodle casserole."

"I like her noodle casserole. The one with tuna, right?"

"Ew, you do not like it. You were probably just starving because you'd gone on a nine-hundred-mile run. Also, you eat everything."

"True," I admitted. "But, Addie, remember, it's my grandma we need to worry about convincing. She's super on board with me living here."

"Which makes absolutely no sense. Why would she send you halfway across the world to be with a stranger? She doesn't even know him."

"I don't think she knew what else to do. On the drive to the airport she told me she's thinking about moving with my grandpa into an assisted care center. Taking care of him is getting to be too much."

"Which is why you should live with *us*." She exhaled. "Don't worry. You just leave Grandma Rachelle to me. I'll take her out to buy some of those butterscotch candies all old people love, and we'll talk about why the Bennett house is your best option."

"Thanks, Addie." We both stopped talking, and the sound of insects and Howard's music filled the brief silence between us. I wanted to crawl right through the phone back to Seattle. How was I going to survive without Addie?

"Why are you being so quiet? Is Gravedigger there?"

"I'm in my bedroom, but I get the feeling that sound travels in this house. I don't know if he can hear me or not."

"Great. So you can't even speak freely. We'd better come up with a code word so I know if you're okay. Say 'bluebird' if you're being held hostage."

"'Bluebird'? Isn't it supposed to be a word that doesn't sound out of the ordinary?"

"Crap. Now I'm confused. You said the word, but I don't know if you meant it. Are you or are you not being held hostage?"

"No, Addie. I'm not being held hostage." I sighed. "Except maybe to the promise I made to my mom."

"Yeah, but do promises really count if you make them under false pretenses? No offense, but your mom wasn't exactly forthcoming about why she wanted you to go to Italy."

"I know." I breathed out. "I'm hoping there was some reason for that."

"Maybe."

I looked over my shoulder at the window. The moon was skimming the dark tree line, and if I hadn't known any better

I would have thought the view was crazy pretty. "I'd better go. I'm using his cell phone, and this is probably costing a fortune."

"Okay. Call me again as soon as you can. And seriously, don't worry. We'll have you out of there in no time."

"Thanks, Addie. Hopefully I can FaceTime you tomorrow."

"I'll be waiting by my computer. How do they say good-bye in Italy? 'Choo'? 'Chow'?"

"I have no idea."

"Liar. You're the one who's always talked about traveling the world."

"Hello and good-bye is '*ciao*.'"

"I knew it. *Ciao*, Lina."

"*Ciao*."

Our call disconnected and I set the phone on the desk, my throat tight. I missed her already.

"Lina?"

Howard! I practically tipped over in my chair. Had he been eavesdropping?

I scrambled to my feet, then opened the door a couple of inches. Howard was standing in the hallway holding a bunch of folded white towels that had been stacked up like a wedding cake.

"I hope I didn't interrupt you," he said quickly. "I just remembered I meant to give you these."

I studied his face, but it was as bland as whipped cream. Apparently being related meant nothing. I had no idea if he'd overheard my conversation with Addie.

I hesitated for a second, then opened the door wider and took the towels from him. "Thank you. And here's your phone." I grabbed it from the desk, then handed it to him.

"So . . . what do you think?"

I flushed. "About . . . ?"

"About your room."

"Oh. It's great. Really pretty."

A big, relieved grin spread across his face. It was definitely the first genuine one of the night, and he looked about a hundred pounds lighter. Also, his smile was kind of lopsided.

"Good." He leaned against the door frame. "I know I don't have the best taste, but I wanted it to be nice. A friend helped me paint the desk and dresser, and Sonia and I found the mirror at a flea market."

Ugh. Now I had the image of him traipsing around Italy looking for stuff he thought I'd like. Why the sudden interest? As far as I knew, he'd never even sent me a birthday card.

"You didn't have to go to all that trouble," I said.

"It wasn't any trouble. Really."

He smiled again, and there was a long uncomfortable pause. The whole night had felt like being on a blind date with someone I had nothing in common with. No, it was worse. Because we *did* have something in common. We just weren't talking about it. *When are we going to talk about it?*

Hopefully never.

Howard bobbed his head. "Well, good night, Lina."

"Good night."

His footsteps faded down the hall and I shut and locked the door again. My nineteen hours of travel had worked its way to the center of my forehead, and I had an insane headache. Time for this day to be over.

I put the towels on my dresser, then kicked off my shoes and took a flying leap onto the bed, sending sprays of decorative pillows in every direction. *Finally.* The bed was as soft as it looked and the sheets smelled awesome, like when my mom had sometimes hung ours on the line to dry. I wriggled under the covers and switched off the lamp.

Loud laughter erupted from downstairs. The music was still at full blast, and either they were doing the dishes or playing a loud round of indoor croquet, but who cared? After the day I'd had, I could fall asleep anywhere.

I had just drifted into that murky half-sleep phase when Howard's voice brought me back to consciousness.

"She's really quiet."

My eyes snapped open.

"I don't think that's surprising, considering the scenario," Sonia answered.

I didn't move a muscle. Apparently Howard didn't think sound traveled through open windows.

He lowered his voice. "Of course. It was just kind of a surprise. Hadley was so . . ."

"Lively? She really was. But Lina might surprise you. I wouldn't be a bit surprised if she turned out to have some of her mother's oomph."

He laughed quietly. "'Oomph.' That's one way to put it."

"Give her a little time."

"Of course. Thanks again for dinner—it was delicious."

"My pleasure. I'm planning on posting up at the visitors' center tomorrow morning. Will you be in the office?"

"In and out. I'd like to be off early so I can take Lina into town."

"Sounds good. Night, boss." Sonia's footsteps crunched down the gravel driveway and a moment later the front door opened and then closed again.

I forced my eyes shut, but it was like I had soda pop running through my veins. What had Howard expected? That I'd be overjoyed about moving in with someone I'd never met? That I'd be superexcited about living in a cemetery? It's not like it was a big secret that I hadn't wanted to come here. I'd agreed only when my grandma had pulled out the big guns: *You promised your mom.*

And why did he have to call me "quiet"? I *hated* being

called quiet. People always said it like it was some kind of deficiency—like just because I didn't put everything out there right away, I was unfriendly or arrogant. My mom had understood. *You may be slow to warm up, but once you do, you light up the whole room.*

Tears flooded my eyes and I rolled over, pressing my face into my pillow. Now that it had been more than six months, I could sometimes go whole hours pretending to be okay without her. But it never lasted long. Turns out reality is as hard and unforgiving as that fire hydrant Addie and I had run into.

And I had to live the whole rest of my life without her. I really did.

Chapter 3

"LOOK, THAT WINDOW'S OPEN. SOMEONE MUST BE HERE."

The voice was practically in my ear and I sat bolt upright. Where was I? Oh. Right. In a cemetery. Only now it was saturated with sunlight, and my bedroom was 890 degrees. Give or take a hundred.

"Wouldn't you think they'd have signs telling you where to go?" It was a woman's voice, her accent as tangy as barbeque sauce.

A man answered. "Gloria, this looks like a private residence. I don't think we should be poking around—"

"Yoo-hoo! Hello? Anyone home?"

I pushed off my covers and got out of bed, tripping over a smattering of decorative pillows. I was still fully dressed. I'd been so tired that pajamas hadn't even crossed my mind.

"Hell-ooo," the woman trilled again. "Anyone there?"

I gathered my hair into a bun so I wouldn't scare anyone, then went over to the window to see two people who matched their voices *exactly*. The woman had fire-engine-red hair and wore high-waisted shorts, and the man wore a fishing hat and had a massive camera around his neck. They were even wearing fanny packs. I stifled a giggle. Addie and I had once won a costume contest dressed as Tacky Tourists. These two could have been our inspiration.

"Hell-o," Real-Life Tacky Tourist said slowly. She pointed at me. "Do you speak-a the English?"

"I'm American too."

"Thank the heavens! We were just looking for Howard Mercer, the superintendent? Where can we find him?"

"I don't know. I'm . . . new here." The view caught my eye and I looked up. The trees outside my window were a rich, velvety green and the sky was maybe bluer than I'd ever seen. But I was still in a cemetery. I repeat: Still. In. A. Cemetery.

Tacky Tourist looked at the man, then back up at me, settling her weight into one hip like *You can't get rid of me that easily.*

"I'll check to see if he's in the house."

"Now you're talking," she said. "We'll be around front."

I unzipped my suitcase and changed into a tank top and running shorts, then found my shoes and headed downstairs. The main floor was pretty small and, besides Howard's bedroom, the only room I hadn't seen yet was the study. I knocked just in case, then pushed my way inside. The walls were lined with framed Beatles albums and photographs, and I stopped to look at a picture of Howard and a few other people throwing buckets of water on a huge, gorgeous elephant. Howard was wearing cargo pants and a safari hat and looked like the star of some kind of adventure nature show. *Howard Bathes Wild Animals.* He obviously hadn't spent the past sixteen years sitting around missing my mom and me.

"Sorry, Tacky Tourists. No sign of Howard." I headed for the front, all ready to tell The Tackys I couldn't help them, but when I walked into the living room I jumped like I'd stepped on a live wire. The woman was not only waiting for me out front, but she'd pressed her face up against the window and was peering in at me like an enormous bug.

Over here. Over here! she mouthed, pointing to the front door.

"You've got to be joking me." I put my hand to my chest. My heart was going like a million beats per minute. You'd think life in a cemetery would be a lot more . . . dead. *Ba dum tss!* My first official cemetery joke. And first official eye rolling at own cemetery joke.

I pushed the door open and the woman trundled back a couple of inches.

"Sorry, darling. Did I startle you? You looked like your eyes were going to bug out of your head." She was wearing one of those stick-on name tags. HELLO, MY NAME IS GLORIA.

"I didn't expect you to be . . . looking in." I shook my

head. "I'm sorry, but Howard's not here. He said something about having an office; maybe you could go look for him there?"

Gloria nodded. "Uh-huh. Uh-huh. Well, here's the problem, doll. We only have three hours before the tour bus comes back for us, and we want to be sure we see everything. I just don't think we have the time to be traipsing all over looking for Mr. Mercer."

"Did you see the visitors' center? There's a woman who works there who might know where he is."

"I told you we should try that," the man said. "This is a *home.*"

"Which one's the visitors' center?" Gloria asked. "Was it that building near the entrance?"

"I'm sorry, I really don't know." Probably because the night before I'd been way too panicked to notice anything but the army of headstones staring me down.

She raised an eyebrow. "Well, I hate to inconvenience you, *darlin'*, but I'm sure you know this place better than a couple of tourists from Alabama."

"Actually, I don't."

"What?"

I sighed, casting one more hopeful glance back into the house, but it was as quiet as a tomb. (*Ack!* Second cemetery joke.) Guess I was going to have to jump headfirst into this whole living-in-a-memorial thing. I stepped out onto the porch and pulled the door shut behind me. "I don't really know my way around, but I'll try to help."

Gloria smiled beatifically. "Grah-zee-aye."

I walked down the stairs, the two of them following after me.

"They sure do keep this place up nice," Gloria observed. "Real nice."

She was right. The lawns were so green they looked spray-painted, and practically every corner had a grouping of Italian and American flags surrounded by patches of *Wizard of Oz*–worthy flowers. The headstones were white and sparkly and didn't look nearly as creepy in the daylight. But don't get me wrong. They were still creepy.

"Let's go this way." I marched toward the road Howard and I had driven in on.

Gloria nudged me with her elbow. "My husband and I met on a cruise."

Oh, no. Was she going to tell me their life story? I slid a quick glance at Gloria and she smiled engagingly. Of course she was.

"He'd just lost his wife, Anna Maria. She was a nice lady, but real particular about how she kept house—one of those who puts plastic on all the furniture? Anyway, my husband, Clint, had passed a few years earlier, so that's why we were both there on the singles cruise. They had great food—just mountains of shrimp and all the ice cream you could eat. You remember that shrimp, Hank?"

Hank didn't appear to be listening. I sped up and Gloria did too.

"There were a bunch of horny old dogs on that boat, just nasty things, but lucky for me, Hank and I were assigned the same table for dinner. He proposed before the ship had even docked—that's how sure he was. We got married just two months later. Of course, I'd already moved in, but we really rushed things because we didn't want to be, you know . . ." She paused, looking at me meaningfully.

"What?" I asked hesitantly.

Her voice fell an octave. "Living in sin."

I looked desperately around the cemetery. I either needed to find Howard or someplace to vomit. Maybe both.

"First order of business was ripping all the plastic off that furniture. A person's got to live without their buttocks sticking to the darn sofa. Right, Hank?"

He made a guttural noise.

"This is sort of like a second honeymoon for us. I've wanted to visit Italy my whole life, and now here I am. You sure are a lucky duck, living here."

Quack, quack, I thought.

The road curved and a small building appeared just ahead of us. It was right next to the main entrance and had a giant sign that said, VISITORS CHECK IN HERE. Easy to confuse with VISITORS, FIND THE NEAREST HOUSE AND THEN YELL THROUGH THE WINDOWS.

"I think this is it," I said.

"Told you," Hank said to Gloria, breaking his silence.

"You didn't tell me anything." Gloria sniffed. "You just followed me around like a lost puppy dog."

I practically ran for the building's entrance, but before I could reach for the handle, the door swung open and Howard stepped out. He was wearing shorts and flip-flops, like he planned to catch a flight to Tahiti later.

"Lina. I didn't think you'd be awake yet."

"These two came looking for you at the house."

Gloria stepped forward. "Mr. Mercer? We're the Jorgansens from Mobile, Alabama. You probably remember my e-mail? We're the ones who wanted a private, *special* tour of the ceme- tery? You see, my husband, Hank, has a real love for World War II history. Tell them, Hank."

"A real love," Hank said.

Howard nodded thoughtfully, but the corners of his mouth twitched. "Well, there's just the one tour, but I'm sure Sonia would be happy to take you. Why don't you two head inside and she'll get you started."

Gloria clapped her hands. "Mr. Mercer, I can hear you're a Southerner yourself. Where are you from? Tennessee?"

"South Carolina."

"That's what I meant. South Carolina. And who is this lovely young woman who came to our aid? Your daughter?"

He paused for a nanosecond. Just long enough for me to notice. "Yes. This is Lina."

And we just met last night.

Gloria shook her head. "Glory be. I don't think I've ever seen a daddy and his daughter look quite so different. But sometimes it's like that. I got this red hair from my great-aunt on my mother's side. Sometimes the genes just skip a few generations."

We both looked at her skeptically. There was absolutely no way Gloria's red hair had come from anywhere but a box, but you had to admire her commitment.

She squinted at me, then turned to Howard. "Is your wife Italian?" She pronounced it "Eye-Talian."

"Lina's mother is American. She looks a lot like her."

I shot him a grateful look. Present tense keeps things a lot less complicated. But then I remembered his and Sonia's conversation on the porch, and I turned away, sucking my grateful look right back into my eyeballs.

Gloria put her hands on her hips. "Well, Lina, you just fit right in here, don't you? Look at those dark eyes and all that gorgeous hair. I'll bet everyone thinks you're a local."

"I'm not a local. I'm just visiting."

Hank finally found his voice. "Gloria, let's shake a leg. If we keep chatting like this, we're going to miss the whole dang-blasted cemetery."

"All right, all *right*. No need for strong language. Come on, Hank." She gave us a conspiratorial look, like her husband was a little brother we were all being forced to hang out with, and then she opened the door. "You two have a good day now. A-river-dur-chee!"

"Wow," Howard said when the door had closed behind them.

"Yeah." I folded my arms.

"Sorry about that. People don't usually go to the house. And they're usually a little less . . ." He paused, like he thought he could come up with a polite word to describe the Jorgansens. Finally he just shook his head. "Looks like you're headed out for a run."

I looked down at what I was wearing. It was such a habit to get dressed this way I hadn't even thought about it. "I usually go first thing."

"Like I said, you're welcome to run through the cemetery, but if you want to get out and explore, just head out those front gates. There's only one road, so you shouldn't get lost."

The visitors' center door opened again and Gloria poked her head out. "Mr. Mercer? This *woman* in here says the tour only lasts thirty minutes. I specifically requested two hours or longer."

"I'll be right in." He glanced at me. "Enjoy your run."

As he walked away I impulsively stepped forward so I could see both our reflections in the glass door. Gloria may be ridiculous, but she hadn't been afraid to point out the obvious. Howard was well over six feet tall with strawberry blond hair and blue eyes. I had dark features and had to buy all my clothes in the petites section. But sometimes genes just skip a few generations.

Right?

I jogged out the front gates of the cemetery and crossed through the visitors' parking lot. Right or left? I guess it didn't matter. I just needed to get away from the cemetery for a while. *Left. No, right.*

The road that ran past the memorial was only two lanes, and I stuck to the strip of grass along the side, picking up my pace until I was almost at a sprint. I could usually outrun disturbing thoughts, but this one was pretty hard to shake. *Why don't I look anything like Howard?*

It was probably just one of those things—I mean, lots of people look nothing like their parents. Addie was the token blonde of her family, and there was this guy I'd grown up with who was taller than both his parents by the sixth grade. But still. Shouldn't Howard and I look at least a *little* bit alike?

I kept my eyes glued to the ground. *You'll adjust in no time. He's really a nice man.* That from my grandmother, who as far as I knew had never even met Howard. At least not in person.

An enormous blue bus went whooshing past, sending a blast of hot air into my face, and when I looked up, I gasped. *What the . . . ?* Was I running through a scene from an Olive Garden menu? It was so *idyllic*. The road was lined with trees and curved gently past rustic-looking houses and buildings painted in soft, buttery colors. Patchwork hills stretched out into the distance and there were honest-to-goodness vineyards behind half the houses. So *this* was the Italy people were always talking about. No wonder people were always losing their minds over it.

Another vehicle came roaring up behind me, honking loudly and jolting me from my Italian moment. I sprang away from the road and turned to look back. It was a small red car that looked like it was really, really trying to come across as more expensive than it was and as it neared me it slowed down. The driver and his passenger both had dark hair and were in their early twenties. When we made eye contact, the driver grinned and started honking again.

"Calm *down*. It's not like I'm in your way," I said under my breath. The driver slammed on his brakes, like he'd somehow managed to hear me, then came to a stop right in the middle of the road. Another guy, maybe a year or two older, rolled down the window of the backseat, a big grin on his face.

"*Ciao, bella! Cosa fai stasera?*"

I shook my head and started running again, but the driver just pulled ahead a few yards, coming to a stop on my side of the road.

Great. After four years of running I knew all about this breed of guy. I don't know who told them that "out running alone" was code for "please pick me up," but I'd learned that telling them you weren't interested wasn't enough. They just thought you were playing hard to get.

I crossed to the other side of the road and turned toward the cemetery, taking a second to tighten my shoelaces. Then I inhaled deeply, hearing an imaginary starting pistol in my mind. *Go!*

There was a shout of surprise from the car. "*Dove vai?*"

I didn't even look back. If properly motivated I could pretty much outrun anyone—even Italian men in cheap red cars. I'd scale a fence if I had to.

By the time I got back to the cemetery the guys had passed me twice more and then given up, and I'm pretty sure even my eyelids were sweating. Howard and Sonia were standing with their backs to the gate, but they both turned quickly when they heard me. Probably because I sounded like an asthmatic werewolf.

"You weren't gone long. Are you okay?" Howard asked.

"I . . . got . . . chased."

"By who?"

"A car . . . full of guys."

"They were probably just smitten," Sonia said.

"Wait a minute. A car full of guys *chased* you? What did they look like?" His jaw tightened and he looked toward the road like he was considering charging out there with a baseball bat or something.

It kind of made up for the *She's so quiet* comment.

I shook my head, finally catching my breath. "It wasn't really a big deal. I'll just stay inside the cemetery next time."

"Or you could run behind the cemetery," Sonia said. "There's a gate that leads out behind the grounds. Those hills would probably give you a great workout, and it's beautiful back there. And there'd be no cars to chase you."

Howard still had steam curling out of his nostrils, so I changed the subject. "Where are the Jorgansens?"

Sonia grinned. "There was a bit of a . . . conflict. They opted for the self-guided tour." She pointed across the cemetery to where Gloria was marching Hank past a row of headstones. "Your dad was just telling me he wants to take you into Florence for dinner tonight."

Howard nodded, his face finally decompressing. "I was thinking we could walk around the Duomo and then get some pizza."

Was I supposed to know what that was? I shifted from one foot to the other. If I said yes, I'd be agreeing to what was sure to be an awkward dinner alone with Howard. But if I said no, I'd probably be stuck here in the exact same scenario. At least this way I'd get to see the city. And the Duomo. Whatever that was. "All right."

"Great." His voice was enthusiastic, like I'd just told him I really *really* wanted to go. "It will give us a chance to talk. About things."

I stiffened. Shouldn't I be allowed some sort of grace period before I had to deal with whatever big explanation Howard had in store for me? Just being here was already putting me into overload.

I turned to wipe the sweat off my forehead, hoping they wouldn't see how upset I was. "I'm going back to the house."

I started to walk away, but Sonia hurried after me. "Would you mind stopping by my place on your way? I have something that belonged to your mother, and I'd really love to give it to you."

I stepped sideways, putting an extra six inches between us. "Sorry, but I really need to take a shower. Maybe some other time?"

"Oh." The space between her eyebrows creased. "Sure. Just let me know when you have a minute. Actually, I could just—"

"Thanks a lot. See you around."

I broke into a jog, Sonia's gaze heavy on my back. I didn't want to be rude, but I also *really* didn't want whatever it was she had for me. People were always giving me things that belonged to my mother—especially photographs—and I never knew what to do with them. They were like souvenirs of my previous life.

I looked out over the cemetery and sighed. It's not like I needed any more reminders that things had changed.

Chapter 4

AS SOON AS I GOT INSIDE I HEADED STRAIGHT FOR THE kitchen. I had a feeling that if asked, Howard would give the standard *mi casa, su casa* speech—probably with Italian pronunciation—so I skipped the asking and went straight to raiding the fridge.

The top two shelves of the refrigerator were packed with things like olives and gourmet mustards—stuff that makes food taste good, but isn't actually food—so I rifled through the drawers, finally coming up with a carton of what looked like coconut yogurt and a thick loaf of bread. I was pretty much devastated to not find any lasagna leftovers.

After devouring half the bread and practically licking the bottom of the yogurt carton (hands down the best yogurt I've ever had), I looked through the cupboards until I found a box of granola that said CIOCCOLATO. Jackpot. Chocolate spoke to me in any language.

I ate a huge bowl of the granola, then cleaned the kitchen

like a crime scene. *Now what?* Well, if I were still in Seattle I would probably be getting ready to go to the pool with Addie or maybe pulling my bike out of the garage and demanding we go get one of those triple chocolate shakes I pretty much lived on. But here? I didn't even have the Internet.

"Shower," I said aloud. Something to do. And besides, I really needed one.

I went upstairs and grabbed the stack of towels from my bedroom, then went into the bathroom. It was incredibly clean, like maybe Howard scrubbed it every week with bleach. Maybe that was the reason he and my mom hadn't worked out. She'd been unbelievably messy. Like once I'd found a Tupperware of pasta on her desk that had been sitting so long it had turned blue. *Blue.*

I pulled back the shower curtain but had no idea what to do next. The showerhead was tiny and flimsy-looking and underneath it were two nozzles that read C and F.

"Cold and frigid? Chilly and frosty?"

I turned on the F and let it run for a few seconds, but when I put my hand under the stream it was still ice-cold. *Okay. So maybe C?*

Exact same results, maybe half a degree warmer. I groaned. Were freezing showers part of what Howard had meant when he'd said Italy wasn't on the cutting edge of technology? And what choice did I have? I'd traveled for a full day and then done

one of the hardest speed workouts of my life. I *had* to shower.

"When in Rome." I gritted my teeth and jumped in. "Cold! Cold! Ahh!"

I grabbed a bottle of something off the edge of the tub and rubbed it over my hair and body, rinsing and jumping out of there as fast as I could. Then I grabbed the entire stack of towels and started wrapping myself up like a mummy.

There was a knock on the door and I froze. Again. "Who is it?"

"It's me, Sonia. Are you . . . all right in there?"

I grimaced. "Um, yeah. Just having some water issues. Does this place not have hot water?"

"We do, it just takes a while. At my house I sometimes have to let the water run for a good ten minutes before its ready. C stands for '*caldo*.' It means 'hot.'"

I shook my head. "Good to know."

"Listen, I'm sorry to bother you again, but I just wanted to tell you that I left the journal on your bed."

I froze. The *journal*? Wait, I'd probably just misheard her. Maybe she'd said "the gerbil." A gerbil would be a totally thoughtful gift. And if I were giving someone a gerbil I would definitely put it—

"Lina . . . did you hear me? I brought you a journal that—"

"Just a minute," I said loudly. Okay, she'd definitely said "journal." But that didn't mean it was any journal in particular. People gave each other journals all the time. I quickly dried off and got dressed. When I opened the door Sonia was standing in the hallway holding a potted plant.

"You got me a *new* journal?" I asked hopefully.

"Well, an old one. It's a notebook that belonged to your mother."

I slumped against the doorway. "You mean like a big leather one with lots of writing and photographs?"

"Yes. That's exactly what it's like." Her forehead scrunched up. "Is it something you've already looked at?"

I ignored her question. "I thought you were just going to give me one of her photographs or something."

"I actually do have a photograph of hers, but it's hanging on the wall in my guest bedroom and I don't have any plans to part with it. It's a close-up of the Wall of the Missing. Quite a beautiful shot. You should come see it sometime."

Apparently the Wall of the Missing was a big deal around here. "Why do you have one of her journals?"

My voice came out kind of bad-cop-sounding, but she just bobbed her head. "She sent it to the cemetery back in September. There wasn't a note, and the package wasn't addressed to anyone, but when I opened it I recognized it right away. When she was living at the cemetery she carried that journal around everywhere."

Living at the cemetery?

"Anyway, I thought about giving it to your dad, but your mom had always been kind of a taboo subject. Whenever I brought her up, he got . . ."

"What?"

She sighed. "It was hard on him when she moved out. Really hard. And even after all these years, I was nervous about bringing her up. Anyway, I stalled for a couple of days, and then your dad told me about the plan for you to come stay here. That's when I realized why she'd sent the journal."

She gave me a funny look and suddenly I realized that I'd been slowly gravitating toward her. We were only like five inches apart. Oops. I sprang back, and questions started flying out of my mouth.

"My mom lived at the cemetery? For how long?"

"Not very long. Maybe a month or so? It was right after your dad got the job. He'd just barely moved into this house."

"So they were like, *together* together? It wasn't like a one-night stand between friends or something?" That was Addie's theory.

Sonia cringed. "Uh . . . no. I don't think it was . . . that. They seemed very in love. Your dad adored her."

"So then why did she leave? Was it because she was pregnant? Howard wasn't ready to be a dad?"

"No. Howard would have been a great dad—I thought . . ."

She put her hands up. "Wait a minute. Haven't they talked to you about what happened? Your mom didn't explain things?"

I dropped my head. "I don't know anything. I didn't even know Howard was my dad until after my mom died." Great. Now I was going to cry. Losing my mom had turned me into a human faucet. The regular hot/cold kind.

"Oh, Lina. I didn't know. I'm so sorry. I assumed they'd talked to you about what happened. To be honest, *I* don't even really know what went wrong. It seemed like their relationship ended pretty suddenly, and then your dad never wanted to discuss it."

"Did he ever talk about me? Before now?"

She shook her head, her long dangly earrings swinging back and forth. "No. I was pretty surprised when I heard about you coming to live here. But you really need to talk to Howard. I'm sure he'll answer all of your questions. And maybe the journal will too." She held the flower pot out to me. "I went into town early this morning and your dad asked me to pick these up for you. He said your room was missing flowers and that violets were your mother's favorite."

I took them from her and studied them suspiciously. The flowers were deep purple and had a subtle scent. I was ninety-nine percent sure my mom hadn't had any special feelings for violets.

"Would you rather I keep the journal for a while? It sounds like it's a lot to process. Maybe you should spend some time talking to your dad first."

I shook my head. Slowly at first, and then more forcefully. "No, I want it."

Technically a lie. I'd packed up the rest of her journals several months earlier when I'd finally given up on the idea that I'd ever be able to read them without falling apart. But I had to read this one. She'd sent it to me.

I blinked a couple of times, then put on my best *I'm in control now* smile for Sonia, who was looking at me with the expression of a hapless bystander trapped in a hallway by an emotionally unstable teenager. Which she was.

I cleared my throat. "It'll be nice. I can read about what she did while she was in Italy."

Her expression softened. "Yes, exactly. I'm sure that's why she sent it. You'll be experiencing Florence just like she did, and maybe it will be a nice connection."

"Yeah, maybe."

If I could make it past the first page without falling apart.

"Lina, it really is great having you here. And stop by anytime to see that photograph of your mother's." She walked to the top of the stairs and then looked back. "I meant to tell you, it's best to water violets from the bottom. Just fill up a saucer and set the whole pot in there. That way you won't overwater. They could probably use a drink right away."

"Thanks, Sonia. And I'm, uh . . . sorry for all those questions."

"I understand. And I really liked your mother. She was pretty special."

"Yeah. She was." I hesitated. "Would you mind not mentioning this conversation to Howard? I don't want him to think I'm . . . uh . . . mad at him or something." *Or instigate any awkward conversations that aren't strictly necessary.*

She nodded. "My lips are sealed. Just promise me you'll talk to him. He's a great guy, and I'm sure he'll answer any questions you have."

"Okay." I looked away and there were a long few seconds of silence.

"Have a nice day, Lina."

She went down the stairs and out the front door, but I just stood there staring at my bedroom door. It was practically glowing with urgency. Cue panic.

It's just one of her journals. You can do this. You can do this. I finally started making my way down the hall, but at the last minute veered toward the stairs, the violets teetering dangerously.

I had some seriously thirsty violets on my hands. Sonia had said so. I'd just take care of that first. I plummeted down the stairs, then looked through the cupboards twice before finding a shallow dish big enough for the flower pot.

"Here you go, buddy." I filled the dish with an inch of tap water (F) and set the pot inside. My violets didn't seem particularly interested in having company, but I sat down at the kitchen table and watched them anyway.

I wasn't stalling. Really.

Chapter 5

JOURNALING WAS KIND OF MY MOM'S THING. WELL, A LOT of things were kind of her thing. She also liked hot yoga and food trucks and really terrible reality TV shows, and once she'd gotten really into the idea of homemade beauty products and we'd basically spent a month with coconut oil and mashed avocado all over our faces.

But journaling . . . that was a constant. A couple of times a year she'd splurge on one of these thick artists' notebooks from our favorite bookstore in downtown Seattle, and then she'd spend months filling it with her life: photographs, diary entries, grocery lists, ideas for photo shoots, old ketchup packets . . . anything you could think of.

And here was the strange part: She let other people read them. And even stranger? People loved to. Maybe because they were creative and hilarious and after you read one you felt like you'd just taken a trip through Wonderland or something.

I walked into my bedroom and stood at the foot of my

bed. Sonia had left the journal right in the center of my pillow, like maybe she was worried I wouldn't notice it otherwise, and it was weighing down the bed like a pile of bricks.

"Ready?" I said aloud. I was definitely not ready, but I walked over and picked it up anyway. The cover was made of soft leather and had a big gold fleur-de-lis in its center. It didn't look anything like her journals back home.

I took a deep breath, then cracked open the cover, half expecting confetti to come shooting out at me, but all that happened was a bunch of brochures and ticket stubs fell out onto the floor and I got a whiff of something musty. I picked up all the papers, then started flipping through the pages, ignoring the writing and focusing on the photographs.

There was my mother standing in front of an old church with her camera slung over her shoulder. And there she was grinning over a gigantic bowl of pasta. And then . . . *Howard*. I practically dropped the book. Okay, of *course* he was in her journal. It's not like I'd appeared out of thin air, but still. My mind totally resisted the idea of the two of them together.

I studied the picture. Yep, it was definitely him. Younger, longer-haired (and was that a *tattoo* on his upper arm?), but definitely Howard. He and my mom were sitting on stone steps and she had short hair and Old Hollywood lipstick and this *I've been swept off my feet* kind of look.

I sat down on my bed with a *thud*. Why hadn't she just

told me her and Howard's story herself? Did she think that her journal would do a better job? Was she worried I wasn't ready to hear their story?

I hesitated for a moment, then shoved the journal in the drawer of my nightstand and shut it with a loud *slam*. Well, I wasn't ready.

Not yet.

A car alarm burst into full vibrato somewhere in the cemetery and the sound rained down on my head like a thousand tiny Glorias. *This headache brought to you by Jet Lag & Stress.* Thanks, Italy.

I rolled over and looked at the clock on the wall. Three p.m. Which left me with so much time to kill, it was ridiculous.

I slowly got out of bed, then went over to my suitcase and made a halfhearted attempt at organizing my things— shirts in the right-hand corner, pants in the left, pajamas over there. . . . I'd done a horrible job packing, and it was all basically a jumble. Finally I settled on putting a couple of pictures of my mom and me into my room's empty frames, then laced up my shoes and headed for the front porch.

I didn't have a plan of where to go, so I just sat on the porch swing and rocked for a while. I had a good view of the memorial. It was a long, low building with a stretch of engravings that I would bet money went by the name of Wall of the Missing. Out in front of it was a tall post with a statue of an angel holding an armful of olive branches. Two men stood taking pictures in front of it, and one of them noticed me and waved.

I waved back but jumped up and headed for the back fence. I really didn't have it in me to handle another Jorgansen situation.

The back gate was easy to find, and as I headed out I realized that Sonia hadn't been kidding—the hill behind the cemetery was *steep*. For the second time that day, sweat dripped down my back, but I forced myself to keep running. *I* will *conquer you, hill*. Finally I reached the top, my legs and lungs on fire. I was just about to keel over when a *thud-thud* noise made my neck snap up. I wasn't alone.

There was a boy playing with a soccer ball. He was my age, maybe a little older, and he was at least three months overdue for a haircut. He wore shorts and a soccer jersey and was juggling the soccer ball back and forth from knee to knee, singing quietly in Italian to whatever was playing on his headphones. I hesitated. Could I sneak away without him noticing me? Maybe a tuck-and-roll-type escape?

He looked up at me and we made eye contact. *Great*. Now I had to keep going or look like a weirdo. I nodded at him and walked quickly along the path, like I was late to a meeting or something. Totally natural. People were probably always hurrying off to important meetings on the top of Italian hills.

He pulled off his headphones, his music blaring. "Hey, are you lost? The Bella Vita hostel is just down the road."

I stopped. "You speak English."

"Just a little bit-a," he said with an exaggerated Italian accent.

"Are you American?"

"Sort of."

I studied him. He sounded American, but he looked about as Italian as a plate of meatballs. Medium height, olive skin, and a distinct nose. What was he doing here? But then again, what was *I* doing here? For all I knew, the Tuscan countryside was crawling with displaced American teenagers.

He crossed his arms and scowled. He was imitating me. Rude.

I dropped my stance. "What do you mean by 'sort of American'?"

"My mom's American, but I've lived here most of my life. Where are you from?"

"Seattle. But I'm living here for the summer."

"Really? Where?"

I pointed in the direction I'd come from.

"The cemetery?"

"Yeah. Howard—my dad—is the caretaker. I just got here."

He raised an eyebrow. "Spooky."

"Not really. It's more of a memorial. All the graves are from World War II, so it's not like there are burials going on." Why was I defending the cemetery? It *was* spooky.

He nodded, then put his headphones back on.

Guess that was my cue.

"Great to meet you, mysterious Italian-American. Guess I'll see you around."

"I'm Lorenzo."

I blushed. Apparently Lorenzo had sonic hearing. "Nice to meet you, Lo-ren—" I tried to repeat his name but got stuck on the second syllable. He'd made this rolling sound with the *R* that my tongue refused to do.

"Sorry, I can't say it right."

"That's okay. I go by 'Ren' anyway." He grinned. "Or 'mysterious Italian-American,' that works too."

Argh. "Sorry about that."

"What about you? Do you go by 'Carolina,' or do you have a nickname too?"

For a second I felt like I was in a dream. A weird one. No one but my mother or teachers on the first day of school ever called me by my full name. "How do you know my name?" I said slowly. Who *was* this guy?

"I go to AISF. Your dad came in to ask about enrollment. Word spread."

"What's AISF?"

"The American International School of Florence."

I exhaled. "Oh, right. The high school." The school I'd theoretically attend if I decided to stay longer than just the summer. *So* theoretical. Like not even in the realm of possibility.

"It's actually kindergarten through high school, and our classes are really small. There were only eighteen of us last year, so new students are a big deal. We've been talking about you since January. You're kind of a legend. One guy, Marco, even claimed you as his biology partner. He totally bombed his final project and he kept trying to blame it on you."

"That's really weird."

"You don't look anything like I thought you would."

"Why?"

"You're really short. And you look Italian."

"Then how'd you know to speak to me in English?"

"Your clothes."

I looked down. Leggings and a yellow T-shirt. It's not like I was dressed as the Statue of Liberty or something. "What's so American about my outfit?"

"Bright colors. Running shoes . . ." He waved his hand dismissively. "Give it a month or two; you'll totally get it. A lot of people here won't go anywhere unless they're wearing something Gucci."

"But you're not wearing Gucci or whatever, right? You're in soccer clothes."

He shook his head. "Soccer clothes are exempt. They're about as Italian as they get. Plus, I *am* Italian. So everything naturally looks stylish on me."

I couldn't tell if he was joking or not.

"Weren't you supposed to transfer to AISF in February?" he asked.

"I decided to finish out the school year in Seattle."

He took his phone out of his back pocket. "Can I take a picture of you?"

"Why?"

"Proof that you exist."

I said "no" at the exact moment he took the picture.

"Sorry about that, Carolina," he said, sounding very unsorry. "You should really speak up."

"You're saying my name wrong. It looks like 'Carolina,' but it sounds like 'Caro*leen*a.' And I go by 'Lina.'"

"Carolina Caroleena. I like it. Very Italian-sounding."

He put his headphones back on, then tossed his ball in the air and started playing again. Ren definitely needed some etiquette classes or something. I turned to walk away, but he stopped me again.

"Hey, do you want to come meet my mom? She's basically starving for American company."

"No thanks. I have to get back soon to meet up with Howard. He's taking me into Florence for dinner."

"What time?"

"I don't know."

"Most restaurants don't even open until seven. I promise we won't be gone that long."

I turned back toward the cemetery, but the thought of facing Howard or the journal again made me shudder. "Is it far?"

"No, just right over there." He pointed vaguely at a grouping of trees. "It will be fine. And I promise I'm not a serial killer or anything."

I grimaced. "I didn't think you were. Until now."

"I'm way too scrawny to be a serial killer. Also, I hate blood."

"Ew." I looked back at the cemetery again, mentally weighing my options. Emotionally challenging journal? Or visit with a socially inept potential serial killer's mother? Either option was pretty grim.

"Okay, I'll come with you," I relented.

"Nice." He tucked his soccer ball under his arm and we headed for the other side of the hill. He was only about a head taller than me and we both walked quickly.

"So when did you get here again?"

"Last night."

"So you're pretty much jet-lagged within an inch of your life right now, right?"

"I actually slept okay last night. But yeah. I kind of feel

like I'm underwater. And I have maybe the worst headache of my life."

"Wait until tonight. The second night is always the worst. Around three a.m. you're going to be wide-awake and you'll have to think of weird stuff to keep yourself occupied. Once I climbed a tree."

"Why?"

"My laptop was out of commission and the only other thing I could come up with was playing Solitaire and I suck at that."

"I'm really good at Solitaire."

"And I'm really good at climbing trees. But I don't believe you. No one is good at Solitaire unless they cheat."

"No, I really am. People stopped playing games with me when I was in like second grade, so I taught myself how to play Solitaire. On a good day I can finish a game in like six minutes."

"Why did people stop playing games with you when you were in second grade?"

"Because I always win."

He stopped walking, a big grin on his face. "You mean because you're really competitive?"

"I didn't say that. I just said I always win."

"Uh-huh. So you haven't played a game since you were like seven?"

"Just Solitaire."

"No Go Fish? Uno? Poker?"

"Nothing."

"Interesting. Look, that's my house. Race you to the gate."
He broke into a run.

"Hey!" I took off after him, lengthening my stride until I
caught up and then passed him, and I didn't slow down until
I hit the gate. I whirled around triumphantly. "Beat you!"

He was standing a few yards back, that stupid grin still on
his face. "You're right. You're totally not competitive."

I scowled. "Shut up."

"We should play Go Fish later."

"No."

"Mah-jongg? Bridge?"

"What are you, an old lady?"

He laughed. "Whatever you say, Carolina. And by the
way, that isn't really my house. It's that one over there." He
pointed to a driveway in the distance. "But I'm not racing you
there. Because you're right—you'd win."

"Told you."

We kept walking. Only now I just felt stupid.

"So what's the deal with your dad?" Ren asked. "Hasn't he
been the caretaker at the cemetery for like forever?"

"Yeah, he said it's been seventeen years. My mom died, so
that's why I came to live with him." *Ah!* I mentally clamped

my hand over my mouth. *Lina, stop talking*. Bringing up my mom was a surefire way to create awkwardness around people my age. Adults got sympathetic. Teenagers got uncomfortable.

He looked at me, his hair falling into his eyes. "How'd she die?"

"Pancreatic cancer."

"Did she have it for a long time?"

"No. She died four months after we found out."

"Wow. Sorry."

"Thanks."

We were quiet for a moment before Ren spoke again. "It's weird how we talk about that. I say 'I'm sorry' and you say 'thanks.'"

I'd had that exact thought maybe a hundred times. "I think it's weird too. But it's what people expect you to say."

"So what's it like?"

"What?"

"Losing your mom."

I stopped walking. Not only was this the first time anyone had ever asked me that, but he was looking at me like he actually wanted to know. For a second I thought about telling him that it was like being an island—that I could be in a room full of people and still feel alone, an ocean of hurt trying to crash in on me from every direction. But I swallowed the words back as quickly as I could. Even when they ask, people don't want to hear your weird grief metaphors. Finally I shrugged my shoulders. "It really sucks."

"I bet it does. Sorry."

"Thanks." I smiled. "Hey, we just did it again."

"Sorry."

"Thanks."

He stopped in front of a set of curlicue gates and I help him push them open with a loud *creak*.

"You weren't kidding. Your house is close to the cemetery," I said.

"I know. I always thought it was weird that I live so close to a cemetery. And then I met someone who lives *in* a cemetery."

"I couldn't let you beat me. It's my competitive nature."

He laughed. "Come on."

We walked up the narrow, tree-lined driveway, and when we got to the top he held both arms out in front of him. "Ta-da. *Casa mia*."

I stopped walking. "This is where you *live*?"

He shook his head grimly. "Unfortunately. You can laugh if you want. I won't be offended."

"I'm not going to laugh. I think it's kind of…interesting." But then a tiny snort slipped through and the look Ren shot me pretty much blew my composure to pieces.

"Go ahead. Get it all out. But people who live in cemeteries really shouldn't be throwing stones, or whatever that saying is."

Finally I stopped laughing long enough to catch my breath. "I'm sorry. I shouldn't be laughing. It's just really unexpected."

We both looked back up at the house, and Ren sighed wearily while I did my best not to insult him again. Just this morning I'd thought I lived in the weirdest place possible, but now I'd met someone who lived in a *gingerbread house*. And I don't mean a house sort of loosely inspired by a gingerbread house—I mean a house that looked like you could possibly break off a couple of its shingles and dip them in a glass of milk. It was two stories high with a stone exterior and thatched roof lined with intricate gingerbread trim. Candy-colored flowers blanketed the yard, and small lemon trees were planted in cobalt-blue pots around the perimeter of the house. Most of the main-floor windows were stained glass with swirling peppermint patterns, and there was a giant candy cane carved into the front door. In other words, picture the most ridiculous house you can imagine and then add a bunch of lollipops.

"What's the story?"

Ren shook his head again. "There has to be one, right? This eccentric guy from upstate New York built it after making a fortune on his grandmother's fudge recipe. He called himself the Candy Baron."

"So he built himself a real-life gingerbread house?"

"Exactly. It was a present for his new wife. I guess she was like thirty years younger than him, and she ended up falling for a guy she met at a truffle festival in Piedmont. After she left him, he sold the house. My parents just happened to be looking, and of course a gingerbread house was just the right kind of weird for them."

"Did you guys have to kick out a cannibalistic witch?"

He gave me a funny look.

"You know . . . like the witch in Hansel and Gretel?"

"Oh." He laughed. "No, she still comes to visit on major holidays. You meant my grandmother, right?"

"I'm so telling her you said that."

"Good luck. She doesn't understand a single word of English. And whenever she's around, my mom conveniently forgets how to speak Italian."

"Where's your mom from?"

"Texas. We usually spend summers in the States with her family, but my dad had too much work for us to go this year."

"So that's why you sound so American?"

"Yep. I pretend to be one every summer."

"Does it work?"

He grinned. "Usually. You thought I was American, didn't you?"

"Not until you talked."

"That's what counts, though, right?"

"I guess so."

He led me to the front door and we walked inside. "Welcome to Villa Caramella. '*Caramella*' means 'candy.'"

"Holy . . . books."

It was like a librarian's worst nightmare. The entire room was lined with floor to ceiling bookcases, and hundreds—maybe thousands—of books were mashed haphazardly into the shelves.

"My parents are big readers," Ren said. "Also, we want to be prepared if there's ever a robot uprising and we need to hide out. Lots of books equals lots of kindling."

"Smart."

"Come on, she's probably in her studio." We made our way through the piles of books to a set of double doors that opened to a sunroom. The floor was shrouded in drop cloths and there was an ancient-looking table holding tubes of paint and a bunch of different ceramic tiles.

"Mom?"

A female version of Ren lay curled up on a daybed, yellow paint streaked through her hair. She looked about twenty years old. Maybe thirty.

"Mom." Ren reached down and shook her shoulder. "*Mamma*. She's kind of a deep sleeper, but watch this." Bending close to her face, he whispered, "I just saw Bono in Tavarnuzze."

Her eyes snapped open and in about half a second she'd scrambled to a standing position. Ren cracked up.

"Lorenzo Ferrara! Don't *do* that."

"Carolina, this is my mom, Odette. She was a U2 groupie. Followed them around for a while in the early nineties while they were on tour in Europe. Clearly she still has strong feelings for them."

"I'll show you strong feelings." She reached for a pair of glasses and slipped them onto her nose, giving me a once-over. "Oh, Lorenzo, where did you find her?"

"We just met on the hill behind the cemetery. She's living here with her dad for the summer."

"You're one of us!"

"American?" I asked.

"Expatriate."

"Hostage" was more like it. But that wasn't the sort of thing you told someone you'd just met.

"Wait a minute." She leaned forward. "I heard you were coming. Are you Howard Mercer's daughter?"

"Yes. I'm Lina."

"Her full name is 'Carolina,'" Ren added.

"Just call me Lina."

"Well, thank the heavens, Lina—we need more Americans here. Preferably *live* ones," she said, waving her hand dismissively in the direction of the cemetery. "I'm so glad to meet you. Have you learned any Italian?"

"I memorized like five phrases on the flight over."

"What are they?" Ren asked.

"I'm not saying them in front of you. I'll probably sound like an idiot."

He shrugged. "*Che peccato*."

Odette grimaced. "Promise me you'll never use even one of those phrases in this house. I'm spending the summer pretending to be somewhere other than Italy."

Ren grinned. "How's that working out for you? You know, with your Italian husband and children?"

She ignored him. "I'm going to get us some drinks. You two make yourselves comfortable." She squeezed my shoulder, then walked out of the room.

Ren looked at me. "Told you she'd be happy to meet you."

"Does she really hate Italy?"

"No way. She's mad that we can't go to Texas this summer, but every year it's the same thing. We get there and she spends three months complaining about the terrible food and all the people she sees wearing their pajamas in public."

"Who wears their pajamas in public?"

"Lots of people. Trust me. It's like an epidemic."

I pointed to the table. "Is she an artist?"

"Yeah. She paints ceramics, mostly scenes of Tuscany. There's a guy in Florence who sells them in his shop, and tourists pay like a gazillion dollars for them. They'd probably have a conniption if they found out they're done by an

American." He picked up a tile and handed it to me. She'd painted a yellow cottage nestled between two hills.

"This is really pretty."

"You should see upstairs. We have a whole wall of tile that she's replacing one by one with the ones she's worked on."

I set the tile down. "Are you artistic?"

"Me? No. Not really."

"I'm not either. But my mom was an artist too. She was a photographer."

"Cool. Like family portraits and stuff?"

"No. Mostly fine-art kinds of stuff. Her work was displayed in galleries and at art shows, places like that. She taught in colleges, too."

"Nice. What was her name?"

"Hadley Emerson."

Odette reappeared, carrying two cans of orange Fanta and an opened sleeve of cookies. "Here you go. Ren goes through about a pack of these a day. You'll love them."

I took one. It was a sandwich cookie with vanilla on one side and chocolate on the other. An Italian Oreo. I bit into it and a choir of angels started singing. Did Italian food have some kind of fairy dust that made it way better than its American counterparts?

"Give her more," Ren said. "She looks like she's going to eat her arm."

"Hey—" I started, but then Odette handed me the rest of the cookies and I was too busy eating to properly defend myself.

Odette smiled. "I love a girl who can eat. Now, where were we? Oh—I didn't really introduce myself, did I? I swear, this place is turning me into a savage. I'm Odette Ferrara. It's like 'Ferrari,' but with an *a*. Pleased to meet you." She extended her hand, and I wiped crumbs off mine so we could shake. "Can we talk about air-conditioning? And drive-thru restaurants? Those are the two things I've been missing most this summer."

"You never even let us eat fast food when we're in the States," Ren said.

"That doesn't mean *I* don't eat it. And whose side are you on anyway? Mine or the Signore's?"

"No comment."

"Who's the Signore?" I asked.

"My dad. I have no idea how they ended up together. You know those weird animal friendship videos, where a bear and a duck become best friends? They're kind of like that."

Odette cackled. "Oh, come on. We're not *that* different. But now I'm curious. In that scenario, would you consider me the bear or the duck?"

"I'm not going there."

Odette turned to me. "So what do you think of my Ren?"

I swallowed and handed the rest of the cookies to Ren, who was eyeing them like they were *his precious*. "He's . . . very friendly."

"And handsome, too, isn't he?"

"*Mom*."

I felt myself blush a little. Ren *was* cute, but in that kind of way that you don't really notice at first. He had deep brown eyes fringed with ridiculously long lashes, and when he smiled he had a little gap between his front teeth. But again, that wasn't the sort of the thing you told someone you just met.

Odette waved her hand at me. "Well, we're so glad to have you in town. I'm pretty sure Ren has been having the most boring summer of his life. I told him just this morning that he needs to get out more."

"Come on, Mom. It's not like I just sit home all day."

"All I know is that once a certain *ragazza* went out of town, you suddenly had no interest in going out."

"I go out when I feel like it. Mimi has nothing to do with it."

"Who's Mimi?" I asked.

"His crush," Odette said in a stage whisper.

"Mooom," Ren growled. "I'm not nine."

A phone started ringing, and Odette began pulling papers and art supplies off the table. "Where in the . . . ? *Pronto*?"

A little girl appeared in the doorway wearing a pair of ruffled underpants and black dress shoes. "I pooped!"

Odette gave her a double thumbs-up and then walked into the house, speaking on the phone in rapid Italian.

Ren groaned. "Gabriella, that is so embarrassing. Get back in the bathroom. We have company here."

She ignored him, turning to me instead. "*Tu chi sei?*"

"She doesn't speak Italian," Ren said. "She's American."

"*Anch'io!* Are you Lorenzo's girlfriend?" she asked.

"No. I just met him when I was out for a walk. My name's Lina."

She studied me for a minute. "You're kind of like a *principessa*. Maybe like Rapunzel because of your crazy hairs."

"It's *hair*, not hairs, Gabriella," Ren said. "And it's not nice to tell someone their hair is crazy."

"My hairs *are* crazy," I confirmed.

"Do you want to see my *criceto*?" Gabriella ran over and grabbed my hand. "Come now, *principessa*. You will really like him. His furs are so soft."

"Sure."

Ren put his hand on her shoulder. "Carolina, no. And, Gabriella, she doesn't want to. She has to leave soon."

"I don't mind. I like kids."

"No, seriously, trust me. Going into her room is like stepping into a time warp. Before you know it, you'll have been playing Barbies for like five hours and you'll be answering to Princess Sparkle."

"*Non è vero*, Lorenzo. You're so mean!"

Ren answered in Italian, and Gabriella gave me a betrayed look and then ran out of the room, slamming the door behind her.

"What's a *criceto*?"

"In English . . . a hamster, I think? Little annoying animal, runs on a wheel?"

"Yep. Hamster. She's cute."

"Sometimes she's cute. Do you have any brothers or sisters?"

"No. But I used to babysit a lot for a family in my apartment building. They had triplet boys who were five."

"Whoa."

"Whenever their mom left, she'd say, *Just keep them alive. Don't worry about anything else.*"

"So you tied them up or something?"

"No. The first time I babysat I wrestled them, and after that they loved me. Also, I always came over with my pockets full of fruit snacks." At my mom's funeral, one of the boys asked where I'd been and his brother said, *Her mom is sleeping for a really long time. That's why she can't play with us anymore.*

My throat tightened at the memory. "I'd better get going. Howard might wonder where I am."

"Yeah, sure." We walked back through the living room and Ren stopped at the front door.

"Hey, do you want to go to a party with me tomorrow?"

"Um . . ." I looked away, then quickly bent to tie my shoe-lace. *It's just a party. You know, the things normal teenagers go to?* Losing my mom had somehow made social events feel like a quick jaunt up Mt. Everest. Also, I was doing an alarming amount of self-talk these days.

"I'll have to ask Howard," I finally said, straightening back up.

"Okay. I can pick you up on my scooter. Around eight?"

"Maybe. I'll call you if I can go." I reached for the door-knob.

"Wait. You need my number." He grabbed a pen from a nearby table, then cupped my hand in his, writing his number quickly. His breath was warm, and when he finished, he held my hand for just a second longer.

Oh.

He looked up at me and smiled. "*Ciao*, Carolina. I'll see you tomorrow."

"Maybe." I stepped out of the house and left without looking back. I was afraid he'd see the sparkly smile plastered across my face.

Chapter 6

THE WHOLE REN-HAND-HOLDING THING HAD LAUNCHED A teeny butterfly in my stomach, but all it took was two minutes in the car with Howard for the butterfly to fall flat. It was just so *awkward*.

Howard had these big comb marks in his freshly showered hair, and he'd changed into a pair of slacks and a nicer shirt. I'd missed the memo on dressing up and was still wearing my T-shirt and sneakers.

"Ready?" he asked.

"Ready."

"Well, then off to Florence. You're going to love the city." He popped a disc in his CD player (who was still using CDs?) and AC/DC's " You Shook Me All Night Long" filled the car. You know, the official soundtrack of Ignore How Uncomfortable Your First Father-Daughter Outing Is.

According to Howard the city was only about seven miles away, but it took us like thirty minutes to get there. The road into town was packed with scooters and miniature cars and every building we passed looked old. Even with the weird atmosphere in the car, excitement started building up in me like steam in a pressure cooker. Maybe the circumstances weren't ideal, but I was in *Florence*. How cool was that?

When we got to the city Howard pulled down a narrow, one-way street, then pulled off the most impressive feat of parallel parking I'd ever witnessed. Like he would have made a great driver's ed teacher, if he weren't so into the whole cemetery thing.

"Sorry about the long drive," he said. "Traffic was bad tonight."

"Not your fault." I practically had my nose pressed against the window. The street was made of gray crisscrossing square stones and there was a narrow sidewalk on either side. Tall pastel-colored buildings were smashed close together and all the windows had these adorable green shutters. A bike flew past on the sidewalk, practically clipping my side mirror.

Howard looked at me. "Want to take the scenic route? See a little bit of the city?"

"Yes!" I unclicked my seat belt and then jumped out onto the street. It was still hot out, and the city smelled slightly of warm garbage, but everything was so interesting-looking that it was completely okay. Howard started up the sidewalk and I trailed after him.

It was like walking through a scene from an Italian movie. The street was lined with clothing stores and little coffee shops and restaurants, and people kept calling to one another from windows and cars. Halfway down the street a horn beeped politely and everyone cleared out of the street to make way for an entire family crowded onto a scooter. There was even a string of laundry hanging between two buildings, a billowy red housedress flapping right in the middle of it. Any second now a director was going to jump out and yell, *Cut!*

"There it is." We turned a corner and Howard pointed to a sliver of a tall building visible at the end of the street.

"There's what?"

"That's the Duomo. Florence's cathedral."

Duomo. It was like the mother ship. Everyone was funneling into it and we had to slow down even more the closer we got. Finally we were in the middle of a large open space, and I was looking up at a gargantuan building half-lit by the setting sun.

"Wow. That's really . . ." Big? Beautiful? Impressive? It was all that and more. The cathedral was easily the size of several city blocks and the walls were patterned in detailed carvings of pink, green, and white marble. It was a hundred times prettier and more impressive and *grander* than any building I'd seen before. Also, I'd never used the word "grander" in my life. Nothing had ever required it before.

"It's actually called the Cathedral of Santa Maria del Fiore, but everyone just calls it the Duomo."

"Because of the domed roof?" One side of the building was capped with an enormous orange-red circular roof.

"No, but nice catch. '*Duomo*' means 'cathedral,' and the word just happens to sound like 'dome' in English, so a lot of people make that mistake. The cathedral took almost a hundred and fifty years to build, and that was the largest dome in the world until modern technology came around. As soon as I get a free afternoon, we'll climb to the top."

"What's that?" I pointed to a much smaller octagonal building across from the Duomo. It had tall gold doors with carvings on them, and a bunch of tourists were taking pictures in front of them.

"The baptistery. Those doors are called the Gates of Paradise, and they're one of the most famous works of art in the whole city. The artist's name was Ghiberti, and they took him twenty-seven years to make. I'll take you on a tour of that, too." He pointed to a street just past the baptistery. "Restaurant is right over there."

I followed Howard across the big open space (*piazza*, he told me) and he held the restaurant's door open for me. A man wearing a necktie tucked into his apron looked up from behind his stand and stood a little straighter. Howard was like two feet taller than him.

"And tonight, how many?" he asked in a nasally voice.

"*Possiamo avere una tavolo per due?*"

The man nodded, then called to a passing server.

"*Buona sera,*" the server said to us.

"*Buona sera. Possiamo stare seduti vicino alla cucina?*"

"*Certo.*"

So . . . apparently my father spoke Italian. Fluently. He even rolled his *R*s like Ren. I tried not to stare at him as we followed our server to our table. I literally knew nothing about him. It was so weird.

"Can you guess why I like it here?" Howard asked as we settled into our seats.

I looked around. The tables were covered in cheap paper cloths and there was an open kitchen with a wood-fire pizza oven blazing away. "She's Got a Ticket to Ride" was playing in the background.

He pointed up at the ceiling. "They play the Beatles all day every day, which means I get two of my favorite things together. Pizza and Paul McCartney."

"Oh, yeah. I noticed the framed Beatles records in your office." I gulped. Now he was going to think I'd been snooping. Which technically I guess I had been.

He just smiled. "My sister sent those as a gift a few years ago. She has two boys, ten and twelve. They live in Denver and they usually come out every other summer or so."

Did *they* know about me?

Howard must have had a similar thought, because there was a moment of silence, and then we both suddenly got superinterested in our menus.

"What do you want to order? I always get a prosciutto pizza, but everything here is good. We could get a few appetizers or—"

"How about just a plain pizza. Cheese." Simple and quick. I wanted to get back out in Florence. And keep this dinner as short as possible.

"Then you should order the Margherita. It's pretty basic. Just tomato sauce, mozzarella, and basil."

"That sounds good."

"You're going to love the food here. Pizza here is in a whole different category from the stuff back home."

I set my menu down. "Why?"

"It's really thin and you get your own large pizza. And fresh mozzarella . . ." He sighed. "There's nothing like it."

He honestly had a dreamy look in his eyes. Did my more-than-a-friend love for food come from him? I hesitated. I guess it *would* be a good idea to at least sort of get to know him. He was my father after all.

"So . . . where's 'back home'?"

"I grew up in a small town in South Carolina called Due

West, if you can believe it. It's about a hundred and fifty miles from Adrienne."

"Is Due West where you rearranged all the traffic barricades and caused a traffic jam?"

He looked at me in surprise. "Your mom told you?"

"Yeah. She told me lots of stories about you."

He chuckled. "There wasn't a lot to do in Due West, and unfortunately, I made the whole town pay for it. What other stories did she tell you?"

"She said you used to play hockey and that even though you're pretty even-tempered, you used to get in fights on the ice."

"Proof." He turned his head and ran his finger across a scar that disappeared under his jawline. "This was one of my last games. I couldn't seem to keep it under control. What else?"

"You guys went to Rome and the owner of a restaurant thought you were a famous basketball player and you guys got a free meal."

"I forgot about that! Best lamb I ever had. And all I had to do was take pictures with the kitchen staff."

Our server came over and took our order, then filled our glasses with fizzy water. I took a big swig and shuddered. Was it just me, or did carbonated water feel like liquid sparklers?

Howard crossed his arms. "Forgive me for stating the obvious, but I can't believe how much you look like Hadley. Did people tell you that all the time?"

"Yeah. People sometimes thought we were sisters."

"That doesn't surprise me. You even have her hands." My elbows were resting on the table, one arm crossed over the other, and Howard suddenly jerked forward a couple of inches, like he'd gotten snagged on a fishing hook.

He was staring at my ring.

I shifted uncomfortably. "Um, are you okay?"

"Her ring." He reached out and almost touched it, his hand hovering an inch above mine. It was an antique, a slim gold band engraved with an intricate scrolling pattern. My mom had worn it until she'd gotten too thin to keep it on. I'd been wearing it ever since.

"Did she tell you I gave her that?"

"No." I pulled my hand to my lap, my face heating up. Had she told me *anything*? "Was it like an engagement ring or something?"

"No. Just a present."

There was another long silence, which I filled with unprecedented interest in the restaurant's décor. There were signed photographs of what were probably very famous Italian celebrities hanging all around the restaurant, and several aprons had been tacked to the wall. "We All Live in a Yellow

Submarine" was playing overhead. My cheeks were boiling like a pot of marinara sauce.

Howard shook his head. "So do you have a boyfriend at home who is missing you?"

"No."

"Good for you. Plenty of time to break hearts when you're older." He hesitated. "This morning I was thinking I should make a call to the international school to see if anyone in your grade is around for the summer. It might be a good way to see if you're interested in going to the school."

I made a noncommittal sound, then took a special interest in a nearby photograph of a woman wearing a tiara and a thick sash. Miss Ravioli 2015?

"I wanted to tell you, if you ever need someone to talk to here—someone other than me or Sonia, of course—I have a friend who lives in town. She's a social worker and she speaks English really well. She told me she'd be happy to meet with you if you ever need, you know . . ."

Great. Another counselor. The one I'd seen at home had pretty much just said mm-hmm, mm-hmm, over and over and asked me, *How did that make you feel?* until I thought my ears were going to melt. The answer was always "terrible." I felt *terrible* without my mom. The counselor had told me that things would slowly start to feel better, but so far she was wrong.

I started tearing up the edges of the paper tablecloth, keeping my eyes off the ring.

"Are you feeling . . . comfortable here?"

I hesitated. "Yeah."

"You know, if you need anything, you can always just ask."

"I'm fine." My voice was gravelly, but Howard just nodded.

After what felt like ten hours, our server finally walked out and set two steaming pizzas in front of us. Each of them was the size of a large dinner plate, and they smelled unbelievable. I cut a piece and took a bite.

All weirdness evaporated immediately. The power of pizza.

"I think my mouth just exploded," I said. Or at least that's what I tried to say. It came out more like "mymogjesesieplod."

"What?" Howard looked up.

I shoveled in another bite. "This. Is. The. Best." He was right. This pizza belonged in a completely different universe from the stuff I was used to.

"Told you, Lina. Italy is the perfect place for a hungry runner." He smiled at me and we both ate ravenously, "Lucy in the Sky with Diamonds" filling in for conversation.

I had just taken an enormous bite when he said, "You're probably wondering where I've been all this time."

I froze, a piece of crust in my hand. *Is he asking what I think he is?* This couldn't be the big unveiling moment—you don't go around telling your children why you weren't around while stuffing your face with pizza.

I snuck a glance up. He'd set his fork and knife down and was leaning forward, his mouth set in a serious line. *Oh, no.*

I swallowed. "Um, no. I haven't really wondered." Lie with a capital *L*. I stuffed the piece of crust into my mouth but couldn't taste it.

"Did your mother tell you much about our relationship?"

I shook my head. "No. Just, uh, funny stories."

"I see. Well, the truth is, I didn't know about you."

Suddenly it seemed like the whole restaurant got quiet. Except for the Beatles. "The girl that's driving me mad, is going awaaaayyyy . . . ," they sang.

I swallowed hard. I had never even *considered* that possibility. "Why?"

"Things were . . . complicated between us."

Complicated. That was exactly what my mom had said.

"She got in touch with me around the same time she started getting tested. She knew she was sick, just not with what, and I think she had a feeling. Anyway, I want you to know I would have been there. If I'd known. I just . . ." He rested his hand on the table, palm-side up. "I guess I just want a chance. I'm not expecting miracles. I know this is hard. Your grandmother told me you really didn't want to come here, and I understand that. I just want you to know that I really appreciate having this chance to get to know you."

He met my eyes, and suddenly I wished with all my heart that I could evaporate, like the steam still curling off my pizza.

I pushed away from the table. "I . . . I need to find the bathroom." I sprinted to the front of the restaurant, barely making it inside the restroom before the tears started rolling.

Being here was awful. Before today I'd known exactly who my mother was, and she certainly wasn't this woman who loved violets or sent her daughter mysterious journals or forgot to tell the father of her child that—*oh, by the way, you have a daughter!*

It took all three minutes of "Here Comes the Sun" to get myself under control, mostly deep breathing, and when I finally cracked the door open, Howard was still sitting at the table, his shoulders slumped. I watched him for a moment, anger settling over me like a fine dusting of Parmesan cheese.

My mother had kept us apart for sixteen years. Why were we together now?

Chapter 7

THAT NIGHT I COULDN'T SLEEP.

Howard's bedroom was upstairs too, and the floorboards creaked as he walked down the hall. *I didn't know about you.* Why?

The clock on my bedroom wall made an irritating *tick-tick-tick.* I hadn't noticed it the night before, but suddenly the noise was unbearable. I pulled a pillow over my head, but that didn't help, plus it was kind of suffocating. There was a breeze blowing through my window and my violets kept swaying like Deadheads at a concert.

Okay. Fine. I switched on my lamp and took the ring off my finger, studying it in the light. Even though my mother hadn't seen Howard in more than sixteen years, she'd worn the ring he'd given her. Every single day.

But why? Had they really been in love, like Sonia had said? And if so, what had torn them apart?

Before I could lose my nerve, I opened my nightstand drawer and felt for the journal.

I lifted the front cover:

I made the wrong choice.

A chill moved down my spine. My mother had written in thick black marker, and the words sprawled across the inside cover like a row of spiders. Was this a message to me? A kind of precursor to whatever I was about to read?

I mustered up my courage, then turned to the front page. Now or never.

———

MAY 22

Question. Immediately following your meeting with the admissions officers at University of Washington (where you've just given official notice that you will not be starting nursing school in the fall) do you:

A. go home and tell your parents what you've done

B. have a complete panic attack and run back into the office claiming a temporary lapse in sanity

C. go out and buy yourself a journal

Answer: C

True, you will eventually have to tell your parents. And also true, you purposely timed your appointment so the office would be closing as you walked out. But as soon as the dust settles I'm sure you'll remember all the reasons why you just did what you did. Time to walk yourself into the nearest bookstore and blow your budget on a fancy new journal—because as scary as this moment is, it's also the moment when your life (your real life) begins.

Journal, it's official. As of one hour and twenty-six minutes ago I am no longer a future nursing student. Instead, in just three weeks I will be packing up my things (aka, whatever my mother doesn't smash when she hears the news) and boarding a plane for Florence, Italy (ITALY!), to do what I've always wanted to do (PHOTOGRAPHY!) at the Fine Arts Academy of Florence (FAAF!).

Now I just have to brainstorm how I'll break the news to my parents. Most of my ideas involve placing an anonymous call from somewhere in Antarctica.

MAY 23

Well, I told them. And it somehow went even worse than I expected. To the casual observer, The Great Parental Fallout would have sounded something like this:

Me: Mom, Dad, there's something I need to tell you.

Mom: Good heavens. Hadley, are you pregnant?

Dad: Rachelle, she doesn't even have a boyfriend.

Me: Dad, thanks for pointing that out. And, Mom, not quite sure why you jumped straight to pregnant. [Clears throat] I want to talk to you about a recent life decision I've made. [Wording taken directly from a book called Savvy Communication: How to Talk So They'll Agree.]

Mom: Good heavens. Hadley, are you gay?

Dad: Rachelle, she doesn't even have a girlfriend.

Me: [Abandoning all attempts at civilized conversation.] NO. What I'm trying to tell you is that I'm not going to nursing school anymore. I just got accepted to an art school in Florence, Italy, and I'll be there for six months studying photography. And . . . it starts in three weeks.

Mom/Dad: [Prolonged silence involving two trout-like open mouths.]

Me: So . . .

Mom/Dad: [Continue gaping]

Me: Could you please say something?

Dad: [weakly] But, Hadley, you don't even have a decent camera.

Mom: [regaining voice] WHATDOYOUMEAN-YOU'RENOTGOINGTONURSINGSCHOOO . . .

[Neighborhood dogs start howling]

I'll spare you the lecture that followed, but it basically boils down to this: I am throwing away my life. I'm wasting my time, my scholarship, and their hard-earned money for six frivolous months in a country where the women don't even shave their armpits. (That last tidbit was contributed by my mother. I have no idea if it's true or not.)

I explained to them that I will pay for the entire thing. I thanked them for their contributions to my education. I assured them that I'll keep up on my normal grooming routines. And then I went up to my room and bawled my eyes out for at least an hour because I am SO SCARED. But what choice do I have? The second I had that art-school acceptance letter in my hand I knew I wanted it more than I've ever wanted anything. I'm going because it feels scarier not to!

I set the journal down. A straight-up monsoon was happening in the general vicinity of my face, and the words kept running together in a big, blurry mess. *This* was why I couldn't read her journals. They made me feel like I was overhearing her talking on the phone to a friend and then when I looked up from the page and she wasn't there . . .

Pull it together. I rubbed my eyes ferociously. She'd sent me this journal for a reason, and I had to find out what it was.

JUNE 13

It seems like a bad omen to be leaving on the thir-teenth, but here I am. Chilly good-bye from Mom, then Dad dropped me off at the airport. Hello, unknown.

JUNE 20

I'M HERE. I could write fifty pages about my first week in Florence, but suffice it to say, I am here. FAAF is exactly what I pictured: tiny, cluttered, overflowing with talent. My apartment is right above a noisy bakery and my mattress might be made of cardboard, but who cares when the world's most gorgeous city is right out-side my window?

My roommate is named Francesca, and she's a fashion photography student from northern Italy. She wears all black, switches effortlessly in and out of Italian, French, and English, and has been chain-smoking out our win-dow since she the moment she arrived. I adore her.

JUNE 23

First free day in Italy. I was looking forward to a lazy morning involving a fresh jar of Nutella and some bread from the bakery downstairs, but Francesca had other plans. When I came out of my room she instructed me to get dressed, then spent the next thirty minutes arguing enthusiastically with someone on the phone while I sat waiting for her. When she finally hung up she insisted I had to change my shoes. "No sandals. It's after eleven o'clock." She made me change twice more. ("No dark denim after April." "Never match your shoes to your handbag.") It was exhausting.

Finally we were out on the street and Francesca started giving me a speed-dating version of Florence's history. "Florence is the birthplace of the Renaissance. You <u>do</u> know what the Renaissance is, don't you?" I assured her that everyone knows what the Renaissance is, but she explained it anyway. "A third of the population died in the bubonic plague in the 1300s, and afterward Europe experienced a cultural rebirth. Suddenly there was an explosion of artistic work. It all started here before trickling out to

the rest of Europe. Painting, sculpture, architecture—
this was the art capital of the world. Florence was one
of the wealthiest cities in history . . ." and on and on
and <u>on</u>.

She was weaving in and out of the streets, not even
taking a second to make sure I was following, and
then suddenly I saw it. THE DUOMO. Intricate, colorful, Gothic Duomo. I was completely winded, but
even if I hadn't been, it would have taken my breath
away.

Francesca put out her cigarette, then led me to the
Duomo's side entryway and told me that we were
climbing to the top. And we did. Four hundred and
sixty-three steep stone stairs, with Francesca pogo-
ing up the steps like her stilettos had springs. When
we finally got to the top I couldn't stop taking pictures. Florence spreads out like an orange-tinted
maze, towers and buildings jutting up here and there,
but nothing as tall as the Duomo. There were green
hills in the distance, and the sky was the most perfect shade of blue. Francesca finally stopped talking
when she saw how in awe I was. She didn't even get
mad when I reached my arms out wide, feeling the

wind and this new feeling—this freedom. Before we headed back down I gave Francesca a giant hug, but she just peeled me off her and said, "All right, all right. You got yourself here. I just took you to see the Duomo. Now let's go shopping. I've never seen a sadder pair of jeans. Really, Hadley, they make me want to weep."

"No way," I whispered to myself. What were the chances that I'd read this entry on the day *I'd* seen the Duomo for the first time? I ran my fingers over the words, imagining my twenty-something-year-old mom running to keep up with tyrannical, springy Francesca. Was this part of the reason my mom had sent her journal? So we could experience Florence together?

I marked my place and switched off the light, my chest heavy. Yes, hearing her voice was the emotional equivalent of a damaged ship taking on water. But it felt good, too. She'd *loved* Florence. Maybe reading her journal would be like seeing it with her.

I'd just have to take it in small doses.

Chapter 8

I HAVE TO TELL ADDIE ABOUT THE JOURNAL. THE NEXT morning I tumbled down the stairs without even changing out of my pajamas. Ren had been totally wrong about the jet-lag thing. Once I'd finished reading the diary entries, I'd tucked the journal under the covers with me and then slept a solid thirteen hours. I felt like a well-rested hummingbird.

Right before I escaped up to my room, Howard had told me he'd leave his cell phone out for me, and I was ridiculously grateful that I didn't have to ask him for it. If last night's drive home were a book, it would have been titled something like *The Longest, Quietest, Most Miserable Ride Ever,* and I really wasn't looking forward to a sequel. The less interacting, the better.

Back in my room I closed the door, then powered up the phone. Country code first? Area code? Where were my instructions? After three tries, the phone finally started ring-ing. Ian answered.

"Hello?"

"Hey, Ian. It's Lina."

A video game blared in the background.

"You know . . . the one who lived with you for five months?" I prompted.

"Oh, yeah. Hi, Lina. Where are you again? France?"

"Italy. Is Addie there?"

"No. I don't know where she is."

"Isn't it like two a.m. there?"

"Yeah. I think she stayed over at someone's house. We're sharing a phone now."

"I heard. Could you tell her I called?"

"Sure. Don't eat snails." *Click.*

I groaned. Ian's track record meant that my message had a less-than-zero chance of ever getting to Addie. And I *really* needed to talk to her—about the journal, about what Howard had told me, about . . . everything. I paced around my bedroom like my grandma's OCD cat. I really didn't feel ready to go back to the journal again, but I also *really* couldn't just sit around thinking. I quickly changed into my running clothes, then went outside.

"Hi, Lina. How'd you sleep?"

I jumped. Howard was sitting on the porch swing with a stack of papers on his lap and dark circles under his eyes. I'd been ambushed.

"Fine. I just woke up." I propped my foot up on the banister and gave my shoelaces total and complete concentration.

"Ah, to be a teenager again. I don't think I saw the morning side of a sunrise until I was in my late twenties." He stopped swinging and sort of stumbled into his next sentence. "How are you feeling about what we talked about last night? I wonder if I could have told you that in a better way."

"I'm not upset," I said quickly.

"I'd really like to talk to you more about your mother and me. There are some things she didn't tell you that—"

I yanked my foot off the banister like I was a Rockette. "Maybe another time? I'd really like to start my run." *And I want to hear my mom's side first.*

He hesitated. "Okay, sure." He tried to meet my gaze. "We'll take it at your pace. Just tell me when you're ready."

I hurried down the steps.

"You got a phone call at the visitors' center this morning."

I whipped around. "Was it Addie?" *Please be Addie.*

"No. It was a local call. His name was strange. Red? Rem? An American. He said he met you yesterday while you were out running."

A handful of confetti rained down on me. *He called?* "Ren. It's short for 'Lorenzo.'"

"That makes more sense. He said you're going to a party with him tonight?"

"Oh, yeah. Maybe." The whole Howard/journal thing had done an awesome job at crowding everything else out of my brain. Was I feeling gutsy enough to go?

Howard's forehead creased. "Well, who is he?"

"He lives nearby. His mom's American and he goes to the international school. I think he's my age."

His face lit up. "That's great. Except . . . Oh, no."

"What?"

"I started grilling him because I thought he was one of the guys who chased you when you were out running. I think I might have scared him."

"I met Ren behind the cemetery. He was playing soccer on the hill."

"Well, I definitely owe him an apology. Do you by chance know his last name?"

"Ferrari or something? They live in a house that looks like gingerbread."

He laughed. "Say no more. The Ferraras. How lucky that you ran into him. I didn't realize their son was your age or I would have tried to arrange for you guys to meet. Is the party with your other classmates?"

"*Potential* classmates," I said quickly. "I'm not sure if I want to go."

His smile just increased in wattage, like he hadn't heard me. "Ren wanted me to tell you that he can't make it until eight thirty. I'll make sure dinner is ready before then so you have plenty of time to eat. And we should look into getting you a cell phone—that way your friends won't have to call at the visitors' center."

"Thanks, but that would probably be overkill. I only know one person."

"After tonight you'll know more. And in the meantime you can just give people my number so they don't have to call the cemetery line. Oh, and good news. Our Internet connection is finally sorted out, so FaceTime should work great." He set the papers on the porch. "I need to head down to the visitors' center, but I'll see you a little later. Enjoy your run." He turned and went into the house, whistling quietly to himself.

I squinted after him. Was *Howard* my mom's wrong choice? And what about the party? Did I really want to go meet a bunch of strangers?

"What about this?" I walked up to my laptop and twirled around so Addie could see what I was wearing.

She leaned in, her face filling the screen. She'd just woken up and her smudged eyeliner was kind of making her look like a blond vampire. "Hmm. Do you want me to be nice or do you want me to be honest?"

"Is there a possibility that you could you be both?"

"No. That shirt looks like it's been wadded up in the bottom of a suitcase for three days."

"Because it has."

"Exactly. My vote is the black-and-white skirt. Your legs are killer and that skirt is maybe the only thing you have that doesn't look awful."

"Whose fault is that? You're the one who talked me into binge-watching *America's Next Top Model* instead of doing my laundry."

"Listen, it's all about priorities. One of these days I'm going to grow ninety inches, and then I'm totally going to be on that show." She sighed dramatically, attempting to wipe some of the makeup off her eyes. "I can't believe you're going to a *party*. In *Italy*. I'm probably just going wind up stuck at Dylan's again night."

"You like going to Dylan's."

"No, I don't. Everyone just sits around talking about all the stuff we could do, but then no one makes a decision and we end up playing foosball all night."

"Look on the bright side. He has that downstairs freezer full of burritos and churros. Those are pretty good."

"You're right. Eating mass-produced churros totally sounds better than going to a party in Italy."

I picked up my computer, then flopped onto my bed, setting it on my stomach. "Except I don't like going to parties, remember?"

"Don't say that. You used to."

"And then my mom got sick and no one knew what to say to me anymore."

She set her mouth in a line. "I honestly think some of that's in your head. People just don't want to say the wrong thing, you know? And you have to admit you shut people down a lot."

"What do you mean? I don't shut people down."

"Um, what about Jake?"

"Who's Jake?"

"Jake Harrison? Hot senior lacrosse player? Tried to ask you out for like two months?"

"He didn't ask me out."

"Because you kept avoiding him."

"Addie, I could barely go thirty minutes without talking about my mom and crying. Think he would have been into that?"

She frowned. "Sorry. I know it's been rough. But I think you're ready now. In fact, I'm making an official prediction: Tonight you will meet and fall in love with hottest boy in all of Italy. Just don't fall so in love that you don't want to come home again. It's already been the longest three days of my life."

"Mine too. So, black-and-white skirt?"

"Black-and-white skirt. You'll thank me later. And call me as soon as you're home. I want to talk more about the journal. I think I'm going to hire a film crew to start following you around. Your life would make awesome TV."

"Lina! Dinner is ready."

I looked at myself in the mirror. I'd gone against Addie's advice and settled on my favorite jeans. And I was way too nervous to eat.

I guess there's a first for everything.

"Did you hear me?" Howard called.

"Coming!"

I put on some lip gloss and smoothed my hair one last time. I'd had to spend a solid forty-five minutes with a flat iron, but at least now my hair looked like a normal person's. Not that that was any sort of guarantee. If someone looked at it funny, it would assume its natural craziness in about half a second. *You're sort of like Medusa,* Addie had once told me helpfully.

Howard met me at the bottom of the stairs and handed me a giant bowl of pasta. I could tell he was making a big effort to make things feel less tense, and so far it was working.

"You look nice."

"Thanks."

"I'm sorry about dinner being so late. We had an issue with maintenance. I thought I was going to be working all night."

"That's okay." I set my bowl down. "And thanks for dinner, but I'm actually not all that hungry."

He raised an eyebrow. "Not hungry? How many miles did you run today?"

"Seven."

"Are you feeling okay?"

"I guess I'm kind of nervous."

"I understand. Meeting new people can be nerve-wracking. But they're going to love you."

BEEP! We both looked out the window to see Ren driving up the road on a shiny red scooter. My stomach clenched. *Why did I agree to go?* Was it still possible to get out of it?

"That's the Ferrara boy?"

"Yes."

"He's early. He's not taking you on that scooter, is he?"

"Yeah, I think so." I shot Howard a hopeful glance. Maybe he'd say I couldn't go! That would solve everything. Except, are brand-new fathers allowed to tell you what you can and can't do?

Howard crossed the living room in three long strides, then opened the door. "Lorenzo?"

I hurried after him.

"Hi, Howard. Hi, Lina." Ren was wearing jeans and expensive-looking sneakers. He pulled the scooter back onto a kickstand, then bounded up the stairs, his hand extended to Howard. "Nice to meet you."

"Nice to meet you too. I'm really sorry about the mix-up on the phone earlier. I had you confused with someone else."

"That's okay. I'm just glad to know you're not going to come after me with a chainsaw anymore."

Oh, boy. Howard was really taking his new role seriously.

"Lina, you ready to go?" Ren asked.

"Um, I think so. Howard?" I looked at him hopefully. He was eyeing Ren's scooter, his face grim.

"You been driving that thing for a while?"

"Since I was fourteen. I'm a really safe driver."

"And you have an extra helmet?"

"Of course."

Howard nodded slowly. "All right. Drive carefully. Especially on the way back." He tilted his head toward me. "*È nervosa. Stalle vicino.*"

"*Si, certo.*"

"Um, excuse me. What was that?" I asked.

"Man talk," Ren said. "Come on. We're missing the party."

Howard handed me his cell phone and a twenty-euro bill. "Take this, just in case. The cemetery's number is in there. If I don't answer, Sonia will. What time will you be home?"

"I don't know."

"I can have her back whenever," Ren said.

"Let's say one."

I looked at him. *One?* He must really want me to make friends.

Howard settled himself on the porch swing and I followed Ren to his scooter, where he handed me a helmet from the compartment under the seat.

"Ready?" Ren asked.

"Ready." I clambered awkwardly onto the back, and suddenly Ren and I were zipping down the road, cool air flowing past us. I grabbed tight around Ren's waist, grinning like an idiot. It was like riding on a motorized armchair, superfast and supercomfortable. I glanced back to see Howard watching from the porch.

"Why do you call him 'Howard'?" Ren shouted over the noise of the scooter.

"What else would I call him?"

"'Dad'?"

"No way. I haven't known him long enough."

"You haven't?"

"Just . . . long story." I quickly changed the subject. "Where's the party?"

He paused to signal at the main road, then turned away from Florence. "At my friend Elena's house. We always go there because she has the biggest house. Her mom is a descendant of the Medici, and they have this giant villa. You can always tell when Elena's had too much to drink because she starts telling people that back in the day they would have been her servants."

"What's the Medici?"

"Really powerful Florentine family. They basically funded the Renaissance."

I had a sudden image of a teenage girl in flowing robes. "Did I dress up enough?"

"What?"

I repeated my question.

He slowed for a red light, then turned to look at me. "You look great. We're wearing the same thing."

"Yeah, but you look . . ."

"What?"

"Cooler."

He tipped his head back so our helmets *clacked*. "Thanks."

Chapter 9

THE DRIVE TO ELENA'S HOUSE TOOK FOREVER. FOR-EV-ER. By the time Ren signaled to pull off the main road, my legs were going numb.

"Almost there."

"Finally. I thought we were driving to France or something."

"Wrong direction. Hold tight."

He accelerated and we sped up a long, tree-lined driveway. Where were we? I hadn't seen a single house or building in more than ten minutes.

"Just wait for it. Three . . . two . . ."

We rounded the corner and I exploded. "*What*?"

"I know. Crazy, right?"

"That's a house? Does anyone live in normal places here?"

"What? You don't know people who live in gingerbread houses back home?"

Elena's villa was a palace. The house was several stories

high, and huge—like museum huge—with towers that rose on either side of a large arched doorway. I started to count all the windows, then gave up. It was that big.

Ren slowed down, navigating around a large circular fountain that sat in the center of the tennis-court-size driveway. Then we bumped off the pavement to park next to a bunch of other scooters. My mouth was as dry as the Sahara. Eating churros in Dylan's basement was really more my speed.

"You okay?" Ren asked, catching my eye.

I gave him the world's most unconvincing nod, then followed him past a wall of sculpted hedges to the sort of door you imagined angry villagers storming with torches and battering rams. I was about three seconds from throwing up.

Ren nudged me. "You sure you're okay?"

"Fine." I took a deep breath. "So . . . how many people live here?"

"Three. Elena, her mom, and her older sister, when she's home from boarding school. Elena told me there are rooms that she's never even set foot in, and she and her mom sometimes go days without even seeing each other. They have an intercom system so they don't have to walk across the house every time they want to talk to each other."

"Are you serious?"

"Totally serious. I've never even seen her mom. There are theories she doesn't actually exist. Also, this place is ridiculously haunted. Elena sees a ghost like once a day." He pushed hard on a brass doorbell and there was a loud *clang*ing noise.

"Do you believe that? About ghosts?"

He shrugged. "Elena does. She passes the ghost of her great-great-grandmother Alessandra on the stairwell every night."

Ghosts had never made sense to me. When my mom was gone, she was just *gone.* I'd give anything for it to be otherwise.

Suddenly a loud *bang*ing noise made me shriek. I stumbled back and Ren caught me.

"Relax. It's just the door. It takes a long time to unlock it."

After what felt like ten minutes, the door slowly creaked open and I took a step back, half expecting to be greeted by Great-great-grandmother Alessandra. Instead, a casually dressed teenage girl stepped into the doorway. She was curvy with a diamond stud in her nose and thick black hair.

"*Ciao*, Lorenzo!" She threw her arms around Ren and pressed her cheek to his, making a kissing noise. *"Dove sei stato? Mi sei mancato."*

"*Ciao*, Elena. *Mi sei mancata anche tu.*" Ren stepped back, then gestured to me. "Guess who this is?"

She switched from Italian to English as quickly as Ren did. "Who? You must tell me immediately."

"Carolina."

Her mouth dropped open into a perfect O. "You're *Carolina*?"

"Yes. But I just go by Lina."

"*Non è possibile!* Come!" She grabbed my hand and pulled me inside, kicking the door shut behind her. The foyer looked like something out of a *Scooby-Doo* episode. The hall was dimly lit with a few electric sconces, and tapestries and old-looking paintings covered every inch of wall, and wait—was that a *suit of armor*? Elena was looking at me.

"Your house is really—"

"Yes, yes. Creepy. Spooky scary. I know. Now come with me." She linked her elbow with mine, then dragged me down the hall. "They will be so surprised. You wait."

At the end of the hallway she opened a set of double doors, then shoved me inside. The room was a lot more modern-looking, with a jet-size leather sectional, a big-screen TV, and a foosball table. Oh, and twenty people. Give or take. And they were all looking at me like something that had managed to escape from the zoo.

I gulped. "Um, hi, everyone."

Elena took my hand and held it triumphantly in the air. "*Vi presento,* Carolina. *Ragazzi*, she exists!"

A collective cheer went up in the room and suddenly I was being swarmed.

"You are here. You are really here!" A tall boy with a French accent patted my arm enthusiastically. "I am Olivier. Welcome."

"I won the bet! They all said you'd never show."

"Better late than never."

"*Che bella sorpresa!*"

"I'm Valentina."

"Livi."

"Marcello."

Half of them reached out to pat me. Did they think I was a hologram?

I stumbled backward. "Nice to . . . meet you all."

"Guys, quit mouth-breathing on her!" Ren shoved a couple of people back. "You're acting like you never meet any-one new."

"We don't," a boy with braces said.

They started raining questions.

"How long have you been here?"

"Are you going to AISF in the fall?"

"Why didn't you start school last year?"

"Was that really tall man your dad?"

I took another step back. "Um . . . which one do you want me to answer first?"

They all laughed.

"Where do you live? In Florence?" It was a redheaded girl on my left working on a big wad of gum. She sounded like she was from New Jersey or somewhere.

"My house is kind of near Ren's."

"It's in the American Cemetery," Ren clarified.

I shot him a look. *Way to make me the weirdo.*

He patted my arm. "Don't worry. Everyone here lives in weird places."

They all started chiming in.

"My family is renting a medieval castle in Chianti."

"We live in a farmhouse."

"William lives at the American Consulate. Remember when his sister ran over that foreign dignitary's foot with a Razor scooter?"

An Italian boy with shoulder-length hair stepped forward. "*Ragazzi,* she will think we are very strange. Sorry for all the questions."

"It's fine," I said.

"No, we're weird. We don't meet new people all that often. We're totally sick of each other," a Hispanic-looking girl on my left said.

Suddenly a pair of arms wrapped around me and I was lifted off my feet. "Hey!"

"Marco! Down, boy!" Ren yelled.

"Heel!" Gum Chewer said.

Was Marco a Rottweiler? I wriggled away and turned to see a muscly guy with short black hair.

"Ren, introduce me. Now," he bellowed.

"Lina, this is Marco. Now forget you ever met him. Trust me, you'll be better off."

He grinned. "You're really here! I knew you would come. I knew it all along."

"Wait a minute. Are you my biology partner?"

"Yes!" He pumped his fist in the air, then put his arms around me again and gave me another one of his specialty python hugs.

"Can't. Breathe," I gasped.

"Let her go," Ren commanded.

Marco loosened his grip, shaking his head sheepishly. "Sorry. I'm normally not like this."

"Yes, you are," the dark-haired girl said.

"No, it's this beer." He held his can out to me. "I don't know who brought it, but it's disgusting. It tastes kind of like a urinal, you know?"

"Not really."

"That's okay. I'd offer you a drink, but I just told you it tastes like piss. By the way, you're really cute. Like way cuter than I thought you'd be."

". . . Thanks?"

"Hey! Margo! Who's your papa?" He turned and loped away.

"Wow," I said.

Ren shook his head. "Sorry about that. I wish I could

say it's because he's drunk, but he's actually worse when he's sober."

"Much, much worse," a short boy with glasses chimed in.

"There you are." A cool voice cut through the noise, and I turned and came face-to-face with an exquisitely pretty girl. She was tall and slim with big blue eyes and hair so blond it was almost white. She was looking straight through me.

"Hi, Mimi. Welcome back." Ren's voice was suddenly like three octaves lower.

"I was worried you weren't going to make it tonight," she said in an accented voice. Swedish? Norwegian? Someplace where everyone has good skin and silky, well-behaved hair?

"Everyone says you haven't been around much."

"I'm here now."

"Good. I missed you." She lifted her chin at me, her eyes still fixed on Ren. "Who's this?"

"Carolina. She just moved here."

"Hi. I go by Lina."

She slid her eyes at me for about a millimeter of a second, then leaned in to Ren and whispered something.

"*Si, certo.*" He glanced at me. "Just . . . later. Give me a few minutes."

She walked away, and it was like the whole group exhaled.

"Ice queen," someone whispered.

"She's really gorgeous," I said to Ren.

"Really? I hadn't noticed." He grinned like someone had just offered him a lifetime supply of pink Starbursts. I'd definitely misread that moment at the gingerbread house when he'd held my hand. If Mimi was what he was used to, then forget it.

"Hey, come on. I want to show you something."

"Okay. So . . . see you around?" I said to the rest of the people.

"*Ciao, ciao*," one of them said.

Ren was already halfway across the room.

"Where are we going?"

"It's a surprise. Come on." He held the door open for me. "After you."

I walked out into a dark hall and Ren pulled the door shut behind us. We were standing in front of an enormous staircase.

"Oh, no. Is this where we go to see Elena's great-great-grandmother?"

"No, that's in the other wing. Come on. I want to show you the garden."

He started up the stairs, but I held back. "Um, Ren? It looks creepy up there."

"It is. Come on."

I looked back toward the door. Creepy staircase or overly friendly international teenagers? I guess I'd take my chances with Ren. I hurried after him, my footsteps echoing off the high ceiling. At the top of the stairs Ren pushed open a tall, skinny door and I reluctantly stepped in after him.

"This place is unbelievable," I muttered. The room was packed full of stuff, like the contents of ten rooms had been consolidated into one, and everything was covered in thick, dusty sheets. There was even a gigantic fireplace guarded by the portrait of a stern-looking man wearing a feathered hat.

"Is that for real?" I pointed to the portrait.

"I'm sure it is."

"It looks like something from a haunted house. Like I'm going to turn around and he'll have changed positions."

Ren grinned. "And that's coming from someone who lives in a cemetery."

"I don't think two days counts as 'living.'"

"Over here." He made his way over to a set of glass doors and unhooked a latch, then opened them to a balcony. "I wanted to show you the gardens, but mostly I wanted to give you a break from your adoring crowds."

"Yeah, they seemed kind of hyperactive about meeting me."

"A lot of us have been stuck together since elementary school, so we're crazy excited to meet new people. We should probably work on the whole playing-hard-to-get thing."

"Hey, the hedges are a maze." I leaned over the balcony. The hedges around the front door were actually part of a carefully sculpted pattern interspersed with old-looking statues and benches.

"Cool, right? They have this ancient gardener who has spent half his life pruning those things."

"It looks like you could actually get lost."

"You can. Once Marco wandered out there and we couldn't find him for like three hours. We had to come up here with a spotlight. He was sleeping on his shoes."

"Why his shoes?"

"I have no idea. You want to hear something really creepy?"

I shook my head. "Not really."

"Elena's older sister, Manuela, refuses to live here because ever since she was little she's had this ancestor appear to her. The spooky part is that whenever the ghost appears she's the same age as Manuela."

"No wonder she's at boarding school." I leaned against the railing. "This place is making me feel way better about living in a cemetery."

"Telling ghost stories?"

I jumped, practically toppling over the edge.

"Lina! You're like the Incredible Startled Girl," Ren said.

"Sorry, guys. Didn't mean to scare you." A boy sat up on one of the couches and stretched his arms over his head.

"Hi, Thomas. Spy much?"

"I have a headache. I was just trying to get away from the

noise for a while. Who are you with?" He stood up and lazily made his way over to us.

OM . . . And then I couldn't remember how to end the acronym, because *who looks like this?*

Thomas was tall and thin with dark brown hair and thick eyebrows, and he had this strong-jaw thing going on that I'd heard about but never actually witnessed. And his *lips.* They were pretty much ruining any chance I had of forming words.

"Lina?" Ren was raising one eyebrow. *Crap. Did they ask me something?*

"Sorry, what'd you say?"

The boy grinned. "I just said that I'm Thomas. And I gather that you're the mysterious Carolina?" He had a British accent.

A British. Accent.

"Yes. Nice to meet you. I go by Lina." I shook his hand, doing my best to stay upright. Apparently "weak in the knees" was a real thing.

"American?"

"Yeah. Seattle. You?"

"All over. I've lived here for the past two years."

The door swung open and Elena and Mimi walked in. "*Ragazzi, dai.* My mom will *freak out* it if she finds out you are up here. I had a forty-five-minute lecture after the last party. Some *idiota* left a piece of pizza on a two-hundred-year-old credenza. Come downstairs, *per favore!*"

"Sorry, El," Thomas and Ren said in unison.

"I was just showing Lina the garden," Ren said. "And Thomas was taking a nap."

"Who takes a nap at a party? It's lucky you look like a god, because you're *veramente strano*. Really, Thomas."

Like a god. I snuck another look at Thomas. Yep. Could totally imagine him lounging around on Mt. Olympus.

Mimi linked arms with Ren and everyone walked out except for Thomas and me. Was I making this up, or was he staring at me, too?

Thomas crossed his arms. "A bunch of us made bets on whether or not you'd ever show. Looks like I'm going to be out twenty euro."

"I was supposed to move here earlier this year, but I decided to finish out the school year in Seattle."

"Still doesn't change the fact that you owe me twenty euro."

"I don't owe you anything. Maybe next time you should have a little more faith in me."

He grinned, raising one eyebrow. "I'll let you off the hook this one time."

My bones were roughly the consistency of strawberry jelly. He was so flirting with me.

"Did I hear you live in a cemetery?"

"My dad's the caretaker for the Florence American Cemetery. I'm staying with him for the summer."

"The whole summer?"

"Yes."

A slow smile spread across his face. I was smiling too.

"Thomas!" Elena shrieked from the doorway.

"Sorry." We both followed her out of the room.

So this is what it's like to be normal. Well, sort of normal.

"First concert you ever went to." Most everyone had moved outside to the pool and Thomas and I were sitting with our feet in the deep end. The water was glowing bright blue and either the stars had dropped down to our level or fireflies were everywhere.

"Jimmy Buffett."

"Really? Margaritaville guy?"

"I'm surprised you know who that is. And yeah, it was pretty much a sea of Hawaiian shirts. My mom took me."

We both ducked as a spray of water came our way. Half the party was playing a rowdy alcohol-fueled game of Marco Polo, and Marco kept getting stuck as, well, Marco. It was way funnier than it should have been.

"Okay, favorite movie."

"You're going to make fun of me."

"No, I won't. I promise."

"Fine. *Dirty Dancing*."

"*Dirty Dancing* . . ." He tipped his head back. "Oh, right.

That horrible eighties movie with Patrick Swayze as a dance teacher."

I splashed him. "It isn't horrible. And why do you know so much about it anyway?"

"Two older sisters."

He scooted in to me until our bodies touched from shoulder to hip. It was the exact sensation of licking a nine-volt battery.

". . . So you're a runner, you're from one of the coolest cities in the U.S., you have horrible taste in movies, you once blacked out snowboarding, and you've never tried sushi."

"Or rock climbing," I added.

"Or rock climbing."

Addie, you were so right. I splashed my feet around happily, sneaking another glance at Thomas. I was never going to hear the end of it. Who knew that guys this good-looking even *existed?* And, side note, he'd just slipped his arm around me. Like it was no big deal.

"So why did you move here?" Thomas asked.

"I came to stay with my dad. He's, uh . . . sort of new in my life."

"Gotcha."

There was a *crash*ing noise, and suddenly Ren came careening out of the darkness behind us. "Lina, it's twelve thirty!"

"Already?" I pulled my feet out of the water and Thomas dropped his arm. I stood reluctantly.

"We have to go now. He'll kill me! He'll *kill* me." Ren clutched his hands to his chest and fell over on the grass.

"He's not going to kill you."

"Who's going to kill you?" Thomas asked.

"Lina's dad. The first time I talked to him he said he had a bullet with my name on it."

"No, he didn't." I looked at him. "Wait. Did he?"

"He might as well have." He rolled to his knees, then stood up. "Come on. We have to leave now."

"You have a bunch of grass in your hair," I said.

He shook his head like a dog, sending grass flying. "I was rolling down a hill."

"A Swedish hill?" Thomas asked.

"I didn't ask its nationality."

I groaned. "Is it really twelve thirty? Maybe we could stay for just another twenty minutes or something."

Ren threw his hands in the air. "Lina. Don't you care whether I live or die?"

"Of course I care. I just wish we didn't have to leave."

Thomas stood too, then wrapped his arms around me, his chin resting heavily on my shoulder. "But, Lina, it's so early. I'll be so bored without you. Can't you get an extension?"

Ren raised an eyebrow. "I see things have *progressed* in the last couple of hours."

My mouth would not stop smiling. I turned my face so Ren wouldn't see. "Sorry, Thomas. I do have to leave."

He blew air out of his mouth. "Fine. Guess we'll just have to hang out again."

"*Ciao, tutti*," Ren yelled to the group. "I have to take Lina home. She has a curfew."

There was a chorus of "*Ciao, Lina*s."

"*Ciao,*" I yelled back.

"Wait!" Marcus pulled himself out of the pool. "What about the initiation? She has to do it."

"What initiation?" I asked.

"She has to walk the plank."

Ren groaned. "Marco, that's dumb. We stopped doing that in like seventh grade."

"Hey, you guys made *me* do it, and that was just last year," Olivier protested. "Also, it was November. I froze my balls off."

"Yes, she must do it," another girl chimed in. "It is tradition."

"She is wearing jeans," Elena said. "*È troppo* mean."

"Doesn't matter! Rules are rules!"

Thomas sidled up next to me. "If you jump, I'll jump too."

Cut to mental image of Thomas soaking wet.

I turned to Ren. "How much will you hate me if you have to drive me home drenched?"

"Not as much as you'll hate yourself."

I kicked off my sandals and headed for the diving board.

"New girl's going for it!" Marco whooped.

The whole party broke out in wild applause as I climbed up on the diving board, then bowed. *Is this me?* Too late to wonder. I sprinted down the board, bouncing high and tucking into the world's most perfect cannonball.

I felt the most alive I had in more than a year. Maybe ever.

Chapter 10

SO MAYBE SOGGY SCOOTER RIDING WASN'T MY MOST brilliant idea. By the time we pulled up to the house I was shaking like crazy. Also, the pool had reactivated my hair's natural crazy, and when I took off my helmet, my hair fluffed around my head like a cloud.

"Are you shivering because you're cold or because you're terrified?"

"Cold. Ren, come on. We're an hour late. What's he going to do?"

The front door burst open and Howard stepped into the doorway, his enormous silhouette illuminated against the light.

Now we were both shivering.

"Want me to come in with you?" Ren whispered.

I shook my head. "Thanks for the ride. I really had a lot of fun."

"Me too. See you tomorrow. Good luck."

I waddled up to the door, my jeans sticking to my legs. "Sorry I'm late. We lost track of time."

He squinted at me. "Is your hair wet?"

"They made me walk the plank."

"The plank?"

"It's their initiation ritual. I jumped into the pool."

A faint smile glimmered under his stern look. "So tonight was a success."

"Yes."

"I'm glad to hear it." He looked over my head. "Good night, Ren."

"Good night, Mr. . . . Carolina's dad." He spun his scooter around and took off in a spray of gravel.

"Hello, hello," a woman said as I followed Howard into the house.

Sonia and four other people were sitting on the couches, wineglasses in hand. Jazz music was playing in the background and everyone looked a little tipsy. Apparently Howard was having a party too. Cemetery-style. Maybe later they'd all dive into the little pools in front of the memorial.

"Everyone, this is Lina," Sonia said. "Lina, everyone."

"Hi."

"*Che bella.* You are a beauty," an older woman in cat-eyed-glasses purred.

Howard grinned. "Isn't she?"

"We are old friends of your dad's," one of the men said in deliberate English. "We've known him since his wild stallion days. Oh, the stories we could tell."

"Yeah," the guy next to him chimed in. "He wasn't giving you a hard time about being late, was he? Because maybe I should tell you about the time we went backpacking through Hungary and he—"

"That's enough," Howard said quickly. "Lina went for a little swim, so I'm sure she wants to go upstairs and get changed."

"Pity," Cat Eyes said.

"Good night," I said.

"Good night," they all chorused back.

I clambered up the stairs. I was *freezing*.

"She's the photographer's daughter?" It was Cat Eyes. I froze.

"Yes. She's Hadley's."

Silence.

And . . . yours, too, right? I waited for him to clarify, but someone just changed the subject.

What was *that* about?

I FaceTimed Addie as soon as I was in dry clothes. "You ready to say 'I told you so'?"

"I am *always* ready to say 'I told you so.' Oh my gosh! How was it? Amazing?" She started bouncing up and down on her bed.

I turned down the volume on my computer. "Yes. A-mazing."

"Please tell me you met the hottest of hot Italian guys."

"I did. But he's not Italian. He's British."

She squealed. "Even better! Is he online? I have to stalk him."

"I don't know. I didn't ask."

"I'll look him up. What's his name?"

"Thomas Heath."

"Even his name is attractive." She was quiet for a minute as she typed in his name. "Thomas ... Heath ... Florence ..." She inhaled sharply. "HOLY MOTHER OF HOTNESS. That is the best hair I have ever seen. He looks like a model. Maybe an underwear model."

"Right?"

"Have you seen him without his shirt on? You have to get online and see these pictures. Great. Now you'll never come back to Seattle. Why would you when *Thomas Heath* is—"

"Addie, slow down! It doesn't matter how hot he is. I'm not staying here."

"What do you mean it doesn't matter? You can have a summer fling, can't you? And wow. I mean, really, *wow*. That is one good-looking guy. What's your other friend's name?"

"Ren. But his full name is Lorenzo Ferrara."

"Yeah, you're gonna have to spell that for me."

"His mom said it's like 'Ferrari' but with an *a*."

"Ferrari with an *a* . . ." She bit her lip and typed into her keyboard. "Curly hair? Plays soccer?"

"That's him."

She grinned at me. "Well, Lina, you're two for two. Ren's adorable. So if Underwear Model doesn't work out, you're still in good shape."

"No, Ren's off the table. I met his girlfriend tonight. She's like Sadie Danes, only Swedish. And Photoshopped."

"Shut up. Did you run for your life?"

"Pretty much. She didn't seem all that happy that Ren brought some new girl along."

Addie sighed, falling back on her pillow. "I'm spending the rest of the summer living vicariously through you. And I know the cemetery thing is weird, but now I'm one hundred percent on board with you being there. You have to stay there for at least a little while. Do it for me. Please!"

"We'll see. How's Matt?"

"Still not getting the message that I'm interested. But who cares about him? On a scale of one to ten, how weird would it be if I printed out Thomas's profile picture and had it framed?"

I laughed. "Weird. Even for you."

"Or how about I make a Thomas calendar? 'Twelve Months of British Hotness.' Do you think you could get more pictures of him with his shirt off? Maybe you could spill Kool-Aid or something on him next time you're together."

"Yeah, definitely not doing that."

She sighed again. "You're right. That would be pretty weird. So how's the journal?"

"I'm just about to read more." I hesitated. "Last night was kind of hard, but it was nice, too. She really loved it here."

"And so will you. And so will I. Vicariously."

I shook my head. "We'll see."

"Okay, you get back to the journal. I want to know what her wrong choice was. The suspense is killing me."

"Night, Addie."

"Morning, Lina."

***

JULY 2

Florence is exactly how I thought it would be and nothing like it at all. It is absolutely magical—the cobblestones, the old buildings, the bridges—and yet it's gritty, too. You'll be walking down the most charming street you've ever seen and suddenly get a whiff of open sewer or step in something disgusting. The city enchants you, then brings you right back down to reality. I've never been anyplace that I want to capture so much. I spend a lot of time photographing things that seem uniquely Italian—laundry hanging in alleyways, red geraniums planted in old tomato-sauce cans—but mostly I try to capture the people. Italians are so expressive; you never have to guess what they're feeling.

Tonight I watched the sun set at Ponte Vecchio. I think its safe to say I have finally found the place that feels right to me. I just can't believe I had to come halfway across the world to find it.

JULY 9

Francesca has officially inducted me into her circle of friends. They were all at FAAF last semester too, and they're smart and hilarious, and I secretly wonder if they're being followed around by reality-TV cameras. How can this many interesting people be together in one spot? Here's our cast of characters:

Howard: The perfect Southern gentleman (Southern giant, Francesca calls him), handsome, kind, and the sort of guy who will go marching into battle for you.

He's in a research program studying Florence history, and when he isn't teaching he sits in on a lot of our classes.

Finn: An Ernest Hemingway wannabe from Martha's Vineyard. He pretends to just happen to have a full beard and a penchant for turtlenecks, but we all know he spends half his time reading <u>The Sun Also Rises</u>.

Adrienne: French and probably the prettiest person I've ever seen in real life. She is very quiet and unbelievably talented.

Simone and Alessio: I'm grouping them together because they are ALWAYS together. They grew up together just outside of Rome and are constantly getting into fistfights—typically over the fact that neither of them has ever dated a girl that the other didn't immediately fall in love with.

And finally . . .

Me: Pretty boring. American wannabe photographer who has been giddy since the moment her plane touched down in Florence.

Mine and Francesca's apartment has become the official hangout. We all crowd onto the tiny balcony and have long discussions about things like shutter speed and exposure. Is this heaven?

JULY 20

Turns out you can't learn Italian through osmosis, no matter how many times you fall asleep with <u>Italian for Dummies</u> propped open on your face. Francesca said that learning a language is the easiest thing in the world, but she said it while simultaneously smoking, studying aperture, and making homemade pesto, so she may not have a normal grasp on "easy." I signed up for the institute's beginner Italian class. It's held evenings in the mixed-media room and meets three times a week. Finn and Howard are in the class too. They're both much further along than I am, but I'm glad to have them for company.

AUGUST 23

It's been more than a month since I've written, but I have good reason. I'm sure it will come as no surprise when I say that I've fallen in L-O-V-E. What a cliché! But seriously, move to Florence and eat a few forkfuls of pasta, then stroll in the twilight and just TRY not to fall for that guy you've been ogling from day one! You'll probably fail. I <u>love</u> being in love in Italy. But truth be told, I would fall for X anywhere. He's handsome, intelligent, charming, and everything I've ever dreamed of. We also have to keep things completely secret, which, if I'm totally honest, makes him all the more appealing. (Yes, X. I seriously don't think anyone would read my journal, but I'm giving him a new name, just in case.)

WHAT? I let the book fall onto my lap. It had taken only three pages for Howard to make the leap from squeaky-clean "Southern gentleman" to secret lover X. Apparently I hadn't been giving him enough credit.

I picked up my laptop and FaceTimed Addie again, and she answered almost immediately. Her hair was wrapped in a towel and she was holding a half-eaten freezer waffle. "What's up?"

"They had to keep their relationship a secret." I kept my voice down. It sounded like Howard's guests were on their way out, but there was still some backslapping and "Let's do this again soon" going on outside on the front porch.

"Howard and your mom?"

"Yeah. She talks about them being in the same group of friends, and then suddenly she's calling him by a new name because she's worried someone will pick up her journal and find out that they're secretly dating."

"Scandalous!" Addie said happily. "Why did they have to be secretive? Was he in the mafia or something?"

"I don't know yet."

"Call me back when you figure it out. Crap. I won't be here! Ian's driving me to the car dealership. I'm finally getting my car back."

"That's good news."

"Tell me about it. Last night Ian made me fold all his nasty laundry before he'd take me to Dylan's. Call me tomorrow?"

"Definitely."

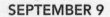

SEPTEMBER 9

Now that I've started writing about my storia d'amore, I might as well tell it from the very beginning. X was actually one of the very first people I met when I arrived in Florence. He gave one of the semester's opening lectures, and afterward I just couldn't stop thinking about him. He's obviously talented, and the kind of good-looking that makes you stumble over words like "hello" and "good-bye," but there was something else—he had this <u>depth</u> to him. It made me want to figure him out.

Lucky for me we were able to spend a lot of time together in and out of class. It's just that we were never alone. Ever. Francesca was either sitting in the corner rattling away on her phone or Simone and Alessio would ask us to weigh in on some ridiculous new argument, and our conversations just never seemed to get all that far. I had this big debate going on my head. IS HE OR ISN'T HE INTERESTED? Some days I was positive he was, and others I was less sure. Maybe I was just reading too much into things?

But I kept catching him staring at me during class, and every time we talked, there was this <u>something</u> between us that I couldn't ignore. This went on for weeks. And then, finally, just when I thought I was imagining the whole thing, I saw him at Space. Francesca calls it the official nightclub of FAAF, but he'd never come with us before. I had stepped outside for a little air, and when I came back in, there he was, leaning against the wall. Alone.

I knew this was my chance, but as I started toward him I realized I had absolutely no idea what to say. "Hi. I hope this doesn't sound crazy, but have you noticed this weird chemistry thing between us?" Luckily I didn't even have to open my mouth. As soon as he saw me, he reached out and grabbed my wrist. "Hadley," he said. And the way he said it—I knew that I hadn't been imagining things.

SEPTEMBER 15

Met X at the Boboli Gardens so we could be alone for a while. It's a sixteenth-century park, kind of an oasis in the middle of the city. Lots of architecture and fountains and enough space to let you forget you're in a city. We both took our cameras, and when we'd captured everything we wanted to, we sat down under a tree and talked. He knows so much about art. And history. And literature. (And everything, really.) The grounds closed at seven thirty, but when I stood up to pack up my things, he pulled me back down and we kissed until a guard made us leave.

SEPTEMBER 20

The only hard part about being in love with X is not telling anyone about it. I know the school wouldn't be okay with us dating, but it's hard to keep something this big a secret. It's torture to spend half our days within ten feet of each other and not even touch.

I'm pretty bad at secret-keeping, and everyone seems to know I'm in love. Part of it is logistics. Most nights we meet up late, and I don't get home until three or four a.m. I told Francesca that I'm out working on my night photography, but she just rolled her eyes and told me she knows all about "night photography."

Part of me wonders if everyone is just pretending not to know what's going on. Are they really that dense? Our relationship is taking place right under their noses!

OCTOBER 9

X and I are starting to get really creative about where we meet. We knew that everyone else would be staying in studying tonight, so we went to Space (one and the same) and after we'd danced until we were exhausted we wandered around the city. X told me he had a surprise for me and we started winding our way through the dark streets until I could smell something amazing—a mixture of sugar and butter and something else. Bliss?

Finally we turned a corner and saw a group of people gathered around a brightly lit doorway. It was a secret bakery—one of a few. Basically, commercial bakers work through the night to produce pastries for restaurants, and even though it's illegal, they'll give you a freshly baked pastry for a few euro.

Only a few insiders know about it, but those who do, well . . . let's just say they're in danger of becoming nocturnal.

Everyone in line was acting really quiet and nervous, and when it was our turn, X bought a chocolate-filled cornetta, a glazed croissant, and two stuffed cannoli. Then we sat down on a curb and devoured all of it. When I got home Francesca, Finn, and Simone were sprawled out on our tiny couches and they all teased me about what kind of night shots I'd gotten. I wish I could tell them.

***

Wow.

First of all, sign me up for a trip to the secret bakery. I didn't even know what a *cornetta* or cannoli was, and I was still practically salivating all over the pages. But most important, what was the deal with all this secrecy?

I flipped back through the entries. Did schools really have policies on students not dating assistant teachers? I could see it being a rule for actual professors, but research students? And my mom had been *smitten*. How was it possible that someone this crazy about their boyfriend had ended up walking out and keeping their child a secret for sixteen years?

I marked my place in the journal, then walked over to the window. It was a gorgeous night. Clouds were drifting past the moon like ghost ships, and now that Howard's friends had cleared out, everything was still and quiet.

Suddenly a blur of movement caught my eye and I froze. What was *that*? I leaned out the window, my heart hammering against my rib cage. A white figure was moving toward the house. It looked like a person, but it was moving way too fast, like a . . . I squinted. Was that *Howard*? On a long board?

"What are you doing?" I whispered. He kicked off hard and went sailing past the driveway, like a seal gliding out to sea. Like it was something he did all the time.

I had to figure this guy out.

Chapter 11

"LINA, YOU AWAKE? PHONE'S FOR YOU." HOWARD knocked on my open bedroom door, and I shoved the journal under the bed. I'd been rereading the entries from the night before. And stalling. Because, yes, I wanted to know what had happened. But I also wanted to prolong the happy part. Sort of like the time I stopped *Titanic* halfway through and made Addie watch the first part over again.

"Who is it?"

"Ren. I've got to get you your own phone. You just hang on to my cell phone for now. I'll use the landline."

"Thanks." I got up and walked over to him. He looked wide-awake and very un-X-like. No evidence of his ghostly night riding. Or sketchy dating practices.

He handed me the phone. "Will you please tell Ren that he doesn't need to be afraid of me? He just set a world record for using 'sir' the most times in a single conversation."

"I can, but it probably won't do any good. You really messed with him that first time you talked."

"I had good reason." He smiled. "See you a little later? I should be off work around five."

"Okay." I put the phone to my ear and Howard stepped out into the hallway. Ciao, *mysterious X.*

"Hi, Ren."

"*Ciao,* Lina. I'm so glad you're alive."

I leaned casually out the door and watched Howard walk down the stairs. He'd made out with my mom in a public park? Totally not the kind of thing you should have to know about your parents. And what had been so special about the way he'd said her name that first time they'd connected at Space? It sounded like a cheesy scene from one of those soap operas Addie's mom pretended not to watch.

"You there?" Ren asked.

"Yeah, sorry. I'm kind of distracted." I closed my bedroom door, then sat on my bed.

"So he wasn't mad?"

"No. He was having a party, and I don't think he even noticed we were late."

"*Fortunato.* Have you gone running yet?"

"No. I was just about to. Want to come?"

"Already on my way. Meet me at the cemetery gates."

I changed, then ran out to meet him. Ren was wearing

a bright orange T-shirt and was jogging in place like an old man. As usual his hair was in his eyes and he looked sort of warm and glowy from the run over.

"How is *this* not American-looking?" I asked, plucking at his shirt.

"It's not American-looking when it's on an Italian."

"Half-Italian," I corrected.

"Half is enough. Trust me." We started up the road.

"So your mom won a LensCulture Award," he said.

I looked at him. "How'd you know?"

"There's this thing called the Internet. It's really helpful."

"Oh yeah, I vaguely remember that from back before I lived in Italy." I'd tried to FaceTime Addie about ten times that morning to update her on the night's reading, but so far I'd just gotten this annoying NO SERVIZIO message over and over. At least now I could use Howard's phone whenever I wanted.

"I found a bunch of articles on her. You didn't tell me she was a big deal."

"The LensCulture jump-started her career. That's when she started doing photography full-time."

"I liked the picture. I've never seen anything like it. What was it called? *Erased?*" He sprinted ahead of me, then wrapped his arms around himself, looking over one shoulder. The photograph had been of a woman who'd just had a tattooed name removed from her shoulder.

I laughed. "Not bad."

He fell back in line with me. "I also saw the self-portraits she did while she was sick. They were pretty intense. And I saw you in some of them."

I kept my eyes laser focused on the road. "I don't really like looking at those."

"Understandable."

The road dipped and I automatically sped up. Ren did too.

"So . . . you hanging out with your friends again soon?" I asked.

"You mean Thomas?"

I flushed. "And . . . others." Priority number one was figuring out what had gone on between Howard and my mother, but that didn't mean I had to let my chance with Thomas go to waste, right?

"It's Marco, right? You really want to see him again, don't you?"

I laughed again. "Maybe."

"Didn't Thomas get your number?"

"I don't even have a number. You keep calling me at the cemetery, remember?" Also, he hadn't asked for it. Probably because he'd remembered his expensive watch *after* following me into the pool.

"I also called you on your dad's cell phone. Even though it was terrifying."

"How'd you even get that number?"

"Sonia. But it took me like an hour to get up the courage to use it."

I sighed. "Ren, you've got to get over that first bad conversation with Howard. I mean, he's a pretty nice guy. It's not like he's going to hurt you for being nice to me."

"Have you ever been yelled at by an ogre for something you didn't do? It's not that easy to get over."

"Ogre?" I laughed.

"People just aren't that tall here. I bet he gets stared at everywhere he goes."

"Probably."

The world's tiniest truck sped past us, sending out a series of staccato beeps. Ren waved. "Hey, do you want to go into town with me tonight? We could get some ice cream or just walk around or something. Maybe like eight thirty?"

"Think Swedish Model would be okay with that?"

I meant it as a joke, but he looked at me seriously. "I think it will be all right."

When Ren arrived to pick me up, Howard and I were finishing dinner. He'd made a big bowl of pasta with fresh tomatoes and mozzarella, and I'd spent the whole meal staring at him like a complete weirdo. *X is handsome, intelligent, and charming.* Except for when you get pregnant with his baby? Then he's suddenly so terrible that you flee halfway across the world and avoid him for the next sixteen years? I'd picked up the journal three different times that afternoon, and each time I'd had to set it back down. It was just so overwhelming.

"Is everything all right?" Howard asked.

"Yes. I was just . . . thinking." Ever since we'd had that talk about *not* talking about my mom, things had been feeling a little better. He was actually pretty easy to be around. Sort of laid-back-beach-guy-meets-history-buff.

I stabbed another forkful of pasta. "This is really good."

"Well, that's in spite of the chef. It's pretty hard to mess up when you have such great ingredients. So what do you think about tomorrow? I can take the whole day off so we'll have plenty of time for sightseeing."

"Okay."

"Where are you and Ren headed tonight?"

"He just said he wants to go into town."

"Lina?" Ren poked his head into the kitchen.

"Speak of the devil," I said.

"Sorry I'm late." He caught sight of Howard and startled. "And I probably should have knocked. Sir."

Howard smiled. "Hey, Ren. Would you like some dinner? I made *pasta con pomodori e mozzarella*."

"*Buonissimo*. But no thanks. I already ate. My mom tried

to re-create a Kentucky Fried Chicken meal and she made this giant pot of potatoes that basically turned to glue. I'm still trying to get over it."

"Ewww."

Howard laughed. "Been there. Sometimes you just have to have KFC." He picked up his plate and walked into the kitchen.

Ren sat down next to me and grabbed a noodle from my plate. "So, where should we go tonight?"

"How should I know? You're the one from Florence."

"Yeah, but I get the feeling you haven't spent much time in the city. Anything you've been dying to see?"

"Isn't there like a leaning tower or something?"

"Linaaa. That's in Pisa."

"Relax, I'm joking. But actually, there is something I want to see. Come upstairs with me for a second." I took my plate to the kitchen, then Ren followed me to my bedroom.

"Is this really your room?" he asked when we stepped inside.

"Yeah. Why?"

"Haven't you unpacked anything? It's kind of bare in here." He opened one of my empty dresser drawers, then slowly rolled it shut.

"All my stuff's over there." I pointed to my suitcase. Everything was piled on top of it, and it looked like there had been some kind of explosion.

"Aren't you going to be here awhile?"

"Just for the summer."

"That's like two more months."

"Hopefully it will be less." I shot a look at the open door. *Yikes.* Was it just me, or had my voice just reverberated through the whole cemetery?

"I don't think he can hear us."

"I hope not." I crossed the room, then knelt to get the journal from under the bed and started flipping through the pages. "I just read about this place . . . Pont Ve-chee-o?"

"*Ponte Vecchio?*" He looked at me incredulously. "You're joking, right?"

"I know I said it wrong."

"Well, yeah, I mean you totally butchered it. But you've never *been* there? How long have you been in Florence?"

"Since Tuesday night."

"That means you should have seen Ponte Vecchio by Wednesday morning. Get dressed. We're leaving."

I looked down at what I was wearing. "I am dressed."

"Sorry. Figure of speech. Get your purse or whatever. We're going now. You have to see it. It's in my top ten most favorite places in the entire world."

"Is it open? It's almost nine."

He groaned. "Yes, it's open. Come on."

I grabbed the money Howard had given me the night

before, then stuffed my mom's journal into my purse. Ren was already halfway down the stairs, but he stopped abruptly at the bottom and I crashed right into him.

Howard was sitting on the couch, his laptop balanced on his knees. "Where are you two headed in such a hurry?"

"Lina's never been to Ponte Vecchio. I'm taking her." Ren cleared his throat. "With your permission, sir."

"Permission granted. That's a great idea. Lina, you'll love it."

"Thanks. I hope so."

We headed for the door, and just as Ren stepped out on the porch Howard said, "I'm keeping my eye on you, Ren."

Ren didn't turn around, but he straightened up like someone had just sent a jolt of electricity down his spine. Howard caught my eye and winked.

Great. Now Ren was never going to relax.

It was a hot night, and Florence seemed twice as crowded as the night I'd gone with Howard. Traveling by scooter was a little faster because we could just drive around stopped cars, but it still took us a long time. Not that I minded. Riding the scooter was really fun, and the cool air whipping past us felt like my reward for surviving such a long, hot day. By the time Ren parked his scooter, the moon had risen round and heavy as a ripe tomato, and I felt like I'd taken a long, cool swim.

"Why's it so crowded tonight?" I asked, handing him my helmet to stow under the seat.

"It's summer. People like to go out. And tourists come in droves. Droves, I tell you!"

I shook my head. "Ren, you're kind of weird."

"So I hear."

"What are we going to see exactly?"

"A bridge. 'Ponte Vecchio' means 'Old Bridge.' It's on the Arno. Come on, it's this way." I did my best to keep up with him as he elbowed his way across the street, and before long we were standing on a wide sidewalk running the length of the river. The Arno stretched black and mysterious in either direction, and the banks were lit up like a runway with strings of glittering lights that stretched and disappeared in either direction.

I gave myself a second to take it all in. "Ren . . . this is really pretty. I can't believe people get to actually live here."

"Like you?"

I glanced at him and he was smiling. Duh. "Well, yeah, I guess so."

"Just wait. What you see next is going to make you want to stay here forever."

People kept pushing us away from each other, so Ren linked arms with me and we headed up the river, stepping over a long-haired guy sitting with his back to the water. He was playing a banged-up guitar and singing "Imagine" in a heavy accent.

"'Ee-magine all da pee-pull,'" Ren sang. "My dad has this book that's supposed to teach English song lyrics to Italian speakers. I think that guy back there could really use it."

"Hey, at least he got the feeling right. He sounds really nostalgic." My arm was kind of heating up where Ren's was interlocked with mine, but before I could think about it, he pulled away and put both hands on my shoulders.

"Ready to swallow your gum?"

"What?"

"Ready to see Ponte Vecchio?"

"Of course. That's why we're here, right?"

He turned and pointed. "This way."

The sidewalk had led us to a small commuter bridge. It was paved with asphalt, and a bunch of tourists were milling around blankets set up with displays of knockoff bags and sunglasses. *So* not impressive.

"This is it?" I asked, trying not to sound disappointed. Maybe it was cooler at sunset.

Ren guffawed. "No. Not *this* bridge. Trust me, you'll know it when you see it."

We headed toward the center of the bridge, and a dark-skinned man stepped out in front of his blanket of stuff, blocking our way. "Young man. You want nice Prada handbag for girlfriend? Five hundred euro in store, but ten euro for you. Make her fall in true love."

"No thanks," Ren said.

I nudged him. "I don't know, Ren. That sounds like a pretty good deal. Ten bucks for true love?"

He smiled, stopping in the center of the bridge. "You didn't see it, did you?"

"See wha—oh."

I ran over to the railing. Stretched across the river, about a quarter mile ahead of us, was a bridge that looked like it had been built by fairies. Three stone arches rose gracefully out of the water, and the whole length of it was lined with a floating row of colorful buildings, their edges hanging over the water. Three mini-arches were cut out of the center, and the whole thing was lit golden in the darkness, its reflection sparkling back up at itself.

Gum officially swallowed.

Ren was grinning at me.

"Wow. I don't even know what to say."

"I know, right? Come on." He looked to his right, then his left, then launched himself over the side like a pole vaulter.

"Ren!"

I leaned over, fully expecting to see him dog-paddling toward Ponte Vecchio, but instead came face-to-face with him. He was crouching on a table-size ledge that jutted out about five feet below the side of the bridge and he looked ridiculously pleased with himself.

"I was waiting for a splash."

"I know. Now come on. Just make sure no one sees you."

I looked over my shoulder, but everyone was too involved in the whole fake-Prada-bag thing to pay me any attention. I climbed over, dropped down next to him. "Is this allowed?"

"Definitely not. But it's the best view."

"It's amazing." Being just a few feet lower somehow cut out the noise of the people above us, and I swear Ponte Vecchio was glowing even brighter and more regal. It gave me a solemn, awestruck kind of feeling. Like going to church. Only I wanted to stay here for the whole rest of my life.

"So what do you think?" Ren asked.

"It makes me think of this time my mom and I drove to a poppy reserve in California. The flowers all bloom at once and we timed our visit just right. It was pretty magical."

"Like this?"

"Yeah."

He shimmied back next to me and we both rested our heads against the wall, just looking. *I have finally found the place that feels right to me.* It was like she was waving at me from just across the water. If I squinted I could almost see her. My eyes fogged up a little, turning Ponte Vecchio's lights into big gold halos, and I had to spend like thirty seconds pretending to have some mysterious Arno dust in my eye.

For once, Ren was being totally quiet and once the crying

jag had passed I looked over at him. "So why is it called 'Old Bridge'? Isn't everything old here?"

"It's the only bridge that survived World War II, and it's really, really old, even by Italian standards. Like medieval old. Those house-looking things used to be butcher shops. They'd just open the windows and dump all the blood and guts into the river."

"No way." I glanced at the windows again. Most of them had green shutters and they were all closed for the night. "They're way too pretty for that. What are they now?"

"High-end jewelry shops. And you see those windows spaced out across the very top of the bridge?"

I nodded. "Yeah?"

"Those go to a hallway. It's called the Vasari Corridor and it was used by the Medici as a way to get around Florence without having to actually walk through the city."

"Elena's people."

"*Esattamente.* That way they didn't have to mix with us commoners. Cosimo Medici was the one who kicked out all the butchers. He wanted the bridge to be more prestigious." He looked at me. "So what was that book you were reading? The one you had under your bed."

You trust him. The words elbowed their way into my head before I even had a chance to wonder. So what if I'd known Ren for only two days? I did trust him.

I took the journal out of my purse. "This is my mom's journal. She was living in Florence when she got pregnant with me and it's all about her time in Italy. She sent it to the cemetery before she died."

He glanced at the book, then back up at me. "No way. That's pretty *heavy*."

Heavy. That was exactly it. I opened to the front cover, looking again at those ominous words. "I started reading it the day after I got here. I'm trying to figure out what happened between Howard and my mom."

"What do you mean?"

I hesitated. Was it possible to condense the whole messy story into a couple of sentences? "My mom met Howard when she was here going to school, and then when she got pregnant, she left Italy and never told him about me."

"Seriously?"

"Once she got sick she started talking about him a lot, and then she made me promise I'd come live here with him for a while. She just never actually told me what went wrong between them, and I think she left me the journal so I could figure it out."

I turned and met Ren's stare. "So last night when you said you don't know Howard very well, it was like a huge understatement."

"Yeah. I've officially known him for . . ." I counted on my fingers. "Four days."

"No way." He shook his head incredulously, sending his hair flying. "So let me get this straight. You're an American, living in Florence—no, living in a *cemetery*—with a father you just found out about? You're even stranger than I am."

"Hey!"

He bumped his shoulder against mine. "No, I didn't mean it that way. I just meant we're both kind of different."

"What makes you different?"

"I'm sort of American, sort of Italian. When I'm in Italy I feel too American, and when I'm in the States I feel too Italian. Also, I'm older than everyone in my grade."

"How old are you?"

"Seventeen. My family lived in Texas for a couple of years when I was really young, and when we moved back I didn't speak Italian very well. I was already kind of old for my grade, and they had to hold me back a year so I could catch up. My parents ended up enrolling me at the American school a few years later, but the school wouldn't allow me to skip forward to the grade I'm supposed to be in."

"When will you be eighteen?"

"March." He looked at me. "So you're really only staying for the summer?"

"Yeah. Howard and my grandma want me to stay longer, but the circumstances are obviously pretty weird. I barely know him."

"But maybe you'll get to know him. Chainsaw aside, I kind of like him."

I shrugged. "It just seems so bizarre. If my mom hadn't gotten sick, I probably still wouldn't know anything about him. She'd always just told me that she'd gotten pregnant young and decided it was best to keep my father out of the picture."

"Until now."

"Until now," I echoed.

"Where will you live when you leave Florence?"

"Hopefully with my friend Addie. I stayed with them for the rest of sophomore year, and she's going to ask her parents if I can stay with them next year too."

He looked at the journal. "So what have you been reading about in there?"

"Well, so far I know that they had to keep their relationship a secret. He was an assistant teacher at the school she was going to, and I guess the school wouldn't have liked it. And she was hard-core about keeping it a secret. Like after they started dating, she stopped writing his name because was afraid someone would read her journal and find out about them. She just calls him 'X.'"

He shook his head. "Scandalous. Well, that's probably your answer right there. Seems like most secret romances have a shelf life."

"Maybe. But when I first got here Sonia told me that my mom lived with Howard at the cemetery for a while, so that's not exactly secretive. And she said that one day my mom just left. She didn't even say good-bye to Sonia."

"Wow. Something must have happened. Something big."

"Like . . . my mom got pregnant?"

"Oh. I guess that would be a big deal." He chewed on his lower lip thoughtfully. "Now you have me curious. Keep me in the loop, would you?"

"Sure."

"So she loved Ponte Vecchio. What other places did she write about?"

I took the journal from him and started flipping through it. "She talks about this club a couple of times, Space."

"Space Electronic?" He laughed. "No way. I was there like two weeks ago. Elena loves it. She knows one of the DJs, so we usually get in for free. Where else?"

"The Duomo, Boboli Gardens . . . He also took her to a secret bakery. Do you know where one is?"

"A secret bakery?"

I handed him the journal. "Read here."

He scanned the entry. "I've never heard of this, but it sounds awesome. Too bad she didn't write down the address—I could totally go for a fresh *cornetta*."

His phone started ringing and he pulled it out of his

pocket and hesitated for a second, then hit SILENCE. It started ringing again right away and he hit SILENCE again.

"Who is it?"

"No one."

He shoved the phone back in his pocket, but not before I saw the name on the screen. *Mimi.*

"Hey, do you want to get a gelato?"

I wrinkled my forehead. "What's that?"

He groaned. "Gelato. Italian ice cream. The greatest thing that will ever happen to you. What have you been *doing* since you arrived?"

"Hanging out with you."

"And you're telling me I only have one summer." He shook his head, then stood up. "Come on, Lina. We've got work to do."

Chapter 12

SO . . . ITALIAN GELATO. TAKE THE DELICIOUSNESS OF A regular ice-cream cone, times it by a million, then sprinkle it with crushed-up unicorn horns. Ren stopped me after my fourth scoop. I probably would have kept going forever.

When I walked in the front door Howard was watching an old James Bond movie with his bare feet propped up on the coffee table. There was an industrial-size bucket of popcorn sitting next to him.

"Movie just started—want to watch?"

I glanced at the screen. Old-school James Bond was swimming toward a building wearing a disguise that basically consisted of a stuffed duck attached to a helmet. Normally I was all over cheesy old movies, but tonight I had other things on my mind. "No thanks. I'm going to get some rest." *And hopefully some answers.*

NOVEMBER 9

Tonight was the best night of my life, and I have a statue to thank for it.

X and I were standing in Piazza della Signoria looking at a statue by Giambologna called <u>The Rape of the Sabine Women</u>. The name confused me because it doesn't match what's going on. It's of three figures: a man holding a woman up in the air and a second man crouching down on the ground looking up at her. There's obviously something distressing going on, but the three of them are graceful, harmonious even.

I told X that I thought the woman looked like she was being lifted up, not hurt, and as usual he knew the story. When Rome was first settled, the men realized their civilization was missing one very important ingredient: women. But where to find them? The only women within striking distance belonged to a neighboring tribe called the Sabines, and when the Romans went to ask for permission to marry some of their daughters, all they got was a big fat no. So in a particularly Roman move, they invited the Sabines to a party, then, partway through the night, overpowered the men and dragged all the women kicking and screaming back to their city. Eventually the Sabines managed to break into Rome, but by that time they were too late. The women didn't want to be rescued. They'd fallen for their captors and it turned out life in Rome was actually pretty great. The reason I was confused by the statue's title is that it is mistranslated in English. The Latin word "raptio" sounds like "rape" but actually means "kidnapping." So really the sculpture should be called <u>The Kidnapping of the Sabine Women</u>.

It was already late and I told X I needed to head home, but suddenly he turned to me and told me he loved me. He said it casually, like it wasn't the first time he'd said it, and it took a moment for the words to seep in. Then I made him repeat it. He LOVES me. Carry me off. I'm invested.

NOVEMBER 10

Went to class this morning on about two hours of sleep. X arrived late, and even though I knew he'd probably gotten even less sleep than I had, he somehow looked perfect. He broke our act-like-friends-in-school rule and gave me a big shiny smile that anyone could see. I wish I could pause this moment and live in it forever.

NOVEMBER 17

Sometimes I feel like my time is divided into two categories: time with X, and time spent waiting to be with X. Since that night in Piazza della Signoria, things have been up and down between us. Some days we get along perfectly, and other days he acts like I really _am_ just a friend. Lately I feel like he's been overly cautious about keeping things secret. Would it be that big of a deal if everyone knew? I think they'd be happy for us.

NOVEMBER 21

When I left for Italy in June, six months sounded like an eternity. Now it feels like it's slipping through my fingers. I only have a month left! The school director, Signore Petrucione, told me they'd love to admit me for another semester, and I would kill for a little extra time to study and be with X, but how would I make that work financially? And would it completely devastate my parents? Every time I talk to them, they bring up nursing school and I can hear that I'm disappointing them.

When I got home from class today there was a letter waiting for me from my parents. They'd enclosed two letters from the university telling me that if I don't return for spring semester I will lose my spot in the program. I basically just skimmed the letters, then shoved them in my closet. I secretly wish it would just be over with.

———❧———

Uh-oh. First signs of trouble. Like those minishakes you feel before an earthquake hits. What were they called? Tremors? I was definitely feeling them in these entries. He told her he loved her, but he wouldn't let her tell their friends about their relationship? Why was he so adamant about keeping things a secret? She didn't seem all that worried about it.

I lay back on my bed and covered my eyes with my arm. Young Howard seemed pretty hot and cold. Had he used the whole secrecy thing as an excuse for not really committing? Had she been way more into him than he was her? That was *crazy* depressing. My poor mom. But then how did that fit in with what Sonia told me about Howard being crazy about her?

I glanced at the photograph on my nightstand. I couldn't stop thinking about that feeling I'd gotten at Ponte Vecchio. After she died a bunch of people had told me my mom would stay close to me, but I'd never actually felt that. Until tonight.

I rolled off the bed and grabbed Howard's cell phone from the dresser.

"*Pronto?*" Ren sounded groggy.

"Sorry, are you asleep?"

"Not anymore. I saw Howard's number on my phone and had a panic attack."

I smiled. "I've commandeered his phone. He said I can keep it until further notice. So I have a question for you."

"You want to know if I'll take you to Space?"

I blinked. "Uh . . . yeah. How'd you know what I was going to ask?"

"I just had a feeling. And I'm way ahead of you. I texted Elena when I got home. She thinks her DJ buddy is working this week, which means we'll get in for free. Want to go tomorrow? I can see if other people from the school want to go too."

Yes. "Ren, that's perfect. And thanks again for taking me to Ponte Vecchio."

"And for introducing you to your new best friend? I think you set a new world record for most gelato ever eaten in one sitting."

"I want to try for another record tomorrow. What was that last kind I had? With the chocolate chunks?"

"*Stracciatella*."

"I'm naming my first daughter after it."

"Lucky her."

———

DECEMBER 6

Got an e-mail from the nursing school stating that they have officially revoked my spot in the program. I tried to file an extension after I got those letters from my parents, but if I'm honest, I didn't try that hard. My parents are upset, but all I feel is relief. Now there's nothing holding me back. When I told X the news, he seemed surprised. I guess he didn't know I was serious about wanting to stay.

DECEMBER 8

Amazing news! The school has offered to let me stay for a second semester at half tuition. Petrucione said I'm one of the most promising students they've ever had (!!) and that he and the other faculty think another semester of study will really help my future career. FUTURE CAREER. Like it's a given! I can't wait to tell X. I almost told him over the phone, but decided to wait to tell him in person. The soonest we can meet up is tomorrow night. I hope I can last that long.

DECEMBER 9

Told X. I think the news kind of caught him off guard, because for a second he just stared at me. Then he lifted me off my feet and swung me around. I'm so happy.

DECEMBER 27

X went home for the holidays, and Francesca saved me from what was almost the longest, saddest Christmas by inviting me to go to Paris to stay in her friend's vacant apartment.

Paris is a photographer's dream. When we weren't out shooting, we hung out on the apartment's balcony, wrapped up in blankets and eating giant boxes of chocolates we claimed to have bought for our families. On Christmas Eve I talked Francesca into going to the ice-skating rink on the first level of the Eiffel Tower, and even though she just sat on the sidelines and complained about the cold, I skated for more than an hour, giddy about how magic it all was.

The only downside was how much I missed X. Francesca brought him up a couple of times, and it took every ounce of willpower I had not to tell her what's been going on between us. It's like we're living a double life—friends in public, lovers in private. I hated spending Christmas away from him. And I'm also feeling worried. How is our relationship supposed to progress if we can't even tell anyone that we're together? Can I survive another six months of secrecy?

JANUARY 20

School is back in full swing, and now that the initial excitement of staying for another semester has worn off, I'm stuck with reality, which basically means calculating and recalculating. Every night I get out my notebook and try out different scenarios. How long can I afford to stay in Italy if I take fewer classes? What if I eat only spaghetti and tomato sauce? What about if my student loan gets approved? (Fingers crossed.) All the answers are pretty grim. I can stay, but just barely.

FEBRUARY 4

Student loan finally cleared today. PHEW. Had a dinner party to celebrate. Weather was perfect (cold and clear), and the food was divine. Even Simone and Alessio were on their best behavior—they had only one argument (a record), and it was just over who got to eat the last piece of caprese. Finn didn't end up coming back for the semester. He was on the fence about it, and at the last minute decided to accept a teaching position at the University of Maine. Francesca put a copy of The Old Man and the Sea in the chair where he usually sat, so at least he's here in spirit. I felt that old familiar weirdness about my friends still not knowing about X and me, but I'm kind of coming to peace with it. He doesn't seem to mind, and it is what it is. It feels out of my control.

MARCH 15

Something weird happened tonight.

Adrienne hasn't been hanging out with us much this semester. She stays in most nights and lately it seems like she avoids us even when we're in class, so tonight a few of us ambushed her at her apartment and took her out to dinner. Afterward, everyone headed over to our apartment, but when we got to the building, she hung back. I finally went looking for her, and when I stepped out of the apartment I saw her standing in the stairwell, talking on the phone and sobbing like her heart had just been snapped in half. I tried to sneak away, but the floorboards creaked, and when she saw me, she gave me a look that froze me to the core. She left without saying good-bye.

MARCH 20

By some horrible stroke of luck, Adrienne and I were paired up for an "Out in Florence" assignment. And I say "horrible" because things have been pretty uncomfortable since the other night.

My idea for the project was to head down to the Arno to photograph fishermen, but Adrienne told me she already had the perfect subject in mind. The way she said it left absolutely no room for discussion, so I just packed up my camera and followed her out into the street. I tried to ask her if she was all right, but she made it pretty clear she didn't want to talk about the other night. Or anything else for that matter. Finally I gave up on conversation and just followed her into the city.

We walked for at least ten minutes in silence and then she turned off onto a side street and went into a small tourist shop. There were two middle-aged men sitting in the corner of the shop playing cards, and when they saw Adrienne, they nodded at her and she just headed for the back of the shop. Behind the register was a doorway with a beaded curtain, and on the other side was a small apartment with a kitchenette and a twin bed. A woman wearing a flowered housedress was sitting in front of a black-and-white TV, and when she saw us she raised her hand and said, "<u>Aspetta. Cinque minuti.</u>" (Translation: "Wait. Five minutes." See, I am learning some Italian.)

While I tried to figure out what we were doing there, Adrienne pulled out her camera and started taking photos of the room and the woman, who didn't seem to notice. Finally Adrienne turned to me and said in her deliberate English, "This is Anna. She is a psychic. Her sons own the shop out front, and during the day she reads cards. No one else will be photographing a Florentine psychic. It is a unique subject."

I had to hand it to her. It was unique. And the setting couldn't have been more interesting: dingy back room, the beaded curtain, smoke from Anna's cigarette curling at the ceiling. So I pulled out my camera and started taking picture as well. Finally the show ended and Anna got up to turn off the TV, then shuffled over to a table pushed up against the wall, gesturing for us to take a seat. After we'd crowded around the table, she picked up a stack of cards and began laying them out one by one in front of her, muttering to herself in Italian. Adrienne set her camera down and was absolutely silent. After a few minutes Anna looked up at us and said with a thick accent, "One of you will find love. Both of you will find heartache."

I was a little bit stunned. I hadn't realized we were getting an actual reading. But my reaction was nothing compared to Adrienne's. She looked devastated. Once she regained her composure she started firing off questions in Italian until Anna got annoyed and cut her off. Finally Adrienne gave her some money and we left. She didn't say a word to me the entire way back.

MARCH 23

All of us went to a lecture at the Uffizi. Howard offered to walk me home, and I found myself telling him about Adrienne and the psychic. For several minutes he didn't say anything. Then he started walking faster and asked if he could show me something. We headed to Piazza del Duomo, and when we got there he led me to the left side of the cathedral and told me to look up. The sun had just started to set and the Duomo's shadow was covering half the piazza. I had no idea what I was looking for—all I could see were the beautifully detailed walls—but he just kept trying to get me to see something. Finally he took my finger and guided it so I was pointing at something jutting out of the cathedral's wall. "There," he said. And then

I saw it—right in the middle of all that beautiful stonework and statues of saints is a sculpture of a bull's head. Its mouth is open and it stares down at the ground like it's looking at something.

He told me that there are two stories about the bull's head. The first is that animals were critical to the building of the Duomo, and the bull was added as a way to honor them. The other story has a bit more Italian flair.

When the Duomo was being constructed a baker set up shop near the building site, and he and his wife sold bread to the stonemasons and workers. The baker's wife and one of the master stonemasons ended up meeting and falling in love, and when the baker found out about their affair he took them to court, where they were humiliated and sentenced to life away from each other. To get revenge, the stonemason carved the bull and placed it on the Duomo in a spot where it would stare down at the baker in his stall as a constant reminder that his wife loved another man.

I <u>love</u> how much he knows about Florence, and it definitely took my mind off the whole Adrienne thing, but now I keep wondering about the timing of the story. Was he trying to tell me something?

———

Howard. The place where she'd written his name was practically glowing. Why had she not called him X? Was it a slipup, or were they on their way to making their relationship public? And was there some kind of connection between Adrienne and the timing of Howard's story?

I stood up and walked over to the window. It was still warm out, almost hot, and the moon was flooding the cemetery like a spotlight. I scooted my violets over, then leaned out, resting my elbows on the windowsill. It was funny, but less than a week in and already the headstones weren't bothering me all that much. They were kind of like people you pass on the street—there, but not really. Like background noise.

A set of headlights appeared over the edge of the trees and I watched as the car snaked its way down the windy road. Why had Adrienne taken my mom to a psychic reading about their love lives? Was it possible she'd been interested in Howard too? Was it maybe him she'd been talking to in the stairwell?

I sighed. So far the journal wasn't clearing anything up. It was just making things more confusing.

Chapter 13

"THERE ARE SO MANY PLACES I WANT TO SHOW YOU IN Florence, it's hard to know where to start."

I glanced at him. Howard and I were headed for the city again, and I was having a really hard time deciding how to feel about him. Maybe because he was blasting Aerosmith's "Sweeeeeeeet Emooooootion" with all the windows rolled down, and his occasional drum-playing on the steering wheel made it really hard to think of him as the mysterious heart-breaker X. Also, he couldn't sing worth anything.

I leaned against the door, letting my eyes close for just a second. I'd stayed up really late thinking about Howard and my mom, and then an incredibly exuberant group of what appeared to be Italian Boy Scouts had come galumphing through the cemetery at the crack of dawn. I'd gotten approx-imately four minutes of sleep.

"Would you mind if we started at the Duomo again? We could climb to the top and you'd see the whole city at once."

"Sure." I opened my eyes. What if I brought up the baker and the bull? Would he remember?

"I thought you'd probably invite Ren to tag along."

"I didn't know that was an option."

"He's always welcome."

"Except he's petrified of you." Which was ridiculous. I gave him a quick look. Regardless of his shady past, Howard looked like he was trying to emulate the perfect 1950s dad. Freshly shaved face, clean white T-shirt, winning smile.

Check, check, check.

He sped up to pass a semi. "I shouldn't have given him a hard time last night. I can tell he's a good kid, and it's nice to have someone I feel safe sending you out with."

"Yeah." I shifted in my seat, suddenly remembering our phone call the night before. "He actually invited me to go somewhere tonight, too."

"Where?"

I hesitated. "This, uh, club. A bunch of people from the party will be there."

"For someone who's been here less than a week, you've sure got quite the social calendar. Sounds like I'll have to restrict all our outings to daytime." He smiled. "I have to say, I'm really glad that you're getting to know students from the school. I called the principal a few days before you arrived, and she said she'd be happy to give us a tour. Maybe Ren would come with us. I'm sure he could answer any questions you have."

"That's all right," I said quickly.

"Well, maybe another time. It doesn't have to be right away." We circled through a roundabout, and then he pulled over in front of a row of shops.

"Where are we?" I asked.

"Cell phone store. You need your own."

"Really?"

He smiled. "Really. I miss talking to people. Now come on."

The shop's windows were coated with dust and when we walked inside a tiny old man who looked like a direct descendant of Rumpelstiltskin looked up from his book.

"Signore Mercer?" he asked.

"*Si.*"

He hopped nimbly off his stool and started rummaging around on the shelf behind the desk. Finally he handed Howard a box. "*Prego.*"

"*Grazie.*" Howard handed him a credit card, then passed the box off to me. "I had them get it all set up, so we're ready to roll."

"Thanks, Howard." I pulled out the phone and looked at it happily. Now I had my very own number to give Thomas. Just in case he asked. *Please let him be at Space tonight. And please let him ask.* Because really? Even with all my parents' drama, I couldn't stop thinking about him.

• • •

Howard parked in the same area he had the night of the pizzeria, and when we got to the Duomo he groaned. "The line is even worse than normal. You'd think they're giving away free Ferraris at the top."

I eyed the line leading into the Duomo. It was made up of about ten thousand sweaty tourists and half of them looked like they were on the verge of a nervous breakdown. I tilted my head back to look up at the building, but there was no sign of the bull. I probably wouldn't be able to find it on my own.

He turned to me. "What do you say we get a gelato first, see if we can outwait the line a bit. Sometimes it's more crowded in the morning."

"Do you know any place with *stracciatella* gelato?"

"Any *gelateria* worth its salt will have *stracciatella*. When did you try it?"

"Last night with Ren."

"I thought you seemed different. Life-changing, right? Tell you what, let's go get a cone. Start the day off right. Then we'll brave the line."

"Sounds good to me."

"My favorite place is a ways away. Do you mind a walk?"

"Nope."

It took us about fifteen minutes to get to the *gelateria*. The shop was roughly the size of Howard's car, and even though it was pretty much breakfast time, the shop was packed to the brim with people happily devouring what I now knew was the most delicious substance on earth. They all looked rapturous.

"Popular," I said to Howard.

"This place is the best. Really."

"*Buon giorno.*" A bell-shaped woman waved at us from behind the counter and I made my way to the front. This place had a huge selection. Mountains of colorful gelato garnished with little bits of fruit or chocolate curls were piled high in metal dishes, and every single one of them looked like they had the ability to improve my day by about nine hundred percent. Chocolate, fruit, nuts, pistachio . . . How was I going to choose?

Howard came up next to me. "Would you mind if I ordered for you? I promise I'll get you another one if you don't like my choice."

That solved things. "Sure. Bad flavors of gelato probably don't exist, right?"

"Right. You could probably make dirt-flavored gelato and it would turn out all right."

"Ew."

He looked up at the woman. "*Un cono con bacio, per favore.*"

"*Certo.*"

She took a cone from the stack on the counter, piled it high with a chocolate-looking gelato, then handed it to Howard, who handed it to me.

"This isn't dirt-flavored, right?"

"No. Try it."

I took a lick. Super rich and creamy. Like silk, only in gelato form. "Yum. Chocolate with . . . nuts?"

"Chocolate with hazelnuts. It's called *bacio*. Otherwise known as your mom's favorite flavor. I think we came here a hundred times."

Before I could catch it, my heart slammed straight down to my feet, leaving me with a massive hole in my chest. It was amazing how I could just be going along, doing okay, and then suddenly—*wham*—I missed her so much even my fingernails hurt.

I looked down at my cone, my eyes stinging. "Thanks, Howard."

"No problem."

Howard ordered his own cone, and then we made our way out onto the street and I took a deep breath. Hearing Howard talk about my mom had kind of thrown me, but it was summertime in Florence and I was eating *bacio* gelato. She wouldn't have wanted me to be sad.

Howard looked down at me thoughtfully. "I'd like to show you something at Mercato Nuovo. Have you ever heard of the *porcellino* fountain?"

"No. But did my mom by chance swim in it?"

He laughed. "No. That was a different one. Did she tell you about the German tourist?"

"Yes."

"I don't think I've ever laughed that hard in my life. I'll take you there sometime. But I won't let you swim."

We made our way down the street. Mercato Nuovo was more like a collection of outdoor tourist shops—lots of booths set up with souvenir stuff, like T-shirts printed with funny sayings:

I AM ITALIAN, THEREFORE I CANNOT KEEP CALM.

I'M NOT YELLING, I'M ITALIAN.

And my personal favorite:

YOU BET YOUR MEATBALLS I'M ITALIAN.

I wanted to stop and see if I could find something ridiculous to send to Addie, but Howard bypassed the market and led me to where a ring of people stood gathered around a statue of a bronze boar with water running out of its mouth. It had a long snout and tusks and its nose was a shiny gold color, like it had been worn down.

"'*Porcellino*' means 'boar'?" I asked.

"Yes. This is the Fontana del Porcellino. It's actually just a copy of the original, but it's been around since the seventeenth century. Legend is that if you rub its nose you'll be guaranteed to come back to Florence. Want to try?"

"Sure."

I waited until a mom and her little boy cleared out of the way, then stepped forward and used my non-gelato hand to give the boar's nose a good rub. And then I just stood there. The boar was looking down at me with his beady eyes and creepy little molars and I knew without asking that my mom had stood right here and gotten gross fountain water splashed all over her legs and hoped with all her heart that she'd stayed in Florence forever. And then look what had happened. She'd never even come back to *visit*, and she never would again.

I turned around and looked at Howard. He was watching me with this kind of sad/happy look in his eyes, like he'd just had the exact same line of thoughts and now he suddenly couldn't taste his gelato all that well anymore either.

Should I just ask him?

No. I wanted to hear it from her.

Conditions at the Duomo had not improved. In fact, the line had gotten even longer, and little kids were breaking down left and right. Also, Florence had decided we could all handle a little more heat, and makeup and sunscreen and all hope of ever cooling off was pretty much dripping off of people's faces.

"Maybe we should have just stayed hoooooome," the little boy behind us wailed.

"*Fa CALDO*," the woman in front of us said.

Caldo. I'd totally recognized an Italian word.

Howard met my eye. We'd both been pretty quiet since the *porcellino*, but it was more of a sad quiet than an awkward quiet. "I promise it's worth it. Ten more minutes, tops."

I nodded and went back to trying to ignore all the sad feelings sloshing around my stomach. Why couldn't Howard and my mom just have had a happy ending? She'd totally deserved it. And honestly, it seemed like he did too.

Finally we were to the front of the line. The Duomo's stones had some kind of miraculous ability to generate cold air, and when we stepped inside it took effort not to lie down on the stone floor and weep from happiness. But then I caught a glimpse of the stone staircase everyone was filing up and suddenly I wanted to weep for a whole different reason. My mom had described walking up lots of stairs, but she'd left out the tiny detail that the staircase was narrow. Like gopher-tunnel narrow.

I shifted nervously.

"You okay?" Howard asked.

No. I nodded.

The line fed slowly into the staircase, but when I got to the base of it my feet stopped moving. Like *stopped*. They just straight-up refused to climb.

Howard turned around and looked at me. He kind of had to hunch over to even fit in the staircase. "You're not claustrophobic, are you?"

I shook my head. I'd just never faced the possibility of being squeezed through a stone tube with a bunch of sweaty tourists.

The people behind me were starting to bottleneck and a man muttered something under his breath. My mom had said the view was amazing. I forced one foot onto the stairs. Wasn't a staircase this narrow a fire hazard? What if there was an earthquake? And, lady snorting nasal spray behind me, could you please give me some *room*?

"Lina, I didn't tell you the whole story of the *porcellino*." I looked up. Howard had walked back down to the stair just above me and was looking at me encouragingly. He was going to try to distract me.

Well played, Howard. Well played.

"Tell me the story." I looked down at the stairs again, focusing on my breathing and finally beginning to climb. There was a smattering of applause from behind me.

"A long time ago there was a couple who couldn't have a child. They tried for years, and the husband blamed the wife for their bad luck. One day after they'd gotten into a fight, the woman stood crying at the window and a group of wild boars ran past the house. The boars had just had piglets and the woman said aloud that she wished she could have a child just like the boars did. A fairy happened to be listening in, and decided to grant her wish. A few days later the woman found out she was pregnant, but when she gave birth she and her husband were shocked because the baby came out looking more like a boar than a human. But the couple was so happy to have a son that they loved the child anyway."

"That story doesn't sound true," a woman behind me said.

I winced. Four hundred more steps?

Chapter 14

THE CLIMB WAS TOTALLY WORTH IT. THE VIEW OF FLORENCE was just as stunning as my mother had described it, a sea of red rooftops under an unblemished blue sky and soft green hills circling everything like a big, happy hug. We sat up there roasting for about a half hour, Howard pointing out all the important buildings in Florence and me working up the courage to climb back *down* the staircase, which turned out to be way easier. Afterward we stopped for lunch at a café and I left Florence with an unsettling realization. Regardless of what I was reading in the journal, I kind of *liked* Howard. Was that traitorous?

Ren's scooter pulled up just after nine.

"Ren's here!" Howard yelled from downstairs.

"Will you tell him I'm still getting ready? And don't scare him!"

"I'll do my best."

I looked in the mirror. As soon as we'd gotten home I'd figured out how to use Howard's arthritic washing machine, then hung a bunch of stuff to dry on the porch. Luckily it was still sweltering outside, so my clothes had been dry in no time. No more crumpled-up T-shirts for me. If Thomas was going to be there, I wanted to look amazing. No matter what my hair insisted on doing. I'd tried the flat iron again, but my curls were feeling extra-rebellious and had basically spat in its face. At least they were mostly vertical.

Please, please, please let him be there. I twirled around. I was wearing a short jersey dress my mom had found for me more than a year ago at a thrift shop. It was kind of amazing and I'd never really had anything to wear it to. Until now.

"Looking sharp tonight, Ren," Howard boomed scarily from downstairs.

I groaned. Ren answered, but I couldn't make out the rest of their conversation except for a couple of "yes, sirs."

After a few minutes there was a knock on my bedroom door. "Lina?"

"Hang on." I finished putting on my mascara, then gave myself one last look in the mirror. This was the longest I'd spent getting ready in ages. *You'd better be there tonight, Thomas Heath.*

I flung the door open. Ren's hair was wet, like he'd just taken a shower, and he was wearing an olive-green T-shirt that set off his brown eyes.

"Hey, Lina. Have you—" He stopped. "Whoa."

"Whoa what?" My cheeks flushed.

"You look so . . ."

"So what?"

"*Bellissima.* I like your dress."

"Thanks."

"You should wear dresses more often. Your legs are really . . ."

My blush spread like a wildfire. "Okay, you should totally stop talking about my legs. And quit staring at me!"

"Sorry." He gave me one last look, then made this stiff forty-five-degree turn to the corner, like he was a penguin that had just been put on time-out.

"I like your hair better curly."

"You do?"

"Yeah. Last night I thought you didn't really look like yourself."

"Huh." My cheeks were on *fire.*

He cleared his throat. "So . . . how's the journal? Have they crashed and burned yet?"

"Shh!"

"He just left to check on something at the visitors' center. He can't hear us."

"Oh, good." I pulled him into the room, then shut the door. "And no. Their relationship is still secret and he seems kind of hot and cold, but for the most part I'm still reading about the good stuff. It's all pretty lovey-dovey."

"Do you mind if I read it?"

"The journal?"

"Yeah. Maybe I could help you figure out what went wrong. And I could find more places to take you to in Florence."

I hesitated for approximately three-tenths of a second. This was *way* too good of an offer to pass up. "Sure. But you have to promise, *promise* me you won't tell Howard. I want to finish reading it before I talk to him about it."

"Promise. So Space doesn't really open until about ten. How about I start reading now?"

"Good idea." I fished the journal out of my nightstand. "It's pretty much half writing and half photographs, so it should go pretty fast. I marked where I left off, so don't read past that." I turned around and he was staring at my legs again. "Ren!"

"Sorry."

I walked over to him, flipping open the front cover. "Look what she wrote on the inside cover."

He made a low whistling noise. "'I made the wrong choice'?"

"Yeah."

"That sounds ominous."

"I think she wrote it as a message to me."

He flipped through the pages. "This should only take me like a half hour. I'm a really fast reader."

"Great. So . . . do you by chance know who is going to Space with us?"

"You mean, will Thomas be there?"

"And, um, other people."

"I don't know. All I know is that Elena sent out a mass text." He looked up at me. "And I think Mimi is coming."

"Nice."

There was a pause, and then we both looked away at the exact same second.

"So . . . I'll be on the porch." I grabbed my laptop and ran out of the room. I sort of hadn't been able to stop staring at him, either.

Weird.

Ren met me on the porch. I'd hoped that the Italian Internet gods would smile upon me and I'd be able to check my e-mail or watch a YouTube cat video or something, but I'd had no such luck. Instead I was lying on the swing, kicking off the banister every so often to keep me moving.

"Your mom reminds me of you."

I sat up. "How so?"

"She's funny. And brave. It's cool that she took such a big risk, dropping out of nursing school and everything. And her photographs are really good. Even though she was just starting out, you can tell she was going to be a game changer."

"Did you see the series of portraits of Italian women?"

"Yeah. That was cool. And you totally look like your mom."

"Thanks."

He sat down next to me. "It's nine thirty. Ready to go to Space?"

"Ready."

"I told Howard we'd honk on our way out. We had a good conversation earlier. I think we really made some progress."

"I told him to be nice."

"Is that why he kept smiling at me? It kind of freaked me out."

LINA'S RULES OF SCOOTER RIDING:

1. Never ride a scooter sopping wet.

2. Never ride a scooter wearing a short skirt.

3. Try to pay attention to light signals. Otherwise, every time the driver accelerates you'll smash into him and you'll have this awkward untangling moment and then you'll worry he's thinking you're doing it on purpose.

4. If by chance you aren't abiding by rule number two, be sure to avoid eye contact with male drivers. Otherwise they'll honk enthusiastically every time your skirt flies up.

Ren turned down a one-way street, then pulled up next to a two-story building with a long line of people wrapped around its perimeter. "This is it." Music pulsed from the windows.

My stomach sank down to my sandals. "This is like a *club* club."

"Yeah."

"Do I have to actually *dance*?"

"Ren!" Elena was attempting to run across the street to us, but her high heels were making it difficult. The effect was sort of Frankenstein-ish. "Pietro put us on the list. *Ciao*, Lina! It is nice to see you again." She pressed her cheek against mine and made a kissing sound. "Your dress is very beautiful."

"Thanks. And thanks for getting us in. I really wanted to see Space."

"Oh, yes. Ren said something about your parents coming here? They're not here tonight, are they?"

I laughed. "No. Definitely not."

"Who's coming tonight?" Ren asked.

"Everyone says they are coming, but we'll see who actually shows up. Don't worry, Lorenzo. I'm sure a certain someone will make it. *Vieni*, Lina." She linked arms with me, then dragged me across the street to the front of the line. Dragging me around was kind of her thing.

"*Dove vai?*" a man in line yelled as we cut ahead of him.

She tossed her hair. "Ignore him. We are much more important. *Ciao*, Franco!"

Franco wore a black T-shirt and was disproportionately muscular on top, like he'd skipped leg day way too many times. He unhooked the velvet cord from a stanchion that blocked the entrance and let us inside.

We stepped into a dimly lit hallway with big racks of clothing. Was this a coatroom?

"Continue," Elena said. "The party is this way."

I kept going, my arms stretched out in front of me, blind as a bat. It was *really* dark. And loud. Finally we emerged in a rectangular room with a long bar on one side. Two different songs were playing—one in English, and one in Italian—and on the far side of the room people sang group karaoke to a third. Everyone was either not talking or shouting to be heard.

"Lina, do you want a drink?" Elena asked, gesturing to the bar.

I shook my head.

"We will wait here for everyone. Once we get in the actual club there is no way to find each other."

"This isn't the club?" I asked.

She laughed like she thought I was being cute. "No. You'll see."

I looked around. Was *this* the room where Howard had uttered his first infamous "Hadley . . ."? I half expected to see him lounging against the wall, a good two heads taller than everyone else. Except this totally didn't seem like his scene. They probably wouldn't let him wear his flip-flops here.

Ren nudged me. "Want to sing karaoke with me? We could pick something in Italian, and I could pretend I don't speak Italian either. It would be hilarious. How about . . . ?"

He trailed off because Mimi and Marco were making their way toward us. Mimi was wearing a miniscule skirt and her hair was pulled back in a long, loose braid. Not a stray Medusa hair in sight. I shot a look at Ren. Did he like her legs too?

Okay, yeah, he did. Someone needed to teach him the art of discretion.

"Hi, guys," Marco yelled. He had exactly one volume. "Lina!" He came at me with his arms outstretched, but I ducked. "Too fast for me, I guess."

"Are you going to try to pick me up every time you see me?"

"Yes." He turned and picked up Elena. "Ask Elena."

"Marco, *basta*! Put me down or I'll feed you to a pack of wild dogs."

"That's a new one." Marco grinned at me. "She's kind of creative with her threats."

Mimi was yelling to be heard over the music. "Ren, why didn't you call me back? I didn't know if you were going to be here or not."

I couldn't hear his response, but she smiled at him and then started playing with the buttons on his shirt, which shouldn't have bugged me, but kind of did. Just because she was into him didn't mean she had to spread her Swedish PDA all over the place.

"Lina?"

I slowly turned around. *Please let it be . . .* "Thomas!"

He was wearing a royal-blue T-shirt that said BANNED FROM AMSTERDAM and somehow looked even better than I remembered. If that was possible. I forgot all about Mimi's button playing.

"Elena said you'd be here. I tried to call Ren to—"

"Hello, stalker." Ren suddenly side checked him, sending him stumbling.

"Ren, what the hell?" he said, straightening up.

"I had like ten missed calls from you."

"All you had to do was answer one."

Ren shrugged. "Sorry, man. I've been busy."

Mimi sidled up next to Ren, staring at me like she had no idea who I was.

"Hi, Mimi," I said.

"Hey." She squinted.

"I'm Lina. We met the other night at Elena's?"

"I remember."

Elena launched herself into the middle of our weirdly

tense little circle. "*Ragazzi*, no more talking! I want to dance."

"Do you dance?" Thomas asked me.

"Not really."

"Me neither. We could just hang out. We could go walk around by the Arno or something. I know this cool place that—"

"No way!" Ren grabbed my hand. "Thomas, you can't rob her of this experience. She's at Space. She wants to get her dance on."

"I don't have that much dance to get on," I protested.

"Sure you do." He lowered his voice. "And come on. This is where it all started, right?"

I nodded, then looked at Thomas. "I'd better stay. I would hate to miss the chance to embarrass myself."

"Worst case you just bust out your *Dirty Dancing* moves. Nobody puts baby in the corner, right?"

"I'm telling you, you know *way* too much about that movie."

"*Ragazzi!*" Elena yelled. "I mean it, let's go!"

We followed her through a narrow doorway, Thomas resting his hand on the small of my back and causing all sorts of ecstatic feelings, and then we were all shoving our way up a ramp into a large room. For a second I couldn't see anything solid—everything was flailing. Then a spotlight washed over us and OMG.

We were in a gigantic room with a ceiling that was at least twenty-five feet high, and it was *crawling* with people, like an anthill, only with designer clothes. There were a bunch of platforms set up throughout the floor, so some people were standing like five feet above everyone else. And they were all dancing. And I don't mean The Shopping Cart or The Sprinkler or any of the other moves that always seemed to dominate the proms back home. They were *really* dancing. Like having-sex-on-the-dance-floor dancing.

Mom, what have you gotten me into?

"Welcome to Space," Ren yelled into my ear. "This is the most crowded I've ever seen it. Probably because it's tourist season."

"Guys, follow me!" Marco put his arms in front of him like a diver, then started cutting through the crowd, all of us trailing behind.

"*Ciao, bella,*" a man hissed in my ear. I yanked my head away. Everyone I brushed past was sweaty. This place was kind of gross.

Finally we were in a little pocket of space somewhere in the middle of the floor and everyone started dancing. Immediately. I guess no one else needed a little warm-up period before they got their groove on?

My palms started sweating. Time for some positive self-talk. *Lina, you are a confident woman and you've totally got this.*

Why don't you try out a sexy version of the Running Man? Or the Hokey Pokey? Just quit standing still. You look ridiculous. And then I made the fatal mistake of looking at Mimi, which made things about a million times worse. She had her arms up over her head and she looked awesome. Like cool-sexy-European awesome. I wanted to crawl into a hole.

"You've got this," Ren yelled, giving me a thumbs-up.

I cringed. *Okay, start moving. Maybe copy Elena? Sway back and forth. Move hips. Pretend not to feel like a total idiot.* I glanced at Thomas. He was doing this awkward back-and-forth step that kind of made me want to melt into oblivion, because *how cute was he?* He couldn't dance either. Maybe I could take him up on a walk through Florence later.

And then something crazy happened. The music was so loud it was like it was pounding and rattling through my bones and teeth and everyone was having such a *good time* and suddenly I was dancing. Like actually dancing. And actually having fun. Well, maybe not as much fun as Ren, who was dirty dancing with Mimi, but *still.* The DJ pulled a microphone close to his mouth and shouted something in Italian and everyone cheered, raising their drinks over their heads.

"He is my friend! *È mio amico!*" Elena shouted.

"Lina, you're doing great!" Ren shouted. Mimi was doing

this crazy hip-rolling thing that looked like it required intense concentration, but when she heard Ren she looked up, sending me the polar vortex of all looks.

I was getting the feeling she didn't like me.

Thomas nudged me with his shoulder. "Have you ever been someplace like this before?"

"No."

"It's weird, you'd have to be twenty-one to get into a club like this in the States." We were so close I could see the tiny droplets of sweat in his hair. Even his *sweat* was sexy. I was officially disgusting.

Ren disentangled from Mimi, then came up on my other side. "Having fun?" He was out of breath.

"Yes."

"Good. I'll be back in a few." Mimi grabbed his hand and they disappeared into the crowd.

Thomas made a face. "He's kind of protective of you, isn't he?"

"It's because of my dad. He keeps messing with him, so Ren's afraid that something will happen to me and he'll be the one to blame."

"Nothing will happen to you—you're with me."

Sort of cheesy, but I grinned. Idiotically. Thomas pretty much obliterated any control I had over my facial muscles.

He raised his chin, looking over the crowd. "There he is. Looks like he and Mimi are *talking*."

I stood on my tiptoes, taking the opportunity to rest my hand on his shoulder. Ren and Mimi were leaning against a wall and she had her arms crossed in front of her chest and looked pissed. But maybe that was just her regular face.

"So they're together, right?"

"Yeah. He's been into her for like two years. Guess persistence pays off, right?"

I nodded. "Right."

"Hey, I have to go call my dad, and then I'm going to get a drink. You want one?"

"Sure, thanks."

He flashed me one of his bone-melting smiles, then disappeared into the crowd.

"Lina, dance with me!" Elena grabbed my hands and twirled me around. "What is happening with you and Thomas? Is it *amore*?"

I laughed. "I don't know. This is only the second time I've ever seen him."

"Yeah, but he likes you. I can tell. He is never interested in anyone, and last night after you left he asked me if I'd gotten your number."

"*Ooh la la!*" Marco said. "New girl and Thomas."

Elena rolled her eyes at him. "You sound like a child."

"Oh, yeah? Could a child do this?" He bent his arms at the elbows and started doing the robot.

"Marco, *basta*! You are awful at that."

"Want me to do the worm?"

"No!"

The song faded into a faster-paced one, and soon the three of us were holding hands and jumping up and down like little kids. No wonder my mom had liked it here. It was pretty fun. Except for the fact that the temperature kept rising. Didn't this place have AC?

"Where's Thomas?" Elena asked. Her bangs were plastered to her forehead with sweat.

"He went to get a drink."

"He's been gone for a long time." She fanned herself. "*Fa troppo caldo*. I am sweating like a pig."

Suddenly the room tilted from under me and I stumbled. Elena grabbed me by the arm. "You okay?"

"I just got dizzy. It's too hot."

"What?"

"I'm too hot."

"Me too!" Marco yelled. "I'm so hot!"

"I need to sit down for a minute."

"Lina, there are couches. There." She pointed to where Ren and Mimi had been standing. "Want me to come with you?"

"No, it's okay."

"I will tell Thomas where you are."

"Thanks." I made my way over to the side of the room.

The couches looked like breeding grounds for some kind of infectious disease, but I was desperate. I suddenly felt like I might pass out.

The first couch was mostly taken up by a scrawny guy sprawled out on his back. He was wearing gold chains and an enormous pair of sunglasses and every few seconds he'd twitch, like a fly had landed on him or something. An older-looking man sat smoking at the other end and when he saw me he smiled and said something in Italian.

"Sorry, I don't understand." I pushed my way past. My head was pounding along with the music. Hopefully there was an open seat somewhere. Otherwise I was going to have to buddy up with the passed-out wannabe rapper.

There's one! I rushed for an open spot, but just as I got there I stopped, because there was a pair of hands on my butt. And not in an accidental way. I whirled around. It was the older guy from the couch. His hair was long and greasy and he smelled, amongst other things, like a dead muskrat pickled in vodka. Or at least, that's what I'd imagine one would smell like.

"Dove vai, bella?"

"Leave me alone."

He reached out and ran his fingers along my bare shoulder and I sprang away. "Don't touch me."

"Perche? Non ti piaccio?" One of his front teeth was gray.

And he was way older than I'd originally thought. Like ten years older than anyone here.

Forget the couch. I turned to run, but he lunged at me and then grabbed me by the arm. Hard. "Stop it!" I yanked my arm back, but he just tightened his grip. "Elena! Marco!" I couldn't even see them anymore. Where was Ren?

I tried to pull away again, but the man grabbed me by the waist and pulled me in to him until my pelvis was smashed up against his. "Let. *Go.*" Head butt? Knee him in the crotch? What were you supposed to do when you got attacked? He grinned, sidestepping every desperate move I made.

How was I going to get out of this? There were people everywhere, but absolutely no one was paying attention. "Help me!"

Suddenly someone grabbed me by the shoulders, pulling me back, and the man loosened his grip long enough for me to wrench my body away. It was Mimi. Looking like some kind of beautiful, pissed-off warrior.

"*Vai via, fai schifo,*" she yelled at the man. "*Vai.*"

He put both hands in the air, then grinned and walked away.

"Lina, why didn't you just tell him to go away?"

"I tried. He wouldn't let go of me."

"Try harder next time. Just call them a *stronzo*, then push them off you. I have to do it all of the time."

"*Stronzo?*" I was shaking all over. It felt like I'd just been dragged through a Dumpster—that had been *revolting*.

She crossed her arms. "What is happening between you and Ren?"

I tried to focus my brain. "I'm sorry, what?" I rubbed at my arms, trying to get the feel of Gray Tooth's skin off of me.

"What's going on between you and Lo-ren-zo?" She spoke slowly, exaggerating her words like she thought I couldn't understand her.

"I don't know what you're talking about." Where *was* he?

She looked at me for a moment. "You know Ren and I are together, right? He's only hanging out with you because he feels bad for you because your mom died."

Maybe it was leftover adrenaline from my run-in with Creepy McCreeperson, but suddenly I blurted out the first thing that came to mind. "Is that why he was ignoring your calls last night?"

Her eyes widened and she stepped toward me murderously. "He was home with his little sister."

"No, he was at Ponte Vecchio with me." *Please let me have pronounced that right.*

"There you are!" Thomas stepped between us, holding a soda in each hand. He took one look at Mimi and wilted. "Whoa. What did I miss?"

"Shut up, Thomas." She turned and flounced away.

"What just happened?" Thomas asked.

"I have no idea."

"Lina!" Ren was shoving his way toward me. "There you are. Do you want to leave? It's like a thousand degrees in here. I think the AC might be broken."

Relief flooded through me and suddenly I was holding back a boiling lake of tears. "Where have you *been*?"

"Looking for you." He leaned in. "Are you okay?"

"I want to leave. Now."

"I need to leave too," Thomas said. "I'll walk out with you guys."

It took us what felt like an hour to get out of there, and when we finally burst out onto the sidewalk we all gulped in the cool air like we'd just emerged from the depths of the ocean.

"Freedom!" Thomas said. "That was like being slowly smothered."

I leaned back against the wall and shut my eyes. I was never going there again. Ever.

Ren touched my arm. "Lina, are you okay?"

I did a half shake, half nod. *Okay?* I could still smell pickled muskrat.

"So, what did you think of Space? Perfect place for a relationship to start?"

"What relationship?" Thomas asked. "Mine and Lina's?"

He gave me a meaningful look, but I barely noticed.

"He means my parents." I took a deep breath. "This old guy attacked me. He grabbed me and wouldn't let go."

"What do you mean? In Space?" Ren whirled around like he thought he could see through the walls. "When?"

"Right before you found me. Mimi rescued me."

"*That's* what was going on," Thomas said. "Are you okay? What a creep."

"Are you hurt?" Ren asked.

"No. It was just awful."

Ren looked furious. "Why didn't you yell for me? I would have destroyed him."

"I had no idea where you were."

Thomas's phone started ringing and he looked down at it and groaned. "My dad keeps calling. We have family in town and I told him I wouldn't stay out long." He looked up at me. "But I'm not leaving without getting your number."

"Oh. Sure." I'd practiced for this, but when I went to tell him my new number, I forgot and had to look at the paper I'd written it on.

"Great. I'll call you tomorrow." He gave me a big hug, then clapped Ren on the shoulder. "See you around."

"Later." Ren turned to watch Thomas walk away and I used the opportunity to wipe my eyes. My mascara was everywhere.

"His shirt was really stupid, don't you think?"

"What?"

"'Banned from Amsterdam.' No one gets banned from Amsterdam. That's the point."

"I wouldn't know."

"I'm really sorry about what happened in there. I shouldn't have left you alone." He looked at me closer. "Wait a second. Are you crying?"

"No." A giant tear rolled down my face. And then another.

"Oh, no." He put his hands on my shoulders and looked me in the eyes. "I'm so sorry. We'll never go there again."

"I'm sorry. I feel really stupid. That guy was just so disgusting." But that was only half the reason I was crying. I took a deep breath. "Ren, why did you tell Mimi my mom died?"

His eyes widened. "I don't know. It just came up. She was asking why you moved here and I just told her. Why? Did she say something?"

"You know, you don't have to feel sorry for me. It's not like I need you to read the journal and drive me around everywhere. I can figure this out on my own. I get that you have a life."

"Whoa, what? I don't feel sorry for you. I mean, it's sad that you lost your mom and everything, but I hang out with you because I like to. You're . . . different."

"Different?"

"You know, like we talked about last night. We're alike, you know?"

I ran my arm across my face. Because that was totally going to help the mascara situation. "Promise?"

"Yeah, I promise. What brought that on?"

"Mimi—" I stopped. Did it matter? She was just a jealous girl. And every time Ren saw her he acted like he'd just won the lottery.

"Mimi what?"

"Never mind. Can we go to Piazza Signoria? I want to see that statue."

Chapter 15

WE WERE QUIET ON THE DRIVE TO THE PIAZZA. IT WAS after eleven and the city felt different. Sort of emptied out. Like me, after an embarrassing postclubbing cry fest. Ren pulled his scooter up to a curb and we both got off.

"This is it?"

"This is it. Piazza Signoria." He was looking at me like I was a box of highly fragile dishes, but I *was* still covered in snot, so I guess he was justified.

I walked out into the piazza. One side was lined by a large fortress-looking building with a clock tower, and in front of that was a fountain with a statue of a man surrounded by smaller figures. A handful of people were milling around, but for the most part it was empty.

"What's that building?" I asked.

"Palazzo Vecchio."

"Old something . . . Old palace?"

"*Esattamente.* You're getting good."

"I know. I recognized the word 'old.' I'm practically fluent."

We smiled at each other. My eyes felt like water balloons, but at least I wasn't sniveling anymore. Sheesh. I was lucky Ren hadn't abandoned me at the nearest taxi stand.

"So what happened here again?" Ren asked.

"This is the first place he told her he loved her. They were looking at a statue. Something with 'rape' in its name."

"Oh, right. *The Rape of the Sabine Women*. I think it's under that roofed area."

We made our way across the piazza, passing a bunch of other statues along the way, then walked under an arched entryway into what was basically a large patio filled with sculptures.

I recognized it right away. "There it is."

The Rape of the Sabine Women was made of white marble and sat high on a pedestal, the three figures intertwined in one tall column. I walked around it slowly. My mom was right. No one looked *happy* per se, but they were all connected and they definitely complemented each other. They were also all naked and their muscles and tendons were bulging out all over the place. Giambologna hadn't been kidding around.

Ren pointed. "Look how the woman is looking back at the other man. She definitely didn't want to go. And that guy on the ground looks totally spooked."

"Yeah." I folded my arms, looking up at the statue. "Is it

just me, or is this a weird spot for Howard to tell my mom he loved her?"

"Maybe it just kind of happened. He got caught up in the moonlight or whatever."

"But he was studying art history and he'd just told her the whole backstory. I'd be surprised if it didn't have some kind of significance to him."

Ren hesitated. "Speaking of Howard . . . I have to tell you something."

"What?"

He took a deep breath. "I sort of asked him about the secret bakery."

I whirled around. "Ren! You told him about the journal?"

"No, of course not." He pushed his hair out of his eyes, avoiding my gaze. "It was when you were getting ready. I made up this whole story about my mom finding a secret bakery when she first moved here, and then I asked him if he knew where one was. I was going to surprise you and take you there tonight after Space."

Finally he looked up at me with big, soulful eyes, and I sighed. It was like trying to be mad at a baby seal. "Did he tell you where it was?"

"No. That was the weird thing. He said he'd never been to one."

I squinted at him. "What? And you described it to him?"

"Yeah. I tried to be vague so he wouldn't know I was talking about his date with your mom, but he acted like he had no idea."

"So he didn't remember taking her there?"

He shook his head. "No, it was more than that. It was like he'd never even heard of Florence's secret bakeries."

"*What?* That doesn't seem like something you'd forget."

"I know, right?"

"Was he lying?"

"Maybe. But why would he?" He shook his head again. "For the past couple of hours I've been trying to come up with a reason why he'd forget about the bakery, but so far I have nothing. No offense, but your parents' story is kind of sketchy."

I put my back to one of the columns, then slid to the ground with a *thud*. "You're telling me. Why do you think I'm reading the journal?"

He sat down next to me, then leaned in until our arms touched. "I really am sorry, though."

I exhaled. "It's okay. And you're right. Something *is* weird. I've been thinking that all along."

"Maybe you should ask him about something else from the journal. Like a test."

"Like *The Rape of the Sabine Women*?" We looked up at it.

"Yeah. See what he does when you ask him about that."

"Good idea." I looked at the ground. Now it was my turn

to hesitate. "So . . . I did something I should probably apologize for too."

"What?"

"Back at Space, Mimi and I kind of got into this . . . argument, and I told her that you were ignoring her calls when we were at Ponte Vecchio."

His eyes widened. "*Cavolo*. I'm guessing that's why she called me a *cretino* and left?"

"Yeah. I mean, I don't know what a *cretino* is, but I'm sorry. Thomas told me you've liked her for a long time, and I hope I didn't mess things up."

"I'll call her when I get home. It'll be okay." He sounded like he was trying to convince himself.

I took a deep breath. "Hey, you know if you can't hang out with me anymore, I understand. It seems like it's kind of complicating things for you."

"No. It's good complicated." He pulled out his cell phone. "It's almost eleven thirty. Back to the cemetery?"

"Yeah. I should get back to the journal."

"And the man of mystery."

When I got home Man of Mystery was, inexplicably, taking a pan of muffins out of the oven.

"You're baking?"

"Yes."

"It's almost midnight."

"I specialize in late-night kitchen disasters. Also, I thought you might want a snack when you got home, and my blueberry muffins are legendary. And by 'legendary,' I mean 'edible.' Sit down."

It was a command. I pulled out a chair and sat.

"So where did you go tonight?"

I hesitated for a second, then plunged in. "Space. It's a club near the Arno."

He chuckled. "That place is still around?"

Phew. At least he remembered Space. "Yes. Have you been there?"

"Lots of times. Your mother did too."

I leaned forward. "So you guys like . . . went together?"

"Many times. Usually on nights we should have been studying. I don't know what it's like now, but it used to be the place to go for international students. Lots of Americans." He transferred a couple of the muffins to a plate, then set it on the table, pulling up a chair.

"Space was kind of grimy. I didn't like it very much."

"I never really did either. And I'm not much of a dancer."

So I had him to thank for my dancing skills.

I took a muffin and broke it open, steam curling up toward my face. *Now or never.* "So, Howard, I have a question for you. You know a lot about art history, right?"

"Yes." He smiled. "That's one thing I know plenty about. You knew I was teaching art history when your mom and I met, right?"

"Right." I looked down at my muffin again and took a deep breath. "Well, Ren and I went for a drive after Space, and we stopped in this piazza. Piazza della Signoria? Anyway, there was an interesting statue, but we didn't know the history of it."

"Hmm." He stood up and grabbed a butter dish off the counter, then sat down again. "Lots of statues there. Do you know who it was by?"

"No. It was in this open-air gallery. Kind of like a covered patio. You can just walk in."

"Oh, right. Loggia dei Lanzi. Let's see . . . there are the Medici lions, and the Cellini . . . What did it look like?"

"It was of two men and a woman." I held my breath.

"Woman being carried away?"

I nodded.

He smiled. "*The Rape of the Sabine Women.* That one is actually pretty interesting, because the artist—Giambologna—didn't even think of it as a real piece. He just made it as an artistic demonstration to show that it was possible to incorporate three figures into one sculpture. He didn't even bother to give it a name, and then it ended up being the work he's best known for."

Okay. Interesting, but not quite the story he'd told my

mom. I tried again. "Do you know if my mom ever saw it?"

He cocked his head. "I don't know. I can't remember ever talking to her about Giambologna. Why? Did she tell you about it?"

I can't remember. His face was as smooth as a fresh jar of Nutella. He definitely wasn't lying, but was it really possible that he'd forgotten? Had he suffered some kind of head trauma or have a mental block that kept him from remembering details about his relationship with my mom?

Suddenly a new thought tiptoed out of the corner of my mind. What if he *wasn't* forgetting? Or denying? What if . . . ? I sprang to my feet, crumbling the muffin in my hand. "I need to go upstairs."

I ran out of the room before he could ask why.

My mother's words spun through my mind as I climbed the stairs: *Yes, X. I seriously don't think anyone would read my journal, but I'm giving him a new name, just in case.*

As soon as I was in my room I locked the door behind me and fumbled for the journal. I switched on my lamp and started flipping through it.

Howard: The perfect Southern gentleman (Southern giant, Francesca calls him), handsome, kind, and the kind of guy who will go marching into battle for you.

I <u>love</u> being in love in Italy. But truth be told, I would fall for X anywhere.

Howard offered to walk me home, and I found myself telling him about Adrienne and the psychic.

"No way," I breathed.

There was a reason Howard didn't know about the secret bakery or the significance of Giambologna's statue, and why my mom had slipped up and called him by his real name.

He wasn't X.

"Addie, pick up, pick up!" I whispered.

"Hey, this is Addie! Leave a message and I'll—"

"Argh!" I tossed the phone on my bed and started pacing around. Where *was* she? I went and stood at the window. My mom had been in love with someone who wasn't Howard. She'd had this take-over-everything passionate love affair and then she'd ended up pregnant with *someone else's baby*. Howard's. Was *that* her wrong choice? That she'd gotten pregnant with Howard when really she'd been in love with someone else? Was that what had made her flee Italy?

I fell heavily into my chair, then popped back up. Ren would answer! I dove onto my bed, fishing my phone out of the covers and dialing his number.

He answered on the second ring. "Lina?"

"Hey. Listen, I did what you suggested. I asked him about the statue."

"What did he say?"

"He knew all about it, the history and everything. But then I asked him if he'd ever seen it with my mom and he couldn't remember."

"What is his deal? Either he has the worst memory in the world or—"

"Or he was never there," I interrupted impatiently.

"What?"

"Ren, think about it. Maybe he doesn't know about the secret bakery or the confession of love at the Sabine statue because *he isn't X*."

"Oh."

"Right?"

"Ohhh. Well . . . *yeah*. Okay, walk me through it."

"I'm thinking it went something like this: My mom moves to Italy and makes a bunch of friends, Howard included. Then a few months in she falls for this guy X. Something happens, maybe they fight too much, or there's too much pressure because the school has some kind of weird rule about dating, and they break up. Then my mom rebounds with this nice Southern gentleman who probably had a thing for her all along. She gives it a try, but she can't get X off her mind. Then one day she finds out she's pregnant and panics, because she's having a baby with someone she isn't in love with."

"That totally makes sense!"

"I know. And that would explain why we stayed away from him all these years. I mean, he is a nice guy, and from all the stories she told, he was definitely a good friend to her, but you can't just *pretend* to be in love with someone. It would hurt them too badly."

"Poor, scary Howard," Ren breathed.

"And that's why she wrote 'I made the wrong choice.' Maybe that was her big regret. She had a baby with someone she wasn't in love with."

"Except you're that baby. So do you really think she'd have written that in the front of her journal?"

"Oh. Probably not." I sat down. "But, Ren, it's so sad! I mean, the way Howard talks about her, you can tell he really loved her. And she told me all these stories about how much fun they used to have together. But it just wasn't enough—she loved someone else!"

"It's like that old song 'Love Stinks.'"

"Never heard of it."

"You haven't? It's in a bunch of movies. It's about how whenever you fall in love with someone it turns out they're in love with someone else. And it's this big messed-up cycle where no one ends up with the person they want."

"Ugh. That is so depressing."

"Tell me about it." He paused. "Are you going to tell Howard that you know? About X?"

"No. I mean, I'm sure we'll talk about it eventually. But not until I finish the journal. I have to make sure my theory is right."

APRIL 5

Another night of drama. Simone got tickets to a new club near Piazza Santa Maria Novella and our group plus a few other students met up around eleven. I'd been working late at the studio, so I showed up on my own and when I got there the first two people I saw were Adrienne and Howard. They were to the side of the building, and Adrienne was standing with her back to the wall and Howard was leaning in to her, saying something in a low voice. The scene was so intimate that for a moment I didn't understand what I was seeing. I've never seen the two of them even talk one-on-one. What <u>was</u> this?

I went into the club without them noticing and found the rest of the group, and then the two of them came in separately, acting like nothing had happened. Then things really got weird. Partway through the night Adrienne called Alessio a liar—something about him breaking his promise to go with her to an art exhibit—and for some reason that really set Howard off. He told her that she was the last person on earth who should call someone a liar, and that if she had any shred of dignity she'd come out with the truth. Adrienne hissed back that it was none of his business. Then Simone stepped in and told them to both calm down.

Guess I'm not the only one with secrets.

APRIL 19

X has been out of town for a full week, but he gets home tomorrow. TOMORROW. I haven't been able to think about anything else. After class I told Francesca that I needed to find <u>The Dress</u>. You know, the once-in-a-lifetime dress guaranteed to make anyone fall in love with you. (Or in my case, make me look amazing when I tell him my big news.)

Francesca was the perfect person to ask, because when it comes to shopping she has the patience of a saint. It took us five hours, but we finally found it. It's an off-white sundress, very feminine, with a sweetheart neckline and a skirt that falls just above the knee. Francesca even talked me into getting a haircut. Who knew cutting off a few inches of useless hair could give you cheekbones?

And what's my big news, you ask? Earlier this week Petrucione asked me if I'd be interested in staying on through August to assist with the upcoming semester. I'll be paid and get an extension on my student visa, which means I will be here until the end of the summer!!

APRIL 20

Woke up early this morning ecstatic to see X and there was a message on my phone. He decided to extend his time at the conference he's attending and won't make it until Monday. That's when I had a brilliant idea—I'll surprise him in Rome! Even if he's attending seminars all day, at least we'll be in the same city. I can spend my days touring. Express trains take only ninety minutes, so if I catch the four p.m. train this afternoon, I'll be waiting for him at his hotel when he's done for the day. I can't wait to see the look on his face!

APRIL 21

This is my third attempt to sit down and write about what happened in Rome. I can't believe I'm writing this, but it's OVER.

I was never able to find X's conference online, so when I arrived I called his cell phone and told him I was at the train station with some great news. Right then an announcement started on the station's overhead speakers, and when things finally quieted down, I realized that something was wrong. He told me to wait right where I was.

A half hour later he came charging into the train station, and something was definitely wrong. I asked him if he wanted to sit in one of the station's cafés, and for the next twenty minutes I just listened to him talk. Bottom line: He feels like his work has gotten stagnant, he needs some new creative space, and he's decided to leave the school and pursue another job in Rome. Oh, and we're over.

Over.

I just sat there, his words swirling around me. It was like my mind couldn't process it. And then it all hit me. This was the end. He was breaking up with me.

Suddenly I couldn't hear his excuses anymore, only the hard truths. I'd spent nine months lying to my friends. I'd strained ties with my family. I'd completely changed my life to be closer to him, and our relationship had never been to him what it was to me. I had the fleeting thought that I could talk him out of it—tell him that I'd figured out a way to stay in Florence even longer—but even in that brief moment of denial I knew it was useless. When someone walks out of a relationship, there's nothing you can do to keep them there.

X was still talking when I stood. I said good-bye to him in a normal voice, like I hadn't just been shattered into a million pieces, then went to the counter and bought a return ticket on the very next train. I hadn't even been in Rome for an hour. I never even got to wear my dress.

APRIL 22

Woke up this morning thinking I'd had some kind of nightmare, but just like the last few days, reality was waiting for me to get my bearings so it could knock me down again. My eyes were so swollen from crying myself to sleep that I had to sit with a cold washcloth over them before I looked acceptable enough to go to class. The whole weekend I'd been holding on to a tiny shred of hope that X would be in class this morning, but of course he wasn't. Can it really just be over? Nothing has ever hurt this badly. Nothing.

APRIL 25

It turns out that Francesca knew all along. Last night after dinner she put her arm around me and told me that X wasn't worth it, and he never had been. I was so surprised. Did everyone know?

MAY 2

This morning Petrucione announced that X has resigned from his position. I felt a huge relief—not because he's officially gone, but because someone said his name. I didn't let people in on the relationship, and so now I can't let them in on my heartache. I feel so alone. Talking to Francesca doesn't help. If I bring him up, she says bad things about him, and I end up feeling worse. Florence is the perfect place to fall in love, which means it's also the worst place to be heartbroken. Some days I just want to go home. Should I even stay through summer?

———————

"Mom," I whispered. Her sadness was smeared across the journal like paint that had never had the chance to dry. How was it possible that she'd had her heart smashed to smithereens in a Rome train station and never even *mentioned* it to me? Had I even known this woman?

I scanned through the last few entries again. No doubt about it, X had been a serious jerk. I especially hated that he'd told her he needed "new creative space." What kind of a line was that? And it was *awful* that she hadn't seen the end coming, especially when it was so obvious from the outside that the relationship wasn't going anywhere. Reading those last few entries had been like watching a train wreck in slow motion.

And then there was Howard. I rested my finger on the entry about him and Adrienne. He'd definitely had something going on behind the scenes too. Had he and Adrienne been dating and broken up just before my mom and X? Had both my parents been interested in other people and just sort of fallen together for a while? Is that why they hadn't lasted? And what had been so special about X, anyway?

I wanted to keep reading, but my eyelids insisted on doing this slow downward drag. Finally I gave up, tucking the journal into the nightstand and switching out the light.

Chapter 16

"I NEED YOUR HELP." I'D WOKEN THAT MORNING WITH a brilliant idea, and even though I'd waited until a socially acceptable hour, I'd still had to practically drag Ren out of his bed. Now we were sitting on his front porch and he looked only about thirty percent awake.

"Couldn't it have waited?" He was wearing black sweat-pants and a faded T-shirt and, like usual, had to keep shaking his hair out of his face. It was probably just the morning light, but he looked cute. Like way cuter than someone with bed head should.

He caught me staring. "What?"

I quickly looked away. "Nothing. I just need your help with one last thing."

"Listen, you know I'm all about this Howard-Hadley mystery. But can't I take a nap first?"

"No! Ren, why are you so tired?"

"I was on the phone with Mimi until like three."

The sun was suddenly way too bright. "Was she really mad about what I said last night?"

"Yeah. It was pretty ugly." He sighed. "But let's not talk about that. What do you need help with?"

"Could you give me a ride to FAAF?"

"Your mom's school?"

"Yes. I called them this morning. They moved to a new location a few years ago, but I want to go and see if I can get any info on Francesca."

"Fashion police Francesca?"

"I think she's my best bet for tracking down X. Turns out she knew about him all along."

"Whoa, slow down. We're tracking down X? Why?"

"Because my mom had this whole life I didn't know about, and I want to know what was so great about X that she couldn't get over him and had to break Howard's heart."

"But wait. That's still just a theory, right? What if that isn't the reason she left Italy?"

I groaned. "Ren, come on. Don't you want to know who the mysterious X is? He was so awful when he broke up with her. It totally destroyed her. I just want to know what the big deal was. I think it will help me understand it all better."

"Hmm." He yawned and dropped his head onto my shoulder.

"So will you help me?"

"Of course I will. When do you want to go?"

"As soon as possible." His skin was warm and he had that puppy-dog sleeping boy-smell.

"You smell good," he said, echoing my thoughts.

"No, I don't. I ran six miles this morning and haven't showered yet."

"You still smell good."

Apparently that tiny little butterfly was alive and well. And it was definitely making the rounds. I quickly moved away.

Don't. Think. About. Ren.

I ran hard back to the cemetery. I had enough to think about without complicating things with some stupid crush on one of the best friends I'd ever had. Also, he was dating a Swedish supermodel. With anger issues. And let's not forget that I'd just given my number to the best-looking guy I'd ever met.

When I got to the house my heart practically fell out of my chest. Howard was sitting on the porch swing with a cup of coffee, looking like *such a nice guy*. It was cosmically unfair that the whole "Love Stinks" cycle had left him alone in a cemetery with his terrible muffins and old music. It made me want to buy him balloons or something.

"Good morning, Lina."

"Morning."

He gave me a funny look. Probably because I was looking at him like he was an injured baby duck.

"I was just at Ren's," I offered.

"Do you two have any plans today?"

"Yeah, he's coming to get me in a little bit."

"For what?"

"Uh, I think we're just going to get some lunch or something." *Should I invite him?* Wait. We weren't actually going to lunch.

"Fun. Well, I was thinking that if you two are up for it, we could go to a movie tonight. One of the nearby towns has an outdoor theater that plays films in their original language, and this week they're showing one of my favorites."

"That sounds great!" I cringed. All I needed were pompoms and a megaphone. *Tone it down. It's not like his heart was broken recently.*

He squinted at me. "Glad you like the idea. I'll ask Sonia, too."

"Sure."

I hurried into the house, and when I snuck a glance back at him, pity welled up in me so fast it almost overflowed from my eyeballs. He'd loved my mom. Was it too much to ask that she just love him back?

"You said 'Piazzale Michelangelo,' right?" Ren yelled to me.

"Right. They said park there and then head south."

"Okay, it's just up ahead."

It had been a quick scooter ride and I'd been careful to sit an extra inch or two back so we weren't brushing legs or anything. Or at least not that often.

"Someone's going to meet with us at FAAF, right?" he asked.

"Right. I didn't tell them why we're coming in, but they said someone from admissions would be in the office."

He started following behind a line of tour buses, one of them so big it probably moonlighted as a cruise ship. Piazzale Michelangelo was a whirlpool of tourists. They all looked hell-bent on getting their money's worth.

"Why are so many people here?"

"Best view in the city. As soon as this bus gets out of our way you'll see it." The bus slowed and Ren zipped around it and suddenly we had this big panoramic view of Florence including Ponte Vecchio, Palazzo Vecchio, and the Duomo. I mentally patted myself on the back. Five days in and I already recognized half the city.

Ren veered off the road and pulled into a parking spot roughly the size of my suitcase. We squeezed our way out.

"Where to?" he asked.

I handed him the directions. "The woman at the school said it's easy to find."

Famous last words. We spent the next thirty minutes

wandering up and down the same streets, mostly because everyone we asked gave us entirely different sets of directions.

"First rule of dealing with Italians," Ren growled, "they love giving directions. Especially if they have no idea what they're talking about."

I was noticing that Ren sort of had an *I'm only Italian when I feel like it* policy.

"And they use lots of hand gestures," I added. "I thought the last guy was directing a plane. Or maybe an orchestra."

"You know how to get an Italian to stop talking, right?"

"How?"

"Tie their arms down."

"This is it!" I stopped walking and Ren plowed into me. We'd passed by the building at least five times already, but this was the first time I'd noticed the miniscule gold sign above doorway. FAAF.

"Did they think people would be reading their sign with binoculars?"

"You're grumpy."

"Sorry."

I hit the buzzer and there was a loud ringing noise followed by a woman's voice.

"Pronto?"

Ren leaned in. *"Buon giorno. Abbiamo un appuntamento."*

"Prego. Terzo piano." The door unlocked.

Ren looked at me. "Third floor. Race you."

We simultaneously tried to shove each other out of the way, then went pounding up the stairs, bursting into a large, well-lit reception area. A woman wearing a tight lavender dress startled and stood up from behind her desk. *"Buon giorno."*

"Buon giorno," I answered back.

She glanced at my sneakers and switched to English. "Did you call about meeting with our admissions officer?"

"I beat you," Ren said quietly.

"No, you didn't." I caught my breath and took a step forward. "Hi. Yes, I did call. But I was actually hoping to ask you about one of your past students."

"I'm sorry?"

"My mom was a student here about seventeen years ago and I'm trying to track down one of her old classmates."

She raised her eyebrows. "Well, I certainly can't give out any personal information."

"I just need to know her last name."

"And like I said, I really can't help you."

Argh.

"What about Signore Petrucione? Could he help us?" Ren asked.

"Signore Petrucione?" She folded her arms. "Do you know him?"

I nodded. "He was the director when my mom was attending."

She stared at us for a moment, then turned and skulked out of the room.

"Wow. She was a real ray of sunshine," Ren said. "Think she's coming back?"

"I hope so."

A moment later the woman walked back into the room, followed by an energetic-looking old man with wiry white hair. He was dressed stylishly in a suit and tie, and when he saw me, he did a double take. *"Non è possibile!"*

I glanced at Ren. "Um, hi. Are you Signore Petrucione?"

He blinked. "Yes. And you are . . ."

"Lina. My mom was a student here and—"

"You're Hadley's daughter."

". . . Yes."

"I thought I was seeing things." He crossed the room, extending his hand. "What a surprise. Violetta, do you know who this girl's mother is?"

"Who?" She looked determined to be unimpressed.

"Hadley Emerson."

Her mouth dropped open. "Oh."

"Lina, come with me." He glanced at Ren. "And bring your friend."

Ren and I followed Petrucione down a hallway into a small office cluttered with photographs. He sat down, then gestured for us to do the same. I had to move a box of negatives off of my chair.

"Lina, I was so sorry to hear about your mother. It was so tragic. And not just because of her contributions to the art world. She was a wonderful person, too."

I nodded. "Thank you."

"Who is this?" He gestured to Ren.

"This is my friend Lorenzo."

"Nice to meet you, Lorenzo."

"You too."

Petrucione leaned forward, resting his elbows on his desk. "How lovely that you're here visiting Florence. And what a delight that you stopped at FAAF. Violetta said something about you asking for information about your mother's classmates?"

I took a deep breath. "Yes. Well, I've been trying to learn a little bit about my mom's time at school, and I was hoping to get in touch with one of her old friends."

"Absolutely. Which one?"

"Her name is Francesca. She was studying fashi—"

"Francesca Bernardi. She's another one who made quite a name for herself. Had a spread in *Vogue Italia* last spring." He tapped his head with two fingers. "I never forget a name.

Let me have Violetta check our alumni records. I'll be right back." He got up and rushed out of the office, leaving the door cracked a few inches.

"How old is that guy?" Ren whispered. "Didn't your mom say he was like two hundred years old? And that was back then."

"Yeah, she did. So I guess that makes him two hundred and seventeen?"

"At least. And he's superenergetic. He'd better slow down on the espressos."

"Should I ask him about X? They kept it a secret from the school, but I could ask if they had anyone quit their job partway through my mom's second semester."

"Yeah, do it."

I glanced over at the wall and my eye snagged on a photograph of an old woman looking directly into the camera. I stood up and walked over to it. "My mom took this."

"Really? How do you know?"

"I just do."

Petrucione bounded back into the room. "Ah, I see you found your mother's photograph."

"I can usually recognize her work." By the way it made my heart hurt.

"Well, it's certainly unique. She had a real gift for portraits." He handed me a piece of paper, and we both sat back down. "I've written down Francesca's full name and included the number to her company. I'm sure she'll be very happy to talk to you."

"Thank you; this is really helpful."

"You're so very welcome." He beamed at me.

I'd thought I'd just get the info and get out, but suddenly I didn't want to leave. "What was my mom like? When she was here?"

Petrucione smiled. "Like an exclamation mark in human form. I'd never seen anyone so excited to be doing what they were doing. This school is very selective, but even so we'll occasionally have a floater slip through—that's what we call students who are kind of lukewarm but have enough natural talent to get accepted. Your mother wasn't like that. She was full of talent—drenched in it, really—but that's only one part of the equation. You have to be talented *and* driven. I think she could have been successful by her drive alone." He smiled. "All of the students liked her. I remember her being very popular. And once she played a joke on me. She took this very abstract photograph of a section of Ponte Vecchio and turned it in as an assignment. I'd seen enough photographs of Ponte Vecchio to last me a lifetime by then, and I'd warned the class that if anyone dared to use that bridge as their inspiration I'd fail them on the spot. But she did it, and of course I loved the photograph, and only afterward she told me what it was. . . ." He chuckled, shaking his head.

A warm, gooey feeling bubbled up inside of me. I *loved* it when people who really knew my mom talked about her. It was like holding her hand for one tiny second.

Ren met my gaze. *X*, he mouthed.

"Oh." I took a deep breath. "Mr. Petrucione? I have one more question."

"*Prego.*"

"My mom mentioned that there was a . . . male faculty member or teacher or something who resigned partway through her second semester. Do you know who that could be?"

The room's happy vibe evaporated with a *poof*. Petrucione suddenly looked disgusted, like someone had just offered him a plate of dog poop or something.

"No. I don't."

Ren and I exchanged a look. "Are you sure?"

"Positive."

I shifted in my seat. "Okay. Well, he might not have been around for long. I think he ended up taking another job in Rome and—"

He stood, raising his arm to cut me off. "I'm sorry, but we've had a lot of faculty come and go. I don't remember." He nodded at us. "It was such a pleasure to meet you. If you're ever in town again, please stop by and say hello." His voice was still kind, but final. Definitely final.

He wasn't going to talk about X.

"Thanks for your help," I said after a moment, getting to my feet.

As Ren and I passed by Violetta's desk, she jumped up and gave us a smile as wide as the Arno. "It was *such* an honor meeting you, and I'm so happy we could help. Have a *wonderful* day."

"...Thanks."

As soon as the glass door sealed shut behind us, Ren raised an eyebrow. "What was that about?"

Chapter 17

"PETRUCIONE DEFINITELY KNEW WHO WE WERE TALKING about. Did you see that look he got on his face?"

Ren nodded. "Yeah, couldn't miss it. And he'd said like five seconds before that he doesn't forget people's names. He just didn't want to tell us."

"Hopefully we'll have more luck with Francesca." I dialed her number, then pressed the phone to my ear. "It's ringing."

"Pronto?" It was a man.

"Um, Francesca Bernardi?"

He answered in rapid Italian. "Um, Francesca?" I said again.

He *tsk-tsked.* Then the phone started ringing again and a woman picked up. *"Pronto?"* Her voice was low and smoky.

"Hello, Francesca?"

"Si?"

"My name is Carolina. You don't know me, but you knew my mom. Hadley Emerson?"

Silence. I made a face at Ren.

"What?" he whispered.

"Carolina," she said slowly. "What a surprise. Yes. I knew your mother. She was a dear friend."

My heart sped up. "I'm just trying to learn a little bit more about her . . . studies in Florence. You were her roommate, right?"

"Yes. And a messier woman never lived! I thought I was going to be buried alive in her rubble."

"Yeah . . . that was always kind of an issue. Could you maybe answer some questions for me about her life in Florence?"

"I'm sure I could, but why are you asking me? Hadley and I haven't been in touch in ages."

"Well . . ." I hesitated. I never knew how to break the news to people. It was like opening a dam. You never knew what they were going to hit you with. "She died. A little over six months ago."

Francesca gasped sharply. "*Non ci posso credere.* How?"

"Pancreatic cancer. It was pretty sudden."

"Oh, my poor dear. *Era troppo giovane, veramente.* I would be happy to talk about your mother. After she finished her program she dropped off the side of the world. None of us were able to get in touch with her."

"Do you . . . ?" I grimaced. "This will sound weird. But do you remember if she was dating anyone?"

"Oh, the love life of Hadley Emerson. It was like a romance novel. Your mother was in love, yes, and I think half of Firenze was in love with her. I always knew who was right for her—we all did—but then there was that Matteo causing a mess and ruining things."

"Matteo?" I croaked. I hadn't even had to push; she'd just dropped his name into my lap.

Ren looked up sharply.

"Yes. Our professor."

"Professor," I whispered to Ren. Well, that cleared up the whole secrecy thing.

". . . He had her very confused, and I was so angry that she'd hurt our friend. . . ." She trailed off. "I feel like I'm telling old secrets."

"What's Matteo's last name?"

She paused. "I believe it was Rossi. Yes, that sounds right. But I shouldn't even mention him. That man was a waste of time for everyone, especially your mother." She sighed. "We all wanted to save her from him. He was charming. Very handsome. But controlling. He thought he could find talent and take it on as his own. It was quite the scandal when he was fired."

"Fired?" *So much for "creative space."*

"Yes. But that's all old news." Her voice lifted. "Do you know who would be a great person for you to talk to? Howard Mercer. He was another classmate of ours, and he works at a at least a case full of those giant sugar-dusted muffins, but all the café consisted of was a bunch of ancient-looking desktop computers and a group of angry people waiting in line for a turn to delete their junk mail. It was crazy disappointing.

Ren shifted from one foot to the other. "Sure you don't want to just go home and use my computer?"

"No. I want to find Matteo right away." My phone chimed and I pulled it out of my purse.

> Want to go to a party with me tomorrow night? It's for a girl who graduated last year. Band, bar, fireworks . . .
> –Thomas

I braced myself for a stampede of stomach butterflies, but nothing happened. In fact, I think a tumbleweed might have blown by. I looked at Ren furtively. *Lina, you've got to pull it together.* Why did he look so good to me today? Was it just because he was the only person I knew who'd be willing to join me on a wild-goose chase for my mom's ex-boyfriend?

"Who is it?" Ren asked.

"No one."

"So, Lina . . ." His mouth drew down in a cute worried look. *No, not cute.* "Petrucione obviously didn't want to talk about Matteo, and Francesca wasn't a fan of him either. Do you really think it's a good idea to track him down? What if he's a jerk?"

"He was definitely a jerk. But yes, I want to meet him. He was a huge deal in her life, and she must have wanted me to know about him—otherwise, why would I have her journal? I just feel like finding him is a big part of figuring all this out."

He nodded, still looking unconvinced. "Okay. But 'Matteo Rossi' is a pretty common name. It's like looking for Steve Smith in the States."

"We'll find him," I said confidently. "Think: We've already been pretty lucky today. Number one, we found the school—"

"That was a miracle."

"... And number two, once we were in there, you thought to mention Petrucione. If you hadn't, I think Violetta would have thrown us out on the street." On the other side of the room a woman stood up from her computer. "Hey, look! I think one just opened up."

I sprinted over to the computer, Ren at my heels, and we both squished into the chair.

"Want me to search sites in Italian?" he asked.

"Yes. Last we know he moved to Rome, so he's probably still here."

"What should I search for?"

I pulled the journal out of my purse and started flipping through it. "Matteo Rossi Fine Arts Academy of Florence?

Matteo Rossi photographer Rome? Just mash up everything we know about him."

He typed it all in, then started scrolling down the screen, pausing every few seconds to read. I tried to read too, but none of my five Italian phrases made an appearance.

"Nothing. Nothing. Nothing . . . Something? What about this?"

"What?"

He clicked one of the search results. "Looks like an ad. In English."

COMBINE YOUR LOVE OF TRAVEL WITH YOUR PASSION FOR PHOTOGRAPHY.

Join renowned photographer and gallery owner Matteo Rossi on a journey through Rome that will change the way you see the world. Offering several photography workshops throughout the year, Rossi will take your hobby to the next level.

"Ren, you found him! That's got to be him."

"Let's look at his website." He clicked on the link at the bottom of the ad and the website loaded piece by excruciatingly slow piece.

"Ugh. This is taking forever," I groaned. It was like watching the ice age in slow motion.

"*Pazienza*," Ren said.

Finally the website dragged itself onto the screen. It was monochromatic with a big gold banner at the top that read ITALY THROUGH THE LENS.

I grabbed the mouse from Ren, then scrolled down to read the huge amount of text on the site. Every paragraph was translated into both English and Italian, and it was pretty much all a bunch of mumbo jumbo about how unbearably happy and successful you'd be once you paid Matteo a bunch of money for the opportunity to sit at his feet. This guy was unbelievably annoying.

Ren pointed to a link at the bottom. "Bio page. Try that."

I clicked. Then we waited. And waited. Another full ice age came and went. Finally a black-and-white headshot of Matteo loaded and I leaned in to take a look.

And that's when I stopped breathing.

Chapter 18

THE ROOM SUDDENLY FELT EXACTLY LIKE THE WOOL sweaters that my great-aunt used to send me every Christmas. Hot. Itchy. Asphyxiating.

My hands were shaking, but I managed to click on the image to make it bigger. Olive skin. Dark eyes. Hair that had been cut short and then gelled within an inch of its life, because otherwise he was going to have to spend half his day trying to keep it under control.

I would know.

"Oh my gosh. Ohmigoshomigoshomigosh. I think I'm going to throw up." I started to stand up, but the room whirled around and Ren grabbed me and pulled me back into the chair.

"Lina, it's okay. Everything's okay." His voice sounded like it was coming from underwater. "This is probably just a coincidence. I mean, you look a lot like your mom, too. Every-one says so."

"Ren, she never said that he was my father."

"What?"

I spun around. "My mom never said that Howard was my father. All along she talked about him like he was just her best friend."

His eyes widened. "*Davvero*? So why did you think he was?"

"Because of my grandma. She said that Howard's my father, and my mom never told me that because she wanted me to give him a chance without being mad at him." I put my hand to my heart—it was trying to knock down my ribs. "Obviously I don't look anything like Howard, and Ren, *look*." We both looked at the screen again.

"There's got to be some kind of explanation. Maybe . . ." He trailed off.

There was absolutely no room for "maybe."

"And ever since I got here people have been telling me I look Italian. You said so when we met on the hill. Oh my gosh. I'm Italian. I'm *Italian*!"

"Half-Italian. And, Lina, calm down. Being Italian isn't the end of—"

"Ren, do you think he knows? Do you think Howard knows?"

He hesitated, looking at the picture again. "I don't know. He has to, right?"

"Then why is he going around introducing me to people

as his daughter? Oh, no." I doubled over. "The night we went to Elena's he had people over and I overheard one of them ask if I was 'the photographer's daughter' and he said yes. He didn't say I was his, too."

"But he told me he's your dad. That first time we talked. And Sonia says he is too, right?"

"So either they're all lying or they believe it." I put my head in my hands. "Ren, what if only my mom knew? What if that's the reason she sent the journal? So that I would know the truth even if no one else did?"

Ren grimaced. "Would she do that? That seems pretty . . ."

Mean? Insensitive? Pick one.

I shook my head. "I don't know anymore. Ever since I started reading the journal I've been wondering if I even really knew her." I looked at the screen again. "Just last night I was thinking that she and Howard had to get together really soon, because my birthday is in January. But I guess there's no rush. She must have already been pregnant when she moved in with him."

"So now what?"

I took a deep breath. "We have to call Matteo. I have to go meet him."

"Whoa, Lina, that sounds like a bad idea. Why don't we go talk to Howard first? Or at least finish the journal."

"Ren, please! I think it's what my mom wanted me to do. And I can't face Howard like this. I can't. Is that Matteo's number at the bottom?" I grabbed my phone and tried to dial it, but my hands were shaking too badly.

"I'll do it." He took the phone from me. "Should I just call the number to his gallery?"

"Yes. See when it's open. And where it is. How will we get there? Can we drive your scooter to Rome?"

"No, we'll take a train. They run all day." He leaned forward, the phone pressed to his ear. It was ringing.

Ren drove as fast as he could all the way to the train station, me clinging to him like a lunatic monkey. We'd looked up the train schedule online and had found an express train leaving in twenty-six minutes. We'd made it there in twenty-four.

"We made it. We made it," I panted.

Ren collapsed into an empty seat. "I've . . . never . . . run . . . that fast."

I pressed my fingers into my ribs. I had a horrible side ache. "What . . . were the chances . . . that a train . . . was running right now?"

He took a second to catch his breath. "They go all day, but this is one of the fast ones. And we need fast. Because if my parents find out I'm taking you to Rome to meet some random guy, they'll kill me. And Howard will drop me in a boiling vat of oil."

"Matteo isn't some random guy. And Howard . . ." I

groaned. "This is so awful. He's already had his heart broken by my mom, and now he's going to find out he doesn't have a daughter, either."

Just then the intercom came on at an earsplitting decibel, and we both clamped our hands over our ears as a man made a long announcement in Italian. Finally the announcement stopped, then there was a screeching sound, and the train slowly began to move out of the station. *This is happening. This is really happening.*

"You have the journal, right?" Ren asked.

"Right." I pulled it out of my purse. "I'm going to read the whole way. How long until we get there?"

"Ninety minutes. Read fast." He propped his feet up on the seat across from us, then leaned back, shutting his eyes.

"Ren?"

He opened his eyes. "Yeah?"

"I promise I'm normally boring."

"I doubt that."

MAY 9

The semester is wrapping up. Simone and Alessio finished early. They managed to get jobs working together at a museum in Naples, and we're all just relieved they won't have to split up. Who would they fight with? Adrienne finished early too, but she left without saying good-bye.

Now that our group has dwindled to just the three of us, Francesca, Howard, and I spend so much time together that we joke that Howard should just save money and move in with us. Classes are done, but we technically have a couple of weeks before we have to turn in our final projects, and I've already started assisting Petrucione.

I feel like I've come to the end of an era. The past year has held some of my best moments but also some of my worst. I haven't heard a single word from X since that day in the train station, and now that the sharp edges of that day have dulled, I keep asking myself the same question: How could our relationship have meant so much to me and so little to him?

May 12

For the past few weekends Howard and I have been renting a car and dragging Francesca on outings to

Tuscan hill towns. We have very specific roles: Howard drives and DJs, I read aloud from a travel book, and Francesca sits in the back and complains. We have so much fun, and I'm so glad to have them for a distraction. Sometimes I even forget about X for a while.

MAY 13

Francesca was just offered a position as an assistant to a prominent fashion photographer in Rome. If she takes it (and she will) she'll start in less than a month. Howard has been interviewing for jobs too. He told me he'll do whatever it takes to stay in Italy. Janitor with a PhD in art history, anyone? We've always been kindred spirits about Florence. While the rest of our friends sat around complaining about the city's tourists and how expensive everything is, we were the ones pointing out stained glass windows and trying every strange flavor of gelato we came across.

I hate to admit it, but even though I still love Florence with my whole heart, it has become a sad place to me as well. Everywhere I go I see places I went with X, and it's like I can hear echoes of our conversations. I spend hours wondering why our breakup was so sudden. Did the school find out? Did he meet someone else? But it's useless to think about. I could wonder forever.

MAY 14

Only about a week left on my project. Petrucione has recommended a few art schools for portrait photography, and he said that if I can round out my portfolio I'll have my pick of any program I want. Trying to feel as enthusiastic as I should about it. Part of me is ready for the next phase, and part of me wishes I could just stay in this city forever.

MAY 15

Howard must be sick of me blowing him off to work on my portfolio, because he blindsided me on my way out of the studio and told me he was taking me to see the Florence American Cemetery and Memorial. He's been working there as a volunteer for the past few months (add WWII history to his long list of interests) and was recently approached about applying for the position of live-in superintendent. The current superintendent had a stroke earlier this month, and they're scrambling to find someone to replace him. I can't imagine a more perfect person for the job—or a more perfect place for Howard. He said it's a long shot and tried to act nonchalant about it, but I could tell how badly he wants the job.

MAY 18

What is wrong with me?? One day I feel like I'm moving along just fine, and other days I'm so weepy and emotional I may as well be standing in that train station in Rome. I stay up late working most nights, but even if I don't I still can't sleep. Every time I close my eyes I just think about X. I know I should be getting over him by now, but I just wish we could have one more conversation. In a moment of weakness I tried his phone number, but it had been disconnected. I know it was for the better, but I was still so disappointed.

MAY 20

Howard was offered the job! Francesca and I took him out to his favorite pizza place to celebrate, and when we got back to our apartment, Francesca scurried up the stairs, leaving Howard and me standing outside. I was about to say good night, but he started hemming and hawing and then out of nowhere invited me to stay with him at the cemetery for the rest of the summer. He made it sound so easy: Finish up your grad school applications. Stay in my spare bedroom. Spend a little more time in Florence. What an offer! I said yes before he even finished asking.

MAY 22

Today was my last official day as a student at FAAF. I'm planning to take the weekend off. Then I'll start assisting Petrucione on Monday. Francesca and I spent the afternoon packing up our apartment. I never thought I'd say this, but I'm going to miss my cardboard mattress and all those noisy bakery customers. So many good things happened to me here!

Francesca left an hour ago. Her internship starts in two weeks, and she's going to visit her parents first. I helped drag all nine of her bags down to the street, and then we just hugged. She claims she never cries, but when she pulled back her eyeliner was a tiny bit smudged. Hopefully she makes good on her promise to visit Howard and me soon.

MAY 24

Well, it's official. I am now a resident of the Florence American Cemetery and Memorial. All the stress of ending the school year must have hit me, because yesterday I was so exhausted that I could barely even get out of bed. The previous superintendent left the place fully furnished, so Howard's been able to jump right into the job. The spare bedroom is perfect for me, and Howard said he doesn't mind if I cover the walls with photographs.

MAY 26

The cemetery is gorgeous, and even though I should be spending all my free time working on my grad school applications, I keep taking breaks to wander through the headstones. The Wall of the Missing is especially interesting. How is it that they were living, breathing people and all of a sudden they were just gone? This morning I was photographing it and the assistant superintendent, Sonia, joined me and we had a nice long talk. She's a lovely woman. Smart, like Howard, and so dedicated to working here.

MAY 30

This has been such a great week. After we're done working for the day, Howard and I cook, watch old movies, and go for long walks, and it just feels so <u>perfect</u>. Sometimes Sonia joins us, and we sit around playing cards or watching movies or just talking. I don't know how to explain it exactly, but for years I've felt like I was looking for something—like I wasn't quite in the right place. But here with Howard, that feeling has evaporated. I don't know if it's the city, or the peacefulness of the cemetery, or having so much time to work on my photography, but I've never felt more at ease. There's something very healing about this place.

May 31

This morning I showed Petrucione some of the photos I've taken at the cemetery. There's one spot in the northwest corner that gives a perfect view of the grounds, and I've been taking pictures there at different times of day. It's amazing to see the change in light and color as the day progresses.

I guess it makes sense, but living in a cemetery has me thinking often about death. There's an order here that doesn't exist in real life, and I find it strangely comforting. Maybe that's the beauty of death. Nothing is messy anymore. Everything is sealed up and final.

Sealed up and final.

"Ugh," I said aloud. She was so *wrong* about that. How

could anything be final when you left people behind and didn't even tell them your secrets?

"What's up?" Ren asked. "Anything new?"

"She moved in with Howard at the cemetery. But they're just friends. She had to have been pregnant by then." I shook my head. "Matteo has to be the one."

"Can I catch up?"

I handed him the journal, then leaned back, watching the scenery fly past our window. We were driving through a postcard of green countryside and rolling hills, and it was so pretty and picturesque I wanted to scream.

Why had she told me this way?

Chapter 19

BY THE TIME THE TRAIN CAME TO A STOP I HAD ENOUGH adrenaline running through me to power a small island. Not that any of the other passengers cared. They were taking their sweet time gathering up their magazines and laptops, and I stood blocked in the aisle, jiggling nervously.

Ren nudged me with his shoulder. "You sure you want to do this?"

"I have to."

He nodded. "When we get out let's head straight for the curb. If we beat the rush we can get a cab and be there in like ten minutes."

Ten minutes.

Finally the line started moving and Ren and I hurried off the train. The station had a high ceiling and was even more crowded than the one in Florence.

"Which way?" I asked.

He turned around in a circle. "I think . . . that way. Yeah."

"You up for running again?"

"Let's do it."

He grabbed my hand and we sprinted toward the exit, dodging people like they were pitfalls in a video game. *Ten minutes. Ten minutes.* My life was about to change. *Again.* What happened to normal, boring days?

There were a bunch of cabs waiting out on the street next to the taxi stand, and Ren and I jumped into the first one available. Our cabdriver had a thick mustache and a cologne problem.

Ren read him the address.

"*Dieci minuti,*" the cabdriver answered.

"Ten minutes," Ren translated.

Breathe. Breathe. Breathe. He was still holding my hand.

Word to the wise. Unless you have no choice—like maybe you're being chased by a pack of rabid spider monkeys, or you've run away to a foreign city to track down your mysterious father—never, ever get into a cab in Rome. Ever.

"Ren, I think this guy is going to kill us," I whispered.

"Why? Because we almost just got into our second head-on collision? Or because he keeps trying to pick fights with other drivers?"

"*Dove hai imparato a guidare?*" our driver yelled at another driver. He leaned out the window and made a gesture that I'd never seen but definitely got the gist of.

"I think my life is flashing before my eyes," I said.

"How is it?"

"Exciting."

"Mine too. Although I have to admit, it got way more exciting five days ago when you ran up to me on the hill."

"I didn't run up to you. I was actually trying to avoid you."

"Really? Why?"

"I thought it would be awkward. And then it was."

He grinned. "And look at us now. Spending our last few minutes on earth together."

The driver swerved over to a curb, then threw the car into park before coming to a complete stop. Ren and I flew into the seats in front of us.

"Ow!" I rubbed my face. "Do I have a nose anymore?"

"A flat one," said Ren. He was crunched up on the floor like a balled-up piece of paper.

"*Siamo arrivati,*" the cabdriver said pleasantly. He glanced at us in the rearview mirror, then pointed to his meter. "*Diciassette euro.*"

I dug some money out of my purse and passed it forward, and then we climbed out onto the sidewalk. The second I closed the door, the cab screeched back into traffic, causing about four other cars to slam on their brakes and contribute to what was basically a grand orchestra of honking.

"That guy shouldn't be allowed to drive."

"Pretty standard. He's actually one of the better cabdrivers I've had. Look, there's the gallery."

I whirled around. We were standing in front of a gray stone building with gold lettering on the door:

ROSSI GALLERIA E SCUOLA DI FOTOGRAFIA
ROSSI GALLERY AND PHOTOGRAPHY SCHOOL

Rossi. Lina Rossi. Was that actually my name? Crap. It had an Italian *R*. I wouldn't even be able to pronounce it.

"Come on." Before my nerves could get the better of me, I marched over to the door and pressed the buzzer.

"*Prego,*" a man's voice said through the speaker. *Matteo?* The door unlocked with a loud *click.*

I looked at Ren. "You ready?"

"Who cares about me? Are *you* ready?"

"No."

Before I could think, I shoved the door open, launching myself into a large, circular-shaped foyer. The room was made of shiny tile, and there was a huge light fixture with about ten different pendant lights jutting out of it like jellyfish tentacles. A blond man wearing a dress shirt and tie sat behind a curved silver desk. He was young and American-looking. Definitely not Matteo.

"*Buon giorno*. English?" he said in a bored voice.

"Yes." My voice echoed.

"I'm afraid you've missed the class. It started more than a half hour ago."

Ren stepped up next to me. "We're not here for the class. I called a couple of hours ago about meeting with Matteo? My name is Lorenzo."

"Lorenzo Ferrara?" He studied us for a moment. "I guess I didn't realize that you were quite so young. Unfortunately, Mr. Rossi is upstairs teaching a class. His class times vary, and I can't promise that he'll have the time to meet with you afterward."

"We'll wait anyway," I said quickly. *Mr. Rossi.* For all I knew he was standing right above me.

"And what is your name?" the man asked me.

"Lina . . ." I hesitated. Would Matteo recognize my last name? "My name is Lina Emerson."

Ren shot me a look, but I just shrugged. The point was to tell Matteo who I was, right?

"Very well. I can't make any promises, but I'll let him know you're here."

His phone rang with a loud *brrrrnng*, and he snatched it from the desk. "*Buon giorno. Rossi Galleria e Scuola di Fotografia.* Good morning, Rossi Gallery and Photography School."

"Let's look around," I said to Ren. I was crazy jittery. Maybe a tour of the gallery would keep my mind off of what was about to happen.

"Sure."

We walked under an arched doorway into the first room. The room was made of exposed brick, and all four walls were covered with framed photographs. A large one caught my eye and I walked over to it. It was a shot of an old graffiti-covered building in a big city, like New York City or somewhere, and one wall read, TIME DOESN'T EXIST, CLOCKS EXIST. There was a big looping handwritten signature in the bottom right corner: M. ROSSI.

"That's pretty cool," Ren said.

"Yeah, my mom would have loved his style." Correction. She *had* loved his style. My sweat glands immediately went into overdrive.

Ren wandered ahead a few feet, and I headed in the other direction. Most of the photographs were by Matteo, and they were really good. Like *really* good.

"Lina? Could you come here for a second?" Ren's voice was purposely calm, like when you need to tell someone they have a massive spider on their back but don't want them to freak out.

"What?" I hurried over to him. "What is it?"

"Look."

It took me a second to realize what I was looking at, and

then I practically jumped out of my skin. It was a photograph of *me*. Or at least, the back of me, and I even remembered when my mom had taken it. I was five years old and I'd piled up a stack of books so I could watch out the window for our neighbor's pony-size dog, with whom I'd had an intense love/fear relationship. I was wearing my favorite dress. I looked at the tag. *Carolina*, by Hadley Emerson.

"How did he get this?" Suddenly I felt light-headed. "He knows about me. This isn't going to be a surprise."

"Are you sure you want to stay?"

"I don't know. Do you think he's been waiting for me to show up?"

"Excuse me." It was the man from the foyer. He was looking at us like he thought we might try to shove one of Matteo's massive photographs into my purse. "Do you two have any questions?"

About a million. "Um, yeah. . . ." I gave the room a desperate glance. "Are all of these . . . for sale?"

"Not all of them. Some are part of Mr. Rossi's private collection."

"Does he have anything else by Hadley Emerson?" I pointed to the photograph.

"Hmm." He walked over and took a look at *Carolina*. "I can check, but I believe this is the only one. Are you familiar with Hadley Emerson's work?"

"Uh, yeah. Sort of."

"Let me check our system and I'll let you know."

He walked out of the room and Ren raised his eyebrows. "Not exactly the most observant, is he?"

"What am I going to say to Matteo? Do I just tell him straight out who I am?"

"Maybe you should wait to see if he recognizes you."

A door opened overhead and suddenly there was a thundering of voices and footsteps. Class was out. My breathing went into overdrive. This was a mistake. It was too fast. What if he didn't want to be a part of my life? What if he did? Would he be as awful as the guy in my mom's journal?

I grabbed Ren's arm. "I changed my mind. I don't want to meet him. You're right. We should talk to Howard first. At least I know my mom trusted him."

"You sure?"

"Yes. Let's get out of here."

We raced out of the room. About a dozen people were making their way into the foyer, but we quickly skirted around them, and I reached for the doorknob.

"You two. Wait there!"

Ren and I froze. *Oh, no.* Part of me wanted to walk right out onto the street, but another even bigger part wanted to turn around. So I did. Slowly.

A middle-aged man stood at the top of the staircase. He

wore an expensive-looking shirt and slacks, and was shorter than I'd thought, with a carefully groomed beard and mustache. His dark eyes were fixed on me.

"Come on, Lina, let's go," Ren said.

"Carolina? Please come up to my office."

"We don't have to go," Ren said quietly. "We can just walk out of here. Right now."

My heart was pounding in my ears. Not only had he called me "Carolina," but he'd pronounced it right. I grabbed Ren's hand. "Please come with me."

He nodded. Then we slowly made our way toward the staircase.

Chapter 20

"PLEASE, HAVE A SEAT." MATTEO'S VOICE WAS POLISHED, with only a hint of an accent. He walked behind a half-moon desk and gestured to two chairs that looked exactly like hard-boiled eggs. Actually, come to think of it, *everything* in his office looked like something else. A large clock shaped like a cog ticked noisily in the corner, and the rug looked like it was supposed to be a map of the human genome or something. The whole room had this overly colorful modern vibe that didn't seem to mesh with the man standing in front of us.

I lowered myself uneasily into one of the hard-boiled eggs. "What can I do for you?"

Okay. Just tell him? How do I start?

"I—" I made the mistake of glancing at Ren, and suddenly my throat sealed up like a Ziploc bag. He gave me a worried look.

Matteo cocked his head. "You two speak English, correct?

Benjamin told me you wanted to meet me. I'm assuming you have questions about my programs?"

Ren cast a glance at my frozen expression, then jumped in. "Uh . . . yes. Questions about your programs. Um, do you have any classes for beginners?"

"Of course. I teach several entry-level courses through-out the year. The next one begins in September, but I believe it is already full. All of that information is available on my website." He leaned back. "Would you like to be put on the waiting list?"

"Yeah, that sounds good."

"All right. Benjamin can help you with that."

Matteo slid his eyes at me, and suddenly I could feel every nerve ending. Was he pretending not to know, or did he not see it? I felt like I was standing in front of a mirror. An older, male mirror, but a mirror just the same. His eyes lingered on my hair for a moment.

"Can you recommend a good camera for a beginner?" Ren asked.

"Yes. I prefer Nikons. There are several good camera shops in Rome, and I'd be happy to give you the owners' contact information."

"Nice."

Matteo nodded and there was a long silence.

Ren cleared his throat. "So . . . those must be pretty pricey."

"There's a range of prices." He crossed his arms and glanced at the cog clock. "Now if you'll excuse me . . ."

"Do you collect a lot of photographs from other photographers?" I blurted out. Both of them looked at me.

"Not many. But I travel a lot, and I make it a point to visit studios and galleries everywhere I go. If I find something especially moving, I buy it and display it in my gallery, along with mine and my students' work."

"What about the Hadley Emerson photograph? Where did you buy that?"

"That one was a gift."

"From who?"

"Hadley." He looked straight into my eyes. Like a challenge.

All of the air whooshed out of me.

He pushed back from his desk. "Lorenzo, why don't we go to the reception area and ask Benjamin about placing you on the waiting list. Carolina, before you leave I'd be happy to show you the other Emerson photograph I have in my possession."

I rose clumsily from my chair and Ren grabbed my arm. "Why isn't he recognizing you?" he whispered.

"He is. He knew my real name and he's saying it right." No one ever said my name right. Unless they'd heard it before.

We followed him down the stairs, my heart pounding in

my throat, and Matteo stopped at the desk. "Benjamin, will you please assist Lorenzo in being added to the wait list for the next beginners' course?"

"Of course."

"Carolina, the photograph is in the next room. Lorenzo, we'll meet you back here."

We looked at each other. *Okay?* he mouthed.

Okay.

Okay, okay, okay.

"Right this way." Matteo walked briskly into the next room and I followed after him, my mind scrambling like a bad TV connection. What was happening? Did he just want to talk in private?

He walked up to the far wall, then pointed to a photograph of a young woman, her face half in shadow. Definitely my mom's.

"You see?"

"Yes." I took a deep breath, keeping my eyes focused on the photograph for courage. "Matteo, I'm here because I'm—"

"I know who you are."

My head snapped up. He was looking at me like something that had attached itself to the bottom of his shoe. "You're your mother in a pair of skinny jeans and Converse sneakers. The real question is, what are you doing here?"

"What am I . . . doing here?" I took a step back, fumbling

to pull the journal out of my purse. "I read about you in my mom's journal."

"So?"

"She was . . . in love with you."

He laughed bitterly. "In *love*. She was a stupid child, in love with her instructor. She'd had no exposure to life outside of that small town she came from, and when she got here she thought her life would be transformed into some sort of fairy tale. But regardless of what her fantasies were, I was her teacher, nothing more. And whatever ideas you have in your mind, you'd better erase them immediately, Carolina." He spat out my name like a rotten piece of fruit.

Heat spread through my body. "It wasn't *nothing*. You dated. You kept it a secret from everyone and then you broke up with her when she went to visit you in Rome."

He shook his head slowly. "No. Those are lies. She spun an elaborate fantasy about us being in a relationship and then went so far as to believe it herself." His lips curled in an ugly smile. "Your mother was unbalanced. A liar."

"No, she wasn't." My voice echoed through the room. "She wasn't delusional. She didn't make up your relationship."

"Oh, really." His voice rose. "Ask anyone who was there. Did any of them ever see us together? Have you ever spoken with anyone who confirmed her story?"

"Francesca Bernardi."

He rolled his eyes. "Francesca. She was your mother's best friend. Of course she believed her. But did she ever actually see us together? Did she have anything more to go on than your mother's ridiculous fairy tale?"

Did she? A merry-go-round of thoughts started whirling through my head. Francesca had *sounded* sure. . . .

"I didn't think so. But since you've made the effort of coming here, I'll tell you exactly what happened. Your mother was struggling with her course work and asked if I would tutor her outside of school. At first I was happy to help, but then she started calling me at strange hours. During class she would stare at me, then leave things on my desk for me to find. Sometimes it was lines of poetry; other times it was photographs of herself." He shook his head. "At first I thought it was just a crush, harmless. But then she became more intense. One night she came to my apartment and told me she'd fallen in love with me. She said her life would have no meaning if we weren't together. I tried to be kind. I told her that as her teacher a relationship simply would not be allowed. I told her she'd be happier dating people closer to her own age. Like that Howard Mercer."

Howard. I flinched, but Matteo didn't notice. He was looking past me, like he was watching the scene unfold on a big-screen TV.

"That's when she snapped. She started screaming, telling me that she was going straight to the school director to tell him I'd taken advantage of her. I told her that no one would believe her. And then she pulled out a journal—*that* journal, I'm guessing—and told me that it was all there. She'd filled it with a fantasy—a vision—of what she'd wished had happened between us, and told me she would give it an unhappy ending and offer it up as proof.

"The next day I requested a meeting with the school director, and we agreed that even though I'd committed no fault, it was best for me to resign. Later I heard she began sleeping with any man who looked her way. I'm guessing you're a product of that." He met my eyes, and a cold burst of air moved through me. "I wanted nothing to do with your mother, and I want nothing to do with you."

"You're a *liar*." My voice trembled. "And a complete coward. Look at me. I look just like you."

He shook his head slowly, a pained smile on his face. "No, Carolina. You look just like *her*. And whatever poor man she suckered into her pathetic imaginations." In one quick motion he stepped forward, snatching the journal out of my hands.

"Hey!" I tried to grab it back, but he whipped around, blocking me with his shoulder.

"Ah, yes. The famous journal." He began flipping through it. "I guess she called me X? Clever, wasn't she? 'The only hard part about being with X is not telling anyone about it' . . . 'Sometimes I feel like my time is divided into two categories: time with X, and time spent waiting to be with X' . . ." He turned around, fanning the pages lazily. "Carolina, you seem like a smart girl. Does this sound real to you? Does it seem likely that your mother was in a relationship that she managed to keep entirely secret?"

"She didn't make it up."

He glanced down at the book. It had fallen open to the front cover, and he held it up to me. 'I made the wrong choice.' You see? Even in her craziness she knew that faking this journal was wrong. She was so talented, but *folle*. I hate to tell you this, Carolina, but science has proven that the parts of the brain responsible for creativity and madness are the same. At least you can take comfort in the fact that it wasn't really her fault. Your mother was a genius, but her mind was weak."

Suddenly all I could see was hot, boiling red. Before I could think, I lunged at him, twisting the journal out of his hands and running for the foyer.

"Lina?" Ren looked up from the desk. He had a clipboard in front of him. "Are you okay?"

I pulled the door open and burst out onto the sidewalk, Ren chasing after me. I turned and ran up the street, my legs heavy as sandbags. *Her mind was weak.*

Finally Ren caught up to me, grabbing my arm.

"Lina, what happened? What happened in there?"

A wave of nausea washed over me and I ran over to the edge of the street and started dry heaving. Finally the feeling passed and I sank to the ground, the pavement hard under my knees.

Ren was kneeling next to me. "Lina, what just happened?"

I turned and pressed my face into his chest and suddenly I wasn't just crying. I was *sobbing*. Like splitting-at-the-seams, exploding-into-a-million-pieces, falling-*apart* crying. The weight of the last ten months was dumping down on me, and I couldn't do a thing about it.

I cried and cried and cried. Hot, noisy tears that didn't care who was watching. The kind of crying I'd never done in front of anyone.

"Lina, it's okay," Ren said over and over, his arms wrapped around me. "It's going to be okay."

But no, it wasn't. And it never would be. My mom was gone. And I missed her so much I sometimes wondered how I was breathing. Howard wasn't my father. And Matteo . . . I don't know how long I cried for, but finally I felt my feet reach the bottom, my last few sobs coming out in shudders.

I opened my eyes. We were both still kneeling on the ground, and I was smooshed into Ren, my face buried in his neck, his skin hot and sticky. I pulled back. Ren's shirt had a giant soggy puddle on it, and he looked mortified.

This was *so* much more than he'd bargained for.

"I'm sorry," I said hoarsely.

"What just happened?"

I wiped my face, then pulled him up to standing. "He said my mom made it all up. She was obsessed with him and she wrote a fake journal to get him in trouble with the school."

"*Che bastardo.* That's not even that good of a story." He looked at me closer. "Wait. You didn't believe him, did you?"

I hesitated for a moment, then shook my head hard, my hair sticking to my wet cheeks. "No. At first it scared me. But that wasn't her. She never would have hurt someone she loved."

He exhaled. "You scared me for a minute."

"I just can't believe that she loved *him*. He was horrible. And Howard is so . . ." I looked up.

Ren's face was like six inches away from mine, and suddenly we locked eyes and I wasn't thinking about Matteo and Howard anymore.

Chapter 21

IT WASN'T A LITTLE KISS. NOT LIKE YOUR FIRST PECK OR like the time you made out with your junior high boyfriend behind the movie theater. It was throw-your-arms-around-his-neck, bury-your-fingers-in-his-hair, why-haven't-we-done-this-before kissing straight through all the salt on my face. Ren circled his hands around my waist and for five seconds everything was perfect, and then—

He pushed me off him.

Pushed.

Me.

Off.

Him.

I wanted the sidewalk to swallow me up.

He wouldn't look at me.

Seriously, why hadn't it swallowed me up yet?

"Ren . . . I don't know what just happened." He'd been kissing me back, hadn't he? *Hadn't* he?

He was staring at the ground. "No, no. It's okay. I just don't think that the timing's the best, you know?"

TIMING. My face went up in flames. Not only had he just had to peel me off of him, but he was being *nice* about it. *Lina, fix this.* Words started pouring out of my mouth.

"You're right. You're totally right. I think I just got carried away after what happened in there—it was really emotional, and I think I just redirected and . . ." I squeezed my eyes shut. "We're just friends. I know that. And I've never, ever, ever thought of you as anything more."

Does it count as a lie if you're denying something you've only fully admitted to yourself for about a minute? Also: One too many "evers" there. But I was going for believable.

Ren's gaze shot up, meeting mine with literally the most unreadable expression on the planet. And then he was gone again. "It's okay. Don't worry about it."

Why, why, why did I do that? I slumped against my door of the taxi. Ren was sitting as far away from me as was physically possible, and he was staring out the window like he was trying to memorize the streets or something.

Couldn't I have a repeat? Go back twenty minutes to when I hadn't already lost my head and kissed my best friend who had a girlfriend and clearly didn't want *me*? Back before I'd noticed how much I loved his shaggy hair and sense of humor or the fact that even though I'd known him for less than a week I somehow felt comfortable sharing all my crazy history with him?

Oh my gosh. I was so in love it hurt.

I pressed my fingers into my chest. *You've known him like five days. There's no way you can be in love with him.* Totally rational.

Totally not true.

Of course I was in love with Ren. He was exactly himself, and I was exactly *my*self when I was with him. And all of that would be perfect if he felt even close to the same. But he didn't. I glanced over at him, and a flash of pain moved through me. Was he even going to talk to me again?

The cabdriver was eyeing us in his rearview mirror. "*Tutto bene?*"

"*Si,*" Ren answered.

Finally the driver swerved to pull up to the train station and Ren handed him a wad of cash, then practically jumped out of the cab, me following miserably after him.

We still had to get back to Florence. A whole train ride, and then the scooter ride, and then ... *Oh, no.* After that I'd be back in the cemetery. With Howard. I couldn't let myself think ahead that far. It made me feel like I was going to hyperventilate.

Ren slowed down for a second so I could catch up. "Our train leaves in forty-five minutes."

Forty-five minutes. Aka forever. "Do you want to sit down?"

He shook his head. "I'm going to go get something to eat." *Alone.*

He didn't say it, but I heard it.

I nodded numbly, then walked over to a nearby bank of chairs, falling down in one of the seats. What was *wrong* with me? For one thing, you don't sob all over someone and then immediately try to kiss them. For another, you don't kiss someone who has a girlfriend. A gorgeous one. Even if you thought he *might* be into you.

Had I completely misread him? Had he really been spending all this time with me because he was just a good friend? What about all the times he'd held my hand or told me he liked me because I was different? Didn't that mean something?

And what about *Matteo*? My father was literally the worst person I'd ever met. I had no doubts my mom had kept me away from him on purpose, so why had she sent me all the clues I needed to find him?

I needed a distraction. I pulled the journal out of my purse, but when I opened it, the words wriggled across the page like bugs. There was no way I'd be able to concentrate. Not when things felt like this.

Ten excruciating minutes later Ren walked up carrying a big bottle of water and a plastic sack. He handed them both to me. "Sandwich. It's prosciutto."

"What's that?"

"Thinly sliced ham. You'll love it." He sat down next to me and I unwrapped the sandwich and took a bite. Of course I loved it. But it was nothing compared to how I felt about Ren.

And yes. I'd totally just compared the only guy I'd ever felt this way about to a ham sandwich.

Ren reclined back in his chair, stretching his legs in front of him and crossing his arms over his chest. I tried to catch his eye, but he just kept staring at his feet.

Finally I exhaled. "Ren, I don't know what to say. I'm really sorry I put you in that situation. It wasn't fair."

"Don't worry about it."

"I mean, I know you have a girlfriend and—"

"Lina, really. Don't worry about it. It's okay."

But it definitely didn't *feel* okay, and there was maybe a cyclone right in the center of my chest. I leaned back in my chair too and closed my eyes, sending him telepathic messages. *Sorry I dragged you to Rome. Sorry I kissed you. Sorry I messed this up.*

Thirty-five minutes without talking.

No, thirty-one. Because we'd had that one horrible exchange and then I'd gone to the bathroom and stared hatefully at myself in the mirror for like two minutes. My eyes were all puffy and I looked destroyed. I *was* destroyed. I'd lost

Ren and I was about to lose Howard, too. There was no other choice. I had to make sure Howard knew he wasn't my father, no matter how badly I wished that he were.

"Train's here," Ren said, standing up. He headed for the platform and I followed after him. *Ninety more minutes.* I could do this, right?

The train was crowded, and it took us several minutes to find a seat. Finally we found two empty spots across from a large older woman who'd put a bunch of plastic bags in the space between us. A man took the seat next to her and Ren nodded at them, sliding into the window seat, then closing his eyes again.

I took the journal out of my bag and wiped it on my jeans, hoping to get rid of any lingering Matteo cooties. Time to dive back into the story. I had to get my mind off of Ren.

———∾———

JUNE 3

Tonight Howard let me know in his gentle way that he knew about X all along. It made me feel ridiculous. Here I thought we were so sneaky, but it turns out most everyone knew. I found myself telling him everything about the relationship—even the bad parts. And there were a lot of bad parts. The problem was that when things were good with X, they were SO good that I forgot about all the rest. It was such a relief to talk about it, and afterward Howard and I went out onto the porch and talked about other things until the stars came out. I feel the most peaceful that I have in a long time.

JUNE 5

Today I am twenty-two. I woke up this morning with absolutely no expectations, but Howard was waiting for me with a gift—a thin gold ring that he bought from a secondhand shop in Florence almost a year ago. He said he didn't know why he bought it; he just loved it.

The thing I love about it most is that it has history. The man who sold it said it belonged to an aunt of his who had fallen in love but was forced by her family to join a convent. Her lover had given her the ring and she'd worn it secretly her entire life. Howard said the shopkeeper made up a story to add some value to the piece, but it really is pretty and somehow fits perfectly. I was feeling exhausted, so instead of going out to dinner tonight like we'd planned, we stayed in and watched old movies. I barely even made it through the first one.

JUNE 6

Tonight Howard and I were sitting on the swing on the front porch, my feet in his lap, and he asked me a question: "If you could photograph anything in the world, what would it be?" Before I could even think about it I blurted out "hope." I know, cheesy, right? But I mean hope as in <u>stillness</u>, those moments when you just know that things are going to work out. It's the perfect description of my time here. I feel like I've hit the snooze button, and I'm taking a breath before I face whatever comes next. I know that my time is slowly ticking down here, but I don't want it to end.

JUNE 7

I want to record every minute of what happened today.

Howard woke me up just before five a.m. and told me he wanted to show me something. We hiked back behind the cemetery, me half-asleep and wearing pajamas. It was still gray out, and it felt like we walked for hours. Then finally I saw where we were going. Ahead in the distance was a small round tower. It was old-looking and completely on its own, like something that was waiting to be discovered.

Once we got to it, Howard led me to the entrance. There was a small wooden door that had probably been put there to keep out trespassers, but had broken down with time and weather. He moved it out of our way, and then we both ducked under the doorway and followed a spiral staircase out to the top of the tower. We were just high enough to get a view of everything around us, and I could see the tops of the cemetery's trees and the road that leads to Florence. I asked him what we were doing there, and he told me to just wait. And so we did. We stood there without talking as the sun rose in the most amazing pinks and golds, and before long the whole countryside was awash in color. I felt this sudden ache—it had been cold and dark for so long, and then suddenly, slowly, it wasn't.

When it was full daylight I turned around. Howard was watching me, and it was like I was suddenly seeing him for the first time. I walked over to him and suddenly we were kissing like we'd kissed a million times before. Like it was the most obvious thing in the world. When he finally pulled back we didn't say a word. I just took his hand and we went home.

JUNE 8

I keep thinking about what it was like to be with X. When I had his attention it was like a spotlight was shining on me and everything in the world was right. But the second he looked away I was cold and alone. I tried to find the word for "fickle" in Italian, and the closest I came up with was "volubile." It means "turning, whirling, winding." I was attracted to that whirlwind feeling in X, but it also left me feeling uprooted. I thought I wanted caprice and fire, but it turns out that what I really want is someone who will wake me up early so I don't miss a sunrise. What I really want is Howard. And now I have him.

JUNE 10

Francesca came for a visit yesterday. Maybe I'm just not used to her anymore, but in the course of three weeks she'd somehow managed to become an exaggerated version of herself. Her stilettos were a half-inch taller, her clothes were even more fashionable, and she was smoking a record amount of cigarettes.

After dinner we sat around talking. I thought Howard and I were doing a great job of hiding this new thing between us, but as soon as he went to bed Francesca said, "So it happened." I tried to play dumb, but she said, "Please, Hadley. Don't patronize me. I don't know why you think you have to keep all your relationships secret. I could tell the second I walked in that something had happened between the two of you. Now tell me all the details. Subito!"

I told her about the past few weeks—how peaceful and healing they've been. And then I told her about the morning at the tower and how perfect everything has felt for the past few days. When I finished she sighed dramatically. "It's like a favola, Hadley. A fairy story. You've fallen in love for real. So now what will you do? Aren't you returning to America?" Of course I had no answers for her. I've submitted my portfolio to several schools and should hear back from most of them by the end of summer. Yesterday, on a whim, I asked Petrucione if he'd ever consider hiring me as an assistant teacher, but he silenced me with one look and then told me I was too talented to waste any more time.

That's when Francesca told me. At first all she said was, "He contacted me." I asked who, but by the way my heart was beating I knew who she meant. "He found me working on a set in Rome. His excuse was to congratulate me on my internship, but I knew the real reason. He wanted to find you." For a moment I couldn't think of a single thing to say. (He was trying to find _me_?) "He said that you'd changed your phone number and now that you're no longer enrolled at the institute, your school e-mail doesn't work." I'd never considered that I might be unreachable. I had about a million thoughts running through my mind, and Francesca was watching me carefully. "I didn't give him your information, but I took his. Hadley, I think it would be a mistake, but I didn't want to play God. If you want to contact him I have his new phone number. He said he's had a change of heart. That he has something he wants to tell you." Then she handed me a business card. His name was embossed on it in large letters and his new phone number and e-mail were spelled out like a trail of bread crumbs.

That night I could hardly sleep, but it wasn't because I was conflicted. It was because I was so sure. X could appear on a white stallion carrying a dozen roses and a perfectly crafted apology, and I still wouldn't want him. I want Howard.

"How's the journal?"

I looked up. Ren's expression was way more relaxed than it had been at the station, and my heart sprouted a tiny pair of wings. *Forgiven?* I tried to meet his eye, but he looked away again.

I dropped my gaze. "It's okay. And I was really wrong about something."

"What?"

"Howard wasn't just the rebound. She fell in love with him." I tilted the journal so he could see the page I'd been looking at. "What does this mean?"

After the entry about Francesca's visit there was an entire

page scribbled with the words "*sono incinta*" over and over.

"*Sono incinta.* It means 'I'm pregnant.'"

"That's what I thought."

I looked sadly at the page. I know it pretty much meant self-annihilation, but I almost wished she weren't pregnant. Her fairy tale had just blown up.

Chapter 22

JUNE 11

<u>Sono incinta. Sono incinta. Sono incinta.</u> Would it feel different if those words were in English? I'M PREGNANT. There. I can barely think. This morning I puked up my breakfast like I have every day for the past week, and as I was flushing the toilet a horrible thought occurred to me. I tried to brush it off, but then . . . I had to know. I've always been sort of irregular, but had I been more irregular than normal? I walked to the pharmacy but forgot my English-Italian dictionary and had to go through this horrible pantomime to tell them what I needed, and then I rushed home and took the test and—positive. I went back for two more. Positive. Positive.

They were all positive.

JUNE 13

For the past two days I've barely come out of my room. Francesca left yesterday, and now every time Howard knocks on my door I pretend to be asleep. I know I need to leave here. Howard loves me. And I love him. But that doesn't matter anymore, because I'm pregnant with someone else's baby. I know I have to tell X, but the thought of it makes me want to die. What will he say? According to Francesca he's been looking for me, but I know for a fact that he wasn't looking for this. And the timing is so unbelievable. Is it a sign that Matteo and I were meant to be together? But then what about this time with Howard? Three days ago I wrote that he was the one for me. And now <u>this</u>.

I want to tell Howard so badly, but what do I say? I have called my mother and hung up twice. I keep dialing Matteo's phone number but only getting a few digits in. I'm giving myself until tomorrow night and then I have to decide something. I can't even think.

June 14

I called Matteo. He's working in Venice and I'm going there to meet him. I can't tell him over the phone.

JUNE 15

I'm on the train now. Howard insisted on giving me a ride there, and even though I didn't tell him why I was going, I think he knew. Tears just kept running down my face, and the last thing he said was, "It's okay. Please be happy."

As soon as the train pulled away I started crying so hard that everyone around me stared. I've gone over this again and again in my mind, and everything points to Matteo. I'm having his child. I have to put Howard out of my mind. I have chosen Matteo. <u>Fate</u> has chosen Matteo. Our baby has chosen Matteo. He has to be the one.

JUNE 15—LATER

Venice might be the worst place in the world for a pregnant woman. Of course it's beautiful.

One hundred and seventeen islands connected by boats and water taxis and those striped-shirt gondoliers paddling tourists around for ridiculous fees. The Floating City. But it smells horrible, and the water lapping against everything makes me feel like I'm going to topple over at any second. As soon as the train arrived I dried my tears, then forced myself to eat a salty piece of foccacia bread. One hour until Matteo and I meet. One hour until he knows. I read that Venice is sinking into the ocean, an inch and a half every century. What if I sink with it?

JUNE 16

We met in Piazza San Marco. As soon as I'd gotten my bearings I left Venice's train station and went straight to the piazza. I was early, so I walked around looking at the Basilica of St. Mark. The Basilica is so different from Florence's Duomo. It's Byzantine-style with lots of arches and a flashy mosaic on the exterior. Part of the piazza had flooded and there were tourists rolling up their pants and wading through the water.

Finally it was five p.m. I realized we hadn't said where to meet, so I just walked into the center of the piazza. Pigeons were everywhere, and I just kept seeing children. A little boy with dark hair and eyes ran past me shouting something, and my first thought was <u>How clever, he speaks Italian so well.</u> Will I have a child that speaks a language I hardly understand?

And then I saw Matteo. (Why call him X anymore?) He was walking toward me in a suit, his jacket in one hand and a bouquet of yellow roses in the other. I just watched him for a moment, feeling everything that this moment meant. Then, before I could say anything, he scooped me up in his arms and pressed his face into my hair. He just said over and over, "I've missed you, I've missed you," and feeling his arms warm and solid around me, I closed my eyes and exhaled for the first time since I found out I'm pregnant. He isn't perfect. But he's mine.

JUNE 17

I still haven't told him. I'm waiting for everything to feel natural between us again. He has been incredibly kind and gentle with me, and we've been spending most of our time walking through the streets of Venice. He is renting a small apartment with a view of a canal, and every half hour or so a gondolier passes below, usually singing to his passengers. Matteo told me he knew he'd made a mistake the second my train pulled away in Rome. He said he saw me everywhere—once he followed a woman who looked like me for half a block before realizing it couldn't have been me. He said he couldn't concentrate and that he'd started spending hours studying the photographs he'd taken when he was with me. He said I'd inspired some of his best work.

He invited me to stay in his apartment with him, but I booked a room in an inexpensive hotel. It's run by an older woman and has just three bedrooms that all share one bathroom. There are lace doilies covering everything and I feel like I'm staying at an elderly relative's house. I haven't taken a photograph in more than three days, which may be a record for me. My mind is just too full. Tomorrow I'll tell him about the baby. Tomorrow.

JUNE 18

I have to write this. It's ugly and brutal, but it hap-pened and I can't leave it out.

I took Matteo to dinner at this gorgeous little restau-rant near my hotel. It was candlelit and quiet and absolutely everything about the moment was per-fect, except when it came time to tell him, I couldn't get the words out of my mouth. Once the bill came, I asked if he'd like to go back to my hotel with me.

My room was messy—my clothes and photography equipment were everywhere—but at least it was quiet and private, and when we stepped into the room I told him to have a seat. He sat down on my bed and then he pulled me so I was sitting next to him. He said he'd been thinking about something for a long time and he believed it was time for us to take the next step.

My heart started beating so fast. Was he propos-ing? Then I looked down at my hand and panicked. I was still wearing Howard's ring. Would I just have to take it off? Can you say yes to someone when you're wearing someone else's ring? But instead of pulling out a diamond, Matteo laid out what basically amounted to a business plan. He said he's tired of making almost no money working for schools, and he wants to start his own business, leading retreats for English-speaking photographers who want to spend time in Italy. He's already booked two tours and he said I'd make the perfect addition. I could help organize travel and accommodations, and once I have a little more experience I could teach photography as well. Then he put his arms around me and said he'd been an idiot to let me out of his sight. It was time for us to join our lives together.

I hadn't let him kiss me until then, and as soon as his lips were on mine the only thought I had was <u>Howard</u>. And that's when I knew things would never work out with Matteo. Pregnant or not, I love Howard. You can't be in another relationship when you feel that way. So I pulled away from Matteo and blurted out the two words I'd come to tell him.

The words hung heavy in the air. And then he jumped up like the bed had burned him. "What do you mean, <u>pregnant</u>? How did this happen? We've been broken up for two months." I explained that it must have happened just before he left and I hadn't known until earlier this week.

That's when he freaked out. He started yelling, calling me a liar and saying there was no way this baby was his. He said I'd gotten pregnant by someone else—probably Howard—and now I was just trying to pin it on him. He started grabbing all my stuff and throwing it around the room—my camera, pictures, clothes, everything. I tried to calm him down, but then he threw a glass bottle at the wall, and when he turned and looked at me, I was suddenly very afraid.

So I lied. I told him he was right, that the baby wasn't his, it was Howard's, and that I never wanted to see him again. I was telling him what I thought he wanted to hear, but it made him even angrier. He said he was going to ruin both of us and that Howard would regret ever coming near me. Finally he shoved past me, then kicked the door open and was gone.

The ring. The denial. The lie.

I was finally getting a clear picture of my mother's life—

like up until now I'd been looking through a fogged-up window and hadn't even known it. I'd had no *idea* she'd been through so much heartache. Honestly, she was freakishly cheerful. Like once our upstairs neighbor left the bathtub running and when it flooded our apartment and ruined a bunch of our stuff, my mom just pulled out a mop and started talking about how awesome it was that we could clear out the room and start fresh.

Had that bouncy, count-your-blessings attitude I'd grown up with just been some kind of elaborate PR campaign? Had she been afraid I'd find out what her pregnancy had forced her to give up?

I closed the journal. I was pretty sure that if I tried to keep going I'd have another massive breakdown, and this time I didn't think even Ren could pull me out of it. And besides, there was no point to reading any more. No matter what my mom did next—flew by hot-air balloon back to Florence, spelled out HADLEY LOVES HOWARD in hundred-foot letters across Piazza del Duomo, sent him a handful of love letters via Venice's plentiful pigeons—it wasn't going to work out. Period. She was going to end up living the rest of her life six thousand miles away with only a slim gold ring to remind her of what she'd lost.

Oh, and me. Otherwise known as the world's most inconvenient souvenir.

I leaned back and closed my eyes, feeling the tiny back-and-forth movements of the train jostling on the track. I was approximately one hundred miles from a man who was about to get his world turned upside down and six inches from another who wanted nothing to do with me.

I literally wanted to be anywhere else.

When our train arrived in Florence it was after four o'clock. Ren had dozed off again, and his phone kept vibrating spastically on the seat next to him like some kind of giant bug. Finally I leaned over and took a look. Text message from Mimi. *Ouch.* Was he going to tell her about me kissing him? If so, I'd better brush up on my street-fighter moves. I was going to need them.

Ren opened his eyes. "Here?"

"Here. Your phone's been going off."

"Thanks."

He checked his messages, his hair hooding his eyes. As everyone around us gathered up their stuff, I picked up the journal and held it tightly in my hands. It had been one of the longest days of my life and I felt like I was wrapped up in a big, sad cocoon. I couldn't believe I had to add to it by going back to the cemetery and telling Howard what I knew.

. . .

The ride back to the cemetery was silent. Brutally silent. Everyone we passed seemed to be in the middle of a lively conversation, which made the blank space between Ren and me even more painful. I was pretty much a wreck. But I was angry, too. Yes, I'd messed up, but did that mean we couldn't even be friends anymore? And why did I have to meet Matteo and lose Ren all in one day? Don't most people get the luxury of spreading their life's drama over a couple of years?

When we finally pulled up to the cemetery a big bus of people was unloading in the parking lot, and they all stared at us like we were part of the attraction. Howard stepped out of the visitors' center and waved to us.

At the sight of him my insides froze and then shattered, but I managed to wave back. Even smile. What was he going to say?

"To the house?" Ren asked.

"Yeah."

He zipped up the road and a few seconds later pulled into the driveway, then turned off the scooter.

I climbed off the back and handed him my helmet. "Thanks for helping me, Ren. It wasn't great, but at least now I have some answers."

"Happy to." It was quiet, and we looked at each other for a

moment. Then he looked down, starting up the scooter again. "I hope everything goes okay with Howard. It's going to be all right. He really cares about you."

His voice sounded like *good-bye* and I felt my throat tighten. "Maybe we could go running tomorrow?"

He didn't answer. Instead he walked the scooter around in a circle so he was facing the road and gave me a little nod. "*Ciao*, Lina."

And then he was gone.

Chapter 23

"SO EXPLAIN THIS TO ME AGAIN. HOWARD ISN'T YOUR father; he just thinks he is?"

"Yes. Or at least I *think* he thinks he's my father."

"You *think* he thinks he's your father?"

"Yes. Either that or he's lying. But I'm kind of leaning toward the former, because it's not like people are super-eager to take in random teenagers. Even if you did love their mother."

"But Howard isn't your father? It's that Matteo guy?"

"*Yes.*" I flopped back on my bed, holding my phone to my ear. We'd been going over this for like twenty minutes now. "Addie, I don't know how else to explain this to you."

"Just give me a second. It's not like it's complicated or anything."

"I know. Sorry." I covered my eyes. "And I still haven't told you the worst part."

"Worse than meeting your horrible jerk of a father?"

"Yes." I took a deep breath. "I kissed Ren."

"You kissed Ren? Your friend?"

"Yeah."

"Okay . . . Well, what's so bad about that?"

"He didn't want to kiss me back."

"No way. Why?"

"He has a girlfriend, and we'd just met Matteo and I was having this big breakdown, which was like the most inconvenient moment to realize how I really felt about him. So then I like jumped on him and he kind of"—I cringed—"pushed me off him."

"He *pushed you off him*?"

"Yeah. And we were still in Rome, so then we had to take a train all the way back to Florence and he didn't talk to me like at all. So to sum things up, I'm all alone in Italy, I have to break the news to Howard that he isn't my father, and now I don't even have a friend."

"Oh, Lina. And to think, ten minutes ago I was jealous of you." She sighed. "What about what's-his-name? Underwear model?"

"Thomas?" *Crap. His text.* "He messaged me earlier and asked me out. Some big party for a girl who graduated from the school."

"Are you going?"

"Probably not. I mean, who knows what's going to happen

once I tell Howard. For all I know he's going to kick me out."

"He's not going to kick you out. That's ridiculous."

"I know." I sighed. "But I doubt he's going to be very happy. I mean, how weird is all this? Honestly, I wish he were my father."

Words I never thought I'd utter.

Addie was quiet for a moment. "When are you going to tell him?"

"I don't know. He's still working, but he wants to go to a movie tonight. If I can work up my courage I'll tell him as soon as he gets home."

She exhaled. "Okay, here's the plan. I'm going upstairs right now to ask my parents if you can move back in. No, I'm going up to *tell* them you need to move back in. And don't worry. They'll say yes."

I spent the next hour pacing around my room. I kept picking up the journal to examine the sliver of pages I still had left to read, but every time I tried to open it I ended up dropping it like I was playing hot potato. Once I read that last entry, it was over. I'd never hear anything new from her again. And I'd know just how badly she'd gotten her heart broken.

I kept going over to the window to watch for Howard, but he and the tour were moving across the grounds like garden slugs. Did they have to stop at *every* statue? And what was so interesting about that corner of the cemetery versus this corner? By the time they finished learning about WWII, WWIII would probably be done and over. Finally, when I thought I couldn't stand one more second of waiting, Howard led the group back to the visitors' parking lot and waited as they boarded the tour bus.

"You ready?" I whispered to myself.

Of course I wasn't.

Howard walked into the visitors' center, and then he and Sonia both came out and started walking toward the house.

Oh, no. I couldn't tell him with Sonia around. Was I going to have to sit on this all night? When they got to the driveway I took the stairs two at a time down to the living room and met them on the front porch.

"There you are," Howard said. "How's your day been?"

Horrifying. "It's been . . . okay."

He was wearing a light blue button-up with the sleeves rolled up and his nose was sunburned. Something I'd never experienced. You know, because I was *Italian.*

"I tried calling your phone earlier, but there was no answer. If we're going to make it to the movie, we'll have to go now."

"Right now?"

"Yes. Is Ren coming?"

"No. He . . . can't make it." How was I going to get out of this?

Sonia smiled. "They're playing a really old movie tonight, a classic with Audrey Hepburn. Have you heard of *Roman Holiday?*"

"No, I haven't." *And could everyone please just stop talking about Rome?*

Under normal circumstances I probably would have enjoyed *Roman Holiday*. It's a black-and-white movie about this European princess who is doing a world tour, but her schedule and handlers are superstrict, so one night when she's staying in Rome she sneaks out her bedroom window to go have some fun. The only problem is that she'd taken a sedative earlier in the night and so she passes out on a park bench and an American reporter rescues her. They end up exploring the city together and falling in love, except then they don't end up together, because she has too many other demands.

I know. Depressing.

I only half watched it because I couldn't stop looking at Howard. He had this big, booming laugh and he kept leaning over to tell me the names of places Audrey and her love interest were visiting. He even bought me a giant bag of candy, and even though I ate all of it I barely tasted it. It might have been the longest two hours of my life.

On the way back Sonia insisted I sit in the front. "So what did you think of the movie?"

"It was cute. Sad, though."

Howard glanced back at Sonia. "You still meeting up with Alberto tonight?"

"Argh. Yes."

"Why argh?"

"You know why. I swore off blind dates years ago."

"Don't think of it as a blind date. Think of it as going out for drinks with someone I really admire."

"Anyone but you and I'd say no." She sighed. "But then again, what's the worst that could happen? I've always said that a terrible date in Florence is better than a good date anywhere else."

Suddenly I realized I knew absolutely nothing about her. "Sonia, how did you end up in Florence?"

"Came here on vacation the summer after grad school and fell in love. It didn't last, but it got me to plant some roots here."

I groaned inwardly. Maybe that was just part of the Italian experience. Come to Italy. Fall in love. Watch everything blow up in your face. You could probably read about it on travel websites.

Sonia met my eyes in the mirror. "You know, people come to Italy for all sorts of reasons, but when they stay, it's for the same two things."

"What?"

"Love and gelato."

"Amen," Howard said.

I looked out my window and put all my attention on keeping the tears from seeping out from under my eyelids. Just gelato wasn't going to cut it. I wanted the love part too.

When we got back to the cemetery Howard dropped Sonia off at her house, then circled back to ours. The headlights swept eerily across the headstones, and the combination of candy and nerves was making me absolutely sick to my stomach.

We were finally alone. It was time to tell him. I took a deep breath. I'd start talking in three ... two ... two ... two ...

Howard broke the silence. "I wanted to tell you again how much it means to me to have you here. I know this hasn't been easy, but I really appreciate you giving it a try. Even if it's just for the summer. And I think you're great. I really do. I'm proud of you for jumping in and exploring Florence. You're an adventurer, just like your mom." Then he smiled at me, like I was the daughter he'd always hoped to have, and my remaining courage melted like an ice cube in the heat.

I couldn't tell him. Not tonight.

Maybe not ever.

When we got inside I made some lame excuse about another headache, then trudged up to my room and threw myself on my bed. I did a lot of throwing myself on the bed these days. But what was I going to do? I couldn't tell Howard, but I also couldn't *not* tell him.

Would it be so awful if I just stayed the rest of the summer and then went home without telling him? But then what about when Father's Day rolled around and he expected a card from me? Or what about when I got married and he thought he was the guy who was supposed to walk me down the aisle? What then?

My phone starting ringing and I jumped off my bed and crossed the room in two flying leaps. *Please be Ren. Please be Ren, please be—*

Thomas.

"Hello?"

"Hi, Lina. This is Thomas."

"Hey." I caught a glimpse of myself in the mirror. I looked like a puffer fish. Who'd suffered some kind of emotional breakdown.

"Did you get my text?"

"Yes. Sorry I didn't answer. Today's been kind of . . . crazy."

"No problem. What do you think about the party? Do you want to come with me?"

His voice was so uncomplicatedly British. And he was talking about a *party*. Like it mattered. I ran my hand through my hair. "What is it exactly?"

"Eighteenth birthday party for one of the girls who just graduated. She lives in the coolest place—almost as big as Elena's. Everyone will be there."

"Everyone" as in Ren and Mimi? I shut my eyes. "Thanks

for asking me, but I don't think I'll be able to make it."

"Oh, come on. You *have* to celebrate with me. I passed my driver's test yesterday, and my dad said I could pick you up in his BMW. And you really don't want to miss this party. Her parents hired an indie band I've been listening to for more than a year."

I tucked the phone between my ear and shoulder and rubbed my eyes. After everything that had happened today, a party seemed laughably normal. Also, it seemed weird to go out with someone when I'd clearly fallen for someone else. But what do you do when your "someone else" wants nothing to do with you? At least Thomas was still *talking* to me.

"Let me think about it."

Thomas exhaled. "All right. You think about it. I'd pick you up at nine. And it's formal, so you'd need to dress up. I promise you'll have a good time."

"Formal. Got it. I'll call you tomorrow."

We hung up and I tossed my phone on the bed, then walked over to the window and looked out. It was a clear night and the moon winked at me like a giant eye. Like it had been watching this whole complicated story play out, and now it was having the last laugh.

Stupid moon. I put both hands on the window sash and practically threw myself on top of it, but the window wouldn't budge.

Fine.

Chapter 24

THE NEXT MORNING I WOKE JUST BEFORE DAWN. I'D passed out on my bed fully dressed, and there was a dish of spaghetti perched on the edge of my dresser, the tomato sauce pooled in oily clumps. Guess Howard had tried to bring me dinner.

Gray hazy light was filtering through my window, and I got up and walked quietly over to my suitcase, rummaging around for some clean running clothes. Then I picked up the journal and crept silently through the house, leaving through the back door.

I made my way toward the back gate. Not even the birds were up yet and dew covered everything like a big, gauzy spiderweb. My mom was right. The cemetery looked completely different at different times of day. Predawn cemetery was sort of muted-looking, like gray had been swirled in with the rest of the colors.

I went through the back gate then broke into a run, pass-

ing where I'd met Ren for the first time. *Don't. Think. About.
Ren.* It was my new mantra. Maybe I'd have it printed on a
bumper sticker.

I shook the thought out of my head, then took in a deep
breath, settling on a medium pace. The air was crisp and
clean-smelling, like what laundry detergents are probably
going for with their "mountain air" scents, and I was crazy
relieved to be running. At least now it wasn't just my mind
that was in overdrive.

One mile. Then two. I was following a narrow little foot-
path worn into the grass by someone who had made this
route a habit, but I had no idea if their destination was the
same as mine. For all I knew, I was headed in the complete
wrong direction. Maybe it didn't even exist anymore, and
then—BAM. The tower. Jutting out of the hill like a wild
mushroom. I stopped running and stared at it for a minute.
It was like stumbling across something magical, like a pot of
gold, or a gingerbread house in the middle of Tuscany.

Don't think about gingerbread houses.

I started running again, feeling my heart quicken even
more as I neared the tower's dark silhouette. It was a perfect
cylinder, gray and ancient-looking and only about thirty feet
tall. It looked like the kind of place where people had been
falling in love for years.

I ran right up to the base, then put my hand on the wall,

trailing it behind me as I circled around to the opening. The wooden door Howard had moved for my mom was long gone, leaving a bare arched doorway that was so short I had to duck to walk under it. Inside it was empty except for a couple of shaggy spiderwebs and a pile of leaves that had probably outlasted the tree they'd come from. A crumbly spiral staircase rose through the tower's center, letting a pale circle of light into the room.

I took a deep breath, then headed for the staircase. Hopefully all my answers were at the top.

I had to walk carefully—half the steps looked like they were just waiting for an excuse to collapse—and I had to do this acrobatic hurtle over the space where the final step had once been, but finally I stepped outside. The top of the tower was basically an open platform, its circumference lined by a three-foot ledge, and I made my way over to the edge. It was still pretty dark and gray out, but the view was stunning. Like postcard stunning. To my left was a vineyard with rows of grapevines stretching out in thin silvery ropes, and everywhere else was rich Tuscan countryside, the occasional house marooned like a ship in the middle of an ocean of hills.

I sighed. No wonder this had been the place my mom had finally noticed Howard. Even if she hadn't already fallen for his sense of humor and awesome taste in gelato, she probably would have taken one look at the view and gone completely out of her mind with love. It was the sort of place that could make a stampede of buffalos seem romantic.

I set the journal down on the ground, then slowly made my way around the platform, scanning every inch of it. I *really* wanted to find some sign of my mom, a stone scratched with H+H or maybe some lost journal pages she'd tucked under a rock or something, but all I found were two spiders that looked at me with about as much interest as a pair of British Royal Guards.

I gave up on my little scavenger hunt and walked back to the center of the platform, wrapping my arms around myself. I needed a question answered, and I got the feeling this was the best place to ask.

"Mom, why did you send me to Italy?" My voice threw off the quiet peacefulness of everything around me, but I shut my eyes tight to listen.

Nothing.

I tried again. "Why did you send me to be with Howard?"

Still nothing. Then the wind picked up and made a whipping noise through the grass and trees, and suddenly all the loneliness and emptiness I carried around with me swelled up so big it swallowed me whole. I pressed my palms to my eyes, pain ricocheting through my body. What if my mom and my grandma and the counselor were wrong? What if I hurt this badly for the rest of my life? What if every second of every day would be less about what I had than what I'd lost?

I sank to the floor, pain washing over me in big, jagged waves. She'd told me over and over how wonderful my life was going to be. How proud she was of me. How much she wished she could be there, not just for the big moments, but for the little ones. And then she'd said she'd find a way to stay close to me. But so far, she'd just been gone. Then gone some more. And all that gone stretched out in front of me like a horizon, endless and daunting and empty. I'd been running around Italy trying to solve the mystery of the journal, trying to understand why she'd done what she'd done, but really I'd just been looking for her. And I wasn't going to find her. Ever.

"I can't do this," I said aloud, pressing my face into my hands. "I can't be here without you."

And that's when I got slapped. Well, maybe not slapped—it was more like a nudging—but suddenly I was getting to my feet because a word was pushing itself into my brain.

Look.

I shaded my eyes. The sun was rising over the hills, heating up the undersides of the clouds and setting them on fire in crazy shades of pink and gold. Everything around me was bright and beautiful and suddenly very clear.

I didn't get to stop missing her. Ever. It was the thing that my life had handed me, and no matter how heavy it was, I was never going to be able to set it down. But that didn't mean I wasn't going to be okay. Or even happy. I couldn't imagine it yet exactly, but maybe a day would come when the hole inside me wouldn't ache quite so badly and I could think about her, and remember, and it would be all right. That day felt light-years away, but right at this moment I was standing on a tower in the middle of Tuscany and the sunrise was so beautiful that it hurt.

And that was something.

I picked up the journal. It was time to finish.

———— ～ ————

JUNE 19

<u>Every new beginning comes from some other beginning's end.</u> I had that song lyric written on a piece of paper above my desk for almost a year, and only today does it actually mean anything to me. I've spent the entire afternoon wandering the streets and thinking, and a few things have become clear.

First, I have to leave Italy. Last September I met an American woman who's trapped in a terrible marriage because Italian law says that children stay with the father. I doubt Matteo will ever want anything to do with our baby, but I can't take that chance.

And second, I can't tell Howard how I feel about him. He thinks I've already chosen someone else, and he needs to keep thinking that. Otherwise he'll leave behind the life he's created for himself for a chance to start things with me. I want that so badly, but not enough to let him give up his dream of living and working in the middle of so much beauty. It's what he deserves.

So there it is. In loving Howard, I have to leave him. And to protect my child, I have to put as much distance between her and her father as possible. (Yes, I think it's a girl.)

If I could go back to one moment—just one—I would be back at the tower, a whole world of possibility ahead of me. And even though my heart hurts more than I ever thought it could, I wouldn't take back that sunrise or this baby for anything. This is a new chapter. My life. And I'm going to run at it with arms outstretched. Anything else would be a waste.

———

The End. The rest of the journal was blank. I slowly turned to the front cover and read that first sentence one more time.

I made the wrong choice.

Sonia had been wrong. My mom hadn't sent the journal to the cemetery for me—she'd sent it for Howard. She'd wanted him to know what had really happened and tell him that she'd loved him all along. And then, even though she couldn't go back and change their story, she'd done the next best thing.

She'd sent me.

Chapter 25

I PRACTICALLY FLEW BACK TO THE CEMETERY. I WAS INCRED-ibly nervous, but I felt light, too. No matter what Howard's reaction was, it was going to be okay. And he deserved to read her story. Right this second.

Daylight had totally transformed the cemetery, taking it from washed-out to vibrant, and I ran diagonally across the grounds, cutting through a batch of headstones and ignoring my blossoming side ache. I had to catch Howard before he started working.

He was sitting on the porch with a cup of coffee, and when he saw me he stood up in alarm. "You aren't being chased again, are you?"

I shook my head, then came to a stop, struggling to catch my breath.

"Oh, good." He sat back down. "Do you always sprint? I thought you were more into long-distance running."

I shook my head again, then took a deep breath. "Howard, I have to ask you something."

"What?"

"Do you know you're not my father?"

For a few long seconds my words hung in the space between us like a bunch of shimmering soap bubbles. Then he smiled.

"Define 'father.'"

My legs gave out and I stumbled toward the porch.

"Whoa, whoa. You okay?" He put his hand out to steady me.

"Just let me sit down." I fell to a seat on the porch step next to him. "And you know what I mean by 'father.' I mean the man who gave me half my DNA."

He stretched his legs out long in front of him. "Well, in that case, no. I'm not your father. But if you go with another definition, meaning 'a man who wants to be in your life and help raise you,' then yes. I am."

I groaned. "Howard, that's sweet and everything, but explain yourself. Because I have spent the last twenty-four hours completely confused and worried about hurting you, and you've known all along?"

"I'm sorry about that. I didn't know you had any idea." He looked at me for a moment, then sighed. "All right. You up for a story?"

"Yes."

He settled in, like he was about to tell a story he'd told a million times. "When I was twenty-five I met a woman who changed everything for me. She was bright and vibrant and whenever I was with her I felt like I could do anything."

"You mean my mom, right?"

"Let me finish. So I met this woman, and I fell completely head over heels in love with her. I'd never felt that way about anyone before—it was like I'd been looking for her all along and just hadn't realized it. I knew I had to do everything in my power to make her feel the same way, so I started by being her friend. I took an Italian class I didn't need just so I'd have some extra time with her—"

"The beginners' class?"

"Shh. Lina, listen. We took Italian together, I sat in on the rest of her classes, and I even worked my way into her circle of friends. But every time I tried to summon the courage to tell her how I felt, I turned into a blob of Jell-O."

"A blob of Jell-O?" I said incredulously.

"Yes. You know, the gelatin—"

"I know what Jell-O is!" Apparently "good guy" does not equal "good storyteller."

"What I mean by that is that I liked her so much it literally tongue-tied me. And then I found out I was too late. While I was bumbling around, carrying her books to class and pretending I liked to go out dancing, some other man had swooped in and carried her off."

"Matteo Rossi."

He flinched. "How do you know his name?"

"I'll tell you later."

He hesitated. "Anyway. I told myself that if this other guy was someone great, someone who really cared about her and made her happy, I would leave it alone. But I knew Matteo, and I knew what he was really like. Unfortunately, your mother was blinded by him for a long time, and even though we tried our hand at a relationship, she ended up choosing him. That's how you came to be—her relationship with Matteo. But when your mom got sick, I was the one she asked to step in. And so I did. Because I loved her." He nudged me. "And you're kind of growing on me too."

I groaned again. "Okay, nice story. But you got some of it wrong, and why did you and my grandma tell me you're my father if it isn't true?"

"I can see now that that was wrong, and I'm sorry. I wasn't planning to at first. Your grandmother and I started communicating after Hadley passed, and a few weeks in I realized that your grandmother assumed I was your father. I knew it wasn't true, but I worried that if I told her the truth, she'd change her mind about sending you, and your mother had made me promise to bring you here. I also thought it might be better for you.

I thought that if you believed I was your father it would make you more likely to come here and give me a chance."

"Except I was a total brat."

"No. Under the circumstances, you were actually pretty great."

"Liar."

He smiled. "I guess I just didn't know what else to do. Your grandfather was already struggling, and I didn't know what the situation was with Addie's family. I was worried you wouldn't have anywhere to go. So when your grandmother asked if she could tell you that I'm your father, I said yes." He shook his head. "I planned to tell you sooner rather than later, but after that night at the pizzeria, I thought I'd let you settle in first. But you don't seem to be much of the settling-in type. I should have known you'd see right through it."

"You're like twice as tall as me. And you have blond hair. We look nothing alike."

"True." He paused. "So now it's my turn. How long have you known?"

"About a day."

"How did you find out?"

I picked up the journal from the steps and handed it to him. "This."

"Your journal?"

"No, it's my mom's. It's the journal she kept when she was living here."

"This is *her* journal? I noticed it looked similar, but I thought it was just a coincidence." He turned it over in his hands.

"She wrote about everything that happened between her and Matteo. Only for most of it she just called him X, so at first I thought I was reading about you. But then you didn't know about the secret bakery."

"Wait a minute. The secret bakery? The place Ren asked me about?"

"Yeah. He was trying to surprise me by figuring out where it was."

"So Ren knows about all this too?"

"Yes. He actually helped me track down Matteo." I looked away. "We, ah, met him."

He levitated like half a foot. "You *met* him?"

I kept my gaze on the ground. "Uh-huh."

"Where?"

"Rome."

He was looking at me like I'd just told him I was actually half-ostrich. "When did you go to Rome?"

"Yesterday—"

"*Yesterday?*"

"Yeah, we took the express train. First Ren picked me up. Then we went to FAAF and I called Francesca—"

"Francesca Bernardi? How did you even know about her?"

"The journal. She told me what Matteo's last name was and we found him online and went to his art gallery and it was . . . well, a disaster."

His mouth was literally hanging open. "Please tell me you're joking."

I shook my head. "Sorry. I'm not."

He rubbed his hand across his chin. "Okay. So the two of you tracked down Matteo. Then what? Did he know who you were?"

"He made up this story about my mom being crazy and faking her journal. It was ridiculous. I mean, we look exactly alike and he just kept telling me that he'd never had a relationship with her. We ended up just booking it out of there."

Howard blew the air out of his mouth. "Your mother would kill me. Here I thought you and Ren were just out eating gelato and going dancing, but you were tracking down your father in another city?"

"Yes. But I won't do that again," I said hastily. "It was kind of a one-time deal. Unless you're hiding something else from me . . ."

"Nothing. All my cards are out."

"Okay, good."

"But where did you get the journal? Did you find it after your mom passed away?"

"No. Sonia gave it to me."

"*Sonia* Sonia? My Sonia?"

"Yeah. My mom sent it in the mail last September and when it got to the cemetery Sonia was worried it was going to upset you, so she held off for a couple of days. But then you told her about the plan for me to come stay here and she thought my mom had sent it for me. But it wasn't for me. It was for you."

Howard held the book up carefully, like it was a bird he didn't want to fly away.

"You should read it."

"Mind if I start right now?"

"Please do."

He slowly opened the cover, stopping at the sight of that first sentence. "Oh."

"Yeah. I'll leave you alone."

Chapter 26

TWO HOURS LATER HOWARD CAME TO MY BEDROOM DOOR, journal in hand. "I finished."

"That was quick."

"Want to go sit on the porch again?"

"Sure."

I followed him downstairs and we settled ourselves on the porch swing. His eyes were kind of red.

"It was hard for me, reading all of that. I mean, she told me bits of it, but I didn't know the whole story. There were so many misunderstandings. Missed connections." He looked out over the cemetery. "She didn't get everything right. For one thing, I never dated Adrienne."

"You didn't?"

"No. Matteo did."

I looked at him blankly.

"Your mother wasn't the only student Matteo was messing around with."

"Ohhhh." Another puzzle piece fell into place. "So is that why you told her the story of the bull and the baker? You were trying to tell her to look closer, because Matteo was two-timing her?"

He grimaced. "Yes, but I obviously wasn't very successful. She had no idea what I meant by that story."

"Yeah, that was pretty cryptic. Did you just make that story up?"

"No, it's real. I think it's pretty unlikely that it's true, but it's one of the legends that has been hanging around the city for centuries. I love stuff like that." He shook his head. "Anyway, I knew that your mom was involved with Matteo. She kept it a secret because she was worried he'd get in trouble with the school, but *he* kept it a secret because he was a dirtbag. I knew he'd had at least a few affairs with students, and from what I'd seen of him, I knew he was bad news. I had my suspicions, and then one day I walked in on Adrienne and Matteo in the darkroom. That night when your mom saw us outside the club, I had been confronting her about it. I wanted her to tell your mother."

"Why didn't you just tell her?"

He shook his head. "Everyone but Hadley knew that I was in love with her, and I knew it would just look like I was stirring things up. I was also pretty sure that Matteo would just deny it and then I would lose your mother's trust. Then once they broke up I couldn't see any reason to tell her. Also, I was kind of a coward. The breakup was my fault."

"Why?"

"Your mom was becoming withdrawn and started saying pretty critical things about herself and her work. So one week when Matteo went out of town for a conference, I called him up and told him that if he didn't stay away from her I'd tell the school."

"And that's when he broke up with her?"

"Yes. And then I went ahead and told the school anyway, and they ended up firing him. Hadley was so heartbroken it was like the color had been sucked out of her. I spent weeks wondering if I'd done the right thing." He pushed off, sending the swing gliding. "But then she seemed to get better. I convinced her to spend a summer here with me, and we were together for a while. But then I lost her again."

"Because of me."

He shook his head, gesturing to the cemetery. "She should have told me. I would have walked out on this in a heartbeat."

"That's exactly why she didn't tell you."

"I know." He sighed. "I just wish she'd let me make that decision. One day with Hadley was easily worth a lifetime in Italy."

"Tell me about it." I studied him for a moment. He loved her. Like *really* loved her. And he'd been missing her for even longer than I had. It made me want to throw my arms around him.

I looked away, blinking back tears. Hopefully my eyeballs would dry out one of these days. Otherwise I was going to be offered a job as spokesperson for Kleenex or something.

"Did you ever try to get her back?"

"No. In my mind she'd chosen Matteo. If I'd known the reason why, it would have been a different story. It wasn't until years later that I found out they weren't together and then only recently that I found out about you. I worried a lot about her, but every time I thought about reaching out, it was like something stopped me. Maybe my pride."

"Or just not wanting to get hurt again. She basically smashed your heart to bits."

He chuckled. "Smashed indeed. And of course, I was eventually able to move on. But having you here . . . well, I've kind of been reliving it."

We were quiet for a minute. The sun had risen full and hot, and my hair was practically sizzling.

He shook his head. "This isn't at all how I'd imagined we'd have this conversation, but I'm glad that things happened the way they did. And now we don't have to worry about Matteo. Your mom was really careful about keeping you away from him, especially once she was successful. She had always wanted to bring you to Italy but was too afraid to until now.

I guess you being close to eighteen made her less afraid of Matteo."

"She probably never thought I'd be the one to go looking for him."

"Never. I think she underestimated you." He chuckled. "I think I did too. I can't believe you went to Rome."

"It was stupid."

"Well, that goes without saying. But it was also pretty brave."

"Ren came with me. He helped a lot." My expression fell. *Ren.*

"What?"

"Ren's not . . . talking to me anymore. I upset him."

Howard's forehead creased. "Did you get in an argument?"

"Something like that."

"I'm sure whatever happened, you two can work it out. He really cares about you. I can tell."

"Maybe." We sat there for a moment, swinging back and forth, when suddenly a thought occurred to me. "Howard, were you trying to tell me something when you told me that weird story about the woman who gave birth to the boar?"

He laughed. "The *porcellino*. I'd better stop doing that. It really doesn't seem to work."

"No."

"All right, yes. I was trying to tell you something. When we went to see the statue I realized it was the perfect symbol.

Even though our circumstances are strange, and we're a bit of a mismatch, I really do want to be a part of your life. We may not be a regular kind of family, but if you'll have me, I'll be your family just the same."

I looked up at him and a thousand feelings swelled up inside me until I was as taut and full as a balloon. My mom had been totally right. No one would ever come close to replacing her, but if I had to choose someone, it would be Howard. She'd just been a few steps ahead of me.

"So what do you say, Carolina?"

I hesitated. I didn't want to rush into anything, but I did know that today it felt right. And that was going to have to be enough.

"Okay." I nodded. "I'm in if you're in."

He gave me one of his lopsided smiles, then leaned back in the swing. "Good. Well, now that we have all that cleared up, what about this Ren business?"

Chapter 27

HOWARD INSISTED I COULDN'T GIVE UP. IF I WANTED TO
see things through, I needed to be good and sure that there
hadn't been some kind of gross miscommunication between
Ren and me.

That's really how he said it. Gross miscommunication.

I shoved my remaining shreds of dignity into the back of
my closet, then called Ren's cell phone. Twice. Both my calls
went straight to voice mail and I did my best to block out the
image of him hitting REJECT.

Finally Howard helped me track down the Ferraras' number, and I called their house.

"*Ciao*, Lina!" Odette trilled. She obviously hadn't been
filled in on the state of affairs.

"Hi, Odette. Is Ren home?"

"Yes, just a moment." She set the phone down. Then there
were some muffled noises. Finally she picked it up again.

"Lina?"

"Yeah?"

"Ren can't talk right now."

I grimaced. "Could you ask him a question for me?"

"What's that?"

"Is it okay if I come over? I need to talk to him."

There was a pause. "Ren? Why are you shakin—" Then she must have put her hand over the mouthpiece, because I couldn't understand anything else.

It was so unbelievably humiliating. My remaining shreds of dignity caught on fire.

When she came back on the line she sounded confused. "Sorry, Lina. He said he's too busy. He's getting ready to go to Valentina's party."

I perked up. "He's going for sure? It's for the girl who graduated last year, right?"

"Yes. I think it's to celebrate her eighteenth birthday."

At least I'd see him face-to-face. I took a deep breath. It was better than nothing. "Thanks, Odette."

"No problem."

I hung up the phone and sent a quick text to Thomas. Then I booked it all the way to the visitors' center. I needed a favor.

When I came bursting into the visitors' center, Howard and Sonia looked up in alarm. They were both going through a stack of papers and Howard was wearing these tiny old-man reading glasses that made him look like a nearsighted lumberjack. I giggled.

He put his hand on his chest. "Lina! One of these days you're going to give me a heart attack."

"Your glasses are so . . ."

"So what?" He drew himself up to his full height and I busted out laughing again.

"Just . . . ignore me. Listen, I really need some help. I'm going to a party tonight and I really need to look amazing. I think it's my best shot at winning Ren back. I need to find The Dress."

He took his glasses off. "The one guaranteed to make anyone fall in love with you?"

"Yes! Exactly. Just like my mom had. Only hopefully I'll actually get to wear it and it will do its job."

"The Dress?" Sonia asked, looking back and forth between us. "I'm sorry, but I'm not following."

Howard turned to her. "Sonia, we'll have to close the cemetery early. Finding a new dress is probably pretty easy, but *The* Dress? It's going to take some time." He winked at me. "And by the way, I remember catching a glimpse of your mother in her version of The Dress. I think I walked into a wall."

Sonia shook her head. "I'm still a little unclear about what we're talking about here, but you know we can't close the cemetery. It's completely against regulations."

"Fine, we won't close it. We'll abandon it for a few hours while the three of us take an emergency shopping trip into Florence."

I bounced up and down. "Thank you! That would be really awesome!"

Sonia still didn't look convinced. "Howard, I'll just stay behind in case any visitors show up."

He shook his head. "No, we're going to need you. You know I'll be completely useless when it comes to shopping. My closet is where things go to die. We need a woman's opinion."

She shuddered. "Your taste is pretty bad. Remember when I made you get rid of that horrible pair of corduroys? They were sprouting *hairs*."

I clasped my hands in front of my chest. "Please, Sonia. I don't even know where dress stores are, and I'm going to need all the help I can get. I have to look incredible tonight. Will you help me?"

She looked back and forth between Howard and me, then shook her head. "I think you've lost your minds. But all right. Pick me up at my house."

"Yes!" Howard and I high-fived. Then I waited outside while he closed up the visitors' center and we both jogged up the path to the house.

On the way into Florence, Howard and I filled Sonia in on our status as not related-sort of related.

She looked shocked. "You're telling me you're not actually father and daughter?"

"Not technically," I said.

"And, Howard, you've known all along?"

"Yes."

She shook her head, then started fanning herself with her wallet. "Only in Italy."

Howard looked at her. "And, Sonia, in the future please don't redirect any of my deliveries. Although in this case I think it worked out okay."

"Cross my heart. I'll never do anything like that again." She turned around so she was facing me. "What time does Ren pick you up?"

"At nine. But I'm not going with Ren. I'm going with Thomas."

"Oh. But I thought that you and Ren . . ." She trailed off.

"You thought me and Ren what?"

Howard glanced at Sonia, then met my eyes in the rearview mirror. "You know how in English we say that people wear their hearts on their sleeves? Well, in Italian, you say *avere il cuore in mano.'* You hold your heart in your hand. Every time Ren looks at you I think of that saying. He's crazy about you."

"No, he isn't."

Sonia chimed in. "Of course he is. And you can't blame him. Look at you. The poor thing can't help himself."

"He has a girlfriend."

"He does?" Howard asked.

I nodded.

"Well, how do you feel about him?"

They both looked at me and I managed to stay quiet for about three seconds before blowing like a volcano.

"Fine. I'm in love with him. I'm completely in love with Ren. Besides Addie, he's the only person I've ever been around who makes me feel normal, and he's hilarious and weird and he has a gap between his front teeth that I love. But none of that matters because he has a girlfriend, and yesterday I must have had a momentary lapse in sanity, because I kissed him and it totally freaked him out. Also, his girlfriend looks straight out of a fashion magazine and whenever Ren sees *me* I'm either sweaty or crying. So now I'm dressing up and going to a party in hopes that I'll get his attention long enough for him to at least talk to me, so I can tell him how I really feel and try to at least salvage our friendship. So there. *That's* how I feel about Ren."

Howard and Sonia both looked stunned.

I slumped back in my seat. "That's why I need the perfect dress."

It was quiet for a moment, and then Sonia turned to Howard. "Is money an object?"

"No."

"Then turn left. I know where we need to go."

Howard drove us straight to a dress shop near the center of the city, and after we'd parked, all three of us got out and ran the three blocks from the parking center. When we burst into the shop, the woman behind the counter looked up in alarm.

"*Cos'è successo?*"

"*Stiamo cercando il vestito più bello nel mondo.*" He turned to me. "She needs *The* Dress."

The woman studied us for a moment, then clapped her hands. "Adalina! Sara! *Venite qui.*"

Two women emerged from the back room, and after going through the same exchange with Howard, they pulled out their tape measures and started measuring my waist and butt and bust and . . . yeah. It was pretty embarrassing.

Finally they started grabbing dresses from all over the store, then hustled me over to a dressing room and stuffed me and the dresses inside. I wriggled out of my running clothes and pulled the first one over my head. It was cotton-candy pink and reminded me of the time I'd thrown up on a Ferris wheel. The second one was yellow and feathery and looked suspiciously like Big Bird's carcass. The third wasn't terrible, but the straps were so big they hovered a full inch above my shoulders, and the party was tonight—I couldn't just take it to a tailor for alterations. I looked at myself sternly in the mirror. *Don't panic.* But my hair panicked anyway. Or maybe that was just how it always looked.

"How's it going?" Sonia called from outside.

"Nothing yet."

"Try this one." She tossed another one over the door and I quickly changed into it. White and poofy. I looked exactly like a marshmallow. On her wedding day.

"Oh, no," I wailed. "None of these are right. What if I can't find it?"

"I brought you to this place for a reason. Let me see if the shopkeeper's oldest daughter is around. She's a dress genie. Be right back."

I stepped up to the mirror and looked at myself again. Not only did I not look forgivable, but I looked ridiculous. There was no way I was going to win Ren back looking like something I roasted at Girl Scout camp.

"Lina?" Sonia knocked on the door. Then the door opened and she and another woman stepped in.

The woman was in her late thirties and had her hair pulled up in a bun with a pencil stuck through it. She looked like she meant business. She gestured for me to spin around.

"No. *Tutto sbagliato*."

"*D'accordo*," Sonia said. "She says this one is all wrong."

"Will you ask her to find me one that's all right?"

"Don't worry. It's what she's good at. Let her work."

The woman stepped forward, cupping my chin in her hands. She turned my face back and forth, studying my features, then stepped back and motioned for me to do another spin. Finally she nodded and held up her hand. "*Ho il vestito perfetto*. Wait."

When she came back she was holding a pinkish-nude-colored dress with embellished lace all over the top and a short flowy skirt. I took it from her, holding it up in front of me.

"This one?" I asked.

"Yes. Thees one," she said firmly. She stepped out of the room, pulling the door shut behind her.

I took off the marshmallow dress and eased the new one over my head. The fabric was smooth and silky-feeling, and it slipped easily over my chest and hips, landing in the exact right spot.

I didn't even have to look in the mirror to know that it was the one.

By the time Thomas pulled up in his dad's car—a silver BMW convertible—I had managed to completely transform myself. Sonia had helped me style my hair so it fell in soft un-Medusa-ish curls, and had loaned me a pair of heels and diamond stud earrings. I'd put on makeup and perfume and had practiced my speech to Ren over and over. *Ren, I have something to tell you.* When I looked in the mirror I almost did a double take. I couldn't believe how Italian I looked.

"He's here," Howard yelled from downstairs.

"Coming!" I took a deep breath to steady my nerves, then teetered down the stairs. Sonia's high heels were really gorgeous but *crazy* high. I miraculously made it to the bottom of the stairs without performing any sort of involuntary gymnastics, and when I looked up, Howard was giving me this misty look.

"You look beautiful. I don't care what Ren's girlfriend looks like. She doesn't stand a chance."

"That would be nice. But I'll be happy if he just talks to me again."

"I'm betting on the former."

There was a knock on the door and Howard crossed the room to open it. "Hello. Are you Thomas?"

"Yes. Nice to meet you."

I clattered over to the doorway.

"Woah! Lina, you look . . ." Thomas's jaw literally dropped. But then he noticed Howard looking at him like he was a deer during hunting season and he quickly cleared his throat. "Sorry. Nice dress. You look really pretty."

"You look nice too." Gray fitted suit. Hair styled messily. I could practically hear Addie spontaneously combusting from here.

"You ready to go?" he asked.

"Ready." I walked over and gave Howard a hug. "How long can I stay out?"

"As long as you want. Well, within reason." He winked at me. "It's going to work out."

"Thanks."

I followed Thomas out to his car and he opened the door for me. "You really do look gorgeous."

"Thanks."

"What did your dad mean by 'it's going to work out'?"

"Uh, I'm not sure." I glanced at my phone for about the millionth time. All afternoon I'd been hoping Ren would call. And all afternoon he'd kept *not calling*.

Thomas got in the front seat and put the keys in the ignition. "Nice car, right?"

"Really nice."

"My dad has a Lamborghini, too. He told me if I have a clean driving record for a year I can take it out sometime."

"Too bad it's not tonight."

"I know, right?" He backed carefully out of the driveway, then took off down the road. "Did you know you have to be eighteen to drive a car in Italy? I think I'm the only one at our school who even has a license."

"Ren will get one next year."

"But he's only a junior."

"He'll be eighteen in March."

"Oh." He pulled out onto the road and accelerated, turning up the music too loud to talk.

I'm sure riding through the Italian countryside in a luxury convertible with a young 007 should have been a magical experience, but it was lost on me. I was too busy mentally rehearsing what I was going to say to Ren. And trying to keep young 007's hands off me.

"Valentina's dad works with my dad, only he's even higher up. I've been to lots of parties at their house and they're always crazy. One year they did this big Japanese dinner and there were women lying on the serving tables. You had to eat your sushi off of them."

"Ew. Really?"

"Yeah, it was awesome." He slid his hand onto my bare knee—again—and I made a big show of rearranging my legs so he'd move his hand. Again. I looked at him and sighed. Any other girl would trade all the gelato in Florence for a chancing to be sitting in my spot. But they weren't me. And they didn't know Ren.

When we finally pulled up to the party, I was shocked. Not because the house looked like Dracula's castle—of course it did—but because of how many people were there. Cars and cabs were all funneling into the driveway while throngs of ecstatic partygoers weaved their way toward the front door. It took us ten full minutes and three leg rearrangings just to wind our way up to the valet station.

When we got to the top Thomas threw his keys to the valet, then made a big show of helping me out of the car. A red carpet was draped on the big stone steps leading up to the entryway and tons of people were making their way inside. I'd been a little worried I'd be overdressed, but everyone looked like they were on their way to some kind of red-carpet premiere. This was definitely a The Dress occasion.

"This is way bigger than I thought it would be," I said, grabbing Thomas's arm before I could lose my balance on the stairs.

"Told you. It's going to be awesome."

"Do all of your friends live in houses like this?"

"Just the ones who throw parties."

The entryway had a long, curving staircase and an extravagant chandelier made of colored glass. A man holding a big stack of papers stopped us.

"Name, please." His accent was as thick as his biceps.

"Thomas Heath." Thomas turned and grinned at me. "And my date."

The man shuffled through his papers, marking Thomas's name. "*Benvenuti.*"

"Do you mind if I check your list really quick?" I asked. "I'm wondering if my friend is here."

"No." He scowled at me, covering the list with his hand. "It is *privato*."

It wasn't like we were attending a party at the Pentagon or something. "I just need to look for one sec—"

"Come on." Thomas grabbed my hand and yanked me away from the list and farther into the house. Everyone was sardine-ing themselves into this big, overly frilly room with high ceilings and like five more chandeliers, and we had to push our way in, tripping over all the fancy dresses and guys sweating into their jackets. All the furniture was moved to the outer edges of the room, and a makeshift stage had been set up in one corner. So far there was just a bunch of instruments up there, but music was playing from speakers around the room at a level that could kill small birds. It was *so* crowded. How was I going to find Ren?

"Lina! Thomas!" Elena emerged from the crowd, grabbing my arm. She was wearing a short gray dress and her hair was pulled up in a high ponytail. "Wow. Lina, you look *bella*. This is the color for you."

"Thanks, Elena. Have you seen Ren?"

"Ren? No. I don't know if he's even coming. Mimi would probably kill him."

"Why?"

Thomas cracked up. "Guys, look. There's Selma." He pointed to a tall middle-aged woman who had climbed onto the stage and was fumbling around with cords. She was wearing a tiara and a hot-pink minidress that was about ten seconds from giving up on keeping her boobs covered.

"Ugh," Elena said, shaking her head. "That is Valentina's mom. She was a supermodel in the nineties, and she displays sexy pictures of herself around the house. I think I would rather die than see my mom's cleavage on a daily basis."

"Your mom's *bionic* cleavage," Thomas said. "We should try to get a good spot by the band. Valentina said they start playing at ten."

Elena shook her head. "I'm waiting for Marco."

"Marco, huh?"

Elena scowled at him. "*Dai.* I just told him I would. It doesn't mean anything."

"Uh-huh."

"Elena, if you see Ren, will you tell him I really need to talk to him?" I asked.

"Sure, no problem." She glanced at Thomas, then leaned in. "Wow. Thomas looks *incredibile*." She pronounced it the Italian way. "Good choice. He is *troppo sexy*. I'm pretty sure every girl who's met him has tried for him. I guess you are the lucky one. It sucks that Ren broke up with Mimi for you, but I totally understand why you are here with Thomas."

Eight hundred exclamation marks went off in my head. "Ren broke up with Mimi? When? Today?"

She frowned. "I don't know. Maybe yesterday? Mimi said she was glad, though. No offense, but Ren can be very strange. He always says whatever pops into his head."

"Yeah, but that's what's so great about him."

She slid her eyes at Thomas. "Yeah, I guess so. See you later. I'm going out front."

"Bye. Just tell Ren where I am if you see him, okay?"

"You okay?" Thomas asked when Elena had left.

"Yeah, sure." Maybe better than okay. Ren had broken up with Mimi for *me*? Then what was all that in Rome? The urgency of my Find Ren mission had pretty much hit the roof.

"Let's get a drink and go over by the stage," Thomas said.

"Sure."

The next couple of hours were incredibly slow. The band was Spanish, and after every couple of sets the drummer got carried away and threw his drumsticks into the crowd, where they had to be fished out again before they could start playing the next song.

Thomas kept disappearing for more and more drinks and Ren kept *not showing up*. Where was he? What if he *didn't* show up? Was this whole The Dress thing actually a curse? If so, I would have come in running clothes.

Finally I excused myself. "Thomas, I'm going to the bathroom. I'll be back in a while."

He gave me an unfocused thumbs-up and I pushed myself through the crowd, doing a quick scan of the party. As far as I could tell, Ren wasn't in the main room. And he wasn't on the front steps or in the entryway, either. Where was he? Finally I decided to actually use the bathroom, but there was a long line, and I kept my neck craned to watch for Ren.

When it was my turn I locked the door behind me, then looked in the mirror and sighed. My dress still looked great, but I was sweaty and I could tell my hair was plotting a mutiny. I pulled it back into a ponytail, then checked my phone again. Nothing. Where was he?

Thomas was waiting for me outside the door. "There you are. We have to hurry. Everyone's supposed to go outside. There's a big surprise."

I gave up on my shoes, taking them off and carrying them as we moved with the crowds toward the back doors. When we finally stepped outside I sucked in my breath. The yard was the size of a football field, and dozens of large white blankets checkered the ground, their edges lit with tea lights. It was nauseatingly romantic. Half the people out there were going to get carried away and start professing their undying love to each other.

"Thomas, you didn't see Ren while I was in the bathroom, did you?"

"No, no, no." He stopped at the bottom of the stairs, putting both hands on my shoulders. "Let's make a pact. No more talking about Ren. I just want to talk about you." He grinned. "And me. Now come on."

He pulled me forward, and I stumbled a little as we made our way across the grass.

"Where are we going?"

"I told you, it's a surprise."

We walked all the way to an empty blanket on the outskirts of the yard and Thomas sat down, loosening his tie and taking off his jacket. His shirt and hair were rumpled and I wished for about the thousandth time that Addie were here to enjoy all this hotness. It was totally wasted on me.

"Now lie down," he said.

"What?"

"Lie down." He patted the blanket.

"Thomas . . ."

"Relax. I'm not going to do anything. Just lie down for a second. I promise I'll stay right here."

I looked at him for a moment, then lay down on the blanket, smoothing my dress around me. "Now what?"

"Close your eyes. I'll tell you when to open them."

I looked at him, then exhaled, half closing my eyes. Did he have to be this gorgeous? It was really complicating my life.

He started counting down slowly. "Twenty ... nineteen ... eighteen ..." By the time he got to "one" I'd been lying there for half a century, and I opened my eyes to the sound of a collective cheer going up from the lawn.

All around us, white paper lanterns lit by candles were rising into the air. There were *hundreds* of them.

Thomas grinned at my stunned expression. "Valentina told me they were doing this. Cool, right?"

"So cool."

We watched quietly for a moment, the lanterns twirling up to the stars like graceful jellyfish. The night was beautiful and magical and *ugh*—I was so miserable I could cry. Here I was in *Italy* witnessing a scene out of a fairy tale, and all I could think about was Ren. Was I going to be like Howard? Heartbroken for life? Was I going to have to buy my own long board and start baking blueberry muffins in the dead of night?

"Told you you'd like it. They're doing fireworks later too." Thomas reclined on one elbow, lowering his face close to mine. A bunch of lanterns were reflected in his eyes and for a second I lost track of why I wasn't into him. And then I remembered.

"Thomas, I have to tell you something."

"Shh. You can tell me later." Before I could react, he rolled on top of me, pressing his lips against mine and my whole body into the ground. For a second it was like Christmas and my birthday and summer vacation all rolled into one, but then it was all so *wrong*. I wriggled out from under him and sat up.

"Thomas, I can't do this."

"Why?" He sat up too, a confused look on his face. This was probably his very first experience with rejection. Poor devil.

I shook my head. "You're great. And so good-looking. But I just can't."

"Because of Ren?"

"Yeah."

"Why'd you even come here with me if you're into Ren?"

"I'm sorry. It was really lame of me. And I should have told you earlier."

He stood up and grabbed his jacket, brushing grass off his pants. "Lucky for you, lover boy's right over there."

"What?" I whipped around. Ren was standing a few yards away, his back to me. I scrambled to my feet.

"See you around," Thomas said.

"Thomas, I really am sorry," I called after him, but he was already on his way back to the house.

I took a deep breath, then scooped up my shoes and half ran over to Ren. He was wearing a navy blue suit and it looked like someone had held him down and given him a haircut.

I touched his back. "Ren?"

He turned around and I felt the shards of my broken heart crumble to dust. He looked so good. Like *so* good.

"Hey." Not even a hint of surprise.

"I was really hoping you'd be here. Could we talk?"

Suddenly Mimi materialized from a nearby group of girls. She was wearing a fitted black dress with cutout panels along the rib cage, and her eyes were outlined in dark liner. She looked like a tiger. I'd never seen anything more terrifying.

She linked her arm with Ren's. "Hello, Lina. How's Thomas?"

"He's okay," I said quietly.

"Ren, let's go back inside. I think the band's going to start again."

"Ren, can I talk to you for a minute?" I asked.

He was looking just past my right ear. "I'm kind of busy."

"Please? It will only be a minute. I just have to tell you something."

"He's busy," Mimi said, tightening her grip on his arm.

He looked down at her hand, then back up at me. "Okay. One minute."

"Seriously, Ren?" Mimi growled.

"It will just be a second. I'll be right back."

She turned and flounced away. That girl knew how to flounce.

"What's up?" Ren asked quietly.

"Will you go for a walk with me?"

By the time we made it to the edge of the yard the lanterns were just tiny little specks in the sky, and I was a hundred percent sure that Ren hadn't gotten over what happened in Rome. He just kept trudging after me like a well-dressed robot, and I felt myself sinking lower and lower. Was this even going to work?

The yard was terraced and we walked down some steps, passing a couple making out against a tree and a group of guys riding around on croquet mallets like they were jockeys. Totally something we'd laugh about. That is, if we were talking.

Finally we came to a white stone bench and Ren sat down. I sat down next to him.

"Amazing party," I said.

He just shrugged.

Okay. He wasn't going to make this easy on me.

"I guess I'll just get right into it." My voice was wobbly. "I've never met anyone like you. You're smart and funny, and really easy to be around, and you're basically the one person I've met since my mom died who I don't feel like I have to act fake around. And I'm really, *really* sorry about what happened in Rome. Kissing you wasn't fair because you have a girlfriend . . . or *had* a girlfriend . . ." I looked at him, hoping he'd clarify, but he didn't say anything.

"Anyway. I didn't know right until that moment how I felt about you, but I should have just told you instead of basically jumping on you. Anyway, what I'm trying to say is, I really like you. A lot. But if you don't feel the same way about me, it's okay. Because you're really important to me, and I hope we can still be friends."

Suddenly a second round of cheering started up on the lawns and there was a hissing noise followed by the *pop* of a red firework exploding across the sky.

It would have been the perfect moment for Ren to gather me in his arms and profess his undying love.

Only he didn't.

I shifted uncomfortably. A few more fireworks went off, but Ren didn't even look up.

"It would be really awesome if you'd say something."

He shook his head. "I don't know what you want me to say. Why didn't you tell me sooner? And back in Rome, why'd you say that you'd never thought of me as more than a friend?"

Crap. I shouldn't have said that.

"I guess I was trying to save face. You obviously didn't want to kiss me, and I was so embarrassed. I was just trying to fix the situation."

He looked up. "Well, you're wrong. I really did want to

kiss you, but I stopped because I was worried you didn't mean it. Meeting Matteo was pretty crazy, and I didn't want things to happen just because you were in the middle of some kind of emotional roller coaster. And then afterward, you told me you *didn't* mean it."

"But I did. That's what I'm—"

He cut me off. "I liked Mimi for a long time. Like two years. I thought about her all the time and then when things finally started happening between us I thought I was the luckiest guy ever. But then I met you and suddenly I was avoiding her calls and trying to think of ways to get you to hang out with me. So the night we went to Space I called her and broke up with her. I didn't know if things were going to work out between you and me, but I really wanted the chance."

He shook his head. "Then we went to Rome. And then all that stuff happened. And now tonight . . ." He stood up. "Why do you think you can be all over Thomas and then come tell me you like me?"

A whole different kind of fireworks exploded behind my eyes. "Why do you think *you* can be all over Mimi and then tell me you liked me all along? You're the one who's had a girlfriend all this time."

"You're right. *Had* a girlfriend. Who I broke up with. And I'm not the one who was just rolling around on the ground with someone else. What am I? Your backup plan?"

I jumped to my feet. "If you'd actually been watching, you would have noticed that I pushed Thomas off me and told him I like you, but forget it. I don't even care anymore."

"Me neither. I'm going back to the party. And you'd better get back to your date." He turned and walked away.

"*Stronzo!*" I yelled.

A heart-shaped firework exploded over his head.

Chapter 28

IT TOOK HOWARD ALMOST AN HOUR TO FIND VALENTINA'S house. For one thing, I didn't know who Valentina was, and for another, I couldn't find anyone who knew the address. Selma and her bionic cleavage were nowhere to be found, and I couldn't find Elena or Marco or anyone else I recognized. Finally I got the bouncer to tell me where I was, but he didn't speak much English and kept guarding his clipboard from me like he thought I was trying to trick him into giving me access. Finally I just forced my phone on him and he gave directions to Howard.

By the time Howard's car pulled up to the driveway all the anger had drained out of me and I was about as perky as a wet noodle. I felt crumpled. No, *bedraggled*, and when I got in the car Howard didn't even ask how it had gone. He could tell by my face.

When we got to the house I threw my dress on the floor, then put on a T-shirt and a pair of pajamas pants and went downstairs. I was on the verge of tears, but I couldn't handle the thought of crying alone in my room. Again. I'd reached my threshold of pathetic.

"We have gelato and we have tea," Howard said when I walked into the kitchen. "Which sounds best?"

"Gelato."

"Excellent choice. Why don't you go sit in the living room? I'll bring you a bowl."

"Thanks." I went and sat cross-legged on the couch, resting my head back against the wall. I'd spent all night looking for Ren and then he'd seen me in the exact moment that Thomas had made his move. What were the chances? Was fate just against us? And had I really called him a *stronzo*? I didn't even know what that meant.

Howard walked in with two bowls. "I got you two kinds, *fragola e coco*. Strawberry and coconut. I'm sorry we don't have *stracciatella*. I can tell it's a *stracciatella* night."

"It's okay." I took the bowl from him, balancing it on my knee.

"Rough night?"

"I don't think things are going to work out with Ren." My eyes teared up. "Not even friend-wise."

"Your talk didn't go well?"

"No. We actually got into this awesome screaming match

and I called him a bad word in Italian. Or at least I think it was a bad word."

"What was it?"

"*Stronzo.*"

He sat down on the chair across from me, nodding gravely. "We can recover from *stronzo*. And remember, it isn't over until it's over. For years I thought things were completely finished with your mother, but we actually started talking again before her diagnosis."

"You did?"

"Yes. She sent me an e-mail and we corresponded for almost a year. It was like we picked up right where we left off. We didn't talk about any of the heavy stuff, just kind of fun banter back and forth."

"Did you ever see each other?"

"No. She probably knew that if I ever saw her again I'd carry her off. No questions asked."

"Like the Sabines." I tried to take a bite of gelato, but it just sort of slid off my tongue, and I let my spoon clatter back into the bowl. "You two basically have the saddest story I've ever heard."

"I wouldn't say that. There was a lot of good."

I sighed. "So how do I get over Ren?"

"I'm the worst person to ask. I fell in love and stayed that way. But if you ask me, it's worth it. 'A life without love is like a year without summer.'"

"Deep. But I'm about ready for summer to be over."

He smiled. "Give it some time. It will be all right."

Howard and I stayed up really late. When I checked my phone I had a three-word text from Addie (THEY SAID YES!!) and Howard and I spent more than an hour discussing the pros and cons of staying or leaving Florence. He even pulled out a lined notebook and made two columns with REASONS TO STAY and REASONS TO GO at the top. I didn't add Ren to the list because I couldn't decide which side he belonged on. Brokenhearted and see him every day? Or brokenhearted and never see him again? Either one sounded incredibly miserable.

Finally, I went up to bed where I spent the night tossing and turning. Turns out there's a reason they call it *falling* in love, because when it happens—really happens—that's exactly how it feels. There's no doing or trying, you just let go and hope that someone's going to be there to catch you. Otherwise, you're going to end up with some pretty hefty bruises. Trust me, I would know.

I must have dozed off eventually, because around four a.m. I woke in a five-alarm panic. Had something just *hit* me? I scrambled to my feet, my heart racing. My window was as wide-open as ever, and a dusting of stars glittered at me from the cemetery's treetops. Everything was as calm and still as a lake. Not a single ripple.

"Just dreaming," I said, my voice sounding supercalm and in charge. It was literally the only part of me not freaking out over the fact that I may or may not have just been woken up by something cold and hard hitting me in the leg.

Not that that made any sense.

I shook my head, pulling back the covers to get back in bed like a rational person, and then I yelped and jumped like half a foot, because there were coins everywhere. Like, *every-where*.

They were scattered across my bed and rug and a few of them had even made it onto The Dress, which was still lying in the world's saddest heap on the floor. I fumbled for my lamp, then bent down to take a look, being careful not to touch any of them. They were mostly copper-colored one- or two-cent coins, but some of them were twenty or fifty cents. There was even a two-euro coin.

My bedroom was raining money.

"What is going on?" I said aloud.

Just then another coin arced through my open window, hitting me square in the face and causing me to do this dramatic tuck-and-cover move that I'd learned in elementary school earthquake drills. But by the time I hit the floor I wasn't freaked out anymore. I knew what was going on.

Someone was throwing money at me through my window. Which meant that either a government official was here to let me know that I'd won the Italian Powerball or Ren was trying to wake me up. Either way, my night had just gotten a whole lot better.

I jumped up and ran over to the window.

Ren was standing about six feet from the house, his arm cocked back to hurl another coin.

"Look out!" I dropped to the floor again.

"Sorry."

I slowly raised myself back up. Ren's jacket and tie were sprawled out on the grass, and he was holding a white paper bag in his nonthrowing hand. I was so happy to see him it made me want to punch his lights out.

I know. Mixed signals.

"Hi," he said.

"Hi."

We just stared at each other. Part of me wanted to chuck The Dress at him and the other part wanted me to let down my Medusa hair so he could use it climb up to my room. I guess it all depended on why he was here.

Ren seemed like he was having an internal debate as well. He shuffled around for a second. "Would you mind coming down here?"

I held out for exactly nine-tenths of a second, then threw one leg over the windowsill and slowly lowered myself out. Some of the bricks were uneven, and I used them as footholds to slowly climb down the house.

"Be careful," Ren whispered, holding his arms out to catch me.

I had to jump the last few feet, and I smashed right into Ren, who did this awkward crumpling thing that left us tangled up on the ground. We both sprang to our feet, and Ren took a step back, looking at me with an expression I couldn't read.

"You could have used the stairs," he said.

"Stairs are for *stronzos*."

He cracked a smile. "You left the party."

"Yeah."

Suddenly a light turned on in Howard's room.

"Howard!" Ren whispered. He looked like he'd just spotted a yeti in the wild. He was never going to get over that first conversation.

"Come on." I grabbed his hand and we ran for the back fence, trying—and failing—to not trip over every single curb we came across. Hopefully we'd never have to resort to a life of crime, because I was pretty sure we'd be the worst fugitives in the world.

"There's no way he didn't hear us," Ren panted when we reached the back wall.

"I think he went back to sleep. Look. His bedroom light is off again."

Minor lie. Most likely Howard had figured out what was going on and decided to let my middle-of-the-night escapade slide. He really was kind of the best. I turned to look at Ren, but I was so nervous that my eyes kept sliding off his face. He seemed to be having the same problem.

"So what did you want to talk to me about?"

He kicked at the grass. "I, uh, didn't tell you earlier, but you really looked amazing tonight. It was your version of The Dress, wasn't it?"

"Yeah." I looked down too. "I don't think it worked, though."

"No, it did. Trust me. So back there . . . at the party." He breathed out. "I was pretty upset when I saw you with Thomas."

I nodded, doing my best to ignore the flicker of hope in my chest. *And* . . .

"I really need to apologize. I was pretty upset back in Rome when you said you'd never, ever, ever, *ever* considered me as more than a friend—"

"I only said 'ever' twice," I protested.

"Fine. Never, *ever, ever.* It was like a slap in the face. And then when it comes to Thomas, I'm a total idiot. He's like a British pop star. How do you compete with that?"

I groaned. "British pop star?"

"Yeah. With a fake accent. He actually grew up near Boston, and when he gets really drunk he forgets about the whole British thing and sounds like one of those guys you see yelling at Red Sox games with letters painted on their beer bellies."

"That's horrible." I took a deep breath. "And I'm really sorry that I told you I'd never, ever, ever—"

"Ever," Ren added.

". . . ever consider you as more than a friend. It wasn't true." I cleared my throat. "Ever. Also, you're not a *stronzo*."

Ren grew a tiny, hopeful smile on his face that immediately transplanted itself onto my face too. "Where'd you learn that word, anyway?"

"Mimi."

He shook his head. "So, did you mean it back there? When you said you aren't with Thomas?"

I nodded. "Are you really not with Mimi?"

"No. I am one hundred percent available."

"Huh," I said, my smile ramping up like ten more degrees.

We looked at each other for another long minute, and I'm pretty sure all four thousand headstones leaned in to hear what was going to happen next. So . . . were we just going to stand around *looking* at each other? What about all that crazy Italian passion we supposedly had?

He took a tiny step forward. "Did you finish the journal?"

"Yes."

"And?"

I exhaled. "I think they were perfect for each other. Things just got in the way. And Howard knew all along that he wasn't my father. He just really wanted to be in my life."

"Smart, scary Howard." He held out the white paper bag he'd been carrying all this time.

"What's this?"

"An official apology. After I left the party I went into Florence and started driving around asking people where I could find a secret bakery. Finally some women walking home from a party told me where to go. For future reference, it's on Via del Canto Rivolto. And it's awesome."

I opened the bag and warm, buttery heaven wafted up at me. A flaky, crescent-shaped pastry was wrapped in white tissue paper. "What is it?"

"*Cornetta con Nutella.* I bought two of them, but I ate the other one on the way. And then I used my leftover change to wake you up."

I reached reverently into the bag, then took a big bite of the *cornetta*. It was warm and melty and tasted like every perfect thing that could ever happen to you. Italian summers. First loves. Chocolate. I took another big bite.

"Ren?"

"Yeah?"

"Next time, please don't eat my other one."

He laughed. "I wasn't sure if you were going to talk to me at all, but I knew food was probably my best bet. Next time I leave you standing alone in the dark like a total jerk, I'll buy you a dozen."

"A dozen at least." I took a deep breath. Now that I had Nutella coursing through my veins I felt invincible. "And just so you know, I meant what I said at Valentina's. You're the one I like. Maybe love."

"Maybe love, huh? Well, that's good news. Because I maybe love you too."

We grinned at each other and then a warm, spicy feeling dripped straight though my core, and I could tell Ren was feeling the same thing, because suddenly we were standing so close I could see every single one of his eyelashes. *Kiss me, kiss me, kiss me.*

He squinted. "I think you have Nutella on your face."

I groaned. "Ren, would you just kiss me alre—"

But I didn't finish because he dove on me and we kissed. Like really, really kissed. And it turns out I'd been waiting absolutely my entire life to be kissed by Lorenzo Ferrara in an American cemetery in the middle of Italy. You're just going to have to trust me on that one.

Finally we broke apart. We'd somehow ended up on the

grass and we both rolled on our backs and lay there looking up at the stars with these big Christmas-morning smiles that should have been cheesy but really were just awesome.

"Can we please count that as our first official kiss?"

"First of many," he said. "But if it's okay with you, I'm not going to forget that one in Rome, either. Before I so rudely interrupted it, that kiss was pretty much the best thing that had ever happened to me."

"Me too," I said.

He rolled to his side, propping himself up on one elbow. "So . . . there's been something I've been wanting to ask you."

"What?"

He pushed his hair out of his eyes. "Have you ever thought about what it would be like to stay here in Italy? Permanently? Now that you have a boyfriend and all that?"

Boyfriend. The stars winked ecstatically.

I propped myself up too. "I was actually kind of working on that earlier. Addie texted and told me that I could live with her family next year, and Howard and I spent a long time talking about it."

"And?"

I took a deep breath. "And I'm staying, Lorenzo."

He gasped. "Did you just roll your *R*? I swear you just rolled your *R*. Say it again."

I smiled. "Lo-ren-zo. I'm half Italian, right? I should be

able to roll my *R*. And come on. I tell you I'm staying in Florence and you get excited that I can say your name?"

"Never been so excited in my life."

We grinned at each other. Then I leaned over and kissed him again. Because that was totally something we did now.

"So you're telling me that not only do you like, maybe *love* me, but you're staying here indefinitely?"

"That's what I said."

"This is officially *la notte più bella della mia vita*."

"I'm sure I would totally agree if I had any idea what that meant."

"You'll be speaking Italian in no time." He interlaced his fingers with mine. "So now that we won't be chasing your mom's ex-boyfriends around, what are we going to do?"

I shrugged. "Fall in love?"

"Way ahead of you." He extended his index finger, lining it up against mine to make a little steeple. "Hey, I just thought of something."

"What?"

"When we're together, we make one whole Italian."

I smiled, looking down at our fingers and feeling my heart grow so fast and big I had to shut my eyes to keep it from bursting out.

He leaned in to me. "Hey, what's the matter? Are you crying?"

I shook my head, slowly opening my eyes and smiling at him again. "No, it's nothing."

But it wasn't nothing. I didn't want to ruin the moment by explaining it to him, but suddenly it was like I had a zoomed-out view of this moment and I never, ever (ever) wanted it to end. I had Nutella on my face and my first real love sprawled out next to me and any minute the stars were going to sink back into the sky in preparation for a new day, and for the first time in a long time, I couldn't wait for what that day would bring.

And that was something.

Acknowledgments

Before *Love & Gelato* I had only a vague understanding of how many people it takes to make a book happen. Turns out it takes lots. Scads. Heaps. Oodles. So here's my best attempt at narrowing that number down.

My first thank you has to go to my parents, and especially my mom, Keri DiSera Evans, for giving me Italy. Those two years expanded my world exponentially and were pure magic. Thank you for never settling for the status quo. You're my hero.

Thank you to my inspirational dad, Richard Paul Evans, who not only led me to the cliff of Authorship, but shoved me over the edge. I can only dream about writing as many books or impacting as many lives as you have. Thank you for not letting me give up. (Thank you, thank you, thank you.) I am doing my best to repay you in hilarious grandchildren.

A special thank you to my son, Samuel Lawrence Welch. I got the news that *Love & Gelato* was going to be a real live book just minutes after you blew out the candle on your first birthday cake, and I still can't believe I get to live out both my dreams at once. Thank you for making sure I took time out to play cars and read silly books. And you're right—pencils should be used for drawing choo-choos, not writing endings. Those can wait. (Also, grown up Sam: Did you need a sign that you can accomplish your biggest, scariest dream? This is your sign. Go for it, Sammy Bean.)

Thank you to my lifelong friend/family member/fairy godmother, Laurie Liss. I've been so lucky to have you in my life and feel even luckier to have you as my agent. I simply couldn't love you more than I do. Thank you for believing in me.

Thank you, thank you to everyone at Simon Pulse, and in particular my brilliant editors Fiona Simpson and Nicole Ellul. This story could not have happened without you. Thank you for being enthusiastic about Lina and Ren, telling me what was and wasn't working (in the kindest way possible), and for helping me to find my voice. I honestly don't know how to thank you for helping me write a book I love. So just thank you.

Thank you to my friends at the American International School of Florence—in particular Ioiana Luncheon, the real live girl who grew up in the Florence American Cemetery. I've obviously thought a lot about you and your runs through the cemetery over the years. Thank you for your help with translating and getting all the facts straight. You were awesome. (Also, an apology to the current groundskeeper at the Florence American Cemetery. I was just the tiniest bit overexcited about my visit and really didn't mean to set off the alarms or ruin your family dinner. I pretty much want to die every time I think about it.)

Also, a heartfelt thank you to the fourteen-year-old boy who asked me on a date while I sat working on my novel in the Millcreek Library. I was having a tough writing day and you totally turned it around. Also, I forgive you for yelling, "She's *OOOLD!*" to your friends. I'm sure you didn't mean that.

And best for last, thank you to my husband, David Thomas Welch. You are immensely talented, kind, and strong, and I have relied on you so much. Thank you for believing I could do this even when I didn't. Thank you for all the extra carrying you did to allow me to fulfill my dream. Thank you for listening to every crazy direction this story could have gone and for allowing Lina and Ren to hang out in our home like they were real people. (They are, aren't they?) But most of all, thank you for choosing me. This December will mark thirteen years since I sat in your car and worked up the courage to say, "Um, hey. Do you maybe want to hang out for a little bit longer?" I'm so glad you said yes.

LOVE & LUCK

To Nora Jane,

the possessor of two exceptionally plucky feet and

a one-dimpled smile that lit up my darkness for

over a year. This one's for you, baby girl.

Dear Heartbroken,

What do you picture when you imagine traveling through Ireland? Belting out drinking songs in a dim, noisy pub? Exploring mossy castles? Running barefoot through a field of four-leaf clovers? Or maybe that old Johnny Cash song: *green, green, forty shades of green.*

Whatever you've imagined, my little lovelorn friend, I can emphatically say *you're wrong.* I'm not saying you won't find yourself singing a rousing rendition of "All for Me Grog" at a little tavern in Dublin, or that you won't spend your fair share of afternoons stumbling through waterlogged castle grounds. But I am saying that this trip of yours will undoubtedly be *even better than anything you've imagined.* Don't believe me? Wait until you're standing at the edge of the Cliffs of Moher, your hair being whipped into a single dreadlock, your heart pattering like a drum. Then we'll talk.

I know you're feeling fragile, turtledove, so let me just lay it all out for you. You are about to fall head over heels in love with a place that will not only heal that little heart of yours, but also challenge you in every way imaginable. Time to open your suitcase, your mind, and, most of all, this guidebook, because not only am I an insufferable expert on all things Ireland, but I'm also an insufferable expert on heartbreak. Consider me a two-for-one guide. And don't pretend you don't need me. We both know there are a thousand travel guides on Ireland, and yet you picked up *this* one.

You've come to the right place, love muffin. The Emerald Isle may not be the only place to mend a broken heart, but it is the best.

Trust me.

PS: On a recent, particularly vibrant afternoon in County Clare, Ireland, I counted forty-seven shades of green. So take that, Johnny.

—Introduction to *Ireland for the Heartbroken: An Unconventional Guide to the Emerald Isle, third edition*

Prologue

WORST SUMMER EVER.

That's the thought I went over the side with. Not *I'm falling*. Not *I just shoved my brother off the Cliffs of Moher*. Not even *My aunt is going to kill me for ruining her big day*. Just *Worst summer ever*.

You could say that my priorities weren't in the best shape. And by the bottom of the hill, neither was I.

When I finally rolled to a stop, my designer dress and I had been through at least ten mud puddles, and I was lying in something definitely livestock-related. But cow pies weren't the worst of it. Somewhere along the way I'd hit something— hard—and my lungs were frantically trying to remember what they were supposed to do. *Inhale*, I begged them. *Just inhale*.

Finally, I got a breath. I closed my eyes, forcing myself to slow down and breathe in and out to the count of five like I do whenever I get the wind knocked out of me, which is way more often than the average person.

I have what my soccer coach calls the *aggression factor*. Meaning, whenever we arrive at a school where the players look like Attila the Hun in ponytails, I know I'll be playing the whole game. Getting the wind knocked out of me is kind of a specialty of mine. It's just that usually when it happens, I'm wearing soccer cleats and a jersey, not lipstick and designer heels.

Where's Ian? I rolled to my side, searching for my brother. Like me, he was on his back, his navy-blue jacket half-off, head pointed down the hill toward all the tourist megabuses in the parking lot. But unlike me, he wasn't moving.

At all.

No. I sprang to my knees, panic filming over my vision. My high heels impaled the hem of my dress, and I struggled to untangle myself, scenes from the cheesy CPR movie they made us watch in health class firing through my head. Did I start with mouth to mouth? Chest compressions? Why hadn't I paid attention in health class?

I was about to fling myself at him when his eyes suddenly snapped open.

"Ian?" I whispered.

"Wow," he said wearily, squinting up at the clouds as he wiggled one arm, then the other.

I fell back into a relieved heap, tears spiking my eyes. I may have shoved my brother off the side of a mountain, but I hadn't killed him. That had to count for something.

"Keep moving; eyes up here." I froze. The voice was British and much too close. "Hag's Head is a bit farther. Ooh, and look, there's a wedding going on up top. Everyone see the lovely bride? And . . . oh, my. I think she lost a bridesmaid. A tiny lavender bridesmaid. Hellooooo there, tiny lavender bridesmaid. Are you all right? Looks like you've had a fall."

I whipped around, my body tensed to unleash on whoever had just dubbed me "tiny lavender bridesmaid," but what I saw made me wish I was even tinier. Not only had Ian and I landed a lot closer to the walkway than I'd realized, but a tour guide sporting a cherry-red poncho and a wide-brimmed hat was leading a pack of enraptured tourists right past us. Except none of them were looking at the sweeping landscape or the lovely bride, who happened to be my aunt Mel. They were looking at *me*. All thirty of them.

You'd think they'd never seen a midwedding fistfight before. *Act in control.*

I straightened up, shoving my skirt down. "Just a little tumble," I said brightly. *Yikes.* "Tumble" was not a typical part of my vocabulary. And whose robotic happy voice was coming out of my mouth?

The tour guide pointed her umbrella at me. "Did you really just fall down that big hill?"

"Looks like it," I said brightly, the thing I actually wanted to say brimming under the surface. *No. I'm just taking a nap in a manure-coated dress.* I shifted my eyes to Ian. He appeared to be playing dead. Convenient.

"You're sure you're okay?"

This time I injected my voice with a heavy dose of *now please go away.* "I'm sure."

It worked. The guide scowled at me for a moment and then lifted her umbrella, making clucking noises to the group, who begrudgingly shuffled forward like a giant, single-brained centipede. At least that was done with.

"You could have helped me out with the tour group," I called to Ian's motionless form.

He didn't respond. Typical. These days, unless he was cajoling me to come clean to our parents about what had happened this summer, he barely looked at me. Not that I could blame him. *I* could barely look at me, and I was the one who'd messed up in the first place.

A raindrop speckled down on me. Then another. *Really? Now?* I shot a reproachful look at the sky and pulled my elbow in next to my face, cradling my head in my arm as I assessed my options. Apart from seeking shelter in one of the souvenir shops built into the hills like hobbit holes, my only other choice was to hike back up to the wedding party, which included my mother, whose rage was already sweeping the countryside. There was absolutely no way I was going to put myself in the line of fire before I had to.

I listened to the waves smash violently against the cliffs, the wind carrying a few snippets of voices over the top of the hill like the butterfly confetti we'd all thrown a few minutes earlier:

Did you see that?

What happened?

Are they okay?

"I'm not okay!" I yelled, the wind swallowing up my words. I hadn't been okay for exactly one week and three days, which was when Cubby Jones—the boy I'd been sneaking out with all summer, the boy I had been in love with for what amounted to my entire teen life—had decided to crush my heart into a fine powder and then sprinkle it out over the entire football team. *Ian's* football team. No wonder he couldn't stand to look at me.

So no. I was most definitely not okay. And I wasn't going to be okay for a very, very long time.

Maybe ever.

The Wild Atlantic Way

Me again, buttercup. Here to give you an extraordinarily important tip as you enter the planning phase of your journey. Read carefully, because this is one of the few hard-and-fast rules you will find in this entire book. You listening? Here goes. *As a first-time visitor to Ireland, do not, under any circumstances, begin your trip in the capital city of Dublin.*

I know that sounds harsh. I know there's a killer deal to Dublin on that travel website you've been circling like a vulture all week, but hear me out. There are a great many reasons to heed my advice, the main one being this:

Dublin is *seductive as hell.*

I know what you're going to do next, sugar. You're going to argue with me that there isn't anything particularly seductive about hell, to which I would counter that it's an excellent place to meet interesting people, and those fiery lakes? Perfect for soaking away stress.

But let's not get sidetracked.

Bottom line, Dublin is a vacuum cleaner and you are one half of your favorite pair of dangly earrings—the one you've been missing since New Year's. If you get too close to that city, it will suck you up and there will be no hope for unmangled survival. Do I sound like I'm being overly dramatic? Good. Have I used one too many metaphors? Excellent. Because Dublin is dramatic and worthy of metaphor overuse. It's full of interesting museums, and statues with hilariously inappropriate nicknames, and pubs spewing out some of the best music on earth. Everywhere you go, you'll see things you want to do and see and taste.

And therein lies the problem.

Many a well-intentioned traveler has shown up in Dublin with plans to spend a casual day or two before turning their attention to the rest of Ireland. And many a well-intentioned traveler has found themselves, a week later, on their ninetieth lap of Temple Bar, two leprechaun snow globes and a bag full of overpriced T-shirts the only things they have to show for it.

It's a tale as old as time.

My firm recommendation (command?) is that you begin in the west, most particularly, the Wild Atlantic Way. Even more particularly, the Burren and the Cliffs of Moher. We'll get to them next.

HEARTACHE HOMEWORK: *Surprise!* As we traipse across this wild island of ours, I will be doling out little activities designed to engage you with Ireland and baby-step you out from under that crushing load of heartache you're packing around. Assignment one? Keep reading. No, really. *Keep reading.*

—Excerpt from *Ireland for the Heartbroken: An Unconventional Guide to the Emerald Isle, third edition*

"YOU WERE BRAWLING. DURING THE *CEREMONY*." WHENEVER my mom was upset, her voice lowered three octaves and she pointed out things that everyone already knew.

I pulled my gaze away from the thousand shades of green rushing past my window, inhaling to keep myself calm. My dress was bunched up around me in a muddy tutu, and my eyes were swollen drum-tight. Not that I had any room to talk: Ian's eye looked much worse. "Mom, the ceremony was over; we—"

"Wrong side, wrong side!" Archie yelled.

Mom swore, swerving the car over to the left and out of the way of an oncoming tractor while I dug my fingernails into the nearest human flesh, which happened to belong to my oldest brother, Walter.

"Addie, stop!" he yelped, pulling his arm away. "I thought we agreed you weren't going to claw me to death anymore."

"We almost just got into a head-on collision with an oversize piece of farm equipment. It's not like I can control what I do," I snapped, shoving him a few inches to the left. I'd spent the last seventy-two hours crammed between my two largest brothers in every variation of transportation we encountered, and my claustrophobia was hovering around a level nine. Any higher and I was going to start throwing punches. Again.

"Mom, don't listen to them—you're doing great. There were a good three inches between you and that tractor," my other brother Archie said, reaching under the headrest and patting her on the shoulder. He narrowed his blue eyes at me and mouthed, *Don't stress her out.*

Walt and I rolled our eyes at each other. The man at the airport car rental desk had insisted that it would take only an hour, two tops, for my mom to get the hang of driving on the opposite side of the road, but we were more than forty-eight hours in, and every time we got in the car, I got the same sinking feeling that rickety carnival rides always gave me. *Impending doom.* I held the airport car rental man personally responsible for all the emotional and psychological damage I was undoubtedly going home with.

Only Ian, whose perpetual car sickness made him the unspoken victor of the front seat, was unfazed. He rolled down the window, sending a cool burst of cow-scented air into the car, his knee doing the perpetual Ian bounce.

There are two important things to know about Ian. One, he never stops moving. Ever. He's the smallest of my brothers, only a few inches taller than me, but no one ever notices that because his energy fills up whatever room he's in. And two, he has an anger threshold. Levels one through eight? He yells like the rest of us. Nine and above? He goes silent. Like now.

I leaned forward to get another look at his black eye. A slash of mud crossed under his ear, and grass peppered his hair. His eye was really swollen. Why was his eye so swollen already?

Ian gingerly touched the skin under his eye, as if he was thinking the same thing. "Brawling? Come on, Mom. It was just an argument. I don't think anyone even saw." His voice was calm, bored even. He was really trying to convince her.

"'Argument' implies that there wasn't any violence. I saw fists. Which makes it a brawl," Walter added helpfully. "Plus, everyone, look at Ian's eye."

"Do *not* look at my eye," Ian growled, his Zen slipping away.

Everyone glanced at him, including my mom, who immediately started to drift to the opposite side of the road.

"Mom!" Archie yelled.

"I *know*," she snapped, pulling back to the left.

I really hurt Ian. My heart started in on a dangerous free fall, but I yanked it back into place. I had exactly no room for guilt. Not when I was already filled to the brim with remorse, shame, and self-loathing. Plus, Ian *deserved* that black eye. He was the one who kept bringing up Cubby—poking me with Cubby was more like it. Like he had a ball of fire on the end of a stick that he could jab at me whenever he felt like it.

Ian's voice popped into my head—the broken record I'd been listening to for ten days now. *You have to tell Mom before someone else does.*

Hot, itchy anxiety crept up my legs, and I quickly leaned over Archie to unroll the window, sending another rush of air into the car. *Don't think about Cubby. Don't think about school. Just don't think.* I was four thousand miles and ten days out from my junior year—I shouldn't spend my remaining time thinking about the disaster scene I was going back to.

I stared hard out the window, trying to anchor my mind on the scenery. Houses and B and Bs dotted the landscape in charming little clumps, their fresh white exteriors accented with brightly colored doors. Lines of laundry swung back and forth in the Irish drizzle, and cows and sheep were penned so close to the houses, they were almost in the backyards.

I still couldn't believe I was here. When you think destination wedding, you don't think rainy, windswept cliff on the western coast of Ireland, but that's exactly the spot my aunt had chosen. The Cliffs of Moher. Moher, pronounced *more*. As in more wind, more rain, more vertical feet to traverse in a pair of nude high heels. But despite the fact that my brothers had to Sherpa my aunt's new in-laws up to the top, or that all of us had sunk to our ankles in mud by the time *dearly beloved* had been uttered, I completely understood why my aunt had chosen the place.

For one thing, it made for great TV. Aunt Mel's traveling camera crew—a couple of guys in their late twenties with exceptionally well-thought-out facial hair—forced us to do the wedding processional twice, circling in on her as the wind whipped around her art deco dress in a way that should have made her look like the inflatable waving arm guy at a car dealership, but instead made her look willowy and serene. And then once we were all in place, it was all about the view, the overwhelming *grandiosity* of it. Big hunks of soft green ended abruptly in sheer cliffs, dropping straight down into the ocean, where waves threw themselves against the rocks in ecstatic spray.

The cliffs were ancient and romantic, and completely unimpressed with the fact that I'd spent the summer ruining my own life. *Your heart got publicly stomped on?* the cliffs asked. *Big deal. Watch me shatter this next wave into a million diamond fragments.*

For a while there, the view had crowded out every other possible thought. No cameras, no Cubby, no angry brother. It was the first break I'd had from my mind in more than ten days. Until Ian leaned over and whispered, *When are you telling Mom?* and all the anxiety pent up in my chest had exploded. Why couldn't he just let it go?

Walter rolled down his window, creating a cross tunnel of air through the back seat. He sighed happily. "Everyone saw the fight. There was a collective gasp when you went over the edge. I'll bet at least one of the cameramen caught it on film. And then there was that group of tourists. They were talking to you, weren't they?"

The Ian bounce stopped, replaced by angry fist clenching. He whirled on Walter. "Walt, just shut *up*."

"All of you—" my mom started, but then she blanched. "Oh, no."

"What? What is it?" Archie craned his face forward, his shoulders shooting up to his ears. "Roundabout," he said in the exact tone a NASA scientist would announce, *fiery Earth-destroying meteorite.*

I anchored myself onto both my brothers' arms. Walter clutched his seat belt to his chest, and Archie reverted into coach mode, barking out instructions. "Driver stays on the inside of the roundabout. Yield when you enter, not when you're inside. Stay focused, and whatever you do, *don't hit the brakes.* You can do this."

We hit the roundabout as though it were a shark-infested whirlpool, all of us holding our breath except for my mom, who let out a stream of loud profanities, and Ian, who carried on with his regularly programmed fidgeting. When we'd finally cleared it, there was a collective exhale from the back seat, followed by one last expletive from the driver's seat.

"Great job, Mom. If we can handle every roundabout like

that, we'll be golden," Archie said, unhooking my claws from his upper arm.

Walt leaned forward, shaking himself free of me also. "Mom, please stop swearing. You're *awful* at it."

"You can't be awful at swearing," she said shakily.

"You have single-handedly disproven that theory," Walt argued. "There's a science to it; some words go together. You can't just throw them all out at once."

"I'm going to throw *you* all out at once," Mom said.

"See, that's good, Mom," he said. "Maybe stick to the clever quips. At least those make sense."

"It's about context. And respect for the form," Ian added, his voice back to calm. I dug my fingers into my muddy skirt. Now I was confused. Was Ian angry-calm or *calm*-calm?

Archie glared at all of us. "She can use whatever combination of words she wants. Whatever gets us back to the hotel safely. Remember what you practice in your business meditations, Mom. *Go to your powerful place.*"

"Great," Ian groaned. "You've invoked the Catarina."

"There's no reason to bring her into this," I added.

Mom scowled at us dangerously. Thirteen months ago my mom had traded in her yoga pants and oversize T-shirts for a real estate wardrobe and a bunch of *Be the Business, Feel the Business* audio recordings from a local real estate guru named Catarina Hayford. And we couldn't even make fun of her for it, because in one year she had outsold 90 percent of her more sea-soned fellow agents, even landing a spot on her agency's bill-boards. This meant that I could be almost anywhere in Seattle and look up to see her smiling imperiously down on me. And with her new busy schedule, some days it was the only time I saw her at all.

"Remind me why I paid to bring all of you to Ireland," Mom snapped, her voice rising.

Walt piped up. "You didn't pay for it—Aunt Mel did. And besides, if it weren't for Addie and Ian's performance back there, that would have been an unbelievably boring wedding, even with that crazy scenery." He nudged me. "My favorite part was the moment when little sis here decided to shove Ian off the cliff. There was this *deliberateness* to it. Like that scene in *The Princess Bride* when Buttercup shoves Wesley and he's rolling down the hill yelling, 'As yooooou wiiiiiish!'"

"Two things," Ian said, his long hair brushing his shoul-der as he looked back. His gaze skipped right over me. "One, great reference, seeing as the Cliffs of Moher is where they filmed the Cliffs of Insanity scenes. And two, did you even *see* what happened?"

Walter drew his breath in sharply. "Why didn't anyone tell me that before we went? You're right. We were totally at the Cliffs of Insanity. We could have done a reenactment—"

"Stop *talking*." I laced my voice with as much menace as I could muster. When Walter got started, he was a human diesel train. Loud and really hard to stop.

"Or what? You'll throw me off a cliff?"

"It was more of a chambered punch," Archie said. "Or maybe a right hook. The technique was actually really good. I was impressed, Addie."

Ian whipped back, and this time his bruised eye stared me down. "She didn't knock me off the cliff. I *slipped*."

"Yeah, right." Walter laughed. "Way to save your ego there, buddy."

I dug my elbows into Walter and Archie's legs, but they both grabbed hold of my arms, locking me into place until I struggled free. "We went down the complete opposite side of the hill. No one was actually in danger."

Walter shook his head. "Lucky break. Auntie Mel would have never forgiven us if you'd ruined her dream wedding by committing *murder*." He whispered *murder* the way the narrator always did in his favorite true crime TV show.

"But could you imagine the ratings on the wedding episode if that happened?" Archie quipped. "HGTV would love you forever. They'd probably give you your own reality show. It would be like international wedding crasher–meets–hired hit man. Or hit woman."

"All of you, *stop*." My mom risked taking her hand off the

steering wheel to massage her right temple. "You know what? I'm pulling over."

"Mom, what are you doing?" I yelled as we bumped off the side of the road, a parade of cars honking behind us. If I had to stay sandwiched in this car for even a minute longer than was completely necessary, I was going to lose it. "There's a whole line of cars behind us. And the shoulder's almost nonexistent."

"Yes, Addie, I know that." She shakily threw the car into park, wrenching us all forward. "This can't wait."

"The fight at the cliffs was one hundred percent Ian's fault." The words screeched—unplanned—out of my mouth, and all three of my brothers turned to stare at me in horror. I had just broken Bennett sibling code rule #1: *Never throw one another under the bus.* Except this Cubby thing was on a whole new level. Maybe old rules didn't apply.

Ian's face tightened in anger. "You're the one who—"

"ENOUGH!" My mom's voice reverberated around the car like a gong. "I don't care *who* started it. I don't care if Addie drenched you with honey and then threw you into a bear den. You're teenagers, practically adults. And I have had it with your arguments. You fell off a hill. In the middle of a wedding."

Bear den? Honey? Mom had a great imagination. Walter started to laugh, but Mom wrenched her neck toward him, and he fell silent. Next she zeroed in on Ian.

"There is one year standing between you and college, and if you think I'm going to put up with how you've been acting, you're wrong. And, Addie, you're sixteen years old and you have all the self-control of a ten-year-old."

"Hey!" I started, but Archie shot his elbow into my ribs, and I doubled over. It was a saving gesture. If I had any chance of surviving this, it was going to involve the subtle art of *keeping quiet*. And Mom was right. As my outburst had just so aptly demonstrated, I did struggle with impulsivity. It got me into trouble a lot.

"You two are so close," Mom said. "The closest of any of you. There were years when I thought that neither of you knew that anyone else existed. What is going on this summer?"

And then suddenly the car was quiet. Horribly quiet. All except for the windshield wipers, which chose this exact moment to become sentient. *This summer, this summer, this summer*, they chanted, sloshing water across the window. Ian's knee slowed, and I felt his stare, heavy on my face. *Tell Mom.*

I raised my eyes to his, my telepathic message just as insistent. *I am not. Telling. Mom.*

"Fine. Don't tell me." Mom slammed her palm down on the steering wheel and we all flinched. "If Dad were here, you know you'd be on the first flight back to Seattle."

Ian and I simultaneously levitated off our seats. "Mom, no! I *have* to go to Italy. I have to go see Lina!" I shouted.

Ian's measured voice filled the car. "Mom, you've got to think this through."

She threw her hand up, deflecting our emotion like one of the backhand shots that ruled her tennis game. "I didn't say you're not going."

"Geez, chill, Addie," Walter whispered. "You almost went headfirst through the windshield."

I sagged back into my seat, panic filtering out of my veins. The only good thing about Aunt Mel's wedding—besides the gorgeous location—was that it had gotten me to Europe, the continent that had stolen my best friend from me at the beginning of the summer.

My aunt had arranged for a postwedding tour of Ireland that was supposed to include all of us, but I'd managed to talk my parents into letting me skip the tour in exchange for a few days in Italy with Lina. I hadn't seen her since she moved to Florence ninety-two days ago to live with her father, Howard, and every single one of those days had felt like a lifetime. Not seeing her was not an option. Especially now, when it was very likely she was the only friend I had left.

Ian slumped forward in relief, twisting the back of his hair into a tight corkscrew. I swore he'd grown his hair out just to give him more fidget options.

"Don't get me wrong," my mom continued. "I should be sending you both back, but we spent way too much on those tickets to Florence, and if I don't have some time away from the two of you and your constant fighting, I'm going to have a breakdown."

A fresh dose of anger hit my system. "Could someone please explain to me *why* Ian's coming with me to Italy?"

"Addie," my mom snapped. Ian shot me a wide-eyed look that said, *Shut up NOW.*

I glared back, our stares connecting. Despite the fact that I definitely should have been *Shutting up NOW,* it was an extremely valid question. Why did he want to come on a trip with me when, by all accounts, he couldn't stand me?

"So here's the deal," my mom said, inserting herself into the middle of our staring match. "Tomorrow morning, Archie, Walter, and I will leave on the tour, and the two of you will continue on to Florence." She spoke slowly, her words lining up like a row of dominoes, and I held my breath, waiting for her to topple the first one.

But . . . she didn't.

After almost ten seconds of silence, I looked up, hope lifting the edges of my voice. "That's it? We just get to go?"

"You're just going to send them to Italy?" Walter asked, sounding as incredulous as I felt. "Aren't you going to, like, punish them?"

"Walter!" Ian and I both yelled.

My mom wrenched herself around again, focusing first on me, then Ian, her spine swiveling seamlessly. At least she was putting all her yoga classes to good use. "You're going to Italy. It will force you two to spend some quality time together," she said, barbing the word "quality." "But there's a catch."

Of course there was. "What?" I asked impatiently, pulling a particularly stabby bobby pin out from its favorite spot in the back of my wilting updo. If it wouldn't completely set him off, I'd stick it in Ian's hair, try to get some of it out of his face.

"Here we go," Ian muttered, just loud enough for me to hear.

Mom paused dramatically, her eyes darting back and forth between us. "Are you both listening?"

"We're listening," I assured her, and Ian's knee bounced receptively. Couldn't he ever just hold still?

"This is your chance to prove to me that you can handle yourselves. If I hear anything bad from Lina's father, and I mean *anything*—if you fight, if you yell, if you so much as look at each other cross-eyed while you're there—both of you are off your teams."

There was a moment of dead air, and then the car exploded. "*What?*" Archie said.

"Whoa, whoa, whoa!" Walter shook his head. "Are you being serious, Mom?"

"We'll be off our teams?" I asked quickly. "Like soccer and football?"

She nodded, a self-satisfied smile spreading like warm butter across her face. She was proud of this one. "Yes. Like soccer and football. And it doesn't even have to be both of you. If one of you messes up, you're both getting punished for it. And there will be absolutely no second chances. One strike, you're out. That's it."

I thought I had no space for fresh panic, but it squeezed in with all the old stuff, turning my chest into an accordion. I leaned forward, putting my hands on the front seats to steady myself. "Mom, you know I have to play soccer this year." My voice was high and stringy, not nearly as reasonable sounding as I'd intended. "If I don't, college scouts won't see me play, and then there's no way I'll get onto a college team. This is the year that matters. This is my *future*."

"Then you'd better not mess up."

Ian's eyes met mine, and I could see the words ping-ponging through his head. *You already messed up, Addie.*

I shot lasers at him. "But—"

"This is in your control. And Ian's. I'm not backing down on this."

As if she needed to add that last part. My parents never backed down on anything. It was one of life's constants: the shortest distance between two points is a line, root beer floats always taste better half-melted, and my parents *never* take back their punishments.

But soccer? That was my way into a good school. Because no matter how hard I tried, my grades were never all that great, which meant I needed to rely on sports to get me into any college with a halfway decent engineering program. It was a long shot, but I had to try.

Plus, *soccer*. I closed my eyes, imagining the smell of the grass, the complicated rhythm of my teammates, the way time disappeared—the rest of life forced to the outer boundaries of the game. It was my place. The only place where I ever truly fit in. And with Lina moving and Ian now hating me, I needed that place more than ever.

Forget future Addie. I needed soccer for present Addie. If I had any chance of surviving post-Cubby life, it was going to be on that soccer field.

Mom tilted her head toward Ian, who was now impersonating a collapsed puppet. "Ian, are you listening?"

"Listening," he responded, his voice oddly resigned. His body language and voice all said *I don't care*, but I knew that couldn't be true. Sports were an even bigger deal to him than they were to me. He was way better at them.

"So you understand that if you *or* Addie do anything wrong, you are off the football team? No second chances, no debating, you're just off?"

"Got it," he said nonchalantly. His hand sank back into his hair, forming a tight knot.

Archie raised one finger in the air. "Not to criticize your wisdom, Mom, but that does seem a tad bit *harsh*. One of them messes up and they're *both* off their—"

"Enough from the peanut gallery," Mom snapped.

"Wait, what?" I startled, the second part of her punishment finally sticking to my brain. "You're saying that if Ian messes up, *I'm* going to be punished for it?"

"Yes. And if you mess up, Ian is going to be punished for it. Think of it as a team sport. One of you blows it, you both lose."

"But, Mom, I have absolutely no control over what Ian does. How is that fair?" I wailed.

"Life isn't fair," my mom vaulted back, a hint of glee in her voice. My parents loved maxims the way other people loved cheese or fine wines.

And how was Ian acting so *chill*? Ever since his first junior football game, where he single-handedly turned the game around and then methodically led them to the championship, football had been Ian's life. Not only was he the starting quarterback on our high school's football team, but he'd already been approached by two different colleges with talks of scholarships. One of them had been right before football camp. No wonder he was acting like he didn't care. He was probably in the process of internal collapse.

You know what Cubby's been doing, right? He's been— Without warning, Ian's words charged into my head, and I had to dive on them before they could gain any ground. I couldn't think about football camp now. Not unless I wanted to go from kind of losing it to *completely* losing it. Not when Italy was on the line.

"Great. We're all in agreement," my mom said to our silence. She turned forward, placing her hands on the steering wheel at a perfect ten and two. "Here's the plan for tonight. When we get back to the hotel, I want everyone to pack up. Walter and Archie, the tour bus leaves at some ungodly hour tomorrow morning, and you need to be ready. Addie and Ian, you are going to change and get cleaned up, and then I am taking you to your aunt's room, where you will apologize profusely and beg for her forgiveness."

"Mom—" I groaned, but she held up a hand.

"Did I say beg? I meant grovel. After that, we're all attending the wedding dinner, where I trust you will all manage to behave like civilized human beings, or at least like mildly trained apes. Then, once we've danced and eaten cake or whatever else my sister wants us to do, we will all go right to bed. And, Addie and Ian, I suggest you both figure out a way to reconcile in a nonviolent manner. Otherwise it's going to be a miserable few days in Italy. I hear that cemetery Lina lives in is pretty small."

"It isn't. It's giant," I blurted out.

"Addie," Ian said, his patience completely spent. "Stop. Talking."

"I just don't get why you—"

"Addie!" the whole car yelled.

I threw myself back into my brothers' meaty shoulders. *Stop talking.* If I wanted to play soccer, I was going to have to keep my focus on two goals: stay on Mom's good side and get along with Ian.

I bit the inside of my lip, Ian's tousled hair on the outskirts of my vision. How had getting along with Ian become a *goal*?

At any other point in our lives, Ian coming to Italy with me would have made perfect sense. He'd always been my partner in adventure. When we were in elementary school, he'd made a game out of finding strange spots around the neighborhood to surprise me with. Once we'd snuck into an abandoned shed full of molding comic books, and another day he'd boosted me up into a massive oak tree littered with initials.

"Field trips," Ian called them. And as we got older, we stuck with the tradition, driver's licenses extending our possibilities. We'd been on one just three weeks earlier.

"Field trip time." As usual, Ian hadn't bothered to knock. He'd just burst into my room, shoving past me at my desk to launch himself onto my unmade bed.

"Not happening. Mom's coworker will be here in an hour, and we will be at dinner," I said, doing my best imitation of Mom. "Also, you're getting my sheets dirty."

I hadn't actually turned around yet, so this was based entirely on speculation. But I knew Ian. Instead of showering and changing like a normal human, Ian almost always jetted straight out of practice the second it was over. The muddy upholstery of our shared car was a testament to that.

I scribbled out my last answer and flipped to a fresh page in my notebook. It offended my very essence to be enrolled in summer school, but I'd barely passed biology, and my parents and I had decided that a second go-around would be a good idea.

Ian flopped around dramatically, making my bedsprings squeak. "Mom is fine with us missing dinner for our important Student Athlete Committee meeting."

"SAC?" I spun around, my chair twisting with me. "Please tell me you did not sign me up for that." SAC was a new and desperate attempt to repair our school's reputation as having the most aggressive (read: mean) spectators in the state.

Ian grinned his signature grin, the one that took over his whole face and let me know that something exciting was about to happen. "Don't worry. I did not sign you up for that. Although if Mom asks, that's where we're going."

I let my pencil clatter onto the desk. "You know they're going to make you do it, though, right? Ms. Hampton said they were going to recruit the school's 'most beloved student athletes,' and I *swear* she was making googly eyes at you when she said it." I placed *my* hand over my heart, doing my best impression of her shaky *falsetto*. "Ian, you shining star of perfection. Save us from ourselves!"

He made a gagging face. "Please, please, please, can *we* *not* talk about football? I'll be in the car." He jumped up and *thundered* out, leaving a muddy body print splayed out on my *white* sheets.

"Ian," I groaned, looking at his imprint. But I grabbed *my* sneakers from under my desk and took off after him. Chasing *after* Ian never felt like a choice—it was like sleeping or brushing *my* teeth. It was just what I did.

The Cliffs of Moher

Every time a traveler goes to Ireland and doesn't stop at the Cliffs of Moher, a banshee loses her voice. That's right, sweet pea, a banshee. We are in Ireland after all. Shrieky ghosts abound. And as your tour guide and now friend, I'm required to tell you that one simply does not *go to Ireland and not see the cliffs*. They're nonnegotiable. Required reading. They are the entire point.

Here's why. The cliffs are gorgeous. Breath-stealing, really. But not in the soft, endearing way of a sunset or a wobbly new lamb. They're gorgeous like a storm is gorgeous— one of those raw, tempestuous ones that leave you feeling awed and scared at the same time. Ever been trapped in a car during a particularly brutal thunderstorm? The cliffs are that kind of beautiful. Think drama, rage, and peace all packed up into one stunning package.

I studied the cliffs for years before I figured out their secret—the thing that takes them from merely scenic to life-altering: *they're beautiful because they contradict themselves.* Soft, mossy hills turn to petrifying cliffs. A roiling sea rages against a serene sky. Visitors stand around in a combined state of reverence and exuberance. Before the cliffs I knew that beauty could be delightful and inspiring. After the cliffs I knew that it could also be stark and miserable.

In fact, the cliffs are an *awful* lot like a certain heart I know. You know, the one that has managed to contain both splintering joy and shattering sorrow and still remain exquisitely beautiful?

Not that anyone asked me.

HEARTACHE HOMEWORK: Let's unleash a little rage, shall we, pet? I want you to find something to throw. A rock? An annoying pigeon? Now name it. Give it the identity of the thing that is bothering you the most about this situation, and then let it fly. Sometimes a little rage is good for the system. After that, I want you to take a deep breath. And then another. Notice how the breaths just keep coming? Notice how they just take care of themselves?

—Excerpt from *Ireland for the Heartbroken: An Unconventional Guide to the Emerald Isle, third edition*

I looked up from my book, fully intending to scowl murderously at Archie, but I made it only halfway before my energy fizzled, landing me somewhere between disgust and disdain. After the day I'd had, I just didn't have any murderous left in me.

Archie, being Archie, took my passivity for an invitation and did a sideways trust fall onto the sofa, launching me and the guidebook off in the process.

"Archie, what the hell?" I growled, scrambling back into place and suddenly panicking over the fact that I was holding a book with the word "heartbroken" in the title.

The book had all but jumped into my arms from the shelf of the tiny library off the hotel ballroom. The library was convenient for a lot of reasons. Along with providing a solid view of my still-raging mother, it smelled like a soothing combination of lavender and dust and was packed full of what appeared to be cast-off books from previous hotel guests. In other words, the perfect place to hide out.

Ireland for the Heartbroken had caught my eye immediately. It wasn't much to look at. The cover was decorated with heart-shaped clovers, and a coffee ring obstructed the too-long title. But the cover didn't matter: I was in Ireland, and I was heartbroken. This book was my soul mate.

"What are you reading?" Archie asked as I attempted to stuff the book behind the sofa's cushions.

"*Little House on the Prairie*," I said, spouting off the first thing that came to mind. As a child I'd been slow to reading, but once I picked it up, I'd read those books until they fell apart. "Also, you shouldn't jump on the furniture. I think this sofa's an antique."

"This whole hotel's an antique." He gestured toward the ballroom stuffed with more antique furniture, glittery chandeliers, and precious crystal than I'd ever seen in my entire life.

But even as a pretentious wedding host, Ross Manor definitely had a magical woodland cottage feel to it, thanks to the lush lawn lined with gnarled rosebushes and the freshly plumped pillows that sprouted golden-wrapped chocolates every night before bed. Even the caretakers were adorable—a white-haired wrinkly couple that were constantly in the process of ambushing guests with offers of tea and biscuits. Walter had dubbed them the *garden gnomes*. It fit.

"How much would Dad hate this, by the way?" Archie said.

"I'm so glad he's not here." Earlier this summer, when news of our aunt's engagement had descended on our house like a particularly expensive swarm of bees, my dad had put his foot down fast and firm. *Your sister collects men like other people collect shot glasses. I am not going to another wedding where we spend a week trying to re-create a fairy tale.*

I leaned forward, doing my quarter hourly Mom check. Right now she was walking around the ballroom spiffing up the floral centerpieces that an hour ago Aunt Mel had begun shrieking were starting in on a "slow dance of death." There was obviously no room for slow dances of death. Not when ratings were involved.

Five years ago my aunt Mel started a home design show that had been picked up by HGTV. That meant that on

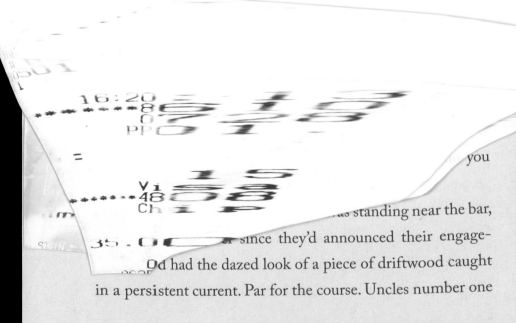

you

standing near the bar,

since they'd announced their engage-

d had the dazed look of a piece of driftwood caught in a persistent current. Par for the course. Uncles number one and two had had that look as well. I'd once heard my dad describe Aunt Mel as a riptide, which made my mom angry and my dad truthful. Mom only got mad when people were telling the truth.

"Probably with her money. And easygoing 'modern eclectic' style," I said, doing an Aunt Mel voice.

"Yeah, but is that really enough? Mom told me she made him lose twenty pounds."

"And shave off his mustache," I added.

"Society should have made him shave off his mustache. It looked like he had a wet rat stuck to his face."

I laughed, my first real laugh in ten days, and it came out creaky, like a door that hadn't been opened in a long time.

Archie flashed me a smile. "Nice to hear that. It's been a while. You've been kind of . . . depressed."

My mood tumbled back down again. He was right. Every time I somehow forgot what junior year was going to be like, Cubby suddenly appeared, landing on my shoulders and sinking my mood a solid three feet. Like now. *How could I have been so stupid?*

"You and Ian do an adequate job of groveling?" Archie asked.

I nodded, grateful for the subject change. "I did. Ian mostly just stood there scowling defiantly."

He groaned. "So in other words, being Ian."

"Exactly." It was just like on the cliffs with the tourists. Me scrambling for an explanation while Ian played dead. At least this time he was upright.

"Speaking of, where is Ian?" Archie asked.

I lifted my chin. "Eight o'clock. Sitting in that throne-looking chair." Ian had come up with the same survival strategy I had: find an out-of-the-way piece of antique furniture to camp out on and pretend you're anywhere other than where you were. Except he'd been texting all night, his face stretched in an expression I could only describe as gleeful.

"Is he *smiling*?" Archie said incredulously. "After everything that happened today? That kid is such a weirdo."

I bit my lip, fighting off my automatic instinct to defend Ian. That's the way our family had always lined up: Ian/Addie versus Walter/Archie. We occasionally formed alliances, but our core allegiances stayed the same. Had I ruined that forever? "He's been grinning at his phone ever since we left the cliffs. Whoever he's texting, it must be good."

"Probably a girl," Archie said.

"Doubt it." Every girl in the world was in love with Ian, but he rarely surfaced long enough to notice them, which left me to fend off all the wannabes who thought that getting close to his little sister was the certain way to his heart. Ha.

Archie plucked at my sleeve. "Seriously, though, sis. This dress. You look like Miss Seattle Real Estate."

This time the glare came without effort. "Come on, Archie. You saw what happened to my dress at the cliffs. I didn't exactly have a lot of options. I had to wear one of Mom's."

"Didn't she have anything less . . . realtory?"

"Um, you've met our mom, haven't you?" I said.

"Briefly. She's the one who's always yelling at us, right? Short hair? Occasionally seen on billboards?"

I shuddered. "We've got to talk her out of those this year."

"Good luck with that. Those billboards are paying my tuition."

"Football is paying your tuition. And Walt's," I pointed out. "And Ian is probably going to be the first college student in history to get paid to play. I'm the only one who's going to need those billboards to help pay for college."

That wasn't self-pity talking; it was truth. My brothers had used up all the *natural athlete* genes, leaving me to do my best with *enthusiastic athlete*. I was good, but not the star. Bad news when your brothers had shrines dedicated to them in the athletics hall.

Archie's face softened. "Hey, don't give up on playing in college so soon. I saw huge improvements in your game last year. You definitely have a shot."

I shrugged. I was in way too wallowy of a mood for a pep talk. "Unless I blow it with Ian."

"You won't. You'll just be with Lina, and Ian will be . . . I don't know. Being Ian."

Being Ian. It was like its own extreme Olympic sport. Music, football, school—all at a higher intensity than everyone else. "Do *you* have any idea why Ian wants to come to Italy with me? Because I don't think he even likes Lina. She lived with us for six months, and he barely even talked to her. Is he just trying to torture me?"

He shrugged. "Little Lina? I'm sure he likes her. She's funny and kind of quirky. Plus, she has all that crazy hair. How long has she been gone again?"

I wanted to say the actual number of days, but I knew that would sound neurotic. "Since the beginning of June."

"And she's staying in Italy permanently?"

My shoulders rounded in on themselves. "Permanent" sounded like a life sentence. "She's staying for the school year. Her dad, Howard, is a serious traveler, so they go all over the place. In October he's taking her and her boyfriend to Paris."

Lina's *boyfriend.* Yet another thing that had changed. Over the past year, Lina had gone through a lot of changes, starting when her mom, Hadley, was diagnosed with pancreatic cancer. A familiar ache ignited in my throat—the one that always flamed up when I thought about Hadley. She had been special, no doubt about it—creative, adventurous, chaotic, and just the right amount of hovering to make you feel cared about but not smothered.

Sometimes I felt like I'd experienced Hadley's loss twice—once for myself and once for Lina. I'd been desperate to drag Lina out of the grief she was floundering in—to the point that I'd made myself sick with worry.

I bit my cheek, fighting back old feelings of helplessness to refocus on Archie and the trip. "It makes way more sense that Ian would choose to visit all the castles and other sites you guys are seeing this week. Aren't you going to the castle where *Braveheart* was filmed?"

Archie perked up, just like I knew he would. Every single one of my brothers could recite that movie by heart. "We are definitely going to the *Braveheart* castle. Walt brought face paint so we can do some reenactments."

Oh, geez. Aunt Mel was going to love that. "See? Ian loves that movie. He used to fall asleep watching it. I think he's coming to Italy just to bug me."

"Maybe he just wanted a little quality time with his sister."

"Right, because he's been spending so much time with me this summer." Archie rolled his eyes, but there was no arguing with my sarcasm. Ian had spent most of the summer locked in his room writing college application essays and driving around on mystery errands, his music blaring. And then I'd gotten involved with Cubby and brought our relationship to a standstill.

Not to mention what happened at football camp.

Suddenly, Archie shifted, his eyes boring into mine. "So, Addie, talk."

There was a serious edge to his voice, and my heart rate climbed to a rickety pace. "About what?"

"What's the deal?"

"With . . . Ian?" I asked uncertainly. *Please tell me he didn't hear.*

Archie shook his head no. My heart clawed its way up to my throat, pushing my voice out in an angry burst. "Well, then I don't know what you're talking about."

"Easy, sis. I'm not the brother you're mad at." He steadied me with his gaze. "I heard what Ian said. Before you pushed him."

My breath caught in my throat, and I scrambled, trying to remember exactly what Ian had said. How much could Archie have pieced together from one whispered conversation? "What did you hear?"

"Are you in some kind of trouble? What does Ian want you to tell Mom and Dad about?"

Archie doesn't know what happened. I flopped back in relief. "I'm not in trouble," I said quickly. So far that was the truth. As long as this thing didn't spread any further than it already had, I was not in trouble. Embarrassed and heartbroken? Yes. In trouble? No. Which was why I was *not* telling my mom.

Archie studied me, his head resting on his hand. "So, what? Does this have something to do with a guy? I'm guessing someone on Ian's team from how pissed off he sounded?"

Was that *incredulity*? My body tensed. "Why, you think it's impossible that a popular football player would like someone like me?" I snapped.

"What? No." He held his hands up defensively, his blue eyes wide. "Addie, I didn't say that at all. Why are you acting so strange?"

Because my heart hurts. Because it actually is *impossible for someone like Cubby to like someone like me.* I kept my eyeballs glued to the green velvet upholstery, scratching my thumbnail against a tear in the seat. Tears burned hot in my eyes. "Did Mom and Walt hear?"

He shook his head. "Mom was secretly negotiating a deal on her phone, and Walt had headphones hidden under his hair. He didn't even know you guys had gone over the side until everyone started freaking out."

At least it was Archie who had heard, and not Walter. Of all my brothers, Archie was the most normal secret keeper, as in he kept most secrets most of the time. It was the other two who were extreme. On the one end was Ian. The second you told him anything, he turned into a human vault—it was the reason I didn't have to worry about him being the one to tell my parents about Cubby. And then there was Walt, the exact opposite. Any time he had a secret to keep, it was like a game of Hot Potato—he just had to throw it somewhere, usually dead center of wherever you *didn't* want it to go.

"If this guy messed with you, I'd be happy to pay him a visit on my way back to campus. Maybe just wait until he's out in the road and do some distracted driving? Back out without looking behind me first? All I need is his name." His tone had gone from his usual laid-back Archie to hyperintense Archie, which was rare.

"*No.* Archie, I do not want you to run over anyone," I said emphatically, just in case his half joke was half-serious.

"You sure?"

"Yes, I'm sure," I wailed. "It's not like it would fix anything."

"It would fix the fact that he's messing with people he shouldn't be messing with."

I put my hands on his shoulders. "Archibald Henry Bennett. Promise me you won't do anything."

"You sure?"

"*Promise* me!" I yelled.

"Fine. I promise."

Oh my hell. Brothers. It was like having a bunch of guard dogs that occasionally turned on you. I was completely exhausted by this conversation. By this whole day. "Well, thanks for the talk, but I could use some time alone," I said, tilting my head ungracefully toward the door. I'd learned long ago that hints get you nowhere with boys—or at least not with the ones I was related to. The more direct the better.

Archie jumped gracefully to his feet and patted me clumsily on the shoulder. "I'm here for you, Addie," he said.

"And I really appreciate it." I tilted my head more aggressively toward the doorway.

"Okay, okay. I'm gone." He jumped up and swaggered out of the room, his to-do list lit up in neon over his head. *Be there for little sister. Check.*

* * *

Once Archie was out of my visual, I grabbed the guidebook and flicked on the library's dusty side lamp. I tried to focus on the words, but Ian kept snagging my gaze. He hadn't moved from his chair once, and he was still laser-focused on his phone, his hair flopping forward to shield his face.

Right after Christmas Ian decided to stop cutting his hair, and no matter how much my mom begged and threatened, he hadn't let up. Now it was almost to his shoulders and a constant reminder of how unfair the gene pool was. My brothers all had my mom's thick eyelashes and wavy dark hair. My grandmother's fine blond hair had leapfrogged a generation, bypassing my dark-haired dad to land on me.

We all had the blue eyes, though, and even from here Ian's were looking bluer than usual, accented by the heavy dark circle around his left eye, courtesy of me. The bruise looked really painful. And final. A punctuation mark on the end of a long, miserable sentence.

Suddenly, a smile split Ian's face, and a mixture of emotions bunched up in my chest. Because here's the thing about Ian's smile: it was always 100 percent genuine. Ian didn't fake anything for anyone—he never had. Get him laughing, you knew you were actually funny. Make him angry, you knew you were actually being an idiot.

I am such an idiot.

Panic bubbled in my chest, and I jumped to my feet, tucking the guidebook under my arm. I needed fresh air. Now.

As soon as my mom got swept into a conversation with the groom's mother, I took off, hugging the side of the dance floor to burst through the doors and into the courtyard.

Outside, I paused to take a few glorious breaths. If I were writing a travel brochure for Ireland, I'd start with what it smells like. It's a combination of just-fallen rain mixed with earth and something else, something secret. Like the extra sprinkle of nutmeg in the top secret French toast recipe my dad and I had spent Fourth of July weekend perfecting.

What if my dad finds out?

Before my mind could dig its fingernails into the thought, I started moving, walking down the stairs past a trickling fountain overflowing with rainwater. Strings of warm, twinkly lights crisscrossed over the courtyard's path, the yellow bulbs making a cheery clinking noise in the spots where they overlapped. Puddles shimmered in the divots in the stone pavement, and the air ruffled in cool, sparkly perfection. How was it possible to feel so horrible in a place that was so beautiful?

I squeezed my fingernails into my palms, a dull ache blooming in my chest. Sometimes I didn't know if I missed Cubby or if I missed the picture I'd put together in my head of the two of us. It was always the same. It would be mid-September, a week or two after everyone's start-of-school jitters wore off. We'd be walking down the hall, him with his arm slung casually around me, lost in one of those conversations where the only thing that matters is the person you're with. Whispers would follow us down the hall. *That's Addie Bennett. Aren't they cute together? I know. I don't know why I never noticed her before either.*

Well, I'd gotten my wish. They'd be whispering all right. But not about what I wanted them to be.

Finally, I made it to an ivy-enclosed alcove on the far side of the garden—an outdoor version of my hiding place in the library—and I attempted to sit cross-legged, cold seeping up through my mom's constrictive skirt. I pulled out my phone, and my heart bounced when I saw a new text message.

WHERE ARE YOU??????????????????

Lina.

Lina and eighteen question marks. I counted them twice to be sure. Aggressive punctuation was never a good sign with Lina. Normally, she texted like a nineteenth-century school-teacher who'd gotten ahold of a smartphone: proper use of capital letters, restrained emoji use, and always a complete sentence. Multiple question marks was the equivalent of Lina standing up in the middle of a church service and yelling cusswords through a bullhorn. She wasn't just angry; she was raging.

I hit respond, quickly typing out an exceptionally vague text. Sorry, can't talk now. Wedding stuff ☹

I was getting good at vague texting. And avoiding phone calls. The frowny face emoji looked up at me judgmentally.

"What?" I snapped. "For your information I have a great reason for not answering her calls."

I wasn't talking to Lina because I *couldn't* talk to Lina. She knew me too well. The second she heard my voice, she'd know something was wrong, and I refused—*refused*—to tell her about Cubby over the phone. If Lina was going to judge me, I wanted to see it in person. There was also the issue of the sheer number of things I had to tell her. She didn't know anything about Cubby, which meant I had to walk her through my entire summer.

I just had to make it to Italy. Once I got there I'd unpack the story and lay it all out, start to finish, nothing excluded.

I knew exactly how it would go. First she'd be shocked, then confused. And then she'd be struck with a brilliant plan for getting me through my junior year while reassuring me that everything was going to be okay.

Or at least that's what I kept telling myself.

The first time Cubby ever spoke to me was four days after we moved to Seattle. I was making waffles. Bribe waffles, to be more specific, and I wasn't having an easy time of it. Archie and Walter had been assigned to unpack the kitchen, and they'd somehow managed to turn it into one large booby trap. I'd taken a baking sheet to the head and dropped an entire carton of eggs when I tripped over a bread maker. But once my first waffle was on the iron, sending delicious spirals of steam into the air, I knew it would be worth it.

I took a deep, satisfied inhale. The waffles needed to be delicious. They were my ticket into the early-morning hangout Ian had expressly banned me from. No one yells Addiegetoutofhere *to someone holding a plate of hot waffles. Not even when they're trying to impress their new friends.*

"You have batter in your hair."

And there they were. The first words Cubby Jones ever said to me. Admittedly, not the most romantic introduction, but I was only twelve. I didn't have a name for the way my attention funneled to Cubby every time he walked into a room. Not yet.

While I swiped at my bangs with a dish towel, Cubby stepped closer, sniffing the waffle air. The second he was within five feet of me, I pinpointed what was different about him. "Your eyes!" I crowed, abandoning my dish towel. Cubby's eyes were two different colors.

His smile slipped off his face. "It's called heterochromia. It's just a genetic thing; it's not weird."

"I didn't say it's weird," I said. "Let me look." I grabbed his arm and yanked him in close. "Blue and gray?" I whispered.

"Purple," Cubby corrected.

I nodded my head. "Yep. I like that one the best. If you were in a sci-fi movie, that eye would be the source of all your powers."

Both of his eyes widened, and then he smiled, a slow, surprised drizzle that started at his mouth and went right up to his mismatched eyes. That was the moment I realized there were two different ways to look at boys. There was the regular way—the way I'd done my whole life—and then there was this way. A way that made kitchens tilt ever so slightly and waffles go forgotten in Mickey Mouse irons.

The sparkler send-off for the newlywed couple was a joke. Not only did my legally tipsy oldest brother attempt—and succeed at—catching one of the rosebushes on fire, but cameraman number two kept missing his shot of the bride and groom. This meant repeating the whole process over and over again until we ran out of sparklers and even the most camera-hungry wedding guests began to bray mutinously.

"Buses arrive tomorrow morning at six thirty sharp," Aunt Mel yelled over her shoulder as Uncle Number Three carried her back into the hotel. The train of her dress dragged behind her, sweeping up bits of confetti and dried sparklers. The send-off had been just for show. They were staying at Ross Manor tonight with everyone else.

"Finally free to go," my mom said quietly, running a tired hand through her hair. Her mascara was smudged, and it made her eyes look blurry.

The rest of us followed behind her, slogging silently up the billiard-green staircase to our floor, then filed one by one into our closet of a room. Despite the fact that there were five of us, including two college football players who were roughly toddler-size versions of King Kong, Aunt Mel had assigned us what had to be the smallest room in the hotel.

Fuzzy floral wallpaper decorated the walls, and my brothers' cots occupied most of the space, so all that was left over was a tiny corridor running along the base of the beds. And of course my brothers had filled that up with their never-ending supply of junk—candy wrappers, tangled-up phone cables, and more sneakers than should really exist in the world. I had a term for it: brother spaghetti.

I managed to claim the bathroom first and locked the door behind me, turning the tub on at full blast. I had no intention of actually taking a bath. I just needed to drown out the sound of everyone crashing around the room. Traveling with my family made my head hurt.

I yanked off the real estate dress, replacing it with an over-size T-shirt and a pair of black pajama shorts, then brushed my teeth as slowly as possible.

"Gotta pee, sis!" Walt shouted, banging on the door. "Gotta pee, gotta pee, gotta pee pee peeeeee."

I yanked the door open to make it stop. "Cute song. You should trademark that."

He shoved past me. "Thought you'd like it."

I picked my way through the room, avoiding half a dozen sneaker land mines before climbing onto the bed and cocooning deep into my blankets. I couldn't wait to sleep. Forget. It had been my main coping skill over the past ten days—ever since Ian had burst into my room to tell me how badly I'd screwed up his life. *His* life. Like he was the one who would have to spend the whole upcoming year avoiding Cubby and everyone who knew Cubby. My stomach twisted as tightly as the sheets.

"So what's the strategy exactly? Wear my T-shirt until I forget it's mine?" Ian's voice pierced through my blankets, and I slowly uncovered my head. Was he talking to me?

My mom was stuffing her suitcase like it was a Thanksgiving turkey, and Archie lay with his face planted on his cot, still wearing his suit. Ian propped himself up on a mountain of pillows, one earbud in, his face pointed in my general direction.

"You gave it to me," I said, aiming my voice for what a sitcom writer would mark as RETORT, SASSY. It was an exceptionally comfortable T-shirt with a black collar and sleeves and SMELLS LIKE THE ONLY NIRVANA SONG YOU KNOW written across the chest in block letters.

"By 'gave it to you,' do you mean you raided my T-shirt drawer and stole the softest one?"

Nailed it. "You can have it back," I said. *Ian is talking to me. Talking. To me.* A flicker of hope sprang into my chest.

"Do you even get the reference?" he asked, punching his top pillow into shape. His hair was in a horrible attempt at a man bun, with bumpy sides and a large chunk hanging out the back. He clearly hadn't watched the *How to Man-Bun Like a Boss* tutorial I'd forwarded him.

"Ian, I sat with you on Fleet Street and listened to the entire *Nevermind* album. How would I not know what it means?" That had been during Ian's Nirvana period. We'd gone on three different Nirvana-themed field trips, including a trip to Kurt Cobain's red-vinyl childhood home. I'd even agreed to dress up as Courtney Love for Halloween even though it required wearing a tiara and no one knew who I was.

"At least you know what it means." Ian flopped grudgingly onto his side. He hesitated, then nudged at his phone, his voice slightly above a whisper. "When are you going to tell Mom?"

I groaned into my sheets. He was bringing it up *again*. Now? When Mom, Archie, and Walt were all within earshot. Not to mention that's what the black eye had been about. One of Ian's teammates had texted him asking about Cubby. And instead of waiting until after the wedding ceremony, when we would be alone, he'd shoved the phone in my face and whisper-demanded that I tell Mom. Our parents finding out was the worst thing that could happen. Why didn't he get that?

"Ian!" I hissed.

He cut his eyes at Mom, then shot me a warning look. I growled in my throat and then slid down under the covers, forcing my breathing to calm. The odds of me *not* exploding on Ian were only as good as the odds of him not bringing up Cubby every chance he got. That is to say, not good.

Time to put a hard stop to this conversation. "Good night, Ian." I slid even farther under the covers, but I could still feel Ian's glare on my back, sharp as needles. A few minutes later I heard him rustle under the covers, the music from his earbuds filling the air between us.

How were we going to survive a full week together?

* * *

The next morning, I awoke to what sounded like the brass section from our school's famously exceptional marching band rumbling with our famously unexceptional drama team. I opened my eyes a slit. My mom was untangling her leg from the alarm clock and lamp cords. "Damn hell spit," she muttered. Or at least that's what it sounded like she muttered. Walter was right. She needed a swearing intervention.

I opened my eyes a half millimeter more. Weak sunlight puddled under the curtains, and Archie and Walter and their extreme bedhead stood next to the door looking all kinds of ambiguous about the state of their consciousness.

"You both have your passports, right?" my mom asked them, finally freeing herself. They stared at her with blank, sleep-coated expressions, and she sighed before swooping in on me in a cloud of moisturizer. "Your cab will be here at nine. The gnomes will knock on the door to wake you up." She pressed her cheek onto my forehead like she used to do when I was little and had a fever. "Promise me you'll work things out with Ian. You two are the best friends you'll ever have."

Way to twist the dagger. "Love you, Mom," I said, scrunching my eyes shut.

She crouched down next to Ian and mumbled something to him, and then the three of them cleared out of the room, banging loudly into the hallway.

It felt like only minutes later when a slamming noise sprang me out of sleep. I sat up quickly, disoriented, but not too disoriented to notice that the entire vibe of the hotel room had changed. Not only did it feel twice as big without Archie, Walter, and my mom, but the curtains were straining against full, brilliant sunlight. The room was silent, highlighting a distinct ruffling sensation hovering in the air. Had someone just been here?

"Ian," I whispered. "Are you awake?"

He didn't budge, which was typical. Ian could sleep through almost anything.

I rolled onto my back and lay still, straining my ears. The hotel's silence was as thick as black pudding. Suddenly, the door to our room pulled quietly shut, followed by an explosion of footsteps down the hall. Someone *had* been in our room. A thief? A European kidnapper? One of the gnomes?

"Ian," I said, tumbling out of my bed. "Someone was just here. Someone was in our room." I reached out to shake his shoulder, but in a highly disorienting moment, my hand sank straight through him.

I yanked off the covers to find a pile of pillows. Had he *pillow ghosted* me? I spun around, checking the rest of the cots. Empty, empty, and empty. "Ian!" I yelled into the silence.

My eyes darted to the door, and what I saw elicited my first real bit of uneasiness. Instead of the two navy-blue suitcases that were supposed to be standing by the door, there was only one. Mine.

I hustled over to the alarm clock, but it stared up at me blankly. Of course. My mom had ripped it out of the wall. I needed to find my phone.

Not under the sheets, not under the complimentary stationery, not in the scattered brochures. Finally, I ran to the windows and flung open the curtains, only to get kicked in the retinas. The countryside was on fire—green and sunlight combining to create an intense glare. Apparently, Ireland did have sunshine, and it was blinding.

I stumbled my way to the door and burst out of the room, my bare feet making staccato echoes down the hall.

Downstairs I did a fly-by inspection of the breakfast room and lounge, but the only form of life was an obese orange cat who'd taken up residence on a velvet armchair. I sprinted out the front door and into the parking lot, and a wave of cold air hit me head-on. Irish sunshine must be for looks only.

The only vehicle in the parking lot was a lonely utility van parked next to a line of rosebushes waving frantic messages at me in the wind. *Where's Ian? Did you miss your cab?*

I needed to pull it together. Even if I had overslept, it's not like Ian would have left for Italy without me. Maybe he was just out for an early-morning walk. With his suitcase?

The distant sound of an engine starting pulled me out of my trance. I took off after it, the shuddering noise getting louder as I headed toward the side parking lot. When I rounded the corner, I skidded to a stop, giving myself a few seconds to process what I was seeing.

The tortured-sounding vehicle was technically a car, but it just barely qualified. It was tiny and boxy—like when a Volkswagen and a hamster love each other *very much*—with a splotchy paint job and a muffler dangling an inch or two off the ground. And striding purposefully toward it, navy-blue economy suitcase in hand, backpack slung over one shoulder, was Ian.

Adrenaline hit me full force. My legs got the message before I did, and suddenly I was charging across the parking lot, my brother in my line of target.

He saw me just before he reached the passenger door, but by then it was too late. I collided with him like I was the Hulk going in for a high five, which was to say, hard. His backpack went flying, and we both hit the ground, tumbling for the second time in twenty-four hours. It hurt in a white-hot, head-pounding kind of way.

"What are you doing?" he hissed, scrambling to his feet.

"What am I doing? What are *you* doing?" I yelled back, jumping up to shake off the fall.

He lunged for his backpack, but I beat him to it, wrapping

the handle around my fingers. "Are you trying to leave with-out me?" I demanded.

"Just go back up to the room. I left a note on the bath-room mirror." He wasn't meeting my eye.

"A *note*? Is this the cab Mom ordered for us? Why is it in such bad shape?"

Suddenly, the passenger window began cranking down in jerky, uneven motions. The sound of an appreciative slow clap filled the air followed by an Irish voice. "Ah, Ian, you've been beaten by a girl! I wish I'd been recording. Would love to see a replay."

"Rowan!" Ian hustled over to the window, his voice much happier than someone who'd just been tackled in a parking lot should sound. He wore the same massive grin he'd had plastered all over him last night during his text sessions.

I dropped Ian's backpack on the ground and ran over, butting him out of the way so I could get a look inside.

"Well, hello there," the driver said. He was Ian's age, maybe a little older, with tousled hair, large grayish eyes, and horn-rimmed glasses that should have been perched on an old man's face but managed to be at home on his. His T-shirt said HYPNOTIZING CAT and featured a large feline with whirl-pool eyes. Definitely not a cabdriver. He smiled, and a dimple appeared charmingly on one side. Until now I'd thought that dimples only came in pairs.

"Who are you?" I demanded.

He stuck his hand out. "I'm Rowan. And you must be Addie." His accent was 100 percent Irish, singsongy with the vowels getting soft and running together like chocolate syrup in ice cream.

I ignored it. His hand and the chocolate syrup voice. But I couldn't ignore the way he was looking at me—like I was something rare and exciting that he'd just discovered in the wild. "How do you know who I am?" I asked.

"I knew Ian has a sister named Addie, and let's be honest, only a guard or a sibling would tackle someone in the middle of a stony car park."

When I didn't match his smile, he dropped his, self-consciously reaching up to push the corners of his glasses up with both hands. "Or at least I'm guessing that's how siblings operate. Also, you look like the mini female version of him."

"Do *not* call me a female version of Ian," I snapped. My first week of high school, at least five of Ian's friends had made it a point to tell me that I looked like my brother with a blond wig, which was not the confidence booster I'd been looking for.

He held up his hand quickly. "Chillax. I didn't mean to annoy ya. I probably wouldn't like it if someone called me a male version of a woman either." The dimple reappeared. "Also, I come in peace. So please don't attack me, too."

Ian quickly nudged me aside. "Sorry about this, Rowan. Minor glitch in the system. Addie, go back up to the room. Your taxi will be here later. And the note will explain everything."

Had he just called me a minor glitch in the system? "What do you mean *my* taxi? It's our taxi. Why are you out here talking to . . . ?" I stopped. I'd been about to say "Hypnotized Cat Guy," but that just sounded rude.

Ian grabbed my arm, pulling me away from the car and lowering his voice so Hypnotized Cat Guy wouldn't hear. "Great news: your wish is granted. I'm not coming with you to Italy. Go upstairs and read the note—it has all the details."

The parking lot revolved once, then twice. He was serious. "You're not coming to Italy? Since when?" I asked dizzily.

He swiped his hair out of his eyes and put a steadying hand on my shoulder. "Since always. I'll meet you in Dublin for the flight home." My mom had only arranged for our flights to and from Italy. The plan was that we would return to Dublin to fly home with the rest of the group. But now it seemed that plan was about to be compromised.

"But . . . why?" I asked desperately.

Rowan's voice pierced the air between us. "I thought Addie was in on this. Why doesn't she know we're going to Stradbally?" I was momentarily distracted. The way he said my name made it sound like it was being played on an Irish fiddle.

"I left her a note," Ian said, his cheeks flushing pink. He shoved his hair out of his face and slid his eyes guiltily at me. "It's easier this way."

"For who?" I shot back.

Rowan leaned toward the passenger window, his eyes concerned behind his glasses. "A *note*? No wonder she just knocked you over. This must look unbelievably sketchy. You meet some random guy and leave for a place she's never heard of?"

I lifted my hands in the air. "Finally, someone's making sense here."

Rowan looked pointedly at me. "Stradbally is a small town near Dublin. But we're headed to a few other sites first. We have to do research for—"

"Stop—stop—stop!" Ian stuttered. "Please don't tell her anything." He shoved past me again and yanked on the car door handle, but it didn't budge.

"Don't tell me what? Ian, don't tell me *what*?" I grabbed at his backpack.

Rowan smiled apologetically at my brother. "Sorry, Ian. According to the previous owner, that door hasn't worked since the late nineties. The lads always just have to climb in through the window."

"Who are the lads?" I asked. As if that were the most important question that needed answering.

Ian hoisted his backpack in and slithered through the

window before reaching for his suitcase. I lunged for it, but he managed to pull it in. "Addie, just go read my note. I'll see you in a few days."

I clamped my hands onto his window frame. They were shaking. "Ian, were you not in the car yesterday? Didn't you hear what Mom said about us not messing up? This is the definition of 'messing up.'"

His shoulders slumped. "Come on, Addie, you said it yourself. You don't want me to come to Italy, and I get it. I even respect it. So you go have your trip, and I'll have mine. The only way we're going to get in trouble with Mom and Dad is if we tell them, and let's be honest, neither of us is going to do that."

"Ian—"

"Just stopping by Electric Picnic," Rowan added in the kind of soothing voice you'd use on a rabid dog. "We'll be done by Monday morning. Nothing to stress about, ninja sister."

"Electric what?" The Hypnotized Cat looked at me pityingly. My voice sounded hysterical. Strangled.

"Electric Picnic. It's the biggest music festival in Ireland. It happens every year. Lots of indie and alternative stuff. But this year is special. Guess who is headlining?" Rowan paused, his smile suggesting that I'd just dangled something warm and cinnamony in front of his nose.

"Not Ian," I answered weakly.

"Yes, Ian," Ian said. "*Definitely* Ian. And you won't even

care because you'll be off in Italy having an incredible time."

"Titletrack will be at Electric Picnic," Rowan said, his tone a clear indicator that we'd both just let him down.

Titletrack. It took me a second, but my mind leapfrogged to a massive poster hanging over Ian's desk. Four guys, four brooding expressions, and an admittedly unique sound that I'd actually started to look forward to on the mornings when Ian drove me to school. "That band you love. From the U.K."

"Now you've got it," Rowan added encouragingly. "Only they're Irish, not British. And Ian's planning to—"

"Okay, Rowan, that's enough. Addie, have a great time in Italy." Ian cranked at his window, but I threw myself on top of it, using all my weight to keep it down.

"Ian, *stop.*" Rowan looked disapprovingly at my brother. "You were just going to roll the window up on her?"

Ian shrank under Rowan's stare, and he dropped his gaze to his fidgeting hands like he was trying to decide something. "Addie, I'll explain it all later. Just make sure Mom and Dad don't find out, and everything will be fine. You'll figure out a way." He took a deep breath, delivering the next part in a rush. "You've been lying to everyone all summer anyway, so this will be easy."

The line was rehearsed. He'd been carrying it around in his back pocket in case of emergency. In case I *got in his way.*

"Ian . . ." Tears prickled my eyes, which of course made

me furious. I couldn't lose it now—not in front of this oddly dressed stranger and definitely not when Ian was already settled in the oddly dressed stranger's car. "Ian, there's no way we'll pull this off. You know they're going to find out that you didn't make it to Italy, and then we'll have to quit our teams."

His gaze collapsed to the dashboard. "Come on, Addie. Sports aren't everything."

"Sports aren't everything?" Now my breath was catching in little bursts in my chest. What was he going to say next? Fainting goats aren't hilarious? "Who are you?"

"This is my only chance to see Titletrack in concert. I'm sorry you don't like it, but I'm going." The edges of his voice set hard and crinkly, his eyes a steely blue. The look set off a chain reaction of panic in me. We had officially entered the Defiant Ian stage, better known as the Never Back Down Ever stage. Unless I did something drastic to stop him, he was going to that concert.

Now or never.

I dove through the window and grabbed the keys out of the ignition, then shimmied out before either of them could process what was happening.

"Addie!" Ian yanked his seat belt off and scrambled out the window. I was already on the other side of the car, the keys imprinting in my palm. "Are you seriously doing this?"

"Wow. You people are really entertaining. Like sitcom-level entertaining." Rowan reclined his seat noisily.

I squared toward my brother. "Ian, you can't do this. You know I have to play soccer if I'm going to get into a good school. Don't ruin this for me."

"Your college plans are not my problem." His voice fell halfway through. He was trying to play the tough guy, but the real Ian was under there, the one who knew how hard I tried—and continued to fail—at school. Sometimes I got the impression that he felt guilty about how easily things came to him, when nothing ever seemed to come easily to me.

We stared each other down, waiting for the other to make the first move. Ian stepped toward me, and I bolted in the opposite direction, using the car as a buffer.

Ian groaned. "Sorry, Ro. Let me just get this out of the way and we can head out. Minor bump in the road."

"Don't you mean glitch in the system?" I asked, purposely making my voice snide. "And 'Ro'? You already have a nickname for this guy?"

Ian shoved his hair back, edging toward me. "I've known him for more than a year."

"How?"

"We met online." Ian lunged at me, but his foot slipped on the gravel, giving me plenty of time to make it around to the other side of the car. He rose slowly, holding his hands up in surrender. "All right, all right. You win."

"Ian, give me some credit. I've fought with you for sixteen

years. You think I don't know that the fake out is your go-to move?"

He just raised his hands higher. "Look, even if Mom and Dad do find out, that just means we're even. I have to deal with the fallout of you messing around with Cubby, and you have to deal with the fallout of me staying in Ireland. Now give me the keys."

"I told you to stop talking about Cubby," I said. "And you being embarrassed in front of your friends is not a *fallout*."

Rowan's voice floated out the window. "Is Cubby your oldest brother?"

"No," Ian said shortly, his eyes on me. "That's Walt."

"Oh, right. Walt." Rowan cracked his door and got out, clutching a jumbo-size box of cold cereal that read SUGAR PUFFS. "Look, guys. As entertaining as this is, we all know you can't keep this up forever. So why don't we head inside and grab a real breakfast?" He shook his Sugar Puffs winningly at Ian. "Or something stronger if you need it. A pint? We could talk it through."

I shook my head. "We aren't old enough for a *pint*. And there's nothing to talk about—"

In a flash of dark hair, Ian slid across the front of the car and clutched my wrist. We settled into a death grip, Ian fighting to wrench the keys from my hands while I curled up like a pill bug, channeling all my energy into keeping my fists closed. Another classic Addie/Ian fight move. In junior high we'd once maintained this position for eleven and a half minutes, and that was over an Oreo. Walter had timed us. "Ian . . . let . . . *go*."

Rowan leaned back against the car, popping a handful of cereal into his mouth. "You two are the best argument I've ever seen for single-child families." He crunched for a moment, then swallowed. "Okay, here's a wild idea. Addie, what if you relinquish the keys to my custody and then join us on our first stop?"

"Not a good idea," Ian said, leveraging his shoulder against mine.

"What do you mean join you?" My elbow plunged directly under Ian's rib cage.

"Addie," Ian groaned. "That hurt."

"That one's my signature move," I said proudly.

"Hear me out." Rowan raised his Sugar Puffs into the air. "The first site is not too far from here. Less than an hour. Addie, you can come with us and learn a little more about what Ian's doing. Then you two can come up with a solid plan to avoid detection by your parents, and then Addie can be on her way. No death matches involved."

First site. Did that mean there was more than one? Curiosity bit into me, but I wasn't about to start asking questions. Not about a trip Ian was *not* taking. And especially not when every bit of my energy was currently being channeled into maintaining possession of Rowan's keys. "We can't risk missing our flight," I said, putting a heavy emphasis on the "we." "Not seeing Lina is not an option."

"Who's Lina?"

"My best friend."

"Oh, duh. The one who moved to Italy."

"What else did Ian tell you about me?" I asked, doubling down on the keys.

"Don't flatter yourself," Ian said. "Believe it or not, we don't spend all our time talking about you."

I spun away and tried to run for the hotel, but Ian executed a half tackle, and the keys flew out of my hands, jangling across the gravel. I scrambled for them, but Ian got there first.

He ran for the car. "Let's go!" he shouted, tossing the keys to Rowan, but Rowan didn't follow. Instead, he carefully placed the keys in his pocket, surveying me seriously. "Just come with us on our first stop. The airport's a straight shot from the Burren. We'll make it in plenty of time."

Burren. Where had I heard that word before? *You know where, buttercup,* a little voice said. Guidebook Lady. Of course.

"Are you talking about the place of stone?" I asked.

He brightened, shoving his glasses up enthusiastically. "You've heard of it?"

"I read about it last night." *Ireland for the Heartbroken* had a whole section on the Burren, right after the Cliffs of Moher entry. What were the odds that Ian's first stop on his not-happening road trip was also in my heartbreak guide? My stance shifted. "You really think we'd make it on time?"

"Absolutely." Rowan flashed me a friendly smile.

Ian made a strangled noise, then positioned himself between us. "Look, Rowan, I appreciate what you're trying to do here, but this is a bad idea." And just in case Rowan didn't get the point, he kept going. "A *really* bad idea. We need to stick to the original plan."

"It is not a *really* bad idea," I protested.

"But we would be following the original plan, just with a minor detour to the airport. It wouldn't put us behind at all." Rowan's voice was slow with uncertainty, his eyebrows bent. He didn't have to say it for us to hear it: *Why are you being such a jerk about this?*

Ian's shoulders sagged, and his right hand disappeared nervously into his hair. "But . . . there's a lot of stuff in your car. Where would she sit?"

"Easy. She's a little yoke. We'll make room." *A little yoke?* Rowan lifted his chin up to me. "You don't mind a tight squeeze for an hour or so, do you?"

I leaned over to look through the back window. Ian wasn't exaggerating. Not only did the car have the tiniest back seat in existence, but it was packed full the way Archie's and

Walter's cars were whenever they left to start a new semester at college. A jumble of clothes, books, and toiletries. For once, being tiny was going to pay off. "I can make it work."

Ian shifted back and forth between his feet, absent-mindedly strumming the zipper on his jacket. He was torn. No matter what he said, he didn't feel okay about abandoning me at the hotel. The big brother was too strong in him. I was going to have to use it to my advantage.

"Look, it makes sense." Rowan held out the cereal box to Ian, but he waved it off. "What you guys need is some time to get used to this idea. Going to the Burren will give us that time."

"This is a bad idea," Ian repeated.

"You already said that." Two scenarios played through my head. Best case, I used the extra time to talk some sense into Ian. Worst case, I saw another guidebook site, and maybe got one step closer to healing my broken heart—that is, if Guidebook Lady knew what she was talking about—before continuing on to Italy alone. My mental Magic 8 Ball tumbled out an answer: *All signs point to yes.*

I took an authoritative step toward Rowan. "I need you to give me the keys."

"Do *not* give them to her," Ian ordered.

One of Rowan's eyebrows lifted, a smile pulling at the corner of his mouth.

"I have to go get my suitcase. And I need insurance that you aren't just going to leave while I'm gone."

"Rowan . . . ," Ian warned.

Rowan nodded thoughtfully and threw them to me in one smooth motion, his grin still playing on his face. His smiles felt like a payday. "Sorry, Ian. She's right: I wouldn't leave us alone in the parking lot either. And I'm a sucker for a well-thought-out argument."

Victory.

Ian shook his hair into his face and crossed his arms tightly. "Addison Jane Bennett, if you are not back down here in five minutes, I will come looking for you."

Rowan's dimple dented his cheek. "Better hurry, Addison Jane."

"Addison Jane Bennett. B-minus in geometry? I thought you were straight As all the way."

I stumbled back into the doorway, hand to my chest. It was early one morning in July, and either I was hallucinating or Cubby Jones was standing in my kitchen looking at my report card.

I blinked hard, but when I looked again, he was still there. Only now he'd deployed the signature grin, one hand still on the fridge. A lot had changed since the morning I'd made him waffles. Cubby's smile didn't go all the way up to his eyes anymore, and something about it looked calculated, like he'd figured out its power and was using it to his advantage. Like now.

"What are you doing here?" I managed to choke out.

He grinned again, then pulled himself up onto the counter in an easy, athletic motion. "Don't try to change the subject. B-minus? What does your honor student brother think of that?"

"I bombed the final," I said, attempting and failing at non-chalant. "And you know report cards are confidential, right? Meant only for the person they're addressed to." I attempted to snatch the paper from his grip, but he held on to it tighter, pulling me toward him before he let go. And suddenly I was twelve years old again, in this very kitchen, looking into his eyes for the first time and noticing that Cubby was different. The memory must have hit him, too, because this time the old Cubby was back, his smile climbing to his eyes.

"So"—he cleared his throat, looking me up and down—"are you going out for a run?"

I quickly crossed my arms over my chest, remembering what I was wearing. A ratty T-shirt and an ancient pair of volleyball shorts that were so short, I only wore them to bed or for quick trips to the kitchen for early-morning Pop-Tarts. Or in this case, quick trips to the kitchen that resulted in running into my long-time crush.

Sometimes I hated my life.

"No run. I'm just, um . . ." I bit my lip nervously, desperate

to get out of there but also desperate to stay. "What are you doing here, Cubby?"

"No one calls me Cubby anymore, Addison," he said, tilting his head slightly.

"Well, no one calls me Addison. And the question stands." I edged toward the hallway, the tile cold under my bare feet. Cubby's stare ignited too many feelings in my stomach—and they tangled into a knot. Why did I have to look so gross? Upstairs, the bathroom door slammed shut.

"I'm picking up your brother. Coach called for an extra practice this morning, and Ian said you had the car today."

"We have joint custody," I said. "This weekend it's mine."

Cubby nodded knowingly. "But you made sure to explain to the car that it isn't his fault, right? And that you both love him very much?"

A laugh burst out of me just as Ian appeared in the doorway. His hair was wet from the shower, and the strings from the two sweatshirts he wore tangled together. He was the only person I knew who ever wore two hoodies at once. How he managed to put them on was an unsolved mystery that I had been attempting to put to rest for several years now.

Cubby lifted his chin. "Hey, Bennett."

Ian nodded at him sleepily, then squinted his eyes at me. "Addie, why are you up so early?"

"I was on the phone with Lina." The time difference meant

I sometimes had to get up really early if I wanted to talk to her.

He looked at my pajamas and wrinkled his face. I didn't have to be a mind reader to know what he was thinking.

"Bye, Addison." Cubby smiled disarmingly, then jumped off the counter, giving me a long look as he followed Ian out.

"Bye, Cubby," I called back, my heart hummingbird-fast. The second he was out of sight I fell against the counter. Why did I always have to act like a lovestruck third grader? I might as well walk around with a T-shirt that reads I ♥ CUBBY JONES.

Suddenly, Cubby's face appeared around the corner. "Hey, Addie, you want to hang out sometime?"

I shot back up to standing. "Um . . . yes?" You'd think that living with so many brothers would mean I'd know how to talk to guys, but I didn't. It just meant I knew how to defend myself. And the way Cubby was looking at me—really looking at me—I had no defense for. It set my capillaries on fire.

Back in the hotel room I set a world record by getting dressed, packing my suitcase, and locating my phone, all in less than six minutes. Once my sneakers were laced, I stuck my head into the bathroom to check for Ian's alleged note. Sure enough, there was a folded-up square of paper wedged into the corner of the mirror, my name spelled out in Ian's miniscule handwriting.

"Ian, come on," I groaned. Chances were I wouldn't even have seen it there.

I jammed the note in my pocket, then wheeled my suitcase to the doorway, pausing when I caught sight of the guidebook peeking out from under my cot. I hurried over and scooped it up. I didn't like the idea of stealing from the gnomes' library, but something about the guidebook's crinkled pages made me feel better. Less alone. And besides, what if Guidebook Lady was telling the truth? What if she *was* an expert on heartbreak? I needed all the help I could get. Maybe I'd figure out how to mail the guidebook back to the gnomes from Italy.

Outside, the car was right where I'd left it and Rowan stood rummaging through the trunk. Now that I wasn't engaged in actively fighting off my brother, I could actually take Rowan in. He was taller than I'd expected and really skinny—like half the size of Archie or Walter. But even so, he definitely had what my mom called "presence." Like he could walk into any lunchroom anywhere and ten girls would look up from their ham sandwiches and whisper, *Who's that?* in identical breathy voices.

Good thing my breathy voice had been scared into permanent hibernation.

"Welcome back." Rowan took my suitcase, tossing it into the trunk.

I pointed to the bumper stickers plastering the back of the car. "Did you pick all of those, or were they a preexisting condition?"

"Definitely preexisting. I've only owned the car for three weeks."

IMAGINE WHIRLED PEAS

THIS CAR IS POWERED BY PURE IRISH LUCK

TEAM OXFORD COMMA

CUPCAKES ARE MUFFINS
THAT DIDN'T GIVE UP ON THEIR DREAMS

"The muffin one is pretty funny," I said, hugging the guidebook to my side.

"I think so too. It may be the whole reason I bought this car. There wasn't a whole lot to love otherwise."

I shook my head. "Not true. This car is equipped with a rare sagging tailpipe. I'm sure people go crazy over those at car shows."

"Wait. Is that a joke, or is the tailpipe actually sagging?" He looked anxiously at the roof of his car, his gaze a solid six feet above where the tailpipe actually resided. Yikes. I think it was safe to say Rowan was *not* a car person.

"Uh . . . that pipe thing?" I said, pointing under the back bumper. "It lets exhaust out of your car. If it starts dragging on the ground, it'll make a loud, horrible noise."

"Oh . . ." He exhaled, a blush spreading across his cheeks. "Actually, I think it was making that noise. On the way here. Especially when the road got bumpy. But Clover makes a lot of horrible noises, so I thought it was just business as usual." He patted the car affectionately.

"Clover?"

Rowan pointed to the most prominent bumper sticker, a large, faded shamrock. "Her namesake."

"How Irish."

"Nothing like a good stereotype," he countered, his mouth twisting into another smile. I wished he'd stop with the smiling. It kept conjuring up memories of another notable smile.

"Time to go." Ian stuck his head out the window, drumming his hands against the side. I don't think he meant for it to, but his excited expression landed squarely on me. "Addie, I cleared you a spot. It will probably work best if you climb in from this side."

I rushed over, eager to keep up the goodwill, but when I looked inside, the glow that Ian's smile had created instantly faded away. He had somehow managed to stack Rowan's items into a teetering pile that almost touched the ceiling. The only actual space was behind Ian's seat, and it was just the right size for three malnourished squirrels and a hedgehog. If they all sucked in.

"Grand, Ian," Rowan said from behind me. "You worked a wonder back here."

He was either a liar or a serious optimist. "Um, yeah . . . a really great job, Ian," I echoed, bracing my hands on either side of the window. I needed to keep things positive. "So how am I getting in there exactly?"

"Tunnel in," Ian said. "You can just climb over me."

"Great." I threw my leg in through the window, managing to keep the guidebook pressed to my side as I climbed onto the middle console.

"What are you holding?" Ian asked, reaching up for the book.

I quickly tossed it into the back seat. "It's a guidebook about Ireland."

"Oh, right. The one you read about the Burren in," Rowan said.

"Right." I hovered, unsure of my next step. Circumventing the pile was not going to be a straightforward process.

"Maybe put your foot on the . . . ," Rowan started, but I was already midfling, Rowan's possessions snagging at every bit of exposed skin on my body. I landed in a heap.

"There was probably a less violent way to do that," Ian said.

Rowan raised his eyebrows. "There was definitely a less violent way to do that. But none quite so entertaining."

Crunchy, sun-faded velvet lined the back seat, which smelled vaguely of cheese. And Ian's seat was so close to mine that my knees barely fit in the space. I jammed my legs in as best as I could, wincing at the tight squeeze, then poked at the pile. "Rowan, what is all this stuff?"

"Long story." He started up the car, pointing to Ian's black eye. "So, are you going to tell me what happened, or will it just be the big mystery of the trip?"

"Ask her." Ian hiked his thumb back at me. "She's the one responsible."

Rowan turned and looked at me appraisingly. "Wow. You always so aggressive?"

"Always," Ian answered for me. Was it just my imagination or was that a thin layer of pride spread atop all that exasperation? Either way, I didn't protest. Rowan thinking I was dangerous might work to my advantage.

"Ready?" Rowan asked. Before we could reply, he hit the gas, accelerating so hard that the pile shimmied, spitting out a handful of records and one dress shoe. A group of birds scattered as we peeled brazenly out of the parking lot and onto the sunlit road, sprays of rose petals shooting out behind us.

Or at least that's what I imagined our exit looked like. There was too much stuff blocking my view for me to know for sure.

* * *

I assumed that once we were on the open road, a few things would be cleared up. For example, what a tourist site in western Ireland had to do with my brother's favorite band. But instead of explaining, Ian produced a massive, scribbled-on map of Ireland that he'd apparently been carrying around in his backpack, and Rowan passed around his box of cold cereal, and the two of them commenced to yell at each other.

Not angry yelling, *happy* yelling, part necessity due to the loud music—because as Rowan explained, the volume knob was missing—and part excitement. It was as if the two of them had been holding back an arsenal of things to say, and now that they were face-to-face, they had to get it all out or risk annihilation. And Rowan was as big of a music nerd as Ian was, maybe even more so. Ten minutes in, they'd covered:

- An eighties musician named Bruce something who was famous for composing guitar symphonies that involved bringing thirty-plus guitarists onstage at once
- Whether or not minimalism is a sign of a truly great musician
- Something called "punk violence," which Rowan claimed (and Ian enthusiastically agreed) was the natural balance to the synth-pop genre that emerged through early MTV
- Why the term "indie" meant nothing anymore now that massive indie labels were churning out artists assembly-line style

I was torn between listening to Ian in his element and trying not to have a panic attack every time I looked at the road. Rowan was the kind of driver every parent dreads. His speed hovered just below breakneck, and he had some kind of psychic method for determining which curves in the road didn't require remaining in his own lane.

But I was the only one worrying. Ian's excited voice climbed higher and higher until it was resting on the roof of the car, and he alternated between his favorite fidget modes: knee bouncing, finger drumming, and hair twisting. Wasn't he supposed to be explaining things to me?

My phone chimed, and I fumbled quickly for it, tuning out their conversation as I pulled up a behemoth text:

(1) Thank you for subscribing to LINA'S CAT FACTS—the fun way to quit ignoring your best friend and learn something feline in the process! Did you know that when a family cat died in ancient Egypt, family members mourned by shaving off their eyebrows? And bonus fact: Did you know you are in danger of having YOUR eyebrows shaved off? BY ME? (Mostly due to the fact that you are arriving in Italy today and I haven't heard from you in A WEEK AND A HALF?) In order to receive double the number of Daily Cat Facts—please continue to ignore me. Thanks again for your subscription, and have a PURRRfect day!

"Oh, no," I whispered to myself. Immediately, Lina's texts began dropping in like fuzzy hair balls. Egyptian family members were just the beginning.

(2) Cats who fall five stories have a 90 percent survival rate. Friends who ignore their friends for longer than 7 days have a 3 percent chance of remaining friends (and then only if they have a really good reason). Thanks again for your subscription, and have a PURRRfect day!

(3) A group of kittens is called a kindle. A group of adult cats is called a clowder. People who stop talking to their best friends for absolutely no good reason are jerks. This is not a CAT FACT. It is just a fact. Thanks again for your subscription, and have a PURRRfect day!

(4) Back in the 1960s, the CIA turned a cat into a tiny spy by implanting a microphone and camera into her ear and spine. Unfortunately, Spy Cat's mission was cut short when she immediately ran out into traffic and was flattened by an oncoming taxi. This reminded me of the time you decided to visit me in Italy and then the week before completely stopped talking to me. ARE YOU EVEN COMING ANYMORE?? Thanks again for your subscription, and have a PURRRfect day!

Guilt twisted painfully in my gut. I had to respond to that one.

So so so so so sorry. And of course I'm still coming to Italy. Explain everything once I'm there.

"Is that Mom?" Ian's voice bypassed Rowan's pile of stuff to hit me in the face. He held a lock of wet and stringy hair near his mouth.

"That is disgusting," I said, pointing to his hair. "And no. It's Lina."

He chomped down on the lock. "What's she saying?"

"How excited she is to see both of us. You know, because *both* of us will be there?" I wiggled my eyebrows at him. Sometimes humor worked really well on Ian.

"Keep dreaming," he said. Guess it wasn't going to work today.

"Addie, you want any cereal?" Rowan shoved his box of Sugar Puffs through the space between the seats.

"No. Thank you." I leaned back, rubbing my thigh. Being crammed into such a tiny space had set my left leg on fire with pins and needles. "So when are you guys going to fill me in?"

"Fill you in on what?" Ian dropped his hair out of his mouth, and it bounced perkily off his shoulder.

"On your master plan." I gestured to the map. "You can start with what the Burren has to do with Titletrack."

Ian's knee shook. "Nice try, sis. We have one hour until we drop you off at the airport, and the deal is you stay quiet until then. So you just sit tight back there, okay?"

I hated when Ian used that condescending tone with me. It only came out when he was trying to leverage his role as big brother. Fifteen months was not a lot of extra experience, but according to him all of creation had happened during that time period. "What deal? No deal was made."

He flipped around, giving me a bouncy smile that caught me off guard. Even with me here, he was happier than I'd seen him all summer. "Your getting in this car was proof that you agreed to our terms and conditions. It was a contractual agreement."

"And let me guess. You're in charge of the terms?" I asked.

"Exactly." He patted my arm patronizingly. "Now you're getting it."

I shoved his hand away. "You know what? Never mind. This is actually really great. Instead of thinking about an Irish road trip that you're not taking, I can spend my time looking at the view and thinking about what a great time we're going to have in Florence."

"Keep dreaming, sis."

Rowan met my eyes in the rearview mirror, the corners of his mouth turning up in an amused smile. I hoped he'd lobby for me—after all, he was the one who'd suggested we use this little side trip as a way to get things out in the open—but instead, he and Ian dove right back into their conversation. The pull of the music was too strong.

I crouched forward to scout for clues on Ian's map. A string of *X*s looped in a crescent along the bottom of Ireland, each site surrounded by a mini flurry of tiny Ian handwriting. Most of the writing was concentrated around six numbered spots:

1. Poulnabrone
2. Slea Head
3. Torc Manor
4. An Bohair Pub
5. Rock of Cashel

And the grand finale, written in large letters:

ELECTRIC PICNIC

Great. I knew an Ian project when I saw one. Any time he found something he was really interested in, he dug in, and no amount of coaxing could peel him away from it. Once he committed, he went all in. That's what made him such a great athlete.

I shimmied his note out of my back pocket.

Addie,

Change of plans. Not going with you to Italy.
Tell Lina and her dad that I had to go home
early for practice. Tell Mom and Dad that I'm
with you. Will meet up with you for the flight
home. Will explain later.

—Ian

Was he serious? I heaved myself forward again, thrusting the paper under Ian's nose. "This was your note? Your big explanation? This doesn't even look like your handwriting! I would have thought you were kidnapped!"

Ian startled, like he'd forgotten I was back there. He probably had. He snatched the note from me. "I was going for brevity."

"Nailed it," I said.

"Let me see it." Rowan took the note and read it aloud, his musical voice making it sound even more cryptic. "Wow, that is bad."

Ian grabbed the paper, stuffing it into his backpack. "I wanted it to be like in war movies where people only have the information they need. That way, when they get captured by the enemy, they can't have the information tortured out of them."

"Tortured out of them?" I said incredulously.

He hunched his shoulders sheepishly. "You know what I mean. I just thought it would be better for you if you didn't have all the facts."

"I still don't have all the facts." I yanked at my right leg, managing to free it from the crevice. If Ian wouldn't tell me what was going on, maybe Rowan would. I fixed my eyes on the back of his neck. His hair was slightly longer at the nape.

"So who are you exactly?" I asked, using my friendliest Catarina-approved voice. She was big on curiosity as a means of persuasion. Start by acting interested.

I don't know if it was my question or sparkly tone, but his eyes flicked toward me warily. "Rowan. We met back at the hotel? You told me my bumper was sagging?"

"That sounds dirty," Ian said.

"It was your tailpipe," I wailed, dropping the act. "Never mind. That part doesn't matter. What I want to know is why you"—I pointed at him—"clearly Irish, and my brother"—I pointed at Ian—"clearly American, are acting like best friends. And don't just say 'online' again. People who only know each other online don't complete each other's sentences."

"Isn't this a violation of the terms and conditions?" Rowan asked, calling upon what Ian had said earlier. Ian gave him a smirk equivalent to a fist bump.

"True, it is a clear violation . . . ," I started, but I paused to think. What I needed was a cohesive argument. It had worked before in persuading Rowan to give me the keys. "Rowan, the thing is that I'm much more likely to be supportive of Ian's plans if I know what is going on."

"Riiiiight," Ian said, dragging out the word.

"I am," I insisted. "I didn't come with you on your first stop just so I could sit back here listening to you guys dissect the music industry." Saying "first stop" felt like a dangerous concession. It suggested the possibility of the road trip.

Rowan took both hands off the wheel to adjust his glasses. "She's right. This is why she's came with us in the first place— to give her some time to get used to the idea."

Or talk you out of the idea, I added silently.

"Fine. Fall for her evil tactics. But don't come crying to me when she makes your life a living hell." Ian fell into a heap against his window. I'd always thought he'd missed his calling by not signing up for drama club.

Rowan lifted his chin curiously in the rearview mirror.

I shrugged. "By all means, continue. I'll let you know when my evil tactics kick in."

His dimple winked at me. "Right. Well, Ian and I talk a lot. Like most days. And we've known each other since last summer. Well, I guess 'known' isn't quite the right word, is it?" No comment from Ian. Rowan continued nervously. "At first I was just familiar with his work. I read his first series of articles, and we started e-mailing from there. And then—"

"You read his first series of what?" I interrupted.

Ian made a barely audible groan, and Rowan's eyebrows knit in confusion. "I'm sorry, but I was under the impression that you two had met? Addie, meet Ian Bennett, esteemed teen music journalist. Ian, meet Addie, parking lot tackler extraordinaire."

Music journalist? I jammed my knees into the back of Ian's seat. "This is a joke, right?"

Rowan cleared his throat. "Um, sorry, but is *this* a joke?"

"Addie, I write articles, okay?" Ian propped his feet up on the dashboard and yanked irritably at his shoelaces. "I used to have a blog, but now I get paid to write articles for online publications."

"Ha ha," I said. "And you also love My Little Pony, right?"

"What are those guys called?" Rowan asked. "Bronies?"

Ian shot me a dirty-as-mud look, and I flinched. He was serious—and hurt. I could see it in the way he jutted his chin out. "Wait. You really do have a blog? Like online?"

"Yes, it's online. Where else would it be?" He scowled.

"But . . ." I hesitated, waiting for the pieces to fall into place, like they usually did. They didn't. "You have a *blog* blog? Like the kind you add entries to?"

"Yeah . . . like a website run by an individual? They're usually pretty informal," Rowan said helpfully, his voice kind. "It's pretty easy to sign up for one."

I blinked a couple of times. Anyone else would have

made fun of me. He was too nice for his own good. "Thanks, Rowan, but it's not the idea of a blog that's tripping me up. I'm just having a hard time believing that Ian has one." The thought of Ian coming home from practice to pour his feelings out in an online diary was so far in the realm of not possible that it technically didn't exist.

"Why can't you believe it?" Ian demanded, his mouth pressed into a tight line. He sounded exactly the way I had when talking to Archie last night. *Why, you think it's impossible that a popular football player would like someone like me?* "Because jocks aren't allowed to do anything but play sports? Thanks for stereotyping me."

"Ugh. Ian, no one's stereotyping you." Lately, Ian had had a huge chip on his shoulder about being seen as The Jock— impossible when he worked so hard to look alternative. And why did he mind the role anyway? It raised him to the level of high school god. "I just don't get how you'd even have time to write. During the school year you're either doing homework or playing sports."

"I make time," Ian said. "And what do you think I've been doing all summer?"

Finally, something clicked into place. Except for when he was at practice, Ian had spent most of the summer stationed at his computer. "Mom said you were working on college admissions essays."

He let out one of those harsh noises that sometimes passes as a laugh. "I have definitely not been working on college admissions essays. Unless you count creating a portfolio for journalism schools as a college application. If so, then yes."

"Journalism school? Does Washington State even have a journalism program?"

Ian slammed his hands on the dashboard, making Rowan and me jump. "I'm not going to Washington State."

"Whoa. Ian, you okay there?" Rowan asked. Ian lifted his chin slightly, as if he was rearing for a fight.

"What do you mean you're not going to Washington State? They scouted you earlier this summer. They're going to offer you a full-ride scholarship," I reminded him. And if this scholarship didn't work out, then another one would. Great grades plus incredible player equals money.

"I don't care about the football scholarship," Ian said, lowering his voice to a simmer.

"Why, because you won the lottery?"

"So fill me in here," Rowan broke in, his voice confused. "You two are obviously brother and sister, but were you separated at birth? Mom took one, Dad took the other? Or did one of you only recently learn English so that's why you've never communicated before?"

The tips of Ian's ears suddenly turned red. "It's pretty hard to communicate with someone who spent their whole summer lying to you."

I grabbed the back of his seat, my ears as red as his. They were our ultimate anger indicators. "Don't try to make this about Cubby. And besides, you're one to talk. You apparently have a whole secret life."

"It's not a 'whole secret life,'" he snapped, imitating my tone. "It was just this summer. And I would have told you if you weren't so busy sneaking around with Cubby."

"You have to stop bringing him up," I yelled.

Rowan tapped Clover's brakes firmly, lurching both of us forward. If we hadn't been the only ones on the road, we would have been rear-ended for sure. "Look, guys," Rowan began, "I get that you're dealing with some issues here, but I've been around enough arguing to last a lifetime. So, Ian, how about you bring Addie up to speed on what is apparently your dual life? I'm pretty curious myself how you've managed to keep this a secret from your family."

"It isn't that hard to keep it a secret. Unless it's about football, no one cares what I do." Ian dropped his shoulders, tension framing his eyes. "Fine. Addie, what do you want to know?"

Where to begin? "What's your blog's name?"

"*My Lexicon*," Ian said.

"How do you spell that?" I pulled out my phone and typed

it in as Rowan spelled. Not only did the blog exist, but it looked way more professional than a seventeen-year-old's blog should, with a sleek monochromatic theme and MY LEXICON spelled out in all caps across the top.

"It's a reference to a Bob Dylan quote," Rowan explained before I could ask. "'The songs are my lexicon. I believe the songs.'"

Ian crossed his arms angrily. "My blog is how I got my gig with IndieBlurb. I do a weekly column with them."

"It's called Indie Ian's Week in Five," Rowan said.

"Indie Ian? That's, like, your handle?" I kept waiting for one of them to crack a smile, but neither of them did. "Fine. What are the five?"

"They're music categories." Ian listed them off on his fingers. "Worth the hype, overhyped, covered, classic, and obscure. Every week I choose a song to fit into each." He exhaled loudly. "Why are you having such a hard time believing this? I've always liked writing. And music. I tried to be on the school newspaper last year, but Coach wouldn't let me do it. He said he didn't want me to lose my focus."

Coach had said that? A flurry of sibling protectiveness roared in my head.

Rowan jumped in. "Ian has a huge following on Twitter. Every time he publishes something, a hashtag goes around—#IndieIanSpeaks. That's how I found him."

"It isn't a huge following," Ian said modestly, but pride ringed the edges of his voice.

"You have ten thousand followers; how is that not huge?" Rowan said.

Ten thousand? Not bad.

Ian shook his hair into his eyes. "No, it's never been ten thousand. Every time I get close, I post something in the 'overhyped' category that offends people, and there's a mass exodus. My tombstone's going to say, 'Always fifty followers short of ten thousand.'" Rowan snorted.

I pulled out my phone to verify the Twitter account. The profile photo on @IndieIan11 was an up-close shot of Ian's eyes, his long hair framing the right side of the square. 9.9K followers. A massive party I hadn't been invited to. Hadn't even been told about.

I gripped the phone hard, a herd of feelings galloping across my chest. At least now I knew why Ian had been so distant all summer. He'd been living a secret online life. "Ian, why didn't you tell me about all this?" I asked.

He shook his head. "Why would I? It's not like you listen to anything I say anyway."

Cop-out answer. "Ian, for the last time, this isn't about Cubby. If Rowan found you a year ago, that means you were music"—I hesitated—"music journaling way before Cubby and I started hanging out."

"'Music journaling.' I like it." Rowan might as well have been wearing a referee jersey. He was desperate to stop our fight.

Ian turned back impatiently. "So tell me again, are you planning to tell Mom about Cubby during or after your trip to Florence?"

"Ian, we've been through this a dozen times. I am not telling her." My words vibrated loudly through the car. How had he even jumped to that? "And it's not my trip to Florence. It's *our* trip."

Even I didn't sound convinced.

The first time I ever lied to Ian, it was about Cubby. It was surprisingly easy.

It was during our last field trip together, and right away I realized something was different about this excursion from the others. Usually, our trips were to my brother's newest and most recent discoveries, but not this time.

"I've been coming here since I got my license," he said, as I aimed the flashlight at the troll's one visible eye, glistening as hard and shiny as a bead. Cars roared above us on the overpass.

Ian climbed up the statue's gnarled hand, settling into the curve between its head and neck. I let my light wander over the statue. The concrete troll was over twenty feet tall, and one of its plump hands clutched a life-size car in its monstrous grip. "Why have I never been here before?"

Ian stretched out over the arm. "I like to come here after practice. To think."

"To think about what? How you're going to dominate at the next game?" I teased.

He made a noise in the back of his throat, quickly changing the subject. "Did you notice how blobby the troll is? It's because people spray-paint him, and the only way to remove the paint is to cover him up with more cement."

"Nice segue," I said. Lately, Ian had been dodging every conversation that had anything to do with football. But tonight I wasn't going to pry. It was nice just to be with him. I felt like I hadn't seen much of him lately.

I tucked the flashlight into my sweatshirt pocket and scrambled up to join him. For a while, we listened to the rhythmic rumbling of cars rushing overhead. Their predictable noises were comforting. I could see why Ian liked it here.

"Where were you last night?" he suddenly asked, and my heart raced faster than the cars on the highway.

I avoided looking him in the eye. "I went to bed early."

He shook his head. "I came into your room to see if you wanted to watch SNL. You were gone on Tuesday night too. How are you getting out? The window? Kind of ballsy to climb out past Mom and Dad's room."

Very ballsy. Particularly for a person who was five foot one on a good day trying to descend a tree whose branches were spaced out at least five feet apart.

"I was probably in the kitchen," I said, surprised by how easily the lie slipped through my mouth. I'd never lied to Ian before, never even really considered it. But then, I guess I'd never had a reason before. A small smile invaded my face. I couldn't help it.

He raised his eyebrows. "So now that I know how you're sneaking out, the question is who are you sneaking out with?"

I pressed my lips together, sealing in my secret. Sometimes it felt like everything I owned had once belonged to one of my brothers, and as much as I loved them, I loved the idea of having something all to myself even more.

After a few seconds Ian let out a long and exaggerated sigh. "Fine. Be that way." He slid off the troll, his sneakers thudding heavily onto the ground. "But you know I'll find out eventually."

Taking me to the troll was Ian's attempt at drawing out my secret: I'll tell you one of mine, you tell me one of yours.

Unfortunately, I wasn't going to be the one to tell him.

Rowan's car raced down the twisted road as I watched Ireland suddenly morph into something remote and ferocious. Roofless stone structures lined the narrow roads, moss blanketing them softly in green. Everything looked abandoned, which for some reason made my internal clock tick even louder. I had less than an hour to convince Ian to abandon his plan.

Luckily, I had a secret weapon. Two weeks ago, my mom and I had driven over an hour north to visit her aunt, and I'd gotten stuck listening to a new Catarina Hayford recording called "Modes of Persuasion." Back then I hadn't thought I would ever need it. But now I needed to draw on the experts. Step one: act curious. "So what exactly does the Burren have to do with Titletrack?"

The bruise under Ian's eye looked at me accusingly. "Listen, Catarina. We're working on a strictly need-to-know basis here. Also, no one invited you, so quit asking questions."

"I was not being Catarina," I snapped. I guess he'd listened to that one too.

"Yes, you were. Rule number one," he said in a surprisingly good impression of Catarina's throaty voice, "act curious."

"I'd ask who Catarina is, but you'd probably both rip my head off," Rowan said.

"You're safe on this one," Ian assured him. "She's a real estate guru who spends all of her free time getting spray tans. She turned our mom into a Seattle real estate mogul."

"I didn't know your mom was in real estate." Rowan slid his eyes curiously at Ian. For someone who was so close to my brother, he knew surprisingly little about him. He hadn't even known Walt's name.

"Rule number two: Never meet the client halfway. Meet them all the way." Ian flicked his hair behind his shoulder and pursed his lips convincingly. "Rule number three: Be realistic and optimistic. The future belongs to the hopeful."

I flicked him on the shoulder. "Ian, stop."

He snorted and dropped the pose, ducking down to look out the windshield. "Rowan, is this Corofin?"

"No. That was the first town. This is Killinaboy. Also, I'm overruling your terms and conditions." Rowan's gaze fell on me, light as a butterfly. "Your sister needs to know what we're doing."

"What? Why?" he asked.

"Because if she knows why you're taking off without her, maybe she'll retaliate less."

"Rowan, believe me. She won't retaliate less," Ian said.

"She can hear you," I reminded them, my gaze snagged on yet another attempt by Rowan to adjust his glasses. The way he pushed them up was the perfect combination of endearing and nerdy. If he didn't seem so clueless about it, I'd think he was doing it on purpose. "And, Ian, I'm starting to like your friend here. Unlike you, he actually considers other people's feelings."

I meant for it to be funny, but I heard my mistake the second it was out of my mouth. Ian took loyalty very seriously—just hinting that he was letting someone down was enough to make him snap.

He twisted around. "Right. Because I never care about your feelings. Because I never, ever stand up for you or help you with school or clean up your mistakes."

My cheeks scalded. Had he just lumped helping me with school in with Cubby? "Did you really just say that?" I demanded.

Rowan verbally threw himself in between us. "Okay, guys. Let's talk about Titletrack. When they first started out, they couldn't get anyone to sign them, so they started posting songs online and performing in pubs around Ireland. Eventually, they talked a radio station into playing one of their songs, and it was requested so many times that it ended up on the top ten charts. After that, labels couldn't ignore them."

There was a long, awkward pause, but the oddly timed description worked. We weren't fighting anymore. Ian sank down into his seat, his chin resting on his chest.

Rowan kept going, probably in hopes of squelching another eruption. "And Titletrack's final concert is in three days. They made the announcement earlier this year and swore they aren't going to do that stupid thing bands do where they retire and then do a bunch of reunion tours."

"I hate that," Ian said, rechanneling his anger.

It was Titletrack's final concert? This was more hopeless than I thought. "So what does the Burren have to do with anything?" I asked again, carefully.

Rowan valiantly picked up the torch again. "So Ian's idea—which was brilliant, I might add—is to visit some of those early places that were important to the band and write a piece that culminates at the picnic. Kind of like following their footprints all the way to Electric Picnic." He paused. "Ian, that's what you should title it!"

"Hmmm," Ian said noncommittally.

"Anyway, the Burren is where they filmed their first music video for a song called 'Classic,' which is, in my humble opinion, the greatest song in the world."

"It is," Ian confirmed. He leaned forward, and his hair fell into a waterfall around his face. "I played it for you on the way to school a couple of times. It's the one that talks about slippery simplicity."

I did remember the song. I'd even requested it a few times, mostly because I liked the way the singer rolled "slippery simplicity" through his mouth like a piece of butterscotch candy.

"Right," Rowan said. "We're going to document the whole trip, Ian posting pictures to his blog and social media. Then, when it's all done, he's going to submit the final article somewhere big."

"*Maybe* I'm going to submit it somewhere big," Ian said quickly.

"What do you mean, 'maybe'?" Rowan's voice sounded

incredulous. "If you don't, I'll do it for you. Your writing is definitely good enough, and I have a whole list of Irish music magazines that would go crazy over it."

"So this is like serious fanboying meets research trip," I said. Each new fact pushed me a little closer toward hopeless.

"Exactly." Rowan punched the air enthusiastically. "And your aunt's wedding? Best coincidence to ever befall planet Earth."

Ian smiled at Rowan, his anger forgotten. Zero to sixty, sixty to zero. It could go both ways. After a lifetime of fights, I should be used to it, but it still caught me off guard sometimes. Especially now, when I'd thought we were headed for another grand mal fight, like the one at the cliffs. "I couldn't believe it," Ian said. "I mean, what are the odds of me being in Ireland during their final concert?"

For Ian? High. Life liked to make things work for him.

I crumpled into the back seat, resignation settling over me in a fine layer. Ireland was enchanting, Rowan was Ian's best friend soul mate, and Ian's favorite band was doing a once-in-a-lifetime show. I'd lost before I'd even begun.

I curled up tightly, hooking my arms around my knees. "I need you guys to be really fast at the Burren. And, Ian, did you cancel your ticket to Italy?"

Ian started to look back but caught himself halfway. "No, but I checked with the airline. They'll just give my seat away when I don't show up." He had enough compassion to keep the victory out of his voice.

Italy and Lina reached out, warm and inviting. Sunshine, gelato, art, scooters, spaghetti, my best friend. I closed my eyes and clung hard to the image. Leaving Ian in Ireland wasn't what I'd had in mind, but maybe it would be good for us. The next hour couldn't go fast enough.

"Fine," I said, falling back dejectedly against my seat. "You win. You always win."

The Burren

Ah, the Burren. *An Bhoireann.* The place of stone. Arguably the most desolate, bleak, miserable excuse of a landscape that has ever graced God's (mostly) green earth. An early admirer said, "There isn't a tree to hang a man, water to drown a man, nor soil to bury a man."

You're going to love it.

But before this love affair begins, let's start with a little Irish geography. Three hundred forty million years ago, the Emerald Isle looked a tad bit different than it does today. Not only were there no pubs or Irish preteens scouring Penneys department stores, but it was covered by water—a great big tropical ocean, in fact, that was absolutely teeming with life. Animals, fish, plants, you name it, all paddling around snapping at one another in certain barbaric bliss. But as every Disney movie has taught us, at some point those creatures had to die (usually horrifically and in front of their children), and as their bones gathered at the bottom of the ocean, an ancient primordial recipe was put into action, one that can be roughly summed up in the following equation:

$$\text{bones} + \text{compression} + \text{millions of years} = \text{limestone}$$

And that's exactly what was formed. Limestone. Ten square miles of it, in fact. And once it was done with its stint as the ocean's floor, that limestone came rising to the surface, forming the bleak, unique landscape your plucky little feet are standing on today. Which brings me to another equation, not entirely related but helpful all the same:

$$courage + time = healed\ heart$$

Spelled out that way, it all seems rather doable, doesn't it, chickadee? I mean, the fact that you've somehow managed to get yourself to the Emerald Isle lets me know we're all good on the courage bit. And as for the time bit? Well, that will come. Minute by minute, hour by hour, time will stretch and build and compress until one day you'll find yourself standing on the surface of something newly risen and think, *Huh. I did it.*

You'll do it, buttercup. You really will.

HEARTACHE HOMEWORK: See those wildflowers popping up from amongst the stone, pet? Don't worry. I'm not going to make an overworked point about beauty in pain. But I do want you to pick a few of those, one for each of your people. And by "your people," I mean the ones you can count on to stand by you as you wade through this. Put yourself in a circle of them and draw on their power. Be sure to pick one for me.

—Excerpt from *Ireland for the Heartbroken: An Unconventional Guide to the Emerald Isle, third edition*

"WHAT AM I LOOKING AT EXACTLY?" I ASKED AS ROWAN eased into a sticky parking lot. The Burren was less landscape and more hostile takeover. At first it was subtle, a few flat rocks cropping up in the fields like gray lily pads, but slowly the proportions of stone to grass increased until gray choked out all the cheery green. By the time Rowan slowed to pull over, we were engulfed in cold, depressing rock. A sign read POULNABRONE.

Guidebook Lady had said the Burren was depressing, but this was over-the-top.

Ian pointed to a small, drab structure in the distance. He was already poised for takeoff, seat belt undone, notebook in hand. "The Poulnabrone is a tomb. It's over two thousand years old."

I squinted my eyes, turning the tomb into a gray blur. "A tomb? No one said anything about a tomb."

Rowan slid the car into park, and Ian launched himself out the window feetfirst, his notebook tucked securely under his arm. "See you there!" he called over his shoulder. His sneakers made wet squelching sounds as he sprinted toward the tomb.

Rowan whistled admiringly, keeping his eyes on my brother. He'd been quiet ever since I'd conceded defeat to the

Titletrack plan. Ian had talked more, but he looked slightly uncomfortable, like he was wearing a shirt with a scratchy tag. Detecting Ian guilt was a subtle art; his natural energy made it difficult.

"He looks like one of those Jesus lizards. You know, the ones that move so fast, they can run on water?" Rowan said.

I heaved myself into the passenger seat. "Promise me you won't tell him that. The last thing we need is for Ian to get a Jesus lizard complex."

His dimple reappeared. "Promise."

The parking lot was one large, sludgy puddle that seeped into my sneakers the second I hit the ground. A thin shroud of clouds covered the sun, erasing even the illusion of warmth, and I wrapped my bare arms around myself. Why had no one bothered to tell me that Ireland was the climatic equivalent of a walk-in freezer? Once I arrived in Italy, I planned to spend my first few hours there baking in the sun like a loaf of ciabatta bread. And talking to Lina.

Lina will know soon. A violent shiver worked its way down my spine.

"You cold?" Rowan asked, looking at me over the top of the car.

"What makes you think that?" I asked jokingly. My teeth were seconds from chattering.

"Maybe the fact that you're shivering like a puppy in one

of those animal cruelty commercials? You have those commercials in the States, right? *For just sixty-three cents a day, you, too, can stop a blond girl from shivering. . . .* They used to be on the television all the time."

"Yep, we have those too." Archie had a soft spot for animals, and when we were young, we used to wait for the commercials to come on so we could call him into the room and watch him tear up. Siblings can be a special kind of cruel. When my dad found out, he'd lectured us on the fact that we were being cruel about an animal cruelty commercial, and we'd all donated a month's worth of our allowance to an animal rescue organization.

I plucked at my shorts. "When I packed, I was thinking about Italy, so all I brought were summer clothes. I didn't realize that Ireland spends all its time in Arctic winter."

"And you're here on a good day. Give me a minute." He ducked back into Clover, and I pulled my phone out of my back pocket. 9:03. I wanted to be at the airport by ten o'clock.

"Hey, Rowan, how long will it take us to get to the airport?" I asked.

"About forty-five minutes."

"Then we'd better keep this trip short. I don't want to cut our time close."

He reemerged, his hair slightly mussed. "Addie, what is this?"

For a second I thought he was talking about the navy-blue sweater he had wrapped around one arm, but then I realized he was holding something in his other hand too. The guidebook.

"Rowan, that's mine!" I staggered toward him, a tidal wave of embarrassment washing over me.

He studied the cover. "Yeah, I know it's yours. Is this the guidebook you were talking about? Why does it say it's about heartbreak?"

"I need you to give that back." I jumped up, and he let me snatch it from him. I pressed it to my side. "Why were you looking through my stuff anyway?"

"I was just trying to find you a sweater, and your book was under the seat. I thought it was one of mine." He took a step closer. "But now you've got me curious."

His eyes were puppy-dog soft, and I felt myself cave. And besides, explaining the guidebook didn't mean I had to spill everything about my heartbreak. "I found this in the library of the hotel. It takes you to important sites in Ireland and then assigns you tasks to do while you're there. It's supposed to help you get over having your heart broken."

"Do you think it would actually work?" The urgency in Rowan's voice made my eyes snap up. He stared hungrily at the guidebook.

"Uh . . . I'm not really sure," I said. "The writer is a little eccentric, but it seems like she knows her stuff. Who knows? Maybe it does work."

"So you're using the guidebook to help you get over Cubby?" he persisted.

Now he wanted to talk about Cubby too? I straightened up to shut him down, but he must have seen it coming because he quickly backpedaled. "Sorry. That was too personal. It's just that I've, uh"—he shoved his glasses up, fidgeting with the rims—"I've actually been through a bit of heartbreak myself." He met my eyes, and this time his gaze pleaded with me. "So if you've discovered some kind of magic guide for getting through it, please don't hold out on me."

The vulnerability in his eyes made my heart well up, and before I could talk myself out of it, I thrust the guide-book into his hands, the words spilling out of me: "Maybe you should try it out. There's a homework assignment for the Burren, and I could help you if you want." I always did this. Any time someone was in pain, I wanted to fix it immediately. "If you want, I'll leave the book in the car for you. Maybe you could stop by the sites on the way to your music festival."

He turned it over in his hands, slowly raising his eyes to mine. "Wow. That's really nice of you." He bit his lower lip. "Also, I'm really sorry about my part in keeping Ian from Italy. If I had known . . ."

I waved him off. "I'll survive. And I really do need some quality time with Lina, so maybe it will be better if Ian isn't there anyway."

He nodded, then lifted the book eagerly, hope crossing his face. "If you don't mind, I think I'm going to give the homework thing a shot."

"Of course not. I don't mind at all," I said eagerly, my insides glowing the way they always did when I helped someone.

"Then I'll see you out there. And here, for you." He tossed me the navy sweater, and I quickly pulled it on. It smelled lightly of cigarette smoke and fell all the way to my knees, but it felt fantastic—like getting a hug the second before you realized you needed one. Now for the Heartache Homework. I turned and looked at the gray, bleak landscape.

Wildflowers. Right.

* * *

Lucky for me and my homework assignment, up-close Burren was very different from in-the-car Burren. For one thing, it had a lot more dimension. Yes, flat gray stones covered 90 percent of the ground, but grass and moss exploded up in the cracks between them, bright wildflowers popping up every chance they got.

I walked as far from the tomb as I dared, then collected a handful of flowers. Once I was positive that Ian's back was turned, I placed them one by one in a circle, naming them as I went. "Mom, Dad, Walter, Archie, Ian, Lina, and Guidebook Lady," I said aloud. Too bad only one of them even knew about my heartache.

Okay, Guidebook Lady. Now what? I pulled my arms into Rowan's sweater and turned in a slow circle. How was surrounding myself with floral representations of "my people" supposed to make me feel better?

"How's it going?" I looked up to see Rowan making his way over to me, his grasshopper-long legs carrying him from rock to rock.

"That was fast," I said. "Did you read the Burren entry?"

"Yes. I'm a fast reader." He stopped, remaining respectfully outside the circle. "Is it working?"

"I don't know," I said truthfully. "I mostly just feel stupid."

"Can I come in?" I nodded, and he stepped in, holding out a sunshine-yellow flower. "Here. I wanted to be one of your flowers." He grimaced lightly. "Sorry. That sounded really sappy."

"I thought it was nice," I said, running my thumb over the silky-smooth petals. No guy had ever given me flowers before. Not even Cubby.

I placed Rowan's flower next to Ian's, then—because it felt like I should be doing something—I turned in a slow, self-conscious circle, focusing my attention on each flower, one by one.

When I was back to Rowan's yellow flower, he looked at me expectantly. "So? Anything?"

"Hmm." I touched my heart lightly. It didn't hurt any less, but it actually did feel lighter, like someone had slipped their hands underneath mine to help me with the weight. "I actually do feel kind of different. You should try it."

"Do I have to turn in a circle?" An embarrassed flush bloomed on his cheeks. "Or say their names or something?"

"I think you can do whatever you want. You want some time alone?"

"Yes," he said resolutely. "I think I'd be better without an audience on this one."

I stepped out of the circle and headed over to join Ian at the site. The tomb was about ten feet tall with several flat slabs of rock standing parallel to one another to form the walls, another resting on top to create a roof. Ian's pencil scratched furiously across his notebook. What was there to even write about?

"So . . . this is cool," I said, breaking the silence. "You said this is where Titletrack filmed their first music video?"

He didn't look up from his notes. "Right where we're standing. The quality was so bad. In some parts you can barely hear Jared singing, and the cameraman had a sneezing attack at minute two, but they still got a million views. The song's that good."

He dropped his notebook to his side and we stood quietly, the wind at our backs. The Burren felt solemn as a church, and just as heavy. Guidebook Lady's words broadcasted through my mind. *Courage + time = healed heart. Spelled out that way, it all seems rather doable, doesn't it, chickadee?*

That's where Guidebook Lady was wrong, because it didn't seem doable. Not at all. Especially not when Ian and I could barely talk to each other without spiraling into an argument. I glanced back at Rowan. He was still in the circle, his back to us.

"So you're really not going to tell Mom about Cubby," Ian said, reading my mind like normal. I hated the frustration in his voice—his disappointment always felt heavier than anyone else's.

I shook my head. I knew Ian might be right. Not telling Mom and then having her find out from someone else was a huge risk. But I hadn't managed to even tell Lina—how could I possibly expect myself to come clean to my mother?

Ian's voice rang in my mind. *You know what Cubby's been doing, right?* I stepped away from him, unable to say a word.

Maybe some time apart would be good for us.

* * *

9:21. I spent a few minutes wandering the Burren, and when I finally got to the car and checked the time, my anxiety spiked to a record high. Had we really been here for twenty minutes?

"Guys!" I yelled, waving my arms at both Ian and Rowan. They were standing side by side at the tomb. How had that thing kept their attention for so long? "Guys!"

Ian glanced over, and I tapped an imaginary watch on my wrist. "We need to go. Now."

He languidly pulled his phone out of his pocket before he and Rowan began jogging toward me. I hurried around the back of the car, something unexpected catching my eye.

"Oh, no." The tailpipe now sagged lazily to the ground, the tip completely submerged in a puddle of water. I ducked down to assess the damage.

"Sorry. We lost track of time," Rowan said, his breath heavy as he splashed toward me. "Good thing I'm a fast driver." He caught sight of my crouched form. "Oh, no, did the pipe come loose?"

"I think we lost a bolt. We have to fix it before we leave."

Rowan crossed his arms nervously. "Any chance we could fix it later? I don't want to risk getting you to the airport late."

I fought it, but the practical side of me won out. If the tailpipe were to disconnect as we were driving, that would be it. No workable car. No airport. No Italy and no Lina. I had to find at least a short-term solution.

I jumped to my feet. "As long as we can get it off the road, we'll be fine. What do you have that we could tie it up with?"

Rowan tapped his chin, looking at the bumper stickers as if they might be able to help him out. "Dental floss? I might have a bungee cord somewhere."

I shook my head. "It has to be metal, or it will melt through and we'll have to stop and do it again."

"How about these?" Rowan pulled a pair of headphones out of his back pocket, the cords tangled into a nest. "Aren't the wires inside made out of copper?"

Ian's mouth dropped open. "Absolutely not. Those are Shure headphones. They're, like, two hundred dollars."

"You're offering me your two-hundred-dollar head-phones?" I asked, shocked. I knew Rowan was nice, but this was over-the-top.

He tossed them to me. "They were a guilt present," he said, bitterness ringing through his voice. "Divorce kid perks." His shoulders sagged slightly, and Ian gave him a surprised look, but it was pretty clear Rowan didn't want any follow-up questions.

It was way too generous of an offer, but I had to take him up on it anyway. I had too much at stake. I gave him a nod of thanks, then dropped down to the ground. "Ian, hold the tail-pipe up for me." He obeyed and I crawled halfway under the bumper, water seeping into my shorts as I felt my way around.

I was used to being the family mechanic. The summer after Walter turned sixteen, my brothers and I had a tire blowout on a freeway near our house. I'd dug out the owner's manual, and by the time my dad had showed up, I was covered in grease, and the spare tire was on. Unlike school, cars had just always made sense to me—there was something comforting about the fact that the answer was always just a popped hood or wrench twist away.

The underside of Rowan's car was coated in mud, and it took me way longer than it should have to attach the tailpipe. Nerves were not my friend. What felt like an hour later, I jumped to my feet, anxiety rippling through my center. "Got it. Let's get out of here."

"Maybe you should change before you get back in Rowan's car," Ian said, looking at my clothes. "You look like a mud ball."

"We don't have time," Rowan said, heading for his door. "Hop in, mud ball."

* * *

I was bouncing around the back seat, trying to ignore the fact that the numbers on Clover's dashboard clock were moving at warp speed, when Rowan suddenly let loose with a word that sounded mispronounced. "Feck!"

Feck? I looked up. "What's wrong?"

Rowan pointed out the windshield. "That's what's wrong."

I spiked forward anxiously, and what I saw tied my stomach into a neat bow. About a quarter mile up was a tractor. But not just any tractor—this one was massive, spilling out over both lanes of the road like a giant, lumbering lobster. It definitely wasn't in a hurry. Rowan eased up on the gas and coasted up to it.

"We have to get around it," I said. Were tractors allowed to just take over the road?

Addie, don't panic. Don't panic. We were already late. How was this happening?

"How?" Rowan raked his hand through his hair. "It's too big to even pull over to let us pass. It takes up the whole road."

"There's no way it can stay on the road for long," Ian said calmly, but his knee burst into full bounce. "Rowan, they can't stay on the road for long, right?"

"Well . . . ," Rowan said. He grimaced. "Maybe I should turn around. There's got to be another route to the freeway."

The suggestion made me nervous. Another route sounded messy. And risky. A rumble behind us made us all whip around.

"Feck!" This time it was Ian who yelled it. The tractor's twin was coming up the road behind us. Just as big, just as slow.

"What is this, a tractor parade?" I demanded. Tractor number two was pumpkin orange, and the driver returned our scowls with a cheery wave.

"Great. Tractor buddies," Rowan said.

"I'm going to talk to them." Ian rolled his window down, and before Rowan and I realized what he meant, he'd scrambled out of the still-moving car, stumbling when he hit the ground. "Ian! Get back in here," I yelled. But he ran full speed to the first tractor, mud flipping up behind him.

"Wow. Bennetts don't mess around, do they?" Rowan said.

"Especially not that one," I said.

The driver caught sight of Ian and slowed. He jumped up onto the step, moving his arms animatedly as he talked to the driver.

I was about to climb out after him when Ian jumped off the steps and ran back to us. "He can't get off the road for another ten minutes, but he said there's a shortcut to the freeway. He's going to point when we get close."

"Yes." Rowan sighed with relief.

"Ten minutes?" I said, looking nervously at the clock. It was already 9:39. The procession started up again, sending a splatter of mud onto our windshield.

* * *

The second we hit the freeway, Rowan slammed on the accelerator. "Rowan, drive!" I yelled.

"I'm going as fast as I can," Rowan said shakily. "Addie, I think we can still make it. You aren't checking a bag, right? And maybe there will be a delay."

I wanted to believe him, but the adrenaline coursing through my body wouldn't let me. Flights were never delayed when you wanted them to be. It was only when you had an important connection in an airport that was the size of an island nation that you got delayed. And according to my phone's GPS, we were still a solid twenty miles from the airport. Time was gaining on us. 10:16.

Clover hit a pothole, and the pile of Rowan's belongings slid into my side. I fought it back, my heart a jackhammer. I felt like one of the bottle rockets my brothers and I used to set off on the Fourth of July. Another few seconds and I was going to shoot out of the car's flimsy soft top.

"It's okay, Addie. We're going to make it," Ian said, his fingers wrapped tightly around the grab handle. He'd said it four times now. 10:18. It hadn't really been a full two minutes, had it?

"This can't be happening." The words burst out of my mouth, as frantic as I felt.

This time, no one even attempted to comfort me. We were all in the same state of panicked despair. It had taken us a solid ten minutes to even get to the detour road, and what the tractor driver had failed to mention to Ian was that our "shortcut" was actually a narrow, bumpy dirt road that slowed us to a pace just above tractor speed.

"Airport!" Rowan yelled.

I exhaled in relief. A large green sign read AIRPORT/AERFORT, the Gaelic word accompanied by a picture of a jet. We weren't there, but we were close. So long as I made it to the aiport an hour before my 11:30 flight, I should be fine. Rowan hit the gas like a NASCAR driver, unfortunately timing it with a sudden pothole. We hit the road hard, and suddenly a loud screeching noise erupted from under the car.

"No!" I screamed.

"What? What was that?" Ian's fidgeting was so bad, he could have been dancing a tango.

I turned to look out the back window, but I couldn't see anything. It sounded like the tailpipe was dipping up and down off the road, screeching every time it hit asphalt. The two-hundred-dollar headphones were not going to hold for long.

"Please hold, please hold, please hold," I prayed aloud.

BAM. A clanging noise filled the car, and I shot to the rear window to see sparks flying out the back. The car behind us slammed on its horn and swerved into the next lane.

"No!" I yelled again.

"What? Addie, what?" Rowan said. "Did it fall?"

I crumpled into my seat, tears filming over my eyes. "We have to pull over."

Rowan and Ian both visibly deflated, and Rowan pulled to the side. I jumped out. The shoulder was narrow, and cars passed by much too close for comfort as I ran to the back and crouched down. The tailpipe was barely connected, Rowan's headphones dangling helplessly. How was this happening?

"10:21." Ian's hands fell to his sides, his voice shaky. The misery in his voice said it all. 10:21. There was no way we'd make it on time.

I'd missed my flight. I fell back onto my butt in the mud. A large, shuddery sob worked its way to my throat and stuck.

Ian crouched down next to me and rhythmically patted my back. "Addie, it's okay. We'll get you another flight. I'll pay for it myself if I have to."

"I feel so bad," Rowan said, crouching down on my other side. "I should have accounted for tractors. I can help pay too."

"I can't believe this," I said weakly, tears flooding me. A plane passed overhead, its engines a dull painful roar. Insult to injury. And I knew the real reason I was upset. All this time I'd been counting down to the exact moment that I could unburden myself by talking to Lina, and now that was delayed. My secret pressed hard on the walls of my chest, burning hot. I couldn't wait one more second.

I jumped to my feet, leaving the guys behind as I fumbled for my phone. What was I going to say? *Hi, Lina. Do you have a second? Because not only did I just miss my flight, but I have something important to tell you.* Telling Lina about Cubby from the side of a freeway in Ireland was not what I'd had in mind, but it was going to have to do.

Where would I even start?

If I absolutely had to pinpoint the day things started with Cubby, I guess I'd start with the night he jumped into my car.

I was waiting for Ian after football practice, like I usually did. Rain spattered merrily onto the windshield, and I hugged my knees tightly up against the steering wheel. I refused to turn on the heat on principle alone. It was July. Why couldn't Seattle act like it?

"Ian, come on," I muttered, looking at the school doors. My friend and soccer teammate, Olive, had invited me to her house for one of her famous B-movie showings. She had a way of making the worst movies spectacularly entertaining, and Ian was absolutely going to make me late. Suddenly, a TIGERS sweatshirt appeared in the passenger window, and the door yanked open.

"Finally. What took you so long?" I complained, reaching for my seat belt as he slid into the front seat. "Next time I'm going to leave you."

"You'd really leave me?" I startled at the voice. It was Cubby. Freshly showered, with rosy cheeks and droplets of water clinging to the ends of his hair. He smiled, his bright eyes meeting mine. "You're staring at me like I'm a ghost. Why?"

"Because . . ." My words tried to catch up with my brain. Because I think about you all the time and now you're in my car.

"Um, I guess practice is over?" I finally managed. Brilliant.

He grabbed the seat adjuster, reclining a few inches. "So glad it's over. Practice was brutal." His head dropped, and if I weren't so shocked to have him in my car, I probably would have noticed how spent he looked. Ian had mentioned something about the football coach being exceptionally hard on Cubby this year. I guess it was getting to him. "And Ian might be a while. Coach cornered him for strategizing." He paused, his gaze heavy and invigorating all at once. "Do you still want to hang out? We could go somewhere."

A hot spiral formed in my stomach. Is this really happening? Do things you daydream about actually happen?

"Where?" I asked, careful to keep my voice even.

He looked out the passenger window and traced his finger over the fogging glass. "Anywhere."

It took all my effort not to slam my foot on the accelerator. When it came to Cubby, that was my real problem. I never stopped to think, not even once.

"I missed my flight. My parents can't know and Ian and I got in a fight and there were tractors and Ian's going to a festival and Lina I missed my flight." Instead of the calm explanation

I'd planned on, everything came out in one big tumbling blob, my words piling on top of each other.

"Addie, slow down," Lina said sternly. "I need you to slow down."

"What's going on?" It was Ren, Lina's boyfriend, in the background. He was always in the background these days. Did they ever spend time apart? I wished it didn't bug me so much.

"Just a minute." She shushed him. "I'm trying to figure that out. Addie, what is going on with you?"

"I told you. I—I just missed my flight." Tears poured from my closed eyelids, and my voice sounded as shaky as Rowan's car.

She blew into the phone, sending hot static into my ear. "Yeah, I got that part. But I mean what is going on with you? You've been avoiding my calls for the past week and a half, and now you're standing on the side of the road having a breakdown. This isn't just about the flight. Or the wedding. Why have you been avoiding me?"

Cubby dropped down like a marionette, swinging in the space between us. Of course I hadn't fooled Lina. She'd always had this sixth sense about when I needed her. Half the time I didn't even need to call; she just showed up.

And evasion wasn't going to work. Not when she'd cornered me like this. I took a deep breath. "Lina, there's something I need to tell you. About this summer. I was going to tell you as soon as I got to Florence, but—"

"Is this about Cubby Jones?" she asked impatiently.

"I— What?" I cringed, my shoulders shooting up. Had word really spread to Italy? "Who told you?"

Now Lina's voice was all business. "No one told me anything. You've been hiding something since July. Every time we talked, you were just barely holding back. And then you kept casually dropping his name, like, 'Oh, remember when we were in pottery class and Cubby's pot exploded in the kiln?' Not that great of a story, Addie."

My head fell into my hands. I'd never been very good at lying, doubly so when it was to someone I loved. Walter claimed I was the worst liar in the world. My dad claimed that was a compliment. "Yeah, I guess I was sort of trying to tell you. But not really."

There was a long pause, and I pressed the phone closer to my ear, desperately trying to read her silence. Could silence sound judgmental? I turned to look at Ian. He and Rowan both slouched miserably against the car, Ian's hands deep in his pockets.

"So which airport should I fly into? Shannon or Dublin?"

It took me a moment to realize what Lina was saying.

"Wait. Did you just ask which airport you should fly into?"

"Yes." She exhaled impatiently. "That makes the most sense, right? You just told me that you missed your flight and your parents can't know, so obviously I'm coming to you."

"You'd . . . fly here?" I'd clearly missed the jump somewhere. "But how would you . . . ?" I brushed away the fresh flood of tears staining my cheeks.

Lina made another impatient noise that was distinctly Italian-flavored. "Listen to me. I have tons of frequent flier miles, and Ren does too, and we've both been dying to visit Ireland. I'll just tell Howard that you need me. You stick with Ian, and I'll get to you as fast as I can."

I shut my eyes, letting Lina's plan unfurl. I stay with Ian. Lina comes to me. Maybe our parents don't find out. Maybe I still play soccer. Maybe I figure out a way to make Ian stop looking at me like I'm a burr hitchhiking on his sock. It was the best possible plan for the scenario.

"Are you sure?" I managed. "Flying to Ireland is not a small deal."

"Flying to Ireland is not a huge deal, not when friendship is involved. And, Addie, it's going to be okay. Whatever it is, it's going to be okay."

I wanted to tell her what this moment meant to me, but the words dammed up in my throat. She'd come through with a solution I hadn't even considered. It made me feel bad about ever having doubted her.

"Thank you," I finally managed between tears.

"You're welcome. Sorry you don't get to taste gelato, but at least we'll be together. That's the important part, right?"

"Right." I opened my eyes to a brilliant swath of sunlight. A small pink bubble formed in my chest. Precarious, but hopeful all the same.

* * *

"No. Absolutely not." That was all it took for Ian to snuff the spark in my chest. "This is my trip. Our trip. It's once-in-a-lifetime. We've been planning this for months now." Ian edged toward the car protectively. Rowan had managed to find a wire hanger in the trunk, and I'd used it to refasten the bumper.

"Which is why I'm in this position to begin with," I snapped back. Every time a car went by, I felt like I was about to get sucked onto the road. "If you hadn't messed with the original plan, then none of this would be happening." My voice was high and whiny, but I didn't care. His trip had cost me Italy. "Do you think I wanted to miss my flight?" Though the more I thought about Lina's plan, the more it made sense. Our best chance of surviving this trip unscathed was to stick together.

"Ian, come on. . . . It does make a lot of sense. Don't your chances of not getting caught go way down if you're together?" Rowan asked, echoing my reasoning. I looked at him gratefully, but he was completely zoned in on my brother.

Ian kicked at the ground angrily. "Fine. *Fine.* But listen to me. This is my trip. No fighting. No Addie drama. No stuff about Cubby. Got it?"

"I do not want to talk about Cubby!" I yelled. "You are the one who keeps bringing him up." A large truck whooshed by and blew my hair around my face.

"Whoa." Rowan stepped between us, palms up in stop signs. "We need to establish something right away. I'm completely for this new plan, but I'm not spending the next few days trapped in the middle of whatever's going on between you. If we do this, there has to be a truce. No fighting."

To my surprise, Ian calmed almost immediately, his mouth turned down apologetically. "You're right. Addie, I won't talk about Cubby if you won't."

Really? It was that easy? "Okay," I said warily.

"Okay?" Rowan's eyes darted back and forth between us. "So . . . everyone's good?"

"Good" was a little generous, but I managed a nod and so did Ian. It may have been a forced truce, but it was a truce. It would have to be enough.

* * *

We were fifteen minutes into the new plan, the road spooled out in front of us, everyone still slightly shell-shocked, when one aspect of my life suddenly became startlingly clear: I needed a restroom. Immediately.

I elbowed my way into the front of the car. "Rowan, could you please stop next chance you get? I really need a bathroom."

Ian whirled around, his face tense. "But our next stop isn't until Dingle."

"How far is that?" I asked, looking down at his map. Dingle was a finger-shaped peninsula that reached out into the Pacific Ocean, a good hundred miles away. Definitely beyond the capacity of my bladder.

"Are you joking?" I ventured.

He set his mouth firmly. He wasn't joking. "We have this trip all mapped out. The tailpipe and tractors have already put us way behind."

"Ian, that's crazy. The last time I had access to a bathroom, I thought I was going to Italy. Either you let me have a bathroom break or I pee on the back seat."

He threw a hand up dismissively. "Great. Pee back there. It will be like the coffee can incident on the way to Disneyland."

"Ian!" I growled. The coffee can incident may be a part of Bennett road trip lore, but that didn't mean I had any interest in hearing about it all the time. Why couldn't my brothers ever let anything go?

"What's the coffee can incident?" Rowan asked, his eyes hinting at a smile.

"What do you think?" I snapped.

"You get the basic elements, right?" Ian said. "Road trip. Coffee can. Girl who—"

"Ian!" I threw my arms around the seat to cover his mouth. "Tell Rowan that story and I swear that I will never speak to you again."

Ian's laugh rumbled through my hands, and he pulled them off, but the mood already felt softer. At least the coffee can story was good for *something*.

"I actually need to put a call in to my mom, so a stop would work great for me. How about we stop in Limerick?" Rowan pointed to a sign. LIMERICK: 20 KM.

"Perfect," I said gratefully. I could handle twenty kilometers.

* * *

Turned out that twenty kilometers of grass-sprouting Irish road was very different from twenty kilometers of, say, any possible other road, and by the time Rowan pulled off the road into a gas station, I had to pee so badly, I was practically immobilized.

"Outoutoutout!" I yelled.

Ian turned, his hand on the headrest. "You have five minutes. And this is the absolute last stop before Dingle."

"Just move!" I pleaded.

Ian jumped gracefully out of the car and beelined for the convenience store. I did my best to follow, but halfway out I lost one of my shoes, and when I tried to reach for it, I lost my balance and belly flopped onto the ground, which was not ideal for the bladder situation.

I rolled to my side. Rowan's sweater was studded with gravel, and my elbow screamed in pain.

"Addie, are you okay?" Rowan sprinted around the car to help me up. "Where's your shoe?"

"No time," I managed. My bare foot throbbed as I sprinted for the store, but my bladder was now giving me the twenty-second countdown. This was no time for protective footwear.

Inside, I wasted a good five seconds stumbling through the aisles of unfamiliar junk food before realizing there was no restroom inside. Finally, I hurried up to the register. An older woman with braids wrapped around her head had her hip to the counter. "I told her, marry him or don't. But don't come crying to me—"

"Hi, love," the clerk said, latching his gaze onto me eagerly. *Save me*, his eyes pleaded. "What can I do for you?"

"Wheresthebathroom?" I didn't have time to space out the words; the situation was too desperate.

He understood the urgency, barking out directions in admirable alacrity. "Toilet's outside, around back. Just that way."

I sprinted past Ian filling up a basket with neon-colored caffeine bombs. My stomach was literally sloshing. Finally, I made it to the back, but when I yanked on the handle of the women's restroom, it didn't budge. "Hello?" I called, banging my fists on the door.

"Occupied," replied a cheery Irish voice.

"Could you hurry up, please?" I jiggled the knob desperately. I was going to pee my pants. I was absolutely going to pee my pants.

Suddenly, the men's room door shifted, and I hurled myself at it just as a bearded man stepped out. "Oh. Men's room, love," he said nervously.

"I'm American," I said, like that explained things. *I'm American, so I don't have to follow gender conventions.* He seemed to accept it as a valid explanation—either that or he thought I was crazy—and he darted out of my way. I quickly locked the door and turned around. Even in the awful lighting, the floor was *disgusting*. Damp and covered in wet toilet paper slime. I instinctively clamped my hand over my nose and mouth.

"Addie, you can do this," I instructed myself motivationally.

I had to. My only other option was to wait it out in the back of a clown car until Dingle.

By the time I'd hopped my way through the bathroom and then back out again, Rowan was at the car, his phone pressed to his ear. I quickly darted back into the store and picked up the largest box of Sugar Puffs I could find and carried it to the counter. The clerk's situation hadn't changed much.

"—so I told her, if she wants to live in a trash heap, that's fine. She just can't expect us to—"

"Can I point you to the milk?" The clerk lunged to take my cereal, almost losing his Santa Claus–looking spectacles in the process. How long had he been trapped there?

I shook my head. "Thanks, but I'm on a road trip. We wouldn't have anyplace to store it."

Interest sparked in his eyes. "I took a road trip or two myself back when I was your age. Where are you headed?" The braided-haired woman made a little huffing noise, shifting her bags from one hand to the other so I'd be sure to know what an inconvenience I was being.

"Right now we're going to Dingle, but after that we're going to a music festival."

"Electric Picnic?" he asked.

"You've heard of it?" Rowan and Ian had said Electric Picnic was a big deal, but I had no way of knowing if they meant big deal in their alternative music world or big deal in the real world. Real world it was.

"Absolutely. I'll pray for your parents." He winked. "I've

never been myself, but my daughter went last year. I get the feeling I heard only a very censored version of what she did there. But, of course, you know the stories."

His eyes crinkled at the edges. "People getting married in unicorn costumes, outdoor hot tubs made from old claw-foot bathtubs, rave parties in the forest, a sunken double-decker bus . . . petting zoos made entirely of three-legged animals. That sort of thing. Everyone's in costume and acting badly."

Was he joking? He didn't look like he was joking. Plus, who could come up with a list like that on the spot? I stared at him in horror.

"You hadn't heard the stories," he said, his eyes crinkling even more.

This brought the need for secrecy to a whole new level of desperation. My parents would flip. It was one thing to sneak off to see a bunch of no-name sites in Ireland, but it was quite another to sneak away to a wild party. Getting caught would probably require them to come up with an entirely new category of punishments.

"Well, I didn't mean to scare you." He laughed at my expression. "Keep your head and you'll be fine. Is there a particular music act you're going to see?"

I nodded, regaining my footing. *Keep your head.* So long as Cubby Jones wasn't involved, I could handle that.

"My brother's going to see his favorite band. They're called Titletrack."

"Titletrack! Their final show," the woman interjected, clutching her hand to her chest. "You lucky, lucky girl, you!"

I turned to her, aghast. *She* was a fan? "I love that first song of theirs—Aaron, what's it called, the one with the music video in the Burren?"

"'Classic,'" the clerk said. "We're definitely fans around here."

"We're actually on a Titletrack road trip. I just left the Burren."

"A Titletrack road trip!" She looked like she was about to faint. She yanked on one braid. "What a *wonderful* idea. Aaron! Isn't that a wonderful idea?"

"Wonderful," he replied dutifully.

"Yes, my brother is a huge fan. He's right . . ." I turned to point at Ian, but the store was empty. "Uh-oh, I'd better go. Thanks so much for the advice."

"Stay hydrated," the man called after me as I rushed through the door.

"Take hand sanitizer!" the woman yelled. "And be careful out on the peninsula. Big storm coming today. One of the worst of the summer."

"Thanks," I called over my shoulder.

The second I stepped outside, Rowan's voice punched

me in the ears. "Mum, I told you, I'm not ready to talk about this. You said I had until the end of the summer, and that means two more weeks. And if you want to talk about Dad, call him. . . . Mum, *stop*." He hung up, then whirled around, his expression leaping with dismay.

My first instinct was to bolt, but instead I stood there stupidly, clutching my cereal box, resting my bare foot on my shoed one. I probably looked like I'd been eavesdropping. I mean, I had been eavesdropping. It just hadn't been on purpose. And now I was curious. What was Rowan not ready to talk about?

"Hey, Addie," Rowan said weakly. "Been there long?"

Please say no was written in a thought bubble over his head. I shook my head as I handed him the cereal. "Not long."

His face drooped sadly. *Fix this*, my inner voice demanded. My inner voice had a lot to say about other people's feelings. I looked around, trying to think of a way to lighten the mood. "So . . . remember when I belly flopped out of your car?"

His face instantly brightened. "On average, how many times a day would you say you dive into parking lots?"

I looked up at the gray sky, pretending to think. "Three. Today's a slow day."

His smile increased, then he looked down, kicking a rock toward me. "You know, Addie, you aren't at all what I expected."

"Hmmm," I said, folding my arms. He had a slight smile, so I was pretty sure he'd meant it kindly, but I wasn't positive.

"'Hmmm,' what?" he asked.

I shrugged my shoulders. "That was one of those compliments that could easily be an insult. Like 'Did you do something different with your hair? It looks so nice.' Meaning it looked like crap before." Rowan's mouth twitched into a smile. I was talking too much. I steered us back on course. "If you don't mind me asking, what *did* you expect?"

His dimple deepened. "Someone more average. I can see why Ian talks about you so much."

Surprise flooded me. "He told you about me? But I thought you guys didn't talk about a lot of personal stuff."

"Just the important things," Rowan said. "He told me you two are very close. Which is why I'm a little confused that you guys are, uh . . ." He flourished his hand.

"Fighting all the time?" I filled in.

"It was a little surprising," he admitted. He folded his arms, dropping his gaze down again. "Anyway, I'm glad you came out here, because I have something to show you." He reached through the window into the back seat and pulled out the guidebook. "While you were in there, I checked the sites against Ian's map, and a lot of them are pretty close to each other. A few of them even double up with Titletrack sites. And guess what? One of them is on the Dingle Peninsula, which is where we're headed next!"

He handed me the guidebook, flipping open to an entry

marked DINGLE PENINSULA. I clutched the pages tightly.

"What about Ian?" I said, glancing back toward the store. "I don't know if you've noticed, but every time my love life comes up, someone starts yelling."

"Really? I hadn't noticed." He grinned a cute, lopsided smile that transplanted onto my face. "I'll handle Ian. Look, I technically could do the guidebook on my own. It's just that it feels a little . . ." He twisted his mouth. "Pathetic. But if we do it together . . . Maybe it's dumb."

"It's not dumb," I said quickly. My flower ceremony at the Burren hadn't exactly been the life-changing experience I'd hoped for, but I did like the thought of having some dedicated time to cope with Cubby. Plus, Rowan was really putting himself out there—there was no way I was going to leave him hanging.

I pitched my tone to sound more enthusiastic. "I mean, why not? Worst case, we see some interesting places. Best case, I leave Ireland with an unbroken heart." *Yeah, right.* I didn't believe it for a second.

His face split into a huge smile. "Thanks, Addie. You work on finding your shoe. I'll work on finding Ian. I'm sure I can talk him into this."

He took off across the parking lot at a happy sprint, and I turned to watch him. Was it possible that I'd managed to find the only person in the world who was more heartbroken than I was?

The Dingle Peninsula

If Ireland were a cake, and you the nervous recipient of something coming out of my oven, I would serve you a thick slice of Dingle. Tart, sugary, chewy Dingle.

It's a combination of absolutely irresistible ingredients—crushed velvet hills, roads disappearing into milky mist, jelly bean–hued buildings crammed together on winding roads—all blended and whipped together into a ladyfinger-shaped peninsula that you're going to want to dunk into a cold glass of milk.

Now, I know what you're wondering, dove: *What does this idyllic bit of perfection possibly have to do with the pathetic state of my heart?* I'm so glad you asked. And, my, aren't you catching on nicely?

It's about the circle, love. The process. At some point (maybe it's already happened?), you're going to wrestle your heartache into a sturdy brown box and then lug it all the way to the post office, where you'll drop it off with a huge sigh. *Glad that's over*, you'll think. *Such a relief.* You'll skip back home, your heart as airy as cotton candy, only to realize—with horror—that that heavy brown box is sitting on your front door. It was delivered back to you. Return to sender. Shipping incomplete. *But I just did this,* you'll think. *I already dealt with it.*

I know you did. But you're going to have to do it again. Contrary to popular belief, getting over someone is not a one-time deal.

It might be helpful to look at the process of heartache like you would a peninsula. One with a long, looping road carrying you past a myriad of delights and wonders. Grief requires you to circle around the issue at hand, sometimes passing by it many, many times until it is no longer the destination but just part of the landscape. The trick is: do not give in to despair. You are making progress, even if some days it just feels like you're going in circles.

HEARTACHE HOMEWORK: Find Inch Beach, then walk out into the water as far as you dare. You'll get cold. Then colder. Then numb. And when you can't stand the cold for one more second, I want you to stand the cold for one more second. Are you surviving this moment of discomfort? Have there been other moments of pain or discomfort that you thought you couldn't survive and yet you did? Interesting, pet. Interesting.

—Excerpt from *Ireland for the Heartbroken: An Unconventional Guide to the Emerald Isle, third edition*

THE STORM HIT JUST AS WE ENTERED THE PENINSULA.
And by "hit," I mean came at us as if we were trespassers
that had to be forcibly shoved back to the mainland. There
was no buildup, either: one second it wasn't raining, and
the next raindrops pummeled the roof so loudly, they
may as well have been on the inside my skull. Rain slid
down our windows in heavy sheets, and Rowan kept over-
correcting against the wind. "It's really bucketing down,"
he said nervously.

"Hey, Rowan. I think we need to pull over," I said, gesturing to Ian. Ian balled up against the window, the green tint of
his face highlighting his black eye. I'd seen Ian throw up more
times than I could count, and he was exhibiting four out of
five of the warning signs. Puke was imminent.

"I'm not sick. I just . . . ," Ian started, but he couldn't even
make it through the sentence before gritting his teeth.

"Pull over the next chance you get," I instructed Rowan,
grabbing the empty cereal box and shoving it into Ian's hands.

Ian was the poster child for motion sickness, but he was
also the poster child for stubbornness. He never wanted
to admit that things made him sick, which meant he was

constantly doing things that made him sick. None of us had sat next to him on a roller coaster in years.

"Just a little Irish holiday weather. I'm sure we'll be through it in no time." Rowan attempted nonchalance, but the wind blew at us again and he gasped, jerking the wheel as Ian doubled over.

"Ian, you okay? You never told me you had motion sickness."

"I don't," Ian answered. "I must have eaten something bad at the wedding."

Sometimes I thought my brothers were incapable of admitting to weakness. "Rowan, he's lying. This is an ongoing condition. A windy road during a storm is the worst possible scenario."

I turned away from Ian's scowl and pressed up to my blurry window, focusing on the view. Even without the storm's theatrics, the Dingle Peninsula was Ireland 2.0—the drama factor turned on and cranked as high as it would go. We were still on a narrow two-lane road, but everything had been pumped up to Dr. Seuss level. On our left, neon green mountain peaks disappeared into pudding-thick clouds, and to our right, a thick nest of rain rested on top of the ocean.

Ian's phone chimed. "Oh, no. Text from Mom."

"What does it say?"

He attempted to swivel his queasy face toward me, but the motion made him shudder. "She wants us to check in when we land. I'll text her back in a few hours."

Suddenly, a gush of wind blasted Clover, bumping us off the road and into the shoulder. And this time, Rowan's choice of language was a bit more potent than "feck."

"Rowan, you got this?" I asked. He cranked frantically at the steering wheel, trying to regain equilibrium, but the hardest gale yet caught us on the opposite side. For a nanosecond, Clover favored her left two wheels. Ian lurched for the cereal box, dry heaving.

I gagged. I could see Ian puke a million times and never get used to it. I patted him clumsily, keeping my face averted. "It's okay, Ian. It's okay."

"Now I'm pulling over." Rowan pulled over to the foot-wide shoulder, then threw the car into park, collapsing over the steering wheel. Ian rolled his window down, sending in a spray of rain as he stuck his head outside.

"Well, that was traumatizing," I said, taking a few deep breaths of my own.

Suddenly, the car began vibrating. "What—" Ian started, his eyes wide, but just then a massive tour bus sliced around the corner.

"Hang on," Rowan warned. I pulled Ian inside, and we all braced for death as we watched the bus narrowly miss our front bumper. A large swell of water slammed into the car. We all screamed, haunted-house style.

"We are all going to die!" I wailed, once we'd all stopped

screaming. Water trickled in through Ian's window, and he quickly rolled it up.

"Death by tour bus." Rowan sighed.

Suddenly, a terrible non-storm-related thought popped into my head, and I grabbed the back of Ian's seat. "Ian, there's no way we're going to run into the wedding tour, right? Didn't Aunt Mel say they're touring western Ireland?"

Ian made a little *X* with his fingers, which I guess was supposed to mean "no." "I hacked into Mom's e-mail and printed out a copy of their itinerary. We aren't going to be anywhere near them."

"Hacked?" I said. "By that do you mean you used her password?" Our mom either didn't know or care that you're supposed to change your passwords often. Archie had figured it out one December, and we'd been using it to track our Christmas presents ever since. "Can you imagine if we ran into them?"

Ian shook his head. "It's impossible. I scheduled our trip to make sure there was no possible way for us to run into them. Also, I don't know if that's our biggest concern right now," he said, pointing to the sky. His face was shamrock green.

Suddenly, a shot of ice-cold water trickled down my back, and I catapulted forward. "Cold!" I screamed, water pouring down from my window. The inside of my window. "Rowan! The car is leaking."

He arched back just as the stream transformed from a trickle to a gush. "No! Max said the new top was fine."

"What top? Who's Max?" I asked, like details would solve the fact that it was raining in the back seat.

"The guy who helped me repair—"

"It's my window too!" Ian yelped, his pitch identical to mine. He grabbed his handle, frantically trying to roll up his already-rolled-up window.

"Ian, that's not going to help," I said.

Rowan turned the key and jetted onto the road, and Clover responded by giving up on any attempt at being waterproof. Water flooded in through every possible crevice. We sped over a small bridge, water flowing in at full speed as we pulled into a tiny two-pump gas station.

Ian frantically rolled down his window and stuck his head out, gasping like a beached flounder. I was soaked. Water pooled in the seat of my shorts, and my hair hung in stringy clumps.

"Did that really just happen?" Rowan fell back against his seat.

"Addie, how do we fix it?" Ian asked.

Mechanic Addie to the rescue. I reached up to wiggle the roof, and beads of water tumbled in. "Do we care about pretty?" I asked.

Rowan tapped his hand on the dashboard. "Does it look like we care about pretty?"

"Valid," I said. "We need tape. Really strong, thick tape."

Rowan nodded vigorously. "Tape. Got it. I'll just pop in the shop and ask." He grabbed a beanie from the cup holder and pulled it on as he sprinted for the gas station.

"We almost just drowned in a Volkswagen," Ian said, drumming his fingers on the dashboard. "Can you imagine the obituary? Killer car traps trio—"

"Ian." I reached over to still his restless fingers. I had a theory that Ian had spent a previous life as a hummingbird. Or an athletic coffee bean. "What's up with Rowan's mom?"

He glanced back, his eyebrows bent. "What are you talking about?"

"Back at the gas station I overheard him yelling at her. He said something about making a decision before the end of the summer."

"Really?" Ian tucked a strand of hair into his mouth and chewed thoughtfully. "I don't know very much about his family. I didn't even know his parents were divorced until he brought it up back at the Burren."

"Are you serious?" This was so my brother. All of my brothers. I wanted to know everything about my friends—right down to the name of their first pet and what toppings they liked on their pizza. Lina claimed to remember our first sleepover as more of a police interrogation. My brothers, on the other hand, seemed to need only a few similarities to form a bond. *You like football and tacos? Me too.*

Ian followed a bead of rain down the windshield with his finger. "Rowan and I don't talk a lot about stuff like that."

I rolled my eyes. "Because you're too busy talking about Titletrack?"

"No." He blew his breath out loudly. "I mean, of course we talk about music, but most of the time we talk about deeper stuff, like about things we care about and what's bugging us. Stuff like that."

I couldn't help but grin. "So you're saying that you and Rowan talk about your feelings?" Once Archie had asked me what Lina and I could possibly have to talk about on our multi-hour phone conversations and I'd finally told him, "How we're feeling." Now every time she called, they made fun of me. *How's Lina? How are her feelings?*

"Yeah, I guess so," Ian admitted. He flashed me a look that I recognized immediately. Eyes open and vulnerable—it was what I saw before he revealed something about himself. "Have you ever wished you could have someone see you without all the other layers? Like, not how good you are at sports or school or being popular, or whatever, they just see you?"

I wanted to grab him by the shoulders and yell, *Are you kidding me?* Of course I'd felt that way. That was the defining feeling of my life.

Ian had felt that way? This was news to me. "Like I could

just be Addie instead of being Archie's/Walter's/Ian's little sister?"

"Exactly," Ian said.

Suddenly, I realized something—Ian was talking to me like he used to, like Cubby wasn't hanging out in the bruise under his eye. I chose my next words carefully, not wanting to break the spell. "But the label thing is just part of being human, right? We like to categorize people, so everyone gets labels slapped on them whether they're right or not." I'd never thought about it that way before, but it was true. We even labeled ourselves: Bad at math. Flirt. Clueless.

"They're never right," Ian said, a hint of venom in his voice. "Labels aren't big enough for people. And once you try to categorize someone, you stop looking for who they actually are. That's why I like talking to Rowan so much. We're friends but completely out of context. I never thought someone I met online could be such a close friend, but I really needed a friend, and he was there."

I waited for him to crack a smile on the *I needed a friend* part, but he just dropped his gaze to his lap, his knee bobbing. If Ian felt friendless, then the rest of us were doomed. We could barely go anywhere without someone yelling his name and wanting to talk about the football season—kids, adult, everyone.

"I didn't know you were feeling that way," I said carefully. "You could have told me."

His hair whipped back and forth. "You were busy—with Lina and soccer and ..." Cubby. He didn't have to say it. We both averted our gazes. "So Rowan told me about the guidebook."

"And?" I said, careful to keep my voice neutral.

"And I care about him and I care about you, so if you guys think it will help you, then fine, I'm up for it." He twisted around, his eyes fastening earnestly on mine. "But you know that following some guidebook around isn't actually dealing with what happened, right? It isn't going to make it go away."

My anger flared up, hot and bubbly. "And telling Mom is? Getting our parents involved will just make things get bigger."

"It's already getting bigger," Ian said, mounting his big-brother soapbox. "Addie, at some point you're going to have to deal with it. Don't you want it to be on your own terms? Admit it. You're in over your head."

I wasn't just in over my head; I was gasping at the bottom of the pool. But there was no way I was going to admit that. "I told you back at the Cliffs of Moher, I am done talking about this," I snapped.

"Well, I'm not. Not until you do the right thing," he insisted.

The right thing. The right thing had been to listen to Ian and trust my gut, and ditch Cubby the second things had started to feel off. But I hadn't done that, had I? It was too late now. "Ian, stop!" I shouted.

"Fine," he breathed, falling back against his seat moodily. Why did he have to ruin the moment? For a second there, things had felt almost normal between us.

* * *

I didn't have to see the sign to know we were in Dingle, because Guidebook Lady's description was spot-on. It was *Alice in Wonderland* meets Ireland—a mash-up of charm and color spiked with whimsy. Stores with names like Mad Hatters and the Little Cheese Shop lined the road in every color on the neon spectrum: tangerine, cotton-candy pink, turquoise, and lime. Rowan snaked carefully through the flooded cobblestoned streets, talking a blue streak the entire time.

"Dingle is a huge draw for Irish teenagers. Every summer they come here for Irish camp. You learn Irish language, dances, that kind of thing. The peninsula was pretty cut off from the rest of the world for a while, so a lot of people here still speak Gaelic."

The talking had started as soon as Rowan came out of the gas station with the tape and picked up on the tension between Ian and me. He was obviously someone who tried to bury conflict underneath a lot of words—even if we'd wanted to get a word in edgewise, we couldn't have.

"That's cool," Ian finally said, hedging his way into a rare silence. Our argument had sapped the energy out of both of us. Ian was crunched up into a little ball, buried in his phone, and I was slumped against my window, my anger dissolving into sadness.

"So . . . you're sure you guys are okay?" Rowan asked the quiet car.

"Rowan, we're fine." My voice came out more forcefully than I meant it to, and a shadow covered his face. Ian shot me an annoyed look. Poor Rowan. He hadn't asked for this. I straightened up, swallowing my tone. "Sorry about that, Rowan. Thanks for filling us in on the history. So what's this next Titletrack stop about?" I snuck a glance at Ian's map. "Slea Head?"

"Ah, this one's kind of brilliant," Rowan said, doing the double-handed-glasses move. "When Titletrack first started, they signed with a tiny record label called Slea Head Records. It doesn't exist anymore, but the place it was named after does. It also happens to be one of my favorite places in Ireland."

"Because of Irish camp, right?" I said, to prove that I had been listening to his monologue.

"Right." He beamed.

The road led us through town and onto a windy road that thinned until we were sandwiched between a hill and a cliff. Thick, fluffy fog billowed on the road, and the ocean all but disappeared into the distance. We kept traveling farther and farther out onto the peninsula, and just when I thought we'd drive straight into the ocean, Rowan bumped off the road, stopping at the base of a steep hill where a goat trail snaked its way up to the top.

"Here?" I said.

"Here," Ian confirmed, his knee starting in on one of its specialty spastic dances.

"Too. Much. Wind," Rowan grunted, struggling against the door. Finally, he managed to pry it open, dousing us all with a salty spray of rain.

"Please tell me we're not going out there," I said, but Ian was already scrambling over the console, following Rowan out into the mist, and I followed quickly behind. It's not like the situation inside the car was much drier.

Outside was wet and freezing, and the view was even more intense. The water shimmered a deep turquoise, and a thick afghan of clouds rested on gently sloping hills. All the colors looked oversaturated, especially the green. Before Ireland, I thought I knew what green was. But I hadn't. Not really.

"This way," Rowan said, pointing to the unbelievably slippery-looking goat trail. It rose up a steep hill, disappearing into the mist. Ian bounded forward without a second of hesitation, Rowan close on his heels.

I may as well have been climbing up a sheet of glass. My

usually lucky Converse sneakers were completely useless in this situation, and I ended up on all fours, digging my fingers into the mud and pretending not to notice slugs nestled in the grass.

Up top, Rowan was waiting to haul me up the last few feet, and I stumbled, finally upright, onto the grassy clearing. Nearby, smooth black rock plunged into the water at a forty-five-degree angle, the ocean wild and frothy in front of us.

"People surf here!" Rowan yelled to us over the wind. I looked down in disbelief, watching the water throw itself against the cliff. He shrugged. "Extreme people."

"Good thing Aunt Mel didn't see Slea Head; she would have moved her wedding here," I said to Ian, but he was bent over his notebook again, scribbling furiously through the rain.

I stepped toward the edge, the wind blasting me like a challenge. "Careful," Rowan said.

I extended my arms out wide, feeling the way the wind fought and supported me at the same time. Rowan grinned, then mimicked my stance, the two of us standing like *T*s, spray hitting us full force.

He touched the tips of my fingers with his. Rain speckled his glasses. "I feel like we should yell."

"Yell what?" I asked.

"Anything." He took a deep breath, then let out a loud "Harooooo!"

"Harooooo!" I echoed. My voice sailed out over the water,

overlapping with Rowan's. The sound made me feel alive. And brave. I wanted to feel this way all the time.

"What are you guys doing?" Ian dropped his notebook and stepped next to me, the wind whipping his hair into a frenzy.

"Yelling," I said.

Rowan pointed his chin to the curtain of fog. "Know what's out there?"

"The Loch Ness Monster?" Ian guessed.

"America," Rowan said. "This is the westernmost point of Ireland. It's the closest you can get to the States while still being in Ireland."

I squinted out into the horizon. America. No wonder I felt so good here. There was an entire ocean between me and my problems.

Ian bumped his shoulder into mine—intentional or not, I didn't know—and for a second the three of us stood there, the wind pushing as hard as it could and us pushing back. Together. For one second, I imagined what it would be like if this were real life. Me and Ian against the pressure of everything back home.

I wanted this to be real life, not a detour.

The summer had been full of detours, usually of the nocturnal kind.

It was just after eleven p.m. when I snuck out the back door, creeping through the yard and running down the sidewalk to

Cubby's car. His face shone blue, lit up by his phone in the dark, and his radio played softly. I slid into the passenger seat, quickly pulling the door shut behind me.

"What would your brother think of you sneaking out with me?" Cubby's voice was its usual laid-back drawl, but a thin line of nervousness etched the surface.

"Ian? Good question. Are you going to tell him?" I asked, pointing my finger at his chest.

"Nope," he said, grinning.

Ian didn't know I was out. He also didn't know about the postpractice drive Cubby and I had gone on, or how during the drive Cubby's hand had just casually made its way over to my knee, as if that was where it had always belonged. And I didn't push his hand away either. I wanted it there.

There were a lot of reasons I wasn't going to tell Ian, but the main one was this: Over the past few years my brother's voice had taken on a specific quality whenever he talked about Cubby. Like he'd just taken a bite of bitter chocolate. And tonight was not about Ian's approval or disapproval. It was about me.

Me and Cubby.

"You're sure you want to stay here?" Ian asked skeptically. We sat parked in front of a peeling, burnt-orange building that looked more like a prison than a hostel. Chains tethered the wrought-iron furniture to the porch, and bars lined the windows. "Are they trying to keep people out or in?"

"I think it looks nice," I said. "Very . . . homey. Authentic." Rowan and I exchanged a look. It had taken some convincing to get Ian to agree to stay in Dingle overnight. He'd wanted to keep going, but our guidebook stop was at a place called Inch Beach, and this was not exactly beach weather. There was also the minor issue of hypothermia, which was starting to feel like more and more of a possibility.

There was still one problem, though: Dingle was in high tourist season. And that meant no vacancy—except for the Rainbow's End Hostel, whose way-too-cheerful, Flash-heavy website claimed to ALWAYS HAVE AVAILABILITY!!!! Now, having seen the hostel and all of its charm, I understood why.

"Somewhere over the rainbow," Rowan deadpanned. "How Irish is that?" He took the key out of the ignition.

"Come on," I added. "Anything has to be better than driving in that storm."

"And you get to work on your article," Rowan joined in. "I'm sure you have plenty of material after visiting the Burren and Slea Head."

"True," Ian admitted. "It would be nice to keep up on my writing. That way it isn't a huge job at the end. Plus, I need to post to my blog."

"Perfect! Let's go," I said. Half a day in Clover, and already every bit of me ached. I couldn't get out of the back seat fast enough.

For someplace named Rainbow's End, the interior was surprisingly lacking in color. All except for brown. Brown floors, brown carpet, brown linoleum, and a brass light fixture missing two out of five bulbs. Even the smell was brown: a mixture of burnt toast and the lingering of a pot roast.

I made my way up to a rickety wooden desk. Papers cluttered its surface, and a cup of coffee sat on top of a grubby three-ring binder.

"Hello?" I called out. Brown swallowed up my voice.

"It doesn't look like anyone is here. Maybe we should try somewhere else," Ian offered.

"There is nowhere else. Believe me, we tried." I bypassed the desk and headed down a dark hallway. Light trickled from underneath a door. "Hello?" I called, pushing it open slightly. "Anyone here?"

A guy with a mass of curly white-blond hair sat playing a video game, his dirty feet propped up on the table in front of him. A large pair of headphones encased his ears.

"Excuse me?" I reached out to tap his shoulder, but just before I made contact, he whirled around, crashing noisily to the floor.

"Are you okay?" I scrambled to help him up.

"Okay? Not terribly." He yanked the headphones off. He

was in his late teens or early twenties, furiously tan, and built small and muscular like a rock climber. His accent was decidedly not Irish. Was it Australian? British? He smiled wide, and his white teeth contrasted sharply against his tanned face. "How are you going?"

How are you going? What was the correct answer to that? Good? To Electric Picnic?

He didn't wait for me to figure it out. "So sorry about the mattresses. I know they're utter crap. But I guess that's why we have such an affordable rate. And be honest, you didn't come all the way to the Emerald Isle to sleep anyway, right? You're here to explore."

I raised my eyebrows, completely lost. "I think you're mistaking me for someone else." Someone he'd spoken to before.

His eyes widened. "Oh, no. You aren't with the German group, are you? Forget what I said about the mattresses. Sleeping at the Rainbow's End is like sleeping on a cloud." He sang the last part.

"Nice save," I said. "Do you have space for three people?"

He clapped me on the shoulder. "Didn't you see the sign? We always have availability. I already told you about the mattresses, but let me sell you on the good parts of our humble Rainbow's End. We have a killer nightlife here. Party out front after dark every night, heaps of people, amber fluid, everything you could ask for." He winked, erasing my ability to tell if he was joking or not. "I'm Bradley, by the way. Welcome to the Rainbow's End, the most westernly youth hostel in Europe."

"I'm Addie." I shook his hand. "You didn't by chance write the content on the website, did you?"

He bobbed his head enthusiastically. "That I did, Addie. That I did. Built the whole thing in forty-eight hours. That thing is pretty bodgy, but it does a lot of my work for me, which means I get to spend my afternoons surfing."

"Do you surf at Slea Head?" I asked.

"What kind of crazy do you think I am?" He folded his arms and gave me an appraising look. "Why do you look like you floated here? You weren't out walking in the storm, were you?"

"Driving. Our car isn't waterproof."

"Ah," he said, like he knew all about it. "I'm not supposed to let anyone in until after evening, but this looks like an emergency. You could use a hot shower."

"Yes, I could," I replied gratefully.

He grabbed a grimy white binder from the table and began flipping through pages full of names and phone numbers. The hostel's record book, I assumed. "Where are you from?"

"Seattle. Well, that's where my brother and I are from. The other guy we're with is from Dublin." A loud creak erupted behind me, and Rowan and Ian poked their heads in. Bradley immediately launched himself at them. "You must be brother. And other guy. I'm Bradley." He shook their hands enthusiastically. "But why aren't you two as wet as this one? I thought your car wasn't waterproof."

Rowan grimaced. "The back leaks the most."

"And the back is where I sit," I filled in.

"Way to be gentlemanly," Bradley said brusquely, his gaze drifting back and forth between them.

Ian yanked at his sweatshirt strings, his cheeks slightly pink. "She wasn't supposed to come; we weren't prepared."

"Yeah, yeah, save it." Bradley waved them off. "Now come sign the book while little sister takes a shower." He turned to me. "Bathroom is past the bunk room. Towels are in the closet next to it." I was out of the room before he even finished his sentence.

* * *

Despite the bathroom's questionable cleanliness, the shower felt life-changing. I changed into a fresh set of clothes and wandered back into the lobby, tugging a comb through my hair. Bradley sat paging through a dog-eared copy of *Encyclopedia of Surfing*. When he saw me, he slow clapped. "Huge improvement. Huge. You look one hundred percent less like a boiled rat."

"Thank you," I said, biting back a smile. "I wasn't aware

that I ever looked like a boiled rat, but that's an incredible compliment. Do you know where the guys are?"

He nodded his head to the dining room. "Bouncy one's in there, trying to track down the Internet signal. Good luck to him. Sad guy is in the bunk room."

Sad guy?

"Sad guy is here," Rowan interrupted, walking into the room.

Ouch. "Oh, sorry, bloke. I meant, um . . ." Bradley back-pedaled.

Rowan ignored him. "Addie, you ready to go to Inch Beach? It looks like it's clearing up out there."

"Already?" I turned to look out the window. A patch of blue beamed brightly among the gray clouds. "That was fast."

Bradley dropped his book. "Weather turns pretty quickly around here." He straightened up, dropping back into a sales pitch. "And might I interest you two in renting bicycles for the small fee of three euro apiece? I can also toss in the best free tour guide Dingle has to offer." He extended his arms out wide. "Me."

Stretching my legs on a bicycle sounded like perfection. "That's a great idea! Rowan?"

He hesitated, keeping his eyes firmly away from mine. "Bikes would be great. I have no interest in getting back in that wet car. But . . . I've spent some time on the peninsula, so I think I can manage the tour guide role." He didn't want an audience for the Heartache Homework. Rowan was really taking this seriously.

"Ahhh," Bradley sang, looking between us.

"We're just doing this guidebook thing," I said quickly. My cheeks boiled even though I had nothing to hide.

"Guidebook thing, is that what the kids are calling it?" Bradley winked. "No worries. I know when I'm not wanted. Bikes are around back in the shed. You can have them on the house. Just don't tell my uncle Ray. And you'll come to the party tonight, right? People start gathering on the porch at about nine o'clock."

Party? I'd forgotten about the party. "Maybe," Rowan answered for us.

"We'll be there," I said. Bradley winked, then took off down the hall.

Rowan exhaled slowly. "That guy is too much."

"I like him." I studied the fresh T-shirt Rowan had changed into. This one featured a cat holding a piece of pizza in one hand and a taco in the other. A purple-and-black galaxy played out in the background.

"I think I like this one even more than the hypnotized cat," I said, pointing at it.

"Thanks." He lifted the familiar coffee-stained book into the air. "Ready for an adventure?"

"You mean am I ready to walk back out into the cold?" I flourished my hand toward the door. "Why not?"

* * *

Poststorm Dingle had a completely different temperament. The heavy clouds had thinned into a soft haze, and water lapped restfully against the edges of the cliffs. We rode past a marina filled with colorful bobbing boats and signs about a local hero, a dolphin named Fungie, who, according to Rowan, had been visiting tourists for decades.

"We're here," Rowan called back to me. We coasted off the main road, our bikes picking up speed as we curved down to a small inlet.

"Wow," I said.

"I know, right?" Rowan said.

The sand at Inch Beach sparkled a deep gray, the sun kissing it with a touch of glitter. The tide was low, and silver ruffles of water unfurled lazily onto the shore. Out on the water, sunlight fragmented into kaleidoscope shapes. Stress melted from my shoulders, and my lungs opened up. I took the first deep breaths I had in days.

Next to the sand was a small, sea-glass-green building with SAMMY'S STORE stenciled on the side. Large swirly script read:

Dear Inch must I leave you
I have promises to keep
Perhaps miles to go
To my last sleep

It reminded me of a paper I'd written for English last year about the similarities between Robert Frost's "Stopping by Woods on a Snowy Evening" and Emily Dickinson's "A Bird, came down the Walk." I loved Emily Dickinson. She didn't get things like capitalization and punctuation right, but it didn't matter because you could still hear exactly what she was saying.

As we made our way toward the beach, two messy-haired kids emerged from the store holding ice-cream cones and chasing each other in a feisty game of tag. Their mom played along, lifting the young girl up in the air once she caught up with her.

"She reminds me of my mom." I nodded toward the woman. The girl now sat comfortably on the mom's shoulders, the little boy speeding around them in a circle.

Rowan pulled his beanie over his ears. "How so?"

"The way she's running around with them. She played with us. Lots. Even when it meant she didn't get other stuff done." My mom had never been a picture-perfect type of mom—the kind with a clean kitchen floor or a PTA résumé. But she was excellent at building blanket forts, and when she read to us, she did all the voices. Plus, she was just always there. Her going back to work had rocked me more than I'd thought it would.

"She sounds really great," Rowan said, shoving his hands into his pockets. "Once, I was talking to Ian, and your mom came in to talk to him about school. I could tell she really cared."

"She does." *So why aren't you telling her about Cubby?* a little voice inside my head asked. I brushed it away.

"So what's your family like?" I asked carefully. I'd have to be deaf to miss the longing in his voice.

"Ha," he said unhappily. "It's just the three of us—my mum, my dad, and me—and we're a mess, that's what we are. Sometimes I wish there were more of us, to spread the misery around."

In my experience, that wasn't how misery worked. Or happiness, for that matter. Both tended to expand until everyone had an armful.

I dug my big toe into the sand. "I'll bet there are lots of perks to being an only child." The words felt false as they slid off my tongue. Not that being an only child couldn't be great—I was sure it had its pluses and minuses just like every family situation—but I didn't even know who I'd be without my brothers. Especially Ian.

"I guess so," he said very unconvincingly. He straightened up, squaring his shoulders to the horizon. "You ready to do this?"

The wind heard its cue, skipping off the water and blasting us with cold air. I had officially given up on being anything but frozen on this trip. "What Guidebook Lady wants, Guidebook Lady gets."

We headed toward the water, our toes sinking in the cold sand. When a cold wave slipped over our ankles, we both looked at each other in shock. "Cold" didn't even begin to describe it. It needed a more dramatic word, something like "arctic" or "glacial." Maybe "arcticglacial."

"We've got this," Rowan said, extending his hand to me. Before I could overthink it, I grabbed tight, his hand warm and comfortable in mine as we plunged into the water.

"So, back to the guidebook. What's your thing?" Rowan asked. "What's something you survived that you thought you couldn't?"

"Losing Lina's mom to cancer." I was surprised by how easily the words bypassed my filter. I didn't usually talk about that experience with anyone but Lina. I'd tried a few times, but I found out pretty quickly that most people don't actually want to know about the hard things you've been through. They just want to look like they care and then move on to the next subject as quickly as possible. Rowan felt different.

He looked up, his gray eyes stricken. "I didn't know her mom died. How long was she sick?"

"Only a few months. It was so disorienting. One minute she was running us around town looking for the best fish taco, and the next . . ." I trailed off. The water tingled against my shins. Whenever I thought about those months after Hadley's diagnosis, I remembered the sounds. The beeping hospital machines. The whooshing of the ventilator. How quiet Lina's apartment was in the afternoons when I brought her her homework. I was supposed to be the go-between, delivering homework both ways, but the teachers all knew the score, so they never cared that I rarely brought any back.

The water inched above my knees. "I don't know if Ian told you, but Lina moved in with us right after the funeral. She was really shut-down. She even stopped eating, which is a huge deal, because she loves food more than anyone I know. I ended up getting really obsessed with cooking shows because the only way I could get her to eat was by making things I knew she couldn't possibly turn down."

"You can cook?" Rowan said hungrily. "What did you make for her?"

A tall wave slammed into our knees, sending a spray of salt water into my face. I wiped my eyes on the neckline of my shirt. It was taking every ounce of my willpower not to turn and run out of the water. "Triple chocolate cupcakes. Bacon-wrapped asparagus. Wild blueberry pancakes with whipped cream. Gourmet mac 'n' cheese . . . That one was probably my best. It had four kinds of cheese plus bacon and truffle oil."

Rowan moaned. "I haven't eaten anything but Sugar Puffs since I left Dublin yesterday."

"I thought you loved Sugar Puffs."

"I do love Sugar Puffs," he said adamantly. "But I love bacon and truffle oil more." He looked down at the water, then squeezed my hand. "How's this? We far enough?"

For a second I didn't know what he was talking about, but then I realized water was up past my midthigh, waves kissing the hem of my shorts. "Can you feel your legs?" I asked.

He grimaced. "What legs?"

"This is worse than being in the back seat of Clover." We dropped hands, and I skimmed my fingers across the water's icy surface. Rowan's turn. "What about you? What's the hardest thing you've survived?"

"This year." No hesitation. And no eye contact. Which for most people meant door closed.

But me being me, I had to at least try the knob. "This year, because of your breakup?"

He exhaled, then wiggled his shoulder like he was trying to shake off his mood. "Is this too depressing? I know you're going through your own heartache; I don't want to burden you with mine."

"You aren't burdening me," I said, telling the truth. I liked that he felt like he could talk to me. We were a support team of two. "And what was your girlfriend's name, anyway? Or . . . sorry, girlfriend? Boyfriend?" I shouldn't assume.

"It was actually a goldfish," he said seriously. "We dated for a whole year, but every few hours she forgot who I was and we had to start over."

"Oh," I said, adopting his serious tone. "That sounds challenging. Did the goldfish have a name?"

He hesitated for a second and his smile faded. "It's my parents," he finally said. "They're getting divorced."

"Oh." I didn't know what to say. His answer was not what I was expecting, but it shouldn't have surprised me so much. Heartache came in all sorts of flavors. "I'm really sorry," I said.

"Me too." He gave me a rueful smile. "If they could get past their issues, I think they'd actually be pretty great together, but . . ." He trailed off, shivering violently. I suddenly became acutely aware of the cold. He gave me a lopsided smile, his eyes not quite meeting mine. "I think I'm about to succumb to hypothermia."

"That means we have to stand here for one more second," I said. *Are you surviving this moment of discomfort? Have there been other moments of pain or discomfort that you thought you couldn't survive and yet you did?*

"Now!" I said, turning back to shore. We ran. My legs were so frozen, I could barely feel them churning the water to white, but Rowan's warm hand found its way back to mine, and suddenly I felt that same lightening sensation I had back at the Burren.

It was possible that Guidebook Lady was onto something.

* * *

Bradley was not exaggerating about the nightlife at the Rainbow's End. Music blared from a miniature speaker, and every light blazed. More people than I'd seen on the entire peninsula were crowded onto the porch and steps. Someone had built a fire in a garbage can, and flames licked the edges of the metal.

"The Rainbow's End's infamous nightlife," Rowan said, skidding to a stop. The way back had taken us twice as long since we had to pedal uphill, and my shaky legs meant sore muscles tomorrow. "Any sign of Ian?"

"No, but there's our host." Bradley sat holding court in an anemic-looking lawn chair. He'd paired a too-small button-up shirt with a tee featuring Jesus on a surfboard. Bradley caught sight of me and waved, gesturing dramatically to the seat next to him.

The seat of honor. Part of me wanted to coast on the calm feeling I'd carried back from Inch Beach by going straight to bed, but Bradley kept waving his hands excitedly at me.

"I'll take the bikes back," Rowan said, grabbing my bike handlebars. "Better get over there. We don't want to keep the king waiting."

As I made my way over to Bradley, Ian suddenly appeared at my side, latching on to my arm. He wore double hoodies, and his hair looked more tangled than usual. "Where have you been?" he asked urgently.

I shook him off. "Inch Beach. Didn't Rowan tell you?"

"I didn't think it would be all day."

"All day? We were only gone for a few hours." Suddenly, I realized that Ian was rocking back and forth from his heels to the balls of his feet, which was Ian speak for *I have something to spill.*

My heart fell. Not another text. Please not another text from back home. "Ian, what is it? What's going on?"

He set his mouth in a grim line. "Mom called."

"And?" Huge rush of relief. That was manageable. Mom was manageable. "What did she say?"

"She wanted to talk to Howard."

Yikes. I hadn't even thought about that. "Oh, right. We should probably come up with a plan of what to say next time she calls."

He rocked onto his heels again, spitting the rest out. "I got nervous and I had Bradley pretend to be Howard."

"What?" I yelped so loudly that a cluster of long-haired girls looked up from the fire. "You asked Bradley to pretend he was Howard? Please tell me you're joking."

He grabbed for his hair, twisting the same snarled piece. "It actually wasn't too bad. His American accent was sort of . . . questionable, but I think she bought it."

"No," I whispered. This was a disaster. Less than a day in, and Ian was already jeopardizing us. We were never going to pull this off. "Ian, what were you thinking? You should have waited to talk to me."

He threw his arms up defensively. "She kept calling and calling. You know how she is about the persistence thing—I think Catarina warped her brain. I had to improvise. And besides, you said you were stopping at a site, not leaving for the whole night."

The accusation in his voice was too familiar—*You know what Cubby's been doing, right?* "This isn't my fault, Ian," I snapped. "It was your decision to stay in Ireland, not mine." I shoved past him, heading for the porch steps.

"Addie!" Bradley called. "Did you hear I talked to your mom?"

"Sorry, Bradley, now's not a good time." I stomped into the building and made a beeline for the bunk room, collapsing onto my bed. I was exhausted. And starving.

But instead of leaving the room to forage for food, I dug my phone out of my pocket and searched for Indie Ian. I wanted to see for myself what this trip—and the possible end of our sports careers—had been about. Two articles came up automatically: "Is the Garage Band Dead?" and "I Went to the Mall. Here's What Happened."

"Here it goes," I said aloud.

Two sentences in and I fell headfirst into the world of garage bands. The article blew me away. Ian's voice rang through loud and strong, but with an extra gloss, like it had been coated with furniture polish and set out in the sun to shine. It was well written and intellectual but approachable, too, packed full of personality and enough enthusiasm to make me actually care.

I quickly pulled up the second article, "I Went to the Mall. Here's What Happened." This one was about him wandering around the mall near our house reviewing the music played in individual stores. When had he done that? The only time I'd ever seen him at the mall was when our mom dragged us at the beginning of the school year.

I dropped my phone to the bed, my chest heavy. There was a whole part to Ian that I'd never known existed. One that he hadn't told me about. That he'd chosen not to tell me about.

You did the same thing, my brain nudged silently.

I hadn't told Ian about Cubby; he'd found out all on his own. And then he'd confronted me immediately.

"Addie, not him. Anyone but him." Ian's voice startled me so much, I almost fell back out the window. It was two a.m., just a few days after our field trip to the troll, and he was sitting at my desk in the dark, his headphones pushed down around his neck.

I recovered just in time, stumbling into the room and turning to pull the window most of the way shut. Cubby's car was already gone. "What do you mean? Not who?" I said, pulling my shoes off and tossing them onto the floor. I'd taken to wearing running sneakers at night—it made the climb easier.

"I just saw you get out of his car." Ian stood, sending my desk chair spinning. "Addie, not him," he repeated, his face pleading.

A slow fury built in my center, surprising me with its intensity. Why did he think he got a say in who I dated? "Ian, I get that Cubby's your teammate, but you don't get to tell me whether or not I hang out with him."

He pulled his headphones off his neck, balling them into his fist. "Addie, I'm with him a lot. I hear how he talks about girls. You don't want to hang out with him. Believe me."

But I didn't want to believe him. And so I didn't.

I can usually count on sleep to polish out the hard edges of whatever I'm worrying about—like a broken bottle tumbling through waves to become sea glass. But I spent the night as jagged as they come.

The mattresses were, as promised, utter crap, and a little after one a.m. the entire party, including Ian and Rowan, descended on the bunk beds in a stampede. Finally, morning came, and I woke to light filtering softly through the barred windows. I rolled to my side. An orchestra of different snores and breathing patterns wafted through the room. Most of the beds still contained lumps of people. Everyone's, that was, except Ian's.

I jumped to sitting. Ian's and Rowan's beds were empty,

the sheets and pillows removed. Even their bags were gone.

"Are you kidding me?" I yelped into the silence.

They'd left me. Again. Even Rowan. I hurled myself out of bed, stumbling over a child-size backpack propped up against my bed before crashing loudly into a bedpost.

"Hallo?" a startled voice said from the top bunks.

"Sorry." I raced barefoot out into the hall and into the dining room, colliding face-first with Ian, who, of course, was holding a steaming hot mug of something.

"Addie!" he yelled, the drink sloshing everywhere. "Why are you running?"

The relief was so intense that I nearly folded in half. I rested my hands on my knees, waiting for my heart to slow. "I thought you left me."

"Left you? What would possibly make you think that?" He opened his eyes wide and then snorted, laughing at his own joke.

Laughing. He was laughing. Had he forgotten about last night's fight? He grabbed a handful of napkins from the kitchen table and swiped at the spill on his shoes.

"Yes, really funny. So, so funny." I jabbed him in the shoulder. His black eye looked a little better today. The outer edges were already fading to a dull green.

"What's so funny?" Rowan asked, joining us in the hallway.

"The fact that I now have PTSD over being left behind,"

I said. Rowan's hair was nicely rumpled. Today's cat shirt featured a bespectacled cat with the words HAIRY PAWTER.

"That's not new," Ian said. "You did that every time one of us graduated to the next level of school. I thought you were going to have a breakdown when I graduated from elementary school to junior high."

"Ian, shut up," I demanded, but I relaxed a little. His tone was still teasing. "Why are you in such a good mood, anyway?"

He held up his phone. "I'm only two followers away from ten thousand. Everyone loved the photos of Slea Head and the Burren."

"Ian, that's great," I said, meaning it. I wanted to tell him how much I'd liked his articles, but covered in coffee at the Rainbow's End didn't feel like quite the right time. I wanted it to be special.

He nodded happily. "Hopefully, the next stop will put us over the edge. Get dressed—we're leaving in five."

"How about six?" I asked. Rowan caught my eye and grinned.

"Five," Ian said. "Don't push me, sis."

Killarney National Park

Are you enjoying the wooded delights of Ireland, love? Have you noticed the trees standing in tight communal bunches, branches locked together in an embrace of mutual affection and appreciation? Does it remind you of me and you? The way we just *get* each other?

Me too, pet. Me too.

Muse with me for a moment—have you ever stopped to think about how much work a tree represents? How many steps it's gone through to get to where it is today? Take one of those mammoth trees outside your window, for example. Their ancestors had to migrate to our bonny island. Birds and animals carried seeds like hazel and oak across land bridges that once connected Ireland to Britain and Europe. Other seeds—the light ones, like birch and willow—arrived on a puff of air. And that was just the beginning. Once they were here, those tiny seeds had a lot of work to do. All the growing, stretching, reaching.

Makes me think about all the work you're doing.

What work? Heartache, love. The aching of the heart. And unlike so many other tasks, it's one only you can do. No delegating or shortcuts allowed. We humans love to try to circumvent pain. We want a shortcut, a trapdoor, something that will slurp us up and spit us out on the other side, no sticky messiness necessary.

But the sticky messiness is required. The process is built into the name. If you want to get through heartache, you're going to have to let your heart, you know, ache. And no matter how many distractions you pile on—cartons of ice cream, shopping binges, marathon naps—you can't outsmart heartache. It has nowhere to be, nothing to do. It will just stand there, buffing its nails, waiting until you're ready.

It's a persistent little devil.

So let's get to work, sugarplum. Let's quit drowning our pain in music and credit card bills and cyberstalking. Let's confront it. Let's own it. You've got a job to do, and the sooner you get to work, the sooner you can get back to frolicking through a forest like the sparkly little forest nymph I know you to be.

HEARTACHE HOMEWORK: Ready to do the work, love? I thought so. Find a tree that speaks to you and nestle up at its base. And then, when you're good and comfortable, name the thing that hurts the most about this heartache of yours. Don't flinch. Don't look away. Just face it. Why the tree, you ask? Because trees are exceptionally good listeners, of course.

—Excerpt from *Ireland for the Heartbroken: An Unconventional Guide to the Emerald Isle, third edition*

"WELL, THIS SUCKS," ROWAN SAID FROM THE OTHER SIDE of the tree.

"Agreed," I answered. We'd decided to use the same mossy-trunked tree, him on one side, me on the other. And so far, the Heartache Homework was making my heart feel . . . achy. Which I guess was the point. Looking right at heartache was like looking at the sun. It burned.

I shivered, rubbing at my goose bumps. My clothes were soaked again. A night in the Rainbow's End carport hadn't done the magic we'd hoped for. Clover's back seat had morphed subtly from soggy to mushy, and even though Bradley had donated a few towels to what he called Operation Keep Addie from Looking Like a Boiled Rat, my shorts were soaked through before we even hit the main road.

I was also dealing with some extra stress. Lina had found a flight that would get her and Ren into Dublin by tomorrow evening, and Ren had even managed to secure three tickets to Electric Picnic so we could all go to the concert together. Seeing the e-mail sent insecurity ricocheting through me. What if I didn't like Ren? Or worse, what if he didn't like me? Could a boyfriend and best friend coexist if they didn't like each other? And if not, who got the ax?

I wrapped my arms around myself and looked up through the trees, trying to refocus my mind. The forest was absolutely drenched in moss. Every surface and every branch dripped and glistened with it, softening everything to a green glow.

"We'd better do this before Ian gets back," I said. We'd convinced him to take a walk, but I doubted he'd be gone long. He was antsy to get to the next Titletrack site.

"Okay, you first. What's the worst part of your heartache?" Rowan asked.

Mine was a hard call. Was it public humiliation? Letting my brother down? An unexpected answer rose to the surface. "I didn't listen to myself. There were so many red flags, but I ignored them. I let myself down." I exhaled slowly, sadness coating me from head to toe. "What about you? What's the worst part?"

Rowan shifted, crunching some twigs. "Knowing I don't have any control over the situation."

"I might steal that one."

Rowan hesitated again. "You can tell me to shut up, but what happened exactly? Did you break up with him, or did—"

"It was him." I pressed my head against the bark, my heart sending out another pulse of ache.

Rowan absorbed my silence for a moment, then stood and crunched his way around the tree, sitting next me. "Hey,

Addie, you know I'm here for you, right? Like if you need to talk?"

I met his eyes. They were big and liquid, ready to absorb whatever ugliness I had for them. And suddenly the whole ugly story rose up until it was pushing against the back of my teeth. I did need someone to talk to about it all, but I'd been telling myself the story for ten days now, and it had become pretty clear what part I played in it: loser girl who throws herself at a guy because she's desparate to keep his attention. Not exactly flattering. Or friend-attracting.

"Thanks, Rowan, but I think I'm done here," I said, climbing quickly to my feet. At the car, Ian narrowed his eyes at us. "Why do you guys look so mopey?"

He was right. The time in Killarney National Park had really brought my mood down. I'd always heard you were supposed to distract yourself from heartbreak—not zero in on it. Why was Guidebook Lady so insistent on digging into heartache?

"We don't look mopey," Rowan said. "We're sad. They're two different things."

"Well, this isn't going to help," Ian said, tossing me his phone. "Text from Mom. That woman is relentless."

"Great," I groaned. I pulled up the text.

How's Italy? How are things with Addie?

"Well, at least she actually seems to think we're in Italy," I said.

He shook his head, unconvinced. "Or she's testing us."

I wrote back, Hey Mom, this is Addie. Things are going great!! Italy is so beautiful and WARM. You were right, we just needed some time together!!!! Really feeling some great sibling vibes!!

I regretted the text the second I hit send. It sounded like it had been written by a deranged cheerleader. A deranged cheerleader who was obsessed with the fact that her body temperature hadn't been normal in days. If Bradley's cameo hadn't tipped her off, this would. She wrote back immediately: Had no idea Howard was Australian. How interesting!

Ridiculous. Either she was laying a trap, or spending so much time with Aunt Mel was warping her brain. She knew Howard was American—it was a requirement for running the American cemetery.

I was so absorbed in trying to decipher my mom's text that it took me several minutes to realize that Ian and Rowan were now arguing.

"Ian, I'm being serious. I can't get caught." Rowan's hands were as tense as his voice, and his eyes darted nervously to the rearview mirror. I turned to look behind me, but the road was empty except for a long, fuzzy strip of grass growing through the middle of it. Roads had no chance here—Ireland liked to swallow them whole. "I just don't think we should risk it."

Ian's mouth settled into a hard line. "Rowan, it took us three weeks to track down where the Red Room is. And you just want to throw that all away?" He jabbed his finger accusingly. "I thought you were a fan."

"Whoa," I said, perking up. Those were fighting words. But they didn't seem to ruffle Rowan.

He shook his head soundly. "Stop acting the maggot. Not wanting to see it and not wanting to get caught are two different things."

This sounded interesting. I abandoned Ian's phone and scrambled forward to read the next site on the map. "What's Torc Manor?"

Rowan inclined his head slightly toward Ian. "Should I tell her, or do you want to?"

"Be my guest," Ian said, dropping his head back down to his map. Back at the Rainbow's End, he had peeled the tape off his window, and now he had his right hand out, fingers spread in the wind.

"I'm waiting," I prompted.

Rowan sighed heavily, then met my expectant eyes. "Torc Manor is a summer house that used to belong to the drummer's uncle. They recorded an entire album in the sitting room there."

"It's called the Red Room," Ian added, taking over. Whenever he was excited about a story, he had to get involved in the telling. "They went in thinking the album would be more upbeat and kind of poppy, but the room was full of heavy drapes and carpet, and all the fabric absorbed some of the sound and completely changed the way the songs came out. After that, they started producing songs that had that same moody vibe. They even re-created the same atmosphere in real recording studios with pillows and things. The room changed their whole musical direction."

This was exactly the kind of musical fact that Ian loved to geek out over. Thanks to Ian, I knew tons of odd music trivia—things like Paul McCartney hearing the melody for "Yesterday" in a dream, and Bill Wyman being asked to join the Rolling Stones solely because he had access to an amplifier. No wonder Ian's knee had graduated from bouncing to marching. Seeing something as iconic to him as the Red Room was his dream come true. "Okay . . ." I studied Rowan's grim face, allowing the "dot-dot-dot" to settle. Then I jabbed him in the shoulder. "So what's the problem here? Why are you so nervous?"

Rowan exhaled, giving his glasses a shove. "I just don't want to get caught trespassing. School's about to start, and if I get in any kind of trouble with the law, I'll get expelled."

"'Trespassing' is such a harsh word," Ian said, a grin swallowing his face whole. "I prefer 'unlawful entry.'"

Trespassing? I transferred my jabbing finger from Rowan to Ian. "No way. Priority number one is keeping Mom and Dad from knowing about our side trip. Which means we are not doing anything that could potentially involve police."

"No one is going to call the police." Ian tugged on his hair. "Why are you guys being so dramatic? All we're going to do is drive in there, snap a few photos, and get out. The owners will never even know we were there."

"Until photos of their house show up online and then they remember that you heckled them with e-mails for a full month." Rowan dragged his eyes away from the road and tapped his chin in mock-thoughtfulness. "What did that last e-mail from them say? Oh, yes. I believe their exact words were, 'Come near our property and we will not hesitate to notify the authorities.'"

"But they didn't say which authorities," Ian said, his smile still plastered on his face. "Maybe they meant the town water authorities. Or the leading authority on climate change."

Oh, Ian.

This plan—whatever it entailed exactly—was so my brother. One part danger, two parts music trivia, three parts rebel. Add a handful of jalapeños and some marshmallows and we had ourselves the perfect Ian recipe. Nothing I said was going to matter. May as well conserve energy—I might need it for running. I tried to send Rowan an abandon-all-hope shrug, but his eyes locked onto the road.

"'Look for a mossy, broken-down fence a few kilometers past the bent speed limit sign,'" Ian read from his phone. He stuck his head out into the wind, and his hair puffed into a large dandelion. "Addie, did you see that sign back there? Did it look kind of bent to you?"

"It was a Guinness advertisement," I said.

"But, Ian, what about the fan who got arrested?" Rowan hadn't known Ian long enough to understand what he was up against. "The break-in wasn't that long ago. You know the owners are going to be on high alert. They're probably sleeping with shotguns under their pillows."

"A fan got arrested?" I flicked the back of Ian's head. Was the fan part of his brain completely overriding the common-sense part?

Ian's smile only grew. "That was a whole year ago, and that girl was a mega stalker. You don't just walk into a stranger's house. Not when they're home."

"Because you only walk into a stranger's house when they're not home?" I clarified.

"Oh, she did more than walk in." Rowan pulled his glasses off and wiped at his eyes in a move that made him look like an old, tired businessman—but because it was Rowan, a cute, old, tired businessman. "She made a ham-and-banana sandwich in the kitchen and then ate it while rolling around on the carpet. The owners were sleeping upstairs, and she woke them up."

"Ew," I wailed. "Ham and banana? Is that a Titletrack thing or an Irish thing?"

"Definitely not Irish," Rowan said, a wry smile crossing his face. "Haven't you heard? All we eat are potatoes and beef stew."

Ian clasped his hands prayerlike in front of him and pushed his lower lip out in a pout. "Come on, guys. I promise not to make a gross sandwich and roll around on the carpet. No one will see us; no one will know."

I shook my head disgustedly. "Ian, the lower-lip-pout thing stopped working about ten years ago."

He pooched it out even more. "The lower lip pout is successful at least seventy-three percent of the time. How do you think I passed Español last year? Señora Murdock can never resist it."

I shook my head impatiently. "Quit trying to change the subject. Rowan's telling you that he doesn't want to go to Torc Manor, which means we are not going to Torc Manor."

"That was the bent speed limit sign!" Ian shrieked, hurling his body partially out the window. "We're almost there. Rowan, we have to, have to, have to go."

"Fine." Rowan's gaze swiveled back and forth from my brother to the road. "But listen to me. I cannot get caught. *Cannot* get caught. My parents are already in a constant state of stress. I can't stir the pot by getting in trouble."

"That's it!" Ian yelled.

Rowan hit the brakes, and Ian all but threw himself out

the window, extending his face toward the tall, ivy-covered fence. An oversize NO TRESPASSING sign cozied up to an even larger BEWARE OF DOGS sign.

I pointed to the image on the sign. "What a cute snarling shadow dog."

Ian waved me off. "That sign's a fake. Half the time people put those up when all they really have are goldfish."

"Rowan has a goldfish," I said.

His mouth twitched. "Had a goldfish. *Had*, Addie."

"Look, as long as we stick to the plan, we'll be fine. We already know that the room is ground level and faces the backyard. It will probably take me ten seconds to find. Rowan, all you have to do is drive in and wait. I'll do the rest."

This was train-mode Ian. I couldn't stop him. Rowan couldn't stop him. A slab avalanche couldn't stop him. Our best bet was to do exactly what he wanted—get in there, get a photo, and run.

"Fine." Rowan sighed, rolling his eyes to the ceiling.

Ian bounced giddily, pulling his notebook out. "Thanks, Rowan. I really owe you."

Rowan put the car into reverse. "Yeah, you really do."

"What about me?" I asked, yanking my legs out of the crevice behind the passenger's seat. Over the course of the day, I had reached a new and alarming mental space where I now accepted my legs being asleep as normal.

Ian petted me on the head. "Thanks, Addie. I really owe you, too, I guess?"

I shoved his hand away. "No, I mean what do you want me to do while you take photos of the inside of someone's house? Go with you?"

"No. It will be better if you stay right where you are. Guard Rowan's stuff." He tried to pet my head again, but I ducked out of the way.

I was about to insist on going with him, but when I straightened up, Ian had already moved into his pregame routine, a ritual I'd seen just shy of a million times. First he tied and retied his shoes—once, twice, three times—then he cracked his neck back and forth, finishing with a firm shoulder shake.

Watching him soothed me. If anyone could outrun an angry shadow dog, it was Ian. If he weren't the quarterback of the football team, he'd be the running back. He was the fastest sprinter on the team.

There was also the semicomforting fact that Ian was unequivocally lucky. If, for instance, the owners saw us and decided to shoot our car with flamethrowers, Clover would choose that exact moment to hit a pothole, and Ian would be launched from the car at just the right second, tumbling into soft grass and surviving the ordeal completely unscathed. It was Rowan and me who would end up crispy.

* * *

"Where is he? It's been donkey's years," Rowan hummed under his breath. Our eyes met over the clock on the dashboard. I wasn't sure about donkey's years, but it had been a lot longer than the two minutes Ian had promised before he'd disappeared out the window. Now we were both impersonating him, jiggling anxiously.

Torc Manor was trying very hard to be charming, and the ingredients were all there: a steeply pitched roof, white-trimmed windows, well-kept flower garden. But the longer we sat there, the more I realized there was something eerie about it too. Thick white sheets shrouded the patio chairs, and the surrounding trees grew in a wild tangle, filling the sky with branches and making the afternoon feel much darker than it actually was.

At least Ian was right about no one being there. There weren't any signs of life—no cars in the driveway, no shoes at the door, and no noise. Even the birds and insects were quiet.

Suddenly, Rowan ducked low. "Did you see that?"

My heart skittered as I followed his gaze to the upstairs window. But the curtains were drawn; no movement anywhere. "See what?"

"I thought I saw something. A flash of white." He cleared his throat. "Sorry I'm being a dope. I'm not that great at stress."

Ian suddenly materialized at the car window, startling

me so much that I flung my arm into Rowan's chest, hitting him with a dull thud.

"Oof," he wheezed.

"Sorry, Rowan," I said. This was not an isolated incident. Startled Addie equaled flailing Addie. Once, during a particularly intense cinematic moment, I'd showered an entire row of moviegoers with popcorn. Now I had my snacks doled out to me at movies.

Ian crossed his arms, reveling in a self-satisfied smile. "Why are you so jumpy? I told you, no one's here."

I looked at the house again. I couldn't shake the feeling that we were being watched. "Can we get out of here? This place creeps me out."

Ian shook his head. "The windows back there are too high. I need you to come with me so I can lift you up."

Instinct told me to hijack the car and get us out of there, but reason told me to go along with Ian's plan and get it over with. Also, I liked the fact that he was asking me for help. It felt pre-Cubby. "Let's just make it quick."

Ian dragged me around back. The back lawn was carefully maintained, with a wall of well-tamed rosebushes. Wind rippled through the trees, making a low shrieking noise. "I think it's that one," he said, pointing to a large window.

"Let's check." He knelt down so I could climb onto his shoulders, then wobbled to a stand. I leaned in, careful not to touch the spotless window. "Impressive," I said. "You found the Red Room on the first try."

"I did? What does it look like?" He bobbed around happily, and I had to grab his hair to keep from falling off.

"It looks . . . red." Heavy red drapes drooped down to the oxblood carpet, tufted sofas and chairs rounding out the remaining hues of red. Even the portrait over the mantel depicted a redhead holding an armful of poppies.

He handed me his phone, but between the glare and my proximity, all I could see in the image was my own reflection. "Can you move to the right? The glare is really bad over here."

Ian moved, stumbling on a garden hose but catching his balance quickly. This time the image was perfect. I took a stream of photos, capturing as many angles as I could. "These are going to turn out great."

"Addie, thank you so much. This is really great of you!" The excitement in his voice narrowed the chasm between us.

"I read your articles," I said, holding tightly to the small bridge between us.

The swaying underneath me immediately stopped, and his shoulders tensed. My opinion still mattered to him. "And?"

"They were incredible," I said simply. "Really, really incredible. You're meant to write about music."

He squeezed my ankle. "Thanks, Addie. That means a lot. I've wanted to show you for a long time, but at first it was nice to keep it secret, because it was less pressure. And then this summer . . ." He hesitated.

A long, clunky silence filled the air, and I suddenly felt desperate to keep the camaraderie going. I missed the easy parts of our friendship.

"Ian, maybe you're right. Maybe I should tell Mom." The words ran out of my mouth faster than I could catch them. *Oh, no.* Why had I just said that?

"Really?" Ian's voice bounced off the house, his relief heavy as an anchor. "You have no idea how happy I am to hear you say that. Telling Mom is the right thing. That's what being an adult is, you know? You have to own up to your mistakes."

Mistakes. I felt myself bristle at the word. But I couldn't afford to get angry; I needed to focus on letting him down gently. "Ian, listen . . ." I steadied my fingertips on the glass and took a deep breath. But before I could speak, something caught my eye and I looked up. A woman stood at the glass, a vein bulging in her pale forehead, her face as close as my reflection. Her mouth stretched open in a wordless howl.

"Aaaaaah!" The scream ripped out of me and I hurled my body backward.

"Addie!" Ian tried to catch me, swiveling back and forth. I lost my balance and fell onto my back, hitting my head on something solid. A rock? Black polka dots invaded my vision.

"Addie, are you okay? Why did you scream?" Ian stood over me, his eyes tight with panic.

"Because—" My brain felt too confused to explain.

Suddenly, the porch door slammed, bringing me back to coherence. "Brutus, Marshall, get them!" The sound of scrambling erupted across the patio, followed quickly by barking.

"Addie, we have to run!" Ian yanked me to my feet, dragging me behind him as he charged for the car.

Rowan's phone was pressed to his ear, and his eyes widened when he saw us. "What happened? What—?"

"Just drive!" Ian stuffed me in headfirst, then jumped in behind me, and Rowan dropped his phone, tearing down the drive as two of the largest dogs I had ever seen threw themselves at our back tires.

* * *

Even though the dogs stopped dead at the edge of the property, Rowan spent the next ten minutes driving like a madman, swerving through lanes and overtaking every car he possibly could.

My hands would not stop shaking. Seeing the woman in the window reminded me of a game I'd played in elementary school called Bloody Mary. A group of us would turn off all the lights in the girl's bathroom and then chant *BLOO-DY MAR-Y* into the mirror in hopes that her ghost would appear. Nothing scary ever happened except for the occasional appearance of the crabby old janitor who came in to shoo us out. I'd always wondered what I'd do if a face actually appeared, and now I knew: crumple into a ball and wait for Ian to rescue me.

"Follow my finger," Ian commanded, moving his index finger left to right. "Do you feel dizzy? Nauseated?"

"Ian." I slapped his hand away. He was running through concussion protocol. All the student athletes had been required to attend a meeting on it back in March.

"What about sensitivity to light?" Ian shined his cell phone flashlight directly in my eyes, and I quickly blocked the brightness with my hands.

"Ian! Forget a concussion. You're going to blind me." I pushed him back into the front seat and carefully touched the back of my head. "It hurts, but it's just a bump." I winced, feeling the goose egg already forming. "No concussion."

"Good." Ian nodded, pointing to his black eye. "Call it even?"

I shrugged, and Clover flew over a bump and soared through the air.

"She didn't see me, right?" Rowan kept saying. "We're positive that woman did not see me?" His phone had been ringing ever since he'd dropped it, and he stuck his hands down between the seats, groping around.

"Rowan, how would she have seen you? You were in

the car the whole time," Ian said cheerfully. At least he was happy; he had his photos to keep him going. "Addie, these are incredible."

I knew his sunniness wasn't just about my excellent photo-taking skills—it was about what I'd said right before diving into the flower bed. *Maybe I should tell Mom.* What had possessed me to say that? It was only going to make things worse. I carefully touched the back of my head, wincing again.

"Tackling people in parking lots, surviving head injuries . . ." Rowan sounded amused, his worry about being seen lifting. "Addie, I have a new nickname for you, and I think it fits perfectly." He met my eyes in the mirror, pausing dramatically. "Queen Maeve."

"Who's that?" I asked.

"She's a famous Irish queen. Part myth, part real. And she was a warrior. I'll find a picture." He hit silent on another incoming call and then passed his phone to me. Ian crowded in close to look. A blond, long-haired woman sat slumped over on a throne, like someone was trying—and failing—to entertain her. Her foot rested on a golden shield.

"She seems . . . cool," I said, trying to disguise how flattered I felt. I'd always identified with characters like this. The limp-noodle princesses never felt right—who wanted to sit around in a tower all day?

Rowan took his phone back, nodding. "They buried her

standing up; that way she's always waiting for her enemies. The best part is that her tomb keeps getting bigger because any time someone hikes up the hill where she's buried, they take a rock with them and add it to the pile." He quickly turned his head back to me when he said, "So she's always getting stronger."

I loved the sound of that.

Just as I was about to thank him, Rowan's phone started ringing again, and I quickly handed it back to him. He angrily hit the silence button.

"Who keeps calling?" Ian asked, his nose just a few inches from the photos.

"My mum." The words spat out of his mouth, too vehement for either of us to ignore. It was the same tone he'd had when he was on the phone at the gas station.

Ian's eyes quickly found mine. "Everything okay?" he asked.

Rowan shook his head roughly. "I'm not her friend. I'm her kid. She can't keep coming to me with her problems." His foot pressed heavily on the accelerator, and suddenly we went from flying to jetting, the scenery rushing past.

Ian and I exchanged a worried look. The speedometer was rising. We were still in the okay range, but very high speed could be in our immediate future.

I tapped him lightly on the shoulder. "Uh . . . Rowan.

You're going pretty fast. Do you need a break? I could drive for a while."

"Or I could," Ian offered, his hands twisting nervously. "I can't promise I won't drive us into a wall, but I could try."

"I'm the only one with a license to drive here." Rowan let up slightly, but he was still going way over the speed limit. His hand gripped tightly around his phone.

"Rowan, let me take that for you." I reached forward, gently prying his phone away. "I think you and your phone need some time apart." I tossed it discreetly to Ian, then rested my hand on Rowan's shoulder. "Hey, Rowan, I don't know what's going on exactly, but you aren't alone. We're here for you." It was almost exactly what he'd said to me back in Killarney.

A long moment of silence unspooled, and then Rowan sagged forward, his speed slowly ticking down. Ian looked at me with appreciative eyes.

"Sorry, guys. My parents are putting a lot of pressure on me. It's been a really tough year. I just . . ." His voice wobbled.

Ian's eyes met mine again, and the message was clear. *Help him.*

"Um . . ." I glanced down, my eyes landing on the guidebook. "What if we add an extra guidebook stop? There's a castle between Killarney and Cobh. It's a little bit off our trail, but it sounds really interesting."

"Blarney Castle?" Rowan's voice instantly perked up.

"That's a great idea. I could really use some time to decompress."

"Uh . . . ," Ian broke in. "I obviously want you to have some time to decompress, but I'm worried that another stop will make us late to Cobh. It took me a month of e-mailing to get the owner of the pub there to respond, and then she said she only had a one-hour window. I really don't want to risk it."

Why was he being so clueless? Could he not tell the level of despair Rowan was in?

"He really needs a break," I said, shooting daggers at Ian through my eyes. "We'll be fast. Also, how many Irish people have you been cyberharassing this summer?" Poor people. When he fixated on something, Ian could be relentless.

"Only two," Ian muttered, the tips of his ears glowing red.

"We have plenty of time. And back there you did say that you owe me." Rowan looked at Ian expectantly.

Ian hesitated, a clump of hair disappearing into his mouth before he relented. "Okay. As long as we're fast, it should be fine. I just don't want another tractor situation."

Rowan and I shared a victorious smile in the mirror.

The Blarney Stone

There comes a moment in every heartbroken traveler's life when she find herself dangling upside down from the top of a castle, lips planted on a saliva-coated rock, and she thinks, *How on earth did I get here?*

Let me assure you, this is a perfectly natural part of the heartbreak process.

The place? Blarney Castle. The saliva-coated rock? The Blarney Stone, a hunk of limestone with a sordid history and the propensity for attracting more than three hundred thousand visitors a year. Rumor has it anyone who locks lips with the magical stone will find themselves endowed with "the gift of gab"—the ability to talk and charm their way out of just about anything.

I'm not entirely sold on the gab bit, but I do know two things the Blarney Stone is excellent for: communal herpes of the mouth and discussions about rejection. Let's delve into rejection, shall we?

Because you're a human and because you're alive, I'm going to assume that you've faced your own Blarney moment. A time when you've put yourself out there—vulnerable, dangling—but instead of the blessed reciprocity your heart yearned for, all you got was a slimy stone that did *not* in fact create any oratorical prowess.

Been there. And I know exactly how that feels. I also know it's tempting to believe that you're the only person who's been left hanging. But you're not. Oh, you're not. In fact, the pain of rejection is so common, it's served as the inspiration for roughly half of history's art (and, I would argue, acts of lunacy). And yet when it happens to *you*, it feels like something brand-new. Like the world has cooked up the worst thing it could think of and then called you in for dinner.

That's love for you. Universal and yet *so damn personal.* Solidarity, sister. Anyone who hasn't gotten hurt is either a liar or a robot, and we all know that liars and robots make for terrible friends. Also, robot uprisings. Can we talk about the fact that we don't talk about them enough?

HEARTACHE HOMEWORK: You know what you're going to have to do, don't you, pet? Climb the castle, plunge into a gaping hole, and kiss the damn stone. Embrace the communal germs. They're there to remind you that you are not alone.

—Excerpt from *Ireland for the Heartbroken: An Unconventional Guide to the Emerald Isle, third edition*

AS USUAL, IRELAND HAD NO INTEREST IN KEEPING TO OUR time frame. Roadwork cluttered the road into Blarney—mostly construction workers yelling jovially to one another as they set up unnecessary-looking traffic cones. The castle wasn't much better. The site was stuffed full of tourists and the variety of ways they'd gotten themselves there.

After twenty long minutes behind a cranky row of tour buses, Ian threw his hands up. "How about I park, and you guys get out and do your thing?"

"Don't you want to see the castle?" I asked, craning my neck to get a glimpse. The castle managed to give off the impression of being both imperious and decrepit, a spindly old lady in a crown.

Ian stuck his head out the window. "Seen it."

Rowan laughed. "All right, Ian. Take the wheel." Rowan and I both jumped out, and Ian slid into the driver's seat.

"Watch out for roundabouts," I said.

"Ha ha, very funny. I'll probably have moved two feet by the time you get back." He lowered his voice, addressing me. "Keep it quick?"

"Of course."

Rowan and I took off together, following signs that explained the Blarney Stone's location at the tip-top of the castle. We crammed our way inside, shoving through giant picture-taking masses to get to the swirling staircases.

I started up first, and I must have climbed fast because when I got to the top, I had to wait several minutes for Rowan to emerge. When he finally popped out of the staircase, he was breathing heavily, a light sheen of sweat on his forehead.

"It wasn't a race, Maeve," he said, throwing his arm around me and collapsing dramatically.

I liked hearing my new nickname again. "I've been conditioning this summer." I couldn't quite extinguish the pride in my voice. I'd missed only two workout days the entire summer. The plan was to be as ready as possible for college scouts.

"Just to be clear, you know you just ran up a hundred flights of stairs to wait in line to kiss a manky stone, right?"

"No . . . *we* just ran up a hundred flights of stairs to kiss a manky stone," I corrected, enjoying the chance to try out some Irish slang. At the front of the line, a Blarney employee carefully lowered a woman backward into a stone cutout, her upper body disappearing into the hole. "Look how much fun that is. You get to hang upside down."

"A bit of a thrill seeker, eh?" Rowan said, his gray eyes shining.

"One hundred percent." My brothers called me a thrill junkie, which was decidedly more negative. But it was the truth. Heights, roller coasters, the bigger the better.

Rowan grimaced. "I'd expect nothing less from you. But sorry, Maeve, what I'm trying to say is that there is no 'we' in this enterprise. My mouth is not going anywhere near the Blarney Stone."

"Why? Is it a height thing?" I stood on my tiptoes to see over the wall. Besides the Cliffs of Moher, the top of Blarney offered the best panoramic view I'd had so far. Down below was an ocean of subtly shifting green, people scattered like colorful confetti. It even gave me the same sensation as the cliffs—I felt free, disconnected from all the heaviness waiting for me down below.

Rowan joined me on tiptoe, even though he could see over the ledge just fine. "Heights aren't the problem, Maeve." He shoved his glasses up. "Look, I'm sorry to be the one to tell you this, but locals really mess with Blarney Stone. They pee on it, spit on it, all kinds of stuff. Trust me, you don't want to kiss it."

I wagged my finger at him, a breeze blasting over the top of the castle. "Do you need me to reread the guidebook entry to you? Those communal germs are the whole reason we're here. And besides, I grew up sharing a bathroom with three brothers. Being afraid of pee is not an option."

Rowan's eyebrows shot up amusedly, just the way I knew they would. I liked surprising him. And besides, it was completely accurate. Once when I was in elementary school, I'd gotten so fed up with the situation that I'd drawn a bunch of arrows plus the words IN HERE on the toilet seat in permanent marker. My mom had laughed for a solid hour.

"Queen Maeve, your bravery knows no limits. If you kiss the pee stone, I kiss the pee stone. You have my undying allegiance." Rowan swept into a low bow.

"Thank you, my lord," I said, bowing back.

* * *

When it was finally our turn, even my daredevil instinct faltered slightly. The cutout the stone was located in was really just a hole, the long drop down to the lawn safeguarded with just three metal bars.

The worker beckoned to me. "Ready for the gift of gab, love?" He wore a cap, and his collar was pulled up against white stubbly whiskers.

"Ready," I said resolutely, ignoring the way my stomach spiraled. Rowan gave me a reassuring smile.

I sat quickly on the ground, shimmying back until my butt was on the edge. The hole felt cavernous behind me, wind gushing up through it.

"All right, then. Lean back, hand on each bar, back, back,

all the way back," the man chanted rhythmically, like he must have done a million times before. I followed his instructions until I was completely upside down, the man's hands firmly on my waist. Blood rushed to my head along with Guidebook Lady's words. *Because you're a human and because you're alive, I'm going to assume that you've faced your own Blarney moment. A time when you've put yourself out there—vulnerable, dangling— but instead of the blessed reciprocity your heart yearned for, all you got was a slimy stone.*

Cubby's face appeared, and a dart of pain traveled from my heart to the rest of my body. But instead of forcing the feelings away, I sat with them. Or dangled with them, I guess. Just like I had in Killarney. Again, none of the pain went away, but they did shift over slightly, revealing something that had been hidden. My feelings—my heartache, embarrassment, pain, all of it—weren't me. They were something I had to go through, but they weren't me any more than a pair of sneakers or a T-shirt was me. I was something else entirely.

"Kiss the stone, love," the man called down patiently, breaking me out of my epiphany.

Right. I planted a quick kiss on the stone. It was, in fact, manky. And oddly empowering. I kissed it again, this time for Rowan.

"Success!" Rowan grabbed my hand to help me once I was upright. "You okay?"

"A little dizzy." I wasn't sure what to do with my new realization. It wasn't like I could just throw off my heartache like a sweaty jersey. But could I look at it in a new way? As something that didn't define me?

I looked up at Rowan. "You don't have to kiss the stone. I did it for you."

He grinned. "And now you have truly earned my undying allegiance." He kept a steadying arm around my shoulders as we made our way back to the staircase.

Back on ground level, I was just about to try to put my revelation into words when a voice shot through the crowd, spearing my attention. It was the kind of voice you couldn't ignore. Bossy. Female. American.

My feet froze to the ground. That couldn't be . . .

"All right, people, listen up. Cameramen are going first. The rest of you? Single file. I need one good shot and then we're moving on to the next site. We're already behind, so I need you to make this speedy."

"No," I whispered.

"What?" I felt rather than saw Rowan turn toward me. I couldn't move. Twenty feet away, just past a long steel bench, my aunt Mel stood in full camera makeup.

"No," I said more forcefully. Aunt Mel shifted to the left, yanking at her perfectly tailored blazer, and a second heaping of panic poured over me. It was Walter. And my mom. Walter must have sensed my gaze, because suddenly he looked up, his eyes locking on mine. A single thought erupted in my brain. *Run.*

There was no time to warn Rowan. My feet pounded the pavement, and I rounded the corner of the castle so quickly, I slipped on mud. I needed a solid hiding place, somewhere I could gather my thoughts. Someplace . . .

Like that. I spotted a small opening in the bottom of the castle and hurtled toward it, ducking under the low doorway and stumbling up two steps to a small room. It was barely the size of a walk-in closet, dark except for a thin shaft of light working its way through a chink in the wall. I sank to my knees, adrenaline rushing through my body. Now what? I had to warn Ian.

"Addie?" My heart seized, but luckily it was just Rowan in the doorway, a serious frown crowding his features. "I know we haven't known each other long, but there's such a thing as common decency. You don't just tear away from your travel partner with no explanation."

Common decency? Travel partner? Rowan reverted to the role of stuffy English professor when he was angry. Before I could assign this particular trait the label of "cute," I grabbed his sleeve and pulled him in, our bodies colliding clumsily as he stumbled up the steps. The ceiling was much too low for him, and he ended up in a half stoop over me.

"My mom's out there. The whole wedding party's out there," I stammered.

His jaw dropped—I'd never seen anyone's jaw actually drop before—and he turned to gape at the doorway. "Which one was she? Did she see you?"

"No, but Walt did. We have to find Ian, and we have to get out of here." I crouched down to the ground, trying to still my trembling legs.

"I'll text him right now." He started for his phone, but just as he pulled it out, a second voice boomed into the cave, sending me toppling and Rowan's phone clattering.

"Addie?"

I sprang to my feet. Walt's eyes were as wide as I'd ever seen them, and he blinked unsteadily into the darkness. "I thought I was going crazy. I saw you, but you're supposed to be in Italy and . . ." His gaze snapped down to Rowan, who was still hunting for his phone, and suddenly Walt's face switched into Big Brother Mode. "Who the hell are you?"

"Walt!" I threw myself at him just as he charged Rowan, managing to pin him back against the wall. This was escalating way too fast.

"Whoawhoawhoa." Rowan stumbled backward, holding his phone up like a shield. "I'm her friend."

"Everyone, listen!" I yelled at the top of my lungs. It was a risk, but it worked.

I stepped back from a now-still Walter. "Walt, this is Rowan. He's Ian's friend. He's safe."

"But . . . but you're not in Italy." Walt's voice shot up to dog whistle levels. If he could hear how he sounded, he'd be mortified. "Mom thinks you're in Italy. *Everyone* thinks you're in Italy."

"And that's how it has to stay. Mom can't know we're in Ireland. You have to keep this a secret." I leaned in to emphasize my point and got hit by a solid wall of fragrance. Walt had a lot of things going for him—he was sweet and uncomplicated, and he could be extremely thoughtful. But he was not good at cologne regulation. Which was unfortunate, because he also really, really loved cologne.

"Addie, what are you thinking?" His piercing voice lifted another octave, raising my anxiety with it. If I didn't derail him, he was going to run out and ruin everything. Time to deflect.

I waved my hands in front of my watering eyes. "Walt, your cologne! I thought Mom said you couldn't pack any."

"I only did two spritzes," he protested. "Two spritzes and a walk-through. That's what you're supposed to do. Why can't any of you get that?"

Rowan suddenly piped up, catching on to my plan. "That's got to be a John Varvatos. What is it? Artisan Acqua?"

The shift was instantaneous. "Artisan Blu," Walter said, his mouth twisting into a grudging smile. "You wear it?"

Varvatos to the rescue. Rowan nodded vigorously as the tension in the cave lowered. "I've noticed that sometimes I have to water mine down a little because its one of the stronger scents. Might be worth a try." Rowan was a master at argument disruption. My mom would adore him. I just hoped she wasn't about to meet him.

Walt dropped his hands to his sides, his voice now calm. "Addie, why aren't you in Italy?"

Insert plausible/convincing/nonincriminating explanation here. Minor problem: I was not good on my feet. Maybe if I just started talking, something brilliant would come out. "We stayed because of Ian. He's . . ." I hunted through my brain for some sort of lifesaver, but nothing emerged.

"They stayed because Ian's doing research for a college admissions essay." Rowan to the rescue again. "I'm a student mentor from Trinity College. Ian hired me to help him write the perfect paper. Right now we're researching famous historical sites."

Not bad. Too bad Walt was never going to buy it. People were always falling for Walt's laid-back-surfer-guy act, but it was just that—an act. Despite his lack of cologne awareness, Walt was most definitely not clueless. He had straight As and was working toward an accelerated degree in chemical engineering.

"But Ian doesn't need a college admissions essay," Walt

said, unconsciously flexing his left biceps. "He could fail his whole senior year and still get into any sports program in Washington. Why is he wasting time writing a paper?"

I automatically jumped to Ian's defense, my voice coming out in a snarl. "Maybe he likes writing." *This is what Ian meant.* Any time the subject of his future came up, it was automatically wrapped in a helmet and shoulder pads. Suddenly, a new idea popped into my head. One that might actually work. I quickly softened my voice. "Ian's trying to get into Notre Dame or Penn State. They have stricter admissions rules, so the paper matters."

"Penn State?" Walt whistled admiringly. "You're right, he might need something a little extra to get admitted there."

"Exactly!" My voice was way too amped-up.

"So . . . why is this a secret?" Walt asked, doubt edging its way back into his voice. He looked Rowan up and down, and Rowan straightened, lifting his chin slightly, maybe in an attempt to look more professional.

"He really wants to surprise Mom and Dad," I added quickly. "Can you imagine how excited Dad would be if Ian played for Penn State? And it was so hard for Ian to get matched up with a good . . . student adviser. He was really lucky to get Rowan."

Walt still looked a little unsure, but he nodded slowly. "All right, I've got you, sis. Your secret is safe with me."

"Thanks, Walt, I really appreciate it. Now, I think you'd

better get back to the group; we don't want them to notice that you're gone."

He sighed wearily. "Remind me to never travel with Aunt Mel again. The last two days have been a nightmare." He tilted his head at Rowan. "Nice to meet you, man. Take good care of my brother and little sis."

"She's pretty good at taking care of herself, but I will," Rowan said.

Walt gave me a quick, strong-smelling hug, then ducked back out of the room.

"That wasn't so bad, right, Maeve?" Rowan collapsed back against the cave.

I fell back next to him. "Thanks for jumping in with the college admissions story. I think it may have worked."

It may have worked short-term, but it definitely wouldn't work long-term. Secret keeping simply wasn't a part of Walt's chemical makeup. I'd just activated a ticking time bomb.

* * *

We waited as long as my adrenaline would allow—about seven minutes—while Rowan texted Ian and then traded me his hoodie for the navy sweater so I could cinch it around my face. Under the circumstances, it was the best disguise we could muster. We crept carefully out of the cave and then ran full speed, me praying fervently that no one from the group was watching the grounds too closely.

Back at the car, Ian was a solid mess of nerves, so bouncy that he could barely get the window down. We both ducked low, Rowan attempting to tear out of the parking lot. "They weren't supposed to be here until tomorrow," Ian said. "I checked the itinerary."

"Sounds like they aren't following the itinerary."

"I can't believe you saw Walt," he moaned. "Of all people, Walt." My thoughts exactly.

"Maybe it will be okay." I was trying to emulate the yoga instructor who sometimes came to our pregame practices to help us with visualization. Her voice was smooth and melodic and always worked to calm my nerves. "Rowan came up with a great story about you staying in Ireland to work on a college admissions essay. Plus, he promised to not tell Mom."

"Addie, he's Walter."

I abandoned the yoga teacher voice. "I know he's Walter. What do you want me to do about it?"

"Guys, remember the sibling treaty? No fighting?" Rowan hunched over the steering wheel, looking anxiously at the road. We were stopped at a crosswalk, a flood of people blocking our exit.

"I just can't believe this happened." Ian's leg bouncing slowed, and he slumped dejectedly against the side of the car.

Suddenly, my phone chimed and he whipped back around. "It's Mom, isn't it? Walt lasted a whole ten minutes."

"It's not Mom," I said, my relief quickly replaced with confusion. It was from one of my soccer teammates, Olive, and was in her signature all caps.

DID IAN REALLY GET KICKED OFF THE TEAM????
EVERYONE IS TALKING ABOUT IT AND FREAKING OUT!!!!

What?

I looked up, meeting Ian's nervous gaze. "Who is it?" he asked, his voice drum-tight.

"It's ... Lina," I said, making a split-second decision to lie. Olive prided herself on always knowing what was going on, but this text couldn't be true. And bringing up some stupid rumor would probably just make Ian angrier. "She's just confirming her flight."

The crosswalk finally cleared and Rowan surged forward. "Tomorrow evening, right? And they're going to take the train to the festival?"

I nodded, my head too cloudy to form words. What had kicked off this rumor? And of course people were freaking out. Ian was the star player—the MVP. If he got kicked off, there'd be riots in the street.

I rubbed my thumb over the screen, and an uncomfortable thought popped into my head. One of my parents' favorite phrases: *Where there's smoke, there's fire.*

Something had started this rumor. What was it?

* * *

Once we cleared Blarney, the road became extra twisty, relegating Ian to his balled-up position against the car door. I'd been studying him carefully since Olive's text. Part of me wanted to shove my phone under his nose and ask him what it was all about, but the other part was afraid of opening another door—who knew what kind of ugliness was on the other side?

Rowan's voice pierced the silence. "Addie, do you know what this light on the dashboard means? It just turned on."

I set the guidebook down and scrambled forward to get a look. The temperature gauge was all the way up to the red *H*, and a small orange indicator light glowed next to it. I almost wished I didn't know what it meant.

"It's bad news, isn't it?" Ian said, watching my face.

"The car is overheating." I rose to look at the hood. At least there was no steam. Yet.

"Is that a big deal?" Rowan asked, tapping his thumb nervously on the steering wheel.

"Only if you want to keep your engine." His complete lack of car knowledge was almost endearing. "Almost" because it kept getting us into trouble. "Pull over, but don't kill the ignition."

Ian spun his carsick face away from the window, his voice wobbly. "Addie, we don't have time to pull over. My interview appointment is in an hour."

"Then we definitely don't have time to break down on the side of the road. We need to stop. Now."

"Just do it." Ian sighed, admitting defeat. I was the final word in car maintenance, and he knew it. Even our car-ogling dad had started asking me for advice on his old BMW.

Rowan pulled up alongside a line of trees. I crouched down near the hood, coming face-to-face with a small, steady trickle of liquid. I stuck my hand under, and a drop of green goo landed in my palm. "Great," I muttered, wiping my hand on my shorts. The guys squatted down on either side of me.

Ian clenched his fists nervously. "What is it? What's that green stuff?"

"It's antifreeze. Max probably overfilled the radiator, which causes too much pressure, and then you end up with leaks and your engine can't cool itself."

"I'm going to kill him." Rowan punched his fist into his hand. "And then I'm going to get my money back and kill him again."

"So now what? We tie up the radiator with a hanger? Plug it with bubble gum?" Ian asked, tugging anxiously at the ends of his hair. "Because missing the interview is not an option.

Miriam is a huge deal in the music world. The fact that she agreed to see me was a complete—"

"Ian, I get it," I interrupted, trying to think up a quick solution. I'd once seen a car show host crack an egg into a steaming radiator, allowing the heat to cook the egg and plug up the hole. But we didn't have any eggs, and it would probably gum up the engine anyway. "How far are we from Cobh?"

Rowan shielded his eyes to look up the road. "Maybe twenty kilometers?"

I jumped to my feet. It was never a good idea to drive on an overheating engine, but if we sat around waiting for a tow truck, we would definitely miss Ian's appointment. Was it worth the risk?

I looked down at Ian's still-clenched fists. It was either Clover or Ian. One of them was going to blow. I mentally flipped through the *Auto Repair for Dummies* book I kept on my nightstand. It was the only book that simultaneously stuck to my brain and made me feel calm. Something was clearly wrong with me.

"Ian, go turn on the heat. We're going to idle for a few minutes. Rowan, I need you to pop the hood and find me some water. I'll refill the radiator and we'll watch the gauge the whole time. And, Ian, find us a mechanic shop in Cobh. We need to drive directly there."

His smile filled up the entire road. "Done."

Cobh

Cobh, pronounced COVE. Or as I like to call it, the town of LISTEN TO YOUR UNCLE. NO, REALLY, LISTEN TO HIM.

Yes, there is a story, honey bun. But first, context.

Cobh is a good-bye kind of place. See that dock down by the water? It was the stepping-off point for 2.5 million Irish emigrants. It was also the site of one rather famous good-bye: the *Titanic*. You've heard of it? The Unsinkable Ship made its final stop in Cobh, adding and subtracting a few passengers before slipping off into the icy Atlantic and infamy. I'm going to tell you about one of the lucky passengers.

Francis Browne was a young Jesuit seminarian with an uncle who had a flair for gift giving. His uncle Robert (bishop of the spiky cathedral you see in the center of town) sent him a ticket for a two-day birthday cruise aboard the *Titanic*. The plan was to start in Southampton and end in Cobh, where he'd disembark, enjoy a slice of chocolate cake, and spend some quality time with good old Uncle Rob.

It was a great plan. And a thrilling ride. Along with snapping more than a thousand photographs, Francis did a good deal of schmoozing. One wealthy American family was so taken with him that they offered to pay his full voyage to America in exchange for his company at dinner. Hurray! Ever the dutiful nephew, Francis sent a message to his uncle asking for permission to stay aboard and received this rather terse reply: GET OFF THAT SHIP.

Francis and his iconic photographs got off that ship. Arguably, it was the most important decision he ever made.

All this in preparation for the rather terse and important message I have for you, my jaunty little sailor: GET OFF THAT SHIP.

What ship? You know what ship, love. It's the one you built back before the water got cold and the sailing treacherous. The one you stocked full of optimism and excitement and *look what's up ahead—this is so thrilling!* When hearts get involved, heads like to join in too, creating hypothetical futures full of sparkling water and favorable tides. And when those futures don't work out? Well, those ships don't just drift away on their own. We have to make a conscious effort to pull up anchor and let them go.

So get off the ship, dove, and send it out sea. Otherwise, you run the risk of allowing the thing that once carried you to become the thing that weighs you down. Solid land isn't so bad. Promise.

HEARTACHE HOMEWORK: Find some reasonably sturdy paper and draw your ship, pet. The plans, the dreams, all of it. I don't care how bad you are at drawing. Just get it all down. Now we're going to have ourselves a little send-off party. Use the PAPER BOAT FOLDING 101 instructions at the end of the book to create a tiny vessel. Fold that future of yours into a boat, and then put it in the water. Let the water do the rest.

—Excerpt from *Ireland for the Heartbroken: An Unconventional Guide to the Emerald Isle, third edition*

WE PULLED INTO COBH A HOT, SWEATY MESS. TO DRAW heat from the engine, we'd had to keep the car's heater on full blast, and by the time we made it to the auto shop, we were all dripping in sweat. And I only got hotter when the mechanic—a vaguely tuna-fish-smelling man named Connor—took one look at me and predecided that I couldn't have any idea what I was talking about. "I'll just have a look myself," he said.

"There's a hole in the radiator," I insisted. "I already found it."

His mouth twisted into a patronizing smile. "We'll see."

Before I could blow up, Ian yanked me toward the door. "We'll be in touch."

We hustled down the waterfront streets, carrying our bags past candy-colored row houses with lines of laundry out back. Ships bobbed against the wooden docks like massive rubber ducks, and a spiky stone cathedral stood tall and commanding, its steeple piercing the clouds.

The church was surrounded by visitors, and as we approached, bells suddenly split the air, their song surprisingly cheerful for such a grim-looking structure. "Wow." I skidded to a stop, my neck craning up toward the bell tower.

"Man down," Ian called over the clanging, circling back to

grab my elbow. "Those bells mean we're supposed to be there by now. You can stare at churches later."

"We have to come back for our homework anyway," Rowan said, pointing to the harbor.

"Fine." I sighed, slinging my backpack up higher on my shoulder and breaking into a run.

Au Bohair Pub was hard to miss. The two-story structure had been painted a startling robin's-egg blue and was sandwiched between a lime-colored hat shop and a cranberry-colored bakery. Even this early in the day, it had a festive, game-day feel, music and people spilling out onto the sidewalk in front of it, a collective cloud of cigarette smoke hovering in the air. When we got to the edge of the crowd, Ian ran up to a man standing near the doorway wearing worn denim overalls. "Do you know where I can find Miriam?"

"Miriam Kelly?" He smiled wide, revealing corncob-yellow teeth. "Stage left. She's always stage left. Just make sure you don't bother her during a set. I made that mistake once."

Ian nodded nervously, shoving the handle of his suitcase into my hand. "Addie, could you just . . . ?" He shot through the doorway, disappearing in a crush of people.

"Nope, don't mind at all," I called after him. It wasn't like I already had my suitcase to deal with. The man gave me an amused smile.

"Here, let me help you," Rowan said, absentmindedly

shuffling the guidebook from under my arm and disappearing just as quickly as Ian had.

"Really?" I muttered, grabbing hold of the bags. I bumped clumsily through the entryway, running over toes and sloshing people's drinks as I went. It was only when I'd squeezed into the middle of the room that I took a moment to look around. Wooden tables littered the floor, and the walls were almost completely eclipsed by music posters. A well-stocked bar stood in one corner of the room, customers filling every inch of remaining space.

"Ian!" I called. He and Rowan stood on tiptoe, staring hungrily at the stage. "Stage" was a bit too grand of a word for it. It was actually a small wooden platform, just a foot or two off the ground, that was somehow managing to accommodate a large tangle of musicians, their various instruments belting out a decidedly Irish tune.

I mashed my way over to them. "Could have used a little help."

Neither of them acknowledged me. They were too busy fanboying. Hard.

"That's Titletrack's first stage," Rowan was saying, his glasses practically fogging up with excitement. "This place is lethal. So, so lethal."

"I can't believe we're here," Ian said. "We are standing in the first place Titletrack ever performed."

I wriggled between them to get their attention. "Remember when you left me with all the bags?"

"Is that my baby music journalist?" a raspy voice boomed from behind us.

We all spun around, coming face-to-face with a short, round woman wearing thick spectacles and a shapeless brown dress, her hair pulled back into a tight knot.

"Um . . . are you . . . ?" Ian managed.

"Miriam Kelly." She yanked him in for a hug, patting him enthusiastically on the back. "You made it! I was worried you'd stood me up."

Ian cleared his throat, trying and failing to get over the shock of the most important woman in Irish music looking like the kind of person who baked banana bread and crocheted afghans in her spare time. "Um . . . ," he said again.

Suddenly, she dropped her smile, pointing a finger at him seriously. "So, tell me, Ian, is the garage band really dead?"

"You read his article!" I crowed, recognizing the title from when I'd read it back at the Rainbow's End.

She turned her bright eyes on me. "Of course I have. This young man left me five voice mails and sent an ungodly number of e-mails. I either had to turn him over to the guards or arrange a meeting. You must be the little sister."

"I'm Addie," I said, accepting her firm handshake. "And this is our friend Rowan. He's a huge fan of Titletrack too."

"So, so nice to meet you." Rowan pumped her arm, his face splitting into a smile. "Such an honor."

"An Irishman amongst the Americans. I like it." She turned back to me. "Addie, your brother here is quite the writer. I was very impressed."

"You—you were?" Ian's face lit up like a birthday cake, and he stumbled back a few steps. I'd never seen a compliment hit him so hard, and on the field they rained down on him constantly. "Thank you," he choked out.

Miriam slapped him heartily on the back. "And I love that you're so young. When you get to be my age, you realize that age has nothing to do with what you can accomplish—if you've got it, you've got it. Why wait until you grow up? And then once you're all grown-up, why stop? Or at least that's my motto."

Forget Titletrack. We should start a fan club about *her*.

She kept going. "I want all of you to find a table. I've been on the road all summer, but they let me back in the kitchen today and I made my famous Guinness beef stew. Bruce Springsteen claims it changed his life."

"Bruce Springsteen?" Ian looked like he was about to collapse.

She tapped her chin with one finger. "Or was it Sting? Funny, I sometimes get those two confused. I'll tell the kitchen staff you're here—see you in two jiffs." She bustled away, leaving ripples of shock in her wake.

"Ian, that was savage!" Rowan enthused.

Ian turned to me, his eyes round. "I just talked to Miriam Kelly."

"No, you were just *complimented* by Miriam Kelly," I pointed out, pride bubbling up in my chest. Whenever Ian was this happy, it always spread to me.

* * *

Miriam had ushered Ian to a table near the small stage, so Rowan and I chose another one closer to the door, in an attempt to give Ian some space for the interview.

"So why is Miriam such a big deal?" I asked, keeping one eyeball on Ian. His face had settled on a subtle shade of cranberry, and so far he'd dribbled stew onto his T-shirt and dropped his pen twice. If he was going to be a music journalist, he was going to have to work on the starstruck thing.

Rowan nodded. "She's like an informal talent director. At first she was just booking people to play here at her pub, but after she pushed some of the biggest acts in Ireland, all the record companies started hiring her to scout talent. Fifteen years ago, she heard Titletrack playing at a university contest and invited them here for a summer. It's how they started building up their fan base."

I dug my spoon into my bowl. "She's also an incredible chef." Miriam's Springsteen stew was a mixture of carrots, potatoes, and gravy topped off with two big ice-cream scoops of mashed potatoes. It was so rich and warm that I wanted to crawl straight into the bowl.

"Hey, did you read the guidebook homework yet?" Rowan asked, nudging the book across the table to me. "We have to build a paper boat and put it in the water."

"Are you going to do it or are you going to bail again?" I teased, flipping open to the Cobh section.

"Look, as long as it doesn't involve body fluids, I'm in."

"Fair." I leaned back in my chair happily. I was stuffed, and relaxed for the first time in days. The live music had been replaced with a Queen album that I recognized from when my dad cleaned out the garage, but mostly all I could hear was Ian. He kept dropping his head back and laughing.

When was the last time I'd seen him laugh so hard? Over the past few years, he'd gotten more solemn, which was probably football-related. You'd think that being the star player meant you got special treatment, but if anything it seemed to make the coaches harder on him. And he took his games so seriously. I didn't even have to check the schedule to know when a game was coming up because he always became quiet and moody for a few days beforehand.

Thinking about football reminded me of Olive's message, and I glanced down at my phone, a pit forming in my stomach. DID IAN REALLY GET KICKED OFF THE TEAM???? The text was obviously something I had to deal with. If rumors of Ian were flying around back home, then he deserved to know about them. *But what if it isn't a rumor?* my brain asked quietly. I quickly shushed it. Of course it was a rumor. Ian would have to set the school on fire before they'd do something as crazy as kick him off the team.

Regardless, I needed to tell him about it the next chance I got. The last thing our relationship needed was another secret.

I glanced over at Ian, and he met my gaze, waving us over. At their table, Ian's bowl sat half-full, the lines of his notebook packed full of his cramped writing. His face glowed with excitement. "Guess what? Miriam said we can stay here tonight."

"Are you serious? Where?" Rowan turned like he expected a bed to appear on the bar.

Miriam smiled, pushing her chair back. "Upstairs. We keep a few rooms to rent out, usually for the talent. Jared must have stayed in that main bedroom for an entire month. Which reminds me, he still owes me for that month, the gobshite. I think he can afford it now, don't you? I'm going to give him a call."

"Jared?" Rowan's mouth dropped open. "Lead singer Jared? He stayed here? And you *have his number*?"

"Of course I do." She shrugged lightly, looking at Ian.

"Let me know when your article is finished. If you'd like, I could forward it on to Jared."

"You—" Ian choked on his own words, his face reverting to a deep vermilion. "I—"

He gasped, and I whacked him on the back. "Ian, breathe."

Miriam raised her eyebrows at him. "Ian, you'll be okay. Once you've been in the business as long as I have, you figure out that musicians are just people. Interesting people, but people just the same." She turned to me. "Speaking of interesting people, let's talk about you, Addie."

My face attempted a copycat of Ian's. Miriam's attention felt sparkly, and a little too heavy. "What about me?"

She poked her finger at me. "I hear you are *quite* the mechanic. That's a talent. Maybe not one I can book, but a talent just the same. Ian said this trip wouldn't have worked without you."

Happiness bloomed in my chest. "Ian, you said that?"

He shrugged, a hint of a smile on his face. "Well, it's true, isn't it?"

Rowan piped up. "If it weren't for Addie, we'd still be dragging our tailpipe across Ireland. She even saved us today. Right after Blarney, my car started overheating and she managed to get us to the mechanic shop down the street."

Miriam sighed. "Let me guess, Connor Moloney's place? I hate to say it, but that man is as useless as a chocolate teapot." She crossed her arms. "So, mechanic. What do you have to say for yourself?"

What did I have to say for myself? "Uh, cars are just something I enjoy."

"And that you're *good* at," she insisted.

"I call her Maeve," Rowan said. "Because the first time I saw her, she was tackling Ian in a parking lot. She's like a warrior queen."

Now I was really blushing. "Sorry, *why* are we talking about this?"

"Because we need to!" Miriam pumped her arm. "We need more warrior queens around here. Especially ones that own up to their power." She leaned in, studying my embarrassed expression. "Addie, you know what I do, right? For work?"

I nodded uncomfortably. "Yeah . . . you book talent."

"Wrong." She jabbed a finger at me, her voice rising into an enthusiastic crescendo. "I *empower*. I find people who are out there singing their songs, and I put a microphone in front of them and make sure the world is listening. And you know what? I want to do that for you, Addie."

What was she talking about?

Before I could figure it out, she leapt to her feet and wrapped her arm around mine, dragging me up to the stage.

"Hey, Miriam, I don't sing. Or play anything." Or do stages. Unless it was on a field, I hated being in the spotlight.

I desperately tried to wrench away, but she just yanked me up onto the platform, positioning me in front of a standing microphone. Ian and Rowan watched with wide eyes, but neither of them attempted to rescue me. Traitors.

"Pat! The microphone!" Miriam yelled.

One of the bartenders ducked under the bar, and suddenly the mic stand crackled to life. Miriam shoved it into my face. "Go on, Addie. Tell the nice people what you did."

I looked at her in horror. True, the pub wasn't nearly as crowded as it had been earlier during the live performance, but there were still plenty of people, and every one of them looked up from their tables, amused smiles etched on their faces. They were clearly used to Miriam's antics.

"Go on," she insisted, giving me a nudge. "Tell the nice people your name and how badass you are. Making a declaration can be very powerful."

Do I really have to do this? Right as the thought entered my mind, her arm constricted around me like a boa. There was no way she was letting me off this stage. I cleared my throat. "Um, hello, everyone. My name is Addie Bennett."

"Queen Maeve!" Ian shouted from the audience, his hands cupped around his mouth.

I blushed straight down to my toes. Once this was over, I was going to murder him. "So . . . Miriam wants me to tell you that for the last couple of days I've been on a road trip. Our car keeps breaking down, so I've been fixing it. And . . . that's it." I hastily shoved the microphone back toward Miriam's hands and attempted to dive off the stage, but she grabbed hold of the back of my shirt.

"Wait just a minute, Addie. You know what I like to see? A woman who knows her strength. A woman who owns the fact that she is smart and creative, a woman who can *get things done*. Addie, you are a powerful woman." She grabbed my hand and raised it over our heads, victor-style. "Go on, Addie. Say it."

I cringed. "Say what exactly?"

Rowan and Ian grinned at each other. They were loving every minute of this.

"Say, 'I am the hero of my own story.'"

"I'm the hero of my own story," I said quickly.

"No, no, no. Louder. Open up the diaphragm. Really belt it out."

Was she not seeing the irony in forcing someone to declare how powerful they were? *Just get this over with*, I told myself.

I took a deep breath and yelled right into the microphone, "I am the hero of my own story!"

"Yes! Again!" Miriam shouted.

This time I really let loose. "I AM THE HERO OF MY OWN STORY."

"Good girl." Miriam dropped my arm, her face glowing with perspiration.

It actually did feel good to yell. It would probably feel even better if I believed it.

* * *

"So that was weird," I managed, dragging my and Ian's suitcases over to the staircase. As soon as Miriam had dismissed me from the stage, Ian had jetted off, intent on seeing our rooms.

Rowan grinned. "You stood on a stage and yelled to a bunch of strangers about what a hero you are. What's weird about that?"

I attempted to slug him, but the suitcases made it impossible.

Rowan grabbed one from me, shuffling it over to the stairs. "I'm going to run over to the mechanic shop, make sure Connor can have our car ready by morning. Can you believe Electric Picnic is tomorrow?"

"No." I couldn't believe it. Had the past few days dragged or flown? "I'll stay here. It's probably better if Connor and I don't see each other again."

He flashed me a smile. "Too bad. I was hoping to see Hero Maeve in action."

"Ha ha." I followed Ian up the stairs, the weight of the suitcases sending me bumping back and forth between the walls.

Finally, I made it to the top, dropping everything into a heap.

"I can't believe this." I followed Ian's voice through the doorway. The room's ceiling was slanted, and two twin beds crowded the far wall, the fading light streaming in from a single octagon-shaped window.

Ian was writhing around on the nearest bed. "Which bed do you think Jared slept in? This one?"

"I have no idea," I said, averting my eyes. Ian's dedication to Titletrack bordered on embarrassing. I fled for the next room, taking way longer than was necessary to set up my suitcase next to the bed. Olive's text was burning a hole in my pocket. I had to talk Ian. Now.

When I walked back in, Ian had switched to the other bed, his arms tucked under his head, a peaceful smile on his face. Was I really going to do this? *I am the hero*, I thought ruefully.

"Thanks for getting us here," Ian said before I could open my mouth. "It really means a lot."

"Oh. Sure," I said, lowering myself onto the other bed. "So, Ian, there's something I need to talk to you about."

"Me too!" He rolled onto his stomach, reaching for his notebook. "I wanted to tell you that you should tell Mom about Cubby as soon as you possibly can. Maybe even before we get home. If you want, I could distract Archie and Walter at the airport while you tell her."

"*What?*" I felt the bridge between us collapse in one fell

swoop. Now he wasn't just insisting that I tell her, but he was dictating the time and place, too?

He sat up. "I think you should tell Mom about Cubby before—"

"Ian, I heard you," I said, falling against the closet door behind me. "But I'm not ready to tell Mom yet. Not that soon."

He slammed his notebook shut. "But you said I was right about telling Mom. When we were at Torc Manor."

"I said *maybe* you were right. I never said I was going to do it for sure."

Ian jumped to his feet and began pacing furiously. "You have got to be kidding me. Addie! Why not?"

"Because I'm not ready. If I want to tell Mom, I'll tell Mom." And even though I knew it would cause an explosion, I couldn't help but add the last part. "And besides, what happened with Cubby is none of your business."

"None of my *business*?" He stopped in place, his eyes shining angrily. "Addie, I would be thrilled if that were actually the case, but we both know it isn't true. It became my business the second I walked into the locker room."

My throat tightened. The locker room. Any time I tried to conjure up the scene of Ian walking in, of my *brother* being the one to stop Cubby, my brain grabbed a thick set of curtains and slid them shut.

"How was I supposed to know Cubby would do that?" My mouth was dry.

He pointed at me. "Because I warned you about him. I told you he was bad news." It was the same fight we'd been having all summer. It made me feel tired, right down to my bones. "Addie, for once, just listen to me. You can't keep this a secret anymore. You have to tell Mom the first chance you get."

"Stop telling me what to do!" I exploded, my heart hammering in my chest. "And who are you to talk about secrets, *Indie Ian?*"

I spat the name off my tongue, and his eyes hardened. "Don't turn this on me."

"Why not?" I opened my arms out wide, encompassing the room. "Secret Irish friend. Secret writing career. Secret college plans." I needed to pause, reel it in, but I was too angry. I reached into my pocket and then thrust my phone in his face. "And this. What is this about?"

He yanked the phone from my hands, his posture deflating as he read Olive's text. "How does she know?" he said quietly.

His words stopped me in my tracks, sending my brain spiraling. "Wait, are you saying it's true? You got kicked off the team? Why didn't you tell me?"

He tossed the phone onto the bed. "It was because of you, okay? I'm off the team because of *you.*"

No.

I backed out of the room, my hands shaking as a mountain formed in my chest, heavy and brand-new.

Now his voice was pleading. "Addie, I got kicked off the football team. Mom and Dad don't know yet, but I can't keep it a secret forever. You have tell Mom. You have to tell her about the photo, and about Cubby passing it—"

"Ian, *stop!*" I yelled, clamping my hands over my ears. My body spun around, and suddenly I was running, the steps rising up to meet me, Ian at my back.

* * *

I made it all the way down to the harbor before I slowed. My chest was heaving, the tears making it hard to breathe, and I fell heavily onto an iron bench, the cold slats pressing into my spine.

Here's the thing that shouldn't have happened this summer, not to me, not to anyone. After weeks of Cubby asking, I'd sent him a topless photo of myself. I hadn't felt completely okay about it because one, all his joking about it had started to feel uncomfortably like pressure, and two, no matter how many times I swatted at Ian's warning, it refused to stop buzzing in my head. *I hear how he talks about girls. You don't want to hang out with him.*

But Cubby and I had been together all summer. Didn't

that mean I knew him better than Ian did? Didn't that mean I could trust him? And besides, maybe this was how you went from secret late-night meet-ups to walking down the halls of your high school together. You took a leap of faith.

So I'd hit send. Even though my hands were shaking. Even though the buzzing in my head got even louder.

And then two days later, Ian had come home from football camp and all but thrown himself through my bedroom door, angry tears pooling in his eyes. *You know what he's been doing, right? He's been showing everyone your photo. Why didn't you listen to me?*

I'd been too stunned to even ask what happened next, but now I knew. After Ian walked in on Cubby passing my photo around to the entire varsity team, he'd fought him. Of course he had. And then he'd gotten kicked off the football team. And the fact that I hadn't meant to involve my brother—hadn't meant to let my life spill over into his— didn't matter, because that came with being family. Whether you wanted them to or not, your actions always affected the entire unit. I took a deep, shuddery breath. I needed to tell Ian why I hadn't listened to him. The real reason. He deserved to know.

A few seconds later I heard his footsteps behind me, just like I knew I would. "Addie . . . ," he started, but I whipped around, forcing the words out before they could retreat.

"Ian, do you know how hard it is to be your little sister?"

He froze, a searching expression moving over his face. "What do you mean? This summer excluded, I've always felt like we had a great friendship."

"We have." I shook my head, groping for the words as he slid onto the bench next to me. "What I mean is, do you know how hard it is to be *Ian Bennett's* sister?"

He shook his head almost imperceptibly. "I don't understand."

"You're the star of our high school. Star of the football team. The star athlete in a house *filled* with star athletes." My voice wavered, and I picked a spot in the ocean to stare at, steadying my gaze. "You're good at school, and sports, and writing . . . and of course you were right about Cubby. You were completely right. And deep down I knew it all along."

Ian dug his hands into his hair, his face confused. "Then why—"

I cut him off again. I really needed him to listen. "Ian, I was with Cubby this summer because I wanted someone to *see* me. Really see me. And not just in comparison to you three." I took a deep breath. "I just wanted to be someone other than Bennett number four—the one who's just mediocre."

"Mediocre?" Ian's eyes widened in disbelief. "Why didn't you ever tell me you felt that way?"

"Why should I have to tell you? It's so embarrassingly

obvious." A bird hopped happily over, a french fry clamped in its beak. "And, Ian, I'm really sorry that I sent the photo, but—"

"Whoa, whoa, whoa. Back up." Ian's hands shot into the air. "You think I'm mad at you because you sent the photo?" He looked me square in the eye, his knee bouncing. "Addie, that's not what this is about. Sending a photo was your decision. It's your . . . body." We both grimaced. This was firmly out of the realm of brother-sister conversations. At least it was for us.

"Sorry," he said quickly, blush forming on his cheeks. "I don't know if I'm saying this the right way, but what I mean is that I wasn't mad that you sent the photo. Your picture getting passed around the team wasn't your fault—Cubby's the one who did that." He kicked at a loose pebble on the sidewalk. "I was mad that you didn't trust me when I told you to stay away from him. I've been around Cubby for years. I've seen how he's changed, and I just wanted to protect you."

Tears prickled my eyes, and I leaned over, resting my elbows on my knees. The knot in my chest felt like it would never unravel. "Ian, I'm so sorry about football," I whispered.

He exhaled slowly. "Okay, now it's my turn to come clean on something else. I didn't mean what I said back there in the room. I was just angry. And trying to make a point."

I shot up quickly. "You mean you're still on the team?"

He shook his head. "No, I am one hundred percent off the team. What I mean is that's on me, not you."

"So it wasn't about the photo?"

"Well . . ." He hesitated. "I wouldn't say that exactly. But more happened than just me confronting Cubby in the locker room. I mean, I definitely lost it that day. But it was all the other fights that put things over the edge."

"Fights?" My head snapped up. "As in plural? How many did you get into?"

He hesitated. "I'm not really sure. And I'll be honest, at first they were about you, guys making stupid comments to get under my skin. But then it was like I just snapped. I couldn't handle my teammates anymore, and everything set me off. Coach kept giving me warnings and then . . ."

He straightened up, throwing his shoulders back. "But it's okay that I got kicked off, because I hate football. Always have, always will."

"What?" I ripped my gaze from the ocean. Enjoying writing more than football was not the same as *hating* football. And he couldn't hate it, could he? Not when he was so talented. "Like you hate practice or . . . ?"

He shook his head, sending hair into his face. "No, I hate *football*. All of it." His eyes met mine. "I hate practice, I hate games, the pep rallies, the banquets, the uniforms . . . I hate how people treat me differently—like I'm special just because I'm good at this one thing. And it's been this way for so long. Once everyone figured out I was good, it was like someone threw this big football blanket over me—no one could see anything else. Everyone just wanted me to fall into this stereotype, and it just never . . . fit."

I had never even considered that Ian didn't like football. Suddenly, it all fell into place: the rush out of practices, the grumpiness before games, how hard he worked to not talk about football when it was all anyone else wanted to talk about. It had been right in front of me all along. "Ian, I had no idea. That must have been . . ."

"Awful?" he said, his eyebrows dropping.

"Awful," I repeated. "Why didn't you tell me?"

He shook his head. "I didn't want to disappoint you. Everyone gets so excited about me playing, and you were always at my games and . . ." He exhaled loudly. "I want to be like you and Archie and Walter. When you're on the field, it's like you turn into who you really are. You have so much fun. I've never felt that."

"But you feel that way with writing. And Titletrack," I said.

"Exactly," he said. "That's why this trip was so important to me. I thought that if I could maybe write something really incredible, maybe get it accepted into a large magazine, Mom and Dad would be less upset about my quitting football."

I pressed my lips together, barely containing my smile.

"So you're saying that you have something you need to tell Mom and Dad?"

He groaned, but a smile pierced his face too. "I know. Don't bug me about it, okay? I'm getting there."

"Are you kidding me? I am *definitely* going to bug you about it. At least as often as you bugged me."

"There you guys are!" Rowan suddenly appeared next to the bench, startling us. "I had no idea where you went. I ended up asking one of the bartenders, and he told me . . ." He stopped, his eyes drawn to my tearstained cheeks. "Wait, what's wrong? Did something happen?"

"You could say that." Rowan had the guidebook in his hand, and seeing it sparked an idea. "Hey, Ian, do you want to do the Cobh homework with us? I actually think it might help you."

"Good idea," Rowan said. "I bet you'll like this one."

Ian yanked his hair back, securing it with an elastic from his wrist. "I don't know. Do I have to talk to a tree? Or kiss something?"

I shook my head. "We're supposed to draw something that didn't work out the way we hoped it would. Then we're going to fold our papers into boats and send them out to sea."

"Hmmm," Ian said, but from the way his eyes landed on the book, I knew he was interested.

"I was looking for you because I wanted to do the homework before it gets dark. I even asked for paper back at the pub, but all they had were these." Rowan handed me a stack of old fliers advertising a show by a local violinist.

"Good enough for me." I handed them each a paper, and then we spread out, sitting on the ground with our drawings in front of us. Mine came easily. It was Cubby and me, walking down the hallway, his arm slung around me, admiring whispers coming from all directions.

The drawing itself was terrible, barely a level above stick figure, but getting it all out shifted something inside. Again, the pain was still there, but some of the weight traveled down through my pencil, solidified into something I could look at. Something I could let go of.

We gathered at the edge of the water, following Guidebook Lady's instructions for the Anti-Love Boat, and as I set my boat into the water, I let myself imagine for one more second what it would be like if things had gone differently. If Cubby had cared about me the way I'd cared about him. And then I let it go, watching as the waves carried it out to be dissolved by salt.

And when it was gone? Ian and Rowan were still beside me. Solid. It meant more to me than I'd thought it would.

* * *

There was a storm in the night, a gentle pattering that infiltrated my dreams and infused the late-morning sky with a bright peachy hue. Before getting out of bed, I rolled onto my back and stared up at the spiderweb cracks in the ceiling, testing out my new feeling of lightness.

The knot was still in my chest, but Ian and I being on the same team made everything seem easier.

I got dressed and then wandered into the boys' room to see them sprawled out on their beds, Rowan wearing a pink T-shirt depicting a cat riding an orca and Ian poring over his map.

I pointed to Rowan's shirt. "How many of those do you have?"

"Not nearly enough. And good morning to you, too," he said, his dimple making me smile.

I pointed to Ian's map. "One more stop before Electric Picnic?"

He grinned, bouncing off the bed. "Rock of Cashel. I can't believe the concert is *tonight*."

"I can't believe *Lina* will be here tonight." I was still nervous, but now that the tension had eased between Ian and me, telling Lina suddenly felt much more doable.

Rowan lifted his phone. "Connor says we can pick up the car after ten. Anyone want to stop for breakfast first?"

"Me," Ian and I said in unison.

Miriam had left bright and early to drive to Dublin for a meeting, so after saying good-bye to the staff, we rolled our suitcases down to Main Street, stopping at a cobalt-blue coffee shop with BERTIE'S: FREE TEA WITH EVERY ORDER spelled out across the window in gold stick-on letters. Inside, a small bell jingled overhead, and we ordered eggs and toast from a woman standing behind the counter.

I wanted to watch the ocean for as long as possible, so while we waited for our toast and eggs, I chose a table near the window, wrapping my hands around my hot mug of mint tea.

Outside, tourists streamed past us on the sidewalk, and I watched them absentmindedly, spooning sugar into my cup and tuning out Rowan and Ian's conversation to think about Lina. I hadn't seen her in more than three months. What was tonight going to be like? Would we just pick up where we left off? Would we have to get used to each other again?

Our server had just set our plates in front of us when suddenly one of the passersby snapped me out of my peppermint-infused daze. He was tall with wide shoulders, a massive pair of headphones, and an undeniable swagger that reminded me of . . .

"Walter!" I squeaked. He glanced in the window and stopped dead, his gaze on Ian.

"NO." Ian dropped his spoon into his mug, sending hot water splattering. My instinct was to dive under the booth, but Walter's glare traveled from Ian straight down to me, and suddenly we were making eye contact. Furious eye contact.

"Is this seriously happening again?" Rowan groaned. "This island is way too small."

"Who is he?" our server asked, holding a pitcher of water in her hand. Walter pressed his face to the window, his breath steaming up the glass. "Is he dangerous?"

"Moderately," I muttered, jumping to my feet.

Walter pushed his headphones off and marched for the door, his lips already moving in an angry diatribe that we were privileged to be a part of the second he opened the door. "—two are the worst!" he yelled. "Here I am doing my best to forget that Addie appeared out of nowhere at Blarney Castle, and now you're here EATING BREAKFAST." He roared "eating breakfast" like it was at the top of a list of offenses people could commit against him. Secrets did not look good on Walt.

"Sir. Calm down," the server ordered, wielding her serving tray like a shield. "Can I interest you in a nice cup of tea? Maybe one of our soothing flavors? Chamomile? Lemon lavender? It's on the house."

"He's not a big tea drinker, but thanks," I said politely.

"Walt, stay calm," Ian commanded, edging away from the window. "Where's Mom?"

Walt yanked his headphones away from around his neck. "What are you even doing here?"

I gestured to Ian. "Rowan and I told you back at Blarney Castle. We're working on Ian's paper."

He shook his head disgustedly. "BS. I talked to Archie about it, and he thought it sounded made-up too. You don't need to go to a foreign country to do research for an admissions essay. Which makes you a liar," he said, thrusting his finger at Rowan. "Do you even wear John Varvatos cologne?" Rowan grimaced slightly but said nothing.

"You told Archie?" Ian demanded, bouncing to his feet. His map was on the table, and he quickly shuffled it aside.

Walter scowled. "Of course I did. I had to tell *someone*."

I shot a nervous look out the window. He hadn't answered Ian's question. "Where's Mom?" I repeated.

"At the cathedral. I talked her into letting me skip it."

The cathedral was only two blocks away. How close had we come to running into them?

Walt lasered in on Ian. "Now, for the last time, what are you doing in Ireland?" The server cowered at his tone, and I gazed longingly at my plate of fluffy eggs. Breakfast was not going to happen. And Walt wasn't going to believe any more of our lies. Time to come clean.

"Ian, just tell him." I sighed.

Ian grabbed a wad of napkins and mopped up the splattered tea. "We're going to a music festival called Electric Picnic to see my favorite band, Titletrack, do their final show. I had it planned all along. Addie intercepted me on the way out, so that's why she's here too."

Walt's eyebrows shot to the ceiling. "I knew it! I knew you were lying. So that makes international mentor here—"

"Ian's friend," Rowan piped up. "And fellow Titletrack fan. And I actually do wear John Varvatos. The Artisan Acqua scent is my favorite." Walt eyed him critically. He had to quit taking his scents so seriously.

Ian started again. "Walt, this is the plan. After the festival, we're going to meet you in Dublin to fly—"

"Just stop!" Walter threw his arms up and backed quickly toward the door. "Don't tell me any more. Just be safe and stop running into us."

"Deal," I said eagerly.

"You guys obviously aren't sticking to the itinerary," Ian pressed. "Where are you going next?"

"I don't know. Some rock place?"

"Rock of Cashel?" Ian slammed his fist onto the table. "But that's where we're going."

Rowan shook his head. "It's a really common tourist spot. I'm not surprised."

"Well, you're not going there anymore," Walt said, his Adam's apple protruding. "Because if you guys show up there, it's over. I'm barely keeping it together as is."

"Walt, please." I pressed my hands into a prayer. "You have to keep it together. I can't get kicked off the soccer team. Just don't tell anyone else." Out of all the siblings,

Walt and I were the ones who loved sports the most. He had to understand.

"What do you think I've been doing since Blarney Castle? I'm trying to help you guys out." He stumbled over to the door, looking out at the street before pushing it open. "They'll be at the cathedral for maybe twenty more minutes. You'd better get out of here. Fast." He shot out onto the sidewalk, the door slamming behind him.

"Now what do we do?" I asked, edging away from the window.

"Well, we're not going to Rock of Cashel." Ian's face fell in disappointment. "That was going to be a huge part of my article."

Rowan pushed his glasses up his nose. "Actually . . . I might have a place better than Rock of Cashel. It's a little bit of a detour, but it's close to Stradbally. And if the rumors are true, this place may have something to do with Titletrack."

"Really? What is it?" I asked.

He smiled at me. "It's a secret."

Secret Fairy Ring

I'm not exaggerating when I say "secret," pet. This next stop is pure off-the-beaten-path gold. An experience that you can stash in your carry-on and pull out when the jerk in 23A starts bragging about all the under-the-radar local places he visited on his trip. (Not that you asked.)

In general I'm all for the wander-till-you-find-it method of travel, but in this case, winging it just isn't going to cut it. Not when there's magic involved. Follow the map I've included on the next page to a T, then meet back here.

You make it? I knew you would. Such a capable duck.

Now, before you start slogging your way through that unassuming clump of trees on the east side of the road, I'm going to lay out a few ground rules. Fairy Etiquette 101. And I don't want to sound too dramatic, but your compliance or failure to follow these rules may alter your entire destiny.

So, you know. Comply.

Rule #1. Tread carefully.

Fairies need a place to dance their fairy dances and hold their fairy tea parties. And if they're Irish fairies, well, then they also need a place to plot the certain demise of anyone who has ever so much as looked at them cross-eyed. Which leads me to my next rule.

Rule #2. Don't make the fairies mad.

Irish fairies have the reputation of being just the teensiest bit vindictive. Like steal-your-baby, burn-your-barn-down vindictive. Irish fairies don't mess around, and you shouldn't either. Speak gently, don't tread on the flowers, and do your best to entertain only the kindest of thoughts.

Rule #3. Leave the fairies a gift.

I would suggest something tiny as well as either beautiful or delicious. Coins, honey, thimbles, fish tacos, your neighbor's firstborn . . . all excellent choices.

Rule #4. Make a wish.

Showing up to a fairy's home and not making a wish is like showing up to a junior high dance and refusing to do the Electric Slide. Not only is it unprecedented, but it's also rude. Also, be aware that real-life fairies act less as dream granters and more as dream *guiders*—helping you to figure out what it is your heart truly wants and then nudging you all along the way toward it. So listen closely, pet. You may hear something that surprises you.

HEARTACHE HOMEWORK: Fill in your wish here. I promise not to look.

_____

_____

_____

_____

—Excerpt from *Ireland for the Heartbroken: An Unconventional Guide to the Emerald Isle, third edition*

CLOVER'S ENGINE WAS COOL AS A MINT JULEP, HER tailpipe reattached with something a bit more trustworthy than a hanger. We'd sprinted for the mechanic shop, pooled our money to pay for the repairs, then torn out of Cobh like mobsters on a bootleg run. We'd been in such a rush that I'd even skipped the *I told you it was the radiator* gloat speech I'd mentally prepared for Connor.

After Walt run-in number two, it was becoming increasingly clear that Mom finding out was much less a question of *if,* but *when.* I held tight to my final sliver of hope. Maybe he wouldn't tell. But Walt had been on the verge of spontaneous combustion—anyone could see that. Every time a vehicle pulled onto the road behind us, I spun around, expecting to see Aunt Mel's tour bus bearing down on us, my infuriated mom in the driver's seat.

"Do you think Mom knows by now?" I asked, watching the trees whoosh by. "What about now?"

"Addie," Ian groaned, but a smile hovered just under the tension in his voice. Sometimes, joking was the only way to make it through. Particularly when you were about to get caught for sneaking away on a European road trip and in the process lose the thing you cared about the most. I glanced up at Ian's tangled hair. Well, maybe soccer didn't matter the *most*. But the fact remained, we'd begun the trip with the express hope that our parents would never find out, and now we were hoping to make it just a few more hours so we could go to the concert.

My, how the mighty had fallen.

It helped that Lina and Titletrack were already pinpoints of light on the road ahead. My stomach twisted in anticipation.

"I still say Walter isn't going to tell on you," Rowan offered. He was driving a solid twenty kilometers over the speed limit, cutting straight through turns, but now that we were on day three I didn't even bat an eye. He was actually a very alert driver, and the safe feelings I had around him transferred to being in his car. Ian, on the other hand, was channeling his inner Kermit the Frog, his face a dusky green.

I gestured to Ian. "Better ease up. This one isn't looking good."

"I'm fine," Ian insisted, but then in a rare moment of honesty he backtracked. "Nope, you're right. Not fine." He glanced over at Rowan. "I still don't get what this guidebook stop has to do with Titletrack."

Rowan beamed. "You'll see." Whatever the connection, he was very proud of himself over it. Sunlight kept blasting on and off and through our windows, and every time it hit his face, a constellation of freckles lit up on the bridge of his nose. It was oddly mesmerizing.

Finding the fairy ring was not a terribly straightforward process. Instead of regular directions, Guidebook Lady's map used landmarks like "rock that looks like David Bowie in 1998" and "barn the color of sin" to guide us. We had to circle around the road a few times and google David Bowie just to get within striking distance.

Finally, we pulled over, crossing the road to a clump of trees that looked incredibly unpromising. By this point, Ian was a bundle of nerves. Pukey nerves. Hopefully, all the U-turns would be worth it.

"What is a fairy ring anyway?" Ian asked, stepping off the road and into the mud.

"Fairy rings are actually ring forts," Rowan said. "They're the remains of medieval farms. People used to dig moats and then use the earth to make circular barriers. Their remains are all over Ireland. But for a long time people didn't know what they were, so they came up with magical explanations."

I didn't need any more convincing. "Let's go." I marched for the forest like I knew what I was doing. I hesitated for a moment before plunging into the mud. It had the consistency of extra-sloppy peanut butter. My Converse were not going to survive this trip. Ian groaned, sludging his way forward.

Rowan slogged up next to me. "You know what we're looking for, right? It's a raised circular wall, either made of stone or—"

"Like that?" I pointed to a rounded bank draped with patches of grass and moss, and we all hurried over.

But finding the fairy ring and getting into the fairy ring were two very different situations. The bank was about five feet tall and reminded me of a vertical Slip 'N Slide.

"How should we . . . ?" Rowan started, but Ian charged up behind us, summiting the ledge in four big steps. "I guess like that."

"Whoa. What is this place?" Ian shouted once he'd made it over the bank.

"Ian, no yelling!" I said, breaking my own rule. "You'll make the fairies mad."

"You think I'm scared of fairies when *Mom* is out there?" He hesitated, his voice settling reverently. "Seriously, though. What is this place?"

Rowan and I exchanged a look, then hauled ourselves up as quickly as possible. But as usual, Ian had made it look easier than it actually was. I fell backward twice, both times losing my balance and tumbling into the mud.

"Need a little help, Maeve?" I glanced up to see Rowan biting his cheeks.

"Are you *laughing*?" I demanded.

"No way. I'm much too scared of you for that. I was just standing here wondering if I've ever seen anyone fail so badly at climbing a five-foot hill."

"It's my shoes. I'm supposed to be riding around Italy on a scooter, not hiking through mud." I attacked the hill again, this time allowing Rowan to help haul me up.

Once I had my balance I leaned in close. "Okay, tell me the truth: Is this really a Titletrack site, or were you just trying ease Ian's devastation?"

"It really is." Rowan was one of those rare people who was even cuter up close. His gray eyes were flecked with blue, and a constellation of freckles danced across his nose, lit up by the sun.

"Guys! Look at this."

I tore my gaze from Rowan, instantly forgetting about the freckles. All around us, tall, beautiful trees echoed the circle, their branches reaching over to form a protective umbrella over the ring. But it was the light that got me. Sunlight had to filter through so many layers of leaves that by the time it reached the ring, it cast a warm, lucky glow.

If fairies lived anywhere, it had to be here.

Without breaking the silence, Rowan and I slipped carefully down the bank and into the ring. At ground level, everything was a notch or two quieter, the wind moving silkily through the grass. Small, shiny trinkets covered a gray stump in the circle's center: three gold thimbles, a silver lighter, two pearl-inlaid bobby pins, and a lot of coins.

"Wow," Rowan whispered quietly. He reached into his pocket, coming up with a handful of coins and a foil-wrapped stick of gum.

Real-life fairies act less as dream granters and more as dream guiders—*helping you to figure out what it is your heart truly wants and then nudging you all along the way toward it. So listen closely, pet. You may hear something that surprises you.*

I shuffled through my pocket, emerging with a handful of coins left over from paying for our spilled eggs at the coffee shop. I handed one to Ian. "We have to make wishes, and then place these on the stump as an offering."

"Just like Jared did," Rowan said triumphantly.

Ian's eyes grew wide, and not because Rowan's voice was over the fairy-approved decibels. "*Jared* came here?"

Rowan nodded, finally letting his smile break loose. "This morning I was reading more about Titletrack's early days, and I came across this old interview where Jared told a story about stopping at a fairy ring near Cobh. He was actually on his way to Kinsale, which is farther south, but he happened to stop at Au Bohair for lunch, and he met Miriam."

I bounced happily on my feet. "He stopped to make a

wish, and the rest is history. You really think this is the fairy ring he stopped at?"

Rowan shrugged. "I can't really know, but he said it was close to Cobh, and this is pretty much the only main road from Dublin. And here's the part I really liked about the story. Instead of wishing to become a famous musician, he said he asked the fairies for 'the next thing he needed.' A few hours later he met Miriam, and *then* the rest was history."

"Rowan, this is perfect!" Ian yelled, disregarding the fairies' delicate ears. He pointed to the stump. "This is the real beginning of Titletrack. Right here."

Rowan splayed his arms out proudly. "Didn't I say I'd deliver?"

I squeezed his arm. "Nice work, Rowan."

"All right, then, time for wishes," Ian announced. "If it worked for Jared, it'll work for us. Rowan, you found this place, so you go first."

Rowan strode over to the stump and carefully placed his gum next to a bobby pin. As he set it down, something about his posture changed. Opened up. There was a long, quiet pause, and when he spoke, his voice was quiet and clear. "I wish my mom and dad would let go of each other."

I suddenly felt like a trespasser, stumbling upon a private moment. Ian and I exchanged a quick glance. Did Rowan need a moment alone? I began edging backward, but Rowan's voice held me in place.

"My entire life they've always fought." He turned back toward us, his face even. "Bad fights. Even in public. Once we were out to dinner and their fighting got so bad that someone called the guards." He shuddered lightly. "I was so relieved on New Year's when they told me they were getting a divorce, because I thought, *Finally. It's over.*

"But it isn't over. They don't live in the same house anymore, but in some ways they're just as connected to each other by anger as they were by marriage. And now I'm always in the middle—I can't get away from it." He gestured toward the car. "They want me to choose who to live with for the school year. That's why all my stuff is packed into Clover. I still don't know which one. Both places sound miserable."

My heart thickened. "Rowan . . . ," I started, but I didn't know where to go from there. Sunlight spilled over him, highlighting all the layers of his sadness. I'd never thought of connection that way—that hatred could be just as binding as love. My chest ached for him.

"I'm so sorry," Ian said. "I didn't know you were going through all this. I would have tried to help."

"You did help; you just didn't know it." Rowan dug the toe of his sneaker into the ground. "I needed someone who knew me outside of my family context. And I'm sorry I kept harping on you guys about your arguing—it just kept triggering me. I know your mom can be hard on you, but you look out for each other, and I can tell your family is the real deal." He looked up, his eyes open and vulnerable. "I just wish I had what you have."

My feet carried me to him, my arm slipping around his back. "Rowan, you do have us. We're here with you, and we'll be here as long as you need us."

Ian flanked his other side, the three of us looking down at the stump. I carefully set a coin down. "My wish is for Rowan," I said, measuring my words. "I wish that Rowan will be happy, and that he'll know he's not alone."

"Me too," Ian said, setting his coin next to mine. "My wish is for Rowan."

Rowan didn't thank us. He didn't have to. Over the past three ridiculous days, Rowan had been carrying us, holding steady through our fights and bitter remarks. This was about thanking him.

Finally, Rowan broke the silence. "I think that helped. Anyone feel like going to Electric Picnic?"

"I guess," I said nonchalantly, and Ian grinned. "I don't really have any other plans."

We were exiting the muddy bank when my phone chimed. Ian stiffened. "Oh, no. Did Walt spill?"

I lifted the screen to my face. It was Olive.

ADDIE, ARE YOU OK? NOW EVERYONE IS
TALKING ABOUT CUBBY AND A PHOTO OF YOU.

No. I froze, willing the letters to rearrange, willing the message to mean something other than what it meant. My breath turned shallow, my hands clammy.

Olive's "everyone" was bigger than most people's. She was one of those rare people who managed to fit in with every social group on the high school spectrum, as comfortable with the other soccer players as she was the debate team. If she said everyone, she meant *everyone.*

Ian's face flushed as he studied my expression. "Addie, what? Is it Mom?"

I managed to hand him the phone, and his face tightened as he read the text. "Oh, no."

* * *

I cried for a solid twenty-five minutes. The tears just wouldn't stop coming. Rowan and Ian took turns giving me concerned looks, but I could barely register them.

Everyone knew. *Everyone.*

Worse, what if everyone had seen?

Ian and Rowan kept trying to ask me if I was okay, but I was inside a bubble, completely separate from them.

Finally, Ian put his energy into texting one of his teammates.

"My coach found out, Addie," he said nervously. He was looking at me like I was something brittle. Breakable. Did he not realize I was already shattered?

"How?" My voice didn't sound like mine.

"I don't know how. *I* didn't tell him. Not even when he cornered Cubby and me about what the fight was about. But now he's found out. And ..."

"And what?" My throat felt stuffed full of cotton. I couldn't even swallow.

Ian's knee ricocheted off the seat. "And there's talk that Cubby will be suspended from the team. Maybe more. It's still just rumors, but I think that's how this thing got out."

This thing.

This thing that was *me*. And my heart, and my *body*, all on display for anyone to throw rocks at. How big was it going to get? How long until Mom found out? Dad? I huddled in the corner of Clover, so miserable that my tears dried up. Both Ian and Rowan tried consoling me, but it was no use. I could already hear the whispers in the hallways. Feel the glances of boys who'd seen more of me than I'd ever show them. Teachers would know. My coaches would know. I wanted to throw up. Especially when my phone started dinging with messages from my teammates, some concerned, some just curious. **Did that really happen?**

Finally, I silenced my phone and stuffed it under Rowan's pile. What else could I do?

* * *

The closer we got to Stradbally, the tighter my body crunched into a ball. I knew we were just about there when traffic turned bumper-to-bumper and small white arrows directed us to a dirt road lit with fairy lights.

We filed slowly onto the fairgrounds in a long parade of cars, people yelling to one another and music pumping loudly from every car stereo. It reminded me of the high school parking lot every morning before the first bell rang. Home suddenly pressed in on me so tightly that I could barely breathe.

"We made it," Rowan said, meeting my eyes. His enthusiasm was a solid 98 percent lower than it should have been. Even Ian looked docile, his body remarkably still.

Ian glanced back at me and then pointed to an open field blooming with makeshift shelters—tents, caravans, teepees—all crammed together like one giant circus. "Pretty cool, right?" he asked, his voice soft. "And think, Lina will be here soon. It will all be better then."

Or worse, I silently added, my stomach twisting. Just a

couple of hours ago I'd felt good about telling Lina, but hearing from everyone back home had changed that.

Names of the designated camping sites glinted in the dimming sunlight. They were all accompanied by cartoon drawings of famous people: Oscar Wilde, Janis Joplin, Andy Warhol, and Jimi Hendrix. A man with a bright red vest ushered us into our parking spot, and Ian sprang out, stretching his arms. "I can't believe we're finally here."

"It does seem like it took us a lot longer than three days to get here," Rowan added. That I had to agree with. The Rainbow's End Hostel and Inch Beach felt like a lifetime ago.

I climbed out too and numbly followed the guys to the will call booth to pick up my ticket. Inside the gates, my first thought was *chaos*. The grounds were packed to the brim, people walking and riding and cruising around in some of the strangest outfits I'd ever seen. Lots of face paint and costumes ranging from leather capes to tutus. And music was everywhere, the separate melodies twisting together into a tight braid. Even the guys looked overwhelmed.

Finally, Ian turned to smile at us. "I say we do a big sweep, take it all in, and figure out where Titletrack is playing. Sound good?" He looked at me hopefully. What he was really saying was, *Let's distract Addie.*

"Sounds great," I said, attempting to match the glimmer

of hope in his voice. I'd been through a lot to get here; the least I could do was try to enjoy it.

Even with the costumes and overcrowding, Electric Picnic started out fairly normal, with all the usual festival ingredients: stages, food stands, eight billion porta-potties, kids screaming on carnival rides, tarot card readers ... but the longer we walked, the more I began to feel like I'd stepped into a carnival fun house.

The first truly strange sight we stumbled upon was the sunken bus. A bright red double-decker bus angled into the mud, its bottom half almost completely submerged in a ditch. Next was a human jukebox, an elevator-size structure housing an entire band taking requests. Then a trio of college-age guys ran by wearing muddy sumo wrestler costumes.

"Did that just happen?" Rowan asked, watching them in disbelief. The one in the back wore a glittery tutu fastened around his waist.

"Did *that*?" Ian asked as a man rode by on a bicycle made out of a piano.

"I feel like I just fell down a rabbit hole," I said, wishing it were enough to distract me from the phone buzzing in my pocket.

The smell of cinnamon wafted over toward us, and Rowan sniffed the air. "I'm starving. Whatever that is, I want it. Anyone else hungry?"

"Me," I said, surprising myself. Normally, when I was this upset, I had no appetite, but carnival food did sound good. Plus, my mom claimed that most of life's struggles could be cured with butter and sugar. I was willing to give it a try.

"You guys go ahead and eat," Ian offered, pulling his notebook out of his backpack. "I'm going to try to find the stage Titletrack will be performing on. See if I can get some pictures."

"Want me to get you something?" I asked.

"Nah. Meet you back here," Ian hollered, taking off, he and his man bun blending in with the herd of music lovers.

Rowan and I wandered the food trucks, finally settling on a waffle truck that put my waffle attempts to shame. I ordered the Chocolate Cloud—a Belgian waffle drizzled with a mixture of white and dark chocolate—and Rowan ordered the Flying Pig, a combination involving bacon, caramel, and fluffy crème fraîche.

Our order took a long time, and when it was finally ready, we posted up at a mostly empty picnic table and ate slowly, in a silence that I was grateful for. Most people would probably try to talk me out of how bad I was feeling, but not Rowan; he just sat next to me, occasionally offering me bites of bacon. By the time our plates were scraped clean, the day was starting to look worn-out, the edges of the sky taking on a gold hue.

I drummed my fingers on the table. "Where is he?"

"Ian?" Rowan asked, licking some crème off his fingers.

"It's been a while. I thought he'd be back by now." I squinted into the crowd. The direction he'd gone in was dark and fairly empty, clearly not where Titletrack's stage would be.

"Probably lost track of time," Rowan said, leaning in. "I don't know if you know this about your brother, but he gets pretty excited about things he's passionate about."

A snort escaped my nose. "Really? I hadn't noticed."

His dimple appeared. "There it is, Maeve."

"There what is?" I assumed he was pointing out another weird costume, but when I looked up he was studying me.

"Your laugh." He glanced down, fiddling with his napkin. "Hey, Addie, I know what it's like to have the world fall down around you. . . ."

He trailed off, and I clutched my fork, hoping he was about to say something like, *Your friends will suffer from collective amnesia and no one will even remember the photo*, or *I'm actually a time traveler come to save you from your past*, but instead what he said was, "Today is a bad day, but it won't always be this bad. I promise."

I nodded, my eyes fogging up. I knew he was right, of course. Bad things knocked people off their feet all the time, and they got back up and kept moving. But right now I had a mountain in front of me, plus a whole pocketful of texts, and I had no idea how I'd reach the summit.

I shifted at the table, my eyes seconds away from giving the Irish rain a run for its money, but just then Rowan reached over, his hand as warm and comforting as it had been back at Inch Beach. "And what you said back at the fairy ring? About you and Ian standing next to me? That's true for you, too. I know I can't fix this, but I am here for you."

His eyes were earnest behind his glasses, and a pinpoint of calm suddenly dropped into my center, slowly rippling outward. Life could be so unexpected—I was supposed to be eating spaghetti in Italy, yet here I was, finishing up a waffle in the cold drizzle of Ireland, with a new friend I knew I could rely on. "Thanks, Rowan. That means a lot."

Rowan broke eye contact, his hand leaving mine as he looked over my shoulder. "Ian's back."

I stood up quickly, but before I could turn around, a hurricane of curly hair hit me so hard, I almost fell over.

"Lina!" I yelled, and in response she hugged me to the point of asphyxiation, my face planted in her lemon-scented curls. "Lina. I can't breathe," I managed.

"Oops. Sorry." She stumbled backward, and I laughed for no reason other than I was so relieved to see her, I almost couldn't stand it.

"Lina, you look amazing!" I said. She really did. Italy

looked good on her. Her skin was a dark olive color, and instead of her trying to tame her hair the way she always had, it fell loose around her face in bouncing, voluminous curls. Maybe it was the wild familiarity of her hair that got me, but suddenly I was blinking back tears. *Please don't let me start crying within the first few seconds of seeing her.*

"I can't believe I'm here. What *is* this place? Back at the entrance there were two guys running around inside a big rolling plastic ball." Lina stepped back, catching sight of Rowan. "Are you Rowan?"

"That's me," Rowan said, shaking her hand. I waited for him to do the Lina stare. All guys did it—between her hair and her big eyes, she was a lot to take in—but he just smiled politely and then glanced over at me. "I can see you why you two are friends. You're both really good at making an entrance."

She grinned and put her arm around me. "We do our best."

Ian suddenly appeared, deep in conversation with a guy roughly Lina's height, a mess of dark, curly hair crowning his face. "Ian found us near the fairy woods," Lina explained.

"Ren?" I asked the curly-haired stranger. His nose was exceptionally Italian, and when he smiled, a small gap between his front teeth instantly put me at ease.

Ren yanked me in for a hug. "So nice to meet you. I've heard things."

I knew what he meant, but I still stiffened slightly. *Not*

those things, I instructed myself. He didn't mean the text messages, or Cubby. But it was too late; panic crept through my center, and suddenly my head spun. Telling Lina had been hypothetical for so long, and now the moment was here.

Of course, Lina zeroed in on my uneasiness. "Addie? Are you okay?"

I'd better just tell her now. Get it over with. I swallowed nervously. "Lina, can we talk in priv—"

"I just found a Titletrack museum in the woods," Ian interrupted, sidling up next to me. "I don't know who made it, but you guys *have* to see it." And before I could protest, he was suddenly dragging Lina and me in the direction he'd come from, Rowan and Ren trailing right behind.

I tried to dig my heels in, but his momentum was too much. "Ian, *stop*. I need to talk to Lina. I need to tell her about . . . ," I trailed off, hoping he'd take the hint.

Instead he sped up, taking us to a jog. "Sorry, but this really can't wait. The concert starts in less than an hour."

Lina's curls were bouncing in time with our pace, and she wrenched her neck back to look at the guys. "Everyone keeping up?"

"*Ma certo,*" Ren answered affirmatively.

And that's when I realized that it wasn't just Ian pulling me along—it was Lina, too. She was just as intent on getting to the museum as Ian was.

"What is going on?" I demanded. "Why are we all running?"

"Just trust us," Lina said, squeezing my arm, and then all four of them looked at me with big Cheshire-cat smiles.

This was officially getting weird.

* * *

Ian finally stopped in a clearing underneath a canopy of decorated trees. Old CDs hung by strips of ribbon, swaying gently in the evening breeze, and fairy lights snaked around tree trunks and branches. A collection of candles sat flickering on an old tree stump that reminded me of the one in the fairy ring.

"What is this?" I asked, stopping in my tracks.

"Sorry, Addie. I know you were really looking forward to a Titletrack museum, but that's not what this is." Ian grinned at me, then turned to Lina. "Did you bring the ceremonial garb?"

"Of course." She unhooked her arm from mine and then dropped her overstuffed backpack to the ground, pulling out four long white pieces of fabric and tossing them to everyone.

I stared as everyone began twisting the fabric into haphazard togas. "Are those sheets? What's going on?"

Ian knotted his over his shoulder. "We're putting on our ceremonial garb."

"What ceremony?"

"And this is for you." Lina pulled a long, plum-colored

shawl from the bottom of her bag and draped it carefully around me, pulling my ponytail out from under it.

I grabbed the bottom edge and held it up to the light. Intricate mandalas swirled through the pattern. "Where have I seen this before?"

"It was my mom's. She wore it to all of her gallery nights; she said it made her feel royal."

My heart quickened. "Lina, this is special. You really want me to wear this?"

"No, I want you to keep it." She straightened the shawl so it sat evenly on my shoulders, and I bit the inside of my cheek, holding back my protest. Every bit of me wanted to refuse the gift, but I couldn't; it was too meaningful. "Thank you," I said, my voice wobbly.

"You're welcome. Now let's go. Attendant?" Lina gestured for Rowan, who quickly moved to my side, escorting me to the twinkling tree stump.

"Rowan, will you tell me what's going on?" I whispered. "Did you know about this?"

His dimple lit up in the twinkling lights. "Sorry, Maeve, but I was sworn to secrecy. What I can tell you is that this is not a Titletrack museum."

Ian gestured to the stump. "Everyone, grab a candle so Addie can stand up there." His hair looked extra tangly, the hood of his sweatshirt poking out over the top of his toga.

I shook my head quickly. "Oh, no. We are not re-creating Au Bohair." The stump was completely entrenched in lights, and even though we were on the edge of the grounds, plenty of festivalgoers still milled around us, a few already stopping to watch.

"Relax. You don't have to say anything. We'll be the ones doing the talking. So climb up," Ian said firmly.

"Why?"

He exhaled loudly. "Can you please not fight me for once? Please?"

It was the extra "please" that got me. I climbed up and then turned to face my friends. They'd formed a half circle around me, their candles casting strange shadows on their faces. It looked like I was about to be initiated into a cult. Or sacrificed. "What is going on?"

They shared a conspiratorial grin. Then Ian nodded at Ren. "Okay, master of ceremonies. Start us out."

Ren cleared his throat and then let loose, his voice booming through the trees. "Ladies and gentlemen. Stradballas and stradballees. We have before us a fair maiden—"

"Ren, don't improvise," Lina interrupted. "Just go with the script. What we talked about."

"*Nessun problema.*" He cleared his throat again. "On this fine summer day, there was a group of people who loved someone and wanted her to know they had her back. And so they held the first ceremony of Queen Maeve. Here at Stradbally, in full view of many."

"In full view of many" was right. The crowd was growing by the second, no doubt hoping for a show. Ren gestured theatrically, raising his voice to the tops of the trees. "And so, like Queen Maeve of old, we have put her in a high place and will honor her by building her up, one rock at a time."

Suddenly, I noticed a pile of fist-size rocks at their feet, and I realized what this was about. They were re-creating Queen Maeve's growing tomb—the one Rowan had told me about back when he first dubbed me Maeve. "Wait a minute. Whose idea was this?" I asked.

"Ian's," Lina said.

Ian shook his head. "We all get some credit. Rowan gave you the nickname, I came up with the ceremony, Lina brought all the supplies, and Ren is master of ceremonies."

"Ian called me right before we left for the airport," Lina filled in. "I only had fifteen minutes to prepare."

"My mom helped," Ren added. "She has a surprising number of fairy lights at her disposal."

"This is . . ." I bit my lower lip, not sure what to say. My eyes were already burning with tears. "So what do I do?" I managed.

"Just stand there." Ren turned to Lina. "You're up, *principessa*."

Lina picked up the rock closest to her, stumbling on her toga as she stepped forward.

"A good friend is like a four-leaf clover. Hard to find, lucky to have." She paused, weighing the rock in her hand. "I didn't make that up. I saw it on a T-shirt at the airport." She turned slightly, addressing the group. "For those of you who don't know, my mom died last year. Her illness was very sudden, and it took her much too fast." Her voice trembled, but she looked up, locking her eyes on mine and lowering her voice a bit. "Remember right at the end, when my mom couldn't breathe on her own anymore and they knew it was only going to be a few hours?"

I nodded. The memory was etched into my mind. I would never forget answering that phone call. Lina had been crying so hard that I couldn't understand her. All I knew was that I had to get to the hospital. Fast. The old familiar clamp moved over my throat.

Lina exhaled, making the flame on her candle jump. "It was four in the morning, and even though I'd known this was coming, I suddenly felt like it was all brand-new. Like the diagnosis and treatments and everything had just been some elaborate joke. My grandma was there—she was crying so hard, and my mom was hooked up to all these monitors. It was the first moment that I truly understood that I was going to lose her." Tears were running down her face, but she didn't bother to wipe them away. Ren slipped his hand onto her back. "But do you know what I remember most about that night?"

I shook my head, not trusting my voice.

"You. Less than ten minutes after I called you, you came running down the hallway to her room. All the nurses were yelling at you to stop, but you didn't care—you just came running straight up to me. And you'd left your house so fast, you hadn't even put on your shoes." She paused, her eyes glittering. "That's what I'll always remember. You running barefoot down the hall, the nurses yelling as they chased after you. That's who you really are, and I'll never forget that when I needed you the most, you literally didn't wait a single second. You just showed up." She stepped forward, placing the rock at the base of the stump. "All hail Queen Maeve. My best and fastest friend."

We were both crying, tears washing down our cheeks. I'd never considered that that terrible night could hold something other than just pain. Something that Lina would carry with her as a comfort.

"Me next." Ren picked up a rock and stepped forward, squeezing Lina's shoulder. "Has everyone tried Starbursts?"

The abrupt shift in subject made me laugh. There was some general nodding, most of it from outside our circle, and I kept my eyes on Ren, trying not to notice that the crowd was now three people deep. Lina had once confided in me that Ren had the kind of looks that grew on you—the longer you knew him, the cuter he got. I suddenly saw exactly what she meant.

He continued. "Well, I love Starbursts. Whenever I'm in the States, I eat them nonstop. And you know how there's a social order to them? Like you dump out a bag and you eat all the pinks first, then the reds and oranges, leaving the yellows for when you're really desperate?"

Where was he going with this? I glanced at Lina, but she just smiled.

"Anyway, the point is, Addie, you're a pink. Everyone knows you're a pink. Actually, scratch that. You're next-level. You're that limited-edition kind that had all pinks. And I know that because when Lina needed you, you were there." He set his rock down. "All hail Queen Maeve. The pinkest of pink Starbursts."

"Thanks, Ren," I whispered. My body didn't seem to know how to handle what was happening. Laugh? Cry? Enjoy? I was going to go with enjoy.

Next, Rowan stepped forward, his rock resting by his side. The stump made us almost eye-level, but he didn't meet my gaze, and his nervousness wafted onto me. My heart began pounding even harder.

He exhaled. "Okay. Pink Starburst is always tough to follow, but here goes." He rocked anxiously on his feet, a move that looked Ian-inspired. "Three days ago, I was sitting in my broken-down, crappy car when I saw this girl tackle her brother in a parking lot. I thought she was surprising. And different. So I talked her brother into letting her come with us, which ended up completely ruining her plans." He looked up guiltily, shuffling his feet.

"But then the next three days were incredible, because I found out she was more than just feisty. She was smart. And loyal. And completely incapable of dressing weather-appropriate. And we talked about things I'd never talked about with anyone. And even when our car flooded, and we got chased by guard dogs . . . I just kept thinking, *I wish this week would never end.*"

He lifted his chin, looking me straight in the eye. "And I wanted to tell you that you don't need that guy back home. You don't need anyone, unless you want them. You're enough all on your own. You're more than enough. You're Maeve."

A warm, peaceful feeling settled on my shoulders, light as a second shawl. This was the thing that I'd lost track of this summer. That being chosen—or not chosen—was not the thing that made me valuable. I was valuable regardless. I was enough, all on my own. I wanted to climb down and rest my head on his shoulder, but instead I just ducked my head. "Thank you, Rowan," I whispered.

"You're welcome. All hail Queen Maeve." He bent to lower the rock, softening his voice so only I could hear. "I wish I didn't have to say good-bye to you tomorrow."

"Me neither," I whispered back.

Lina met my eye gleefully over the top of Rowan's head, unable to contain her smile. I smiled back.

Rowan returned to his place, and Ian stepped forward, holding up his candle to his open notebook, a string of words marching across the page. He'd prepared something. I straightened up.

"You know that question Mr. Hummel likes to ask at the beginning of the semester? 'If a tree falls in the forest and no one is around to hear it, does it make a sound?'"

I nodded. It was one of those problems designed to make your brain run in circles.

His candle bobbed. "Well, the first time I heard that question it made me think of you. Because my whole life it's felt like unless you were there—helping me blow out my birthday candles, cheering me on in the stands, out on our field trips—whatever I did didn't actually matter. That it didn't count. You're the only person who knows my whole life—who's been there with me through everything. Which makes you my life's witness." He lowered his notebook to his side. "So what's the answer? If a tree falls in a forest and your little sister isn't there to hear it, did it make a sound? I'm not really sure. I'm just glad we're in the same forest." He set his rock down, then stepped back with the others. "All hail Queen Maeve, my best and oldest friend."

Tears puddled under my chin, and I stood looking at Ian,

his eyes forming a shiny mirror, reflecting all the things he saw in me. Then one more voice chimed in, this one in my mind. *What about you, buttercup? What do you see in yourself?*

I looked hard. I saw a lot of things: bravery, compassion, perseverance, insecurity, even fear. But rising out of all of it, I saw Maeve. Her hair shone, and she held a shield, her throne solid behind her. And suddenly it was me on the throne—my robe thick and soft around me.

The upcoming year was going to be hard, no doubt about it. And maybe even the year after it. But I was strong enough. And brave enough. I was Maeve, and I was going to make it.

I jumped off the stump and let my friends encircle me in a warm, tight cocoon.

* * *

Everyone who wasn't already on the lawn in front of Titletrack's stage was headed there, streaming from every possible crevice. It wasn't just our main event—it was everyone's main event.

A muffled, faraway noise sounded over a loudspeaker, instigating a dull roar from the crowd and making us all quicken our pace. Ian bounded ahead, his toga trailing in the mud. None of us had bothered to change out of our ceremonial garb; there wasn't time. It actually made us fit in more with the rest of the festivalgoers.

"I'm going to find us a spot." Ian disappeared into the crowd.

"I hope we can find him when we get there." I held tightly to Rowan's hand, partially to keep us from getting separated and partially because once the group hug had ended, it had just happened. I couldn't get over the way our hands fit together. Like they'd been sitting on opposite ends of the globe just waiting for the chance to meet.

The crowd was turning brutal, bordering on absurd. We'd just survived a near-collision with a man on a bike wearing a peacock costume when a high-pitched choking noise that sounded vaguely like *oh, no* erupted from behind me.

"Lina, what's wrong?" Ren asked.

"Addie." Lina put her hand on my back, her voice still choked. I turned to meet her wide eyes, but instead got snagged on something moving rocket-fast toward me through the crowd. Was that . . . ?

It was.

The rocket was my mother.

"Oh, no," I choked, echoing Lina. *Run*, my brain advised, but even in my panicked state I knew that was a terrible idea. Running would just mean pursuit.

My mom was next to me in a matter of milliseconds. "Hello, Addison. Lina." Her pitch had reached new and terrifying depths. "You'd better start talking. Fast."

"How did you . . . find us?" I stammered.

The answer to my question appeared to her left. Walter. Followed swiftly by Archie, who held a massive bag of cotton candy. "Walter, you told her?" I yelled.

He held his hands up in protest. "It wasn't me. It was Archie. He got the secret out of me, and then he told Mom."

"Hey!" Archie tried to hit Walter in the face with his cotton candy, but my mom grabbed it midswing. "Don't blame it on me."

"No more talking." Mom turned back to me, her face set in a hard stare. Not many people knew this, but back in her college days she'd been one of the top roller derby contenders in the state. It was times like this that I knew exactly why she'd skated under the name Medusa Damage.

"Addison, you are supposed to be in Italy. *Italy*." While I fumbled for an answer, she turned to Lina. "Does Howard know you're here?"

"Rowan, go warn Ian!" I whispered, taking advantage of the momentary distraction. He nodded and then sprinted into the crowd, no doubt thrilled to escape Medusa.

Lina nodded, her head bobbing one too many times. "Nice to see you, Mrs. Bennett. And yes, he does know. He booked my ticket." She shoved Ren forward a few unwilling inches. "This is my boyfriend, Ren."

"Hello there," Ren managed. "Really great to meet you."

He withered under her gaze, and I jumped to the rescue. "Mom, I can explain. This concert is really important to Ian—"

She lifted her hand angrily, silencing me. "Where is Ian?"

Now what? The last thing I wanted to do was unleash Mom on Ian. What if she didn't let him see the concert? "Um . . . I'm not really sure."

"Boys!" My mom snapped her fingers, and Archie and Walt jumped to attention. "You two are the tallest people in this crowd. Find him."

Walt stood on his tiptoes, craning his neck over the crowd, and Archie ran over to a music speaker and began climbing.

"Yeah, I don't think that's allowed," Lina said, just as a security guard made a beeline for him.

"Man bun in a white toga. Straight ahead," Archie shouted as the security guard dragged him back to ground level.

"Why are you guys wearing togas anyway?" Walter asked.

Suddenly, a loud cheer erupted in the distance, followed by a jangling strain of music. My heart somersaulted. "Mom, the concert is starting. I don't have time to explain why, but this is the most important thing that has ever happened to Ian. You have to let him see it."

My intensity caught even me off guard. Catarina would be proud. *Rule number four: Be passionate. No one can argue with passion.*

My mom stepped back slightly, her perfectly shaped eyebrows lifting. "Sounds like you two are getting along again."

I nodded. "Better than ever."

She hesitated, then gestured to Archie and Walter. "Everyone, follow me." Needless to say, we all complied.

Even though Rowan had provided him with a few minutes of warning, the sight of our approaching mother drained all the blood from Ian's face. "Mom," he choked. It was the only way either of us could seem to greet her.

"Ian," she said coolly. "There are a lot of things I want to say to you right now, but your sister claims that this is the most important thing in the world to you. So I'm giving you tonight." She pointed one finger at his chest. "But after the concert? You will both undergo extensive questioning and will most likely be grounded for the rest of your lives. Understood?"

"Understood. Thank you, ma'am," Ian said, shooting me a grateful look. In our family, "ma'am" was code for *I know you're going to pummel me into a fine pulp, and I respect you for that.* My mom nodded approvingly.

Rowan stepped forward, wringing his hands nervously. "Mrs. Bennett? I'm Rowan. Nice to meet you."

She tilted her head. "Ah. The Irish tutor."

"He's my friend," Ian said.

"And mine," I added.

"So then tell me, friend Rowan, why are we standing here when Titletrack is about to perform onstage, all the way up there?" She lifted her chin toward the front of the writhing mass of bodies. "How are we going to even see?"

"That is a problem," Rowan said. "We probably should have arrived a lot earlier. Like, yesterday."

Ian bit his lower lip, his face clouding, and defiance rose in me. *Oh, no.* I had not been through everything I'd been through just to stand at the back of a concert watching my brother crumple into a ball of disappointment.

But before I could come up with a solution, my mom clapped her hands together. "All right, people. Form a chain. We're going in."

"Going in where?" Ian asked. "Those people look like they've been here all week."

"Ian, don't argue with me. For all you know this is your last living act, so you might as well enjoy it." A glimmer sparkled in her eye as she surveyed the crowd, and suddenly I remembered the stash of vintage records she'd kept in the attic for as long as I could remember. The proverbial apple had not fallen far from the tree.

"Do I need to speak louder?" she asked when none of us moved. "Form a chain."

All the non-Bennetts went wide-eyed with disbelief as we obediently grabbed one another's hands.

"Ready?" Mom turned resolutely to the wall of people in front of her, Medusa Damage revealing herself in all her terrifying splendor. "COMING THROUGH."

"Hey, watch it!" a guy in a blue hat yelled at her as she jammed her elbow into him.

"No, *you* watch it," she snapped. "I'm about to ground these children for the rest of their underage lives because of this concert. The least they can do is enjoy it."

"Damn," Blue Hat's friend said. "Carry on."

"Has anyone ever told you that you're your mother?" Rowan whispered, his hand tight in mine. "I don't know who's scarier, Maeve or Mother of Maeve."

"I'm going to take that as a compliment," I whispered back.

It took us nearly the entire opening act, but my mother and her elbows managed to get us near the front, even clearing out a small pocket of space for us to stand all together. Once she stopped assaulting them, people sealed in, cinching us tightly together.

"Mom, that was amazing," Ian said, his face rapturous. "Thank you."

"I'm not saying you're welcome, because that would sound like I'm condoning this," she snapped. But the glint was still in her eye.

I did my best to settle into the crowd. My entire body felt bruised and sticky from colliding with so many Titletrack fans. Everyone was sweating. The temperature inside the crowd was at least ten degrees higher than on the outskirts.

Laser lights spilled over the stage, bathing us in bright red, and then four silhouettes appeared onstage as if by magic. "That's them!" Ian shouted, grabbing my arm as tightly as a tourniquet. "Rowan! Addie! That's them!"

"Ian, ease up!" I yelled, but my voice got sucked up into the vortex of screaming.

The first chords started up, and I recognized the song immediately. "Classic." The one that had been made into a music video at the Burren. At first Ian looked too stunned to react, and then instead of smiling, a large tear zigzagged down his red-lit cheek. "What's wrong?" I shouted.

He squeezed my arm again, his fingernails forming half-moons in my skin. "We're here," he said simply.

The rest of the band joined in with the song, filling my ears and anchoring me to Ian and this moment. And suddenly I was thinking about a different aspect of my future. In one year, my big brother would leave for college, and we'd be separated for the first time. What would life be like without Ian by my side?

I tried to picture it, but the only thing that sprang to mind was the road we'd followed to Electric Picnic, Ian singing along to Titletrack, Ireland green and mysterious outside our windows.

The only thing I really knew was what I had to do next.

Before I could lose my moment of certainty, I reached across Ian, tugging gently at my mom's sleeve. "Mom, after the concert is over, I need to tell you something. Something important." She swiveled her gaze from the stage just as Ian reached down to squeeze my hand.

The road narrowed and then got wider, then disappeared into the distance, too far for me to see what was ahead. And I just let it.

Love & Luck

You've come a long way, pet. Pettest of pets. You can't imagine the pride that's swelling up in my considerable bosom right at this moment to know that you have not only explored the Emerald Isle, but your broken heart is now MENDED. You are completely better, over-the-moon, one-door-closes-ten-more-open, beauty-in-the-pain better.

Right?

Right?

Let's cut the crap, pet. Because now that we're reaching the end of our time together, I feel it's time for me to come clean. I don't want that heart of yours to mend. And I never did.

What? Was she actually evil this whole time? No, pet. Heavens, no. Stick with me for a moment.

Do you know what I love most about humans, pet? It's our utter, dogged stupidity. When it comes to love, we never learn. Ever. Even when we know the risks. Even when it makes much more sense to relocate to individu-alized climate-controlled caves where our hearts have at least a fighting chance at remaining intact. We know the risks of opening our hearts up, and yet we keep doing it anyway.

We keep falling in love and having babies and buying shoes that look incredible but feel like death. We keep adopting puppies and making friends and buying white sofas that we know we're going to drop a slice of pizza facedown on. We just keep doing it.

Is it ignorance? Amnesia? Or is it something else? Something braver?

You opened this book because your heart was broken and you wanted it fixed. But that was never the cosmic plan. Hell, it was never *my* plan. Hearts break open until they stay open. It's what they were made to do. The pain? It's part of the deal. A small exchange for the wild, joyful mess you'll be handed in return.

I hate good-byes, so instead, allow me to hand you one last thought, a small Irish charm to clip to your charm bracelet. Did you know that each leaf on a clover stands for something? They do, pet. Faith, hope, and love. And should you happen to find one with four leaves? Well, that's the one that stands for luck. So, my love, I wish you all of those things. Faith, hope, love, and luck. But mostly, I wish you love. It's its own form of luck.

—Excerpt from *Ireland for the Heartbroken: An Unconventional Guide to the Emerald Isle, third edition*

Epilogue

IAN PULLED SMOOTHLY INTO A PARKING SPOT, TURNING off the ignition but leaving the music on. It was Titletrack, of course. Ever since we'd gotten home we'd been playing it non-stop, the songs overlapping in the hallway between our bedrooms, sometimes competing, sometimes meshing together. It had made a hard week a lot more bearable.

There had been a lot of upset. I'd wanted everything out in the open, so as soon as everyone was reunited, I called for a family meeting, where I laid it all out. My brothers had to be forcibly held back from storming Cubby's house, and my dad was silent and teary for a terrible ten minutes, but they'd all stood by me. And one glimmer of benefit: my news had paved the way for Ian's. His quitting football was just a firework next to my atomic bomb.

I flipped down the visor to check out the dark rings under my eyes. Jet lag combined with nerves had made for a lot of sleepless nights. Last night I'd ended up calling Rowan and staying on the phone until two a.m. watching a terrible movie he'd found on YouTube about a Celtic warrior princess named Maeve, who slashed everyone who got in her way. I think he was trying to pump me up.

Ian lowered the volume. "So, Christmas, huh?"

My cheeks warmed. I swear he could read my thoughts sometimes. "What about it?"

"A certain Irishman told me there are only sixty-eight days until his Christmas break starts. We're good friends and all, but that countdown has nothing to do with me. It's about you."

"Stop. Now." Just like I'd thought, once the situation had been ironed out, my mom and Rowan had bonded almost instantaneously. And now he was coming to visit. Every time I thought about seeing him again, a small, careful butterfly fluttered its wings in the center of my chest.

We looked out the windshield, neither of us in a hurry to leave the car. Was it just me, or had the student body magically tripled? For a second my vision tilted. How many of them know about my photo?

Probably a lot of them.

"Maeve, you ready?" Ian finally asked, the sound of his drumming fingers breaking through my thoughts.

"Yes," I said, sounding surer than I felt. *Act in control.*

"Don't worry, Addie. I'm here for you," he said, like he

hadn't heard me. "I'm going to walk you to all your classes. I already checked your schedule. My homeroom is in B hall and yours is in C, so meet me at the front office. And if anyone says anything to you, you tell them—"

"Ian, I've got this," I said more forcefully. "We just survived a road trip across Ireland in a broken-down car. I think I can handle walking into high school."

"Okay." Ian went back to drumming, his eyes serious. "I know you've got this, but if there's ever a moment when you don't, you've got me. And it doesn't matter what anyone else says. You're Maeve."

"I'm Maeve," I repeated, allowing the nervousness in his voice to extinguish mine. Was it possible that he was more worried for me than I was worried for me? I leaned on that feeling.

Outside, we pulled on our backpacks. Mine was extra heavy, because along with my textbooks, it had rocks in it. Four of them to be exact. It had been a last-minute call, but I liked the way their weight pressed into my shoulders, grounding my feet into my sneakers, my sneakers into the ground. Plus, TSA had had a complete fit about my traveling with them. I might as well put them to use.

We started across the parking lot, Ian sweeping the crowd anxiously.

"Ian, relax." I broke into a jog and fell into step beside him.

"I'm completely relaxed," he protested, but a clump of

hair found its way into his mouth. That habit, unfortunately, looked like it was here to stay. We reached the bank of doors, and he stopped, ignoring the crush of students as he rocked nervously onto his heels. "Ready, Maeve?"

It was a good question. Was I ready?

This summer had shown me that I was a lot of things. I was messy, impulsive, occasionally insecure, and sometimes I did things that I regretted—things I couldn't undo. Like not listening to my brother. Or handing over my heart to someone who couldn't be trusted with it. But despite all those things—no, *alongside* all those things—I was Maeve. Which meant that regardless of how ready I did or did not feel, I was going in anyway. This was my life, after all.

You'll do it, buttercup. You really will.

"I'm ready," I said firmly. I looked into Ian's blue eyes, gathering one last shot of courage. Then we grabbed the door handles and pushed in. Together.

Acknowledgments

Nicole Ellul and Fiona Simpson. Did you all get that? NICOLE ELLUL AND FIONA SIMPSON. The timing of this book was just a hair shy of cataclysmic, and there were many, many moments when you threw me on your backs and carried me. Thank you for your graciousness, support, wisdom, and overall awesomeness. I consider you the Goddesses of Editing. (Would it be embarrassing if I had crowns made?)

Mara Anastas. Thank you for your patience, support, and enthusiasm. I dream of having Mara energy.

Simon Pulse. You are an exceptional group of people sending exceptional books out into the world, and it is a PRIVILEGE to publish with you. *Thank you.*

Sam. Somewhere in the tornado of 2016/2017, you marched up to me and said, "Mama, I see you. And I *like* you." Not only did that line inspire a major theme of this book, but it also struck me as one of the most profound things one person can say to another. To be seen in your messy hair in your messy kitchen, by a very small and very honest person, and be deemed *likable*? It's the entire point. I see you, Sammy. And man, do I ever like you.

Nora Jane. Every second you're here makes the world better. I could compare you to a pink frosted cupcake or a perfect chocolate éclair, but that would be silly. You're a little girl, not a confection! (Although it's easy to see why one would make the mistake.) Thank you for sharing your baby years with *Love & Luck*. And I cannot even begin to tell you how much it thrills me that 90 percent of your tantrums involve wanting to be read to. I love you, Bertie Blue.

Liss. Have I ever told you that you are in my top five women I look up to? You are. Sometimes when the world gets scary, I square my shoulders and march in, attempting that unique Liss combination of simultaneously loving hard and not giving a damn, which is exactly what I've watched you do for the past twenty years. Thank you for keeping me on track.

Ali Fife. This is where I should thank you for dropping everything to spend seventy-two hours on an Irish road listening to me attempt to swear, but I'm going to skip that and talk about another day. It was also in the 2016/2017 haze. Life had been uphill for such a tremendously long time, and

I was worn out in every possible way a person could be worn out. I found myself literally lying on the floor, with no idea how I was going to get up off it. And who walked through my door? You. I didn't even have to call. You just showed up, surveyed the mess my life was in, and *stayed*. For several days. Who does that? You. Thank you for doing that for me.

The women in my postpartum depression support group at the Healing Group. Even if I never run into any of you again, I will never, ever forget that rock-bottom morning when you surrounded me and gave me the strength I needed to walk out of the room and face being a mother for one more day. Thank you.

Mary Stanley. For providing wisdom and irreverence and large boxes of tissues. Also, for being the first person to whom I ever said the words "I am an artist."

The Children's Center. For giving me hope when mine had run out.

Preschool Moms Gone Wild. The friends I didn't know I needed until we crash-landed at the same picnic table. Thanks for making Motherhood 2.0 less lonely, and for making me laugh harder than just about anyone. I think you are all divine. (When are we getting our tattoos?)

Andrew Herbst. For knowing things about cars and patiently coming up with ways for me to ruin them. (Hey, we've been friends for a long time now!)

Eli Zeger. The inspiration for Indie Ian and his articles. Thanks for the phone call. You are *such* a good writer—I can't wait to see where your talent takes you. Everyone, look him up on Twitter, @elizeger.

Roisin & Ross. I think the flight attendant who switched our seats was acting under divine influence. Thank you for teaching me the ways of Irish teens and for being so eager to help! Also . . . congratuations on your engagement!

The Army of Nannies. Dana Snell, Hannah Williams, Sarah Adamson, and Malia Helbling. Thank you for carrying my babies when my arms weren't enough.

My family. Rick, Keri, Ally, Abi, Brit, McKenna, Michael. Thank you all for showing up in your own ways. I am so blessed.

DAVID. My love, my peace, my strength. For a year and a half, we had an ongoing conversation that consisted of me saying, "I can't—this is too much," and you responding with, "You can—this is what you're here for." You are *far* more than I deserve, and I'm hanging on tightly to you anyway.

And this last one's just for me, but it needs to be here. Thank you to the little girl on the raft. New deal: you lead, I follow. I can't wait to see where we go next.

About the Author

JENNA EVANS WELCH was the kind of insatiable child reader who had no choice but to grow up to become a writer. Her first novel, *Love & Gelato*, was a *New York Times* bestseller, a 2017 YALSA's Teens' Top Ten title, a 2016 Goodreads Choice Award nominee for Young Adult Fiction, and a selection for the 2017 Texas Lone Star Reading List. It is currently being published in more than eighteen countries. When she isn't writing girl-abroad stories, Jenna can be found chasing her babies or making elaborate messes in the kitchen. She lives in Salt Lake City, Utah, with her husband and two children. Find her online at www.jennaevanswelch.com.

Praise for *Healing Rage*

"[*Healing Rage*] is a book of enormous scope that helps us to become more curious about our rage and better equipped to use it wisely. Ruth King's compassion and generosity of spirit will leave you feeling like she's right there with you on the journey to a fuller and more courageous life."

—Harriet Lerner, Ph.D, author of *The Dance of Anger*

"A classic . . . filled with the passion, earthiness, and wisdom of a self-described wounded healer. . . . This is a book that can change your life."

—Alice Walker, Pulitzer Prize winner for *The Color Purple*

"A wonderful, wise and inspiring book. I feel the heartbeat on every page. Ruth's compassion and generosity of spirit will inspire us to do our own homework toward a fuller and more courageous life."   —Sue Bender, author of *Everyday Sacred*

"Ruth King has done the unthinkable. She has written a book that empowers women to embrace their pain, confusion, and rage in a way that opens a pathway to liberation, healing, leadership, and vision. This is a powerful, wise and timely message—a brilliant piece of work."   —Lynne Twist, author of *The Soul of Money*

"King has articulated the painful history, patterns, and traps of a raging heart and offers the skillful means for liberation in their very midst. This is revolutionary work."

—Jack Kornfield, author and cofounder of
Spirit Rock Meditation Center

"The psychology of our age is characterized by aggression. The antidote is an experiential process that utilizes the energy for healing. This book provides methods for transforming vital energies into positive, creative, life-enhancing endeavors for individuals, institutions, and societies."

—Cecile McHardy, anthropologist and Radcliffe Institute
Fellow, Harvard University

HEALING
RAGE

*Women Making
Inner Peace Possible*

RUTH KING, M.A.

GOTHAM BOOKS

GOTHAM BOOKS
Published by Penguin Group (USA) Inc.
375 Hudson Street, New York, New York 10014, U.S.A.

Penguin Group (Canada), 90 Eglinton Avenue East, Suite 700, Toronto, Ontario, Canada M4P 2Y3
(a division of Pearson Penguin Canada Inc.); Penguin Books Ltd, 80 Strand, London WC2R 0RL,
England; Penguin Ireland, 25 St Stephen's Green, Dublin 2, Ireland (a division of Penguin Books Ltd);
Penguin Group (Australia), 250 Camberwell Road, Camberwell, Victoria 3124, Australia (a division
of Pearson Australia Group Pty Ltd); Penguin Books India Pvt Ltd, 11 Community Centre, Panchsheel
Park, New Delhi–110 017, India; Penguin Group (NZ), 67 Apollo Drive, Rosedale, North Shore 0632,
New Zealand (a division of Pearson New Zealand Ltd); Penguin Books (South Africa) (Pty) Ltd, 24
Sturdee Avenue, Rosebank, Johannesburg 2196, South Africa

Penguin Books Ltd, Registered Offices: 80 Strand, London WC2R 0RL, England

Published by Gotham Books, a member of Penguin Group (USA) Inc.

Previously published as a Gotham Books hardcover edition

First trade paperback printing, September 2008

10 9 8 7 6 5 4 3 2 1

Gotham Books and the skyscraper logo are trademarks of Penguin Group (USA) Inc.

The Library of Congress has catalogued the hardcover edition of this book as follows:
King, Ruth.
Healing rage : women making inner peace possible / Ruth King.
p. cm.
Originally published: Berkeley, CA : Sacred Spaces Press, c2004.
Includes bibliographical references.
ISBN 978-1-592-40314-1 (hardcover)   978-1-592-40406-3 (paperback)
1. Women—Psychology. 2. Anger. 3. Self-evaluation. 4. Self-management (Psychology).
5. Peace of mind.   I. Title.
HQ1206.K468   2007
155.6'33—dc22   2007014138

Printed in the United States of America
Set in Minion
Designed by Victoria Hartman

While the author has made every effort to provide accurate telephone numbers and Internet addresses
at the time of publication, neither the publisher nor the author assumes any responsibility for errors, or
for changes that occur after publication. Further, the publisher does not have any control over and does
not assume any responsibility for author or third-party Web sites or their content.

To

My family

My world family

May every one of us become more curious and less frightened of rage. May manifestations of rage be acknowledged as pain and treated with the greatest compassion possible. May we look at one another's rage, recognize ourselves, and fall in love with what we see. May our good deeds open our hearts in ways that heal the roots of suffering throughout the world for all beings.

CONTENTS

FOREWORD

We live in a world where humanity continues to suffer terribly because we don't know how to deal with anger, hatred, rage, injustice, oppression, and conflict between people and between nations. Yet we also know from the beloved examples of Dr. Martin Luther King, Jr., and Gandhi, Dorothy Day and Sojourner Truth, from Buddha and Jesus, and from our own heart's deepest wisdom, that there is another way.

Ruth King has dedicated much of her life work to understanding the fiery energies of rage, hatred, and fear, and defining ways to respect, understand, and transform these into a positive power in our lives. She has articulated the painful history, patterns, and traps of a raging heart and offers the skillful means for liberation in their very midst. This is revolutionary work.

As a Buddhist meditation teacher, I was first simply trained to mindfully experience and tolerate these energies. But beyond meditation I then struggled with a need to face them head-on, work with them, and express them without creating more suffering. In this book, Ruth teaches and encourages us to be brave, wise, alive, and compassionate, to both honor our rage and its causes and use them to heal ourselves in the world.

May these teachings and practices bring all who read this book relief from suffering and a clear, strong, and wise heart.

Jack Kornfield
Spirit Rock Meditation Center
2004

INTRODUCTION

From Hole to Whole*some*

I've been enraged all my life, but for half of my life I didn't know it. Before I knew I was enraged I considered myself to be a high-functioning professional woman. With a background in clinical psychology and organization development, I worked at some of the most prestigious Fortune 500 companies coaching leaders in how to make effective business decisions and develop high-performing teams. I was educated in some of the most highly regarded institutions of human development. I trained other consultants and was considered a master designer of group development, diversity, and leadership training programs.

While my work was respected, I had a problem with every *authority figure* I worked with. In my opinion, *they* didn't know what they were doing, *they* never gave me enough credit, *they* always fell short of making the mark, and *they* always needed me—whether they knew it or not. Yet you would have been in for the fight of your life had you told me that I was enraged. What I came to realize was that I had unconsciously chosen a high-powered consulting profession to guarantee me the privilege of pointing out to people in authority how wrong they were, and instead of being abused—as I had been as a child—I was well paid, which meant I was *finally right*!

In the prime of my superficial success, I underwent open-heart surgery for a prolapsed mitral valve, a congenital heart condition. I'll never forget how I felt waking up from surgery. I was cold, clammy, and half dressed. An invasive tube ran down my throat and was held in place by tape across my mouth. I felt silenced. There was a blinding light above my head, and needle marks spotted my arms and chest. A large, impersonal machine appeared to be forcing me to breathe. I felt controlled. There were loud sounds from monitors that looked like angry gray monsters. The enormous weight that once lived inside my heart was now on my chest burying me alive. I felt trapped. I panicked and tried to move, but alarm bells alerted the medical personnel and a slew of them filled my room in an instant. Terrified, I thought: *This must be hell!*

Good Morning! Welcome Back! Their eyes and voices were kind as they busied themselves adjusting monitors, bags, needles, and my bedding, and patting the sweat from my brows. *You are doing just fine, Miss King. You are going to be just fine!* I couldn't speak, but my eyes were screaming: *Who the hell are you people? What have you done to me? Get me out of here! I want out, out!* I was frightened, but even more I was angry. You see, I had sworn long before never to let anyone have this much control over me. Yet, these strangers, whom I considered enemies at the time, not only had control over my heart, they had more access to my heart than I did. It was like a nightmare. Dr. Welder, a squat-looking young man, entered:

> We have good news, Miss King. We did not have to replace your heart valve. We were able to repair it. This means there is nothing artificial about your heart—it's all yours! In no time, you'll be as good as new!

But he was wrong! Little did I know, lying in this stark white, ammonia-scented intensive care unit, that this rude awakening marked the beginning of a profound journey from open-heart surgery to an open heart.

During the helplessness and haunting stillness of my recovery, I found myself remembering the war zone of my childhood. I grew up during the height of the Civil Rights Movement in a working-class family with my mother as head of our household. I was the fifth of eight children, the first six of us each one year apart in age. We lived in a thriving neighborhood in South Central Los Angeles. Many families on 43rd Street east of Central owned their homes. Ours, like the others, was a handsome, tidy, single-story, Craftsman-style house with a large front porch.

Success in our community was defined as being obedient, getting a job with the county (instead of being on county assistance), and making it through the day without being harassed by the police. You could not be softhearted. You had to be tough to survive, know how to follow the invisible mind maps of *the enemy*. Having feelings was dangerous, being called a bitch was a compliment, and going to church was more important than being a Christian.

My mother was active in the Civil Rights Movement. Ironically, she fought against police brutality yet would beat us kids as if we were disobedient slaves. She was an advocate for fair housing while confining us to our rooms to maintain control, where life felt as small as the twin-sized bed that I shared with my sister. Mom also worked for voting rights, but seemed indifferent to our cries. Martin Luther King's "I Have a Dream" speech, espousing freedom and self-determination, was recognized in our house as the zenith of Black pride, while at the same time, my mother's harsh parenting practices remained routine and unquestioned. I don't recall being hugged or kissed, or feeling special as a child. What I remember most is how controlled I felt, and that I could not venture more than twenty-five feet from our house—the length of the concrete sidewalk that defined our front yard.

The most vivid war for me as a child was not the Vietnam War that was taking the lives of many young men I grew up with, or the

Watts riots that exploded in our immediate community. The most traumatic war for me was a war of emotions whose battleground was in my heart. The weapons were emotional neglect and physical abuse, and the enemy was my mother, whom I loved.

My silent mantra as a child was: *I can't wait to get out!* An older sister got pregnant and left home by the time she was fifteen. I followed her example, thinking more about my freedom than the responsibilities of raising a child. I denied any fear and was determined never to need my family again. After graduating from high school, I immediately took a secretarial job with the County of Los Angeles. When my father, a successful plumber, was shot to death by his girlfriend days before the Watts riots broke out, I don't recall feeling much emotion at his funeral. I can't say I knew him. I was seventeen and divorced. I don't think I even had a heart back then. I only remember how tightly I held my two-year-old son while our procession of cars was stopped several times by the National Guard as we carried my father's body across town to the cemetery.

In the loud silence of my surgical recuperation and in the years that followed, I realized that while I had physically walked away from the traumas of my childhood, I still carried them with me. The cruelties and disappointments were thriving, sheltered inside my body, mind, and heart. I did not know how to love and was too afraid to learn. I was beginning to acknowledge that I had spent most of my life running from unbearable pain and shame. Heart surgery had opened up not only my heart, but also my consciousness in such a way that my truth wouldn't leave me alone. I was awakened not only to how I had been harmed, but how I had harmed many people, including myself, and especially those I loved.

Prior to my heart surgery, I was unaware that I was *pregnant* with rage, that there was a rage child growing inside me who refused to be ignored and silenced. Open-heart surgery introduced me to rage by shocking me back into my terrified body. Surgery was only the tip of the iceberg, the beginning of a meltdown toward a deeper, more spiritual journey. Little did I know that my childhood mantra—*I can't wait to get out!*—was more than a mantra. It was my fate. I longed to live wide open, liberated from all forms of oppression, especially those that were self-imposed. It was during my recovery from heart surgery that I began to acknowledge that dancing with the heat of rage, my own and others, was not only my nature, but also my service.

Since that time, more than thirty years ago, I've realized a deeper awareness of rage and its wisdom. Along this journey, ancestors, elders, family members, therapy, world travel, and teachings from wisdom traditions have guided me. After years of what has been a soul-satisfying, magical, and, at times, difficult journey, I've come to understand my heart condition not only as an expression of unresolved and suppressed rage—some of which I inherited and maintained out of an unconscious loyalty to my family—but also as a sacred initiation into the riches of rage.

My journey revealed that rage deserved my attention and respect, and that I could not be fully emancipated until I healed my relationship with my parents, especially my mother. It wasn't enough to *know* I had suffered. I needed to return to that suffering, face it head-on with love, and leave it in the past where it belonged, before I could move forward and genuinely connect with other people and life itself. I recognized that I did not need to continue a legacy of hatred out of blind allegiance and block my chances to give and receive kindness.

I came to know intimately the roots of my parents' suffering—something I, too, carried and passed on to my son and others who dared to love me. I had more than an intellectual understanding of the love and challenges my parents endured raising us—I had a *felt* sense of it, and it was important for me to dignify not only my journey with rage, but also my parents'.

Gradually, I learned to forgive myself for not being able to change my past, but also for not being able to accept it. It took every ounce of my newly repaired heart to move from righteous rage to a more balanced truth. It was then that I could realize that my parents' suffering was not all that I had inherited. I had also inherited their prideful independence, ferocious determination, intelligence, a bias for justice, humor, music, and the ability to know and tell the truth. The pain of my past had undeniably and ironically contributed to tremendous strength and potential in my life, including the courage to write this book. Most importantly, I came to honor this journey as a life's work and service. I know in my bones the delicate power of being human— everyone has the capacity to hurt *and* love *and* heal.

Healing rage is *heart* work that requires courage and kindness, and many women, like me, seek guidance in reclaiming the positive energies that are distorted by the oppression of rage, and want to utilize the enormous power of rage as a vehicle for healing. This need led to the establishment of Bridges, Branches & Braids, an organization that began in 1992 for women to explore the pure character of rage through workshops, seminars, life coaching, and retreats. Through the Celebration of Rage™ retreat, women learn how to put rage in sacred perspective. We discover how we disguise rage, and are guided inward to deal directly with those aspects of ourselves that are unwanted. Through emotional release, art, ritual, and storytelling, we learn how to feed ourselves when our souls are starving. Women realize that the rage that feels larger than life—so intense that to face it we fear it might destroy us or someone else—is really the emotion of a small, hungry child, one that needs to be validated and nurtured. More profoundly, we discover that we are much more than the accumulation of events that have happened to us—we have full agency over our lives. We learn how to accept and forgive ourselves, and that we can heal through our own awareness without the permission, recognition, or approval of others, and be at peace in our own skin.

Women from many parts of the world have participated in the Celebration of Rage™ retreats, each completing detailed pre- and post-retreat questionnaires about their rage history, and each being personally interviewed. The collective insight from the lives of these courageous women contributes immeasurably to this book. At the same time, the cases presented in *Healing Rage* are fictionalized composites based on information shared during coaching sessions and retreats, as well as information from my own personal experiences. I have obtained the assistance of individuals to include helpful information about their experiences. Actual names and some key elements of the stories have been altered to maintain confidentiality and to honor the relationships we have forged in our work together. While *Healing Rage* is based on findings from women, its wisdom extends to, and equally benefits, male readers as well as young adults.

The basic assumption of *Healing Rage* is that unresolved rage from childhood trauma is still locked in our bodies and minds. This blocked energy manifests as *disguises of rage* in our adult lives—ways we cope with life while denying an intimate experience with living. These disguises become such an ingrained part of our existence that we forget that the origins are rage. While our disguises of rage attempt to protect us from the pain of our past, they more often re-create the past and perpetuate the very suffering we seek to avoid. Unresolved rage has been passed on from one generation to the next, contributing to rage inheritances that collectively plague the world, and each of us—whether we know it or not—is charged with transforming this legacy.

Our world is diminished by an ignorance and misuse of rage. Race and class oppression, conformity, greed, media violence, political corruption, indifference, war, abuse of the poor, abuse of the earth, and abuse of women and children are our society's ways of expressing rage, and we are our society. When we hate—any *one* or any *thing*—it is the same as stabbing ourselves in the heart. Regardless of our circumstances, however much we may deny, rationalize, or empathize with the traumatic conditions of our childhood and present lives, in every moment we have the power to feel, release, and transform rage, without harming others or ourselves. This work is not easy, just necessary!

You may have purchased this book because you realize that rage is interfering with your relationships and quality of life. Perhaps you are suffering a loss, or struggling with an illness. You may be seeking to understand an aspect of yourself that you are ashamed or frightened of. Understandably, you may be afraid of or bewildered by the rage that is all around you, and seek ways to turn within for refuge. Whatever the reasons, the fierce truth of rage is calling you to take a courageous step toward greater self-awareness, inner peace, and wholesome service.

The title *Healing Rage* was chosen with careful consideration. For some people, *healing* implies that something is wrong that needs to be right. Here, the word is used more to point toward a need for sacred attention and intention. In this work, healing is about remembering who we are and what we deeply know. It is about learning how to work with our minds in ways that relieve suffering. Healing is also about cultivating a tolerance for peaceful liberation. This means allowing the discomfort often associated with rage to inform us for the benefit of a healthier life and future, and it may even mean that we give up a bit of comfort for more consciousness.

The process of *Healing Rage* is not a quick fix, nor is it an attempt to eliminate rage from our lives. Rage isn't going away. We will continue to be triggered by conditions that give rise to it. These conditions are both outside and within us. Rather, this is a journey of profound introspection that allows our most enraging and shame-provoking experiences to heal us.

Healing Rage is an invitation to wild awakenings and deep beauty. When we embrace this truth, we reveal fully to ourselves, and to the world, our exquisiteness and infinite potential. Let us begin—bring your own light, and a mirror!

PART ONE

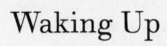

Waking Up

1

The Birth of Rage

Rage is an oppressed *child* emotion housed deep within our bodies, minds, and spirits. Throughout this book, I will refer to her as our inner *Rage Child*. We tend to react to our rage child as an emotional enemy to be eliminated, a fire to be feared. More accurately, our rage child is a natural resource of misused energy, and she exists whether we acknowledge her or not. She is the daughter of our traumas, the twin of our shame, the burden of our denied histories, the foreign language of our emotional pain, and the wisdom that helps us heal.

Our rage child is at once a young and old emotion: *young* because she is tied to our personal childhood traumas that have been suppressed; *old* because she is an accumulation of unresolved anger and shame, some of which has been passed on for many generations. Few of us realize how much rage we have and how rage controls our lives. We feel trapped in a revolving door of conflicting emotions—victims of our own and others' rage, yet socialized to be ashamed of our natural response to it. Sadly, we tend to turn rage inward, against ourselves. We fail to understand that the ongoing, often subconscious struggle to repress rage causes suffering and drains our life force. *Whether we are ignorant or aware does not change the fierce truth that most of us are enraged—with good reason—and the fires of rage continue to burn within us with or without our acknowledgment or permission.*

RAGE, NOT ANGER

Rage and anger are often regarded as the same emotion, but they are distinct experiences. Anger is primarily associated with a current injustice, dislike, or disappointment—a driver cutting in front of you without signaling, a disagreement at work, annoyance at a clerk who forgot to give you correct change, an argument over who said what. We have some control over what we are experiencing, and some ability to leave the situation or create a more desirable outcome.

Rage is an accumulation of anger, an experience that is primarily physical and rooted to unresolved or unknown traumas that shamed us in childhood. Rage is a visceral and instinctive response when we feel we have little or no control over what is threatening or harming us.

When we are enraged our experience is *beyond* anger and rarely brings healing relief. We will discover in the following chapters that anger (referred to as *Defiance*) is one of six disguises of rage. Many of us do not act out or show our rage and anger. These are feelings that we experience within, at times may express outwardly, but more commonly hide or deny. Over time, we become capable of hiding our experiences of rage and anger from others, and even from ourselves.

TRAUMA GIVES BIRTH TO RAGE

Trauma gives birth to rage—an experience of severe emotional shock that causes substantial and lasting damage to our psychological well-being. Trauma is experienced as being intensely overwhelmed by a perceived threat or actual harm. Trauma can be a single incident of devastating loss, violation, or injury, or a chronic atmosphere of fear and neglect.

The traumas that give birth to rage typically occur in our families between the ages of birth and twelve years of age. This birth takes place within our mind and body and significantly influences the rest of our lives. As children, we are often not immediately aware of our experiences of rage but are more likely to feel confused, frightened, and hurt. Rage, naturally born in the face of trauma, becomes problematic when our vulnerability goes unaddressed, and it has a cumulative effect on our development as we grow older. While traumatic experiences give birth to rage, it's not the trauma that devastates us most profoundly as children. *Rather, it's the ways in which our traumatic experiences are responded to that have the most enraging and lasting impact.*

The following are several types of traumas that give birth to rage in childhood: *emotional neglect, emotional abuse, verbal abuse, loss,* and *physical violence and sexual abuse.* Read through them and notice which ones resemble your childhood experiences.

Emotional Neglect

Many of us discover that we are enraged because we did not feel loved *enough* as children. We came from an environment in which there was food and shelter, clothing, even toys, sometimes two parents, a house, and a dog, *but* . . . Emotional neglect results from experiences where parents and other authority figures were gravely unresponsive, or there was a lack of priority or awareness of our emotional needs. The trauma of emotional neglect occurred when there was a chronic atmosphere in which:

- You felt ignored or invisible—not seen, heard, or valued.
- Your parents were unavailable or there were broken promises.

- There was an absence of touch and tenderness.
- You were given things instead of time and attention.
- You were talked at, not talked to, or not made to understand things.
- You were treated as if you didn't (or shouldn't) have needs beyond what was provided.
- You were responsible for parenting your siblings and/or your parents.
- You were attended to only if you were ill.
- You felt something was wrong but no one would talk about it.
- You spent significant time hoping, longing, or wishing things could be different.
- You felt unwanted.

Sadly, these seemingly *normal* examples of neglect are nevertheless traumatizing, and they contribute to children growing into angry and guilty adults. Lizbeth shares her experience of emotional neglect in this way:

> I was able to piece together the story of my birth from distant relatives. Apparently, when my mother was pregnant with me, my father had also impregnated his girlfriend, a woman he loved and wanted to marry. But my mother would not divorce him. While my mother was in labor with me, my father was with his girlfriend who was also in labor, but she died giving birth to a stillborn child. I imagine my father was grief-stricken from this loss—a loss I feel I always shared. He was unhappy and made everyone else unhappy. He always acted like he hated my face and he had nothing to do with me. I guess I reminded him of how stuck he felt with my mother and me, and the child and love of his life he lost. It didn't help that I looked just like my father, something my mother always reminded me of. Neither my mother nor father ever talked about this but I knew—I could feel that I was unwanted.

When we come from emotionally neglectful families, we often feel guilty about our feelings. We live with doubt and shame, and cannot understand why we feel empty, unlovable, and unloving.

Emotional Abuse

An atmosphere of chronic fear and anxiety resulting from emotional abuse and violation of boundaries is perhaps the most common form of childhood trauma reported by women. Frequent situations include:

- Your parents withheld loving emotions to distance themselves from you or punish you.
- You were taught to hate or belittle races, economic classes, ethnicities, cultures, genders, and others who were not like you.
- You were distrusted and questioned—there was an automatic assumption that you had done something wrong.
- You were treated as an object of service to authorities.
- You were praised for or expected to do things you felt incapable of doing.
- You were humiliated if you made a mistake, didn't have the answer, or didn't measure up.
- You were smothered, overpowered, or overcontrolled.
- You were praised more for what you did instead of who you were.
- You could not have your own dreams, restricted from what you passionately felt or desired.
- You were expected to tell all, show all, and prove all.
- You witnessed someone you loved be abused or violated and were unable or too frightened to stop it.
- You felt confused and received conflicting messages—*Make sure your sister doesn't fall* but *don't touch her.* Or *I hate your father,* and *you look just like him.*

- You could not show any intense emotions or naturally express your feelings without being silenced or punished.
- You were socially isolated.
- One or both of your parents were jealous of you.
- You had to be the caretaker of your parents' moods, emotions, or well-being.

Emotional abuse is by far the most common and pervasive form of abuse that gives birth to rage. Sheryl experienced emotional abuse from the age of eight to twelve, a stage in which she was challenged with defining her self-worth:

> Mom always talked about not wanting to live and she would threaten to kill herself whenever we got into an argument. I would get home from school and she would be passed out on the couch and my first thought was that she had killed herself. I spent a lot of time worrying about how she might kill herself. I didn't know whether to feel mad or sad. And I couldn't tell anybody. I feared for a long time that my anger would be the cause of her death.

Emotional abuse leaves us angry, helpless, and hopeless. We distrust others and our own value as people.

Verbal Abuse

Verbal abuse is a form of emotional abuse that involves a deliberately hostile intention. Verbal abuse creates an atmosphere of cruelty and fear that corrodes self-worth. You know you were verbally abused if you were given these kinds of messages:

- You're nothing.
- You're worthless.
- You're stupid.
- You're fat.

- You're black.
- You're skinny.
- You're ugly.
- Get out of my face.
- I should have aborted you.
- You're always fucking up.
- Something is wrong with you.
- You can't do anything right.
- You're a bitch, just like your mother.
- I'm gonna kick your ass.
- Shut up.
- I'll kill you.
- I brought you into this world and I will take you out.
- I hate it when you act just like your father. I got rid of him and I will get rid of you.

When we are verbally abused or live in a climate of intense dislike as children, we are ashamed of existing. We question our worth, and we feel disinterested in caring for others and ourselves. We feel helpless and powerless in our lives, both ashamed and enraged, and don't see why anyone would love us.

Loss

Other incidents of shock and emotional trauma include the loss of love and loved ones to death, divorce, betrayal, or abandonment. These can include:

- You lost your parents or your parents died.
- You experienced the death of a significant caretaker or sibling.
- Your parents separated or divorced.
- You witnessed or felt responsible for the death of someone.
- You felt betrayed or abandoned by a care provider.
- You lost an animal, friend, home, limb, or item of significant

value through death, illogical and unexpected removal, destruction, or disappearance.

- Your family moved around often and you lost friends or felt unsure of yourself, constantly having to adjust to new situations.
- Something terrible happened that you could not stop or control.
- You had to live with a prolonged or terminal illness.

Mildred shares a childhood experience when she emotionally lost her father:

> My father absolutely adored me until I reached puberty. He accidentally walked in on me in the bathroom and I was nude. I was twelve and I'll never forget the shock on his face. From then on I felt completely abandoned by him. He no longer held me, talked to me, or played with me. I would scream at him trying to understand what happened, and he would just leave the room. The cost I paid to become a young woman was the loss of my father. I was confused by his release of me and to this day I long to sit on his lap and laugh again.

When we can't understand the loss of what we desperately rely on, we naturally feel abandoned, hurt, confused, and angry. We learn to distrust love. We feel lost and struggle to make sense of our world.

Physical Violence and Sexual Abuse

Physical violence and sexual abuse toward children are all too common traumatic experiences that give rise to rage. This form of abuse is a bodily violation of extreme humiliation and devastation. It is a precursor to long-lasting issues that profoundly affect our relationship to power in others and within ourselves. You suffered physical violence and sexual abuse if:

- You were beaten, slapped, or shoved by your parents, guardians, and others who were older or had more control.

- You felt sexually obligated or forced through rape, incest, or molestation.
- You were sexually or physically violated by someone known or unknown outside of your family.
- You were emotionally raped, forced to tolerate sexual language, pornography, or to witness sexual activity.
- You felt you needed to respond sexually or violently to be loved.
- You felt physically or sexually vulnerable due to poor boundaries or a lack of protection.

When we are physically or sexually abused as children by those we love, trust, or rely on, we carry a shame so deep in our bones that it silences our voices, numbs our bodies, warps our thinking, and closes our hearts, sometimes for a lifetime. Vanessa shares her experience of incest as a child:

> I had to manipulate my mind into believing I didn't hurt. I wanted to tell but I didn't want to get in trouble, and I didn't want my Mom and Dad to argue. I was also afraid of what my friends would say or what anyone would say if the word got out. I was terrified of my Dad. He told me he loved me but he also told me he would hurt me if I told. I kept it a secret to protect my Mom and the family. When I finally did tell my Mom, her response was: You have ruined my life and this family! How could you do this to me? That was the day I lost my Mom, my family, and everything that mattered. Now he has my Mom and they are a family, and I have nothing.

When we are physically and sexually abused, we distrust our instincts and we especially distrust loved ones. We feel damaged, torn from the truth we embody and terrified to reclaim it. Life feels unsafe, and intimacy is both longed for and feared.

FROM RAGE CHILD TO RAGE WOMAN

When we are taught or forced to deny what we feel while traumatic things are happening in childhood, we grow into troubled adolescents facing problems that childhood did not prepare us for. We are more likely to distrust others, doubt ourselves, and feel guilty and inferior—all of which we must attempt to hide.

As a teenager, the emphasis is on becoming an adult—too often becoming something or somebody else. Often we are told how to think and feel instead of how to discover who we are. For many of us, we enter an oppressive and hostile world of inadequate education, economic hardships, quick-to-jail programs, drugs, sensationalism of violence in the mass media, and a pervasive atmosphere of disrespect and high control. Then we are expected to act like responsible adults. Some of us try, but understandably, we often fall short. We begin to experience failure all around us—within and outside of our families.

As teenagers, we are often thought of as lazy, crazy, and disobedient. But it is closer to the truth that we are afraid of the speed and greed in our lives—afraid that we can't keep up. The adults in our world seem overwhelmed in the face of our disguised pain and helplessness. Ashamed of our hidden inadequacy, we rebel, often caving to the temptations of drugs, sex, and rock and roll—*and* alcohol abuse, teenage pregnancy, suicide, homicide, and depression.

Many of us struggle with body image and sexuality, and an intense need to belong. Pressure to be sexual can make it difficult to choose to be simply touched and hugged. Our reactions to peers can range from feeling shut down and depressed to being overly sexual. While this is true for many of us during adolescence, those of us who have been physically and sexually abused will often cave to sexual pressure to belong, when it is physical and emotional intimacy that we long for.

As we enter adulthood, challenged with complexities of intimacy, sexuality, work, family, and partnerships, life can feel like a chronic, low-level threat. We feel things we don't understand, say things we don't feel, and do things we don't mean to do. Our fear and shame become even more exaggerated when we feel isolated, confused, or threatened. We often avoid our feelings because *feeling* is dangerous— providing a faceless reminder of our inability to be safe and stay in control. There is a frightening instinct operating within us that we don't trust or comprehend. Oddly, we often find ourselves in situations similar to those of our early childhood, wondering why they seem to repeat themselves again and again in our lives.

Some of us become parents to flesh-and-blood children who are forced to share emotional space with an unacknowledged sibling— our denied rage child. As mothers and oftentimes the heads of households, the family is where we commonly control and reenact unresolved rage. Predictably and often innocently, we traumatize our children, by passing on these messages:

- Make me proud.
- Never disappoint me.
- You should be grateful.
- You have it better than I did.
- Always be happy and polite.
- Never show anger.
- Never embarrass me.
- Never disagree with me.
- Never make me angry.
- Always put me first.
- Never be afraid or never show fear.

Sadly, when we become parents without an awareness of our own personal rage, we tend to re-create the same traumas we experienced as children, thus giving birth to another generation of rage. We pass on our legacy of abuse while disowning the pain and shame of our rage child.

Childhood trauma is not the only disturbance associated with rage. Certainly there are social, environmental, and political traumas—past and present—that surround us and profoundly affect our lives, yet our programmed response to trauma and to rage is well established by the time we reach young adulthood. We often discover as adults that it is easier if not more satisfying to fight social, environmental, and political battles than to face up to the shame-filled, deeper roots of childhood rage.

In our adult lives, we often search for ways to tell the truth about what happened in childhood, but even as adults, we distrust or deny our experiences and fear the consequences. Unknowingly, we continue to traumatize ourselves by re-creating the scenes that harmed us. We inherited this dilemma from people we loved and trusted, and, while it secretly shames and haunts us, it was and still is what we know best and what we do out of an unconscious loyalty to our parents and ancestors. Despite our painful journeys, many of us succeed materially. However, success is not to be confused with healing.

OUR RAGE INHERITANCE

We usually think of our rage as belonging exclusively to us, yet you may have thought, in the heat of an enraging encounter: *Hmm . . . what I'm feeling right now seems larger, louder, and older than the present situation!* The truth of the matter is that all of us are part of a much larger tapestry of familial and ancestral rage. We are all recipients of a rage inheritance.

A rage inheritance is a bequest of unresolved rage from our parents and ancestors. This includes generations of unresolved rage from institutions of influence, such as the family, law, politics, education, and religion, as well as from social constructions such as ethnicity, race, class, gender, and culture.

One way to understand our rage inheritance is through the laws of cause and effect, which state that nothing exists on its own, everything has come from earlier circumstances. For example, we each are alive because our parents met at an earlier time. We did not just appear, nor do we exist without a long lineage. As infants, we learned by imitation. We mirrored and reacted to our parents, as our parents learned from theirs, in an unbroken line of unconscious loyalty.

Particular patterns of fear, shame, and rage are taught by one generation and passed to the next. Like it or not, our parents and ancestors are with us even when we don't know them, don't like them, or don't remember them. Many of the ways we are and the things we do reflect this inheritance, including our appearance, gestures, talents, movements, habits—and the ways in which we relate to rage.

Whatever our parents and ancestors could not or would not resolve is gifted to us to transform—this is our karmic reality and our challenge. We are usually unaware of our rage inheritance. Shame, secrecy, and complicity serve to obscure and more deeply embed these patterns. We innocently embody the unresolved generational rage and pass it on to the next generation. When our rage inheritance is unknown or ignored, we subconsciously collude in contributing to a society of ignorance, war, greed, indifference, hatred, violence, and abuse. This recycling of rage continues until we can heal the traumas that caused them.

BELOVED IS THE RAGE CHILD

One story that profoundly illuminates generational rage is the Pulitzer Prize–winning novel *Beloved*, by Toni Morrison. Inspired by an article about a runaway slave, Margaret Garner, Morrison tells a complex and poetic story of motherly love expressed through child murder. The novel's main character, Sethe, has endured a life of brutality and pain at the hands of white slave owners. She kills her own infant daughter, slitting the baby's throat, to prevent her from being stolen and raised as a slave. Years later her daughter reappears as a ghost spirit—Beloved. Sethe's entire life is altered as she becomes obsessed with being forgiven and loses herself in Beloved's insatiable hunger and rage. Beloved's anguish is expressed in two questions: *Why'd you hurt me? Why'd you leave me?* Sethe's sincere response: *It wasn't like that child. I loved you. I always loved you, baby!*

A child does not understand the tough choices a mother must sometimes make, nor can a child comprehend how any harm could be a gesture of love. In a child's mind, it simply means *you don't love me.*

Many of us were confused by mixed messages of childhood love and harm and were forced to silence (or kill) our rage in order to survive. But this rage never leaves us despite our best efforts. Like Beloved, we want to ask our mothers, parents, or guardians—*Why did you hurt me? Why did you leave me?* Our ancestors had these questions, our children have these questions, and most importantly, our rage child is asking us these questions.

We may or may not have visible whip marks on our back like Sethe, or scars on our necks like Beloved, but we have all been scarred, and we have all scarred others. And we all have ways of ensuring that harm never befalls us again, even if it means hurting others and ourselves. The pain and hurt that created our rage are desperately searching for liberation.

How do we help our inner rage child—our Beloved—understand the choices we have made to survive? How do we help her comprehend that our most horrible acts were the best choices we knew to make at the time? How do we forgive ourselves for harming ourselves, and for the shame, fear, and self-hatred we have swallowed from our past?

We begin to heal rage when we discover within ourselves that we are all like Sethe—women who have had to make difficult choices, *and* had mothers, fathers, guardians, and ancestors who harmed and loved us. As mothers and women, our pasts haunt us, and at times we feel unlovable and unforgivable. We are all akin to Beloved—we embody a rage child that we have killed, silenced, misused, neglected, or abandoned, a child spirit within that demands answers. We are all like Sethe's other children who were traumatized by their sister's murder—terrified children in adult bodies, ashamed to be seen or helped, running away from love because we are afraid it will kill us. We are all like Sethe's lover, Paul D—starving for love yet overcome by temptation. We are all like the slave hunters—ignorant of our self-serving pursuits and entitlements and unaware of the pain we cause others and ourselves. And we are all like the community of women who comforted and sustained Sethe—despite our pain we are capable of inspiring and transforming others and ourselves.

Rage is inevitable. No matter what we do, our hearts will break and we will hurt others and be hurt time and time again. Healing invites us to honor our beloved rage child as that part of us that is in pain and in need of our kind attention and care.

2

Into Rage, Out of Body

THE BODY/MIND SPLIT

When we experience trauma in childhood, our minds can't make sense of what is occurring. Because we are emotionally underdeveloped, the body absorbs the full blow of our trauma. As a result the body becomes a dreadful war zone that we must escape in order to cope with the intolerable pain we feel. Because we are children, we cannot physically escape, but we can attempt to escape mentally by a psychological process known as *splitting*. Splitting protects us from remembering and experiencing our traumas. It is a necessary psychological defense when, for example, we love and are dependent on those who abuse us. Denise, suffering from physical abuse and emotional neglect, shares:

> I remember when I was about six years old, my father beat me
> and a few hours later, took me out for ice cream, acting as
> though nothing had happened. Things like this happened a

lot. Sometimes I'd have obvious bruises on my face and arms. People would frown at us and I felt odd, embarrassed, and special at the same time.

A child's confusion when she loves her abuser is in itself traumatic, forcing a split between body and mind. Denise's bafflement does not mean that rage was not felt; it means that love was felt more. In that moment of innocence, rage was not conscious or immediately accessible. Denise knew her father must love her and ice cream was proof of his love. She grew to conclude that love included beatings.

When we are both loved and abused by our guardians, we become confused and learn to distrust what we feel. Because we are dependent on their care, we accept their reality over our own and grow doubtful of what we deeply know to be true.

When our minds and bodies split in the face of trauma, like Denise we separate the feelings in our body from the thoughts in our minds. When we split in this way, the release of rage is interrupted and becomes trapped in the body as we take our minds elsewhere—to a safer place.

Since the onset of our traumas, our body has contained and concealed the pain of rage. We move through our adult lives unaware that we are pregnant with rage. It's as if there were a rowdy party occurring inside our body. Granted, every now and then we might smell a bit of marijuana, or stumble over a few empty liquor bottles, notice that the car has new dents, or that there are clothes lying around that don't belong to us. But we don't *think* much about it and we don't *feel* any of it. Anyone or anything that threatens to put us in contact with this pain is avoided or discounted. We convince ourselves that there's no problem, but the body knows otherwise, and eventually the evidence of our rage bleeds through our mind's defenses.

The body/mind split can be most painful and confusing in matters of intimacy. Intimacy threatens to reveal what we attempt to hide, so we avoid it. Our body has a keen recollection of any physical or emotional trauma suffered at the hands of a loved one. When our early experiences of touch are associated with trauma, we become frightened and ashamed. We find ourselves both avoiding and craving touch. Either way, fear is blocking the intimacy we crave and deserve.

The split can be readily observed in situations where women tolerate physical and sexual abuse at the hands of a loved one for long periods of time. In many of these relationships, the body seeks physical intimacy but settles for abuse, while the mind makes excuses for our situation. The irony is that abuse can be the closest we've ever come to intimacy. These contacts are not intimate, but rather painful and shaming, yet they awaken us to older memories of love. Abuse also forces us to feel, and temporarily reassures us that we live in a body. Over time, physical needs become distorted, boundaries blurred, and abuse from others and ourselves becomes normal—something we cannot live with or without. We don't realize that these are reenactments of childhood trauma that keep our mind and body separate.

Many of us react to the body/mind split by becoming obsessed with how we look, correcting imperfections that no one else sees, while others hide their bodies, fearing intense discomfort from unwanted outside attention. The bottom line is that too many of us don't like what we see when we look at ourselves and hope the pain we feel never shows. Some of us do like what we see but don't feel who we are.

When touch is what has traumatized us in our early years, many of us avoid touching ourselves, or even taking a good look at our own bodies. For example, thousands die each year from breast cancer because we avoid breast self-examination. We miss out on the wisdom our bodies bestow.

We all crave the intimacy of touch—tender contact—but many are confused about the differences between physical and sexual intimacy. Consider, for example, the sexual hunger of many teenage girls. People are quick to label such behavior as sexual addiction when it is more often a longing for tenderness. Somewhere along the way, we have learned that sex is what you do when you want contact. There-fore, we feed our bodies sex, which leaves us only temporarily satisfied because our deeper yearning is for something much more intimate.

The body/mind split is further culturally sanctioned when society benefits from our woundedness. Often, more value is placed on those whom our bodies please than on who we are as human beings. Con-sider the profits of prostitution and the oppressive commercialization of our bodies as entertainment, titillation, and targets of violence. In some cultures, women are punished or even killed for exposing skin, and female genital mutilation is considered a condition of survival and social acceptance. When we are objectified in this way, we split body and mind in order to survive—mentally focusing on one reality while our bodies are experiencing another.

The body/mind split plays a crucial role in our lives as long as we are ashamed of our wholeness, and understandably, we often are. In fact, we are willing to do just about anything to avoid reexperiencing the shame of childhood traumas.

THE RAGE/SHAME DUO

Just as mothers have a psychological bond with their children, rage has a psychological bond with shame—its twin emotion. What makes rage such a volatile emotion is its kinship with shame. While we looked to our mothers for protection, shame looks to her sister emotion, rage, for protection, and vice versa.

Rage and shame are locked in a complicated, symbiotic struggle. Like many twins, rage and shame are mistaken for each other, and, like many siblings, they compete to have their conflicting needs met. For example, rage wants freedom to tell the truth, while shame wants protection and safety. Shame wants to hide, collapse, retreat, and sur-render in the face of conflict, while rage wants to fight, force, and per-sist. Rage wants to stay awake and alert, while shame would prefer to be asleep and sluggish.

Rage and shame incite each other—when one is active, it invariably triggers the other. When rage becomes activated, for example, we can lose control and overexpose ourselves. Being exposed can make us feel vulnerable and ashamed. The vulnerability of this shame in turn incites a protective storm of rage. Here's how Phyllis experienced it:

> An important project at work was not going my way and I was so enraged about it, I had to get out of there. I took a walk to a nearby mall. While admiring a well-dressed mannequin in the window, I noticed my face reflected in the glass. I saw myself as wounded—frightened, vulnerable, and vulgar. I felt embarrassed and horrified. The next thing I knew, I was in the store and within one hour, had charged my credit card up into the thousands. Later I was enraged that I had, once again, put myself in debt.

Phyllis initially felt rage but saw shame reflected in the glass window. Her shame was intolerable, so her righteous rage provided a needed excuse for Phyllis to purchase enough clothing to cover the shame she was attempting to deny. Later feeling guilty, she became enraged toward her own guilt. Phyllis reminds us that rage and shame trigger each other in an incessant duo.

Another result of the Rage/Shame Duo is a subconscious process known as *projecting* (discussed further in the "Solving Rage Riddles" chapter). Here we give over an unwanted part of ourselves to another without that person's knowledge (or our own). That person, in our mind, lives out this unwanted part, which in turn provides a continuing target for our projection of rage. Joyce shares it well:

> I've been dating Paul for four years and his life is a mess. He can never get his act together and his world is chaotic. I go crazy around him. If I didn't tell him what to do, he wouldn't know, and he'd drag us both down the tubes. I know I'm critical of him but he's such a child. Why do I have him in my life? Why can't I seem to stop tormenting myself over how he is? And why is it that everyone I get close to is like this?

Upon further exploration, Joyce realized that her biggest fear is returning to the chaotic world of her childhood, where anytime she made a mess she was verbally or physically abused. Joyce's adult world is one in which she controls things so tightly that nothing is ever out of place. Determined not to feel shame, Joyce becomes her raging parent abusing her partner as she was abused in childhood. Paul, unknowingly, represents the chaotic and shaming world of her childhood—a world Joyce cannot leave behind. When Joyce is projecting her shame onto Paul, she is relinquishing her responsibility and her power to transform her own emotional pain pattern.

Our intertwined experiences of rage and shame represent a complex emotional language. For some women, it is safer to feel rage than shame. For others, it is safer to feel shame than rage. But for too many, it is never safe *enough* to feel. For this reason, we wear disguises of rage.

PART TWO

The Six Disguises
of Rage

3

Determining Your
Disguises of Rage

WHAT ARE DISGUISES OF RAGE?

Many of us go through our lives maintaining a good front. We may have all of the trappings—good job, higher education, and material gain, yet we have an inherent discontent with our lives that won't go away. We manage to look okay from the outside, hiding those periods of despair when we feel everything caving in on us by keeping to ourselves. We express confidence on the surface and feel fear or dread underneath. We know we feel chaotic and on the edge, but we hide it, sometimes beautifully, even from ourselves. This is accomplished by wearing disguises of rage.

Disguises are our rage child's armor—the coats we wear year round to cope with the chill of life, even on a warm day. They are our ways to be in control of a chronically frightening life. Disguises keep our body and mind experiences split so that we can manage the intolerable threat of shame that may awaken traumatic childhood memories. Disguises also serve as symbolic templates of older stories of rage that require our attention. These templates were established during childhood and continue into our adult lives with slight modifications until we transform them. They have played a significant role in our survival but they interfere with our healing. We continue to wear our disguises because we perceive these obscure expressions of rage as being safer and more acceptable than truth itself.

DETERMINING YOUR DISGUISES OF RAGE

To determine your disguises of rage, select from the following statements those that most commonly represent your life pattern or instinctive response to the world. Avoid selecting statements that may reflect actions you have taken only occasionally, and choose instead those that are your typical life pattern, thought, or tendency—even if you do them less and less.

For example: Esther blew up at a salesperson who flirted with her when she was purchasing a car. This action could be characteristic of Statement #31: *I have a quick temper*. However, this action was new for Esther, not a life pattern. What is more characteristic of a life pattern for Esther is Statement #28: *I have difficulty setting boundaries and asking for what I want*. For Esther, Statement #28 would be an appropriate selection.

Take your time and read through all of the statements before making your selections. For each statement, place an X in the appropriate column: *Yes, this has been a lifelong belief or tendency!* or *No, this has not been a lifelong belief or tendency!*

SELF-ASSESSMENT

Characteristics of Disguises of Rage	Yes, this has been a lifelong belief or tendency!	No, this has not been a lifelong belief or tendency!
1. I am vindictive toward others who cross me.		
2. I become incapacitated, speechless, or feel small in the face of disapproval or anger.		
3. I do only what is required and resent additional expectations others have of me.		
4. I do everything I can to keep others from becoming upset.		
5. I overindulge and live beyond my means.		
6. I am unaware of being afraid.		
7. I become angry with others when I feel hurt, disappointed, or need time to myself.		
8. I doubt myself and hope others will take care of my emotional and financial needs.		
9. In general, I feel emotionally heavy, hopeless, and cynical.		
10. I feel intense frustration when I can't do anything to pull someone out of sadness or depression.		
11. I find it difficult to rest, be still, be quiet, or do nothing.		
12. Others accuse me of being bossy, insensitive, self-righteous, and selfish.		
13. I believe that most powers-that-be are inadequate and fall short of my expectations, and must pay for what they have done or not done.		

Characteristics of Disguises of Rage	Yes, this has been a lifelong belief or tendency!	No, this has not been a lifelong belief or tendency!
14. I expect that exceptions will be made for my hard luck.		
15. I isolate or distance myself from others to avoid talking or having to engage in day-to-day life.		
16. I must take care of others first, and if there is time left over, I will care for myself. I feel like I must sneak time to care for myself.		
17. I generally feel hungry for more (time, money, fun, knowledge, sleep, chocolates, etc.).		
18. I must take charge of people, places, and situations or else things will get screwed up.		
19. I believe that most rules restrict my life.		
20. In conflict, I become confused and find it hard to know what I want.		
21. I feel unable to exert energy toward what is important to my health and well-being.		
22. I give so that others will not be upset. If others are upset it is because of something I've done or not done.		
23. I overwork, spend, drink, drug, eat, sex, TV, etc.		
24. I generally feel entitled to express my anger toward others.		
25. I feel I must fight to protect myself or others will take advantage of me.		
26. I often feel inadequate and unqualified.		

Characteristics of Disguises of Rage	Yes, this has been a lifelong belief or tendency!	No, this has not been a lifelong belief or tendency!
27. I routinely question the purpose or point of my life.		
28. I have difficulty setting boundaries and asking for what I want.		
29. I put myself at financial risk by gambling, spending, rushing, or investing.		
30. When challenged or confronted, I become demanding, critical, and judgmental.		
31. I have a quick temper.		
32. I have a history of financial insufficiency or instability.		
33. I over-relate or identify with my pain, illness, and despair.		
34. I pretend to be perfect and positive no matter what is happening.		
35. I take on more than I can handle, then resent the weight of my responsibilities.		
36. When others disappoint me, I can appear heartless and often will distance or leave (the job, relationship, friendship, etc.).		

There are three types of disguises, which we will discuss at length in the next chapters, each comprising two disguises of rage:

- Fight Types—*Dominance* and *Defiance*
- Flight Types—*Distraction* and *Devotion*
- Shrink Types—*Dependence* and *Depression*

Typically we have one, maybe two predominant disguises of rage that we established in childhood with overlapping traits from the other disguises. To determine your primary disguises of rage, transfer the statement numbers you marked in the first or "Yes" column to the matrix below. Total each column in the matrix. Your total in any given column can range from 0–6. Your higher numbers will most likely represent your disguises of rage.

Defiance	Dependence	Depression	Devotion	Distraction	Dominance
1	2	3	4	5	6
7	8	9	10	11	12
13	14	15	16	17	18
19	20	21	22	23	24
25	26	27	28	29	30
31	32	33	34	35	36
Totals	Totals	Totals	Totals	Totals	Totals

A shortcut for determining your primary disguises of rage is to reflect on how you went about completing this exercise. For example, you probably wear a *Devotion* disguise if you found yourself saying: *I'm all of them depending on the situation!* You are likely to wear *Defiance* if you were thinking: *Why should I put myself in one or two categories? You're not the boss of me!* If you checked "Yes" to most of the statements other than the *Dependence* statements, you lean in the direction of wearing the *Dependence* disguise. You have tendencies of *Distraction* if you didn't bother with the task and instead fast-forwarded to the next section of the book. If you just didn't feel up to the task, you may wear the *Depression* disguise. And you are sure to wear *Dominance* if you skimmed the questions and found that most of them didn't apply to you, and in fact was a waste of your time. If you fall into more than two of the disguises, that's okay, too! It does not matter—what matters is that you keep reading!

There is yet another way to determine your disguises of rage. Give the assessment to two or three loved ones or close friends and ask them to complete it for you. There is one catch: You must promise to continue to be their friend even if you don't like what they see or say. Relationships have been known to deepen when friends complete the assessment for each other.

HIGH-CONTROL AND OUT-OF-CONTROL TYPES

Disguises of rage can further be understood when placed along the dimension of high control and out of control. The *High-Control and Out-of-Control* range has to do with how certain disguise clusters relate to anger, guilt, and shame. Refer to your Disguises of Rage Self-Assessment scores to determine where you are located on the spectrum of *High Control and Out of Control.*

High-Control Types

DOMINANCE, DEVOTION, AND DEPRESSION
Those of us who wear the *Dominance* and *Devotion* disguises share high control in our effort to conquer and escape. We need to be needed by others, we know what's best for them, and we need to clone others in our image. We are focused, perfectionists, and generally faultless. *Dominance* and *Devotion* disguises have different experiences of shame. The *Dominance* disguise tends to experience more rage than shame, whereas the *Devotion* disguise tends to experience more shame than rage.

The third high-control disguise, *Depression*, seeks control by forcing others to rescue us and provide us with energy. The *Depression* disguise's control is less verbal and more concealed, but nonetheless communicated, i.e., through withdrawal, silence, or suicide attempts or thoughts. *Depression* and *Dominance* share withdrawal as a form of control, whereas *Devotion* is more likely to control by holding tightly to others.

Out-of-Control Types

DEFIANCE, DISTRACTION, AND DEPENDENCE

The *Defiance, Distraction,* and *Dependence* disguises share the characteristics of being impulsive, entitled, and insatiable. We want immediate gratification and approval from others. Others owe us their undivided attention! We can be self-indulgent saboteurs. What distinguishes us out-of-control types is our experience of shame. Those who wear the *Defiance* and *Distraction* disguises are likely to experience more rage than shame and feel others are at fault, whereas people who wear the *Dependence* disguise feel guilty and resentful for not being in control, and are likely to experience more shame.

SHADOW DISGUISES

Disguises of rage are distortions of reality, extremes that have opposing forces that are feared, avoided, desired, and ultimately realized. Consider them shadow disguises—those aspects of ourselves that we dislike in others but are hidden or even denied parts of ourselves. For example, each *high-control* disguise has an *out-of-control* disguise as its shadow that it avoids experiencing, yet relies upon to navigate events in the world, and the reverse is also true, as indicated by this chart:

High Control	Out of Control
Dominance avoids experiencing Dependence	Dependence avoids experiencing Dominance
Devotion avoids experiencing Defiance	Defiance avoids experiencing Devotion
Depression avoids experiencing Distraction	Distraction avoids experiencing Depression

For example, *Dominance* is terrified of becoming dependent, while *Dependence* avoids taking control of her own life. *Devotion* cannot tolerate the harshness of *Defiance*, while *Defiance* believes that pleasing others is manipulative and violates freedom. *Depression* finds herself paralyzed in the speed of distraction, while *Distraction* dreads the stillness of *Depression*.

As with any extreme, we inevitably find ourselves on the other side of something equally painful and terrifying. This dynamic becomes even more complex when we consider that we wear more than one disguise of rage, or more mind-boggling when we understand that we wear many of them.

The following chapters and descriptions of disguises of rage are not intended to simplify or categorize our complex lives. Rather they are attempts to reveal our deceptions of rage and invite us to reexamine what might ordinarily be considered normal or justified behavior.

4

Fight Types—
In the Ring with Rage

Dominance and *Defiance*—at a Glance

Fight types lead with anger when we feel attacked, trapped, or caught off guard. We have high control needs, readily confront conflict, pretend to be unafraid, deny or ignore shame, and feel faultless—*Somebody must pay!* We seek justice and reprisal, and would say that what we do *is for your own good!* Fight types become angry to divert the embarrassment of losing control and the terror of being truly intimate with another. Intimacy is a high risk that threatens the exposure of shame. We are distrustful and have a low tolerance of tenderness.

As children, we were expected to follow the rules without question. Obeying the rules and not causing problems were more important than having feelings and knowing the reasons for those feelings. Only people in authority had any power or could be seen and heard. Fight types create boundaries that keep what they most need at bay. It is difficult to grasp that fighting is more a plea for respect and kindness—a denied longing for our vulnerability to be seen and our significance affirmed. There are two fight types—*Dominance* and *Defiance*.

	Dominance	Defiance
Core Characteristics	Controlling Critical Judgmental Detached Independent Privileged Seeks power and status Intolerant of imperfection	Angry Blaming Hostile Defensive Cynical Self-absorbed Seeks justice and reparation Intolerant of rules/ prohibitions
When Triggered, Acts	Rejecting Withholding Superior Demanding Unforgiving Cruel Ruthless Needs to be right	Difficult Belligerent Entitled Confrontational Vindictive Hateful Revengeful
Fears	Insignificance	Unimportance
Ashamed of	Needing tenderness	Needing validation
Defense Postures	Distance from others Becomes critical to deny the need for intimacy	Blames others Becomes belligerent to deny the need for intimacy
As a child	Felt overcontrolled or ignored Had to learn things the hard way on her own Expected to behave as an adult	Felt overcontrolled or overindulged Given too much freedom or not enough Expected to do as she was told, or else
Emotional Challenges	Trust Significance	Trust Respect
Shadow Rage Disguise	Dependence	Devotion
Wisdom	Discernment	Truth-telling

DOMINANCE DISGUISE OF RAGE

We know we wear the *Dominance* disguise of rage when we have a life pattern of control. Sometimes we control others, but mostly we will do everything we can not to be controlled. Controlling is our way of keeping shame under wraps. We consider ourselves top dog—a self-appointed judge, which gives us the privilege to evaluate the character of others while we determine our level of emotional investment. Operating from the arrogance of our mental courthouse, we judge what is right and wrong. We have tendencies toward greed and power. Our views are as razor-sharp as they are narrow. We bring unreachable standards to our relationships and hold others accountable to them.

We are deliberate, efficient, and skillful in getting what we want. While we are capable of making good decisions, our self-interest is often at the expense of others, and our critical nature causes others to feel inept and worthless in the process. We prefer positions where we can judge, control, and direct others—roles that keep us apart and elevated from others. We choose to be right over being liked, and prefer to be alone instead of dealing with what we consider to be the incompetence of others. We use our strength to keep people at a distance and even separated from one another. We generally avoid joining groups and have a low need for inclusion. We despise groupies, considering them copycats and chameleons. We are more a loner or creator of our own circumstances. Regardless of where we are, we are in charge, at least of ourselves. If we do not have the official role, we claim it. We believe that if we are not in control, others will make a mess that we will eventually have to clean up.

We do not have a conscious relationship with fear. We are likely to be oblivious as to how we enrage and frighten others. We appear indifferent to our contribution to problems. We deny that we have needs. We may not overtly invest in building intimate relationships because we deny we need them. We have convinced ourselves that we do not need others when we are honestly more ashamed of needing them. We deny this need because what accommodates intimacy is a loss of control, and to lose control is to feel ashamed, and to feel ashamed is to remember what must always be forgotten—early childhood traumas, where we felt powerless. We rarely if ever say "I'm sorry" because it assumes we *need* to be forgiven.

The nature of our relationships is driven by how much control we have over cloning others in our image. We have an intolerance of imperfection—anything that is not to our liking. The rage rules we insist on in most relationships are:

Dominance Rule #1: Don't challenge or disobey me!

Dominance Rule #2: Don't try to change me!

Dominance Rule #3: Don't accuse me of being incompetent, needy, or helpless!

Dominance Rule #4: Don't expect me to regard you as higher or better than me in any way!

Dominance Rule #5: Don't expect me to explain or apologize for what I do!

When anyone breaks these rage rules and takes a stand against us, we become aggravated, impatient, and determined to prove them wrong. In response, others may become frightened and attempt to reduce the tension. They may not feel they have a choice other than giving us what we want because of the influence we have or the dependency they have on us.

Generally we feel entitled to express rage toward others, but our disguise of *Dominance* hides the hurt we feel from being misunderstood and disappointed. When others resist us, we feel ineffectual—like a failure. We are puzzled and don't understand why anyone wouldn't want to be like us. Shameful feelings lurk as the conflict persists unresolved to our satisfaction. To avoid the threat of shame, we strike out, punishing the other person through physical abuse, or by physically leaving the situation, i.e., the job, the relationship, the community, the room, etc. If it is not possible to sever the relationship physically, we emotionally detach, having nothing else to do with them. We become silent, cold, controlled, and dismissing, allowing the intensity of our rage to fill the air with mysterious discomfort and fear. We feel righteously indignant, and swear never to forgive, reserving the right to use our power against them in the future.

Underneath this bravado, an older rage wound has been awakened. We are terrified of feeling insignificant, a horror that must be obliterated to escape the shame of helplessness rooted in a childhood where we were severely controlled, and had to obey the rules or else bad things happened. Bad things *did* happen, and we were hurt when we asserted ourselves. Being obedient and following the rules were more important than having feelings, and we recognized and resented that only adults had a right to be seen and heard. We dislike that we were not able to feel significant as a child. We in no way forgave our parents for not valuing or protecting us, and we vowed never to feel helpless and hurt again. As adults, we still carry that unresolved rage, making sure we have everything we need, and never depending on anyone unless it is under our terms. While we long for tenderness and a respectful affirmation of our existence, we distrust it. We would prefer to take control than to risk drowning in shameful feelings of dependency, smallness, and helplessness—there is nothing in between. We cannot forgive and forget, and will do everything we can to feel important and safe, including hurting others.

A DAY IN THE LIFE OF BETH—*DOMINANCE*

I'm at the gym by 6:30 every morning, you know. Mom taught me long ago to stay in shape! She's eighty-three now and looking better than she feels. Oh, that reminds me. I have to take her fresh flowers when I leave here. She informed me recently that it's my time to take care of her, not that I haven't been doing that for most of my life. I don't even have a life because of her. I guess it's not the time to tell her what I truly feel given she's in that rest home dying of cancer. Of course I'll take care of her. It's my duty—my cross to bear.

Sometimes I take my sixteen-year-old daughter with me to the gym, but lately she prefers to be with her friends. She told me she was interested in locating her real parents. She seemed to emphasize "real"! Hell, she has everything a child could want—great school, fine clothes, money for frivolous things, and me. She's completely ungrateful.

I had this meeting at work this morning with my Diversity Council. The employees seemed preoccupied, angry, and afraid given the impending war, and I've been concerned about productivity and my executive bonus. I wanted to get the employees' minds off war and on work, so I asked my Council to discreetly go around and encourage employees to refocus, you know, on work. How could a request so simple result in such outrage? Hell, you give them a task and they complain. What good are they?

Elizabeth had the nerve to ask me how I felt about the war and if I were willing to guarantee people's jobs if sales went down. The rest of those assholes let her go on and on, talking down to me. Elizabeth thought I should be the one out there asking folks how they felt and talking about how I felt, and telling people they had nothing to worry about. Where does she get off? She disrespected my position as a vice president of the company paying her salary!

My only response to Elizabeth and the other spineless members of the Council that allowed her insubordination was that this was obviously a task too difficult for the Diversity Council. I then excused myself from the meeting. Elizabeth was still shouting at me as I left the room. I was irritated but not angry. I couldn't understand why she was so upset, and assumed the silence of the others meant she was their voice. I kept my cool but I was disappointed in all of them. I kind of felt sorry for them, actually. I went to my office and spent the rest of the afternoon drafting a letter to all employees informing them that if productivity did not return to a level matching last year's projections, drastic measures would be taken, including layoffs. I'm sure that this approach will get people focused on work, not war.

I picked up my daughter from school and she didn't speak to me all the way home. Once at home, she stormed off to her room slamming her door. I marched right behind her demanding that she tell me what was wrong. Before I knew anything I had slapped her and was telling her how selfish and disrespectful she was. She burst into tears and I didn't know what to do, I just knew I felt manipulated, so I left.

When I told my husband that I felt our daughter was moving away from me, he had little to say. He seemed careful not to say anything that would upset me, but everything he says upsets me. He asked me if I'd asked her what she was feeling. How ridiculous! Of course I'd asked her. Does he think I'm stupid? I get so little from him it's hard to see the point in taking anything of significance to him. He just wimps out. I'm not upset with my daughter, just confused. What is her problem? She's got everything she needs. Why is she being such an ungrateful brat? And why should I keep trying to make her life better? Hell, what has she done for me lately?

How do I feel? Kinda numb, empty, and alone.

JOURNALING QUESTIONS

1. What thoughts, feelings, memories, or sensations did you experience while reading about *Dominance*?
2. What aspect of this disguise is alive in your life?
3. Who or what does this disguise remind you of?
4. What does *Dominance* teach you about rage and the need to heal?

THE WISDOM OF DOMINANCE—DISCERNMENT

When our disguise is not ruling our world, we open more to our wisdom. The wisdom in the *Dominance* disguise of rage is discernment, discriminating awareness. Our instincts have afforded us good judgment, courage, autonomy, and clear vision. We are comfortable with our power and use it to transform our worlds. We have an inherent sense of fairness and can recognize whether a social structure is sound or weak. We will not be oppressed nor will we oppress others.

We are naturally able both to see the big picture and hold true to it with understanding and compassion.

LETTING GO

We are beginning to let go of the *Dominance* disguise of rage when:

- We can acknowledge that we are hurt and afraid.
- We become less controlling and judgmental of others and ourselves.
- We become genuinely open to what we don't know and what others can teach us.

We are on track when we acknowledge that we long to know:

- How do I love without feeling like a fool?
- How do I stay connected with others and myself when I am hurt and disappointed?
- How do I allow the good and bad in others and in myself?
- How do I say "I'm sorry" or "It was my fault"?
- How do I stop contributing to rage legacies of war, greed, oppression, indifference, and self-interest?

DEFIANCE DISGUISE OF RAGE

We know we wear the *Defiance* disguise of rage when we have a life pattern of anger and battle. Sometimes we battle outwardly with another person, place, or thing. Other times we battle within our mind or against our body. Anger is our way of keeping others, including ourselves, from noticing the shame we are feeling.

We are quick-witted and charged with energy. We can often see and feel what is wrong before others can, and put a voice to it. We prefer roles where we can have freedom, protect others and ourselves, and inflict punishment where needed. We are as quick to defend those who are less fortunate as we are to abuse them. We have strong convictions and low impulse control. While we have keen instincts, our anger blocks us from knowing what we need and getting what we want. We are quick to complain but slow to solve problems. We resent clearly stating our thoughts and feelings to others, when, in our minds, *"They should already know!"* When we are not understood, we feel rejected and become agitated. And out of this frustration and embarrassment for needing others' understanding, we become even angrier than before.

We are unable to see how we distort reality and fan the fires of our rage. When triggered, we are like a rebellious child on military duty in a solo war shooting a machine gun too large to hold. We can be belligerent, impatient, and blind to other points of view—unaware of the pain we feel and the pain we cause others. Because of this blindness, we are unable to take responsibility for our actions.

In our mind, we have paid dearly for the privilege to abuse others, just as we were abused. As a justifiable warrior in a dangerous world, we are not aware of how we create battles because we are longing for a more just outcome. However, there is never a time when we feel justice is done—somebody must pay again and again for the lost battles of our past.

We believe most people with power don't deserve it; they only abuse it. They are inadequate and fall short of our expectations. If given the chance, we believe they would take advantage of us, therefore they are the enemy. The enemy must pay for violating, exploiting, deceiving, and humiliating us and others with less power, and it is our job to see that justice is done.

In the heat of our battles, we expect the enemy to surrender while we are still firing shots—to come out with her hands held high above her head, fall on her knees, and apologize for firing the first bullet and wounding us, and to do this over and over again, for this is the apology we never received as a child. The irony is that victory in our battles never occurs. While we unconsciously long for acceptance from our enemy, we don't trust it when we receive it, and in our self-righteous aggression to defend our convictions, we become the enemy we most despise.

We are terrified of tenderness. Relationships require us to remove our battle gear, yet being disarmed makes us an obvious target for abuse. Our fears are utterly appropriate given the confusion of childhood abuse, neglect, and abandonment by those we loved and relied on. We associate love with pain. Intimacy challenges us to believe that someone could genuinely care for us, yet our survival instinct has taught us otherwise. The rage rules we insist on in relationships are:

Defiance Rule #1: Don't blame, threaten, or inconvenience me!
Defiance Rule #2: Don't place demands or expectations on me!
Defiance Rule #3: Don't expect me to forgive you!
Defiance Rule #4: Don't make a mistake! You won't get away with it!
Defiance Rule #5: Don't expect me to follow the rules!

When anyone breaks these rage rules, we become suspicious, unforgiving, and intimidating. We feel justified to fight—attack, blame, criticize, and if necessary, abuse, when we are, in fact, afraid and disappointed. We overreact to disappointments without recognizing that we are hurting and hungry for connection. We pretend to be unaffected and smug while denying our pain. In our guardedness, we distrust expressions of compassion and kindness that may come our way.

We come from childhoods where we felt we were victims of a disadvantaged war, unprepared for battle. We were silenced, threatened, and abused by authority. It was then that we made an agreement with ourselves that when we grew up, we would never be violated again. As adults, we are still armed for war. We carry feelings of being humiliated, disrespected, and devalued. *Defiance* has become a way of hiding our shame of needing to be loved. It diverts us from the rage we feel toward our own helplessness, and the longing to be honored and respected. Yet, we are unable to discern that not everyone is the enemy. We are the last one to know that some wars have ended, and that there are new ways to survive that allow us to remove our armor, rest in our own skin, and heal.

A DAY IN THE LIFE OF ANTOINETTE—*DEFIANCE*

I was late so I didn't have time to pick up my double espresso at my favorite coffeehouse. The damn bridge was backed up again, so I did what made sense to me under the circumstances—I drove in the car pool lane.

I was driving along, feeling like a free woman, singing "Respect" with Aretha on the radio. And would you believe I got pulled over by the police! I kept my cool and said nothing, but in my head, I was saying, "This asshole!"

I was pissed off that the officer asked me to turn my radio down so he could take his time telling me how wrong I was. He goes to his car to write me a ticket and it takes forever! He seemed to be enjoying wasting my time, as if I had nothing else to do. Hell, why did he think I was speeding in the first damn place?

When he finally decided to "free me from jail" I drove away screaming in my car and beating the steering wheel. I started screaming at the rubberneckers who were staring at me, turning the bridge into a stadium parking lot. Damn, women are always targets. The police would have never acted that way toward a man, I'm sure of it. I'm going to fight this ticket. It's pure discrimination.

Of all the days, the meeting started on time—thirty-five minutes ago. Everyone stopped and looked at me, just like the rubberneckers on the bridge. I wanted to scream, "What am I? Flypaper for freaks?" Instead, I took my seat without saying a word. My manager rolls her eyes my way, as if to say, "This is the third time this month you've been late." I say to myself, "Hell, I know how to count!" I'm in no mood to be messed with.

The meeting was a bore, as usual. It's amazing we get anything done. I looked at Ralph and visualized putting duct tape over his mouth. Then there was Frances talking on and on. I wanted to say, "I can see your point, but I still think you're full of shit." I couldn't seem to erase the sarcastic grin on my face and noticed that I was slowly turning my head as if to say, "What a circus!"

As my manager closed the meeting, I wondered, "Who in hell appointed her queen?" I silently found a million things wrong with her. I added this million to yesterday's list. It took all of my control not to say, "Thank you. We're all inspired by your worthless point of view." Instead, I sat silent with a hostile smirk that kept others at bay—they knew not to ask so I didn't have to tell. I left the meeting feeling like my time had been wasted. I thought, "Damn, and I got a ticket for this? These are a bunch of idiots."

My secretary stopped me in the hall. She wanted to talk about how I'd been treating her. Abrasive was her word. Why in hell is she so wimpy? She has such low self-esteem. Men don't have to apologize for being bastards, but women always have to apologize for being bitches. What's the difference, they both start with "b"! I didn't have time for her nonsense so I told her, "Get over it!"

Later, I completed several work deadlines while drinking a bottle of wine. My partner finally came home. What I really wanted was for her to notice that I had a difficult day and hold me, to tell me everything would be okay tomorrow—let's love today away. But looking at her not looking at me, I was convinced that wouldn't happen. Hell, who needs her anyway? Before I knew it I was screaming at her "You're late! Where have you been?" She quietly turned around and left the house again. I went to bed angry, hurt, and misunderstood. I tossed all night and pretended like I was asleep when she came home at 4:00 A.M. I don't know when I went to sleep. I woke up feeling like I had had a horrible dream only to realize it was my life and had been for many years.

JOURNALING QUESTIONS

1. What thoughts, feelings, memories, or sensations did you experience while reading about *Defiance*?
2. What aspect of this disguise is alive in your life?
3. Who or what does this disguise remind you of?
4. What does *Defiance* teach you about rage and the need to heal?

THE WISDOM OF DEFIANCE—TRUTH-TELLING

When *Defiance* is not ruled by a pressing anxiety for justice, its bright, warrior spirits can show up with more heart. When there is injustice in our environment, we are the first to feel it. When we, or others, are suppressed or constrained, our spirit rebels. As our rage child heals, these deep instincts can be an even greater gift. Truth-telling, courage, freedom of expression, and choice flowing from a compassionate heart—these are the necessities of our spirit. Our keen sense of justice can give us a life of independence and self-respect, and be a gift that unites the world.

LETTING GO

We are beginning to let go of the *Defiance* disguise of rage when:

- We become less armored—vindictive, angry, and accusatory—and more considerate of how we negatively and positively affect others.
- We can embrace the human frailties of others and ourselves.
- We can experience our truth instead of defending it.

We are on track when we acknowledge that we long to know:

- How can I love and be loved without hurting others and myself?
- What would happen if I didn't have to prove I was right?
- How do I fight for justice and not suffer?
- How do I say "I'm sorry" and mean it?
- How do I stop contributing to rage legacies of violence, hatred, abuse, and disrespect?

5

Flight Types—
On the Run from Rage!

Distraction and *Devotion*—at a Glance

Those of us who are Flight types find ways to escape the intense and painful truth we embody. We don't rock the boat. We are more likely to give in to avoid conflict. We feel *I must pay,* then we harbor silent resentment. We may live beyond our means, spending recklessly or borrowing money, even giving money away. We reveal little of our true selves to others. Instead, we become generous to distract others when we are feeling unworthy and inadequate. We tend to have poor emotional boundaries, and can be targets of use and abuse. We are guilt-driven and impulsive, and occasionally have surprising outbursts of rage that shame us back into being overly nice. Flight types exert tremendous effort outside of themselves. We are image conscious, wanting to be seen as good servants. We over-function to avoid *feeling* in general, and feeling alone, exiled, or abandoned in particular. It is difficult to grasp that pretending and serving are more accurately petitions for acceptance and ways to guarantee that we will always be seen, special, and needed. There are two Flight types—*Distraction* and *Devotion*.

	Distraction	Devotion
Core Characteristics	Incessant Urgent Compulsive Consumptive Envious Hedonistic Seeks immediate pleasure by overindulging Intolerant of stillness	Accommodates Avoids Over-functions Guilt-ridden Resentful Denies the truth Seeks significance by pleasing Intolerant of separation
When Triggered, Acts	Pretender, denies problems Self-indulgent Performs Jealous rages Needs to be seen	Martyr, guilt-inducing Self-sacrificing Pleases Hurt rages Needs to be needed
Fears	Inadequacy	Unworthiness
Ashamed of	Needing nourishment	Needing admiration
Defense Posture	Overindulges in tasks or material acquisitions Self-defeating to avoid intimacy	Clings by accommodating others Self-sacrificing to avoid intimacy
As a child	Frightened and anxious Felt trapped and confused Performed for praise Expected to be better than others	Doubtful, voiceless, guilty Felt unworthy of love Pleased for praise Expected to put others first
Emotional Challenges	Intimacy Stillness	Self-respect Independence
Shadow Rage Disguise	Depression	Defiance
Wisdom	Free will	Harmony

DISTRACTION DISGUISE OF RAGE

We know we wear *Distraction* as our disguise of rage when we have a life pattern of searching, seeking, reaching, and achieving for more. Most of our energy is invested in the external world. We are intellectual and charismatic and we know how to make others feel good. We generally play leading roles in life. We prefer independent and solo acts where our starring role is clear. Politics, technology, sales, and public speaking are well suited for our disguise. We have great vision and can be bored with here-and-now reality. We are more in touch with our intellect than our emotions. Therefore, we can come across as smart, sarcastic, humorous, and unkind in one brief interaction.

We can be intensity junkies, sensation seekers, and adventurers, and can get as lost in a single task as we do in multiple tasks. Many associate us with having various addictions or having an addictive personality. While this may be true, all of us, regardless of our disguises, may struggle with addictions, not just those of us who wear *Distraction*. We will typically have several activities we partake in for immediate gratification—eating, shopping, spending, achieving, working, relating, drugging, drinking—anything we enjoy or do well is likely to be done in excess and become a *Distraction*. We are generally good at what we do but not always present in what we are doing. Because we multitask and are obsessive, we tend to overextend ourselves, run behind schedule, and make commitments we cannot keep. Then we resent others when they express disappointment.

Silently, we feel we are worth waiting for. We will arrive to important appointments on time for curtain call, even if we are up all night obsessively working to make things perfect. But more commonly, appointments are changed, travel is rearranged, details are lost—constant chaos is all a part of the fast life. We rush from one appointment to the next seemingly without breathing. We even rush to our meditation practice! We tend to be more concerned with how we perform or appear to others than how we feel within ourselves.

The idea is to speed through life and to maintain this speed as long as we can without limits and often despite consequences. We tend to ignore the sensations of our body and prefer an altered state that allows us to live high above the lows of life. Therefore, our body takes a beating. We are likely to find ourselves shocked and incapacitated with accidents or illnesses because we move too fast to notice early-warning signs.

We are restless, emotionally ravenous, and often excessive. We resist being idle, unaware that we are afraid that in our stillness our memories will devour us. So we keep busy stuffing ourselves with material gains and activities from the outside world hoping it will quiet the inner terror of inadequacy, emptiness, and loneliness. We must be adored; not because we feel adorable, but because we feel empty if we have no proof of our value—a proof we must be able to point to outside of ourselves.

While we bring spontaneous joy to our relationships and entertain those around us with our various talents, few people really know us intimately. We are afraid that if people got too close we would disappoint them and be uncovered as a fraud. While we prefer to be seen as charming, intelligent, professional, and sociable, in conflict we can swing in the opposite direction and become explosive, aloof, or sarcastic. When this happens, the adoration we have grown to rely on from others is threatened. Therefore, the rage rules we insist on in relationships are:

Distraction Rule #1: Don't expect me to sit still and relax!
Distraction Rule #2: Don't expect me to be emotionally vulnerable!
Distraction Rule #3: Don't tell me I'm not perfect!
Distraction Rule #4: Don't expect me to waste time being upset or depressed!
Distraction Rule #5: Don't expect me to have enough of anything!

The *Distraction* disguise takes exception to anything or anyone that attempts to bring us down. We like to keep things informative, not personal. Emotionally we like to tread water with our hopes and dreams rather than deep-sea dive with the truth. We seek knowledge that offers immediate comfort, not necessarily wisdom. For example, we are more likely to write a check toward a problem to avoid any emotional experience of it, or we make a quick decision or comply with a decision to avoid conflict. We have a low tolerance for conflict or discomfort. We want to do something—anything—to relieve the situation and move on.

In relationships, we want to feel good. Typically, we are not aware of problems unless someone else points them out. When this occurs, we are shocked and ashamed of the truth it reveals. We feel flawed, blamed, and criticized. This exposure must be hidden, so we become belligerent to distance ourselves from the shame. Often, we explode in rage, taking this opportunity to complain about the inequities in the relationship, something, up until now, we had ignored or denied. We don't want any problems, period! We want to fast-forward through pain and discomfort and consume the desserts of life in one sensational gorge. Once the conflict has settled, we want to move back into our comfort lane and proceed with life as usual—all is forgotten until the next time someone brings it up.

Those of us wearing the *Distraction* disguise have shameful memories of feeling blamed, criticized, and humiliated for disappointing someone we depended on as children. We felt punished or ignored for not trying hard *enough* and not being good *enough*. Our life depended on how we performed, and often, how we performed was more important than who we were. Wearing the lifelong pattern of *Distraction* means we do everything we can to ignore feelings of emptiness and inadequacy. We are emotionally and often physically rushing through our lives to escape intolerable shame. We obsessively feed our insatiable emotional appetite with fast food while denying the haunting truth of our hunger.

A DAY IN THE LIFE OF CARMEN—*DISTRACTION*

Lately, life has been a whirlwind. My father has been in the hospital for the past four weeks, I've changed jobs twice, and of course, the obvious, I weigh quite a bit more than before. But you know, I just have to roll with it. Besides, I consider myself fabulously full!

My new job is great. I'm the first woman to serve in my position and the only woman on the management team. Everyone expects me to succeed, so I do, but a lot is required. I attend one meeting after another, often in different states. I can usually get by, you know, pull it off without any major glitches. Hell, the meetings only last an hour and then I'm off to the next thing. Sometimes other people want to sweat the small stuff, but I just ignore them. It's no big deal. Well, it shouldn't be. Actually I was doing quite well with all this until yesterday.

In the middle of an important meeting, a horrendous sadness flooded me for no reason and tears began streaming down my face uncontrollably. Everybody froze and looked at me. I politely left the room and it took me several minutes to regroup. I was so happy no one ran behind me to see what had happened. I couldn't have explained it. I was more angry because of the inconvenience, and I worried about what others thought about my quick exit. I was also frightened over this surprise attack of emotions and didn't know how to make sure it would never happen again. I can't remember the last time I cried. Maybe thirty years ago. It's just not me!

On the way home, I stopped by my favorite takeout and ordered enough food for an army. I don't know what got into me but I had to have everything I wanted. When I got home, I felt tangled in my thoughts. I worried about what I did, didn't do, should have done, and shouldn't have done. It was starting to freak me out. I ate and had a few beers, but I was more anxious than usual. My father called from the hospital down in the dumps about his situation. I had to stop what I was doing and put on a happy face to comfort him, but I wasn't in the mood for it, really. When I hung up the phone I felt pure rage and resentment. He's a grown man and expects me to mother him. It makes me want to scream!

I called some of my friends. We usually party together on the weekends. We may overindulge in food, light drugs, and alcohol, but it's not a daily endeavor, more a way to let loose, relax, and give our minds a break. We can afford our habits and we mind our own business. They came right over and we were up most of the night. When I'm with my friends, it's usually my job to entertain them. Sometimes it feels more like work but I seem to make energy for it somehow. Besides it's fun and it beats being alone, especially last night.

But of all the nights, my friend Silvia had to ask me point-blank what was wrong. Why in hell did she do that? I felt she had crawled underneath my skin and was deliberately trying to bring me down. I don't remember how I replied. I didn't have time for that nonsense. Besides, more and more, these friends seem superficial and boring, and I'm feeling less satisfied around them.

I guess I'm a little stressed but I have nothing to complain about, really. I'm healthy, educated, well traveled, and make good money. Hell, I'm a success story! So why, then, do I feel so empty when I'm so full?

JOURNALING QUESTIONS

1. What thoughts, feelings, memories, or sensations did you experience while reading about *Distraction*?
2. What aspect of this disguise is alive in your life?
3. Who or what does this disguise remind you of?
4. What does *Distraction* teach you about rage and the need to heal?

THE WISDOM OF DISTRACTION—FREE WILL

When we begin to slow down, to soften and rest in our yearning, the wisdom of our spirit begins to emerge. We become more balanced, and find that we have been "looking for love in all the wrong places" and return home, to our bodies, to love ourselves first. Our spirit is a natural antenna for freedom, beauty, generosity, spontaneous joy, and inspiration. When we begin to rest in our own fullness, this goodness can find expression in our relationships, our creative work, and in our environment.

LETTING GO

We are beginning to let go of the *Distraction* disguise of rage when:

- We begin to do less and feel more.
- We are less self-indulgent and consumptive and more thoughtful and appreciative of what we have.
- We invest in the well-being of our body.

We are on track when we acknowledge that we long to know:

- How do I do nothing without being consumed by fear?
- Who am I without "things"?
- What happens to me if I stop running?
- What do I have to give back to the world?
- How do I stop contributing to rage legacies of greed, indifference, waste, and class oppression?

DEVOTION DISGUISE OF RAGE

We know we wear the *Devotion* disguise of rage when we have a life pattern of pleasing. Pleasing is our way of dealing with the terror we feel when others are unhappy or express negative emotions. We are protective of those we love and feel responsible for their emotional comforts and discomforts. It's as if whatever others feel is our fault—if it's good, that's our doing. If it's bad, that's our fault and more disturbing.

We pride ourselves on knowing how to help. We enjoy negotiating, interceding, and peacekeeping. We have convinced ourselves that we have a sixth sense about what others need and we are the right person to give it to them. We like to be seen as nice, good, kind, and generous. Maintaining this image is safer than exposing the terror and resentment we feel but don't understand and therefore deny.

We are intuitive, caring, responsible, and strong-minded. People rely on us to bring heart to a situation and be there for them. We are associated with being a caretaker and perfectionist, and we bring a repertoire of comforting interventions to our relationships. While we are capable and in control, our need to make what we consider to be bad emotions better stifles the growth of others. It is difficult for us to understand how being devoted to others is a detour from taking care of or knowing ourselves.

We are convinced that we must first make sure others feel good before we can enjoy our life. This, of course, is an impossible task. Yet we feel guilty and unworthy if we live happily out loud while others are unhappy, especially those we love. This fact is not only enraging but also demanding because we feel we must drop what we are doing to accommodate others. While our devotion to others is genuine, it has a dual motivation. We want to see others feel good because we care about them *and* because their not feeling good has an alarming impact on us. We tend to expend tremendous energy on people and things we don't have control over while limiting the potential of our life experiences.

Those of us who wear the mask of *Devotion* are social beings and invest heavily in relationships. We enjoy the company of others, especially if we can accommodate them in some small or large way. Regardless of where we are, we appear to be gladly helping others, but the nature of our relationships is driven by how much safety we can guarantee. We believe that if we are not keeping things comfortable, others will become upset. Therefore, the rage rules we insist on in most relationships are:

Devotion Rule #1: Don't expect me to stop worrying about you!
Devotion Rule #2: Don't be unhappy!
Devotion Rule #3: Don't push me away or close me out!
Devotion Rule #4: Don't make me feel unneeded!
Devotion Rule #5: Don't expect me to stop trying to help!

When anyone breaks these rage rules, we become terrified that life will get out of control, other people will become upset, and we will be harshly blamed for it. *Devotion* feeds the faulty assumption we carry that if we care for others, we will always be needed and never blamed, criticized, or disappointed. We deny that our generosity toward the emotional needs of others is our way of purchasing their undying gratitude. The problem with this deal is that it is often without the other person's awareness or agreement.

We have poor boundaries. The problems of others become our priorities. We overextend and overcommit because we must please. We typically say *yes* when we want to say *no*, then rationalize the goodness of our *yes* and deny the truth of our *no*. Our habit of self-sacrificing serves its purpose as long as the perception of *good* and *nice* is maintained. The only time there are problems is when others bring them up.

We often suffer physically because our bodies absorb the pain we deny, contributing to us being targets for inner hardening (fibroids, kidney stones, cancer, etc.) and immune deficiencies. We hide our pain, shame, and resentment to deny our own rage and to avoid being a target of rage. We make this sacrifice, both willingly and unwillingly, and therefore, we don't understand why others don't do the same.

When others complain, we feel guilty and responsible, and are quick to apologize. Silently we feel we don't deserve what is happening, but we are unable to defend ourselves. We detest having to feel anything but good. To avert the pain we grin and bear it, and do whatever is necessary to make peace in the moment, at any cost.

We can be sarcastic, and in rare moments we may break down

and explode in a rage of tears, spewing the buried resentments we've long denied while singing the tune of: *After all I've done for you, how could you! Shame on you!* People are shocked to hear the bitterness dripping from our once-soothing lips. Others feel deceived and betrayed by the absence of the happy face that we've worn and they have come to rely on. They say *I didn't know you felt that way*, while we think to ourselves *I didn't know I felt this way either*. But these cruel surprise acts are disguises to mask our shame of failing to please. While our explosions punish our offenders, we feel guilty for hurting them. To compensate, we once again begin to overextend ourselves, and the vicious cycle continues.

Underneath this perceived kindness and service to others lies a burning rage wound. We are terrified of feeling negative emotions and of being a target of them, a horror that must be obliterated to escape the shame and helplessness rooted in a childhood where we felt blamed, criticized, or humiliated for disappointing someone we desperately relied on. As a child, we felt this injustice was our fault. Despite our best efforts, we felt like a failure and vowed to work harder and never to be humiliated again. As a frightened child in an adult body, we are still searching for forgiveness. We believe that if we demonstrate our undying love *enough*, we will be pardoned. We desperately need to please others while denying our desperate need to be pleased. Inside we feel like a *bad* girl, unworthy of being loved. Beneath this shame lives the *enraged* girl, the one we are terrified to bring to light.

A DAY IN THE LIFE OF THERESA—*DEVOTION*

Sometimes I feel like the little old lady who lives in a shoe. Had so many children she didn't know what to do. By this age, I thought my kids would be taking care of me. But it isn't working out that way. My daughter, Tia, and her two kids have been living with me for the past six months. I'm so happy that she has finally left her husband, who was so abusive to her. I worked so hard to help her to see that she needed to leave him. This was her second abusive relationship. I worry sometimes that my relationship with her father affected her ability to make healthy choices. So I'm trying even harder to help out now.

My grandkids are in shock. They are acting out a lot. I know it's hard for them and they are angry. I try to be supportive and show them how much I care, but they don't seem to want to let me get close. The only time they stop fighting is when the TV is on, which nowadays is night and day. I end up hiding out in my room just to get away from the noise of it.

I'm still in shock about last year, when I was away on a work assignment overseas and I let my daughter and my son Ralph stay at the house. I had just refinanced the house to post bail for Ralph. He got into a bit of trouble with the law but he's a good kid. He needed a place to stay, and there was plenty of room, since I was going to be away. We talked about it, and he and Tia agreed to pay the house note. Well, they never did. The house was foreclosed! I was furious at the time. But they swear I didn't explain about the mortgage payments to them. I'm sure I did, but maybe I wasn't clear enough. I guess I should have known that they had too much on their minds to carry that responsibility. Now the house is gone. It's such a blow. I'm struggling to see any silver lining. We're all crammed in this small apartment. I try to tell myself that material things aren't what's most important; it's loving relationships that matter.

One good thing is that Tia is finally getting a divorce. The legal part of it is complicated, and I've been trying to help. When I went to court with her she really froze up in front of the lawyer and judge, so I told them everything she was having trouble saying. When we got home, she started slamming doors and wouldn't talk to me for days. I had to do everything— cook, clean, take care of the kids, and she never offered to help. And then she got in my face screaming about how she was grown and didn't need me to defend her. That really felt like a slap in the face, after all I had done. I really lost my temper, too. But later I felt guilty, and I realized it must be hard on her pride to realize she made such a mess of things. I know the divorce is upsetting, but she really shouldn't take it out on me.

Now Ralph is back in jail. It's the alcohol that keeps getting him in trouble. Tia drinks, too. I'm trying to convince them to cut back. Sometimes, my advice seems to be helping. Other times, not. Their father was an alcoholic. Maybe it's genetic. I can understand the temptation to drink, but I can't let myself do it. There are too many people depending on me.

How can I be surrounded by so much heartache? Seems like nearly everyone I know is in some kind of crisis. Sometimes it feels like such a burden on me. I can hardly take it, but I can't stop. My friends say I shouldn't get so involved, but how do you just let people suffer when you love them?

JOURNALING QUESTIONS

1. What thoughts, feelings, memories, or sensations did you experience while reading about *Devotion*?
2. What aspect of this disguise is alive in your life?
3. Who or what does this disguise remind you of?
4. What does *Devotion* teach you about rage and the need to heal?

THE WISDOM OF DEVOTION—HARMONY

When the fear and emptiness that has driven us begins to ease, our gifts fully emerge—compassion, empathy, intimacy, and belonging woven with kind attention toward our own needs. Deep, loving relationships, with others and ourselves, are the necessity of our spirit. We are highly attuned to the subtle energies around us, both physical and emotional. We have the instincts of a healer—naturally patient, tenderhearted, accepting, and forgiving. Our commitment to harmony makes us one who weaves the fabric of community into a force for good—a quality that naturally overflows from a well-nurtured spirit that maintains levelheadedness and level-heartedness.

LETTING GO

We are beginning to let go of the *Devotion* disguise of rage when:

- We begin to set healthy boundaries for ourselves and maintain them.
- We stop betraying ourselves by pretending to please.
- We start hearing and responding to our own cries.

We are on track when we acknowledge that we long to know:

- How do I love without giving myself away?
- How do I not take responsibility for how others feel?
- How do I take care of myself without feeling selfish?
- How do I allow others to care for me?
- How do I stop contributing to rage legacies of martyrdom, denial, and abusing the feminine?

6

Shrink Types—
Hide and Seek from Rage

Dependence and *Depression*—at a Glance

Shrink types feel overwhelmed with life. We accommodate to avoid conflict then convince ourselves that we don't have a choice. We feel too small emotionally to fight, so we are likely to give up and sabotage ourselves, and then feel ashamed. We can be silent and passive, and live in the shadows of others, supporting them and living vicariously through them. We expect those we support to notice us, represent us, speak for us, and take care of us. We are afraid that if we show our full selves in the world, we will hurt or disappoint others, or we will be harmed. At the same time, we are silently enraged over living small and as imposters. We hide our resentment and, while we try to hide guilt, we are less successful. Our agreement with life is to *shrink*—not exist too loudly or largely. Because we chose to survive, we must manipulate the world around us to intervene on our behalf. It is difficult to grasp that shrinking is more accurately a game of hide and seek, where the job of life is for others to find us and reassure us that life is worth living.

	Dependence	Depression
Core Characteristics	Sweet Childlike Gullible Seductive Cautious Manipulates to be rescued Intolerant of adult responsibility	Bitter Disheartened Indifferent Avoids Withdrawn Manipulates to be seen Intolerant of adult expectations
When Triggered, Acts	Fearful Confused Mute Helpless Insecure Inhibited Needs to be helped Easily influenced	Withholding Indifferent Inaccessible Mopes Hopeless Reserved Needs to be alone Becomes invisible
Fears	Abandonment	Engagement
Ashamed of	Needing to be cherished	Needing to be seen
Defense Postures	Hides own talents to be taken care of Hopes to be rescued Becomes helpless to avoid the shame of being a woman	Hides own talents to avoid intimacy Hopes to be discovered Becomes hopeless to avoid the shame of being seen
As a child	Felt deprived and abandoned Unable to do things on one's own Seen but not heard Had to stay childlike to guarantee love	Felt deprived and deserted Unable to openly grieve losses Unseen and unheard Had to stay invisible to guarantee safety
Emotional Challenges	Independence Separation	Existence Intimacy
Shadow Rage Disguise	Dominance	Distraction
Wisdom	Originality	Solitude

DEPENDENCE DISGUISE OF RAGE

We know we wear the *Dependence* disguise of rage when we have a life pattern of uncertainty. Being uncertain is our way of being certain that someone is always there, for if this were not so, we would feel lost, afraid, and ashamed. We commonly move through life dependent on the support of others, like a child who *could* take its first step but is afraid that once she does, she will never be held again. We prefer the safety of being held to the risk of walking and *maybe* falling. Fundamentally, we are ashamed of standing on our own, so we play life safe and avoid risks that affirm our adulthood.

We *play* at being grown-up—dreaming about how we want to be some day while denying that we *are* grown-up, or dreaming about a better tomorrow when tomorrow was yesterday. We believe that life should be easy, not hard, and that the universe *will* provide. We expect to be cared for and we feel we deserve freedom without effort or responsibility. We are young at heart, thoughtful, and imaginative, and prefer roles where we can be helpful, original, and needed.

Generally, life feels unfair. We feel overburdened and undersupported. We resent the expectations that come with being an adult—earning money, making decisions, being agreeable, being a wife, being a mother, making others happy, knowing what you want, and taking care of yourself. We want to have fun, live in this moment without worrying about the next, but we often find ourselves in emotional and financial distress. While we are capable of generating creative ideas that support our well-being, we seldom feel confident accomplishing them. It is not that we are afraid of succeeding; we are more afraid of losing the affiliation of others if we become self-reliant, so we therefore promote an *appearance* of helplessness. Being helpless is our way to guarantee connection. Unfortunately, it is at the expense of our emotional growth.

We find it difficult to assert ourselves because it might upset someone we rely on and jeopardize their needed support. We don't feel entitled, i.e., *old enough, smart enough, experienced enough, grown-up enough*, to have such power. Instead of risking the disapproval or loss of others we depend on, we smile, voiceless, in insincere compliance, taking the path of least resistance. We make decisions to appease others, believing we must kiss up to them to avoid being left on our own. We feel stuck between needing others to protect us and not knowing what to do for ourselves if they don't. But underneath this disguise of helpless deceit is pure rage and intolerable shame because we feel we must sacrifice freedom in exchange for affiliation. We commonly feel betrayed and disappointed, and terrified of our thoughts. We may become ill or our lives completely explode around us, forcing others to notice and hopefully come to our rescue.

Long ago, survival meant that *children should be seen but not heard*. While we know as adults that this is not true, we still feel paralyzed in this old role we were forced to assume. We perceive our value as located outside of ourselves. We tend to attach ourselves to powerful people, places, and things and serve them with unquestioned and often blind loyalty. These include parents, teachers, religions, schools, children, friends, work, and the like. None of these affiliations are necessarily a problem, but when we use them to hide and avoid the responsibilities of living, we perpetuate our dependence and stunt our growth. In this regard, our loyalty is more a desperate plea to be valued than a true expression of our thinking.

We have convinced ourselves that it is impossible to accomplish what we want without support from others; therefore, most of our relationships are based on how others can help us feel better about ourselves. The rage rules we insist on in most relationships are:

Dependence Rule #1: Don't expect me to know or do what's best for me!

Dependence Rule #2: Don't expect me to get angry, confront conflict, or take a risk!

Dependence Rule #3: Don't expect me to be more confident than those I admire!

Dependence Rule #4: Don't expect me to grow up and stop needing you!
Dependence Rule #5: Don't ignore me or stop taking care of me!

When anyone breaks these rage rules, we are offended and often
may even cry about it. On the inside we feel enraged, terrified, and
helpless. Our biggest concern is being abandoned, so we feel we must
do what we can to make nice and maintain our status of belonging,
which often means keeping silent, *like a good girl.* This compromise
only further contributes to our feelings of shame, which in turn leads
to more rage.

Our relationships tend to be polite but lack intimacy. We are envious of others who appear to have their lives together. We feel small in
comparison to them. What others have is always better than what we
have—they are bigger and better. We are unaware that we seek surro-
gate parenting in most of our relationships. In our mind, it is someone else's job to affirm us. When frustrated, *They should know what I
need!* is a common mind-set. We expect those with power to notice
us and take care of us. We allow others to control us, blindly trusting
that they will spare us the dread of growing wiser. We rationalize our
faith in others, but inevitably, they disappoint us and we feel betrayed
and abandoned.

It feels *right* that others are greater than we are. As a child, we had
to maintain our child status to be loved. We were rewarded for being
a good *little* girl and felt we were punished for being independent. We
lived in intense fear of expressing ourselves, overdoing something,
not knowing how to behave or whom to please. We resented that we
were not affirmed or encouraged to be self-sufficient, and we are still
seeking this affirmation. Yet, to affirm ourselves as capable adults is
to compete with authority, i.e., our parents, managers, etc., and we
don't trust that we can succeed without losing something or someone
of grave emotional or financial importance.

A DAY IN THE LIFE OF PATRICIA—*DEPENDENCE*

I'm doing the best I can but dammmmmmmn! I feel buried alive! The minute I get one problem solved, another one appears. I guess money is my biggest problem. I'm in a lot of debt, but I can usually make a deal with the creditors if I remember to call. My check was garnished recently for back taxes, and they didn't even warn me. I asked the IRS for a break, but they told me "No!" Being nice didn't seem to have any effect on them. Thank goodness my parents helped me out.

My job is overwhelming! I know that they appreciate my loyalty but they don't tell me enough how much they value what I do. Actually, I stopped liking my job years ago when they promoted me into management. It was a major decision—one I didn't really make but went along with because we ran out of time. I didn't know whether to take the position and make them happy or stay where I was and make myself happy. I chose to take the position, and now I wonder if either of us is happy. I don't know.

Recently, my handsome tax advisor suggested I purchase a house. I said yes before I really thought about it. I wanted him to be impressed with my independence and maybe ask me out on a date. That didn't happen. Meanwhile, I had purchased this damn house! My parents helped me out, even packed me up and moved me in, but I'm not sure I even wanted this house, especially on my own. Hell, I thought I'd be married by now with two kids and a white picket fence. Instead, I'm forty, single, depend on my parents financially, and need this job that I don't like so I can pay for this house that I don't want.

It's been a nightmare from day one. The movers promised three times to deliver my furniture from storage but they never showed up. Each time I had to take off work and wait all day. I couldn't pin them down with a time. Well, I didn't try. They were demanding on the phone and I didn't want to fight with them. I just rearranged my schedule but then they never showed. When they finally came, several of my cherished pieces were missing and two items were broken. They didn't offer any compensation. I didn't push for it either. I just wanted them to go away. They finally found my missing furniture. They called me on a Wednesday to deliver on Thursday. Again, I had to change my plans even though it was my birthday. I was afraid to say no. Besides, I wanted it to all be over. My best friend got angry and told me I should have set a time and demanded compensation. He told me I was being a doormat. I felt hurt, like I had been dishonest with myself. I became ill and felt down, and was in bed for the next few days.

I make enough money but creditors always seem to take it before I see it, and I never seem to have enough. I like to shop and eat, but who doesn't? I had a roommate but she moved out after four months. She wasn't very sociable. I'm not sure what I'll do next. I get tired thinking about it. I could sell the house. Maybe I could reduce my monthly payments if I refinanced. Dad did all this paperwork when I bought the house. Maybe he'd be willing to do it again. My Dad! He's the best!

Maybe I need to get away and have some fun. No, too many deadlines at work and I've taken a number of sick days already this year. My food consultant is concerned about my blood pressure and wants me to relax, cook organic meals, and meditate before bed. I'm not doing any of it, really. I start cooking about 8:00 P.M. after checking my e-mails. The rest of the night I watch TV or read the newspaper. Sometimes I'll eat sweets, especially now that I don't have a roommate. By the time I go to bed it's 11:30 P.M. and I'm up at 5:30 A.M. Mom usually calls early in the morning. She says it's the only time she can catch me, but I know it's to wake me up and help me on my way. Mom's the word! My only problem is that I have too many bills to have fun.

JOURNALING QUESTIONS

1. What thoughts, feelings, memories, or sensations did you experience while reading about *Dependence*?

2. What aspect of this disguise is alive in your life?
3. Who or what does this disguise remind you of?
4. What does *Dependence* teach you about rage and the need to heal?

THE WISDOM OF DEPENDENCE—ORIGINALITY

When the veils of fear are lifted, our natural gift of originality shines true. We are cheerful, trusting, and discover with ease the wonders of life. Our spirit enjoys celebration and creativity. We open wide to joy and can laugh at our mistakes. We naturally delight in the oneness of all beings. Playfulness, insight, magic, and inspiration are our gifts and our offerings to the world.

LETTING GO

We are beginning to let go of the *Dependence* disguise of rage when:

• We shift from being confused, doubtful, and helpless to taking control of the details of our lives.
• We begin to trust and act on our own instincts.
• We are being sincere, creative, and more self-reliant.

We are on track when we acknowledge that we long to know:

• What is more important than being an emotional child?
• What truth about myself should I trust more?
• What might I discover by giving myself what I need?
• What would it be like to have all the answers to my own questions?
• How do I stop contributing to rage legacies of fear, helplessness, self-loathing, and abuse of the feminine?

DEPRESSION DISGUISE OF RAGE

We know we wear the *Depression* disguise of rage when we have a life pattern of being unhappy. This disguise of rage is not to be confused with the depression we may feel during various life challenges of acute loss. Situational depression, especially if prolonged, generally has biological implications or may represent a chemical imbalance in the brain, requiring medication or other professional support. The *Depression* disguise of rage is more characteristic of a lifestyle in which we have conditioned ourselves to stamp out all evidence of rage. But along with stamping out all rage, we also extinguish any light and optimism, and without light we feel downhearted, detached, sad, and hopeless. Needless to say, these are painful and despairing tradeoffs.

We are likely to live as shut-ins. We find it difficult to take care of our emotional and physical health. Even when money is not an issue, we tend to collapse when it comes to caring for ourselves. We may have trouble taking care of practical needs like vehicle maintenance, paying bills, or caring for our bodies. We are vulnerable to illnesses that catch us off guard and incapacitate us for long periods of time. Our conversations with others are often about our fatigue or misery, which we are capable of articulating in elaborate detail. Those closest to us often must accommodate our unhappiness.

While we are overwhelmed by our problems, we become deeply upset when it seems like others don't have confidence in us. We complain to others about our troubles then feel undermined by their efforts to help. We want to be rescued yet any rescue attempt confirms our fear of being perceived as needy or incompetent. We often can't face dealing with other people. When around others, we don't always have much to say. Speaking takes effort and draws too much attention to us, neither of which are comfortable experiences. While we don't mind engaging, we are less likely to initiate it or be able to maintain it.

We prefer time alone where we can do whatever we want, have time to think, and dream without ridicule. We don't like the idea of anyone watching us. To be watched is to be judged. We tend to have a strong and vivid internal landscape. We are generally creative and have hidden talents, but we lack confidence in our ability to express or negotiate our needs, and we will often sabotage our potential by avoiding risks.

When we can, we sleep to avoid the hassles of living. We may use drugs and alcohol to help blur our thoughts, numb our despair, and help us fall asleep. We have tendencies toward panic attacks, phobias, and social anxiety. We mentally punish ourselves for the mere suggestion of taking a risk, saying to ourselves: *I've tried that already. This won't work. Nobody cares. I'm too tired.* We are capable but we feel either over- or underwhelmed. We are paralyzed with negativity and hopelessness, and resent the demands life imposes—even those we impose on ourselves.

Depression is our way of shrinking in physical and emotional size to silence the rage we feel for existing. We hide from others, including ourselves. Relationships are avoided because they force engagement and intimacy—both areas of pain and difficulty. We are afraid of the emotional pain, humiliation, and loss that accompany intimacy. At the same time, we are at war with those parts of ourselves that are terrified of becoming sealed off, isolated, unknown, and therefore unloved. We may become sexual to feel alive and to have contact, but the feeling is temporary and often distracts us from a more intimate experience with life. We struggle with our desire to be open enough to be seen and understood while contending with feelings of shame about our depression and physical ills. We often feel like imposters, yet we want to be seen without feeling ashamed and endangered.

While we are highly intelligent, we lack the self-confidence to acknowledge our needs and we lack the ability to ask for what we want. We tend to lose interest and willpower when it becomes necessary to stand up for ourselves. It is common for us to feel extremely tired, even ill, just before we have important work to do, and especially when we have to do things we don't want to do. We will often feel disappointed and betrayed, and become frustrated when others fail to recognize and promote our well-being. In our brooding, we hope to be discovered over our deeper desire to be bold and daring. We ultimately feel ashamed of both failing and *feeling* like a failure. However, a caring sign from others, even a stranger, can give us hope.

When others complain, we feel guilty, as if we are at fault. We detest the expectations others have of us. To avoid conflict we accommodate their needs, and resent them and ourselves for it. Then we try to disappear or become unavailable. While we want to defend ourselves, we do not want to be challenged or confronted, or held to others' standards. The rage rules we insist on in most relationships are:

Depression Rule #1: Don't humiliate me by expecting me to share what I feel!

Depression Rule #2: Don't force me to take risks!

Depression Rule #3: Don't smother or overwhelm me!

Depression Rule #4: Don't disregard or ignore me!

Depression Rule #5: Don't look at me too closely!

When others break these rage rules, we rarely explode. Our first instinct is to withdraw and isolate, but we will do what is expected because we often feel in a bind, responsible to do as we are told and what is expected of us. But we hate it. At times we feel unbearably alone and afraid. We shut down our feelings in an attempt to deaden our pain. We feel sorry for ourselves and may even become preoccupied more with death than with life. We are ashamed that we need to be discovered and rescued from our despair, and worse, we banish anyone who tries to support us. Those of us wearing the *Depression* disguise generally fall short of seriously harming ourselves physically; however, some of us may inflict injuries to our bodies to alter our mood.

Wearing the *Depression* disguise means that as children, we lived in despair and could not fathom the traumas we experienced, nor have we grieved them. We found it difficult to get positive, support-ive, affectionate attention from our caretakers. We thought that if we became sick or surrendered to our despair, we would be sure to be rescued, but we weren't. Even when sick or needy, we often felt we had to care for ourselves. It was then that we convinced ourselves that nothing we did made a difference. Since then, we have negotiated with life moment to moment—deciding whether to live out loud or in hiding. Despite our dark thoughts and feelings, we choose to live. In fact, we make amazing things happen in our lives, often behind the scenes. We choose to live yet we derive little joy from living.

A DAY IN THE LIFE OF AGNES—*DEPRESSION*

I hate my job more than ever since they didn't give me that promotion last week. I'm good at what I do and the kids I work with like me. What's the problem? Okay, I don't have a high need to be social with folks. But that's not why they pay me.

The head of the residential program always chooses me to do those art projects. My colleagues are jealous so they avoid me. Right after they told me I wouldn't be promoted, I spoke up in a meeting. It wasn't easy and my thoughts were not very clear, but I managed to get it out. A colleague exploded telling me I complained too much. I was enraged and thought to my-self: "I knew I shouldn't have said anything. It goes to show you, speaking up is pointless. Nothing can be changed. Why bother." I didn't say anything. I just dealt with it silently and was relieved when we moved on to discuss the next agenda item. But I couldn't wait to disappear after the meeting.

Another colleague told me I should have stood up for my-self. It's true. I didn't speak up. But, guess what—it doesn't make any difference! Nothing does. Nobody seems to notice or care. Why didn't anyone else stand up for me? I know why, because they're all too lame, weak, and stupid. But who am I to criticize them? I am the lamest, weakest, and stupidest of all. Besides, how could I expect them to care if my own husband didn't? He filed for divorce and told everyone I was a complete bore. He seemed to enjoy showing off his new pregnant girlfriend to everyone. He had no idea how devastating this was to me after twelve years of marriage. He got his divorce and a new life. What did I get? Nothing.

My mom worries about me and my kids. She thinks I'm stuck and need therapy. She's been telling me this all my life. She also thinks I should move back home and start fresh. I listen to her and don't say much. The more I tell her, the more meddlesome she becomes. Some of her ideas are good, but it's my life. Hell, I'm too tired to worry about that. Besides, I hate it when others expect me to do more. I just get as far away from them as possible.

Everybody thinks they know what's best for me. I don't understand it. They seem angry and more emotional about my life than I am. Why can't they see what I'm doing? I'm good at what I do and I work hard keeping things together, yet they seem to easily blow my world apart with their worries and expectations. They say they are trying to help me, but I don't feel helped. I feel invisible, controlled, and intruded upon. I avoid them because they only make me feel worse about myself. Considering everything I'm going through, it's amazing I'm doing as well as I am. I know I'm angry about all this, but I'm just not feeling it.

After working that dead-end job all day and running around town picking up the kids, I'm exhausted. We rarely do anything in the evenings and on weekends—I'm too tired. Sometimes I sleep on and off all day. I wake up exhausted and try to grab sleep wherever I can. The kids get stir crazy and on my nerves, but I've taught the ten-year-old to care for the two-year-old so I can get some sleep. It's not their fault I'm tired, but I just can't do anything else. Thank God for TV and takeout.

But it's always been this way. Nothing I do is appreciated. I don't want to stop living but it often feels more attractive than dragging around. The only reason I keep functioning is because I have to—I have to work, so I do. I have to pick up the kids, so I do. I had to divorce, so I did. But that's it. It seems impossible for me to do the things I really want to do. Most of the time I'm just holding on. But I'm afraid that one day, I'll just come to a dead stop, and that will be it—the end. And worse, no one will notice or care. Last night I got really scared, like something bad was going to happen to me, like I might even hurt myself. I think I was having an anxiety attack. I didn't know what to do. I just knew I needed help.

JOURNALING QUESTIONS

1. What thoughts, feelings, memories, or sensations did you experience while reading about *Depression*?
2. What aspect of this disguise is alive in your life?
3. Who or what does this disguise remind you of?
4. What does *Depression* teach you about rage and the need to heal?

THE WISDOM OF DEPRESSION—SOLITUDE

To survive, we have plumbed the depths of sorrow and shame and we know the courage needed to travel there. Our deep waters are a well from which great creativity is drawn. We have a highly attuned ability to discern profound meaning in ways that move the human heart. When the fear and shame that has compelled us begins to lift, our unique insight and counsel can be brought to generous and spontaneous light. Our knowledge of the human heart allows us to naturally empathize with others and to be a wise and intimate friend.

LETTING GO

We are beginning to let go of the *Depression* disguise of rage when we notice that:

- We are shifting from feeling isolated and hopeless to becoming more invested in the quality of our lives and life itself.
- When we are not hiding behind the scenes but being the main character of our lives.
- When we can ask for what we want and be determined to have it.

We are on track when we acknowledge that we long to know:

- Why have I chosen to live?
- What is worth living for?
- Who am I if I let go of my despair?
- What can I create that speaks louder than words?
- How do I stop contributing to rage legacies of despair, dispiritedness, and self-abuse?

PART THREE

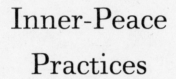

Inner-Peace
Practices

7

Preparing for the Journey

Sacred Practices

It is not rage that harms us—it is our entrapment in the disguises we wear. Disguises are like an intricate work of art, a piece of armor sewn deep into our emotions and our nervous systems, carefully created by a very young part of ourselves determined to live. Having constructed and worn these disguises for our very survival, we have been deeply shaped by them and they are likely to be with us throughout our lives, emerging most strongly at times when we feel threatened.

Our fear and shame of our raw experiences of rage keep us from climbing into our hearts and becoming whole, yet when the compulsion that drove us to wear our disguise is lifted, the shape that is left behind will often reveal our deepest yearnings and our greatest strengths.

There are worlds of experience and ways of being that lie beyond the habits of our conditioning. In the following chapters, we will discover that we are not our disguises—we are much more. We will learn how to examine the clever construction of our intricate disguises with compassion. We will celebrate those parts of ourselves that we have acknowledged, and embrace those parts we have disowned. We will experience the impermanence of rage and live more fully in the present moment. We will discover that we can wear our disguises less often and more lightly, like a loose robe rather than a suit of armor grafted onto our skin, and even learn to lay them aside so that a new curiosity or expanded truth can emerge. The wisdom of rage is fuel—already on fire within us, and these fierce energies have the power to wake us up, transform our lives, and create legacies that liberate the heart.

We begin by placing rage into its natural habitat—an elemental realm—like a season we anticipate and prepare for, rather than a problem we avoid, get a grip on, or try to change. In its natural form, rage simply *is*—neutral, neither good nor bad.

Rage is energy that arises from thought and registers as sensation in the body. In this regard, rage is information—mail delivered that has not been read or translated; an inner fire that flares under predictable circumstances. Rage has healing properties that, when nurtured, help us understand, expand, and mobilize our life's purpose. As we grow wise in our ability to attend lovingly to rage as a sacred messenger, we naturally heal from its warmth and insight. Our challenge is in knowing how to utilize the energies of rage for our own transformation.

At a professional conference on the East Coast, I presented a keynote address on healing rage to women psychologists and asked the audience: *How much time do you spend fighting issues of oppression?* They were confident in their responses. One woman said: *I've spent most of my life fighting racism!* Another one piped in: *I spend too much of my time fighting sexism and homophobia.* We had twenty minutes of voluntary responses to this question, each one topping the previous one. Then I asked them to consider: *What do you imagine you would feel in the absence of oppression? Who would you be if you were not at war? If you were to stop fighting, what would you be doing with your time? What vision do you have of victory? Does your vi-*

sion include peace within yourself and throughout the world? An awkward silence fell across the room, as if an unspoken pact had somehow been violated. One woman spoke her thoughts out loud: *I'd lose a big part of my identity if I stopped fighting, and that frightens me.* This brave woman is describing the terror inherent in giving up a disguise of rage. In such a moment it is difficult to grasp that acknowledging such truth is the literal experience of transforming—what makes inner peace possible.

We may not always experience peace, but peace is always present—it is the white space between the black letters on this page. Peace has to do with where we place our attention. I recall an early winter morning while on a month-long silent retreat. In the middle of the meditation, a rainstorm rocked the hall. I noticed thoughts of anger keeping beat with the rain because I had left my umbrella in my bedroom several buildings away. I became obsessed with worry—*Damn, I'll get soaked going back to my room. I didn't bring the right clothes for a storm. I'm going to miss breakfast if I have to go all the way back to my room, and there won't be any food left for me, and I'm starving—so hungry I could die. How I could make such a stupid mistake, anyway?*

What I did wrong and the resulting *something bad will now happen to me* was all I could think about. My thoughts became so intense I opened my eyes. There before me sat a woman with a soft, pleasing smile on her face, as if she was enjoying the sound of rain thundering through the hall. It occurred to me that rain was what was really happening, and a more peaceful point of focus than my more punishing thoughts of not having an umbrella. Whenever we find ourselves obsessing on thoughts or worry, consider what peace we may be missing in the present moment.

Not only is inner peace possible, it is ever-present and accessible when we can put rage in sacred perspective. This does not mean we never experience rage or other difficult emotions. Rather we can awaken to how peace lives within and is always an available option, albeit one that is foreign to many of us. Not being peaceful is a habit we formed when our focus was more on surviving. It is a habit that can be broken with a practice of self-love.

The process of healing rage is different for each person. Yet it is common for the process to trigger the *Rage/Shame Duo*, and a tug-of-war can erupt in our body and mind. For example, rage wants to come out into the open and tell its story, while shame wants to hide our stories and be safe from danger. As we disrobe our disguises of rage and move closer to ourselves, we may experience a range of emotions that belong to the shame family—fear, ambivalence, help-lessness, confusion, grief, sorrow, regret, obliviousness, innocence, and, at times, nothing at all. It is also possible that we might experience moments of insecurity, hypersensitivity, or agitation.

While the fires of rage can be illuminating, our rage child is best understood in the context of a sacred practice of contemplative self-witnessing, where we can examine our feelings and actions in relative quiet and introspection. A sacred practice allows us to cultivate our deepest intentions of kindness and well-being, and support us in re-garding ourselves and all that is around us with respect. If we want peace in the world, we must practice peace. The operative word is *practice*—becoming aware of how we live true to our intentions and beliefs. The following practices are offered to prepare you for your healing journey. These preparatory practices will be expanded in later chapters. For now, integrate them into your daily awareness.

KEEPING A RAGE JOURNAL

It will be useful to maintain a rage journal to record your experiences. Find a journal that you can carry with you for easy access. As a daily practice, record your feelings and thoughts. Some have found it helpful to record their thoughts at the same time each day. Write down the date and time of each entry. Start with writing a half page each time you record. You may want to expand over time.

Use all of your senses and capture the details of your experiences as clearly and colorfully as possible. Don't inhibit your expression. Draw a picture or symbol, write a poem, or scribble random words. Most importantly, don't edit what you write. After you write on the pages, simply close your journal until the next day. No one should read your journal unless you choose to share it. Throughout this book you will be invited to journal and review what you have written. For now, keep your journal and favorite pen ready!

SETTING SACRED INTENTION

To cultivate a sacred practice with rage, we must be willing to let go of our misery, remember what we love about ourselves, and know why we are here. Our rage child endangers our mind, body, and spirit when we betray ourselves—live untrue to our spirit. She knows that we are much more than our past experiences and the disguises we wear to hide them. Our very life is a path of awakening. When we explore the deeper reasons we are here, we put rage in sacred perspective and open to the light of its wisdom. Ponder the following questions, or feel free to use these questions as a journaling exercise:

1. Do I live true to myself?
2. In what do I place my faith?
3. What values do I live by?
4. What do I love more than I fear?
5. What is worth dying for? Living for?
6. If I knew the date of my death, how would it change how I live?
7. What is my life here to heal?
8. What do my ancestors require of me?
9. How do I live in a way that brings out the best of who I am?
10. How do I use my life to bring goodness into the world?
11. What vision do I have of inner and world peace?
12. How will I know when I am peaceful?

Ask yourself these questions with genuine curiosity. The mere asking invokes a dance with spirit that reveals deeper meaning. Don't expect to have the answers immediately. Rather, allow them to reveal themselves to you in any number of surprising, even auspicious ways—in your significant relationships, disagreements, quiet times, or with strangers, newborns, elders, teenagers, animals, nature, or in your dreams. Also, don't be surprised if you find yourself answering the questions again and again as you deepen your inquiry. The idea is not to have fixed answers but rather to enjoy the dance of inquiry.

CREATING A SACRED SPACE

Just as we may prepare a nursery or special space for a newborn, it is important that you create a space where you welcome your rage child and begin to notice and honor yourself. In this space, you become aware of how your disguises of rage interfere with your sacred intentions, and how to parent yourself like no one else can.

You may already have such a space or practice of contemplation. If so, include your intention to heal rage. If not, create or designate a space—a room or the corner of a room, basement, attic, or even a closet. Personalize this space to your liking with colors, textures, and other items that your rage child might enjoy. Be creative yet purposeful in designing your space. Use whatever works for you. Blanche didn't have a space in the apartment she shared with five other people, but she did take a bath each morning, which became her sacred space with her rage child. She tossed in a rubber duck as a symbol of her rage child and spent a few minutes being mindful of her thoughts and setting an intention of self-care for the day.

If it is not possible to locate a space inside your home, look in your neighborhood for a mature tree, a body of water, or some other peaceful and private place. Wherever you decide to establish your sacred space, make sure it is clean, private, welcoming, and easily accessible. You will want to return to this space regularly. Eventually, you will naturally carry this space within. Any act of self-awareness is a step in the direction of healing rage.

When you enter your sacred space, shift your attention to your healing. Just as when you enter a church, temple, mosque, or synagogue, the same reverence should be given to your sacred place. You may want to begin with a prayer, bow, chant, poem, mantra, song, or spontaneous greeting of respect. You may light a candle or burn a scent. Every action should be mindful, carrying the spirit of love and the intentions of goodwill, discovery, and peace. These intentional acts of kindness toward rage bring warmth and inner peace.

PREPARING A RAGE ALTAR

Within your sacred space, you may want to spread a cloth or have a small table that holds items of significance to you on this journey. Some people refer to this as an altar. Altars have been used for thousands of years in many religious and spiritual practices as useful and pleasing focal points of devotion. Ancestors, family, abundance—anything that you want to keep in your awareness is often worthy of a special place to focus your intention.

Creating a *Rage Altar* is a mindful gesture to welcome your rage child and affirm your intention to be aware of your healing journey. A rage altar can include items of significance to your rage child's history or items that symbolize your rage inheritance, spiritual or religious practice, ancestors, or culture. For example, Delores placed old pictures of herself on her altar next to a picture of Jesus and a childhood birthday card from her mother. Lisa chose to spread a sacred cloth from Israel, a gift from her great-grandmother, as the surface of her altar for rage, and placed baby pictures of herself and her great-grandmother on the cloth. Debra had a pair of bronze baby shoes and a small jar of hair barrettes similar to the ones she wore as a child. Denise's altar contained an image of the Buddha, a picture of herself, and pictures of her family with whom she hoped to reunite.

Should you choose to have a rage altar, you may also want to place on it items from each of four elements—fire, water, air, and earth. For instance, you may light a white candle to represent the spirit of your rage child, ancestors, and the spirits of all those suffering with rage throughout the world. A clear glass of salt or ocean water can symbolize your tears and those of the world from lost innocence, grief, sorrow, and pain. Water can awaken your subconscious and unconscious mind and reveal your purest longings. Air is most symbolized by your breath and may also include incense or fragrances that can inspire spiritual clarity. Rocks, an earth element, can symbolize the bones of your ancestors and can absorb and hold your pain and power. Consider other natural objects as well. Prior to placing any item on your altar or within your sacred space, hold it close to your heart and speak its purpose and your intention.

The idea of an altar is not to make it perfect, but to make it purposeful—a focal point symbolic of your intention to heal. Your intention is what is most important. Don't worry if something does not immediately come to mind. Trust your rage child to inform you of what is needed. Your rage altar will develop naturally over time.

THE *BEING NOW* MANTRA

The *Being Now* mantra is a mental phrase that when repeated invites the body to respond. Here is the mantra: *Deep Breaths, Soft Belly, Open Heart*. The breath always lives in the present moment, and becoming aware of your breath brings you to *Now*. Softening your belly has a grounding effect and makes you aware that you live in your body. Opening your heart invites the entire body to relax and gracefully soften. This harmonizing trio invites your mind and body to join in *Being Now*—being one. Here's how it works:

Take several deep breaths to calm yourself. As you breathe, temporarily suspend your thoughts and feelings. Let your thoughts float like distant clouds. Let your feelings flow like a gentle river. You may say quietly, *I'm okay right now. It's all right now. I'm safe.* Let go as you breathe. Second, allow your belly to soften. As you breathe, bring your awareness into your belly and rest in your core—the space between your belly button and lower back. Breathe from this place and allow your entire body to soften. Finally, focus on the warmth of your heart and allow your heart to open gently like the soft petals of a rose on a sunny day. With each inhalation and exhalation, let your chest become spacious, warm, and more relaxed. Continue breathing in this full-bodied way.

Repeat this mantra throughout the day as often as you can remember it—for example, when you are washing your hands, sitting down to eat, showering, driving, cooking, at the top of the hour, prior to meditating, or prior to speaking. Whatever you are doing, begin to condition your mind and body to listen to and comply with these words.

STARTING A *STILLNESS PRACTICE*

A *Stillness Practice* is a daily routine of self-noticing that prepares the mind for peace. We are already aware, wise, and peaceful—we only need to be still and experience it. Rage is intensified by our confusion and terror, and becomes less intense as we witness and welcome "what is" without distraction, resistance, or over-identification. This requires that we make stillness a practice.

It is best to practice at the same time each day and in the same location—your sacred space. You might begin with ten minutes per sitting twice a day and increase your time as you experience the calm inherent in this practice. It is not important how long you sit but rather how consistently you practice. To begin, sit comfortably and quietly in your sacred space, undisturbed, with your eyes gently closed. Begin by relaxing into the *Being Now* mantra. That's it!

If you have young children and find it difficult to get away for ten minutes, have your children practice with you. Teach them the practice of stillness. Stillness is a natural state. Alice told her four-year-old twins, *Come and sit with mommy. It feels good to be quiet. We can sit and be still like angels. Watch me, and do what I do. Breathe. Close your eyes. And no talking! Okay? When you hear the bell, we will go and have breakfast!* Of course, the twins didn't always follow the rules, but they became accustomed to the routine, and while they didn't always sit still, they learned not to talk or disturb Alice after a while. One of the twins began to enjoy the practice and was more consistent. Your example and sharing of the practice of stillness is a profound yet inexpensive gift for the young people in your life.

A daily practice of stillness allows us to calm our mind and rest in our body. We condition ourselves to be present in our experiences without being controlled by them. We will build on this *Stillness Practice* and learn about meditating in later chapters in this book. For now, just get into the habit of practicing stillness each day.

RECORDING YOUR DREAMS

Our intention to heal often encourages our rage child to reveal herself in our dreams. The dream world is a safe haven for our rage child because she can be outrageous and creative without our conscious control, while also enticing us to seek understanding of her rage riddles. A rage riddle is a story that is imbedded in our dreams that invites us to decode its message and better understand our lives. There is tremendous rage wisdom embedded in our dreams, but we must first strive to remember and record them.

Just before going to sleep, ask your spirit guides to help you wake up, remember, and write down your dreams. Keep a rage journal next to your bed. When you awake, write your dreams as if you are still in them. It does not matter if you do not remember every detail. What you do remember is what is important. Simply write what you are seeing, thinking, doing, and feeling in the dream *in the present tense.*

I write on the right-side pages of my journal, saving the opposite pages for later interpretations. Most importantly, don't change, interpret, or judge what is occurring in your dream, or edit what you are writing. Later we will explore how to interpret rage riddles in dreams. For now, just get your dream on paper!

Healing is the process of becoming more self-aware. We unfold, let go, and discover who we are—who we have always been. We dignify rage when we honor the truth, and we begin by *re*-membering ourselves— looking back to understand our present, then moving forward.

8

Re-Membering—
Looking Back to Move Forward

Now that we have put our rage child in sacred perspective, we can turn our attention to *re*-membering the childhood traumas that gave birth to our rage. *Re*-membering is similar to being an anthropologist, where we excavate or uncover our inner rage experiences to become reacquainted with our fuller selves. This inner history is more accessible to us now that we have begun to put aside our rage disguises and commit ourselves to a relationship with rage.

The first time I led a group of women to Egypt in a journey of *re*-membrance, I recall standing in the inner chamber of the Temple of Philae—Isis Temple, a few miles upstream from Elephantine—feeling the silent stories of my ancestors echo from the walls. The Egyptologist related the myth of Isis and Osiris. Osiris—a powerful and prosperous king of Skondia in northern Egypt—was murdered by his envious brother, Set, a poor king of southern Egypt. Set not only killed his brother, he dismembered him by cutting him into fourteen pieces and scattering his body parts along the whole length of the Nile, hoping the crocodiles would devour them, leaving him to rule. I'm intrigued that it was Osiris's *body* that was dismembered, for it was his physical wholeness that was most feared by his brother. Osiris's mutilation and scattering was intended to strip him of his power. Death alone was not enough. Keeping his body parts separate was a sure way to control his spirit from returning.

Isis, Osiris's beloved wife, a powerful queen and healer, took years to gather his scattered body parts, and she was 99 percent successful. The quick-and-dirty version of the story, I'm told, is that she was unable to locate his penis, so she constructed one of wood, made love to him, and Osiris's spiritual life was conceived in the form of a son, Horus, who grew up to become a king and avenge the wrongs done to his father.

Egyptian mythology is full of mystery and symbolism, requiring years of understanding to decipher its complex meaning. Yet I could not help but wonder, at times humorously, about the absence of the legitimate voice of rage. While the Egyptologist focused on the heroics, I found myself mentally filling in the gaps—the good king dies at the hand of the bad king for the good of his kingdom. It must have been traumatic for Osiris to be manipulated and murdered by his brother and cut to pieces. I can only imagine his terror and helplessness as he lay captive facing his demise. But *what about Isis*? I would think that she was enraged that she lost the love of her life in such a brutal way, and that it took her years to repossess his scattered pieces. And a penis of wood? Talk about the short end of the stick! Who wouldn't be enraged about that!

Making fun of a sacred tale is a cheap shot, yet it makes this point: The most authentic voice one could have in situations like this is rage. Yet as women, for our survival we have depended on both silencing and denying our rage—being politically correct and socially heroic while becoming physically exhausted, emotionally disconnected yet desperate, and spiritually bankrupt.

It's not difficult to understand why we would be afraid to *re*-member ourselves. *Re*-membering evokes feelings of helplessness, anxiety, pain, and shame—emotions that trigger rage. However, we are all Osiris—powerful and innately prosperous, yet traumatized by fear and ignorance and affected by the needs of others to violate and control our body and our lives. Uncountable parts of ourselves have been dismembered—cut off, lost, and scattered along the paths of our lives. Consequently, we have learned how to live without all of our parts. We are all Isis—the beloved healer, capable of *re*-membering ourselves: gathering our lost parts and bringing ourselves back to physical, emotional, and spiritual wholeness, and even able to bring about a blessing in the form of continuation.

Isis was perhaps one of the first anthropologists, aka healer of rage. I'm guessing that she approached her work of *re*-membering very mindfully, careful not to destroy or dismiss any of her discoveries. Similarly, our intent in *re*-membering is not to deny, destroy, or dismiss the details of our memories, but rather to reassemble our history and liberate ourselves from shame and fear to wholeness.

We unearth the pieces of our past not to feel bad or dwell on the horrific details, but rather to examine our traumas *and* how we have come to respond to them. For this task we use an *Empathic Inquiry* to help us *re*-member our traumatic experiences of childhood and to make an explicit agreement with ourselves to put to rest what is already behind us.

EMPATHIC INQUIRY

Take a few weeks to complete the following exercise, allowing plenty of time to *re*-member and reflect on your childhood (up to the age of twelve years). You may want to devote your daily *Stillness Practice* to this task in your sacred space, or respond to these questions whenever the answers make themselves known.

Read all of the questions below before you respond to them. When you are ready, record your answers in your journal without edit or review. Write as much detail as you can recall. If it becomes difficult to write your responses, write about the difficulty you are having.

It is not necessary that you have a complete recollection of your childhood experiences—this would be impossible. It does not matter if what you recall is the absolute truth. It is also not necessary for you to maintain a balanced view, weighing in all the good things your childhood offered. What matters is that through this exercise, you will see the relationship between your past and the present—what you have continued to live even though you thought you left it behind.

Feel free to ignore questions that do not apply, or add questions that you have about your childhood and respond to them as well. You are on a sacred journey, which means much will be revealed. Don't be alarmed if you find yourself recording answers to questions you have not verbally asked. Relax into your *Being Now* mantra. Allow your heart and mind to flow naturally onto your journal pages.

EMPATHIC QUESTIONNAIRE

1. What were the circumstances that surrounded your birth (emotional, political, cultural, social, economical, parental, etc.)?
2. What is your sweetest memory as a child?
3. When did you realize you were special? That you weren't? How did you know?
4. Who were your role models when you were young? Why?
5. What was most important to you as a child? Why?
6. When did your heart first start to close? Why?
7. What did you love most about your father? Your mother? Your caretaker(s)?
8. What pains you deeply to remember?
9. What were you accused of doing that you didn't do?
10. What did you learn about love as a child? From whom did you learn it?
11. What values did you gain as a child from your parents/guardians that help you most in life?

12. What was your earliest experience of letting go? Of being let go of?
13. What happened that should not have happened?
14. What did you want to change but couldn't?
15. What was your greatest loss, failure, disappointment, or misfortune?
16. What physical, emotional, or mental illnesses or anguish do you recall having? How often did you have them?
17. What were you most ashamed of? Most enraged about?
18. What did you have to be an adult about when you were a child?
19. What story can you tell now that you couldn't tell then?
20. What elder/ancestor had the most impact on you as a child? Why?

A *LIFE LINE* TO *RE*-MEMBER

Another way to explore your childhood experiences is through a *Life Line* exercise (diagram below). The *Life Line* is a visual way of recalling your experiences. Here's how it works:

Draw a horizontal line across the middle of a large piece of paper. The space above the line represents positive experiences, whereas the space below the line represents negative experiences.

On the left end of the line, put a 0 indicating your birth, and at the opposite end put a 12, which represents the end of your childhood (or you can go out as far as you like). Indicate the emotional highs and lows of your childhood experiences for each point that corresponds to your ages or the memorable points of your life. You may complete this *Life Line* exercise before you journal your responses to the *Empathic Questionnaire*, or after.

Once you have completed these tasks to your satisfaction, put what you have written aside for a few hours or days. Many feelings emerge when we are *re*-membering our rage, and it is important to

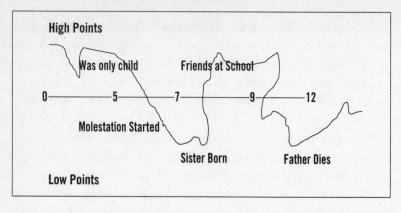

take care of ourselves along the way. If you find yourself feeling overwhelmed by what you are discovering, take a break and let what you know rest in your heart before moving forward. Healing rage is a journey of compassionate self-awareness, not a specific destination. There is no rush—this is a life's work!

UNDERSTANDING YOUR RAGE MEMOIRS

When you are ready, read what you have written slowly and without judgment or criticism, then ponder these questions:

- How do you feel about what you have written?
- What can you celebrate about your survival?
- What still frightens you? Saddens you? Shames you? Enrages you? Why?
- What seems unbelievable? Absolute? Questionable?
- What deal did you make with yourself back then that you still live with today, i.e., via disguises?
- How is your rage today similar to your mother's? Your father's? Your ancestors'? Your culture's?
- What part of your childhood interferes with your healing?
- What other insights can you glean from this exercise?

When you are done, put aside your journal and sit quietly in stillness. Allow some time to go by before you review what you have written. It takes tremendous courage to address the answers to these questions, and a break is well earned. Do something nice for yourself: take a warm bath, get a massage, take a walk in nature, read a juicy romance novel, watch a comedy movie, or spend time with a healthy lover or an uncomplicated friend. The important thing is not to discuss this exercise with anyone, at least for now. Just take a break and allow what you have uncovered to rest and settle within you.

When you are ready, return to your rage journal and review what you have written. Uprooting childhood traumas may evoke emotions. You may feel and remember what you once knew, and reexperience the traumas that made it necessary for you to hide within your disguises. You may experience a deepening, for example, as you feel the difference between your mind *knowing* the truth and your body physically *experiencing* the truth. Or you may find you had one experience writing and another reading what you wrote. When we read our journals, we will often *feel* what we know. This is because the act of writing— finding the right words and adhering to sentence structure—uses our intellect. But when reading what we wrote our emotions are freer to react. All in all, our fierce truth, although long suppressed and misunderstood, is still active and waiting to be liberated.

Re-membering allows us to gently excavate those parts of our past that are hidden, denied, forgotten, and even deplorable, and bring them to light and new meaning. The events of our lives are not mistakes. They have profoundly shaped who we are. All of our experiences are teaching us how to live in outrageous dignity. Take honorable notice!

9

Entertaining Wildness

THE RAGE RELEASE RITUAL

As we continue to disrobe our disguises, our emotions are more readily accessible, yet our understanding and ability to use our rage effectively is still undeveloped. This combination of feeling more but not feeling in control causes anxiety and discomfort.

The most compassionate thing we can do for ourselves at times is to express rage. Think about it this way. Your rage child has recently been released from the prison of your disguises for crimes she did not commit, and her truth is still trapped in your body. She wants her day in court—an opportunity to tell you her version of the story without being silenced, corrected, or polite. She wants to be angry and scream: *This was horrible!* and hear you say, *You're right!* She needs an opportunity to ask: *Why did you hurt me? Why did you leave me?* She wants to share her pain: *This hurts! Please help me! Please protect me! Never abandon me again.* She is that part of you that needs to forgive and be forgiven. A rage release ritual can help us to relieve some of this pressure.

The intention of the rage release ritual is to liberate the pure spirit of rage—to allow your emotions and nervous system to feel release. The goal of the rage release ritual is not simply to blow off steam. With this ritual, you are harmonizing your body and mind without pretense, and allowing yourself to have an authentic experience of rage. You design an experience in which the energies of your rage spirit can be physically released. The idea is to have the experience of completely letting go and losing control in a private and safe space. Energetically, you are creating more inner space to feel more relieved and spacious, to rest momentarily and begin to see and understand yourself more distinctly.

The nature of rage is to engage—to be in contact with something or someone. In many cultures, men are socialized toward high-contact sports, even sexual aggression, both of which can serve as temporary physical and emotional outlets for rage. Quite the opposite, women are socialized to be polite and to serve others. Some women fear that if they release rage verbally and physically it poisons the environs. It is important to know that truth does not harm us—it liberates us. There is nothing we feel that does not already belong to the world and is not in fact a part of the world. For many women, this ritual is the first time in their lives that they can allow themselves to verbally and physically express the full emotional intensity of rage without holding it in, turning it against themselves, or concerning themselves with how someone else feels about it. I have worked with thousands of women, most of whom are absolutely amazed at the breakthrough quality inherent in the physical and verbal release of rage. One woman shares: *Rage is a song I've always sang, just never out loud.*

To heal rage, you must be willing to experience its nature—get close to the heat and be warmed and informed by it. As women, it serves us to understand this part of ourselves to the fullest. Don't worry. Generally, you will need to do this ritual only a few times. It's a way of physically introducing yourself to your rage child. To many, it is like giving birth—you don't like the pain, but you gain so much in return.

The rage release ritual is a powerful way to affirm to yourself that you are capable of physically relieving your own suffering. By no means should you attempt this ritual if you are feeling like you could be a danger to yourself or someone else. If this is the case, seek immediate support from a therapist, crisis hotline, or hospital. There are three conditions you need to accept before proceeding:

1. You are not to physically hurt others or yourself.
2. You are not to destroy property.
3. If you are enraged with a particular person, that person is not present during this ritual. You are not to engage verbally or physically with the person you are enraged with. This time is for you.

This ritual can be practiced as often as needed and especially when you harbor intense feelings or any time you simply want to experiment with inviting your rage child to express her true nature. For example, after completing the *Empathic Questionnaire*, you may want to explode in rage, tears, or both. This would be an excellent time to have a rage release ritual. Other times may include after returning home at the end of a maddening day, or after having a fight with your partner, or after dealing with insane traffic. Most of you do not have to search far for a reason to have a rage release ritual.

Ideally, you will want a space private enough to scream, stomp, curse, cry, shout, kick, rip, roar, and rage! You may want to gather some of the following items:

- A dozen old magazines or telephone books to rip to shreds.
- Several large pillows to pound, scream into, or rest on.
- A large army duffel bag stuffed with old clothes to beat, kick, and punch.
- A belt or a two-foot-long rubber hose for whacking the magazines and beating the duffel bag.
- A large blanket to cover yourself when you want contact.
- A stuffed animal to cuddle with for comfort.

You may need fifteen minutes to an hour for a rage release ritual. If other adults are near, tell them that you may be making some noise, and not to worry. Ask them not to disturb you. Send your kids to a friend's house for a few hours. Send your roommates out for pizza. You need to be able to focus on yourself, and not on other people nearby. You can turn on loud music to encourage the release of rage or to distort your sounds, or you can scream into a pillow. If you cannot get enough privacy at home or in your sacred space, you can take a walk in an open space or drive your car to a private and safe place.

A word of caution: Do not drive while you are out of control with rage. Instead, pull over and let it rip! Automobiles are safe portable containers for rage as long as they are not moving and you do not hurt yourself in the confined space.

A word of encouragement: The more release, the more relief. You are hereby authorized to *"tear the roof off the . . ."* Don't try to be fair, reasonable, or rational during your rage release. It does not matter if what you are saying makes sense or is the truth or a lie. What's important is that you say it—all of it. Be *out*raged: *I fucked up, again! He raped me! That bitch didn't pay me back! He's an asshole! She disrespected me! I hate paying these damn bills! They refused my apology! After all I've done, they fired me! I hate you! I'm sick and tired of being sick and tired! I love you, damn it! He slept with my best friend! She left me! I hate myself!* Whatever!

There is no right way to have a rage release ritual. The idea is to release your rage physically and verbally, rest in the inner space you've created, and deepen your understanding of rage. The process involves the following steps:

1. Retreat to your sacred space and affirm to your rage child that this is her time to come out. Reassure her that you will not harm yourself or others.
2. Invite your sacred spirits to witness and support you in a full release of raging truth.
3. Standing or sitting, take several deep breaths and begin to recall

and speak out loud your incident of rage in vivid and righteous detail. Start softly, and let your voice become louder and louder. It is important to engage your voice in this exercise—to break silence.

4. Allow your rage child to have her way—exploding out of your body and mind—and let her loose! Use any of the materials at hand—ripping paper, beating on the duffel bag, stomping, and screaming. Let her rip!

5. Once you are done releasing rage, wrap yourself in a blanket and rock yourself gently. It is common to cry following a rage release. The *Rage/Shame Duo* is at play, and whenever rage is present, shame follows. The reverse is also true, so don't be surprised if you are resting or crying and want to rage again. Allow that natural dance of rage and shame to unfold.

6. When you have settled, rest with your stuffed animal as you mentally thank your spirit guides, ancestors, and rage child for their support. Practice *Being Now*. Tell yourself that you are healing, and that you are precious and brave. You may even want to take a nap.

When you have rested enough, light a candle, take several deep breaths, and take a few moments to write about this experience in your rage journal. As you journal your experiences from your rage release rituals, write down in full detail what you discovered about your rage child. For example, what did she feel like inside your body? What did she feel like coming out of your body? Describe her size, shape, taste, smell, color, gender, and age. Did she change during your release? What was she saying? What was she doing? What did you discover about her pain? What stories did she tell? What did she want? What was she enraged about? What was she afraid of? What was she ashamed of? Does she have a name? If you were to describe her as an artistic expression, what would it be? Capture these reflections and any other key details about your experience in your rage journal as clearly and in as much detail as possible.

After your ritual, expect to feel a bit vulnerable and tender. Try to arrange things so that you have some time alone, without needing to explain yourself or focus too much on the needs of others. Also, be patient with the people around you.

Don't worry if during your ritual you don't do what you had planned, or you don't feel what you expected to feel. Edith's release was only tears. Barbara mumbled like an infant and could not speak words. Deborah never stopped screaming. Alice's ritual was full of elaborate goddess-like gestures, all in silence. Many women wonder if they have done it right, but there is no right way or right outcome from a release. Patricia shares:

> I really didn't buy into all this. I didn't think for one minute that if I followed these suggestions I'd actually have a release of rage. Was I surprised! I started off being upset about how silenced and stuck I felt in my dead-end job. I walked around in my room cursing and blaming folks at work. I then started stomping and I found my lips mimicking my mother who used to say to me as a child: "The military takes good care of us so shut up and be grateful!" And before I knew it, I was raging at her and every other SOB who felt they had a right to silence me. And it felt great! Afterward, I felt lighthearted and tired, but also clear. I regained the strength I needed to defend myself. When I later read what I had written in my journal, I realized that my job was similar to my childhood, only this time, I could complain, and I could also leave. I've always known this, but now I feel this truth in my body and can act on it.

A rage release ritual is often an experience of relief and discovery. Try not to be critical of how your rage child chose to reveal herself.

Keep in mind that the rage release ritual is not a dress rehearsal for you to eventually go out into the world and confront your targets of rage. Most immediately, you are the primary beneficiary of your rage release ritual because you are the one who is healing. Many have discovered that their rage release ritual has provided them with enough calm that they no longer needed to have direct confrontations with others.

DISCOVERING THE CHARACTER OF RAGE

Once you have experienced two to three rage release rituals, you can begin to discern the character of your rage child. Read through your journal entries and consider the following questions:

1. What is your rage child's name and age?
2. Where does she typically live in your body?
3. What circumstances provoke her most actively?
4. How does she make herself known?
5. What is her most common story or upset?
6. What does she want you to know?
7. What does she want you to do for her? Be specific.

As you continue to practice releasing rage, you open to an experience of yourself that is larger than the stories you tell yourself. For instance, you may experience something old in a new way, or experience something you never dreamed of. The point is to become self-aware, and to allow new vitality to flow into the parts of you that are now open.

We begin to heal by acknowledging that rage is tied to our need for self-compassion and our longing to be free from suffering. The physical and verbal release of rage is not an end in itself. The deeper truth that wants to be revealed is in the expression of pain and shame that we have hidden, inherited, and passed on, and that we are now called upon to dignify.

10

Sacred Agreements with Rage

As our rage child continues to reveal herself, she has the power to run buck wild and work against us if we fail to give her proper attention. Being right too long can actually be wrong. For example, early in my healing journey, I remember a particular session with my therapist. Unknowingly solid in my *Defiance* disguise, I was complaining about the insensitive white men on my job and how I hated them. How they didn't listen and how I felt ignored. How I couldn't understand why, when I pointed out to them how screwed up they were, they mistreated me even more. I was going on and on. My therapist listened with loving ears and observed with loving eyes for quite a while, then she asked matter-of-factly: *Why did you send her to the job?* Stunned, I defensively asked her what she meant. She rephrased her question to my disliking: *Why would you send a child to do a woman's job?*

My first reaction was to get pissed off at my therapist. She obviously didn't understand what I was saying. She was clearly a Black woman. Why should I have to explain what I'm talking about? *She should know.* Sitting there, I was beginning to question her true ethnicity and my judgment for selecting her as my therapist. I felt attacked. She could sense my rage in my agitation—pacing was a dead giveaway. I had a frightened look in my eyes that I get when I realize I've just been hit over the head with truth, but feel too exposed to admit it. Instead, feeling ashamed, I was determined to blame my therapist. This lasted a few more moments.

My second thought was that she *might* be on to something. After all, we had been working together for several months, and she'd been pretty right on target most other times. She kindly went on: *It sounds like such a big job for a small spirit.* We both paused a moment. She then added insult to injury: *I bet she can't even see over the steering wheel when she drives, and she could probably fit into your briefcase. Her clothes are the wrong size and she trips in those big shoes of yours. She sounds ill-equipped for the job. So why do you send her to work?*

Reality slapped me; I felt sober with pure clarity. I didn't know whether to get mad about the big shoes comment or to surrender to the simplicity of her message. Hell, it never occurred to me that my rage and I were not one and the same—that it was just a part of me, not all of me. In that moment, I had once again awakened to my rage child. I sat dumbfounded, processing the truth of her astute observation.

My therapist then asked: *What would it be like for you to make a new deal with your rage child? For example, give this part of you a warm bottle, sing her a song, and put her to bed, then send the wise woman to deal with those wolves—that part of you that is more capable of succeeding?* I thought to myself: *I could do that!* I'll never forget the instant relief and control I felt as I recognized that I was more than my rage. This was the beginning of a sacred agreement with my rage child. Such agreements are particularly helpful as we commit ourselves to living without our disguises of rage.

Disguises are like drugs and we can go through withdrawals without them. They numb us from experiencing the rage we feel toward our own helplessness and the shame we have felt from being dishonored and disrespected.

Following are exercises to help us establish sacred agreements with our rage child. Settle into your sacred space, pull out your rage journal, and enjoy openheartedly setting agreements with your rage child.

APOLOGY

This is your opportunity to explain and apologize to your rage child for imposing adult responsibilities on her as a child spirit. Use this template as a guide when apologizing to your rage child: *I'm sorry for . . . It was my fault that . . . Please forgive me for . . . I forgive myself for . . .* Fill in the blanks and add statements that are most appropriate for you. Speak directly to the heart of your rage child. Here are a few examples:

- I'm sorry for silencing you with drugs.
- It was my fault that I let you drive when I was drunk. I'm sorry I abandoned you and put us in danger.
- Please forgive me for using you to communicate my pain to the outside world. I realize now that your voice belongs first to my ears and heart.
- Please forgive me for ignoring the many ways you have tried to be a close friend.
- I'm sorry for sending you to my job when I should have gone myself.
- Please forgive me for not knowing how to love you. I didn't understand your gifts of truth, clarity, and warmth.

APPRECIATIONS

Appreciations help us let go from the heart and move forward more kindly and humbly. Sharing appreciations are ways you can tell your rage child how grateful you are for the many ways she has contributed to your survival. Look back over your life and notice how an enraging time may have given you much growth and insight. Take your time and be specific as you recall how your rage child has helped you endure and make sense out of life. Here are some examples:

- I appreciate that you are always making a fuss when my boundaries are violated.
- I appreciate how you help me write the truth and remember what happened to me as a child.
- I appreciate how you made me ill and forced me to take a rest.
- I appreciate how you have played a leading role in my activism. Thank you for teaching me how to fight for what is right.
- I appreciate how you kept me alive by staying silent during my rape.
- I appreciate how your energy helps me paint, write poetry, and play the piano.

Capture your appreciations as often as you can recall them, and rest in knowing that your rage child has been on your side, fighting for your well-being, even while being denied by you and ill-equipped for the job. Appreciations help your rage child soften, stop crying, and stop rebelling. Our rage child has not always known what to do with our truth, but with your attention and support, she can rest.

NEW RULES

New rules affirm to your rage child that you are now the parent and she the child spirit, and that things will be both different and better. Most children need structure. They need to have clear parameters and the limits must be directly stated and reinforced. Your rules communicate how you plan to tap the truth of your rage child—to listen to her truth without harming others and yourself. Here you instruct your rage child on how to contact you and how she can best support you. Here are examples:

- From now on, you do not make the ultimate decisions in my life.
- As of this day, I am removing your privilege to drink and drive.
- When I want to talk to you and need your wisdom, I will alert you with five minutes of deep breathing and ten minutes of listening.
- When you want to alert me, you may cause me to perspire. I will get still and listen.
- Starting today, you will take a daily nap lasting from 8:00 A.M. to 5:00 P.M. while I am at work.
- When I get home from work, we can share insights and learn together.
- Sugar, alcohol, and caffeine are not good for you and will be used sparingly.

COMMITMENTS

Commitments are ways of declaring your intention to be a wise, nurturing mother to your rage child, reassuring this fierce spirit of how you plan to take care of yourself so she does not have to resort to disguises. For example, you may celebrate her birthday each year, or determine specific dates and times when you attend to her and nurture your relationship more genuinely. Here are some examples of commitments:

- From now on, you have my undivided attention every morning for ten minutes in our sacred space.
- I commit to talk to you every day and ask how you feel and what you need.
- I commit to practice living without disguises so that you are able to help instead of hurt my life.
- When I'm upset, I'll remember to check in with you and ask your opinion about the situation.

Make commitments that you feel you can keep. Start with one or two commitments and increase them as you become clearer and feel successful.

We are challenged with parenting ourselves as we have never been parented, and loving ourselves as we have never been loved. Love heals rage and sacred agreements are kindhearted practices for building an intimate relationship with your rage child.

After you have completed journaling these agreements, sit quietly in gratitude for all that you have endured, for all that you have overcome, and for all that you will transform. Feel free to add to your sacred agreements as you continue to awaken to your rage child.

11

Solving Rage Riddles—
Looking *In* before Acting *Out*

Healing rage does not mean we eliminate or never feel rage. We will continue to be provoked in the world, thrown off center, and at times will need to dress up in our disguises. Yet each time we react in a knee-jerk fashion to rage instead of responding thoughtfully, we betray ourselves. We give our rage child away, will her truth over to some other power. We deplete ourselves of vital energy before it has fed us, and we feel ashamed because we are vulnerable—overexposed and under-protected.

When we are triggered by the aggression or ignorance of others, an accumulation of anger, shame, and fear can brim over. What we do next is not only crucial but also within our control. Harriet Lerner, author of *The Dance of Anger*, shares: *Anger is a tool for change when it changes us to become more an expert on the self and less of an expert on others.*

To respond outwardly in a responsible way requires that we understand our inner-rage experiences. The following exercises teach us how to examine our thoughts to better understand our rage experiences;

we learn to speak truthfully and mindfully, without harming others or ourselves, and we learn to listen, trust ourselves, and take action on our own behalf.

The benefits of these practices will not be immediately available to us in the heat of a crisis. These practices assume that we will take time to look within ourselves before acting out—scrutinize our rage triggers prior to a crisis and master a more healthy response. Understanding rage requires patience. When we maintain a consistent practice, spend quality time in our sacred space, and keep our rage journal handy, rage ceases to be a problem we overidentify with and overreact to.

TRUTH-TELLING

One of my meditation instructors, Michele Benzamin-Miki, tells the story of a poor Tibetan woman running through the streets screaming, *Thief! Thief!* Everyone in the village runs to her aid intent on protecting her, only to discover she is calling attention to herself—*she* is the thief. I love this story because it invites us to imagine exposing those aspects of ourselves that we disown yet so quickly judge in others. We may not feel much affection, in this case, for a thief, but what we fear even more is being exposed as one—to roam the streets of our hearts proclaiming, *Thief! Thief!* Yet such truth has an immediate effect on our ability to let go and rest within our body and mind.

Truth-telling is best practiced when you have intense feelings of agitation, guilt, frustration, fear, or fury, and you want to understand more deeply, defuse, and own what you are experiencing. Don't try to be logical or reasonable, just be honest. Acknowledge your first thoughts or top feelings.

Sit quietly in your sacred space and listen without judgment or shame. When you have settled your body and mind with *Being Now*, explore the following questions:

Looking In before Acting Out

- What old pain or story does this feeling evoke?
- What does my rage child want me to learn from this situation?
- Does this situation energize or deplete me?
- What might I gain if I let go of my point of view?
- Is this disturbance a priority or a diversion?
- In what ways am I contributing to my own suffering?
- How can I give myself what I need right now?
- What action can I visualize that would build connection and not cause harm?
- Before you take action, consider:
  - What can I do that would foster goodwill and well-being?
  - What can I do that will be respectful?
  - What can I do that will minimize pain and suffering in others?
  - What can I do that will enhance my relationships?
  - What can I do that will acknowledge my contribution to the problem?
  - What can I do that will make my ancestors proud?
  - What can I do that will support my healing intentions?

Ask any other questions you may have that will help you to understand the truth you are feeling. When you feel satisfied with this inquiry, spend a few moments journaling. The point of this exercise is to look within to acknowledge and understand your true experience. We heal by becoming self-aware. Truth-telling is a humbling and humanizing exercise that gifts us with inner comfort and self-respect.

OBSERVATIONS AND INTERPRETATIONS

One way of solving rage riddles is to separate observations from interpretations. An observation is neutral, like a video camera capturing what is seen and heard through its lens. An interpretation poses meaning and influences our feelings about what is being observed. For example:

Observation	Interpretation
She is speaking loudly and frowning.	She is angry with me.
The leadership team is all white.	The leadership team is racist.
He is a Harvard graduate.	He thinks he is better than everyone.

Interpretations often arise from the soil of our rage disguises and represent narrow ways of understanding what is taking place. Many of us fast-forward through our observations as mindlessly as we might operate the remote control of a TV. This impulse is almost reflexive, and common. Slowing down our thinking to observe more objectively causes us to feel more, and feeling more can make us uncomfortable. We feel safer with our hasty interpretations, convincing ourselves that they are the whole truth. Often our interpretations are accurate and valid, but when we suspend them, we open ourselves to the experience of not knowing, or better yet, knowing more. In this spaciousness, we may consider many possible interpretations, including none at all. Often our curiosity will arise in the absence of interpretations, giving us an opportunity to explore new meaning.

Observation	Interpretation	Exploration
She is speaking loudly and frowning.	She is angry with me.	I wonder what she's feeling. I wonder what she needs.
The leadership team is all white.	The leadership team is racist.	Are they aware of the impact of an absence of diversity? Are they seeking more diversity?
He is a Harvard graduate.	He thinks he is better than everyone.	I don't know much about him. I wonder if he liked attending Harvard.

Practice separating your observations from interpretations throughout the day and especially following the truth-telling exercise. Your interpretations may often be accurate, but it is good practice to examine them to ensure that your rage child is not distorting your view. Hers is not the whole truth, nor should her emotional trigger be your first priority. When our interpretations become our only truth, they rob us of energy that would otherwise go toward us connecting more genuinely with others and ourselves.

PAIN AND SUFFERING

Behind rage is pain, not just the stories we tell ourselves. We have feelings about what is occurring, and we use our interpretations to short-circuit or separate from what we are feeling. In other words, we use interpretations not to feel. When this occurs we suffer. Distinguishing between our pain and our suffering provides us with the option to suffer less.

For example, we may accidentally cut our finger while chopping vegetables in the kitchen. Blood is running all over our evening meal. These are clear observations, and we are in pain. However, we suffer when our mind takes over and creates a larger story, or interpretation: *Oh my God, I'm going to bleed to death. I knew this would happen. I hate that damn knife. This will leave a scar. I'm so stupid. How will I play the piano? Why didn't XYZ chop these vegetables? This shit always happens to me,* etc. The interpretations that we lay on top of our original pain cause us to suffer and separate from the experiences we are having in that moment. In our attempt to avoid pain, we create more of it, and we are not taking care of the immediate need. In the above example, the reality is that we have cut ourselves, we are hurting, and we need to take care of ourselves. Dealing with our pain is what is now, and what needs our attention. The rest of the dread is suffering and optional. Similarly, if you saw a child struck by a hit-and-run driver, your impulse would be to comfort the child, not run after the car. In the same way, when we are triggered, we are in pain, and our pain needs our comforting attention. In these moments, we want to stay with our pain and begin to explore what we may need. Let's apply this idea to our earlier examples:

Observation	Pain	Suffering (an interpretation we apply to avoid pain)	Exploration
I cut my finger.	I'm hurting.	I knew this would happen.	Why am I beating myself up? I'm already hurting!
She is speaking loudly and frowning.	I'm frightened.	She is angry with me.	Why am I afraid of people who speak loudly and frown?
The leadership team is all white.	I feel excluded.	The leadership team is racist.	Why is inclusion by white people important to me?
He is a Harvard graduate.	I feel inadequate.	He thinks he is better than everyone.	What is it about Harvard [or higher education] that makes me feel inadequate?

Begin to notice when you are suffering more than you need to. Drop the suffering and comfort the pain. It is our response to what life offers that causes us suffering—not what life offers.

PROJECTIONS AND PERCEPT LANGUAGE

Upon closer inspection of our truth, we ultimately find that what enrages us most is recognizing ourselves in others—often a shocking discovery. For example, let's say our Harvard graduate *does* think he is better than everyone. Why is this important to *you*? Why do you suppose this matter catches *your* attention? The fact that it catches your attention is saying something about you!

This is a psychological concept known as *projecting*, meaning that when you interpret someone as being angry, what you are experiencing is the *angry part of you* reflected in that person. You zoom in on it because it is your projection—an unconscious, feared, or denied part of your experience. Of course, this is not always the case. Sometimes people are wicked, hateful, and violent. However, more often, we see what we fear and deny most, and we see what we expect to see.

We project when we can't tolerate our full selves. We are projecting when we can judge others without recognizing that we, too, behave or have behaved in similar ways, albeit under different circumstances. Individuals, families, communities, and even nations make projections. It is a common, fear-based practice that perpetuates separation and suffering.

Percept Language

Percept is a Jungian-based technique that allows us to experiment with the notion that all that is occurring in any given situation is a projection of our own experience. I was first introduced to this tool while attending a self-differentiation workshop offered by Joyce and John Weir, an elderly couple who had worked together for more than thirty years in the group dynamics community.

The *Percept* technique is simple. It presumes that whatever catches your attention in life is a *part of you.* This technique has been highly useful in understanding rage. Plainly stated, it invites you to add the words *part of me* to every person, character, and object in situations of high distress. Adding the words *part of me* helps you pause, expand your assumptions, and reclaim your projections. You claim each aspect of your own experience and further examine the nature of each aspect independently.

Let's apply the *Percept* technique to an earlier example. Basically, you witness what is occurring (*Observation* and *Interpretation*) and apply the *Percept* language *part of me* to the end of your interpretation, after which you look inward (*Exploration*) to discover the messages your rage child is offering you.

Observation	Interpretation	Percept	Exploration
She is speaking loudly and frowning.	She is angry at me.	She is an angry *part of me.*	What part of me is angry and needs my attention?

Here, we are applying *Percept* to the interpretation of *angry*. It can as easily be applied to the observations of *loudly* and *frowning*—loud *part of me,* and frowning *part of me.* We would explore these parts of ourselves by asking: *In what ways am I afraid of living loudly? What am I frowning on in my life these days? Percept* offers us an opportunity to look within ourselves and explore the gifts that our present circumstances are invoking. Let's explore another earlier example:

Observation	Interpretation	Percept	Exploration
The leadership team is all white.	The leadership team is racist.	The leader *part of me* is a racist *part of me.*	How am I leading in my life? In what ways am I racist?

Percept application does not mean to suggest that what we observe and interpret outside ourselves is all about us and what we project. Life is more complex and clearly there are times when people and situations are hurtful, and their behaviors are not directly related to our personal projections. However, when what we see and feel pierces our hearts and grabs hold of our attention consistently, our rage child is shouting, *Thief! Thief!* and inviting us to reclaim and comfort her.

Percept and Dream Interpretations

The *Percept* technique is also an insightful tool for dream interpretation. Our dreams are rich with rage riddles—messages embedded in the dreams that are ripe for decoding. *Percept* presumes that every character or object in our dreams is a *part of you*. For example, if your mother appears in your dream, the dream is not necessarily about your mother but may be more about the mother *part of you*. You may ask yourself: *What feelings or attributes do I most associate with my mother?* Your response to this question would be what is referenced as a *part of you* in your dream.

The *Percept* application to dreams is simple:

A. Before going to bed, invite your dreams to reveal themselves to you. Commit to wake up long enough to write down your dreams. Have your rage journal and pen near your bedside.

B. Write your dreams in the present tense—as if they are occurring right before you. If you find you cannot recall the entire dream, that's not a problem. Just write any feelings, images, or thoughts that you are having in that moment.

• Note: Go back to sleep if you like. You can do the next steps later.

C. Read through the dream and add *part of me* to the end of key people, places, things, actions, and feelings.

D. Reread your dreams and explore their many meanings.

Marva, disrobing the *Depression* disguise of rage, and grieving abandonment by her father and physical abuse by her mother, wrote the following dream during a Celebration of Rage™ retreat:

A man is captured by the police, hit on the head, and knocked out. They drag him out. Others watch and call the guy a fool for breaking the rule. I'm thinking: Why fight them. You can't win! You are outnumbered.

When Marva applies the *Percept* technique, the dream reads as follows:

A **man** part of me is a **captured** part of me by the **police** part of me, **hit** part of me on the **head** part of me, and **knocked** part of me **out** part of me. The **man** part of me is a **drag** part of me **out** part of me. **Other** parts of me **watch** part of me and **call** part of me a **fool** part of me for **breaking** part of me the **rules** part of me. The **thinking** part of me **asks** parts of me: **Why fight** parts of me. The **outnumbered** parts of me are **always wins** part of me.

After applying the *Percept* technique, Marva solves her riddle of rage by discovering how she has internalized her abuse from childhood and can now transform it. Here is how the *Percept Language* helped in her dream interpretation:

I'm still angry at my father [male, captured] for abandoning me so I abandon myself [knocked out, dragged out] and I abuse myself [hit on head] just as my mother abused me. I witness my abuse [others watch] and don't stop it, and I blame myself [fool] for thinking that I could free myself [breaking the rules]. I feel helpless and hopeless in defending myself [why fight, you can't win, you are outnumbered]. I'm capable of watching/witnessing myself [watch, thinking and asks] therefore I am capable of taking charge and changing my view of self-protection [male, police].

This dream can undoubtedly be interpreted in any number of ways, but what is most important is Marva's interpretation. Marva felt she had a better understanding of her anger and self-abuse, how her past still lived in the present, and that she is capable of redefining how she protects herself.

The *Percept* technique provides simple and often profound insights and can be equally applied to journal entries as well as to other observations and interpretations in your life.

Dreams help us become more aware of our wholeness and of the world we behold. They can show us where we are stuck and what wants to be freed. Once we understand our dreams, we further liberate ourselves. Become acquainted with the active wisdom of rage while you sleep. Discover how your rage child delights and finds complete expression in this subconscious realm of creative freedom.

12

Meditations with Rage

Some people say watch your tongue. No, watch your mind because the tongue does not wag itself!

BHANTE HENEPOLA GUNARATANA

ABOUT MEDITATION

There is no greater gift to our rage child than our willingness to be present with her, and we do this most effectively through meditation. Meditation soothes the hot coals of inner rage and helps us suffer *less*. Through meditation, we teach the mind to ride the energies of rage without battle so that we become aware of what we deeply know and need to heal. When we meditate, we are training the mind to stop feeding a pain pattern—our disguises of rage. We are learning how to stay present, and growing in our awareness that the present moment is worth coming back to and living fully.

Meditation is not recommended here as a way to eradicate our rage, but as a way to become fully present to its energies. Our rage disguises are held in place by a desperate attempt to escape from the intolerable past, and in so doing, we have distanced ourselves from the truth and vitality that is available to us in the present moment.

Meditation is not a quick fix. It asks us to slow down so that we can experience ourselves *lovingly*. There are many benefits derived from a consistent meditation practice. Meditation opens us to levels of consciousness that lie deeper than our intellect. Our disguises fade and our aggression diminishes. Our mind becomes tranquil and more manageable, and we act more wisely toward others and ourselves. Not only does meditation decrease fear and worry, it also reduces our heart rate, blood pressure, respiratory rate, oxygen consumption, perspiration, and muscle tension, and improves our immune system and neurotransmitter function. All this, and it's free! Through meditation, we cultivate inner peace.

In many ways, meditation may seem counterintuitive to healing rage, but it is indeed an act of tremendous self-compassion and respect. While many traditional religions and spiritual paths offer some form of contemplation such as prayer, chants, or song, maintaining a consistent meditation practice is a wholesome and practical way to heal rage.

The following meditations are inspired from the Vipassana Buddhist tradition and are intended to enhance your daily *Stillness Practice* introduced in an earlier chapter. *Vipassana* is a Pali word meaning *insight*, and its goal is liberation through awareness. In Vipassana meditation, compassionate attention is directed to an examination of our inner way of being. This compassionate attention, with practice, sooths the inner heat of rage, and we find ourselves less reactive to what life offers.

GETTING STARTED

It is useful to meditate at the same time and place each day. Start with a short amount of time and gradually increase the time. Hilda Ryumon Baldoquin, a Soto Zen meditation master, suggests to beginners the 5/5/5 Rule: Meditate for five minutes a day, five days a week, for five weeks in a row. Practicing consistently tells the mind that you mean business and reassures your rage child that there is safe space for her development.

Concentration will develop over time. In the early stages of your daily practice, you may experience a range of emotions that distract your concentration. For example, you may become fretful, annoyed, sluggish, sleepy, or numb when you sit still. Don't be alarmed and don't give up. Make sure you are seated comfortably in a chair or on a cushion, as if your flesh were loosely hanging on a straight but relaxed spine.

Your meditation will be affected by what you eat and drink. Avoid meditating on a full stomach. Also, sugar, alcohol, and excessive carbohydrates have an effect on concentration and physical comfort. Become aware of how these substances affect you and use this awareness to make appropriate choices.

Begin and end your meditations with a simple ritual. For example, I begin each meditation by lighting a candle while stating an intention. I then pay respect to my teachers and ancestors by calling out their names. I end with a gratitude prayer dedicating the merit of my good intentions to all sentient beings throughout the world. I then blow out my candle and journal what I am feeling and thinking. That's it! Create a simple yet meaningful meditation ritual that frames your practice. Eventually, such a practice is internalized and carried throughout your day with each breath.

BREATH AWARENESS

Breath gives life to the body. Breathing is the first thing we do when we are born and the last thing we do at death, yet we are seldom conscious of breathing and commonly underutilize our breath. For example, we may inhale and hold our breath too long, causing tension to build up in the body. Or we exhale for too long and experience anxiety, then gasp for our next breath. Or our breathing is shallow, as soft as a whisper, or too fast, like a panting dog. When someone yells at us, we may hold our breath to lessen the intensity of their hurtful words. Too often, and without our awareness, we use our breath to not feel.

Conversely, as we begin to notice our breath, we can notice when we hold on and when we let go. Most profoundly, becoming more mindful of breathing makes our body more alive and reliable, a place to rest and gain tremendous insight. Most practically, our breath is the primary and most affordable tool we have for purifying and reuniting our body, mind, and emotions. Breath keeps open the emotional space that our rage child requires to liberate itself.

Breath Awareness is a useful way to begin and end each day. It offers an immediate way to attune our mind to our body, and to decompress from intense moments. It is a helpful exercise anytime we want to settle ourselves, especially when we feel overwhelmed, frightened, or angry.

To begin this meditation, sit quietly in your sacred space and begin to breathe naturally. You don't need to change your breathing, just become softly aware of it. Notice the sensations of air coming in and going out at the tip of your nostrils. If you do not feel this sensation, notice your chest area expand and contract. Begin to float on the waves of your breath with each inhalation, noticing how and where the body swells. With each exhalation, allow yourself to surrender, let go, and rest in the stillness that presents itself briefly just before your next inhalation. Notice with soft attention where your breath begins and ends in your body—how and where breath touches you. Know that just as there is space between each inhalation and exhalation, there is space in your body between the organs, bones, and joints. Mentally visualize yourself breathing in and out of these spaces, opening to a full breath.

Continue to breathe in and out, concentrating on each phase of your breath—inhaling, floating, exhaling, surrendering, and resting. As you breathe—*in and out, in and out*—the soft rhythm of your breath begins to sing a soothing lullaby to your rage child. As you rest in your body, you simultaneously give your rage child more space to feel relaxed, safe, and at home. The great news about *Breath Awareness* is that it does not require you to go anywhere. It is immediate, constant, and free. It is your private inner*tame*ment. Sit. Breathe. Relax. Notice. Enjoy.

MIND AWARENESS

It's ok to have all these thoughts, just don't believe them!

HILDA RYUMON BALDOQUIN, Soto Zen Priest

The mind's job is to be busy with thought—24/7. The problem is that we often confuse the activities of the mind with the whole truth, rather than an ever-changing moment. A single wave of emotion can feel like the vast ocean at any given time, yet it is still only a wave, to be followed by another wave and another. Emotions are fed by thoughts that believe they are the only reality, but they are simply events of the mind that predictably come and go. What we feel and think changes constantly.

My beloved teacher, Jack Kornfield, tells of being taught to mentally bow to each of his thoughts and emotions as they arise during meditation. This simple and gracious act is a noble way to acknowledge our experiences without becoming entangled or attached to them. As we learn to compassionately witness the activity of the mind, we discover that we can be informed, even entertained, by our thoughts and feelings without the urgency to believe them or act on them.

Mind Awareness meditation is useful at any time you want to be more present with yourself, and especially when you are feeling overwhelmed, anxious, confused, hurt, frightened, or angry. Allow about fifteen minutes. Begin with *Breath Awareness*. Once you have settled yourself, begin to notice what is occurring.

Don't be alarmed if you experience a bombardment of thoughts and feelings. Nothing is wrong! The mind is doing its job. What's important to consider, however, is that the mind's job is not your life! This meditation helps with that distinction. Also, don't try to stop your mind from doing what it is doing. Rather, begin to shift your awareness from *being* the experience that is occurring to *witnessing* it. This subtle shift can be a profoundly liberating experience.

If it feels right, you may want to silently name the thoughts and feelings as they arise—*thinking, analyzing, hate, planning, afraid, happy, sad, worried, angry, bored, judgment, sleepy,* and others. Name your experiences as you are having them with soft awareness—without attachment, judgment, criticism, or stories. Simply return to your breath after each observation.

Mind Awareness meditation is basically about noticing thoughts and feelings, naming them, and returning to the breath. If you become impatient, and start to beat yourself up, acknowledge your experience: *Impatience ... Beating myself up ...* then return to the breath. This is the *mindful* practice—returning to the breath *again and again and again.*

Sometimes our experiences will be liberating, other times frightening, and every experience you can imagine in between. The good news is that our experiences are seldom the same, nor do they last forever. Instead, we experience a constant stream of emotion, thought, and sensation, and this meditation helps us notice and *bow* to them.

Keep in mind that we are not attempting to stop the mind from doing what it does; we simply want to bring kind awareness to it. We are training the mind to bear witness to its experience.

After meditating on *Mind Awareness,* spend some time writing in your rage journal. Consider these questions without judging your experience:

- What thought or emotion predominated my meditation practice?
- Was my primary experience pleasant, unpleasant, or neutral?

• What did my mind attach itself to—a point of view, fantasy, blame, hatred, worry, or nothing at all?

The beauty of the *Mind Awareness* practice is that we cultivate self-acceptance and compassion, and discover that we have the power to witness our experiences without being confused or controlled by them.

BODY AWARENESS

We are more than intelligent minds, we are intelligent bodies, as well. Because we often suffer from a split of body and mind, we are not aware of the subtle interactions of our intelligence. Instead, we over-identify with body or mind in any given circumstance.

For example, when I ask Brenda, *How are you doing?* her immediate response is, *I'm tired and angry with the kids.* I then ask Brenda, *How is your body doing?* To this she replies, *I'd have to think about that.* Therein lies the trap—we too often feel with our mind and not our body. We have raging thoughts that we are not aware of experiencing in our body, or we have intense sensations that we can't explain. Similarly, Charlotte shares vivid details of being raped at the age of twelve. When asked what she is experiencing in her body, she replies, *Nothing.* Like Charlotte, many of us can communicate our experiences while being cut off from feeling them.

While our rage disguises live mostly in our minds, the body is where our rage wisdom lives, and where the truth of the moment lives. To experience our thoughts and feelings, we need to become still, breathe, and allow the sensations to surface.

In *Body Awareness* meditation, we open to a reunion of body and mind by exploring the sensations of our thoughts and feelings. There is a difference between a feeling and a sensation. Feelings are short-cuts, often expressed in thoughts and words: sadness, joy, disappointment, happiness, rage, etc. When we are enraged, our feelings become piercing, and generally there is an object—person, place, or thing outside of ourselves—that is the focus and cause of our suffering. Sensations are more direct experiences from the body: heavy chest, throbbing eyes, stiff lower back, tightness in the back of the head, clammy hands, tight skin, heat, cold, itchy leg, gurgling in the stomach, or sleepy foot. Sensations communicate the raw realness of the moment, and are a more reliable truth than our thoughts and feelings. In *Body Awareness*, we explore beyond our feelings to an awareness of how our feelings are being experienced in the body.

In *Body Awareness* meditation, we practice shifting our attention from the object of agitation—*the other*—to exploring how our feelings are being experienced in the body. This exercise is profoundly useful any time you feel enraged. The beauty of this exercise is discovering that when we are paying *kind* attention to rage, it often ceases to become a problem.

Allow about twenty minutes. Relax into your sacred space. Begin with *Breath Awareness* and acknowledge to yourself that you are safe. Keep in mind that throughout this exercise your breath is your anchor, and you can return to it any time you need to calm yourself.

When you are ready, invite the object of your agitation to reveal itself in full bloom in your mind's eye. See yourself in the righteousness of your frustration and allow this upset to get as large and as intense as it needs to. Breathe to stay present, and take your time. Allow this experience for a while. When you are ready, see yourself turning away from the object of frustration and focusing your attention on your sensations—the way your body is experiencing frustration.

Softly begin to notice your experience in terms of sensations— what is occuring within your body in the absence of thoughts or feelings. For example, you may find yourself thinking: *I'm sad, I'm angry?* If so, direct your attention to the sensations you are experiencing in your body that may be feeding this thinking: *What sensations inform me that I am sad and angry?* Continue this exploration—breathing and bearing kind witness as each sensation arises and passes away.

Take your time and give your sensations your full attention. As you are allowing your sensations to be fully explored, consider sending compassion and kindness to yourself by repeating these phrases:

- *May I be free from suffering and the cause of suffering.*
- *May I experience what life offers with kindness.*
- *May I be free from harming myself and others.*
- *May I be happy loving myself right here, right now.*

Notice how these statements affect your experience—what sensations arise. Continue riding the winds of your breath, allowing your body to be present with you in its unique way. When you are done, gently end your meditation and journal your experience.

Body Awareness meditation helps you discover how your body tells a deeper truth than the mind and its memories. With practice, we heal our mind/body split, gain more access to our rage wisdom, and reacquaint ourselves with resting in our bodies.

Meditation is an invaluable aid to healing rage. When we maintain a consistent meditation practice, we strengthen internal wiring that allows us to carry our full life force peacefully. We learn to rest in our own skin and comprehend all that we behold.

When you become uncomfortable or frightened, remember that difficult emotions are your most profound teachers. The more we can witness our experiences without judgment, the less suffering we experience in our lives. We eventually learn to rest in the ebb and flow of the present moment, experiencing it as pure, often pleasant, and ever-changing. We begin to trust that what feels frightening and intolerable does not last forever.

Through our meditations with rage, we embrace an inner peace that affirms that change is simply our nature—neither good nor bad.

We soften our hold on the faulty assumption that one experience, joy, is always better than another, rage. We discover how to rest in the seasons of rage. We accept gracefully that everything changes all the time within us, within others, and within the world.

We become sensitive to our actual experience of living, and to how it feels to be a seasonal human being. We can feel more love toward others because we understand them, and we understand others because we understand ourselves. The greater this compassion, the more inner peace is possible.

13

Uprooting Your
Rage Inheritance

We are children of a common womb.

Luisah Teish, author of *Carnival of the Spirit*

To uproot our rage inheritance is to turn inward to see baggage we've been hauling, open it up, and shine a light inside. And by shining a light on our rage inheritance—doing our own work of healing—we can create a new legacy.

Our rage inheritance is most often rooted in childhood traumas that were not responded to properly. Stated simply, many of us feel that our rage is rooted in a disconnect from our parents or guardians. Children need the love of their parents. Even if our parents are deceased, many of us still yearn for a closer and more genuine relationship with them. We long to be loved and cherished as their children and respected and acknowledged as powerful people in our own right. Regardless of our independence and worldly accomplishments, we can be perplexed and emotionally disabled by the continuing power of these primary relationships.

The truth is that we can never fully discover, uncover, or understand all the stories that make up our rage inheritance. Many stories may have been lost, and people who are alive may be unwilling to break their silence or shine a light on their own experiences. Yet as we open ourselves to more emotional truth, we may begin to feel the heavy burden of our rage inheritance—a burden whose contents still live in our bones and in our nervous systems, having survived untold generations.

We dwell on things because they are unfinished, and we have an unconscious loyalty to our past that we must make conscious in order to heal. To begin to be at ease within ourselves requires that we be willing to understand our parents' rage histories and rage inheritances, and how they, as humans, have grown to give and receive love. The ultimate reason we want to uproot our rage inheritance is to make an explicit agreement to put to rest what is already behind us, especially those things that trouble the mind. This exercise helps us make sense out of our lives and enables us to make choices that positively affect ourselves and future generations. Uprooting our rage inheritance has four parts.

Part 1: *Imagining*—Because the spirits of our parents and ancestors live inside our bones and in our hearts, we first turn within ourselves and visualize separate conversations with our parents, guardians, and ancestors, to imagine their lives and their rage inheritances.

Part 2: *Conversations with Parents and Elders*—We physically interview our parent or parents, if they are living, and/or the elders in our family, to learn more about their lives and rage inheritances.

Part 3: *Discerning the Gifts of Our Rage Inheritance*—We sort through the information we have gathered—the bones of our inheritance—separating the gifts from those that are to be put to rest.

Part 4: *Amending the Soil of Rage*—We alter our rage inheritance by adding the nutrients of compassion, understanding, patience, and wisdom to our healing intentions.

PART 1: IMAGINING

You begin in your sacred space envisioning yourself asking questions of your parents and ancestors, utilizing the *Rage Inheritance Questionnaire* below, and opening yourself for answers. This visualization can be insightful even if you already know the details of your parents' childhoods, but especially if you don't. You may find that your mind *knows* their histories but has never paused long enough for your heart to *feel* them.

This exercise is also useful to invite the rage wisdom of your ancestors to make itself known. For example, you might have an ancestor whose struggles with rage are similar to your own. Or you may have an ancestor you have called on in times of need. It could be someone your heart went out to because you watched helplessly as they suffered from direct experiences of rage or some other related trauma. Or it may be someone you never knew personally but wanted to know. It may not be a blood ancestor at all but rather someone you felt a kinship with.

You may have lost or never known the stories of your ancestors, yet their spirits are alive nonetheless. You can invite them in and ask them questions about their lives and their rage inheritance, and they will be inclined to answer and pleased to share their insight, for they too have suffered needlessly from family and world legacies of rage. They know the futility of your suffering from their own experiences.

This imagining exercise is a safe dress rehearsal for Part 2, should you desire to physically interview your living parents and/or elders. However, even if you choose not to perform an actual interview, clarifying your questions about your parents' lives and imagining their responses can still be deeply helpful.

To begin, review the *Rage Inheritance Questionnaire* below and select five to seven questions to explore with each of your parents and ancestors. If the questions that you feel are most important are not listed, feel free to create new ones. Consider spacing this exercise out over several

Stillness Practices. For each imagining exercise, allow at least twenty minutes. Keep your rage journal nearby to record your experiences.

Rage Inheritance Questionnaire

As a Child

1. Do you know the circumstances that surrounded your birth?
2. What is your sweetest memory as a child?
3. When did you realize you were special? How did you know?
4. Who were your role models when you were young? Why?
5. What was most important to you as a child? Why?
6. What story did your mother tell you that helped you most in life? Your father? Your caretaker?
7. Have you ever been accused of something you didn't do? What?
8. As a child, how many children did you think you would have as a grown-up? Why?
9. What was the most devastating injustice you personally experienced?
10. What physical or emotional illnesses did you struggle with as a child? Why?

Happiness

11. Why are your hobbies and special talents important to you?
12. What are the lyrics of your favorite songs? Why do you love them?
13. When was the happiest time of your life? Describe it in full detail.
14. What is your most valued personal possession?
15. Who's been your best friend? Why?
16. What do you love about yourself?
17. Who was your most significant love? Why?
18. What were the positive circumstances that surrounded my birth?

19. What did you love most about your mom? Your dad?
20. If you were a painter, what would you paint?
21. What song have you always wanted to write? To sing? To hear?
22. Who was your favorite actor, singer, activist, and role model? Why?
23. What impact has your ability to love had on your life?
24. How has my life changed you?

Disappointments

25. Who or what hurt you the most in life? Why?
26. When did your heart first start to close? Why?
27. What is your earliest experience of letting go? Of being let go of?
28. What were you looking for when you married/partnered (or chose not to)? Did you find it? Why or why not?
29. Why was it necessary to end the relationship with my mom/dad? What would have needed to happen for it to last? What did you learn from this experience?
30. What is your biggest regret/disappointment with your children?
31. How have I disappointed you?
32. What would you hate for any child to experience?
33. What is difficult to hear from your children? Why?
34. Who and what are you unable to forgive?
35. What was your biggest loss? What would you give to get it back?
36. What is your biggest regret?

Challenges

37. What is the most difficult decision you've ever made? What did you learn from it?
38. What is the most difficult decision you *still* must make?
39. How have you been labeled? What would others like to change about you?

40. What is the most significant change you've made in your life? Why'd you do it?
41. What would you hate others to know about you?
42. What is your biggest fear? What is your biggest regret?
43. What physical or emotional challenges do you face? How old are they?
44. What are you most vulnerable about? What pierces your heart?
45. What are you yearning for, wanting in your life right now? Why?
46. How have your children changed you?

Endings
47. What important message have you stressed throughout your life? Why is it important? What difference has it made?
48. Has your life turned out the way you had hoped? How so? Why not?
49. What are you most proud of? Why?
50. What would you change or do over in your life? Why?
51. How do you want to live before you die?
52. What would you like to have forgiven before you die? Who or what would you like to forgive?
53. What would be your ideal way to die?
54. How would you like to be remembered?

Gifts
55. How do you feel about how I have lived my life?
56. How have we contributed to each other's well-being?
57. What lesson do you hope I get from you before you or I die?
58. What encouragement do you have for me?
59. In what ways have you felt loved by me?
60. What gift do you hope I bring to the world?

Once you have selected the questions for which you seek answers, write them in your journal. The following format might be helpful:

Questions for My Father	Questions for My Mother	Questions for My Ancestors
1.	1.	1.
2.	2.	2.
3.	3.	3.
4.	4.	4.
5.	5.	5.
6.	6.	6.
7.	7.	7.

Keep in mind that you are performing a ritual when you investigate the spirits of your parents and ancestors. Your intentions should be pure and steeped in reverence. Your spirit can heal and your life can be enhanced immeasurably when you invite the spiritual wisdom of your parents and ancestors with a healing intention.

In your sacred space relax into the *Being Now* mantra. When you feel grounded, light a candle as you state the name of the person you are inviting to be present. Visualize that person comfortably before you. As you see the person clearly in your mind, silently state your intention. For example, if you are working with your father, you might say to yourself: *Father, I am seeking a deeper understanding of my rage and ask for your support. Can you be with me? Can you share your wisdom and truth with me?* When you feel your requests have been acknowledged, ask one of your questions. Take your time, remembering to breathe fully and stay receptive and soft all over.

Repeat this process until you have asked all of your questions. When you feel complete, journal your experiences. Include the responses to the questions you asked, but especially to those you didn't verbalize. Also record how you felt asking the questions, and include any additional questions you might want to ask later. End your visualization by thanking their spirit and other sacred spirits for being present, and blow out that particular candle.

Once you have begun this exercise, avoid debating, arguing, dismissing, or judging your experiences. Simply allow the questions themselves to deepen your experience. Listen to the responses with your entire body, not just your ears. For example, you may receive a response as a mental image, a memory, a smell or sound, a taste in your mouth, a physical sensation, or nothing at all.

Not getting a response does not mean this exercise is not working. No response *is* a response. Some answers need time to reveal themselves. Stay open to receiving insight and ask the questions again at a later time. The responses to your questions may continue to unfold outside of the *Imagining* exercise. You may get an answer to one of your questions as a thought on your way to work, or in the middle of grocery shopping. A response may arise from something someone else said, or it may occur in your dreams.

For example, during a tour of the temple of Seti I, in Abydos, Egypt, I was minding my own business when a large limestone wall about thirty feet tall by sixty feet long beckoned me. According to my guidebook, this was the "Gallery of Kings." It depicts Seti pointing out to his son Ramses the hieroglyphic names of thirty-four ancestral kings in chronological order. Seti stood tall—like the father I never had, the father I hadn't realized until this moment that I even needed or missed. Ramses stands proud next to his father, affirmed, knowing his legacy of greatness.

A lightning-bolt sensation shot through my heart, knocking me from my feet to my knees. My eyes locked onto the wall as its symbolism unfolded. The proud image of *attentive father* pierced my heart like a healing arrow, responding to a longing that was deeper than any question I could have formulated. Standing in this sacred temple, beckoned by an ancient wall of paternal lineage, I allowed myself to feel the wisdom of my ancestors supporting my healing.

Life mirrors back to us what we need and who we are. Be alert and stay open to the many ways the answers to your questions may appear in your life, and as the answers unfold, capture them like jewels in your rage journal.

You may have had a particularly challenging or abusive relationship with your parents or ancestor spirits. If so, do not feel that you need to invoke them by calling their names. Also, some ancestor spirits may want to come along uninvited, but you may not feel safe or ready to engage them honorably with your highest intentions. You can set boundaries. It is perfectly fine for you to say no to some spirits and yes to others. You are in control of your journey, and at all times you should ensure your safety.

Repeat this visualization in turn for each parent, guardian, or ancestor you choose to work with. Take your time. Allow time for rest, processing, and renewal in between each *Imagining* exercise.

PART 2: CONVERSATIONS
WITH PARENTS AND ELDERS

Once you have completed these *Imagining* visualizations, you may want to take the next step and speak directly with your parents, if they are alive and willing to participate. You can also speak to elders in your family to obtain as much information as you can to understand and uproot your rage inheritance.

It is natural for many of us to feel uncomfortable with this more intimate query. You may say to yourself: *The timing is wrong. No way. The relationship is still too hurtful. Talking with my mother/father about these tender issues is out of the question.* Or, *I'm not comfortable with asking such personal questions.* You're at a critical crossroads. You can proceed with the interviews, noting your fears but not allowing them to deny your opportunity to heal. Or, if you truly don't believe you can conduct an interview without being frightened, hurt, or provoked, delay it for a more suitable time. The *Imagining* exercise (Part 1) has already mentally provided you with an empathic experience with their lives. Should you later decide to speak to your parents, guardians, or elders directly, you can always do so. Should you choose to go forward, here are a few tips on interviewing:

1. Determine the questions you want to ask in advance. Select from the *Rage Inheritance Questionnaire* mentioned earlier, create new ones, or make revisions based on your visualization experiences. Use the following format to organize your thoughts.

Questions for My Father	Questions for My Mother	Questions for My Elders
1.	1.	1.
2.	2.	2.
3.	3.	3.
4.	4.	4.
5.	5.	5.
6.	6.	6.
7.	7.	7.

2. Make a clear request. For example, I asked my mother if she would be willing to answer a few personal questions for me about her life. She agreed and we arranged to get together. It sounds formal but it was a clear request and it was something she could do and *agreed* to do. This was better than me being indirect, then being disappointed when she became suspicious of my motives, or felt caught off guard, and resisted answering.

3. Allow enough time, at least one hour. Err on the side of more time than less.

4. Make the setting private, serene, and comfortable. Do what you can to meet in person. Avoid interruptions. Turn off cell phones, beepers, and other distractions; ask them to do the same. Consider having the conversation in conjunction with a nonthreatening companion activity such as a home-cooked meal, or a leisurely walk. Also consider being in nature. The

openness of nature can absorb the intensity of what is being shared. Sharing near a large body of water or in a spacious park or forest is also a good choice.

5. Let them do the talking. Your job is to become an empathetic anthropologist—gathering information and experiencing the information you gather from their perspectives. This means that you suspend judgment, criticism, and blame. But do ask for clarification when you don't understand what is being said.

6. Keep in mind that you are not there to change them, to be understood, to prove a point, or to like or agree with what they say. You are gathering information to expand your understanding of *their* experiences and how those experiences affected their lives, and ultimately your own.

7. Take notes or, if the person you are speaking with agrees, tape the conversation. A word of caution: Tape the conversation only if it will not interrupt or distract from a real connection. Otherwise, you can record this experience after the conversation in your rage journal.

Gathering this information can often leave you with mixed feelings. For example, you may feel disappointed by what was said or not said. Your mother or father may have avoided questions or offered answers to questions you did not ask—answers you were not prepared for. Or despite your best efforts and objective preparation, they may find themselves unexpectedly resentful, defensive, or even hostile. You may not get the chance to ask the question you most wanted to have answered. You may even be blamed or shamed for causing him or her to feel uncomfortable.

Interestingly, the most puzzling feeling of all can come when the interview turns out better than you imagined, and you now have a wealth of useful information and you don't understand why you hadn't thought of doing this sooner.

Whatever your experience, take these feelings into your *Stillness*

Practice and sit with them—observing them kindly. Let your discoveries rest within you. Allow them to simmer into wisdom. Experiencing and absorbing this information is as important as understanding it.

PART 3: DISCERNING THE GIFTS
OF OUR RAGE INHERITANCE

Discerning your rage inheritance is the act of identifying the pattern or theme that has been passed down to you to heal. You have already prepared to receive this knowledge. Your rage inheritance pattern is embedded in your rage journal (or taped) responses to the *Imagining, Rage Inheritance Questionnaire,* and *Conversations with Parents and Elders* exercises. The next task is to review your notes. When you have reviewed your notes, ponder the following questions.

- How does knowing more about your parents and ancestors affect you?
- What is noteworthy about your parents' journeys? Your elders' journeys? Your ancestors' journeys?
- What disguises of rage did or do your parents wear in their adult lives? What traumas were their disguises rooted in?
- What unresolved rage would you say your parents inherited from their parents?
- What unresolved rage would you say you inherited from your parents?
- How would you characterize your rage inheritance? What themes of rage do you have in common with your parents? Ancestors? Elders?

Once you have had a chance to consider these questions, your rage inheritance may begin to reveal itself—that which has been handed down for you to heal. Awareness of your rage inheritance often deepens your commitment to healing. Susan, unmasking *Devotion* as her disguise of rage, shares:

> My father wears Defiance and has always been verbally abusive toward my mother. He didn't want to talk about this stuff. My mother wears Devotion, and during our conversation she said: "I took it for you kids!" I also learned from Mom that she had come from three generations of women who felt forced to be silent in the face of abusive husbands. But the shameful family secret that everyone lived and feared was that my mother's great-grandmother was beaten to death by her drunken husband, who was never held accountable. While I have felt stuck in a physically abusive relationship for eight years, I had no idea how old the pain was or why it was so intense. I have lived a rage inheritance of "taking a beating" out of blind allegiance to my mother. Discovering this pattern has made healing a priority. Mom may have taken the beatings for us, but I'm stopping the beatings for us.

Rage roots are strong medicine, raw with profundity, potency, and authenticity. Take your time uprooting them. Your rage inheritance may be obvious as you read through and reflect on your journal, or you may need to rest in your *Stillness Practice* for a few days until it becomes clear. Even if you have only a slight indication of a pattern, you are beginning to unearth remnants of your generational legacy that are waiting for your wise attention.

Your rage inheritance discoveries need not be shared with your living parents or elders, for it is not directly their journey. The purpose of this uprooting exercise is to discern the *essence* of your rage inheritance—the unresolved rage of your forebearers that *you* still carry—and to begin to break patterns of generational suffering.

PART 4: AMENDING THE SOIL OF RAGE

Once we have uprooted our inheritance, we can begin to amend our rage soil by adding nutrients that will ensure full-bloom fruition of our healing intentions. This ritual invites us to clearly state our intentions to break the pain patterns of our past. Fundamentally, we want to understand and honor the spirits of our parents and ancestors enough not to repeat and pass on their suffering.

Bring to your *Rage Altar* pictures, artifacts, and mementos of each spirit you are choosing to honor on your healing journey. For example, a rock from their yard, or a special token or treasure they have given you. A piece of fabric that represents your culture could be placed on your rage altar. A glass of water, flowers, and even their favorite foods can be offered as gestures of gratitude and reverence. Have several candles handy, one for each spirit you plan to honor. I associate white candles with ancestor spirits, but you may follow your own instincts and use any color you wish. Also, make sure you have your pen and rage journal on hand.

As mentioned earlier, all items you place on your *Rage Altar* should be placed mindfully with loving intention. These acts of reverence make clear to our parents' and ancestors' spirits that we acknowledge them, and accept our responsibility to transform this legacy of pain.

Sit quietly in your sacred space for several moments with *Breath Awareness* and imagine these spirits joining you in a circle of stillness. Take your time and feel their presence. When the time is right, focus your attention on each spirit separately, light a candle as you state his or her name, and begin to write a letter to this spirit. The letter should describe your rage inheritance and express your intention to transform this pain. You may also include requests for support. Note that you do not need to write a letter to each spirit in this sacred circle. You may write a letter to one or two of them and have the others witness. Always do what makes sense to you.

Once you have completed your letter, place it on your rage altar underneath your lit candle, and sit quietly in *Breath Awareness*. If you begin to sense strongly that a spirit you are addressing does not want to support you on your healing journey, honor it by removing that spirit's letter and symbols, and blowing out its candle. You can try again at a later time if you choose. Your letters can be simple and short. Here are a few examples:

Dear Dad,

We had a difficult life together yet I know you loved me and I certainly loved you—still do. Your rage and drinking got in the way of us loving each other and I have suffered greatly from not having a kind or respectful relationship with you. Just like I know you felt hated by your father, there were many times I felt you hated me, and there are times when I show hatred toward my son, to whom I haven't talked in years. I'm doing what I can to forgive you, and to forgive myself for not being able to change you. I see now that I have continued a legacy of "broken relationships with men." With this awareness, I acknowledge the pain you endured and leave that pain with you as I heal this inheritance in my life and in our family. I bring the best of your spirit with me. My prayer is that my good deeds will help your spirit rest and help me rebuild a loving relationship with my son. I ask you to watch my growth and commitment to love. Thank you, Dad. I feel you with me, and I love you. June

Dear Grandma Della,

I'm your granddaughter. We've never met because you died when you were twenty-six from breast cancer, something I am living with. Some say you were so kind it killed you. Is this true? I don't believe kindness kills. I believe it heals. But I'm so full of rage I'm not sure what's killing me—rage or cancer. Could they be one and the same? Were you, too, enraged, Grandma Della? What about your two older sisters who also died of cancer? I invite your wisdom on my journey. With your kindness, I believe I can transcend our family's legacies of rage and cancer. Your loving granddaughter, Agnes

Hello Mom,

I want you to know that even though I haven't always liked you, I've always loved you. I better understand your coldness and your depression since I've explored the stories of your mother's line. Seems all of them were depressed, like you, like me. I realize that I'm stuck in a cycle much older than myself. Part of it may be genetic, in our blood. Maybe I'll need to struggle with depression during my life. But I want you to know that I'm laying down a part of this: the hiding, the lying, and the meanness. That stops with me. I don't know if you can join me on this journey. But I want you to know that I will always love you. I honor your life and your struggles. While you are alive, I pray that someday we can talk truthfully together. Your daughter, Esther

As you can imagine, these letters were not simple ones to write, but articulating the rage legacy is crucial to heal. The point is that each of them has discerned a pain pattern that they inherited, maintained, and even passed on out of an unconscious loyalty to their parents and ancestors. The soil of these roots is being amended by each of them taking responsibility for transforming this legacy.

Take your time, listening deep within. Be clear about the legacy you behold. The clearer you are, the more responsible you can be. Completing your letters may take several sittings—that's all right. Healing is a journey, not a destination. When you have completed your letters, thank your spirits for joining you and for informing you of your rage inheritance. Stay mindful of your intentions and commitments to heal.

When we amend the soil of our rage inheritance, we honor our ancestors and place our rage in generational perspective. In doing so, we can begin to walk more freely in our own lives, and lift a burden from future generations.

14

Gentling—
Gestures That Ripen the Heart

I heard a story about a young American man who was angry and eager to fight for the freedom of Tibet. He asked the Dalai Lama: *I'm enraged over the injustice of Tibet. It's wrong! What can I do to help?* And the Dalai Lama replied: *Take care of your own heart first. Then come! Gentling* is the practice of comforting our own pain first, and discovering that we can fight with our hearts more readily when we realize that aggression toward others harms us, and gives rise to new generations of rage. *Gentling* includes the following practices: forgiving, gratitude, affirmations, loving kindness, and compassion.

FORGIVING

The act of *Forgiving* helps us unclog the pain of our congested hearts. Healing is not dependent on whether someone forgives or understands us. We need not look outside of ourselves to be forgiven.

Rather, forgiving is an inner peace practice in which we attend directly to the pain of our own suffering.

Forgiving does not mean we condone the behavior of others or ourselves. It means we let go of the blind assumption that we can change uncontrollable situations, and we acknowledge that we have a choice to either hold or let go of our suffering. Forgiving is for our well-being and liberation, and primarily something we do in the privacy of our own heart.

Sometimes we hurt other people unknowingly. For example, we may notice that their reactions to us have changed (withdrawal, anger, or dishonor) but we're puzzled and unclear of our contribution to their behavior. Frustrated, we may feel shut out and not know how to reengage or understand what occurred. Other times, we hurt others knowingly. Feeling justified, we deliberately inflict pain through belligerence, violence, avoidance, or humiliation. Whether we know or don't know how we have hurt or harmed someone, we hurt inside of ourselves. Forgiving ourselves for our actions helps us hurt less.

Forgiving has its own season; therefore, it should not be offered insincerely. For example, if you are feeling angry or hurt over an incident or memory, and you don't feel ready to let go of these emotions, it may not be the right time for you to forgive. But know this: *Bitterness destroys the host.* You are imprisoned by your own thoughts as long as you hold onto them, and they will eventually harm you. Spend time with your rage child—reflect, journal, meditate, get to the root of your pain, or do a rage release ritual. Take care of your own pain. When the season is right for you, you can consider a conscious decision to forgive.

The following forgiveness meditation is rooted in the Vipassana tradition, which emphasizes compassionate attention toward the self. This meditation should be first practiced in the privacy of your sacred space. Once learned, however, it is best mentally practiced as often as possible and whenever you can remember to apply it—while moving from one appointment to the next, in the heat of an argument, dressing in the morning, or just before bed at night.

Begin with *Being Now* to calm yourself. Light a candle or incense to ignite your intention to forgive and invite your spirit guides for support. When you are ready, repeat the following phrases silently to become acquainted with forgiving.

- If I have hurt or harmed anyone—knowingly or unknowingly—I ask your forgiveness.
- If anyone has hurt or harmed me—knowingly or unknowingly—I forgive them.
- For all of the ways I have hurt or harmed myself, I forgive myself.

Pause after each statement and rest within your body. Welcome the thoughts, feelings, and sensations that arise with soft compassion.

These phrases are particularly useful during your *Stillness Practice*, especially as you awaken to the pain and shame your body and mind continue to hold. Sit quietly and breathe deeply. Silently repeat these phrases as the memories and images appear on the screen of your mind or show up in the sensations of your body, but only if you can express them sincerely.

You may discover that various people appear in your mind as you say these phrases. Perhaps they appear because you want to speak directly to them. If this is the case, feel free to personalize these phrases. For example, you may include the name of a person while visualizing them softly in your mind's eye, or you may be specific about the *harm* or *hurt* you are referencing. Here are some examples from other women:

- I forgive myself for leaving you, Mom. And I forgive you for not knowing how to love me.
- I forgive myself for using cocaine and harming myself.

- I forgive you, Bill, for firing me.
- I forgive myself for losing control and exploding in my meeting today.
- I forgive myself for beating my children, Anna and Ray.
- I forgive you, James, for stealing money from me and betraying my trust.
- I forgive myself for putting my children, Janice and Edna, in danger.
- I forgive myself for having an abortion.
- I forgive you, Dad, for abandoning me.

Begin a daily forgiving practice. Start small. Don't be lofty in your statements—keep it simple and sincere. Don't be alarmed if during this exercise you are unwilling to forgive. Kindly and simply say to yourself: *I forgive myself for not being willing to forgive.* Maintain a practice of forgiveness and be patient. Eventually, you will begin to experience the comfort this meditation provides.

Forgiving meditation is for your own liberation. No one else has to be involved. You need only retreat to your sacred space and practice forgiving yourself and others, and release the weight from your heart. However, sometimes the opportunity to forgive presents itself in vivid physicality, inviting your heart to respond directly. Consider the practice of stating aloud: *I'm sorry. It was my fault. Please forgive me. What can I do to help?* Anytime you can genuinely forgive, do so quickly. It brings instant relief.

Forgiving is our nature, an instinct we naturally reclaim as we heal. When we cultivate a forgiving practice, we open wide to inner peace, and outer peace becomes its manifestation.

GRATITUDE

A friend once offered me an exercise that I thought was absurd at the time, but trying it made quite a difference. She suggested that, for the next ten days, I write down ten things that I felt great about doing or seeing each day. For the first three days, I found it difficult to write even three things that I felt good about doing or seeing. By the eighth day, I had more than ten things on my list and it felt wonderful to be on the lookout for them throughout my day. When we pause a moment and notice the miracles that surround us, there is much to be grateful for and celebrate.

Every moment is a divine original, yet our lives are drenched in negativity and worry. If you were to bring sensual awareness to each moment—awareness of contact, taste, smell, sight, and sound—you would burst in aliveness, vitality, and joy, and explode in gratitude. The idea is to practice noticing the shades, gradations, and fine distinctions of your daily life. It's about being on the lookout for simple beauty and pausing to enjoy it. Wild Women Enterprises (www.wildwomen-ent.com) shares this perspective on gratitude:

- If you woke up this morning with more health than illness . . . you are more blessed than the million who will not survive this week.
- If you have never experienced the danger of battle, the loneliness of imprisonment, the agony of torture, or the pangs of starvation . . . you are ahead of 500 million people in the world.
- If you have food in the refrigerator, clothes on your back, a roof overhead, and a place to sleep . . . you are richer than 75 percent of this world.
- If you have money in the bank, in your wallet, and spare change in a dish someplace . . . you are among the top 8 percent of the world's wealthy.
- If you can read this message, you are luckier than the more than two billion people in the world who cannot read at all.

Each day, as often as you can, be grateful! Be grateful for small things and large things, beautiful things and ugly things, good things and bad things, many things and no things. Notice the miracles in your life and celebrate them, then offer your peaceful feelings to all sentient beings throughout the world. Make gratitude a twenty-four-hour practice. It lifts the spirit and ripens the heart, and it costs you nothing other than your kind attention.

AFFIRMATIONS

The mind can be tricky. Pleasant and unpleasant feelings rarely show up at the same place and time. When we are full of unpleasant thoughts—fearful, ashamed, enraged, doubtful, numb, or alone, we can balance our mind with more affirming thoughts—kindness, happiness, harmony, patience, and peace. Affirmations are antidotes to rage disguises, and help us learn that we can choose to uplift ourselves and alter our own inner experiences.

Consider the disguises of rage you wear and consult the following list of affirmations. Feel free to use any of the affirmations listed, or to create ones that affirm your specific qualities. Begin in your *Stillness Practice* with *Being Now,* allowing each breath to open your heart and soften your body and mind. State your selected affirmations slowly, and if necessary repeatedly, allowing each thought to ring true throughout your body. You may want to visualize yourself embodying these affirmations. Enjoy this exercise.

Dominance Affirmations
- I trust life.
- I flow easily with change.
- I am a part of a universal family of love.
- There is always a better way for me to experience life.
- It is safe to let go.
- I trust that the right actions are occurring in my life.
- I declare peace and harmony in my life.
- It is safe to see and experience new ideas.
- I am both powerful and desirable.

- I forgive easily and often.
- I let go of criticism effortlessly.
- I trust in the divine order of life.
- Life supports me.
- I have wonderful experiences with ease and joy.
- My good is everywhere.

Defiance Affirmations

- I am safe and free to love.
- I relax and let life flow naturally.
- I know that life supports me.
- I am free of all frustration.
- I trust that others will do what is right.
- I am kind and gentle with myself and others.
- I forgive others with ease.
- I see through eyes of love.
- I choose thoughts that make me feel good.
- I generously give and receive tenderness.
- I speak with kindness and love.
- I peacefully rest in my mind.
- I create my own experiences.
- I take time to see all sides of an issue.
- There is enough for everyone.

Distraction Affirmations

- I love my body.
- I am at peace with who I am and where I am.
- I enjoy this moment completely.
- I create only peace and harmony in my life.
- I have all that I need.
- This moment is fully satisfying.
- I only take what is offered or what is needed.
- I am deeply centered in my life.
- I am good enough.

- I love and approve of myself.
- I only attract goodness into my life.
- I easily rest in my body.
- I am healthy and happy.
- I am on a sacred journey and there is plenty of time.
- I am at ease with calm thoughts.

Devotion Affirmations

- I am worthwhile.
- I forgive myself.
- I love myself.
- Letting go is easy.
- Saying no feels good.
- I am noticed and appreciated in positive ways.
- I am at peace with all of my emotions.
- I see my own beauty and brilliance.
- I am willing to see and feel my life.
- I am safe.
- I love and approve of myself.
- Self-care is my priority.
- I am free to ask for what I want and receive it.
- I am a worthy priority.
- It is my birthright to have my needs met.

Dependence Affirmations

- I am a powerful woman.
- I am worthwhile.
- I am a success.
- I take charge of my life.
- I am free.
- I have everything I need.
- I live true to my spirit.
- I am safe and secure within myself.
- All that I need I can provide for myself.

- I can go beyond my parents' limitations.
- I have the strength and skill to handle whatever comes my way.
- I am the creative force in my life.
- I know that life supports me.
- I am perfect just as I am.
- I take care of myself.

Depression Affirmations
- It is safe to exist, to be alive.
- I am a beautiful creation.
- My life is sweet.
- My life is a joy.
- I love and cherish myself.
- I forgive myself.
- I create a life filled with rewards.
- Life loves me and I love life.
- I am filled with vibrant energy and joy.
- I create a life I love to live.
- I know that life supports me.
- I enjoy my body.
- My past strengthens me.
- It is safe for me to express my emotions.
- I trust in love and love is all around me.

KINDNESS

As we learn to make room for our overwhelming and shameful experiences, kindness plays a comforting role. Kindness and rage experiences do not generally live in the same moment, and they have an opposite effect on our mind and body. Rage can be hard and restricting, whereas kindness is soft and expanding. Both experiences have their reasons and seasons, yet our rage disguises have conditioned us away from feeling and being kind. Many of us need to relearn how to give and receive kindness and how to be kind to ourselves. Practicing kindness supports our intention to heal, and gives us courage to love our rage.

Loving Kindness, known as *Metta* in the Vipassana tradition, is the active practice of sending love and kindness to ourselves and others. *Loving Kindness* meditation does not fight our rage but embraces the heat of rage lovingly and leaves us softer, more able to rest in our wise bodies. This practice is simple and it does not require us to speak directly to anyone. It is done in silence and can be easily practiced throughout the day whenever we think about it. Traditionally, there are four phrases:

- May we be free from danger.
- May we have mental happiness.
- May we have physical happiness.
- May we have ease of well-being.

Keep in mind that these phrases are not questions—they are offerings that we direct to four audiences: ourselves, our loved ones, all conscious beings, and finally to those who have harmed us and who cause suffering in the world. When we affirm these phrases with feeling and loving intention, we are gifting kindness to ourselves and to the world.

Following is a four-step application of the *Loving Kindness* practice. Read through these instructions, then apply them from your heart. Allow about fifteen minutes for the meditation. Begin in your sacred space. Light a candle and state your intention to give and receive *Loving Kindness*—*Metta*. Invite your rage child and sacred spirits to join you. Begin with *Breath Awareness* followed by *Affirmations* to ground and rest in your body. When you are ready, slowly and silently apply each of the following steps.

Step 1:

We begin by first sending *Loving Kindness* to ourselves, which is often the most alien, the most difficult, and the most needed. In your mind's eye, imagine yourself seated comfortably with your rage child lovingly cradled in your arms. Repeat these phrases or others like them slowly with your well-being in mind, and until you feel the words resting softly in your body:

- May I be well, happy, and peaceful.
- May no harm come to me.
- May I be kind, understanding, and courageous in meeting the difficulties life offers.
- May my actions in the world be motivated by kindness.
- May I be free from suffering.

Step 2:

Invite the faces of dear ones to appear—those closest to you, i.e., parents, teachers, ancestors, friends, and family members. As they appear on the screen of your mind, acknowledge their faces and their spirits in your heart. Repeat these phrases with their well-being in mind:

- May you be well, happy, and peaceful.
- May no harm come to you.
- May you be kind, understanding, and courageous in meeting the difficulties life offers.
- May your actions in the world be motivated by kindness.
- May you be free from suffering.

Step 3:

Next, imagine the billions of people and all conscious beings throughout the world. Consider the people you pass on the streets, the teller at the bank, the new boss or colleague, the ants crossing your path, the fly driving you nuts, communities and nations of poverty, the ignorant, the wealthy, all sentient beings. They, like you, need your *Loving Kindness—Metta,* compassion, and gestures that ripen the heart. Repeat the phrases above slowly and sincerely with their well-being in mind.

Step 4:

Finally, imagine those who have caused harm and suffering to you and in the world. Unfriendly people and those full of pain, greed, or hatred. Those who have innocently or willfully harmed or misunderstood you, others, communities, nations, the earth, and the world at large. Include those you feel have not been in their right mind. Yes, these individuals and institutions also need your kindness. Again, repeat the above phrases slowly with their well-being in mind.

COMPASSION

There are times during our meditations when we will feel our suffering and the suffering of others so deeply that it seems unbearable. Our tendency may be to run away from our experiences by becoming lost in thoughts, or we may overidentify with our suffering by wearing ourselves down with guilt, shame, or hopelessness. We may even terminate our meditation practice prematurely and busy ourselves with something more immediate and pleasant—shopping, eating, surfing the Internet, and even arguing are more preferred distractions than sitting with the suffering we feel. However, the gesture that ripens the heart would be to stay present and open wide to this suffering—without recoiling.

Each of us has a heart that cares deeply about the suffering in our families, our communities, the environment, the nation, and in our own hearts. In the Buddhist tradition, the act of caring and tenderly acknowledging ours and others' suffering is known as *Karuna*, a Pali word for *Compassion*. *Compassion* here is not intended to change or sweeten our experiences. Instead, a *Compassion* practice trains us to kindheartedly acknowledge *what is*.

Compassion is rooted in an acknowledgement that the suffering of others is something we can identify with. It is not to say that we feel their exact pain, but rather we understand that pain is suffering and that our deepest desire is that all beings, including ourselves, are free from suffering. *Compassion*—the gesture of caring genuinely about others and yourself—helps us suffer less.

The application is simple. During any of your *Gentling* meditations, when you feel the emotional pain of others or yourself, bring your heart-filled awareness to the experience. Be mindful of not judging yourself. When you are ready, silently and gently repeat these phrases:

- Whatever it is, it's okay.
- Let me be present. Let me feel it.
- It's okay. This is how it is right now.

What gripes our hearts deeply is when we are unable to help our loved ones who are suffering. Compassion helps us to weather these contractions. You may want to visualize a loved one sitting before you, or you may want to visualize your own mental or physical suffering before you. When you are ready, repeat the phrases above and include the following phrase until you feel more lighthearted.

- I care about your suffering.

It's not always a loved one that causes our suffering. Sometimes our hearts are troubled by a bomb-infested village in a remote part of the world, families that have lost loved ones to senseless crimes, the rape of our environment, or leaders of nations who systematically harm the masses. These *Compassion* phrases apply equally to these situations.

Feel free to carry these statements with you throughout your day—not just during your *Stillness Practice*. For example, a dear friend who lost her mother was sharing her experience with me and I found myself gently saying to her: *I care about your suffering. Whatever it is, it's okay. Let me feel it with you. This is how it is right now, and it's okay. It will not always be this way.* If these words do not naturally come out of your mouth, say them mentally. The effects are often peaceful. My beloved teacher, Bhante Henepola Gunaratana, shares that in the days of the Buddha, phrases like these were used to clean the wounds of the sick just before medication was applied. It is befitting that we use these phrases as a salve for our own mental or emotional healing.

Once you become comfortable with the *Gentling* practices, you can personalize them to more genuinely reflect the care you want to impart to others and yourself.

Gentling Practices are beautiful heart songs we can learn to sing to ourselves and others when comfort is needed. We have the inherent power to give and receive kindness. We simply need to practice doing so. So practice as often as you can. Don't limit it to your *Stillness Practice*. Include these gestures in your thoughts throughout the day, especially when your rage child is triggered. With practice, these gestures bring balance, a poised mind, and soft and spacious awareness to our lives.

PART FOUR

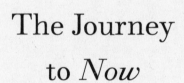

The Journey
to *Now*

15

Rage and Relationships

With a peaceful heart whatever happens can be met with wisdom.

JACK KORNFIELD

The previous chapters were oriented toward becoming familiar with our rage child and the roots of our rage. We will now consider how to maintain healing in our relationships. We will have an advantage if we have established a daily *Stillness Practice* and applied the exercises offered in this book so far.

All of our lives involve friends and loved ones, and our healing affects them immediately and profoundly. As we continue to reclaim our rage, we may discover that we need to negotiate new boundaries in our personal relationships.

Denise, letting go of her *Dominance* disguise, had always complained about being financially responsible for her thirty-five-year-old *Dependence* son, who she felt could never get his life together. The more she complained, the less capable he seemed to become. As Denise moved closer to her own rage, she realized that she was terrified of losing her son and her importance as a mother. She recognized her contribution to the problem, and how she was reacting through her disguise of *Dominance* and its shadow, *Dependence*—complaining, judging, pushing, and paying. With this insight, she set new boundaries with her son, including a phased withdrawal of financial support. During the first few months, her son became depressed. Denise practiced the *Compassion* phrases in her daily *Stillness Practice* as she maintained the financial boundary. Denise noticed that she felt less guilty and less worried, and less provoked into being responsible for his actions. After a few months, her son began to take more responsibility for his life. Denise was finally able to acknowledge and believe that her son was his own person and was responsible for his own life. Maintaining the new boundary had proven beneficial to both of them. Their pain pattern had been transformed.

Changing our own contributions to the problems we struggle with in our closest relationships is difficult, but not impossible. Doing so requires that we care deeply about our own well-being and that of others.

Share your intentions to heal with those closest to you. Let them know how they can support you and themselves. Be aware that others may not understand or want to accept your healing journey. They may resent how you are conducting yourself, and fear that the relationship, as they know it, is lost. Expect resistance, be patient, and stay true to your intentions to heal.

TALKING ABOUT WHAT ENRAGES YOU

The best time to understand rage is not when you are in the heat of a conflict. During these times, the intensity of rage can blind and distort the moment. You may say or do things you don't mean, and feel ashamed and vulnerable—emotions you must quickly cover up with your disguises. Yet, there will be times when you want to talk about something that you find disturbing in another person, and having a framework to organize your thoughts is useful. For example, you may have noticed a pattern forming in your relationship that is causing hurt or frustration, or you may feel yourself growing distant and resentful of the behavior of the other person and want to better understand what is going on.

Maintaining your commitment to healing over your need to be right or to get even is not always easy—just necessary. The following six-step approach is helpful for maintaining balance and integrity when you need to talk about what is enraging you. Consider first trying this approach alone in your *Stillness Practice* as a journal and visualization exercise. When you feel at rest with your responses and can visualize success, you are ready to initiate a discussion about rage. Call and arrange a time. Start with fifteen minutes. When you meet, this is not a time to bring your rage child—she should be otherwise occupied with a nap, not in control of your tongue. If possible sit face to face where you can make gentle eye contact, observe their posture, and hold their hand if appropriate. Use a tone of sincere kindness. Also, you do not need to follow these steps in exact order, but do what you can to include all of them in your conversation.

1. *Affirm what works in the relationship.*

    When we must discuss a difficult concern, the other person is often afraid that the good parts of him or her will go unseen or suddenly have no value, and he or she will be shamed, dismissed, or made to feel insignificant. However, when we start by stating what works and what is truly treasured in the relationship, it helps the ears open and heart soften. There is always something you can genuinely appreciate in another person, and this is a great way to begin. Here are some examples:

    - I value all the fun we've been having together with the kids.
    - Thank you for taking responsibility for our financial needs during this crisis.
    - I treasure our friendship, the ways you affirm me and make me laugh.
    - Our relationship is a high priority in my life.
    - I recognize how you have given more than the rest of us on this project.

- I'm enjoying my work and respect your vision as a leader.
- You are doing a wonderful job of taking care of mom during her illness.
- I respect the choices you have made to improve our lives.
- I'm proud of you for raising your grades in school this semester.

2. *State your concern clearly.*

Be specific about the behaviors you are concerned about. It is useful to mention things that were observable, and your feelings about them. Avoid interpretations. Keep in mind that your concern is not the sum total of the other person's character or experience. Remember to use "I" statements and avoid statements beginning with *you, why, you always, how could you,* and other accusations. It is best if there is no threat voiced in your concern, like *If this doesn't stop, I'm out of here!* While such statements may be tempting and at times appropriate, this kind of demand will drive a wedge into intimacy. Here are some examples of clearly stated concerns:

- It bothers me when you shout, then leave the room.
- I don't like it when you don't respond to my questions.
- When you spend money that overextends our budget, it puts us in jeopardy.
- When you threaten me, I want you to know that it frightens me.
- I know you are angry and I want both of us to feel safe.
- When you tell me I'm wrong, it doesn't help me understand how you feel.

3. *Own up.*

The next step is to acknowledge how you may have contributed to the concern you are voicing. There are few situations in relationships where a problem rests solely on one person. Why? Because you are there! When you own up to how you have participated in the problem, it neutralizes what might otherwise feel like an attack. Take your time and give this some thought. It is at the heart of conflict and often your healing. Examples:

- I recognize I did this very thing last month.
- I know I'm not helping when I scream back at you.
- I get scared and feel caged like I felt when I was a child. Then I blame you.
- I know this is an old pattern for me and I'm working on changing it. Please bear with me.
- You were right to point out that I told a lie, and I apologize for becoming defensive about it.
- I have avoided talking about this. It's difficult for me to explain myself.

4. *Invite engagement.*
   Here you open to further understanding of the situation. Don't be surprised to discover some new things about yourself. When you invite engagement, ask your questions—one at a time—then be silent. Avoid interrupting. Calm yourself by silently repeating *Being Now, Kindness,* or *Compassion* phrases. Stay present and listen with your entire body. Examples:

- How do you see this problem?
- How do you see me contributing to this problem?
- Can you tell me what's going on with you when that happens?
- How can we make things good for both of us?
- What do you want?
- What do you believe I can give you that I haven't already?
- What would satisfy you on this issue?

5. *Make a clear request.*

You may have a request of the person, something that would make things work better for you. Requests should be clear, respectful, specific, and actionable, and move the relationship toward intimacy. Seek common ground. Make agreements, not guarantees. Examples:

- I'd like for us to take a couples' class on healing rage.
- I want you to stop cornering me when you get angry, moving close to me as if you are going to strike me.
- I want you to come straight home from school.
- I want you to speak to me only when you feel you have more self-control.
- I want you to knock before you enter my office.

6. *Extend appreciation.*

It takes courage to talk about concerns related to rage, which is why most people avoid them or handle them poorly. Extending appreciation is an important step. If appropriate, sincerely thank the other person for talking to you about your concern. If the discussion did not end peacefully, use the *Kindness* and *Compassion* practices and appreciate yourself for trying. Examples:

- Thank you. I'm glad we could talk!
- This time means a lot to me. Thank you.
- Our relationship is important to me and I want us both to be happy.
- What you think matters to me.
- This was not easy but we did it.
- I knew we could work this out. We are in agreement.
- I'm committed to us working it out—as long as it takes.
- It may not seem like I'm making progress, but it is courageous of me to keep trying.

Use this technique with children, spouses, partners, coworkers, and others, whenever you can see that connection is more preferable to righteousness. If you both feel you are making healthy progress, you can continue the discussion, but make that action clear: *I know I said fifteen minutes and our time is up. Is it okay with you if we continue?* If you feel stuck, arrange more time later in the day or week. However, it is best to schedule a specific time before you depart. Setting the next time affirms the importance of the concern, and minimizes unspoken feelings of shame, resentment, and fear of abandonment.

A SHORTCUT—ASKING FOR WHAT YOU WANT

We don't always have the luxury to plan a tender time to talk about rage. Sometimes we encounter others whom we don't know and/or choose not to be vulnerable with. In such circumstances, we may not have the desire for an intimate or lasting relationship, yet we want to engage honorably and respect the relationship. Still other times, we may have already talked about our feelings with the person and know that they are trying, and even though they provoke us, we trust the goodness of their hearts. In these circumstances, a shortcut is helpful—*Asking For What You Want!* When you ask for what you want, the key is to be direct and explicit. You also want to keep intense emotions out of your request. Don't elaborate, apologize, be coy, or explain yourself unnecessarily. Make it a simple statement, then be quiet and allow a space for your question to be felt, considered, and responded to. Here are some examples:

- I want you to stop shouting.
- I want a raise of *x* dollars.
- I want to work a twenty-hour workweek.
- I want you to take care of the kids on Monday nights.
- I want to have dinner with you on Wednesday evenings.

- I want you to apologize for XYZ.
- I want us to veto this bill.
- I want your agreement on this proposal.
- I do not want to be disturbed when my door is closed.
- I want out of this relationship.
- I want you to listen to what I am saying without interrupting.
- I want us to go to therapy together.
- I want us to find ways to have more fun together.
- I want a hug!

When you make your request, avoid being seduced into arguing or justifying your request. You might say: *It's a clear statement. Can you support it?* Keep in mind that you won't always get what you ask for, but it is important to know what you want, to ask for it, and to make your request from the heart.

Asking for what you want honors the true character of rage. Regardless of how others respond, stay focused on your desire and take actions that build peace. While it may be uncomfortable to have these discussions, with practice it becomes more natural. Remember: Kindness is our nature.

WHEN OTHERS ARE RAGING

While we have been learning how to comfort our own pain, sometimes this comfort won't come easily or instantly. For example, being face to face with others who are raging can be frightening and can provoke our own rage. While our first impulse may be to dress in the armor of our disguises of rage, we know it is not wise to allow our rage child to be in control. Instead, we may need a "time out" in stillness.

There are other times, however, when we can bear witness to the rage of others without being immediately provoked. We can trust in our knowing—at least in the moment—that we have been invited into a tender zone with a person in pain. Being familiar with this tender zone personally, and having developed some skills in comforting our own rage, we know that a kind heart is required to transform the moment. Despite the disguise of rage we may be witnessing, an enraged individual more deeply longs for acts of kindness, not aggression, disconnection, or withdrawal. It is in these circumstances that we want to practice greeting rage with compassionate awareness and avoiding the temptation to lash out at an abuser who has often been the victim of abuse.

The following information is helpful when others are raging. Remember that you must feel grounded within yourself, and your own rage child has to feel comfortable enough not to react.

Have Boundaries

Only you know when staying present with someone who is raging is a pattern that represents codependence or abuse. In abusive relationships, there tends to be an imbalance in the expression of rage, in which one person rages at the expense of the other, whose self-expression is suppressed, often kept inside. In these scenarios, the person feeling less empowered will often find another target to project rage upon, i.e., her children, coworkers, spouse, partner, even strangers. And often, misguidedly, she expects them to understand and support her outbursts. In healthy relationships, there are fewer rage outbursts because there is more equality and support. If others repeatedly make you a target of their rage, communicate a clear boundary of *No* and stick to it. *No* is an underutilized expression of compassion. Encourage an abuser to seek support elsewhere. If you are the target of consistent rage or abuse, seek help through therapy or a women's organization.

Stay

In healthy relationships, you are in fact building intimacy when you make room for the expression of rage. For many of us, however, when face to face with someone who is raging, our first instinct is to fight, flee, or shrink—to arm up with disguises. I have come to know both in my personal and professional experience that when others are raging, they are intolerably vulnerable from having lost control. Regardless of how it is disguised, rage is a child emotion in desperate search for nurturance. Being left is what our rage child expects and fears most. Yet to have someone *stay* is what the rage child needs. While when enraged we rarely voice this fear clearly, being left can trigger and validate our feelings of victimization while staying could be experienced as compassion in action.

You should *not* stay if you are genuinely frightened or endangered, or if you are in an unbalanced or abusive relationship. If this is not the case, stay. To advance your own journey, the person's rage, and abolish rage legacies, use all of the resources discussed in this book to stay, but only if you can stay in your heart!

Know that your pain and that of the other come from the same well, even though your experiences may appear to be different. By remaining present, it's possible to minimize suffering and discover what you have in common. Here is where your *Kindness* and *Compassion* practices are most helpful. Your compassion and kind attention is often all that is required.

Give Space

The energies of rage take up space, so a raging person should not be crowded into a tight emotional space. As long as you are not in danger, back off and give the one who is raging lots of space. Avoid the temptation to engage. Silently repeat this mantra—*No matter how I might wish things to be otherwise, things are as they are. May I accept this just as it is*—and mentally bow to the pain you are witnessing.

Remember to keep your boundaries. Only you can determine whether your situation is an abusive pattern or an opportunity for growth. Whatever the case, do not permit any physical or verbal attack. Under no circumstances do you deserve to be abused. If the person expressing rage becomes verbally or physically abusive, don't add to it. If possible, take non-harmful measures to protect yourself.

Keep Your Problems Separate

When others are raging, this is not the time for you to bring up all the things that you too are upset about. Don't unload your feelings on their download—let them take up the space. Discuss your issues at a later time—not now. This is also not a time for sarcasm or contempt—verbal or nonverbal—or to try to intellectually understand every word the person is saying. Rage is necessarily messy! Avoid asking clarifying questions like: *How did that happen? Whose fault is that? Why did you do that? You told me . . . I thought . . .*

This is a time to give the other person your undivided, heartfelt, and wise attention. If the person raging is making demands and asking questions of you—inviting you into a tug-of-war, you can respond with brief statements like:

- I want to talk about this, but I'm more interested in hearing what you have to say right now.
- I want to share my thoughts but not when you are upset.
- I want us to talk when we both can listen.
- I hear you. I get it. I didn't realize you felt this way.
- You've got my attention. I want to listen, I want to know.

Put Your Expectations in Check

The raging person is the focus, but she is not the cause of what *you* are experiencing, nor is she responsible for making it better. The raging person should not have such power, so don't give it to her. The reverse is also true: You are not the cause of what the raging person is experiencing or how she is acting, nor should you be responsible for making her feel better. You do not have that power, so don't try to exert it. The point to remember is: Don't expect a raging person to take care of you, especially when inflamed, and don't try to improve or change an inflamed person. Accept them without becoming them and without judging them.

Apologize

Sometimes, we may see that we have done something to hurt the person who is raging. When sincere, an apology can be important medicine to give others as well as yourself. A genuine apology—*I'm sorry! It was my fault! You're right!*—can instantly soften the heart of someone after they are done expressing their rage. You don't want to rush into an apology. When offered too quickly, it can be experienced as insincere—a way to silence the other person, or make things better before rage has had its say. If you cannot genuinely speak an apology to the person raging, or fear that speaking at all is not wise, silently apologize to yourself. For example, you could say to yourself: *I'm sorry for how I have contributed to this problem. I can see how I triggered this. I forgive myself for not being able to do more right now.* This medicine keeps the heart soft and the energetic connection open for intimacy.

We know we are growing wise when, faced with rage, we are focused on our own healing rather than on changing the other person, recognizing not only the other person's rage but also his or her pain. We can learn to look into the hearts of a raging person and empathize with the shame that comes from losing control, and acknowledge that emotionally, we share the same pain.

16

Support on the Journey

As we are liberating ourselves from our disguises of rage and learning how to live in outrageous dignity, it helps to be supported. When we are supported, we can more readily recognize the humanness and universal nature of rage, and balance our perspective. There are as many forms of support as there are people, and the ultimate choice is yours to make. I have listed a few supports particularly helpful in healing rage. Consider incorporating any one or all of them as aids to your healing journey.

SISTER CIRCLES

A great way to be supported on your healing journey is to form a *Sister Circle*. A Sister Circle provides ongoing support for truth-telling and allows the wisdom of your rage child to be witnessed, affirmed, nurtured, and cherished.

If you are already a member of a women's circle, you may want to explore whether an intention to heal rage can be included in the group's activities. Ask if members would be willing to use the methods offered in this book as a guide.

Separate Sister Circles (or Brother Circles for men) are encouraged, as opposed to Sister-*and*-Brother Circles. It has been my experience that the dynamics and effectiveness of groups change dramatically when women and men join together early on the healing rage journey. Often, assumptions are made and fingers are pointed as to who is to blame for rage. Typically in mixed-gender groups, women become too concerned about what men think and become inhibited or angry. And men often expect to be falsely accused and may become indifferent, withdrawn, defensive, or stop listening. This is not to say that similar dynamics are not present when women circle, but women tend to share more common ground in their relationship to rage.

When Sister Circles have met for an extended period of time, it is possible that they are able to incorporate men more successfully, especially if the men have also met in like circles for periods of time. Similarly, women of similar races, ethnicities, sexual orientations, or any groupings in which shared identity helps participants feel safer can circle together and share their common experiences. Regardless of where you land, each woman will bring a unique gift that belongs to all of its members, and everyone will be enriched in turn.

There are rarely any major catastrophes when we join together with clear intention—only lessons. It is my hope that we can move toward circles that include our world family, in which we discover our humanity rather than just our sameness or safeness.

Leadership and hosting should be rotated among members. Starting and ending times should be honored. Meet at least monthly for a minimum of two hours. Weekly or twice monthly is best. The group size can range from as small as two to as many as eight women. You want to keep the size small to build and maintain connections and allow for adequate time for each member to speak. Your commitment should be for at least one year; however, many groups continue because of the deep friendships that result from supporting rage together. Your decision to be in a group means you and the others are willing to accept these responsibilities:

- Meet regularly at an arranged time.
- Listen objectively without judgment or criticism.
- Do not take the rage of others personally, even when it is directed toward you.
- Witness rage without changing or fixing it.
- Do not expect to be attended to when others are actively in rage, thus allowing attention to remain on those who are raging.
- Establish and maintain safe boundaries on commitments, intimacy, and confidentiality.
- Keep time commitments.
- Be intentionally compassionate.
- Be mindful of how disguises manifest themselves.
- Become curious about what you can discover and reclaim in the rage of others.

During your first meeting, openly discuss these guidelines and add or modify them if necessary. The circle's structure should be simple and informal. Rage needs to be witnessed, not fixed. For example, the hostess may begin by inviting each woman to take a minute or two to share how she is feeling, what she has discovered about her rage since the last time you met, and what support she needs from the group. After everyone has shared, apply the tools of this book to address the needs that have been voiced, or tap into the wisdom within the circle and share or create new forms of support.

Be aware that sometimes when people who are healing begin to be vulnerable with one another, distrust or suspicion can arise, along with the impulse to *fight, flee,* or *shrink* to protect us from pain and shame. When this occurs, it is not necessary to depart from the circle or to sever relationships. Often, we are on the edge of a deeper and more genuine connection. Trust is deepened when we risk sharing our concerns without wearing disguises. This requires us to stay with *Being Now*, and cultivate the tools in this book together.

When we can weather the rage storms of distrust, fear, and suspicion, our disguises fade and we form more intimate connections with others. Sister Circles are excellent ways to cultivate a supportive community for our rage child, and to understand ourselves and our impact on others.

Needless to say, consistent and regular attendance is crucial to building trust and group cohesion. Once schedules are arranged, do everything possible to show up. Our rage child expects to be neglected, ill-treated, ignored, and abandoned, and members who attend infrequently may unduly trigger our rage. Make this group a priority for soul searching and you will reap tremendous benefits.

YOGA

Yoga comes from a Sanskrit word that means "union." The goal of yoga is to join our body, mind, and spirit through postures that help tone, strengthen, and align the body. We perform these postures to make the spine supple and to promote blood flow to all the organs, glands, and tissues. This keeps all the bodily systems healthy. A regular yoga practice helps relieve stress, restores balance, rejuvenates the body, clears the mind, opens the heart, and moves us closer to our wise selves.

Yoga is an easily accessible and inexpensive practice that has profound impact on our well-being. You only need comfortable, loose-fitting clothing, a flat floor large enough to stretch out on and raise your arms and legs, and a mat or towel.

There are many types of yoga—Hatha, Ashtanga, Iyengar, Bikram, Vinyasa, Kundalini, Yin, Power, and Restorative, to name a few. Don't let your inability to pronounce these forms of yoga keep you away from this ancient and profound practice. Fundamentally, they all share the goals of health, union, and harmony. It is useful initially to be supported by an experienced teacher or class. Once you have mastered the basic postures with a teacher, you can purchase any number of home-study courses to help you maintain a regular practice. Yoga is a body meditation. It's a graceful way to cultivate inner peace and build strength, concentration, and self-awareness.

THERAPY

On your healing journey, you would be wise to engage the services of a skilled therapist. A therapist can help you examine the origin and dynamics of your rage. Rage can be a messy emotion, and if we are healing, the rage child will not present herself in a clean and polite manner. She wants to be able to rant and rave *and* be welcomed!

I'll never forget the first time I expressed rage in my therapist's office. She was terrified and took what I said personally. Her way of helping me was to quiet me as quickly as possible so that she would feel less uncomfortable. I believe she was also concerned about disturbing her colleagues in the neighboring offices. I felt guilty and confused and angry that I needed to concern myself with her fears *and* my own. We should not have to take care of our therapist or worry about upsetting the folks next door when we are healing rage. It's difficult enough for many of us to express rage, and even harder when we are made to feel guilty about it by our therapists and other teachers.

Within a therapeutic setting, we should have the space and freedom to make an emotional mess and examine its remains. Since rage can be a frightening energy to allow and witness, we must seek safe environments and experienced, knowledgeable professionals to assist in our explorations.

Therapy should not be considered crisis or short-term support but an opportunity for your rage child to unfold gradually and truthfully. Seek a professional who is experienced in working with women and rage and who understands his or her disguises. Choose someone interested in healing the roots of rage, not just supporting you in changing your behavior. Before committing to a therapist, check into his/her background or have a brief telephone conversation. Consider these questions:

- What are your beliefs about rage?
- What work have you personally and professionally done in the area of rage?
- What is your approach to supporting the examination of intense emotions?
- How do you create a safe environment for the expression of rage?
- What has been your experience in working with [Asian, African, White, Hispanic, Bisexual, Transgender, Lesbian, Biracial—fill in the blank] women?

A word of caution: Do not get into a bartering situation with your therapist. For example, do not exchange bodywork for therapy work. This type of arrangement is typically short-lived and often results in an unsatisfying and poorly defined, if not dangerous, relationship. A professional therapist who is experienced in working with rage will not participate in this type of arrangement. He or she will:

- Establish and manage consistent boundaries.
- Balance your need for safety with your need to feel the power of your rage.
- Not protect you from rage but rather encourage you to feel rage in a pure and expressive way.
- Not put you in a position of taking care of his or her needs. The time will be yours!

The result will be that you are the owner and director of this time, with the therapist serving as witness and providing the process and supervision that deepens your awareness and utilization of rage.

Once you have chosen someone to work with, commit to building a relationship over a twelve-month period at least twice a month. Therapy is an excellent way to be supported in deepening your relationship with rage. It is also sacred ground to grieve and to begin to put rage, pain, and shame in perspective with the rest of your life. If you cannot afford the services of a therapist, counselor, or social worker, other lower-cost options include twelve-step programs and reevaluation counseling (also referred to as *co-counseling*). These are widely accessible alternatives to therapy.

INSIGHT MEDITATION

I encourage my clients to attend an Insight [also referred to as Vipassana] meditation retreat. In an Insight retreat, you delve more deeply into the meditation principles introduced in this book. These are silent retreats where you cultivate stillness and a compassionate relationship with your mind and body. You receive instructions on how to be with yourself in kind, forgiving ways, and simply be with things as they are. There are many options for study: two-hour classes, one-day retreats, weekend retreats, or even month-long retreats. These experiences of stillness open us to be more calm in our lives, regardless of what is occurring, and profoundly enhances our healing practice.

Visit the Spirit Rock Meditation Center Web site at www.spiritrock.org to learn about meditation and various study options. For audio and video tapes and books, you may want to visit Dharma Seed at www.dharmaseed.org or Sounds True at www.soundstrue.com. Search the Web or explore what your local community offers.

BODYWORK

Rage is truth born in the body. At the onset of childhood trauma, the complete release of rage was interrupted as we did what we needed to do to protect ourselves. Since then, our bodies have repressed the pain, shame, and fear of rage. As we unmask our disguises, we often reawaken the original pain from the onset of trauma, and this pain wants to be released. For this reason, especially in the early stages of our healing journey, we may feel unexpected physical pain along with the expected emotional pain from digging up old, twisted emotional roots.

When we are uncomfortable or in pain our first impulse is to feel better *immediately*, so we go about the business of soothing ourselves through drugs, food, alcohol, sex, work, or other indulgences and sensations that distract us from feeling. We don't always do this consciously—it's our way of coping. Do what you can to avoid these temptations—they are disguises of rage. The pain you are attempting to silence is not a new problem, but rather an old problem finally releasing itself through your body. It can now complete its cycle because you have committed yourself to healing. Rage naturally releases itself when we open to a physical inquiry, and bodywork supports us on this journey.

The bodywork I would encourage is a touch therapy. Rage naturally wants to liberate itself, and touch puts us in direct contact with rage. With touch, we become aware of what and where we are holding, and how to let go. Touch relieves pain and supports the reunion of body and mind. We can return to a better functioning of our bodies and learn to rest peacefully in our skin.

There is a difference between massage and bodywork. A massage is typically restful and relaxing, and often nonverbal. The goal of a massage is to allow us to feel better through the release of body tension. In massage, we are not necessarily developing a relationship with our body, nor are the benefits intended to last far beyond the course of the treatment, yet it is an excellent way to relax and pamper ourselves. Bodywork, on the other hand, is generally longer term. Through bodywork, the practitioner invites the body to awaken and release, and asks us to examine and understand our experiences.

There are many types of bodywork, including craniosacral therapy,

Reiki, shiatsu, acupuncture, and Rolfing, to name a few. The method I most recommend is the Rosen Method Bodywork. The Rosen Method is a gentle and powerful form of touch. The Rosen practitioner has been trained to notice subtle changes in muscle tension and shifts in breathing. As this process unfolds, you become aware of habitual tension and old patterns are released, freeing you to experience deep muscular and emotional relaxation and greater self-awareness. Says Rosen Method Bodywork founder Marion Rosen: "You become an anthropologist and become your own best discovery!"

Terry, a thirty-five-year-old community organizer wearing the *Distraction* disguise of rage, was in psychotherapy for three years before she acknowledged that her mother's sudden death when she was twelve was not her fault. While she had an intellectual *understanding* of this truth, it was difficult for her body to let go or to feel free of blame. After several sessions with a Rosen bodyworker she was able to *experience* the rage she carried in her body over having been abandoned and was then able to grieve her loss. Through bodywork she was able to move beyond her mental disguises of rage, which had distracted her from transforming this loss. As her body released the pain she had been carrying, she was finally able to grieve and feel relief.

Investigate the various types of bodywork that are available in your area and choose one that best supports your needs. As with most therapeutic processes, committing long-term provides the best results. Ideally, see a bodywork practitioner biweekly, alternating weeks with therapy visits. This combination is a powerful way to enhance self-awareness and well-being.

KEEPING FIT

Caring for your body is an act of self-trust and self-nurturing. You invite your body to work with, not against, you. I know you have probably heard this many times: The body needs to be physical to function well. It is our vehicle—we need to care for its physical structure as well as the fuel we use to run it. This translates into fitness and nutrition.

There is no way around it: Cardiovascular exercises reduce blood pressure and tension, and you need only to exercise twenty minutes three times a week! For example, walking, even at a moderate pace, can transform stiffening blood vessels into pliable ones. Whether you choose walking, running, biking, swimming, or dancing, raising your heart rate for an extended period helps to strengthen your body and its capabilities.

Another component of fitness is nutrition—the fuel we use to run our bodies. You know the saying: *You are what you eat.* It's true! There is a relationship between rage and what you eat and drink. Become aware of how food and other substances alter your mood. Here are a few tips:

- Eat what you love that is also good for you.
- Eat slowly.
- Minimize and decrease white sugar, bleached white flour, dairy, heavy carbohydrates, and caffeine.
- Increase vegetables and fruits.
- Avoid the use of recreational drugs and alcohol.
- Increase your intake of high-quality water.

Our rage child is vulnerable to substances that alter our moods. When we stop over- or under-stimulating our physical body, we become more aware of the moment and increase our ability to rest in our skin.

17

Predictable Joys

Healing rage naturally frees up more inner space for us to feel and be full of life, yet feeling spacious can be frightening. We can be intolerant of our own liberation. To counterbalance these frightening feelings of unknowingness, we can incorporate into our lives experiences that bring instant and predictable joy—encounters that make our entire being soften and at the same time remind us of our connectedness to something larger than our physical selves.

Following are several *Predictable Joys* that I have noticed are especially comforting to our rage child. *Predictable Joys* cost very little, are easily accessed, and place us in the present moment. What brings joy is different for each of us, and it changes. Your task is to partake in as many of these joys as your heart can stand—for the rest of your life— and to be on the lookout for even more of them.

THE JOY OF LAUGHTER

Laughter is the best medicine of all time and provides immediate joy. Research shows that laughter decreases stress hormones, relaxes muscles, enhances our immune system, reduces pain, provides cardiac conditioning, improves our respiratory system, and decreases hypertension. But these reasons are not nearly as pleasurable as the simple and pure joy of laughing.

Make it your priority to find something to laugh about each day. A word of caution—avoid participating in humor at other people's expense. This type of hurtful behavior will erode your own self-esteem and healing. Instead, read cartoons, rent a video, or notice the humor in ordinary life. You may have a friend or relative who is naturally humorous—spend time with that person. Journal humorous stories and insights each day and refer back to them often. Laughter frees up inner space and supports the reunion of body and mind.

THE JOY OF MUSIC

Music travels by air and permeates our senses, creating inner vibrations that regulate our mood. Music affects the release of powerful brain chemicals that have an effect on the rhythm of our breathing, our heartbeat, and our blood pressure. Because music holds such power, we can make use of music as a joy we can count on.

Listening to soothing music can calm even the most troubled minds. It reduces aggression, lifts depression, and improves the quality of rest and sleep. On the other hand, listening to belligerent and violent music may be exciting but may also contribute to hostile, agitated, and harmful states of mind.

Select your favorite sounds and fit them into categories such as: Joy, Bliss, Relaxation, Courage, Beauty, Mastery, Sweetness, Love, etc. When you need to alter your mood, choose from your desired categories. Find a private space to relax and enjoy the sounds. Consider listening as a meditation. Begin with *Breath Meditation*. You might identify a particular instrument or sound and follow its journey throughout the song. You may even imagine yourself being that sound, allowing its vibration to move you or express itself through your voice. Notice what thoughts and feelings arise and ride them. Allow music to take you on a pleasure ride. Kick back and surrender to its predictable joy.

THE JOY OF DANCE

For many of us, it is impossible to feel bad when we are dancing. When we dance, our body and mind work together and we become balanced and harmonious. Dance provides exercise, improves mobility and muscle coordination, and reduces tension. Dance, especially spontaneous and free movements, improves self-awareness and self-confidence, and is an outlet for creative expression and physical and emotional release.

Choose a dance expression that is natural and enjoyable—both are key. If either is lacking, you won't maintain consistency, and in healing rage, consistency is more important than the amount of time you spend.

Linda, a thirty-six-year-old woman putting down her *Defiance* disguise, started a weekly salsa dance class at a local club. She chose this class because salsa was something she enjoyed so much that she would be sure to be consistent. It also offered a wild and joyful freedom that her rage child demanded.

Make a regular playdate with your rage child and dance like nobody's watching. Dance is profoundly pleasurable and predictably joyous.

THE JOY OF HUGS

I get some criticism because I live in California, land of the touchy-feelers. But my motto is: *Hug more and talk less!* For many of us, hugs bring instant and predictable joy! Some of us are afraid of physical contact, but a genuine hug—heart to heart—is a relatively safe form of physical contact, something that can help our bodies to heal. Hugs can break down barriers that words fail to penetrate.

I encourage you to wholeheartedly hug the people you care about when you greet them. Allow your hugs to last a minimum of five seconds! Remember to breathe and enjoy the pure and immediate joy that hugging can provide.

THE JOY OF A CHILD

When those of us who are healing rage make ourselves available to children, we not only witness the subtle unfolding of a child's life, we also awaken to our own. The magical thing about being around a child, especially an infant, is discovering how natural it is to love and be loved. An infant is miraculously one with spirit. Her innocence is pure and her nature unspoiled. When an infant cries, her entire body is involved. Nothing is held back. The same is true when she smiles. Body and mind are one.

You may currently have a child in your life to whom you can open your heart a little wider. Or you may have a niece, nephew, or grandchild you can be close to and nurture. You may also visit an orphanage, homeless shelter, or hospital, or know of a child in your neighborhood. This need not be a time-consuming endeavor but regular enough for you to become acquainted with the child and to enjoy and understand their wondrous ways.

Often our time with a child will help us fill in the blanks of our childhood. We may begin to remember the conditions that gave birth to our rage as well as recall more pleasurable memories. Waking up in this way is a wonderful way to reclaim our own light and innocence. The joy of a child is a gift to all, and an extra benefit to your own rage child, who will delight in interaction with a kindred soul closer to her own age.

Many of us have forgotten that children have wisdom to share. They are not simply here for us to care for. They bring answers to our deepest questions and medicine for our well-being and that of the world. When we invest in the well-being of a child, we discover how to love, how to forgive, and how to live in the moment. Of course it is not always sugar and spice, but it is always real and often joyful.

THE JOY OF A TEENAGER

Teenagers know the truth about their bodies even in the midst of being programmed out of it. They are on fire, candid, often uninhibited, creative, and wise—things we are reclaiming within ourselves. What is often missing from a teenager's life is respectful attention to truth and inner freedom. Teenagers need to be around creative people, and around role models who practice what they preach, and most parents would appreciate this support.

It can be joyous to cultivate a relationship with a teenager and his or her family, and encourage an atmosphere of nonjudgment, creativity, and service. Make an agreement with the family to be of service. Offer assistance with homework, reading, cultural experiences, or exposure to your line of work or special interest. Every teenager should be able to look back on her life and say: *There was this woman who loved me, and I could be myself with her. She saw my potential. She really tried to know me for who I truly was.*

Many teenagers embody those qualities that we have lost and now seek to reclaim—audaciousness, naturalness, timelessness, innocence, and sexual freedom. Enjoy the charge of being around a teen and awaken to who you are. When we take advantage of this predictable joy, we rediscover and advance those parts of ourselves that have always been free.

THE JOY OF AN ELDER

Many of us have difficult relationships with elders in our bloodline. We may have lost them too early, never knew them, or they may still be alive but there may be a painful estrangement due to regret or disappointment. We may even push them to the side or avoid them because we may not be able to tolerate their pain and suffering.

When we feel cut off from our elders, we miss out on the sacred wisdom of their lives and the human experience of aging, death, and dying. Being able to be present with both the joy and complexity of our elders is part of becoming present with our full selves. Just as a child reminds us of our birth, youth, and innocence, many elders embody grace and wisdom that can teach us how to navigate our lives. Unfortunately many elders die alone, with their wisdom unexplored. Being unable or unwilling to draw upon their vast stores of wisdom is a profound disservice to our evolution and dwarfs our experiences of joy.

To experience this joy, identify an elder with whom you want to develop a deeper connection. Perhaps it's your own parents, or an older person in a nursing home or a hospital, a neighbor, or a friend's parent whom you admire. Commit to spending time with them. The *Empathic Interview Questionnaire* may be a helpful tool to apply. Be a good friend and a good listener. Attend to the elder's wisdom fires and heal together. Edith, an inactive writer, writes:

> I just got back from visiting my favorite aunt. It's been over eight years since I've seen her. She's seventy-nine years old and has chronic pulmonary obstructive disease. It was difficult to see her this way and at the same time it felt like a privilege. To my surprise I discovered that my aunt is a talented writer and

poet and has never shared any of her work. She read several of her poems and somehow they were just what I needed to hear. Knowing she is dying made our time precious. I could see how blessed I am to have time, choices, and energy to be creative. Her words were simple: "Don't waste a minute!" I returned home ready to take my writing more seriously. My aunt helped me realize that I have a writing legacy. She was so happy I came. I've been beaming ever since.

While many of us may not have been able to receive such wisdom from our birth parents, there is no reason why we can't obtain elder wisdom from someone else. Keep in mind that there should be mutual respect in your relationship with elders. You do not have to regress or become childlike in the face of elders. Bringing your full woman-self to the relationship is evidence of respect.

Sometimes, our wise elders will come looking for us to impart their wisdom and encourage our healing journey and their own. One such wise elder, age eighty-two, attended a one-day Healing Rage workshop and captivated the hearts of more than sixty women with piercing truth and love:

> I come to you not out of pity, but from pride and pain. I've kept quiet too long about being raped, and seeing my daughters and granddaughters raped by men in our family. I've stood by and said nothing, did nothing, and it happened to practically every girl child. I was so afraid. I just want you to know how sorry I am for being silent. Now that I'm old enough to be your grandmother, I'm sorry that my silence and the silence of people like me have caused you so much harm. And I'm sorry that I've shut down my heart to life for so many years. I've let you down as an elder, as a protector. I came to this workshop because it looked like a good place to heal. I ask for your forgiveness and I want to state in public that I am working on forgiving myself. I think it is important that we tell the truth and free ourselves. I pray that we can all look truth dead in the eye and do what we need to do.

Healing, at its core, is about returning home. There is tremendous healing in returning to our elders and embracing their wisdom, and learning how to live and how to die wisely.

THE JOY OF SACRED INTIMACY

While many of us are sexually active, the true joy of sacred intimacy is rooted in being sensuous and intimate with a lover, and especially ourselves. Our bodies come alive and naturally respond to contact, but many of us are afraid of our bodies. We may have been physically and sexually violated and have become confused about the sacredness of our bodies. Many of us have settled for sex or abstinence when intimacy—touch, presence, respect, and physical and emotional connection—is what we yearn for.

Your task is to embrace your sexual unions as sacred rituals. Make them an intimate endeavor—every time! Lay with your lover heart to heart, and breathe together. Tenderly examine each other's faces with loving eyes. Avoid talking—it's difficult in such moments to talk and feel at the same time. Holding and light caressing is healing, especially if its sole aim is not to become sexual. If you are by yourself, allow the same tenderness toward your own body that you would toward a lover's. Be fully present, soft, and available without fantasy or distraction. Rest and enjoy the oneness that you have created. Don't be quick to fall asleep—take a long time to rest in this pleasure. It is not necessary to be sexual to find joy in sacred intimacy. You need only to partake in this predictable joy as often and as thoughtfully as you can!

THE JOY OF ANIMALS AND PETS

Animals are powerful spirits. Historically, many shamans, deities, and spiritual leaders are portrayed with animals as totems of guidance and protection. In ancient Egypt, the scarab, dog, cat, and asp were a few of many sacred animals that were respected for their wise guidance. In Native American cultures, many animal spirits such as the eagle, snake, buffalo, and wolf are considered medicine for the soul and are depicted in rituals for peace and healing. Many states in the United States, and some countries in other parts of the world, use animal symbols to represent the spirit of the land on their flags. Like children, animals can teach us much about how to live, love, and forgive.

Consider bringing an animal spirit into your life for the pure joy of it. You can have a pet or visit one regularly in the neighborhood. I'm a dog lover. Brandy, my beloved German shepherd for thirteen years, taught me many lessons about unconditional love. She would lie across my feet, panting and smiling as I rubbed her head and chin. Sometimes I would be in awe at the joy in her face as she looked at me. I would talk to her about life and love and would ask her questions like: *How do you love no matter what?* And she would respond by staying beside me and *being* love, teaching me that *being is love!* I witnessed her growth and death and she never stopped loving me. That was many years ago and I still experience much joy at the thought of her.

The spirit of an animal is where the joy lies. Look around and discover the animals in nature that surround you. Relax into the kinship that animals provide. You will find that your animal spirit has something in common with your rage child—it is your presence that matters most. The more capable you are of *being love*, the more capable you are of *being loving*. This is the predictable joy of loving animals and pets—being love and being loving.

THE JOY OF NATURE

The gifts of nature are infinite, varied, surprising, and generous. Many of us live our lives in man-made surroundings, preoccupied with man-made concerns. But our bodies, our senses, and our spirits have a different home, one much older and wilder. Making time for a homecoming with the natural world can fill our nervous systems with relief and joy.

Nature is indiscriminately generous, and she performs miraculously to a revered audience. We need only be present to her predictable joys. Essentially, we want to embrace nature as an extension of ourselves, and invite nature to help us make sense out of our lives. For example, when you question your worth and beauty, it is joyous to admire in intricate detail an unusual flower. See yourself in this flower. Imagine yourself becoming this flower—soft, unique, fragrant, original—the flower of your admiration.

If you feel ungrounded, take some time to be near a mature tree. Notice its full trunk and deep strong roots. Ask the tree any questions that come to mind, for example: *How do you just stand there through all the seasons of life? Teach me how to survive without hiding. Teach me how to stand gracefully.* Imagine yourself being like the tree—old, wise, solid, and grounded, knowing you have a right to exist. Experience the physical power of this natural expression, and listen for an answer to your questions. Imagine *If I were a tree, how would I respond to my question?*

If you feel lifeless and in need of energy to take care of yourself, you may find predictable joy falling asleep in the warm sun and soaking up its rays. If the warm sun is not available, let yourself imagine a radiant sun beaming down on your body, or a beautiful sunset, or a hearth fire. The predictable joy occurs when you allow in more light and become light itself.

If you are hurting because you have a relationship that you cannot mend, invite the earth to join you in transforming your pain. Plant a flower or tree in your yard as a dedication to the person you are unable to relate to. Attend to the flower or tree—love it and talk to it as if it were your loved one.

If you need to grieve but your tears won't flow, take this need to a larger body of water—the ocean, a lake, or a river, and give it over.

Your bathtub will also do. Ask the larger body of water to help you grieve. If you feel overwhelmed, caged, or frustrated, find your way to fresh air and open space.

I take a walk in a park near my home each morning on a long and spiraling path, seldom seeing anyone for miles. One morning, a woman was about a quarter of a mile ahead of me walking alone on the trail. Her pace was fast and she was screaming and cursing at the top of her lungs. I dropped back further on the trail, not wanting to be noticed or to interrupt her self-expression. I mentally bowed to her rage release, knowing she was freeing herself and that the earth and air could hold her.

Begin a practice of noticing the simple pleasures of nature and how they support your existence and reflect your larger essence. Whatever you need, you can find solace and joy in nature.

THE JOY OF ARTISTIC EXPRESSION

When the spider builds its web, it is a mirror image of itself—a beauty we are more likely to pause and admire even if we are afraid of spiders. We can admire the web because of its artistic and unique expression. We are awestruck and wonder: *How is this possible?* We are engaged with the art—the web—not the artist—the spider. Similarly, art provides a natural outlet for our rage child to be seen without being feared.

Our rage child is an artist, and having an artistic outlet is an amazing way to channel passion and express our deepest longings. Too many of us allow ourselves to lie dormant, rather than tapping our creative potential. Art is a resourceful and profoundly meaningful way to transform our rage disguises. Like the spider's web, our artistic talents can reveal and affirm our existence and keep us safe and sane.

Do you long to create a play? Write a poem? Sing jazz? Play the drums? Dance like a wild fire? These art forms, and many others like them, are prayers that allow everything we are on the inside to come out. Consider: *What beauty have I always wanted to manifest?*

Identify a creative project—something your heart would enjoy. Sit in your sacred space and ask your rage child to help you determine the most satisfying paths to creative expression. It can be a project just for you, or one to share with others. Be outrageous and don't worry if it does not make sense. Begin with something simple and silly, not something you need to perfect. For instance, trace the outline of your hand, then decorate it with colors or crafts. Then turn it in any number of directions to see what it reveals. Make up stories about what you see and write them in your rage journal. Just begin and be willing to laugh at yourself. Make room to display your creations just as you would hang the pictures of a preschooler who comes home eager to share his projects.

Teresa had forgotten how much she loved to listen to music. She loved the old Motown sounds and would listen and sing any number of them for hours on end. She always felt lighter and openhearted when she sang. But it wasn't until she began a playful relationship with her rage child that she began to write new lyrics to old Motown tunes, which provided her with much humor, joy, and unique expression. Rochelle, raised as a child in an environment of emotionally distant and austere furnishings, realized through her relationship with her rage child that her attraction to quilting was more than a casual hobby. It was her way to add comfort and texture to her life. This realization made her hobby all the more joyous.

Your disguises of rage may give you clues about your hidden talents. Melanie, healing from the disguise of *Depression,* used her dark times to write poems about depression, giving honor to every detail of her experience. She eventually published a book of poetry that helped others rest and love themselves in dark times. She turned her pain into art and gifted it to the world.

Pay attention to your body's response to rage and explore its meaning through your creative endeavor. Esther, unmasking the disguise of *Defiance,* would impulsively slap her "hardheaded" children when she became angry. During a *Stillness Practice*, Esther recalled that as long as she could remember, she had wanted to grab something hard and change it. Esther found a sculpting class and enrolled. She enjoyed the act of carving and changing the stone, surprised to discover that it was the stone that was teaching her how it needed to be shaped, not the other way around. She was able to translate this experience into the difficulty she was having with her children in that her so-called *hardheaded* children were actually trying to teach her something, and if she looked closely, she might discover a unique treasure not in need of change.

Our rage child is a *fire* spirit—a natural-born artist. Our challenge is to use the fire of rage to illuminate our most heartfelt longings. We naturally feel powerful when our rage becomes tangible and affirmed, even if only for our eyes.

Inescapably, we are both creator and that which is being created. When we partake in an artistic expression, we discover what we need to learn, and learn what we need to discover. Dedicate one evening each month to an artistic project and invite your rage child to participate! The only requirement is that you have fun! You will discover that allowing time for your artistic expression is a soulful and predictable joy!

18

The Journey to *Now*

Rage isn't going away. We will continue to be triggered by conditions that give rise to it. These conditions are both outside and within us. Healing is mostly about compassionate self-awareness—noticing how we contribute to our own suffering and peace. It's not about getting something or changing someone. It's about *you* getting *you,* and *you* changing *you!*

Throughout these pages, you have been encouraged to let go of your disguises of rage, move closer to your own blazing fires, *and* trust that you will be enlightened rather than burned. You have been supported in delving into shameful and disowned aspects of yourself and your family roots, and asked to believe that this painful soul-searching is actually good for you. You have been invited to consider that an intimate relationship with rage can teach you how to love like you have never been loved. You have been told that you are much more than your past experiences, and that the core of who you are has never been touched or damaged by life's circumstances, only strengthened. And you have been given advice on how to utilize your own personal power to rest in and trust the wisdom of your body and be at peace in your own skin. Most importantly, you have stayed with this book long enough to read these pages, and perhaps realize that the journey returns us to *now*.

On this journey, change is often subtle. It may last a few seconds or a lifetime, but the shifts can leave us feeling deeply satisfied. In the early stages, we can expect to continue living a very normal life, but gradually we begin to notice simple yet profound changes in how we relate to rage and those who are raging. We may begin to feel better about ourselves and more attentive. For example, we may be afraid but not feel frozen, or feel the need to blame others for how we feel. As we continue our practice, we do what must be done with less anger, obsession, or compulsion. We can laugh at ourselves and forgive more easily. We can witness our emotions without being controlled by them. And we may begin to notice and anticipate the conditions that give rise to our disguises.

Disguises are like drugs—we go through withdrawal without them. They have served a purpose—they have diverted us from the rage we have felt toward our own helplessness and the shame we have felt from being dishonored and disrespected. As we let go of our disguises of rage, we may feel a new rush of energy. Being less armored can feel as if we are simultaneously experiencing a grave loss *and* a new beginning. Karen, letting go of her disguise of *Devotion*, shares this story:

> I've never felt more alive than I do now. It seems I'm letting go of everything and it's long overdue. My long-dead marriage is now buried. I resigned from the board of the organization I founded. I sold my house and got a smaller one. My youngest daughter graduated and left home. I even lost thirty-five pounds. I feel excited, alone, and at times angry in all this newness, but I don't regret anything that has happened. I sob often, then it occurred to me: All newborn babies cry!

Sadness, even depression, should be expected. It allows us time to grieve and surrender into the deep dampness of shame. Grieving is one way our body rests within our skin. As long as you are not a danger to others or yourself, make space for these feelings. Allow anger, sadness, tears, numbness, agitation, and other emotions to rise and recede without judgment. Avoid the temptation to attach feelings with stories or to overidentify with your experience. Instead, embrace your emotions as if they had no name or history. Allow them to be, without reacting to them. Rest as much as you can and take some time to do absolutely nothing but ponder the intricate patterns of the cracks on the wall. Give yourself a few hours or a few days. Of course, seek support if depression persists. But most often it is likely to be a temporary visitor coming and going throughout your healing.

As we grow wiser in our bodies, we begin to feel more spacious. Our energy is less stuck in self-righteousness or in the shame of our past, and we are more lighthearted and free-flowing in the present. We discover a greater self-trust and spontaneity in our thoughts, feelings, and actions. Our cravings begin to lessen, and our defensiveness and rigidity soften. We are more creative, accepting, and flexible, and we can turn our energy toward improving our lives and those of others.

As we continue to heal rage, our relationships with our children and loved ones will often become more honest. It becomes possible to speak more truthfully without harmful intention, and we like who we are with them. We can claim the power of knowing and giving ourselves what we need.

Susan, fifty years old, disrobing *Dominance* as her disguise and healing from emotional abuse by her father and emotional abandonment by her mother, felt anxious about returning home for the holidays. Her relationship with her parents felt strained, heartless, and detached, and she could not tolerate another year of feeling emotionally distant while being physically close. In our coaching session, Susan created a new ritual. When she telephoned home, her mother answered and she asked that she put her dad on the other telephone. This was her request: *You know that walk we take together every holiday? This time, I'd like for each of you to tell me three things you love about me and I'll do the same for each of you, okay?*

Susan was surprised that they accepted. While she was later thinking of how she would answer this question for each of them, she realized how anxious and vulnerable she felt putting her feelings into words. Asking them the question felt uncomfortable, but responding felt even more terrifying, requiring more from her heart. This anxiety quickly turned to empathy as she realized that if they were experiencing what she was experiencing, it was sure to be a meaningful reunion, and it was. This exercise taught Susan that it was not too late to change her relationship with her parents—she did not have to keep her heart closed, sever her relationship with them, or dread being in their company. She loved them, and she could ask for what she wanted directly by setting an example of the relationship she wanted. At every moment, we have the opportunity to alter our thoughts, speech, and actions.

We won't always be as successful as Susan. Sometimes, it will be necessary to be difficult, independent, insistent, or firm. Our best attempts to be kind or consistent may still result in negative responses. In these inevitable circumstances, we are challenged to return to our *Gentling* practices—accepting the harsh reality of disappointments *and* maintaining an inner and outer practice of kindness. We may begin to trust that everything that happens to us is trying to teach us how to live and learn more honorably.

Over time, we will begin to notice that we fight less with others and ourselves. As we heal, we love ourselves more and need to defend ourselves less. While we may continue to take on certain battles, we are sure to pick our battles more intentionally, staying focused on maintaining equanimity and connection. We recognize more immediately that we don't have to participate in every argument we are invited to join.

The changes we experience may be invisible to the outside world, but they nonetheless have a profound effect on how we feel about ourselves. Life becomes less about what someone else does and more about what we do to affirm ours and others' basic goodness. Joan, letting go of the *Dependence* disguise, shares:

> I was able to be in the hospital, in a really extreme situation, without losing my power. I didn't become enmeshed with my family's negative energy around illness, or devolve into a trauma reaction. Even though the situation was nightmarish, I was an effective advocate for myself, and was able to return again and again to clarity. I can honestly say that there's been a falling away of fear.

People around us may become disoriented, and not know how to relate to us without our disguises. People may bring us their problems to solve, or become angry if they are no longer the center of our attention. Or they may withdraw from us to get our attention. In our rawness, we may at times feel hypersensitive, provoked into assuming our disguise of rage. On the other hand, they may surprise us and take responsibility for themselves instead of projecting onto us. Whatever the responses of others, consider them indications that you are on track with your healing.

Theresa, discarding her *Distraction* disguise, began to change the compulsion to spend, which had resulted in her credit-card debt. Her boyfriend Fred, who was unconscious of his own *Defiance* disguise, became more belligerent, complaining that they no longer had fun together. Theresa was experiencing tremendous confidence in her ability to control her impulses, but Fred was attracted and attached to her impulsivity. Theresa recognized that overspending had been her way of holding on to Fred, and it was not easy letting go of the habit. While she wanted to continue investing in the relationship, she insisted on finding more honest and intimate ways of doing so. They went through several months of adjustment and were able to weather the storm. Their bond eventually became less thrilling and impulsive but more honest and intimate, which led to a deeper and more genuine commitment.

Here's the good news: *It is possible to be fundamentally happy in this life—to live whole and wholesome.* Everything we do to cultivate a loving relationship with rage is an act of courage and cause for celebration. One vision I enjoy is from a story my beloved teacher Jack Kornfield tells about the Babemba tribe of South Africa:

> When a person acts irresponsibly or unjustly, he is placed in the center of the village, alone and unfettered. All work ceases, and every man, woman, and child in the village gathers in a large circle around the accused individual. Then each person in the tribe speaks to the accused, one at a time, each recalling the good things the person in the center of the circle has done in his lifetime. Every incident, every experience that can be recalled with any detail and accuracy, is recounted. All his positive attributes, good deeds, strengths, and kindnesses are recited carefully and at length. This tribal ceremony often lasts for several days. At the end, the tribal circle is broken, a joyous celebration takes place, and the person is symbolically and literally welcomed back into the tribe.

Rage is fuel—transformative energy, the source of our empowerment. Its nature is to liberate us, and its truth mobilizes our deepest, most heartfelt intentions. When we are healing rage, rage can become our ally and teach us how to live *and* love in outrageous dignity. We are free to reveal to ourselves, and to the world, our exquisiteness and infinite potential.

May every one of us become more curious and less frightened of rage. May manifestations of rage be acknowledged as pain and treated with the greatest compassion possible. May we look at one another's rage, recognize ourselves, and fall in love with what we see. May our good deeds open our hearts in ways that heal the roots of suffering throughout the world for all beings. Be well!

ACKNOWLEDGMENTS

Actually, I thought I was done with *Healing Rage* when I self-published in 2004. In my opinion, the book had been wildly successful and I was beginning my next writing project. In May 2006, Laurie Fox read *Healing Rage* while renting my artist studio and felt it belonged in everyone's household—and I agreed. Within months, Laurie, a senior partner with the Linda Chester Literary Agency in New York, had several publishers flirting with an offer. It was right around this time that Alice Walker, the Pulitzer Prize winner for *The Color Purple*, endorsed *Healing Rage*—she thought it was a life-changing "classic." With her blessing, I'm sky-dancing with excitement. Then it got even better. Executive editor Lauren Marino of Gotham Books was eager to add *Healing Rage* to its impressive list of authors and take this self-publication to national exposure. I'm grateful to these powerful women for their auspicious appearance in the life of *Healing Rage*, and for seeing and accepting *Healing Rage* in its purest form—an offering intended to minimize human suffering.

Writing this book was a long, arduous, and amazing journey, and

I received a great deal of support along the way. I would like to thank the creator for the gifts of deep listening and reverence to healing. I am eternally grateful to the roaring whispers of my ancestors whose spirits kept me faithful to this heart work, and to my first love and teacher, my mother, for her songs, soulful wit, determination, and originality.

My work has been deeply influenced and supported by many teachers. Warm regards to Chief Luisah Teish for her ancestral wisdom, and Shaman and Reverend Marguerite E. Bolden for living and teaching through love. Dharma Elder Venerable Bhante Henepola Gunaratana for his fine mind and devotion to service. To my spiritual mother, Dzogchen lineage holder Aba Cecile McHardy, for being the *Friendly Dragon*—seeking me out, biting me with joy, and offering generously teachings of the Vajrayana tradition. I bow in deep gratitude to my spiritual father, Jack Kornfield, for his wise heart, and for being a wisdom weaver of East and West traditions, and for his encouragement and loving attention to my work. Many blessings of thankfulness go to Alice Walker for her integrity, generosity, and wise heart. Also for wise support I am grateful to the Spirit Rock Meditation Center, my Dharma teachers, my family, and especially my *sangha* brother, Jack, and sisters Alice, Arisika, Boli, Marlene, Olivia, Saundra, and Vernice.

I want to acknowledge my clients, who have given me the privilege of their trust, and whose willingness to express rage and understand the unknown in themselves provided me with a wealth of illustrative material for this book. I am thankful to Toni Morrison for *Beloved*, and Alice Walker for *The Third Life of Grange Copeland*—both novels eloquently communicate generational pain and love, and affirm my conception of a rage inheritance. I also want to acknowledge bell hooks for *Killing Rage*, and for her prolific wisdom, and to Harriet Lerner for *The Dance of Anger*, and for being among the first to utilize genealogy in the self-help genre.

This journey has deepened my relationships with friends, family, and life itself, and given birth to a community of genuine support.

Deep bows to Christine Oster, Carol Tisson, Mike Ginn, Alice Walker, Nancy Holms, Hans Henrick, and Suzanne Stevens for offering sacred space for me to write. For continuous support, I'm thankful to Joan Lester, Manly Moulton, Aubrey Pettaway, Eve Robinson, Kathy Ruyts, Monica Wells, and more recently Maeve Richard, Sue Bethanis, Noreen Greenblatt, and especially Penny Terry.

I am further thankful to those who read portions of the original manuscript and provided feedback, especially Jack Kornfield, Alice Walker, Aba Cecelia McHardy, Ondrietta Johnson, Deb McSmith, Claire-Elizabeth DeSophia, Saundra Davis, Erica Kremenak, Ernest Cherriokee, and Cheri Gardner.

A few people deserve special recognition for support during the original publication. I'm grateful to Ayofemi Oseye for providing intelligent and immediate editing, and for being gracious, available, and inspiring. Deep bows to Camara Rajabari for her calm presence and creativity, especially with the original book cover, and to Suzanne Stevens, who has been a beacon of support for many years. Knowing my work intimately, she provided invaluable input that assured the integrity of my writing. While Dr. Delorese Ambrose was the midwife in the first trimester of my writing, Calla Unsworth was the midwife during the final trimester, laboring with me in ritual to shape its structure and ensure translation of thought and spirit. I am grateful for her gentle and generous support, especially in the weary hours. Much appreciation goes to editor Judith Allen, who brought a fine eye for copyediting, inspiration, and faith to the original manuscript, and to Erna Smith, whose joy and generosity reminded me of the importance of my work in the world and in our lives.

I have been blessed by so many that my memory is not nearly as great as the gifts received, yet I am deeply grateful to all of you, named and unnamed, who thought of me kindly throughout this labor of love.

BIBLIOGRAPHY

Bennett-Goleman, Tara. *Emotional Alchemy: How the Mind Can Heal the Heart.* New York, NY: Harmony Books, 2001.

Goldstein, Joseph. *Insight Meditation: The Practice of Freedom.* Boston, MA: Shambhala Publications, Inc., 1993.

Gunaratana, Bhante Henepola. *Eight Mindful Steps to Happiness.* Somerville, MA: Wisdom Publications, 2001.

———. *Mindfulness in Plain English.* Somerville, MA: Wisdom Publications, 2002.

Hay, Louise L. *Heal Your Body: The Mental Causes for Physical Illness and the Metaphysical Way to Overcome Them.* Carlsbad, CA: Hay House, 1994.

Katie, Byron. *Loving What Is.* New York, NY: Harmony Books, 2002.

Kornfield, Jack. *After the Ecstasy, the Laundry: How the Heart Grows Wise on the Spiritual Path.* New York, NY: Bantam Books, 2000.

———. *The Art of Forgiveness, Lovingkindness, and Peace.* New York, NY: Bantam Books, 2002.

———. *A Path with Heart: A Guide through the Perils and Promises of Spiritual Life.* New York, NY: Bantam Doubleday Dell, 1993.

Lerner, Harriet G. *The Dance of Anger: A Woman's Guide to Changing the Patterns of Intimate Relationships.* New York, NY: Harper & Row, 1985.

Levine, Peter A. *Waking the Tiger: Healing Trauma.* Berkeley, CA: North Atlantic Books, 1997.

Levine, Stephen. *A Year to Live: How to Live This Year as If It Were Your Last.* New York, NY: Bell Tower, 1997.

Macy, Joanna. *World as Lover, World as Self.* Berkeley, CA: Parallax Press, 1991.

Miller, Alice. *The Drama of the Gifted Child: The Search for the True Self.* New York, NY: HarperCollins, 1996.

———. *Thou Shalt Not Be Aware: Society's Betrayal of the Child.* New York, NY: Farrar, Straus and Giroux, 1998.

Morrison, Toni. *Beloved.* New York, NY: Alfred A. Knopf, Inc., 1987.

Salzberg, Sharon. *Lovingkindness: The Revolutionary Art of Happiness.* Boston, MA: Shambhala Publications, Inc., 1995.

———. *Faith: Trusting Your Own Deepest Experience.* New York, NY: Riverhead Books, 2003.

Walker, Alice. *The Third Life of Grange Copeland.* Orlando, FL: Harcourt Books, 1970.

———. *We Are the Ones We Have Been Waiting for: Light in a Time of Darkness.* New York, NY: The New Press, 2006.

CONTACT INFORMATION

RUTH KING, M.A., is president of Bridges, Branches & Braids—an organization working with negative energies in positive ways. She offers coaching, workshops, and retreats based on the principles and practices presented in this book, notably Celebration of Rage™. These programs are appropriate for individuals, couples, organizations, health and healing practitioners, and others interested in promoting self-awareness, emotional literacy, and personal development. Ruth King is available for speaking, lecturing, custom retreats, book-club discussions, and life coaching. Visit www.healingrage.com for details, or write to P.O. Box 7813, Berkeley, CA 94707.